Henry Green was the pen-name of Henry Vincent Yorke. He was born at the family home of his parents, near Tewkesbury in Gloucestershire, and was educated at Eton and Oxford. He afterwards worked in the London office of the family business, and frequently visited their works in Birmingham. He married in 1929 and had one son. During the 1939–45 war he served for the duration in the London Fire Brigade. He died in December 1973, aged 68. His other novels are: *Loving*, *Living*, *Party Going* (also available in Picador), *Back*, *Concluding* and *Caught*, together with *Pack My Bag*, an autobiography.

Also by Henry Green in Picador
Loving/Living/Party Going

Henry Green

Nothing
Doting
Blindness

published by Pan Books

All first published by The Hogarth Press
Nothing in 1950, *Doting* in 1952, and *Blindness* in 1926
This one-volume edition published in Picador 1979 by Pan Books Ltd,
Cavaye Place, London SW10 9PG
This volume © The Hon. Mrs Henry Yorke 1977, 1979
ISBN 0 330 25871 0
Set, printed and bound in Great Britain by
Cox & Wyman Ltd, Reading

Contents

Nothing

On a Sunday afternoon in nineteen forty eight John Pomfret a widower of forty five, sat over lunch with Miss Liz Jennings at one of the round tables set by a great window that opened on the Park, a view which had made this hotel loved by the favoured of Europe when they visited London.

He did not look at the girl and seemed nervous as he described his tea the previous Sunday when Liz had to visit her mother ill with flu so that he had been free to call on Jane Weatherby, a widow only too well known to Miss Jennings. It was wet then, did she remember he was saying, so unlike this he said, and turned his face to the dazzle of window, it had been dark with sad tears on the panes and streets of blue canals as he sat by her fire for Jane liked dusk, would not turn on the lights until she couldn't see to move, while outside a single street lamp was yellow, reflected over a thousand raindrops on the glass, the fire was rose, and Penelope came in. Jane cried out with loving admiration and there the child had been, no taller than the dark armchair, all eyes, her head one long curl coppered next the fire and on the far side as pale as that street lamp or as small flames within the grate, and she was dressed in pink which the glow blushed to rose then paled then glowed once more to a wild wind in the chimney before their two faces dark across Sunday afternoon.

'Then you're to be married,' Jane had cried and so it was he realized, as he now told Miss Jennings, that the veil of window muslin twisted in a mist on top of the child's head to fall to dark snow at her heels, with the book pressed between two white palms in supplication, in adorable humility, that all this spelled marriage, heralded a bride without music by firelight, a black mouth trembling mischief and eyes, huge in one so young, which the fire's glow sowed with sparkling points of rose.

'Oh aren't you lucky,' Jane said, 'you sweet you?' but the infant said no word.

It was then he fell, he told Miss Jennings. He had gone on his knees. Not direct onto the floor, he explained. No, he used one of those small needlework cushions women put about a room and the fact was Penelope made no objection when he suggested the ceremony should take place at once. There was a cigar band handy in the ashtray for a ring and he had, he swore it, looked first at Jane who'd only said 'why not then darling?' Thus it is he explained to Miss Jennings that the great mistakes in life are made. And it was Jane, he went on, had called 'wilt thou take this man?' while the little girl stayed agreeably silent, had continued 'for richer or poorer, for better or for worse' right through her own remembered version of the service. Or perhaps Jane had altered the words to make it unreal to herself, Mr Pomfret did not know he said. But the harm was there.

He came out of his description to find Miss Jennings laughing.

'Oh my dear,' she gasped 'you should never be allowed to play with small children. Particularly not little girls!'

'I know, I know,' he said.

'So when did the tears start darling?'

He objected that Jane had not cried then and went on to explain that so soon as this mock ceremony ended and Penelope had flown to her mother's arms he'd taken it all a fatal step forward and asked the child to sit on her husband's knee.

'You see they made an absolute picture,' he explained. 'You know what Janie's eyes are with that wonderful blessing out of the huge things.'

'Well?' Miss Jennings demanded when he paused.

'Just look at the man over there Liz I ask you,' he temporized. 'Where was I? Oh yes,' and went on to describe Penelope's little face buried in Jane's bosom. He'd made a further invitation on which Jane did not call him to order, then suddenly, he said, it broke, there was a great wail came out with a 'Mummy I don't want,' after which nothing was any use, all had been tears.

'I nearly sobbed myself. Oh the blame I had to take! No but seriously you can't think it wrong of me Liz?'

'Are you seeing a lot of Jane these days?' Miss Jennings wanted to be told.

'She's supposed to lunch here this very afternoon,' he answered. 'Which is as much as I ever see her, once in a blue moon, except when you choose to go sick-nursing.'

'Mother isn't often . . .' she began.

'My dear what's come over you,' he interrupted, 'I wasn't serious. No but do look over that man again. Well as you can imagine,' he proceeded 'it's gone on ever since. Whenever I ring I get the latest the child has imagined, she simply never seems to sleep now at all isn't it awful, and the little boy who comes to tea with her quite heartbroken; Liz do say you don't think it was dreadful of me!'

'What man did you mean?'

'Over there with a wig and the painted eyebrows.'

'Oh no how disgusting. But I can't see anyone even remotely like! Well go on. This story of yours begins to amuse me rather, darling.'

'There's no more. But look here Liz you can't think it was indecent can you now?'

'Not a very nice thing after all.'

'But I couldn't tell how she would react to sitting on my knee could I?'

'You should never have married her.'

'Yes but Liz she didn't once in practice settle on my knee.'

'That's not the point dear. Now Jane won't ever hear the last!' Miss Jennings sniffed. 'Well you said she was due and here she comes. We've simply talked her into the room!' Liz made a face as he craned to see Jane.

'Still Dick Abbot,' Mr Pomfret remarked of the man with her. 'Hello there,' he waved. With a great smile and one or two nods that seemed to promise paradise, Mrs Weatherby changed course, made her way between tables to kiss Liz, to lay with a look of mischief and delight between John's two palms a white hand which he pressed as had her own child the imaginary psalter.

The two women greeted one another warmly.

'And how's Penelope?' he asked in his most indifferent voice.

'She's just a little saint,' the mother answered. 'Oh weren't you wicked! I suppose he's confessed to you Liz? Isn't it simply unbelievable!' But she was smiling with great good-nature.

'Have you heard about poor old Arthur?' John enquired.

'Arthur Morris no,' Jane said, her face at once serious, the eyes great and fixed.

'Only a simple nail in the toe of his left shoe,' John told them. 'A small puncture in the ball of the foot. But they've had to take the big toe off and now he's dangerously ill.' He looked up at Jane. Her eyes grew round.

'Oh no,' she said, then began to shake. She was soon helplessly giggling without a sound. Then it spread to Liz and she clapped a hand over her mouth above blue eyes that watered with silent laughter.

'They may even have to amputate the ankle,' he added smiling broadly now.

'His ankle?' Jane cried, a tremor in her voice. Miss Jennings' shoulders began to heave. 'Forgive me I can't help myself. Dick have you heard?' Mrs Weatherby called out and turned around as though the escort must be close behind. He was nowhere near.

'But how rude of Richard!' she exclaimed, serious again at once.

Dick Abbot at that moment was in conference with a youthful seeming creature dressed up in the gold braid of a hotel porter and who turned away to bully a head waiter in white tie and tails.

'Table trouble,' John said.

'I ought to be on my way I suppose,' Mrs Weatherby announced then began her farewell smile. 'Goodbye darlings,' she murmured as if to promise everything again.

'The Japanese do,' Mr Pomfret explained to her back.

'Do what good God?' Miss Jennings demanded.

'They all laugh even when their very own are at death's door. It's nerves. You don't think that dreadful surely? Once Jane starts I've as much as I can do to stop myself.'

'She's rather sweet,' Liz said 'though I say as shouldn't.'

He seemed to ignore this.

'The young don't laugh,' he complained.

'I do, I can't help it,' she said.

'They don't,' he insisted gloomily.

'So what about me?' asked Miss Jennings, all smiles.

'I love you,' he said smiling back. 'That's one reason I love you Liz.'

'Well then? We've been over every one of your other friends haven't we? And lunch Sunday's as much as we ever seem to have. So let's talk about me.'

'Oh don't mention Sunday darling please, that brings up tomorrow, our all inevitably going back to work. Why it's too despairing,' and his voice rose, 'too too awful,' and he flapped both hands, 'like a dip into the future, every hope gone, endless work work work!'

The man in porter's uniform close by hurried across upon these gestures, a head waiter in attendance.

'What is there Mr Pomfret?' he exclaimed. 'Is not everything to your satisfaction?'

Miss Jennings began to laugh helplessly.

'No Pascal, nothing, I'm quite all right. Tell me, who are these other people on all sides?'

The head waiter stepped back.

'Oh Mr Pomfret sir,' he hissed 'they are not your people, they are any peoples sir, they come here now like this, we do not know them Mr Pomfret.'

'Yes Gaspard so I'd noticed,' and he winked his far eye at Miss Jennings. Upon which Pascal spoke furiously to Gaspard who made off.

'For we do not see you often enough these years,' Pascal said to John, bowing low to leave in his turn.

'Thank you, yes that will be all,' Mr Pomfret spoke softly to the retreating back. 'That man's ageless,' he complained to a smiling Liz. He went on 'How old would you say he was?'

'Now how about me?' she demanded.

'Oh about thirty five,' he answered his own question.

'This is outrageous,' Liz said. She was twenty nine.

'But it's true,' John abruptly insisted. 'My daughter keeps a straight face on these occasions, in fact I try Mary all sorts of times and never get a smile out of her.'

'Mary's sweet,' Miss Jennings announced.

'I know,' her father said. 'But she just hasn't that brand of humour or her nerves are over strong. Jane's Philip at twenty is the same. What is it now darling?'

'Thank God I'm too young to have children that age.'

But Mr Pomfret was not it seemed to be diverted.

'If I lay in bed about to be amputated,' he went on 'I wouldn't expect you to laugh of course my dear and naturally Mary couldn't, but I'd lose a certain amount of resistance if I thought our acquaintances weren't roaring their beastly heads off! I'd even forgive you a grin or two,' he said smiling at her.

'That's better,' she said and grinned back. 'You mustn't ever be serious. I can't help but laugh over the solemn way you announce these things.'

'Yet you didn't break out into howls when I told about Penelope.'

'That's different. I mean they make wonderful artificial feet these days.' He laughed. 'No,' she said 'I'm serious. Why it might even get him out of the next war! No, with Penelope, there if you like you did something the young could never bring themselves to do.'

'Don't be absurd Liz,' he said equably. 'You know you would

13

tomorrow, with any little boy dressed up in a top hat and spats for a fancy dress party; in fun of course.'

'But not with a girl. I'll bet Jane's Philip wouldn't! Think of having a son of twenty and a girl of six!'

'That's nothing, you're to have more than that.'

'Oh I'm too old,' she muttered. 'No one will marry me now.'

'Please Liz don't!' he protested. 'In your heart of hearts you know you will.'

'But I'm over twenty nine John.'

'Well when you're fifty you can still have a boy of nineteen with a girl of six months.'

'You are sweet!' She smiled again.

'Then you do think I played Penelope a dirty trick?'

'She's a girl of course,' Miss Jennings answered. 'She really believed you married her so you see she thinks ... how do I know what!'

'I still don't see it Liz.'

'Oh I can't tell, I expect she may just be over-excited. Why don't you ask your Mary?'

'I daren't. She disapproves so.'

'Why d'you say that about her? Oh bother children anyway! Except she isn't a child any more of course. Eighteen if she's a day. It always makes me feel old as the hills when I realize. The time I first knew you she can't have been more than twelve.'

'And you look younger than she does every moment,' he said smiling into Miss Jennings' eyes.

'Stop it John,' she smiled back. 'Mary's a very nice girl, just don't forget, and she's going to have all the young men at her heels in droves.'

'Yes that's as may be. Certainly she'll have to find someone who can look after her, I shan't be able to manage much about setting up house for her husband. Who could these days? But she does disapprove. They all do.'

'I expect they can't help themselves.'

'Yes, and why, that's what no one will tell me Liz when I ask?'

'Perhaps they want to be different from their parents.'

'Poor Julia didn't laugh either,' he said.

'Well if your wife never did then I suppose Mary doesn't laugh especially so as to be different to you.'

'That's rather hard Liz, surely?'

'But you must have been the same with your father or mother once you'd grown up. I know I'd have done anything to be different from both mine.'

'Ah children are a mystery! Just wait until you have yours.'

'Haven't I already told you? It's too late, I'm too old,' she wailed in a bright voice.

He reached across and laid his hand over hers on top of the white tablecloth. Her nails were scarlet. He stroked the bare ring finger.

'Oh I know it's all finished between us where you're concerned but it isn't for me,' she said quite cheerfully.

'Good heavens what nonsense you can talk,' he replied in tones as clear as the skin of their two hands and the gold scrolls on the coffee cups. Looking up at her rather frightened nose he saw a reflection, from an empty wine glass and despatched by the sun in the Park, quiver beside her nostril.

'You're adorable,' he said.

'If you only knew how I wish I were,' she answered smiling.

'Oh look,' he cried. 'Dick Abbot's having one of his upsets with a waiter.'

'Poor Jane, poor Jane,' she replied, in a voice she might have used to speak of Christian martyrs and did not take her eyes from Mr Pomfret's face.

He watched Mrs Weatherby glance about with unconcern, with the especially humble half smile she used when in the same room as with what must have seemed, to her, inferior strangers, while the waiter stood relaxed beneath Abbot's purpling face. Pascal next came over in controlled haste. He stood beside this waiter, bent a little forward, eyes averted while Abbot's mouth worked and the words came tumbling out too far off for John to catch. Then Mr Pomfret stiffened and even Liz turned her head to see. Abbot was half out of the chair, was pointing a palsied finger at his adam's apple, held it there. Jane could hardly ignore this climax and laid a hand as if for reassurance on Pascal's forearm. At least Mr Abbot made gestures with slack wrists as though to brush off flies. Jane smiled again. Pascal bent forward in a torrent of humility, then chased the waiter off.

Mr Pomfret turned back to his girlfriend.

'Poor old Dick! Whenever he gets upset it reminds him of that time at the club when he got stuck with a fishbone. He turned black and ..'

'Now that's quite enough John,' Miss Jennings stopped him. 'In another minute you'll get me laughing and if Jane sees she'll think we're being rude.'

'Well all right then,' he replied in what seemed to be great good humour. 'Now wait a minute, I've paid haven't I? All right then, let's go back to your great bed.'

And they left, an elegant couple that attracted much attention, her sad face beaming.

'My dear I'm so sorry,' Mrs Weatherby said to her companion. Reaching across she laid a hand over his on the white table cloth. Her nails were scarlet. She gently scratched the skin by his thumbnail. Gold scrolls over white soup plates sparkled clear in the Park's sun without.

'It's nothing, only that damn waiter . . .' Mr Abbot muttered, his face alarmingly pale.

'All finished now,' she assured him.

He gave a great sigh.

'Most awfully sorry,' he said at last. 'Can't understand what came over me.'

'So blessed my dear there's still someone to speak to them these days.'

'Terrible thing that half the waiters now don't know what they're serving. But I must apologize Jane. In front of John Pomfret too.'

'I shouldn't let that even enter your head,' she sweetly protested. Yet when he raised his dog like eyes to hers she was looking over to where John and Liz had been.

'See much of him these days?'

'Of poor John?' Her eyes came back on him. To an extraordinary degree they were kind and guileless. 'Why goodness gracious me no! Not from one year's end to another.'

'Can't imagine what people find in the chap.'

'Oh but he has thousands of friends.' She was looking round the restaurant again with her lovely apologetic smile. 'Thousands!'

'Little Penelope care for the fellow?'

'Why yes how funny you should say it, now I come to think, Richard, he did come to tea only the other day, tea with her of course. He's simply sweet with darling Penelope.'

'Only asked because children know you know.'

She brought her eyes back once more to smile full in his great handsome face. She did not say a word.

'Because they size a man up. Instinct or something. Always prefer a child's opinion to me own.'

She gave a light airy little laugh.

'And now,' he went on, raising his voice, 'now this damn waiter,' he said and twisted right round in the chair 'it's got so we'll never be served! Good God I can't apologize enough. Hardly ever see you except luncheon Sundays then this sort of thing crops up.'

Pascal hastened over.

'Have you all gone home man?' Mr Abbot demanded.

'Oh sir, Mrs Weatherby madam, in two minutes, yes sir please,' and Pascal went in pursuit of a head waiter.

'My dear,' Mrs Weatherby smiled. 'Heavens how I love this place! Why I could sit where I am this moment the whole day long.'

'Decent of you,' he said.

'Have you heard about Arthur Morris?' she enquired. When he shook his head she passed on what John had told.

'Good Lord,' he pronounced, entirely grave. 'It's serious all right then. Can't tell where these things'll stop,' he added. 'No telling at all! Well Jane that's bad news you bring there!'

'Isn't it dreadful,' she gravely replied. 'I'll have to try and see him at the clinic.'

'Jolly decent if you would. To cheer the poor unfortunate fellow.'

'You are sweet to be so sad,' she said.

'Then John Pomfret laughed of course?'

'Well darling to tell the utter truth I couldn't help myself even. Oh, I was most to blame.'

'If you did I maintain it was out of common or garden politeness, there you are. Never will understand a man like that though. Good war record, plumb through the desert, all the way up Italy, must have had umpteen fellows killed right beside him. Did he laugh then out there, – eh?'

Mrs Weatherby began to heave without a sound.

'Me being ridiculous again dear?' he asked, at his most humble.

'Only just a very little bit darling Richard. Oh I'm hopeless I know I am,' she said and dabbed at her brilliant eyes with a handkerchief. 'You'll have to forgive, that's all.'

He watched her. His look was adoring.

'Bless you,' he said.

'You are so sweet,' she answered then composed herself.

Pascal and the head waiter hurried over with a trolley crowned by a dome of chromium which between them they removed with a conjurer's flourish to disclose the roast. Abbot watched this closely, leant forward to touch the plate on which they were to serve Jane's portion perhaps to make sure that it was hot and in general was threatening although at first he said very little. Mrs Weatherby, the appreciative audience, greeted this almost magical presentation with small delighted cries, praised everything but told Gaspard to take away the potatoes that he had laid, one by one, around her portion in the loving way a jeweller will lay out great garnets beside the design to which he is to work, before the setting is begun. Pascal conjured these off in what seemed to be despair.

'Sure everything's all right?' Mr Abbot demanded and put out a hand to detain Pascal in case the man had it in mind to flee.

'Simply delicious thank you. Dear Richard do start on yours. Why this is divine, simply melts in one's mouth!'

'Fetch Mrs Weatherby a sharp knife Gaspard now then,' he ordered. 'She can't use what she's got, man! Here give me!' He reached out a hand to Jane.

'No Richard no, you shan't. The veal's too perfect.'

The trolley was withdrawn, Pascal's act over. They ate in silence for a while, appeared to be in contemplation.

'Richard,' she said at last, having dabbed at her red mouth with a napkin, 'I'm worried to death about my Philip!'

'What's the lad up to now?'

'Oh my dear he so needs a father's influence. The dread time has come I'm afraid! I'm fussed dear Richard.'

'If I'm to help I must know more you know.'

'I almost can't find the way to tell you it's all so confusing but there's Philip's whole attitude to women.'

'Playing fast and loose?'

'Oh no I rather wish he would though I fear he is far too much of a snob for that, no no, worse, it's the other, oh dear if I go on like this I never shall explain, oh but Richard what has one done to deserve things? Sometimes I almost wonder if he knows the facts of life even. You see he respects girls so!'

Mrs Weatherby made her eyes very round and large to give Dick Abbot an adorable long glance of woe.

'Good God,' he replied with caution.

'It's not often I wish his father were alive again. You remember how Jim treated me, you're my living witness darling, but oh my dear I have moments sometimes when I'm not sure what to think.'

'You mean he's a . . .?' Mr Abbot demanded lowering.

She broke into a sweet peal of laughter. 'Oh Richard I do love you now and then,' she cried.

'Wish you could more often,' he said, rather glum.

'I'm sorry my dear, there you are. But it's a man about the house he needs I'm almost certain, an older one.'

'No shortage you could marry Jane,' he gruffly said. 'Why there's half a dozen or more would jump at the chance.'

'I couldn't dear. I'd simply never dare!'

'Why on earth not?'

'Because of darling little Penelope!!'

'But good heavens . . .'

'So jealous,' she explained 'such a saint I really believe she would be ill!' Her expression was of admiring love and pride.

'Are you serious?' he asked.

'You don't know what these things can be,' she answered. 'I'm everything to Pen, everything. She often says "mummy I'd simply rather die"! Of course they copy the words out of one's very mouth but I'd never dare.'

'Well then what is wrong with Philip?'

'He just treats girls as if they weren't real.'

'How d'you want him to behave? Chuck 'em about?'

'Oh but he must learn to treat women as human beings.'

'Maybe he does behind your back Jane.'

She gaily laughed. 'My dear I'm almost certain not,' she said. 'No he's so finicky with them.'

'You marry again,' he insisted.

'But I've got used to being alone!'

'I can believe that,' he agreed. 'Besides you wouldn't necessarily be doing it for yourself would you? And after all my dear we can't pay too much attention to the six-year olds. Pen will snap out of it.'

'And one thing that won't snap them out of things, as you call it, is for their poor deluded mothers to remarry.'

'So you'll sacrifice Philip to little Penelope, is that the idea?'

'Richard dear one, how simply diabolically clever you can be sometimes! Oh Lord my horrid problems. But I do apologize, all this must be infinitely dull for you, and just when I'm so enjoying your delicious luncheon.'

'Know what I think? I believe these things settle themselves.'

'Oh but how?'

'Before you realize where you are you'll be in the Registry Office one of these days,' he asserted. 'And after not having asked the children's leave either.'

'Do you really think I could fall in love once more?' she asked.

'I know you can,' he said in a satisfied voice. She made a face.

'Richard,' she grumbled and gave a scared laugh. 'Behave yourself, we were talking of marriage, not anything else, not anything!'

'Like me to have a word with him then, Jane?'

'My dear isn't that too sweet, I do appreciate it, still I very much fear he might not actually listen. Oh I realize how rude this sounds. But he's not normal! No I don't mean that. I mean more he's so old-fashioned! Can you believe it he even gets up to open the door for me!! Because if someone is not in the family then he never seems able to listen.'

'If according to you he'll only pay attention to a stepfather he'll have to wait a bit then, won't he?'

'I don't know what to do. I'm at my wit's end,' she said.

'Thought you maintained you'd never remarry.'

'Why Richard I never uttered a word of the kind!'

'Only man you'll get hitched on to in the end then is your faithful servant,' he said with a sort of forced joviality.

'Richard dear you're quite wonderful! You can't imagine what a solid comfort you are always.' She gave him an exquisitely lingering long smile.

'You wait and see,' he insisted.

'I'll wait,' she promised gaily laughing.

He frowned.

'Wish I could count on that,' he remarked.

'My dear I do apologize,' she said at once. 'How abominably rude that was! But I told you I could never marry again because of little Pen. And I don't think you are being quite kind,' she added with a grave reproachful look. 'Richard I really believe you're almost making fun which doesn't suit you dear. Your sense of humour is not your long suit.'

'I say I'm truly sorry Jane. Fact is everyone's having trouble with their children these days. Only last week John Pomfret button-holed me in the Club about his Mary.'

'I'm miserable I'm such a bore Richard.' She gave him an adorable smile of humility in which there was mischief. For a moment she looked very like her daughter.

'You aren't, good Lord no,' he protested.

'But I am! Anyway I think Mary's such a vulgar child.'

'Flattered to find you can bring yourself to confide in me on occasions,' he said at his most formal. 'Never could make up my mind about her yet,' he said apparently of Mary Pomfret. 'Striking girl though. Why, does Philip see much of her then?'

'My Philip? Certainly not. What's John's trouble over the girl?'

'A bluestocking I fancy. Too taken up with her job. Unfeminine. Properly upset about her old John seemed.'

'But how extraordinary Richard! Why that's just how I worry about Philip. So unmanly and serious for his years. What else did John say?'

'Well you know, one thing or the other.'

'My dear what I do so like about you is your absolute loyalty. Of course if you'd rather not ...'

'Tell you the truth I've pretty well forgotten now.'

'In at one ear and out of the other like when I confide in you over Philip, is that it?'

'Now Jane, you know me.'

'And that's just what I respect you for! It's so perfect to be sure what one pours out won't be all over London the next minute.'

'Oh well,' he said and seemed flattered. 'But you say Philip and Mary never meet. Don't they work along the corridor in the same office?'

'Of course they do my dear. I thought everyone knew.'

'Well then ask Mary what she thinks.'

'But it's just because they talk every day that they don't see anything of each other. Would you take someone out at night when you sat opposite her six hours every twenty four? Really Richard what the world has come to! Besides he's too much of a snob as I said. And thank God for it where that girl's concerned!'

'Don't care for Mary then?'

'I don't see why one should be friends with one's old friend's children do you? Any more than we as children made a fuss of the horrid creatures our parents' friends brought us to play in the nursery. Of course I don't know the way Philip passes his spare time but I've a very good idea he doesn't spend that with Mary! I should hope not indeed.' Mrs Weatherby began to look indignant.

'What's the gal done then Jane?'

'Nothing so far as I know, nothing at all. I couldn't care less. But just because John is one of my oldest friends I don't see why I should like his daughter even if, as you remember perfectly well, at one time I loved her mother, oh so dearly!'

There was a pause.

'Wish I knew something to suggest about Philip,' he said at last.

'Let's not talk about the children any more,' she said, relaxing. 'Did you notice Liz and John had gone? How is that drear sad old affair of theirs have you any idea?'

'Can't imagine Jane. Don't know at all.'

'I believe he's simply sick of her and she clings on in the most disgustingly squalid way.' She laughed gaily again. 'I can't imagine where Liz finds the strength. She's so ill!' She beamed on him. 'Oh dear aren't I being ill-natured all of a sudden! You don't think I'm very wicked do you?' She leaned forward, laid her hand by his. 'I tell you what,' she said. 'We don't want to wait for coffee here. Richard let's have it at your place darling.'

His face showed eager surprise.

'I say, jolly decent of you, why not indeed? Let's go now,' he said and in a few minutes they left. His great face beamed.

Philip Weatherby and Mary Pomfret were sitting in the downstairs lounge of a respectable public house off Knightsbridge.

'Will your parent ever ask a relative to the house?' he sternly enquired.

'Why no, Philip, I don't suppose he does.'

'Nor my mother won't and it's inconceivable.'

'I think Daddy may sometimes.'

'You'd imagine my mother was ashamed of me. You see the position? I can't ring up and say "this is your little nephew here and can I run round for tea?"'

'Poor Philip you must come after the office one day though you'd find us rather dull for you I'm afraid.'

'I'd like very much and it wouldn't be dull.'

'I'll tell Daddy then.'

'Have another light ale Mary?'

'Yes but this one's my turn.'

'Is it? Oh all right.' He took the money she had ready and went over to the bar while she got out a mirror and went over her face. In the way of the very young she did not look round the saloon.

When he came back with their drinks he said,

'D'you think our parents see much of each other still?'

'Now Philip why should they?'

'Didn't you know? They had a terrific affair once.'

'But my dear how absolutely thrilling! I don't believe you.'

'True as I'm here Mary. Arthur Morris told me.'

'How sweet, did they really?'

'I don't think it's sweet in the least.'

'I know but they had their lives to live after all. I mean their time is practically over now you see, so why shouldn't they when they chose?'

'I'm embarrassed by them that's why.'

'Oh Philip are you being fair? What difference does that make?'

'We could be brother and sister for one thing.'

'Only half brother. I don't mind do you?'

'Why should I?' Nevertheless he seemed quite awkward and when she looked at him out of the corner of an eye both hers creased in the tiniest amusement. 'Only it's absurd that we shouldn't know,' he added.

'What makes you think we might be?' she asked. He did not give a direct answer.

'D'you believe there's some special feeling between brother and sister?' he demanded.

'How about you and Penelope?'

'Oh she's too young.'

'I don't suppose there can be unless they live together – have been brought up in the same house,' she corrected herself.

'You don't believe in blood?' he asked.

'Consanguinity, is there such a word?' she answered. 'No more than three types surely? Daddy wore his stamped over a card he hung round his neck during the war on a ribbon he got from me. I thought that marvellous then.'

'I meant heredity,' he said in a severe voice.

'Oh it's all a question of environment now,' she objected. 'I was taught the whole question of heredity had been exploded ages back.'

23

'All the same I'd still like to see my relatives,' he complained.

'Why don't you ask your mother then?'

'She'd think it pansy. Almost told me as much once or twice.'

'But you aren't Philip, no one could pretend you were.'

'One never knows,' he darkly answered.

'Look at you with that Bethesda Nathan at the office.'

'I say, good Lord, what gossips you all are. Who says anything about Bethesda and me?' Obviously he was delighted.

'Of course we all do. Someone as attractive as you,' she said smiling gently full in his face.

'You're making fun,' he complained.

'No Philip don't be absurd. Naturally we gossip.'

'You're laughing at me just like my mother.'

'Now that's not nice and she hoots at everyone after all.'

'Does she? I'd never notice.'

'Every minute. It's her line,' she comforted.

'Anyway there's nothing between Bethesda and me.'

'Perhaps not. What all of us are interested in is whether there may be.'

'Bethesda and I discuss this entire question of relatives,' he told Mary. 'She sees her own the whole time. In fact she's fed up with them.'

'Jews have tremendous family feeling Philip.'

'And why shouldn't they?'

'I say you are touchy! Penelope better grow up quick and take some of these awkward corners off you.'

'Sorry,' he said. 'I'm being a bore.'

'No you aren't at that,' she objected. 'We're having a cosy little argument that's all.'

Yet what she said seemed to silence him. He turned his head away and looked round the room. She stretched her fingers out and tilted them upwards against their table, examined the short nails which were enamelled but not painted. When his eyes came upon a man with two sticks he said,

'Have you heard about Arthur Morris?'

She immediately put those hands away on her lap and smiled upon Philip.

'Who?' she asked, all charm.

'You know that great friend of both our parents.'

'Oh,' she said and seemed to lose interest.

'He's having his toe off.'

'Why ever for?'

Both began to giggle.

'Why does a man have a toe off?' he demanded.

'How should I know?'

'Because it's diseased stupid.'

'Poor man,' she said no longer smiling, in an uninterested voice.

'My mother went to see him the other day,' he told her.

'Well and why not? You don't make out there's something between them on top of her and Daddy?'

'I'm not sure.'

'See here Philip your mother's splendid. Oh I understand she may have a slightly unmarvellous nature at least where you are concerned, but she looks wonderful!'

'What difference does that make?'

'All the difference. She gets so many more offers.'

'But at her age it's disgusting.'

'I never said she accepted them Philip. There are so many must want to take your mother out.'

'Who could?'

'Don't be filthy. Much better her than I should be mauled by one of the men her age!'

'You don't mean to say that antediluvian Arthur Morris . . .?'

'Of course not,' she sharply protested. 'If you go on to others like this you'll be getting me a reputation.'

'I never . . .'

'OK' she said. 'Forget it.' She smiled. 'But suppose you had to have a leg off wouldn't you wish for visitors?'

'Well of course.'

'All right, then don't make out they kiss on top of the cradle they'll have put over his stump.'

'Oh if it was just kissing,' he said in a contemptuous voice.

'How should I know when or where they do the other?' she remarked petulantly. 'I don't mind. If it's Daddy now and some woman good luck to him I say.'

'Yes but your father's a man,' he protested.

'I should hope so indeed,' she replied at which both began to giggle again.

'You're hopeless,' he said.

'I haven't half as much the matter with me as you appear to,' she objected, serious once more. 'Honestly you seem potty about your mother.'

'I wonder if it's why the relatives won't come.'

'No Philip really. You know what their whole generation is!'

'How d'you mean?'

'Well they wouldn't let a little thing like that, I mean of going to bed, what we've just been discussing, make the slightest bit of difference would they?'

'I don't believe it is a little thing.'

'No more do I.'

'That's where the whole difference lies,' he said 'between our generations. Their whole lot is absolutely unbridled.'

'Yes Philip but they are the generation you've just said you want to meet aren't they?' Both laughed gaily at this remark.

'Damned if I can make 'em out at all,' he said. 'You know your father is crazy. Did you hear what he did with little Penelope the other day? When our Italian maid sent her in dressed as a bride for fun, he actually married Pen.'

'Married her!'

'Pretended to of course,' he explained. 'Don't you think it most odd?'

'But Philip what on earth are you saying?'

'Went down on his knees in front of Mamma and from all I can make out ran through some bogus form of church service with the poor old thing. It knocked Penelope cold! She screamed the house down three days. Still she's forgetting now at last.'

Miss Pomfret did not seem impressed.

'If your mother let him, then I'd say she was insane,' she commented.

'Oh I don't know,' he said. 'But I do agree that generation's absolutely crazy.'

'So are little girls, believe you me.'

'And grown ones?' he enquired.

'Now to whom d'you refer may I ask?' she cried delightedly.

'Like when you went up to Derek Wolfram at the party and announced it was time for bed?'

She blushed.

'No but which beast told you?' she demanded.

'Oh that's all over the office,' he announced, at which she began to giggle, he joined in and presently they left, each going their several ways with broad smiles, well content it seemed.

A fortnight or so later Mrs Weatherby was with her son Philip in the sitting room of their flat.

'Dear boy,' she was saying 'I'm really worried about sweet Pen this time!'

'How's that Mamma?'

'She's such a little saint.'

'She always was.'

'Always!' his mother fervently agreed. 'But I fancy if she doesn't soon what Richard calls snap out of it then we shall just have to take her to a psychologist.'

'Mr Abbot? Where does he come into things?'

'My dear,' she replied. 'You must not mind your mother putting her problems to old friends.'

'OK Mamma. But you're about to take matters rather a long way forward surely?'

'Pen doesn't seem to get over it. Oh Philip I'm so distressed. She's just wrapped the whole thing up in her sweet mind!'

'What with? You see I don't understand.'

'I never told you. I don't think one should tell one child the other's secrets. Philip I'd say it must be four weeks ago now. Oh dear doesn't time fly. John Pomfret mistakenly came to tea and Isabella so stupid of her as things turned out dressed my precious Penelope up as a real bride. Then before I could stop him he was down on his knees marrying her with the actual words out of our church service.'

'Which you said over them?'

'My dear wasn't it wicked of him,' she went on, ignoring her son. 'And now she's desperate, yes desperate! I am so worried. I think I shall have to take her along, don't you darling?'

'But psychologists are supposed to dredge back into the past aren't they, and sister's only six?'

'Isn't that just what she needs Philip?'

'My point is it's only the other day.'

'Yet things have already gone so very deep,' she wailed. 'All so hopeless! Though she doesn't say a word. She's been a little brick. I can tell though. Darling she's at breaking point!'

'How do you know Mamma?'

'How do I know? How could I tell with you when you were small?'

'You mean Penelope's really ill?'

'Sick in her mind poor little soul, perhaps even dangerously so. Oh Philip!'

'But look here Mamma . . .'

'No my dear I mean it, I've never been more serious in my life. And thank God your father isn't all over us to complicate matters.'

'Well I don't see why we have to blackguard Father because we're worried about Pen.'

'Don't you? I do. But I'm afraid Philip! I've got to act, rid her of this somehow.'

'You put it down to the what d'you call it, the pretence?'

'I know I'm right!'

'And for that you're going to take her to a trick cyclist Mamma?'

'Don't Mamma me or use that precious slang of yours.' As she said this she sweetly smiled upon him.

'Likely enough the man'll only lead her back to when she used to wet her bed,' he protested.

'Philip I never thought I should have to complain of schoolboy smut in you again' she announced. 'I'm surprised. It really doesn't suit you. And over your own sister please. Philip it's nasty!'

'What is?'

'The way she is taking on, the little martyr. Oh I see what there must be there deep down.'

'How d'you mean?'

'Mind your own business,' she replied darkly. 'Pen's really suffering the sweet.'

'Why after all?'

'She feels wounded. Wouldn't anyone? Oh wasn't all of it gross of him poor well-meaning John, sweet idiot of a man. For I blame myself. Oh yes I can't forget. I've had to give her sleeping draughts every night since that fated afternoon.'

'Now you haven't . . .'

'Well no of course, not actually although she is just in the state I get in when I have to take them.'

'I should show her to Dr Bogle.'

'Dr Bogle?' she cried. 'The man we go to for pills!'

'What's the use of these specialists Mamma?'

'For especial emergencies Philip. Which little girl has ever before been married at six? Tell me out of the whole history of the world!'

'Yes indeed.'

'I can't understand where you get your false insensitive side my dear. She wed poor John in her own mind as sure as if she was actually in church and your father had come back from the grave to give her away, the precious! There you are. And what can you answer to that?'

'You mustn't worry,' he protested.

'Then my dear she made a picture,' his mother proceeded. 'In her long white veil! Somewhere she'd found a lily she was carrying, I can't imagine how unless there were some among the flowers Dick sent me. The shade of that tall lamp was askew so she stood in a shaft of light as utterly sweet as if she had been in the aisle with the sun shining through your father's memorial rose window Philip! So absurd of me my dear but the tears came to my eyes and I really couldn't see. That was the true reason why I couldn't stop it all until too late!'

'She'll recover.'

'But the responsibility dear heart. You know what one comes across with those awful books of Freud's I haven't read thank God.'

'They're completely out of date nowadays.'

'They are? You're sure? Yet there must be something in them when he's been so famous.'

'He wrote about sex Mamma.'

'Well isn't this sex good heavens? Sex still has something to do with marriage even nowadays hasn't it? Rising seven and to have an experience like that, I can't ever forgive myself!'

'Why not run her down to Brighton?'

Mrs Weatherby began to glow at this suggestion.

'D'you know I think I really might,' she said at last. 'What a brilliant idea of yours Philip, just when the weather has been so perfectly vile. Let's see, we could go tomorrow. Oh no I am meeting John. Then Sunday I was to lunch with Dick but I could put him off, that won't hurt Richard. But how will you get along dear?'

'Oh I shall be all right.'

'Why not ask some girl in and have Isabella cook you one of her delicious Italian things?'

'I'll see.'

'I would if I were you.' Mrs Weatherby had become her old self once more. She shone on Philip the whole light of her attention.

'With Chianti. Only it must be white remember. And not Bethesda please!'

When he frowned she laughed.

'Darling you mustn't mind my little teases. Don't bother. I know I'll never be told who. But one thing I am sure of. She'll be a very lucky girl.'

He awkwardly smiled.

'No you must really have pity on the poor fainting souls Philip! Just imagine them sitting by their telephones bored to tears with their sad mothers who're themselves probably only dying to have an old flame in, waiting waiting to be asked, eating their lovely hearts out!'

She leant forward as though she were about to hug him.

'I might,' he said.

'In a little sweat of excitement in their frocks!!' she said turning swiftly away the beautiful innocent eyes soft with what seemed to be love, her great mouth trembling.

His face showed acute embarrassment. She may have sensed this for she changed the subject.

'Do you see much of Mary Pomfret?'

'At the office,' he replied.

'I can't understand someone like John having a girl like it.'

He did not answer. She again went off at a tangent. 'Philip what would you say if I married a second time?'

He jumped up as though he had anticipated this question, walked over to stand at the window with his back to her, a rigid back which she fixed with an apologetic look of ladylike amusement.

'It would be your own affair,' he said at last, indistinctly.

'Yes I expect it could be,' she replied with a small smile. 'But that wasn't quite exactly what I asked. What would you say Philip?' she repeated.

'Me?' he mumbled. 'Why, is there anyone?'

She laughed with great kindliness and then looked at the floor.

'Oh,' she murmured 'we are so queer together. You know this conversation is the wrong way round, I mean it's me should be asking you if there was someone. No of course there isn't just now for me. But suppose one day there still might? Would you find the idea so very horrid?'

He turned round. He seemed all at once to be a schoolboy. She kept her face straight.

'No, I wouldn't mind,' he said.

'I'd've imagined you would have liked that Philip,' she went on. 'Surrounded with nothing but women the whole day long, even at the office from all I can make out.'

'Honest,' he said 'don't bother about me. I'm OK. It wouldn't make a bit of difference.' He smiled.

'These things do happen,' she murmured reproachfully.

'Not putting up the banns then?'

'Don't be so silly dear!'

'Who's it to be Mamma?'

'No but really I shall be quite cross with you in a minute. There's no one. But your mother's not so long in the tooth yet that it mightn't come about. Philip wouldn't you a little bit like to have a stepfather?'

'I don't think you'd marry again just to give me one.'

'My dear how sharp you are sometimes,' she laughed. 'You got me there all right or did you? Not that I don't think of you and you of me, you are simply sweet to me always, bless your heart.'

'Well let me know when and I'll put the wedding march on the record changer. I say look at the time. I must be off.'

'Good heavens yes,' she cried, 'and I've stockings and shoes to get for our little nervous case, the martyr.'

At this she went up to Philip, kissed him with fervour and they both left.

At the same time on the identical day Mary Pomfret sat with her father in their living room.

'What would you say if your devoted parent married a second time?' he asked.

'Oh Daddy how thrilling for you. Who?'

'I don't know wonderful, I was only wondering.'

'Are you sure?'

'You seem very certain someone would agree.'

'Of course!'

'And you wouldn't mind?'

'But is it Miss Jennings?'

'Now wait a minute Mary. I wasn't even making up my mind to ask anyone. Mine is just an idle question.'

'Well are you very discontented as you are then Daddy?'

'What do you mean by that?'

'I can't see why any man ever marries his girl,' she said. He laughed.

'You're dead right,' he answered. 'It often comes as a great surprise.'

'Not to the man; he has to ask.'

'To both,' he insisted. She considered this. Then she said,

'Why did you want to know whether I minded?'

'Surely nothing could be more natural dear? Of course I'd have to know first.'

'Don't I still look after you and the flat all right then?'

'But you are perfect, absolutely perfect.'

'I thought perhaps you might wish for a change.' Her face expressed embarrassment. He yawned.

'My dear,' he said gently 'one doesn't remarry to get a change of housekeeping. Not yet at all events.'

'That's what will happen when that happens in case you don't realize.'

'Oh Mary no. Not at my age!'

'But of course I'd have to go,' she said in a distressed tone of voice. 'I couldn't stay to witness you and your bride.'

'My dear,' he objected 'it would not be so romantic and after all there's room in plenty in the flat for three people.'

Her blue eyes filled with tears she was so young.

'Liz wouldn't like it,' she insisted.

'Now Mary,' he said and seemed alarmed, 'I told you there was no one. I just thought I'd ask to get your reactions. Good Lord you'll be going off one day and wouldn't expect me to stay on here alone.'

'I don't see why not. I mean you can invite in anyone you want can't you?'

'I could be lonely,' he explained with what appeared to be a false voice as he selected a cigarette.

'I'm always here now,' she said.

'But you ought to go out more Mary.'

'How shall I when nobody asks me.'

'They will. I say let's give an entertainment. Why not? Lots of young men for you and hang the expense!'

'Oh I shan't want anyone.'

'Nonsense, that's because you don't know them. You leave it to me darling.'

'No honestly, you have your own friends in if you're dull.'

'Who says I'm dull?'

'Well you've just explained that you'll re-marry, haven't you Daddy?'

'But good Lord one doesn't go through all that again simply because one's dull.'

'Don't you?'

'No,' he said, reached up a hand to where she stood by his chair and pulled her down to kiss an ear. She sat on the arm.

'Anyway I never shall,' she laughed.

'You will,' he said. They lapsed into easy silence.

'It's dark. Wouldn't you like me to put the light on?' she asked.

'No. Let's save money for our party. This fiendish rain!' he commented.

'You must miss your mother?' he said at last. He asked the question once a year and each time got a different answer. On this occasion she replied,

'I don't know. I can't remember her.'

'It must be very dull for you here alone with me.'

She ignored this. 'Who was her best woman friend?' she murmured.

'Jane.'

'Mrs Weatherby?' she exclaimed in great surprise. 'You never told.'

'Oh they were always together,' he assured his daughter. He laughed. 'Never out of each other's pockets at one time.'

'I had no idea, not in the least. Well that does make a bit of difference!'

'How d'you mean darling?'

'I'll look at her quite differently,' Miss Pomfret said in an altered voice.

'She's very nice,' her father assured her.

'You aren't thinking of marrying Mrs Weatherby then Daddy?'

'Now listen, I told you didn't I? There's not a soul, there really isn't. I'm sorry I spoke. It was just a stupid thing one says glibly, then regrets.'

'But marriage might be right for you.'

'There isn't time,' he wailed in his affected voice. He twisted round to smile on her face. 'All this work! We none of us have the leisure to wed! It's too frightful!'

'Oh by the way, talking of her,' she mumbled, 'I told Philip to come round to tea.'

'Not Saturday!'

She frowned. 'No, no,' she said. 'But he seems rather blue at home.'

Mr Pomfret opened wide eyes. He had a question wandering round his mouth. But he shut his lips. Then he asked with indifference,

'How's little Pen?'

'Oh she's all right. She's just spoiled,' the daughter said. 'Why did you never tell me about Mrs Weatherby Daddy?'

'What about her?'

'That she was Mummy's best friend.'

'Oh I must have often,' he yawned.

'No. Never before. And I wonder why?'

'Well I don't say often enough what a wonder you are do I? I suppose the obvious soon gets forgotten. I forgot you didn't know and in case I forget again I'll say this once more, you're wonderful love and no man could have a nicer daughter.' He yawned again.

It was too dark to see the expression on her face.

'Don't get all woolly stupid,' was what she replied. There was a pause.

'How's the job going?' he drowsily enquired.

'Oh much the same.'

'Still scissors and paste?'

'Some of the girls have gone out and bought their own to cut with,' she answered. 'The ones they issue now are quite hopeless. Yes we snip bits out of the newspapers, stick them on folio sheets, and it's still all cabled out to Japan where the press people hardly use any of what we send. It'll go on like that for ever.'

'See much of Philip?' His voice came even lower. She looked down but could make out no more than the dark top of his head. She glanced up at the framed reproductions and in this light they were no more than blurs.

'See him?' she murmured.

'What's that?' he mumbled.

'He's in C Department,' she softly answered, beginning to space out the words, stroking his hair so the tips of her fingers barely touched his head. 'In C Department,' she repeated even softer, as if to sing them both to sleep. 'But yes I see him. Sometimes,' she whispered. 'Sometimes but not often.' A small silence fell. 'Not often,' she went on at last so low she could hardly be heard. Her father began to snore. 'But I do sometimes,' she ended almost under her breath, got up and left him slumbering.

The next day was Sunday. John Pomfret sat over luncheon at the usual table looking out on the Park, with Miss Jennings.

'So I asked her right out,' he was saying in his pleasantly affected party manner, 'I said "would it matter to you if I married again?" '

Miss Jennings appeared to listen with care.

'Oh Liz,' he cried and spread his arms out over two dirty plates on which were soiled knives and forks, two glasses of red wine, and a bottle in its gay straw jacket, 'she made a picture, you know she's a remarkable girl. Mary stood there like an angel, just a Botticelli angel framed in my lovely Matisse over the fireplace, those lozenges of colour perfect as a background for that pretty head. When I think how she's carried on for years without a woman to talk with I feel ashamed and proud Liz!'

'What did Mary say then?'

A faint shade of embarrassment seemed to come over his handsome features.

'Not much,' he replied.

'How d'you mean?' she anxiously asked.

'No man could be luckier in a daughter,' he said. 'Not one moment of worry, nary one. Of course if Jane hadn't quarrelled with Julia before she died I might easily have called on Jane for help. I know I thought of it. But Liz it seemed disloyal to my wife, she would have turned in her poor grave. So I struggle on alone.'

He paused. Miss Jennings appeared incapable of speech. He was gazing through the great window on what looked to be a white sheet of water from which a few black trees in bud leaned against driving rain.

'And it's come out quite perfect,' he proceeded. Miss Jennings blinked. 'I can't say too much in praise of my girl. So I'm going to give a party!'

'A party?' she exclaimed.

'Well she doesn't meet enough people,' Mr Pomfret announced. 'How could the child when she looks after me at night and works all day? I'm not much use to her Liz,' he said. 'My wretched job keeps me pretty well occupied! But Mary never gets a minute off.'

'That makes two in that case.'

'How d'you mean?' he enquired.

'There's Jane going to give a twenty firster for Philip and now you'll have yours.'

'I never heard about Philip's,' he protested. 'As a matter of fact I was to have had drinks yesterday at Jane's but she went off to Brighton with Penelope and Dick Abbot. Jane would have told me then only she never got the chance. Who's she having?'

'Oh all of us I believe John.'

'And some young people too I should hope,' he said. 'So dreadful dull with nothing but us older ones.'

'Speak for yourself,' she protested rather dryly.

'I was,' he assured her. 'In that case I think I shall wait until I see how Jane's comes off. I really can't afford a party, who can these days! Yes I'd rather wait and see. Of course Mary and I will be invited.'

'Did you think of giving a dance with champagne?'

'My dear girl where's the money to spring from? And you can't make out it's expected nowadays!'

'People do. Several get together still,' she explained.

'No that wouldn't go at all,' he decided. 'Only yesterday bless her I asked if there were even anyone Mary specially wanted and she wouldn't have it. No let's see what sort and kind of a show Jane puts on first.'

'And how's little Penelope?' she enquired.

'My dear Liz damn all that silly nonsense is what I insist. The child's just living till she can pick on something new to upset her, you mark my words.'

'I'd've thought it made everything so difficult with Jane.'

'Old Jane's all right,' he said. 'But my God you're lucky not to have children of your own yet Liz.'

'I wouldn't mind,' she muttered.

'Well I must say that's a weight off me now I haven't to give a do for Mary right off,' he announced, visibly taking heart. 'Yes you're lucky all right. Lord the things that keep coming up! No rest at all. Though I've not got anything against the child, please understand.'

'Mary's sweet,' she agreed in a perplexed voice.

He thought of something else.

'How did you come to hear of Jane's party?' he demanded.

'Philip told me.'

'I didn't know you ever saw him,' Mr Pomfret complained with lazy amazement.

'I had to go round to the office. As a matter of fact my business took me to his boss,' she boasted.

'So did you look in on Mary in M?'

'There wasn't time darling and I'm not sure she'd have been over-joyed.'

'Good God Liz what nonsense you can talk. Why Mary'd have loved it! Pity you didn't you know. She's managing marvellously well. No more than a junior in length of service of course but already she's established and doing damned important work too let me tell you. To tell the truth I once knew her chief. I'm always meaning to ring the woman one day to ask. But what holds me back is Mary's face if she got to hear. Oh she's independent Liz, and won't take any manner or means of help. And I respect her for it.'

'Philip was handing round the tea and buns,' Miss Jennings informed him. He burst into laughter.

'Well maybe my dear you did best not to explore further than Department C. You might have come on Mary with a mop and bucket between M and N. No, as for her it's not only what she tells me, which is little enough in all conscience, because I have other sources, I know what I'm talking about. But I'm not far wrong when I say Philip's an ungodly failure. What you told me just now doesn't come one bit as a surprise.'

'Is that really so? I had no idea,' Miss Jennings protested and seemed pleased.

'Don't breathe a word to anyone least of all to Jane,' he implored. 'He's not quite all she's got, there's still little Penelope practising to become St Francis, but it would kill poor Jane all the same. Oh now what made me say any of that! Liz I'm growing crabbed and ill natured in middle age.'

'You aren't,' she said.

'I jolly well am! Oh yes, worse luck! Never mind. Forget it.'

'Good heavens John you remember about nine weeks ago when we were discussing his mother and she promptly came in, well here's Mary with Philip.'

He twisted round in the chair.

'They can't afford this,' he said into the room in a loud voice. Then he saw. They were standing before Pascal, close together in an attitude of humility while the man sneered in their faces. It was plain they were not known.

'Excuse me Liz,' Mr Pomfret asked over a shoulder. He got up.

'Can't have that you understand,' he said and went across. 'Hello there,' he called. Pascal and Gaspard stepped back as he strode to kiss Mary. She seemed to shrink while Philip put on an embarrassed grin. Mr Pomfret shook him warmly by the hand. After some more talk which Miss Jennings watched with a tender smile, Pascal, obsequious again, at once led the young couple away to a good table. As they went John said something to his daughter who sent Liz a startled glance.

When he sat down once more John said, 'Well I only hope he pays.'

Miss Jennings replied, 'Why here she comes.'

Mr Pomfret rose to his feet. 'Fancy seeing you,' Mary greeted Miss Jennings shyly. Her wrist was loose when she took Miss Jennings' hand.

'Oh darling,' Liz cried, 'you look so sweet.'

'You both do look wonderful,' Mary mumbled. Another phrase or two and she made her escape. As he sat down again the father said with satisfaction,

'My girl's got manners. I rather pride myself on that as a matter of fact.'

'She's sweet,' Miss Jennings repeated. 'You didn't expect to see them here then?'

'Those two? My dear Liz I never interfere. But I certainly imagined she was lunching back home this afternoon. Not that she can't do just as she likes of course. I thought she said something about tea. I must have misheard. And I didn't know they ever met.'

There was a pause while he watched his daughter.

'Were you told about Arthur Morris?' she next enquired.

'No? Not more bad news, you can't surely mean? What is it?' he asked turning back to her.

'Now they're having to take the ankle off.'

This time neither laughed or even smiled.

'Good Lord,' he cried 'like so much else it's beginning to be a bad dream. Who's his doctor then? Can't they do anything for him?'

'Poor Arthur isn't it bad luck?' she said.

'Frightful,' he agreed. 'Now what are you proposing to have now? Cheese or sweet or both? Where is Gaspard? First they don't or won't recognize one's own children and then they can't bother to take an order. Here Pascal!' He waved.

'Only coffee for me darling. I must watch my figure.'

'Would you mind if I had just a bite of cheese? Look Pascal you won't give my daughter a table and then there's no one to get us on with Miss Jennings' luncheon! She'd simply like some white coffee and I'll have cheese and biscuits.'

The man hurried off. 'What were we saying?'

'About Arthur.'

'Why,' he protested, 'it's the most frightful thing I ever heard in all my life! Poor old fellow. No knowing where these things'll stop either. And the bill too if you don't mind, waiter. I am sorry to hear that,' he ended.

'It's when a man must wish he'd married,' Miss Jennings said reflectively. 'Having a leg off.'

'Never forget William Smith,' he objected.

'William Smith?' she echoed. 'I don't remember.'

'Perhaps he was a bit before your time. He got into a motor smash, lost both arms and Myra left him.'

'Was he married?'

'But I've just told you! Yes Myra went. And she got her decree on incompatibility of temperament.'

'Perhaps that had been going on a long time John.'

'It's very dangerous to lose a limb when you're married,' he announced. 'Two limbs are almost always fatal. So watch out.'

'Oh I wouldn't think much of a husband who left as soon as I happened to be maimed,' she cried.

'The thing is they do. And damn quick too! Without even a by your leave!'

'No John that's dreadful!'

He let out a great gay laugh.

'It's the way of the world,' he explained. 'Anyway lucky old Arthur isn't married is he?'

'No, but all the same!'

'Forget it I was only joking,' he said.

There was a pause while he fondly smiled and she seemed lost in thought.

'Will she ask me?' she enquired at last.

'Who darling?'

'Jane of course.'

'What to? I can't tell how you mean?' he objected.

'This party she's to give so you can make up your mind whether you'll have one after.'

'Naturally she will.'

'Why darling?' she wanted to know.

'She'd better,' he announced.

'I don't fancy Jane likes me,' Miss Jennings insinuated.

'Ask us without each other?' he protested. 'That would be un-heard of, dear.'

'Have the invitations gone out already John?'

'But most certainly not. Jane doesn't even realize she's giving a party yet, not before she and I have talked it over. And she can't if she won't ask you.'

'John you're being very sweet yet I wonder if Jane really likes me?'

'She loves you,' he roared.

'No, that's going too far,' she insisted. 'You spoil it!'

'You don't understand,' he said. 'She depends on you. She knows very well I wouldn't come if you weren't there and Jane relies on me.'

'And so what do you mean by that, darling?'

'Precisely the little I'm saying. Since her husband died she's never given anything without she had all her old men friends round her, she wouldn't dare.'

'You say she'll invite me only because of you.'

'That's so.'

'Well then it's not very nice is it?'

'Liz darling you're trying to trap me. She adores you.'

'Does she? I don't think I'll come then.'

'Look darling,' he said, 'with this frightful rain this is not one of those days we can take our customary Sunday walk.' He laughed. 'Come Liz,' he said, 'let's get back to bed.'

'Aren't you awful! Oh! I suppose so, all right,' she replied, getting up to go at once, giving a shy smile.

Miss Pomfret waved to her father as he left with Miss Jennings while Philip made as if to rise from his place. When he had settled down again he said,

'Have you heard about this party my mother's to give?'

'Oh Philip but when? And are you inviting me?'

'Of course.'

'How kind! Oh dear how nice.' She beamed upon him. 'When is it?'

'There'll be weeks of talk yet. While she makes up her mind how not to ask a single one of our relations. No at the moment it's to be for my friends, only she knows quite well I haven't any.'

'Surely that's nonsense Philip. What about the men you knew at school?'

'I've lost touch.'

'Well it wasn't so long ago after all?'

'They none of them work in London,' he said in a severe voice as though to discourage questions. 'I don't know where they are now. But she accuses me of behaving as apparently as I used to when she came down to my first school.'

'You'll have to tell me a little more if I'm to understand' Miss Pomfret gently said.

'She was always in the car,' he explained. 'When we passed any of the other chaps I used to duck right down just as if,' and here he copied his mother's emphatic speech ' "just as if they had guns, repeating rifles." '

'And did you?'

'Of course we every one of us did. You don't spend entire weeks with the creatures only to want to see them when you can get away for an hour or so. Besides there was too much chromium plate on the beastly thing. It was vulgar.'

'Oh no Philip.'

'Were you at school?'

'As a matter of fact I wasn't.'

'And I suppose at a girls' establishment you did anything you could to show off?'

'I expect they did,' she meekly replied.

'I used to see the girls out with their parents in hotels Mamma took me to tea,' he muttered. 'But the point, no, part of the point is that Mamma as she accused me of trying to duck every time we passed anyone, suited her action to the words or whatever the phrase may be and bumped her head down on the sofa she was sitting in to show me how I used to behave and smashed one of her eyebrows against a heavy glass ashtray she'd put beside herself.' He laughed.

'Did she hurt her forehead?' Miss Pomfret enquired warily.

'Just a bump,' he answered. 'Sometimes Mamma is rather wonderful.' He was smiling. 'She's so violent.'

'I think your mother's sweet now, Philip!'

'Well the fact is, when she hurt herself it set her off and I got the

41

whole thing again all over. How even at Eton I hadn't any friends, still never saw a soul these days, what was I doing with my life, all that sort of usual trouble. And lastly of course she wanted to know, would she have to have all over again the whole of this wretched experience that had made her so miserably unhappy with little Penelope when Pen grows up.'

'Oh but Philip you aren't really making your mother unhappy are you?'

'It's just the way she speaks you understand. Why, are you the joy of your father's life at the moment?'

She laughed. 'I really believe I am,' she replied. 'How is your kid sister anyway?'

'As well as can be expected. For the time being there's nothing on her mind of course. But even at Eton we didn't want to see each other either. It was torture going to the theatre the night before one went back, there were so many. They even sat right next.'

'You mean you simply couldn't bear to see them again now?'

'Oh no,' he protested. 'Of course it's quite different now. I just don't want to see any of 'em that's all.'

'Well then you needn't.'

'The only thing is,' he said in a rueful way, 'I'm supposed to have this party for my twenty firster.'

'But Philip,' she cried 'in that case you can't not invite your friends.'

'You know what it is with Mamma. The ones she does eventually ask will all come out of her set inevitably in the end. They won't be contemporaries of mine.'

'I could rake up a few girls,' she volunteered.

'I don't mean anything against her,' he said, seeming to ignore Mary's offer. 'I've known this happen before. And of course when Penelope's little time comes there'll be thousands of young men Mamma will have in, all that part of it is in my mother's blood. No, but where I am concerned, she's making an excuse to throw a party of her own. Apart from which one has to be sorry for parents. They had such a lot of money once and we've never seen what that was.'

'I think it's a shame,' she said rather mysteriously.

'If she wants to give her own "do" why shouldn't she? And my twenty firster provides the excuse because I know she can't afford two.'

'But you should have your friends in for your own twenty firster Philip.'

'You don't understand,' he said. 'If I told her that, she's incredibly generous and she'd lend me the flat for the evening and enough money to give another.'

'Then why don't you?'

'Because we can't afford it.'

'I believe you simply won't bother with a party of your own Philip.'

He laughed.

'Well,' she said, 'it's your life after all.'

'But I do wish she'd ask the relations,' he insisted.

'Who've you got specially in mind?' she demanded.

'Uncle Ned,' he replied then rather mysteriously paused.

'What's so thrilling about him?' she asked.

'I see you haven't got the idea,' he said. 'I imagine you either have the feeling or you don't. I just feel a thing for my family that's all. Oh we're nobodies, our names have never been in history or any of that rot, I simply'd like to see them and I don't ever seem to.'

'You can when you're married.'

'How d'you mean?'

'It was what you said the other day Philip about not liking to ring your relations to propose yourself to tea. Well once you marry a girl you'll be able to ask your uncle round as often as you please for him to get to know her.'

'That's quite an idea,' he agreed.

She watched him with an unfathomable expression.

'It's a bit stiff though to have to marry to meet one's uncle,' he protested at last.

'Nothing's easy,' she said. 'Oh nothing's ever easy,' she repeated. A pinched look came over her face. She pushed her empty plate away. 'You get fed up,' she muttered. 'Sick of it all!'

'Why whatever's the matter?'

'I don't know,' she said and looked as if about to cry.

'I say I'm most dreadfully sorry. Would you like to go outside or something.'

'Everything's so hopeless,' she announced in a low voice.

'Are you all right?' he asked.

She appeared to pull herself a little together.

'I don't seem to get anywhere with my life Philip,' she said not looking at him, eyes averted. 'I mean,' she went on and began to speak louder, with some assurance 'I mean now that the only jobs one can land, or the only ones within my reach, are State jobs, well I just can't move on, get promotion, arrive at the top where there's just the one person, you know. In the days there was more private industry one could change around but as I am, I'm no more than in a Grade which I drag about with me like a ball and chain if I apply for another Department.'

'You wouldn't want to go back to the bad old times Mary,' he gently remonstrated. 'Not when we're making this country a place fit to live in at last.'

'A ball and chain dragging at one all the time,' she echoed as if she had not heard him. 'And so it will be the whole of my life. I'll do a little bit better every year and get nowhere in the end.'

'Mary,' he cried, 'you're discouraged!'

'You're telling me?' she asked, showing signs of indignation.

'No but look at all the way we've come the past few years,' he protested.

'Oh yes,' she agreed in an uninterested voice.

'And we're not working for ourselves now,' he went on. 'At least not those of us who are worth anything, like you and me. Besides, if you'll forgive my being personal, you'll marry, have children.'

'Will I?' she said in a small voice.

'Of course you must,' he announced with what was almost impudent assurance.

'I don't think I shall Philip. But suppose I do, what will happen to them? Are they to work through a few Grades until they reach retiring age by which time I'll be dead?'

'There's your grandchildren,' he said not so confidently.

'How d'you know?' she demanded in a loud scornful tone then bit her lip.

There was a pause while he crumbled bread into pellets. He looked at her again. The face he saw seemed even younger, wore an expression of childish obstinacy.

'You were talking of my party,' he tried. 'Why don't you persuade your father to have one for you?'

'Oh Philip,' she protested and gave him a hard, angry look 'one dance doesn't alter everything for ever does it!'

'I know,' he said at last 'I get moments of utter discouragement too.'

'You do Philip?' Her voice was softer.

'Fifty two weeks in the year and we work fifty,' he muttered.

'And they say buy a new hat so you'll feel different,' she agreed.

'But we've got everything before us haven't we?' he moaned as if he were looking down into his own grave.

'Year in year out,' she assented.

'Sometimes it seems hopeless,' he said and in his turn took on an appearance of obstinacy younger even than his years. As she watched him she visibly brightened.

'Cheer up Philip,' she encouraged. 'Things may not be as bad for all that.'

'Here,' he demanded, obviously puzzled. 'I thought you were the one who saw no hope.'

'Oh come on,' she cried. 'Let's not sit here any more, glooming Sunday afternoon away! What about a film?'

'I'd love to if you would,' Mr Weatherby replied, back at his most formal, and in a short time they were off past the small round tables, with older people glancing up at them. As a couple they kept themselves to themselves under scrutiny, and would probably appear bright and efficient to their elders, quite a mirror to youth and the age they lived in.

They hardly spoke again that day, a kind of blissful silence lay between.

The following morning, on the Monday, Mary Pomfret rang up her office to say she was indisposed and took a train to Brighton. Philip did the same. Neither knew what the other had done and they did not see one another on the way down.

Mary went straight to Mrs Weatherby's hotel but Philip strode off in the opposite direction. Soon he came to a pewter sea on which a tramp steamer was pushing its black smoke out in front and he had to lean himself against wind and rain.

Miss Pomfret selected a chair in full view of the lift and not long afterwards when Mrs Weatherby descended she waved, went up to the gates to greet Jane. This lady seemed disconcerted.

'My dear,' she said 'am I supposed to recognize you?'

'Why how do you mean?'

'Are you alone Mary?'

Miss Pomfret laughed and appeared embarrassed.

'I think I must be,' she said. 'I don't see anyone else.'

'My dear you will forgive, you really must, but it was such a queer surprise. No, not so very long ago one never was sure whether to go up to a friend in this wretched uncomfortable place. You see there was no knowing if they wanted to be known. Absurd but there it is.'

'Well I did rather need to see you as a matter of fact.'

'You darling, then it's a visit,' Mrs Weatherby cried although she still seemed wary and once or twice looked over a shoulder. 'Come, where shall we choose for a cosy talk. But what a long way to travel,' and chattering as if delighted she led the girl to a corner from which she could not be observed by anyone passing through the main lounge.

'I was killing two birds with one stone I suppose actually,' Miss Pomfret explained with obvious discomfort. 'Oh no, such a rude way to put it! As a matter of fact there was something I simply had to ask. Something that came up the other day when I talked to Daddy.'

The older woman seemed to pay a great deal of attention to the exact positioning of the diamond clip in the V of her dress.

'You see he said something about my mother,' Mary went on. 'And you,' she added.

Mrs Weatherby sat up very straight.

'It's too wicked the wicked tongues there are,' she cried in great indignation and at once. 'I only hope my dear you won't ever have some such terrible experience you can look back on in your life and be sure that all your poor ills date right from it. Oh I went to my lawyer but he said let sleeping dogs lie, don't stir up mud, better not throw glass stones. I don't know if I did right, yet oh they should have been punished!'

'Please I didn't realize, I'm so sorry,' Miss Pomfret murmured. 'What can it have been?'

'I couldn't possibly tell,' Jane protested. 'I'd rather bite my own tongue off first. And so deceitful,' she wailed. 'People I'd known all my life, thought were my best friends!'

'By the way don't tell Philip I came,' Mary interposed at her most ill assured and nervous.

Mrs Weatherby at once assumed a mantle of tragic calm and decision.

'Then you know everything,' she proclaimed in a low voice.

The two women stared at each other in amazement. Suddenly Jane laughed. A good-natured smile spread across her face but there was still a trace of slyness about the eyes. Miss Pomfret looked small, frightened, and bewildered.

'Then what exactly did dear John say?' the elder asked with a casual tone of voice.

'Only that Mummy and you were great friends.'

'Darling Julia,' Mrs Weatherby assented. 'And you are so like her dear. Simply the living spit! I am very fond of John,' she added then waited rather out of breath.

'You see I've never had anyone tell me about Mummy,' the girl said with an appealing smile.

'But doesn't dear John?'

'Oh you know what Daddy is.'

'Yes I see. I see. What was it exactly you wanted to find out?'

'But everything, how she was like, everything.'

'Of course. Look my angel,' Mrs Weatherby beamed on Mary, 'I'm such a stupid, so you will forget all I said about idle tongues won't you? I thought,' she went on obviously at random, 'you'd heard something about that absurd houseparty. It was in Essex before you were born. But simply invented, every single word made up! I suppose people had much more time on their hands those days which made them so dangerous. Darling Julia!!' She sighed. 'Darling darling Julia and how she would have simply been overjoyed to be sitting looking at you here this instant minute!'

There was pause during which Jane gazed earnestly into Miss Pomfret's face.

'Did you go down to stay in Essex together then in those days?' the girl enquired at last.

'Never once,' Mrs Weatherby replied immediately. 'Put all that right out of your sweet mind. Now promise me. You see my dear you were a little sudden, weren't you, so lovely there by the lift! And I was just a tiny bit upset.'

'Why, is anything wrong?'

Jane gave the girl a shrewd look.

'These beastly servants,' she said. 'Half the time they don't know the dish they're serving. But how selfish of me! What was it you wanted about your dear mother?'

'I'm so ashamed,' Mary excused herself. 'Suddenly turning up like this of course you wouldn't understand at first.'

'But where did you learn how to find me? You are really clever and so sweet with it.'

'Philip said.' At this Mrs Weatherby started. 'Why that wasn't anything awful was it.'

'Awful?' Mrs Weatherby echoed, her response to this colder. At that moment Richard Abbot appeared for a minute on the way out behind his bags but Miss Pomfret had her back towards him. 'Awful?' Jane repeated. 'Good gracious me I should hope not. No it's just that little Penelope is ever such a little bit run down and I always think the wind down here is splendid don't you for all that sort of thing. No we've been like mice,' she added 'like mice, just breathing the air in. We simply haven't seen a soul.'

'She got upset didn't she playing at being married?'

Mrs Weatherby took this with great good humour.

'Well my dear,' she said 'I can at least tell who you got that from. Oh no I'm not blaming, Philip is so sweet with his sister only dear Mary I can speak out to you can't I, but sometimes he does rather overdo things don't you think, makes them to be more than they really are. It's true an old friend came to tea and Penelope dear darling was a wee bit upset after.' Mrs Weatherby paused, seemed to reflect. 'She's so sensitive and jealous. It was one of my dearest friends, we went to dances together, had all the same partners, I've known her for years. And you know how things are. Soon as you have children of your own you'll come upon this very same problem you sweet soul! When they're brought in after tea they expect undivided attention, the wonderful pets, and I suppose Pen thought she was being a trifle neglected.'

'Probably mine will be at my skirts all day long if I have any,' Miss Pomfret commented shyly. 'But did this friend know Mummy too?' she asked.

'We all loved Julia,' Mrs Weatherby answered. 'Why we loved her!'

'Did you know Daddy too then?'

'Of course you angel! It was almost a double wedding. We were never a moment out of each other's houses at one time. Your beloved mother was my dearest friend!'

'Who did you get to love first?'

There was a pause then Jane cried,

'Just listen to you. Isn't that sweet!' And Mrs Weatherby's extraordinary eyes did at this moment fill with tears. So she went on for twenty minutes about Julia's perfections following which, after hardly putting another question, Mary excused herself and left.

Once she was outside the girl hurried back to the station.

Mrs Weatherby had just set her face to rights when she looked up to find her son Philip standing there.

'Good Lord dear boy have you seen Mary?' she cried.

'I had lunch with her yesterday,' he said.

'No just now not an instant ago,' she insisted.

'My sweet Mamma she's in the office cutting out an article on English cherry blossom for the Japanese.'

'What are you down here for then?'

'Oh I thought I'd have a change. To tell the truth I'd something I rather wanted to ask.'

'And you came all the way down to Brighton just for that?'

'It wasn't anything I could mention over the phone. Look here you won't be annoyed will you but am I Father's son?'

Mrs Weatherby went deep red under the make-up.

'Are you what?' she demanded menacingly.

'All right Mamma forget this,' he said in haste.

'What has one done to deserve it?' she claimed in a low voice. She looked closely at his hangdog face. Then she again began to laugh. 'Oh God,' she said. 'Forgive me dearest but what a gowk you are! So you're in love with her isn't that the thing? Or is it more of this damned snobbery? Philip do take your hat off and sit down. You can't stand in a hotel lobby to ask questions like you just have of your very own mother your flesh and blood and remain covered!' He sat at her side. 'There,' she said 'that's better. Are you sure you feel quite all right? Are you contemplating marriage Philip?'

He mumbled no.

'Quite sure?' she asked. 'So this is the reason she wished to see me then,' she added.

'Who?'

'Mary.'

'No Mamma what can she have wanted? You say she's been here?'

'Why all the hurry though dear boy? Good God but you aren't now proposing to elope? With Mary? Oh my dear.' She peered at him with her marvellous soft eyes as though he might be ill. 'Please oh please don't do anything sudden darling, always such a mistake,' she said. She laid a white fat hand on his forearm to restrain him. 'If much happened I'd never be able to look poor John in the face after,' she appealed. 'Promise me! But you're wet,' she cried, 'you're soaked through.' She moved her hand to his forehead. 'It's burning!' she announced. 'That's how it is then, you're in a high fever, don't know what you're doing, oh dear and in a hotel too. Did you see little Penelope?'

'Who Mamma?'

'I'm so worried but this of course explains everything, you've a great temperature. No I've been fussed about the darling if you really want an answer to your stupid question. There are some people here who seemed perfect and I let her run out with their child, the two of them are just of an age. Now look my dear boy you must change at once and have a good hot bath. No arguments please. Oh you'll be the death of me with your pneumonia and your silly insane ideas! Here's the key to my room. Have a really hot bath and sit in my dressing-gown while I see the manager.'

'See the manager?' he echoed.

'To get your clothes dried of course,' she told him. 'You don't suppose I specially bring a change of suits for you when I come away for the weekend and haven't been told that you're to pay me a visit unannounced. If children only knew the worry and responsibility they are to parents.'

'But I'm all right,' he protested.

'You sit there and say that to my face after all you've just asked about me; no I don't want to worry you but you're seriously ill Philip or it would be better for you if you were! Perhaps though in spite of everything you're just insane.'

He sat apparently unmoved.

'I'm sorry, I do apologize,' he said.

'You'll forgive me but your whole generation's hopeless I must say it, so there!' Mrs Weatherby pronounced, still in the low tones she had used all along to voice her indignation. 'You're prudes, there's this and that can't be discussed before you and then you come out with some disgusting nonsense of which you should be thoroughly ashamed. I'm in despair that's all, I'm simply in despair!'

'I had to know,' he said.

'That's quite enough,' she cried. 'Now be off at once and have your bath or I shall be quite cross. No do go Philip or you'll catch your death.'

He went. She settled back like a great peacock after a dust bath, sighing.

*

When Miss Pomfret got back to London she rang Arthur Morris to ask if it would be convenient to call. She arranged to have tea with him at the nursing home.

'This is really nice of you Mary,' he said as she came in. 'Just what your mother would have done. Julia was the kindest woman in the world.'

Miss Pomfret seemed at her brightest.

'Was she? Did you know her well?' she asked, making the question into flattery.

'You see we were all in the one set, went about together, stayed great pals most of the time.'

'Most of the time?' she echoed with an artless expression.

'Well it must be so with your generation,' Mr Morris answered. 'We had our ups and downs. People fall out then come together again. Don't you find that?'

'Me? Oh I haven't any friends.'

'Haven't any friends, a pretty girl like you? Or is there something wrong?'

'Wrong with me!' she cried.

'So you see you've got hundreds of 'em,' he concluded.

'I haven't, honestly. I don't think we meet the number of different people you used to.'

'It may not be quite the same for girls of course but boys still go to Eton don't they?'

'I suppose,' she said. 'Did Mummy know many?'

'Etonians?'

'Don't be idiotic,' she demanded smiling. 'No, people of course.'

'Yes,' he said, 'a beautiful woman like that would have, wouldn't she?'

'And Mrs Weatherby and she got married at the same time?'

'They did,' he replied.

'D'you think Philip and I look like each other?' she asked.

'No I don't.'

'Who were her other friends?'

'Your mother? Well everyone of our lot. You've seen 'em about again and again whenever your father invites them in.'

'He's to give another party now,' she announced.

'Don't tell me that just when I'm stuck here like this!'

'But you'll be out soon?'

'Oh I expect so. When is it?'

'This is funny,' she said. 'You know how cautious Daddy can be. It seems Mrs Weatherby's planning one and he wants to see how hers goes before he commits himself.'

'I don't know why he need,' Mr Morris objected. He hitched himself back against the pillows as though the cradle under bedclothes over his leg were sucking his whole body towards the foot. 'They'll be the same old crowd in the end,' he added.

'And was that the case when Mummy was alive?'

'How d'you mean?'

'Well anyway who were her particular friends?'

'We've all kept together, those who're still alive of course. You've met every single one Mary.'

'Then why ask them to Philip's twenty firster?'

'Is that what Jane's doing?'

'It's what she will do,' the girl replied. 'Oh I've no call to say a word even. But don't you think it rather dim for Philip?'

'I don't know,' he said. 'Nothing's happened yet surely.'

'How d'you mean?'

'I'm still without an invitation and she would be bound to ask me.'

'Still you're in bed aren't you? Oh I am so sorry, how horribly rude! I am beastly.'

'You aren't,' he said. 'But of course she'd send an invite even if I couldn't come. We've all stuck together always.'

'It's not for me to say but don't you think at his twenty firster Philip ought to see more people of his own age?'

'Of course I don't know who is actually to be invited,' he replied. 'Do you mean John's going to ask only his cronies to your party?'

'Oh I've got no one, I don't meet a soul,' she answered. 'You knew Mummy. What would she have done?'

'The same as Jane I imagine.'

'She would have invited her.'

'Yes,' Mr Morris said doubtfully. 'Oh yes, at one time.'

'You see I was told Daddy and Mrs Weatherby had had a terrific affair once.'

Mr Morris seemed uncomfortable.

'Well I don't know about that,' he said. 'We had our ups and downs. One can't be sure of anything. But what would be wrong if they had?' he asked.

'Oh nothing,' she agreed too hastily. 'Nothing in the least. Surely I can be curious when I never knew Mummy,' she pouted, 'don't remember her at all.'

'Yes it certainly can't be easy for you,' he said.

'I've not known anything else and that's easy,' she objected.

Shortly afterwards she left, having learned no more from him.

Later, in time for a glass of sherry, Philip Weatherby sent his name up and was welcomed by Mr Morris.

'Mary's just been,' the older man said.

'I'm back from Brighton as a matter of fact and everyone seems to be asking me if I've come from Mary. I can't understand it.'

'You must be thinking of her all the time,' Mr Morris replied.

'How's that?'

'Did you never notice Philip? You see someone in the street you haven't met for years and the next fortnight you come across them again and again for a bit. You'd better look out, you're falling in love.'

'What's the connection?'

'Forget it I was only joking. There's none of course. Your mother's to give a party I hear.'

'Yes she is.'

'Your twenty firster?'

'No, just a small thing for her friends. I don't see much point in twenty firsters do you? Or bachelor dinner parties before you're married. All that tripe is out of date.'

'Oh I don't know Philip. How about silver weddings?'

'They're different,' the young man announced. 'They're family. There can be some point in those. But I wanted to ask something. D'you think Mr Pomfret's in love with my mother or her with him?'

'Is she feeding him?'

'What on earth are you getting at?'

'Does she ask him continually to meals? Not drinks, meals.'

'Well yes he does come pretty often.'

'It's an infallible sign with women Philip. Do you mind?'

'Me? Why should I? It's none of my business. But look here this is strictly private. Was he very much in love with Mamma once?'

'My dear chap I've no way of knowing.'

'He was supposed to be wasn't he? Didn't you tell me that?'

'That's not evidence,' Mr Morris objected.

'I mean did he ever actually have a child by her?'

Arthur Morris gave the young man a long look before he replied.

'Where is it now if he did?'

'How should I know?'

'Then all you've got is the evidence of your own senses Philip. I wouldn't worry if I were you.'

There was no resemblance physical or otherwise between Mr Weatherby and Mary. Shortly after, without another word on this subject, Philip made his excuses and left with ill grace.

Later that week Philip Weatherby and Mary Pomfret were sitting in the downstairs lounge of the same respectable public house off Knightsbridge.

'They all ought to be liquidated,' he said obviously in disgust.

'Who Philip?'

'Every one of our parents' generation.'

'But I love Daddy.'

'You can't.'

'I do, so now you know!'

'They're wicked darling,' he exclaimed. 'They've had two frightful wars they've done nothing about except fight in and they're rotten to the core.'

'Barring your relations I suppose?'

'Well Mamma's a woman. She's really not to blame. Nevertheless I do include her. Of course she couldn't manage much about the slaughter. And she can be marvellous at times. Oh I don't know though, I think I hate them every one.'

'But why on earth?'

'I feel they're against us.'

'You and me do you mean?'

'Well yes if you like. They're so beastly selfish they think of no one and nothing but themselves.'

'Are you upset about your twenty firster then?'

'Not really,' he answered. 'I wouldn't've had one in any case.'

'Then what is actually the matter?'

There was a long pause.

'It's because they're like rabbits about sex,' he said at last.

'But I don't know the habits of rabbits, do I, except they have delicious noses?'

'You're laughing at me.'

'I am a bit.'

'But you realize I'm right Mary darling.'

'No I don't,' she said. 'And I'm mad about Daddy.'

'Well then what d'you really think about my mother?'

'To me she's very clever and rather sweet, now at all events.'

'Even when she practically broke up your mother's home?'

'Oh no Philip you're not to go on this way about parents. If you continue like it you'll begin to have them on your mind and then there'll be rows and all sorts of unpleasantnesses.'

'But can you stand by and listen to this talk of theirs without putting in a word?'

'Mummy's dead, we'll never know the truth and it's you who're raking a whole lot up or so I think.'

'Oh I didn't have that idea at all,' he protested.

'Yet Philip it can only harm Mummy.'

'When she was the aggrieved party?' he demanded.

'Of course. You must be discreet you really must.'

'I'm sorry. It's natural the whole business should be beastly for you. Forgive me.' He sounded genuine and penitent. She smiled rather sadly.

'You're forgiven,' she said.

But it appeared he was unable to keep off the subject.

'I went to see Arthur Morris the other day,' he began again.

'So did I.'

'You did? Yes I think he said something. I've forgotten. But he made the oddest statement. That when a woman starts to get tired of a man she stops feeding him, having him in for real meals.'

'If that's so then I truly love Daddy because I what you call feed the dear one all the time.'

'We did discuss him as a matter of fact.'

'In what way?' she demanded with signs of irritation.

'As to whether Mamma was still fond of your father.'

'No Philip you shan't go on like this and you simply mustn't discuss Daddy with Mr Morris. I won't have it d'you hear? You're just raking the ashes and I tell you it's most frightfully suspect.'

'I know,' he hastened to explain. 'I see your point. But I can't sleep at night now, I'm getting in a regular state.'

'Oh darling what's the matter?' she asked nervously, and for the first occasion in the evening looked full at him.

'I hope you'll find this absurd, too ridiculous for words, but I've told you before, we might be half brother and sister.'

'So you want to make out whether I'm one of your precious relatives?' she asked with scorn.

'Well yes in a way. Yes I do.'

'Then I'm not!' she said in almost a loud voice. 'I've been making enquiries on my own and we're quite definitely not what you
say.'

'We aren't?' he cried and it was obvious that he was deeply excited. 'You're sure? Certain?'

'Yes Philip.'

'But how? Who can possibly tell?'

'Now I'm not going to have another word about that poor
wretched worry of yours ever again. And you're to promise me
before we leave here!'

'You swear it's true Mary?'

'I do' she said. She got out a handkerchief, blew her nose hard.
'Now will you promise?'

He showed signs of great nervousness.

'All right. Yes. I will,' he said.

She gave him a small smile.

'It's right, what I said. You can trust me,' she averred.

'But you went to find out on your own?' he demanded.

'Now you promised you know,' she reminded him.

'Yes,' he said.

There was a further pause.

'Have another drink?' he asked with enthusiasm at last. 'You
don't want to go on with those light ales. Try a short.'

'I think I'll stick to beer if you do feel like one more,' she replied,
smiling sadly at him. This time she did not offer to pay the round and
sighed as she looked at her face in her mirror while he went to fetch
their drinks.

'Have you heard about little Penelope?' he enquired when he
came back. He laughed in rather a wild manner.

'No.'

'She can't let go of her arm now.'

'What do you mean?'

'She will persist in hugging her own elbow Mary. Holds her left
arm in the right hand all day, even falls asleep like it at night.'

'And how does your mother accept that one?' Miss Pomfret demanded with the first sign of malice she had shown.

'Well I think she's wrong, she takes not the slightest notice

Mamma doesn't. But to my mind it might be really serious.'

'In what way?' the girl demanded in a bored voice.

'You see I got to the bottom,' he replied. 'Cheers,' he said, raising the glass to his lips. She let her drink stand on the table. 'I made Pen come out with it,' he went on. 'You've no idea the passion for secrecy they have at that age.'

'I was one once you know,' she reminded him.

'By now you must have forgotten,' he said. 'Well it seems she saw a war wounded man with a stump for an arm on the front at Brighton without his coat, escaping out of chains or something. So she thinks unless she keeps hold she'll lose hers.'

Miss Pomfret yawned.

'I've told Mamma but she won't catch on,' he continued. 'Mary what do you think?'

'I expect Penelope's doing this to attract attention. Girls usually like attention you know,' Miss Pomfret said.

'But if that's the case she'll go on indefinitely.'

'I suppose she may Philip.'

'That's a grim thought surely?'

'One day she'll marry and then her husband can take over,' Miss Pomfret drily suggested.

'Well you know what my mother is. I can't understand her ignoring this. Oh aren't one's parents and their friends extraordinary! Imagine what I overheard between Mamma and that old Abbot. He was going endlessly on about his war experiences out in Italy. She'd said how wonderful she found white oxen. I expect someone once said those great eyes of hers were so alike. As a matter of fact I distinctly admire her eyes don't you? But anyway he said he'd spent night after night out with them. That made Mamma scream all right. So he came back that a night in a stall with an ox was a damn sight better than out in the open alone under stars. Then she asked did they snore? Would you believe it? And there's worse coming. Because when he didn't reply Mamma said "Do they dream Richard?" Honestly I was nearly sick.'

'I know,' Miss Pomfret agreed. 'They can be frightful.'

Mrs Weatherby was giving Mary's father dinner.

'Oh my dear,' she said, 'when are we ever going to see the sun?' He sighed.

'Is there simply never to be Spring this year?' she insisted.

'The continual rain is too frightful,' Mr Pomfret agreed. 'Well Jane was your trip down to Brighton a success?'

'It helped Penelope and me so enormously John.'

'Did you see anyone?' he incuriously enquired.

'Richard Abbot came over for the day which was sweet of him wasn't it? Oh yes Philip was kind enough to look in.'

'And how's Pen?'

'Ah the gallant angel,' Jane cried. 'She's my one comfort apart from you. She loved Brighton. Just came back with a little thing, only that she has somehow to keep hold on her elbow, but I know a way to manage the little sweet. I'm going to buy her a bag, John, to carry. Now don't you think that a brilliant notion?'

'Well well,' he said, not to commit himself. 'And Philip?'

'Oh no, there I'm in despair,' she announced. 'Simply desperate.'

'Would you like me to talk to him?'

'Dear John I've changed my mind,' she said. 'I think I'd really rather not, that you didn't. It was poor Richard offered himself you remember and put it in my head. Of course I thought at once how much better you would be if you could. But the boy's been so disagreeable, John. Don't remind me of him please.'

'He hasn't been rude to you?'

'Oh no not quite. It's just I think he's insane. Better leave him strictly to his poor mad self. And you? How have you been?'

'As well as may be these hard times.'

'How true that is darling. But then Mary? What's her news?'

'I don't seem to see much of her Jane. One's offspring are a sacred farce.'

'John you don't think this extraordinary feeling they have for snobbery, some of them that is because I'm sure I've not noticed the tiniest trace, even, in Mary, can you suppose it would go oh I can't tell but to absurd lengths with them, even to refusing to marry outside the family.'

'What've you got in mind? The old continental requirement of sixteen quarterings in a husband?'

'No no my dear I wish I had,' she said. 'Or rather I think it quite out of date don't you and in any case I haven't any, that is I can't run to that extraordinary number. But of course in a small way it might simplify things.'

'How Jane?'

'Well naturally not with my Philip,' she explained in a laugh.

'He's got the idea now right enough. Yet I've warned him it might cut both ways, prevent his marrying someone he very much wanted. And again I don't mean Mary, I'm sure the dear child is much too sensible. But oh John I have warned Philip if not once then quite a thousand times. No but the whole picture has grown so enormous in his poor head I really believe he feels deep down inside him that he must, simply must find a wife so close that the marriage could almost turn out to be incestuous John.'

'Incestuous. So you're afraid he'll never start a family is that it?' Mr Pomfret did not appear to take the conversation seriously.

At this point Mrs Weatherby left her place to twitter in bad Italian down the dumb waiter shaft. She was answered by a sweet babble that was almost song.

'Ah these Southerners,' the lady remarked as she sat herself at table again. 'The other day Isabella came to me for half a crown. The last occasion she asked for money was only the whole return fare to go back to Italy to vote in the elections. So I naturally wanted to know what for this time and what d'you suppose she said, why simply to buy a mouse. "Get a mouse?" I said after I'd looked the word up in the dictionary. "Because Roberto" that's our cat "is so lonely" she answered. I screamed, I just yelled, wouldn't you? I can't bear cruelty to animals John dear. But she's so persistent and in the end of course she got her own way! Naturally I kept out of the house for a few days after that and forbade sweet Penelope the kitchen or I said I'd simply never speak to the child again. And then I forgot. Isn't it dreadful the way one does? I went down there for something or other and Isabella showed me. They were both drinking milk out of the same saucer, Roberto and his mouse. John is it sorcery, spell-binding or something?'

He laughed. 'No I'd heard of that before dear Jane.'

'You truly had? Sometimes, lying in my lonely lonely bed at night I wonder if I just imagine I'm alive and all these queer things are true. Because I don't like to say it but Philip is simply very odd. He asks me the most extraordinary questions John.'

'Does he now?'

'Oh I don't want to go into things,' she said in haste. 'Were we like that once dear?' she asked. Then 'are we never to be served?' she demanded with hardly a pause and in the same voice. At which she called from the table an unintelligible phrase in which she displayed great confidence to be answered by an understanding, distant shout.

'Mary's been displaying quite an interest lately,' he suggested.

'Has she? No you know you have really something there in that girl,' she said. 'Mary's such a sweet child.'

'Thank you Jane,' he replied. 'Yes,' he went on, 'she seems quite taken up with the past for the present, no pun intended.'

'What past?'

'Ours of course,' he answered. 'What other could she wish to learn at eighteen? She wants to know the who's who of all our friends and to find out even if you and I didn't see a deal of each other at one time.'

'Well I don't know if I'd care . . .' Mrs Weatherby murmured.

'And you don't imagine I'd blurt I don't know what out to me own daughter?' Mr Pomfret demanded. 'No what's over is over.'

'Maybe for you perhaps,' she responded. 'Oh how must it be to be a man?'

'Trousers my dear are very uncomfortable. I wish I wore skirts. No honestly since my tailor lost his cutter to a bomb in the war I haven't been able to sit down to meals in comfort, it's frightful.'

'Would you like to go out for a minute then since we never seem to be going to get anything to eat?'

'What and leave you on your own darling?' he cried. 'At the mercy of a foreign language you hardly understand?'

'I speak Italian quite nicely now thank you,' she smiled. 'And do you know, I've never had a single lesson.'

'Don't don't,' he wailed. 'When I think of the daily woman who changes every two months and who what she calls cooks for us.'

'My poor John you should have someone to look after you,' Mrs Weatherby said obviously delighted.

'Oh Mary's very good,' he said at once. 'It's not her fault you know.'

'I do realize, who could understand better than me?' she exclaimed. 'If I hadn't always been so quick with languages I'd be in the same boat,' she cried. 'But it's not the children's fault, John. We could travel, try our accents out and they still can't.'

'Mary's very good,' he said 'only she won't get me jugged hare.'

'Jugged hare?' Mrs Weatherby echoed in plain desperation. 'Jugged hare! Oh my dear does that mean you are very difficult about it? Because that's precisely what I'm giving you this evening.'

Her lovely eyes filled with tears. He got to his feet, went round to the back of her and kissed a firm cheek while she held her face up to him.

'My perfect woman,' he said.

'But should I have remembered?'

'You have,' he answered sitting down again. 'My favourite dish.'

'That's just it John oh dear,' she cried. 'You're an expert, you've tried jugged hare in all your clubs and now here's poor me offering it to you cooked by a Neapolitan who probably thinks the jugged part comes out of a jar in spite of all I poured out to her about port wine! And I tried to teach her so hard darling. There's still time to change though. Would you like some eggs instead?'

'But I told you,' he replied eyes gleaming 'you've picked my favourite. Jane this is a red letter evening.'

'I only hope it will be,' she said at her most dry. 'We're still at the stage of just having had the soup. Some more wine John?' and she passed the bottle then went to shout down the shaft.

'*Io furiosa*' she yelled '*Isabella!*'

A long wail in Italian was the answer.

'No don't darling, I can smell it at last,' Mr Pomfret laughed. 'And it is going to be delicious.'

At the same great hotel in which they held their Sunday luncheons Mrs Weatherby reserved a private room to entertain old friends in honour of Philip's twenty firster.

Standing prepared, empty, curtained, shuttered, tall mirrors facing across laid tables crowned by napkins, with space rocketing transparence from one glass silvered surface to the other, supporting walls covered in olive coloured silk, chandeliers repeated to a thousand thousand profiles to be lost in olive grey depths as quiet as this room's untenanted attention, but a scene made warm with mass upon mass of daffodils banked up against mirrors, or mounded once on each of the round white tables and laid in a flat frieze about their edges, – here then time stood still for Jane, even in wine bottles over to one side holding the single movement, and that unseen of bubbles rising just as the air, similarly trapped even if conditioned, watched unseen across itself in a superb but not indifferent pause of mirrors.

Into this waiting shivered one small seen movement that seemed to snap the room apart, a door handle turning.

Then with a cry unheard, sung now, unuttered then by hinges and which fled back to creation in those limitless centuries of staring glass, with a shriek only of silent motion the portals came ajar with as it were an unoperated clash of cymbal to usher Mrs Weatherby in, her fine head made tiny by the intrusion perhaps because she was alone, but upon which, as upon a rising swell of violas untouched by bows strung from none other than the names of unicorns that quiet wait was ended, the room could gather itself up at last.

As after a pause of amazement she stepped through, murmuring over a shoulder *'oh my darlings'* the picture she made there, and it was a painting, was echoed a thousand thousand times; strapless shoulders out of a full grey dress that was flounced and soft but from which her shoulders rose still softer up to eyes over which, and the high forehead, dark wings of her hair were folded rather as a raven may claim for itself the evening air, the chimes, the quiet flight back home to rest.

'How good of Gaspard,' Jane said with an awed voice. At which Philip and Mary entered in their turn. The boy switched on more light.

'No don't,' Mrs Weatherby reproved in the same low tones. 'You'll spoil it all,' she said.

'But it's lovely,' Miss Pomfret murmured.

Pascal sidled through the door which he closed, then turned the lights down again until the room held its original illumination, and there was now the difference made by this intrusion of bare arms and women's shoulders. Mary studied hers in a mirror she had reached. Dressed in black with no jewellery the similar milk white of her face and chest was thinner, watered down beside Mrs Weatherby's full cream of flesh which seemed to retain a satisfied glow of the well fed against Mary's youth starvation. But there was this about the whites of Miss Mary Pomfret's eyes, they were a blue beyond any previously blessed upon humanity by Providence compared with the other ladies present, and it was perhaps to these sweet rounds of early nights that her own attention turned because Jane's were red veined as leaves.

'Is Madame satisfied?' Pascal asked, almost one old friend to another, his false restaurant accent forgotten at this minute.

'Monsieur Medrano you are truly wonderful,' the lady said.

'When I had to sell my precious brooch to give the evening I didn't know – how could I tell . . .' she faltered, and he could see her eyes fill with tears.

'We have done my best for Madame,' the great man answered. 'Madame is more beautiful than ever,' he proudly announced. 'I say to Gaspard, "Gaspard" I said "let all be as never before my friend because you know who will be taking our Parma rooms tonight." '

'No don't – you mustn't – I shall really cry in a moment,' Mrs Weatherby exclaimed from the heart. 'But it is perfect!'

'Jolly good,' her son brought out.

'Ah Philip please not, I'm sorry to be so rude, you see you'll ruin this perfect thing! There do just be content to be an angel and simply place the cards.'

Pascal made small adjustments to napkins folded into linen crowns.

'You did tell the chef about our *soufflé*?' Mrs Weatherby asked eventually.

When the great man replied he used the restauranteur's manner.

'He said it over to me by heart, by heart I made him repeat, Madame. And we have a small favour to ask Madame. We will order orchids for the ladies, gardenias for the gentlemen if you please?'

'But Pascal good Heavens my bill!'

'The management they come to me,' he proclaimed 'they say "it is not often we have with us Mrs Weatherby Medrano". They remember Madame. No no Madame if you will allow us it is on the 'otel,' he said.

'It's too much, children have you heard? Pascal you must thank Mr Poinsetta very specially from me. No I will come tomorrow myself!' She fingered daffodils here and there on the top table, not to disarrange these but almost as though to reassure herself that all were true, to prove to her own satisfaction that she was not bewitched.

'I shall be at call,' Pascal said and sidled out. Mrs Weatherby followed him with her eyes. When the door was quite shut she turned the glance on Mary who was still examining herself in a glass. The older woman stared.

'My dear you look sweet,' she gravely said.

'Doesn't she,' Philip answered from his task.

'Do I?' the girl said and turned to him.

Mrs Weatherby frowned.

'Wonderful,' she echoed. 'And isn't it good of you to come so soon to help. I always feel nervous, distracted before a party I'm giving. And now this divine place has truly done us proud! Philip I wonder if you realize there aren't many women in London they'd put themselves out for in this heavenly way.'

Her son looked up, the seating list in one hand. 'You're telling me,' he said. 'Look Mamma you've a card here,' he waved it, 'and there's no mention of him on my plan. Mr William Smith.'

'Nonsense my dear, poor William's dead these ages past.'

'Well there's his card.'

'Give it here Philip. That must be an old one. Why it's all yellow. How odd and sad,' she tore the thing up into very small bits. She looked about for an ashtray. 'How dreadful,' she murmured. 'Philip you didn't do this to me?'

'Never heard of the man,' he replied with what was obviously truth.

'Mary my dear I wonder if I might bother you,' Mrs Weatherby suggested brightly. 'Such a shame to leave these pieces when everything's fresh! Of course there is behind my daffodils in the fireplace but I rather think not don't you, I never like to look the other side of anything in hotels. Could you be sweet and put them right outside?'

Mary received those pieces, was reaching for the handle, when the door opened and her father's head appeared.

'Well here we are,' he cried at his most jovial. 'Hello my love,' he said to his daughter as she passed him. 'Jane my dear, me dear,' he boomed then strode towards her.

She offered him a cheek. While he kissed she pushed hers just the once sharply back at him. She did the same when he kissed the other side.

'Dear darling John how kind,' she cried. 'D'you think I did right? I said I wouldn't have Eduardo to announce the guests. After all we do all know each other don't we?'

'As long as they find the way dear. I notice Mary has. Until I found her note at home I distinctly thought we were to come on to this together.'

'It's been such true kindness in her to arrive early and help,' Mrs Weatherby insisted. 'No the cloakroom people will tell stragglers where we are. And then I shall send Philip out to round them up. But haven't they done me proud darling?'

'Why but you're the only person out of all London tonight Jane! Even at this sad hotel they realize that.'

'You're such a comfort indeed! Philip have you finished with those cards?' At which Mary Pomfret ushered Richard Abbot through the door. 'Oh Dick!' their hostess cried.

'I say I say,' he said as he advanced and kissed both her cheeks in turn while she pushed sharply twice back, at him. 'Well look at you,' he exclaimed gazing fondly on her. 'Wonderful eh?' he demanded and ended with a 'Simply astounding!'

'But which?' she demanded radiant. 'The room or me?'

'God bless my soul, both. No, here, what am I saying? Dear Jane,' he said, 'could there be a choice? I mean with you standing there! Hello John. Seems we're a bit early aren't we you and I?'

'Darling Richard,' she murmured. 'Oh I'm so lucky!'

Then another male guest entered. Mrs Wetherby greeted him with warmth but gave the man no more than the one cheek which she held immovable and firm under great mischievous eyes.

The party had begun.

Half the guests had put in an appearance before Miss Jennings presented herself looking sadly pretty and also, on closer inspection, quite considerably upset.

As Liz made her way to greet the hostess through a small crowd of company drinking cocktails John Pomfret came forward, as if breasting the calls with which Miss Jennings greeted so many friends in order to give her special welcome. She did not pause but hissed,

'Oh my dear where have you been? I phoned you all day,' and then found herself before Mrs Weatherby, to burst into exclamations, to praise, to receive praises until she had her chance alone for a moment with Jane.

'Darling d'you know what that beastly Maud Winder's said? That I was tipsy at Eddie's dance.'

'But I've never heard anything so frightful in my life,' this lady cried albeit in a careful, restrained voice. 'Oh my dear how criminal of Maud!'

'Isn't it? I think I could hate that woman Jane. Have you invited her tonight?'

'If I'd only been told,' Mrs Weatherby exclaimed with caution. 'What can I say? But Eddie's here and he won't move without her,' as another I could mention without someone else, her wary eye expressed unheard to be taken up silently again and again in tall mirrors.

'Then you could ask him if she told the truth. No Jane I do so wish you would,' Miss Jennings implored with open signs of agitation.

'As though I should even dream of such a thing! Liz your worst enemy, not that you have one in the whole wide world darling would never conceive of anything horrible like that.' Upon which, well out of sight down along a plump firm thigh Mrs Weatherby crossed two fingers.

'But isn't it terrible . . .?' Liz began and had to stand back for a newly arrived couple who came up to go through the shrill ritual of delighted cries at Jane's appearance, at their own reaction to the flattery she repaid with interest, and at the blossoming, the to them so they said incredible conjuring up out of these perfect flowers, of a spring lost once more for yet another year to the sad denizens of London in rain fog mist and cold. When these two had drifted off Miss Jennings was able to start afresh.

'As if I ever did drink, really drink I mean. Oh my dear and I was so looking forward to this heavenly evening!'

'You must put it quite out of your sweet head,' Mrs Weatherby proclaimed with emphasis while she smiled and nodded when she caught a guest's already perhaps rather over bright eye. 'I shall speak to Maud myself. This is too bad.'

'I'm not at her table oh do say not!'

'I wouldn't dream of such a thing you're with us John and me of course,' upon which Miss Jennings with a hint of timidity in her bearing as if she'd just heard yet another insinuation against her security had once more to step back while a second couple paid respect. Then when these two had done with Jane they descended for an endless minute on Miss Jennings until at last they picked their way off towards the drinks.

'My dear can't I get Philip to fetch you just a little one?' Mrs Weatherby asked.

'And leave Maud Winder draw her own conclusions?' the younger woman wailed. 'Because if you had sat us down a place away from each other then I really believe I'd have had to beg you to change round the cards.'

Jane put on a stern look.

'Liz darling you can take these things too far,' she begged. 'Oh what haven't I suffered myself in my time from idle tongues! Why only the other day my own child came to me with some extra-ordinary tale that I'm sure I'd never heard ever but about me of course. Sometimes I think stories of that kind hang about like nasty smells in old cupboards and I'm sure are just as hard to get rid of. Forget all about it, I know I have. The mere suggestion with some-one like you darling is too ridiculous for words. And I always say when I see a man drink cider at meals that means he can't trust himself.'

'Maybe I will have a weak one then.'

'Philip,' Mrs Weatherby waved. 'Philip! Martini or sherry?'

'Oh perhaps a sherry please.'

'My dear boy Miss Jennings has nothing to drink! You must keep moving around you know. Liz would like a sherry and I think I'll try one of those martinis. Oh dear I'll be drunk as a fish wife if I do, but hang it's what I say, might as well be hung for a lamb or whatever the silly phrase is Liz don't you agree, you must!'

'But for one to be said one is when you aren't!'

'Now you promised Liz darling!'

'When I haven't ever in my life,' the young woman persisted.

'Darling,' Mrs Weatherby warned with a hint of impatience.

'Oh I know I'm a bore,' Miss Jennings cried. 'How dreadful and you must please forgive! You see . . .' but yet another pair of new arrivals were making their way and as Jane advanced to meet these she gave Liz one of those long looks of love and expiation for which she was justly famous.

Miss Jennings went after John Pomfret.

'Where have you been all day?' she demanded when she had cor-nered him apart.

'This endless work work work,' he answered.

'Not in your own office, that I do know,' she cried.

'Precisely,' he said. 'Time was one could sit in one's room, do all which had to be done in comparative comfort. But no longer, not now any more!'

'And I did want you so! Must it always be like this?'

'How d'you mean? Liz is something the matter?'

'Just that beastly Maud Winder. She only said I was tight at Eddie's!'

'If she did then she's half seas over now herself!'

'Can the awful woman be here? I don't see her. No John don't be so absurd.'

'But there,' he said of a Mrs Winder who seemed dead sober in quiet conversation with her back to a mirror. 'Tight as a coote.'

'Well talk of the devil,' Miss Jennings exclaimed. 'Really I feel that if it weren't for Jane I ought to go up and slap that silly face. Do you honestly think she's drunk?'

'If she isn't quite now, she has been,' he replied. 'Something must have gone very wrong with her end of Eddie's party which brought her to repeat what she did, if in fact she did.'

'Oh Arthur Morris told me.'

'What a shame old Arthur can't be here.'

'Yes,' she said. 'And a terrible story to insinuate against a girl!'

'Look Liz,' he implored, 'forget the whole of this.'

'You're asking me dear?' she demanded.

'Because I was with you Liz and you were sober as a judge.'

'But that only makes everything all the worse.'

'Naturally it does,' he cheerfully agreed. 'And so now then?'

'Do you truly love me?' she enquired.

'Of course I do.'

'Are you sure?'

'Liz darling!'

'Well perhaps I'll just find myself able to last out,' she said. 'As long as the wretched woman doesn't dare speak to me that is. I could claw her heart right away from her flat chest.'

'Well Liz a wonderful show of Jane's by God eh?' a voice announced behind and she turned to find Richard Abbot. 'Marvellous manager,' he went on. 'Can't imagine how she gets such details organized these days. Upon my soul it's perfectly miraculous!'

'I know Richard,' Miss Jennings replied with an animated look. 'And to see all one's nearest and dearest gathered in one room why it's unique! I do admire Jane so, she's a positive genius.'

'Tell you what,' Mr Abbot propounded. 'A thousand pities poor old Arthur can't be present.'

'I've a wire from him in my pocket this moment wishing us all the best of good times,' John Pomfret said. 'They handed it me outside.'

'Has he telegraphed to Jane I wonder?' Liz thought aloud. 'She would like it because this is her party after all.'

'Oh the wire's for her all right. She doesn't know yet.'

'Then let me take the thing along old boy,' Mr Abbot asked in a proprietary voice. 'Might buck her up a bit. Sure to be feeling a trifle nervous before the curtain rises so to speak.'

'Why certainly,' John responded reaching into his "tails". 'I could have done that myself,' he said with a trace of irony. He handed the envelope over.

'But I say,' Richard Abbot expostulated. 'It's been opened.'

'I told you what was inside didn't I old man?'

'I mean how am I to explain to her?'

'Just tell her it was me Richard.'

'You opened a telegram addressed to Jane?' Miss Jennings demanded.

'I thought there might be a bit of bad news which could keep until the party was over,' he told her in an almost insolent manner.

'Well you can keep the damn thing, break your own good tidings,' Mr Abbot exploded without raising his voice and handed the envelope back. 'Yes by God,' he said then left them.

'He seemed quite upset,' Mr Pomfret remarked.

'I'm not sure I quite like you in this mood,' she warned.

'Oh come off your high horse Liz,' he laughed. 'You know I simply can't stand the fellow, pompous ass that the man is.'

When dinner was well under way, with servants hurrying about the round tables, John Pomfret Liz Richard Abbot and our hostess alone at theirs, the laughing and conversation everywhere at a great pitch, so Jane delighting with all her soul broke out with the following comment on what they themselves had chanced in their own chatter,

'Oh, isn't all this delicious my dears and doesn't it seem only the other day that we were deep in the topic of sex instruction for each other's children and here we are now in an argument about whether they ought to live out in rooms for freedom.'

'Bachelors shouldn't speak up I expect, but part of the idea was the young people might get used to living on what they earn surely?' Mr Abbot genially enquired.

'Darling Richard so unromantic,' Mrs Weatherby crowed. 'Don't you remember John years ago you got in such a state and I was to make a gramophome record for your Mary, oh wouldn't she have hated it, while in return you were to do one for Philip. Then we thought we'd advertise and have a truly immense sale to the public.'

'And I took you to the place in Oxford Street when soon as we got inside a glass box we were tongue tied,' John added.

They all laughed.

'Then what did you do?' Liz demanded.

'Why nothing of course,' Mr Pomfret cried. 'That is the whole beauty of us, we never can seem to do anything.'

Jane dabbed at her eyes.

'What could a woman say to a schoolboy without making him feel such a perfect fool?' she demanded ecstatically. 'But I worried like mad then didn't I John?'

'Bet you couldn't have,' Mr Abbot said adoring.

'Oh yes I did,' Jane assured him. 'Tell me darlings isn't this being such a huge success? Don't you think it was a rather marvellous idea of mine to have them all at tables for four? As long as we insist on a general post with the coffee. You two men must start that ball rolling. Why I can hardly hear myself speak they make so terrific a racket!'

'The greatest fun Jane,' Mr Pomfret assured here. Indeed it would have been difficult for any such party to go better.

'Well I was never told a thing,' Liz said.

'Why you're to stay here of course. I don't intend us to move.'

'I meant about sex Jane.'

'No more was I,' this lady wailed.

'And I've a flat of my own which I can promise hasn't made all that difference.'

'My dear you are between the two generations you fortunate angel! It's these children I'm so worried over. Now John you started the argument. What d'you say to Liz?'

'If our children were all like her we'd not need to discuss anything,' he laughed. 'What's your opinion Richard?' he asked a bit hastily.

'Younger generation's all right I suppose,' Mr Abbot temporized.

'But the sweet ones simply aren't,' Mrs Weatherby beamed at him. 'You know my dear you've been a weeny shade selfish all your life not having children. Though I do love you for it.'

'Know nothing about 'em,' he said.

'Yet you should, a great goodlooking man like you! It's unfair.'

'When I said that, Jane, I didn't infer every parent I'm acquainted with doesn't come to me for advice,' he riposted.

'Good for you Richard,' Mr Pomfret cried. 'You had us there.'

The champagne they were drinking was plentiful.

'And me too,' Liz claimed, as if she would not be left out.

'In that case I expect my dears you two know far more than any of us, mothers and fathers that we are,' Mrs Weatherby laughed. 'We're so ashamed we don't dare ask except, though I say who shouldn't, at some heavenly party like this.'

'Oh no Jane,' Mr Pomfret objected. 'You go too far. Mary's always been sweet. I'm ashamed of myself where she's concerned.'

'But you know very well what I didn't mean darling,' Mrs Weatherby cried. 'Good heavens I simply never mean anything yet all my life I've got into such frightful trouble with my tongue.'

'Certainly going like a house on fire,' Mr Abbot said as he looked around the room.

'Oh aren't I fortunate to have such divine friends,' Jane cried. 'Still, all joking apart my Philip really should take the plunge and launch off into a flat of his own.'

'Can he afford it?' Miss Jennings wanted to be told.

'Gracious me I only meant a little room somewhere. The poor sweet mustn't be expected to fly before he's able to walk should he? Darling Maud Winder who can be so naughty sometimes, her girl is on her own. They all do it now and it might have been everything for us if we had been allowed couldn't that be so John?'

Mrs Weatherby found Richard Abbot gazing at her with a pleading expression.

'What I'm trying to say,' she went on, 'simply is if Philip won't ask girls to the house then he should go somewhere they can just force themselves upon him.'

'And if one fine day you found a mother ringing your door bell whose daughter he'd got in the family way?' Mr Abbot asked.

'Oh my dear don't! But how barbarous of you Richard! Wouldn't that be just the end! Yet I hardly think Philip could. Oh what have I said? I don't mean what's just slipped out at all. I'm sure he's perfectly normal. It's his principles you see. He's too high principled to live!' Mrs Weatherby turned a shy look on John Pomfret. 'What d'you feel dear?' she suggested.

'Well things are different with girls I suppose,' he said. 'I think females ought to share with another woman friend.'

'So does Maud's Elaine.'

'I know Jane,' Liz interrupted 'but how does that alter matters? She's no more than exchanging her mother for a girl her own age.'

'The friend needn't always be in,' Mrs Weatherby said with a look of unease and distress.

'Nor need a father or mother dear.'

'Yes Liz how perfectly right you are as always. But I'm convinced they could arrange for one or the other to be out sometimes! Think of the horrid awkwardness of fixing that up with a parent!!'

'It's worse when the parent has to implore his child not to be home at certain hours,' John Pomfret said, a remark which was received in silence.

'Awkward lives you family people do seem to lead,' Mr Abbot propounded. They all roared their laughter.

'How perfectly wicked of you Dick,' Mrs Weatherby approved.

Pomfret said 'My trouble is I never seem to hear of any girl who wants to share a room or two, do you?'

'Ought I d'you think?' Liz demanded.

'My dear,' Mr Pomfret hastened to assure her, 'I didn't – I mean I wasn't fishing to get Mary in your flat.'

'That just didn't enter my head. What I meant John was, should I still continue to live alone? D'you believe that does make people talk even nowadays?'

'How about me?' Abbot enquired heavily. 'Can my reputation stand it?'

'Now Richard,' Mrs Weatherby remonstrated with some firmness. 'Humour is not your long suit you know. I don't think what you're pretending a bit funny my dear.'

'I can't see why everything should be different for men,' Miss Jennings objected.

'Because they're expected to have women in and I imagine in all my innocence we're not supposed to have men,' Jane said.

'I know that of course,' Liz replied emptying her glass. 'But I still don't see the big blot. If there's no more to it than low gossip then, while dreadful enough of course, should one change one's whole life round just for that?'

'I'd have thought there was a question of children,' Mr Abbot explained. 'Women having babies eh?'

'Richard,' Mrs Weatherby cried in great good humour but in a stern voice. 'Do please don't become coarse! Men can have children too can't they?'

'Dreadfully sorry and all that but girls do saddle themselves with the little things, have done since the start of time.'

'Not Mary though,' Jane said.

'No Richard's perfectly right,' John assured them. 'The danger must be greater as you yourself admitted when you confessed you'd not care to have an outraged mother at your bell, the heavy expectant daughter at her heels. After all Liz you can look after yourself.'

'Can I?' she interjected and was ignored.

'No what we were discussing,' Mr Pomfret went on 'was how to gently ease the fledglings from the downy nest. They have to learn to fly some time. I know Mary will be all right but Jane doesn't want Philip a runner.'

'Darling my boy's not won a race in his life.'

'Wounded bird, broken wing Jane,' Mr Abbot explained.

The young people for Philip's twenty firster consisted of Philip Weatherby Mary Pomfret Elaine Winder and the youth she had brought with her, Derek Wolfram. These four made up one of the round tables.

Elaine had drawn attention to Miss Jennings to ask if her name was what it was. On being assured this could be so, she enquired whether Liz was a particular friend of any present; Philip looked at Mary, had no sign, kept silent, and Miss Winder then continued,

'Well my children,' she said 'the way some women do go on! I saw this with my own sore eyes. Mummy had taken me to a certain party. We brought along a bottle of champagne as a matter of fact which turned out to be a bit of a swindle because no one else had, in fact a woman old enough to be my grandmother just took one of vermouth. There's nothing cheaper surely, I mean you have to pay more for orangeade don't you? Anyway there was this person, Miss Jennings, right next me on a sofa where I'd managed to tuck myself in because there was not a soul for me about, it was one of these so called literary do's, God no! I was listening to a conversation she was having with a type who'd sat himself down between, no friend of mine good Lord, I wouldn't have touched him with a barge pole but anyway there he was and he seemed to know her and that was that when suddenly I heard him say, "can't I get you another drink" and she mumbled something although I didn't take particular notice at the time if you know what I mean. But to cut a long story short,' Miss Winder ended tamely, perhaps rather daunted by the degree the others were paying attention which possibly she was not always accustomed to receive, Miss Elaine Winder said 'well anyway the lady was sozzled and Mummy who was in the doorway, saw her trip over the rug later and be carried off. Properly – no I don't know it may have been rucked up and she'd caught her toe, I can't tell, wish you'd been there Derek, Lord I had a lousy time. I say are we going to dance after?'

These round tables were large enough to allow one couple to talk without the other hearing what passed.

Maybe it was on account of the champagne or possibly because Jane and John seemed to be rather wrapped up in one another but Dick Abbot said to Liz,

'I say you know but you look perfectly ravishing tonight.'

'I do?'

'You certainly are.'

'Well thanks very much Richard,' she responded.

'Makes me feel so embarrassed talking about the younger generation in front of you,' he continued. 'Lord you're a part of 'em yet we go on as if you weren't there. Can't think what you must make of us.'

'You're such a friendly person,' Miss Jennings announced. 'Richard I feel so at home with you!'

'You do? I'm honoured Liz. Nicest thing one can be told, that. But of course I haven't the airs and graces.'

'I don't know what you mean by it! When I find a person's cosy that's all I ask. Because what are we here for? Life's not so wonderful surely that we can afford to miss any single chance – not to help the lame dog over a stile, I don't mean, it seems so disobliging to draw attention in that way somehow, I mean about being lame, as practically no one is except poor Arthur Morris; now where was I – oh yes what I'm trying to explain is we've each one of us simply got to stay careful for each other don't you feel or we're absolutely nothing, I mean lower than the lowest worm that crawls?'

'Always say must respect the next man or Richard you've had it.'

'But I can't get the extraordinary phrase you used about your not having the social graces whatever that may add up to although I believe I understand quite well because of course real politeness which is only fellow feeling, isn't it, is no more than that; all I'm trying to say, you see, is if a person's cosy it's perfection, true manners, what distinguishes us from animals.'

'Jolly though when a cat curls up on one's knee.'

'Yes and then they go spitting in each other's faces soon as the moon is up and they've found a brick wall. Oh one can't trust them

Richard, that is what's so awful but you've only to look into their eyes don't you agree, just like goats?'

'Don't know, you know. I'm very partial to a cat.'

'Well take birds then. What could be sweeter than a robin redbreast yet there's someone been studying them, did you read the book, and they're the fiercest things alive he says, would you believe it?'

'Jungle law,' the man agreed.

'And some of these debs,' she went on. 'Since you were speaking of their generation weren't you? Why I could tell stories but I'm simply not that sort of person. With sleek heads and skins and no knowledge of the world, of how people can count to one another I mean, – well some of them are no better than goats there you are, than farmyard goats.'

'Remember I passed two common women once outside a pub and one said to the other "you filthy Irish git." '

'What's a git then?' she enquired.

'Goat,' he replied.

'How truly curious,' she agreed. 'But you do see this my way?' she proceeded. 'Oh Richard it is so rare to find a man who looks through the surface as you can, deep down to what really's there.' She lowered her voice, glanced over to Jane and John still engrossed in themselves then hitched her chair closer to Mr Abbot's. 'Life,' she continued, 'is not all going back on one's tracks, ferreting out old friends to have a cosy chat with, one simply can't for ever be looking over a shoulder Richard to what's dead and gone. Such a blind view of life. No, you have to look forward, face the future whatever that may bring.'

'No friend like an old friend,' he claimed.

'You're not on to what I mean,' she said. 'Take John now. There are times I could shake him, just shake him. You know what they were once supposed to mean to one another and never will again those two, well as if that wasn't enough he's always going back. He won't admit if you ask him but he's got an idea that once he's had anything in his life he's only to lift his voice to get that back once more and dear Jane's too sweet to let him see.'

'Wonderful woman Jane.'

'Isn't she?' Miss Jennings sighed. She drank down a full glass of wine. 'Too sweet and wonderful. Sometimes. Any other woman would say "Now look John dear I admit we once meant everything to each other and you practically broke your wife's heart over me, but all of it's been finished a long time now, happened many lovers' moons ago and can't come to life again, these little things never do".'

'I say Liz you know, none of my business,' Mr Abbot warned.

'But what does she say?' his companion continued. 'Jane's forever calling Penelope "her little saint" but Jane is the saint if you get me or isn't she?'

'Oh a saint yes undoubtedly.'

'How can Jane put up with him in one of those moods! Now I, I think it's bad for John all this rehashing of what's dead and gone, I try to take his mind off which is the reason I'm such a good influence. I truly am the man's guardian angel.'

'Tremendously lucky fellow.'

'Not but what it can't be a great strain at times,' she murmured with a tragic expression. 'No one in the whole wide world can have the least idea. I get the feeling occasionally, oh to tell the utter truth because I know you are like the grave it is more than that, I wouldn't say quite often but continually I have to lug poor John back to the present by main force and I'm not very strong. It wears me out.'

'Shouldn't let yourself get upset like this, a splendid little woman like you young enough to be his daughter.'

'I suppose it's like so many men,' she gave judgement aloud, 'who imagine no girl can look at a male older than herself. But you're wrong, think of history, anything! As a matter of fact to tell you a little secret about me which I truly trust you not to breathe, I've always been attracted to older men.'

'Have you by Jove!'

'Yes, isn't that strange. But I don't like little old men, they have to be great big hussars if they are older. So now you know!'

'Not for me,' he said. 'I go for the young ones.'

'Oh no you can't mean little girls,' she cried. 'Pig-tails and tunics!'

'I say what must you think Liz,' he expostulated. 'Nothing of the sort. I should hope not. No to tell the truth it's young women of your age, young but old enough to be women if you get what I mean.'

'Jane,' she enthusiastically cried, 'Richard's just paid me the sweetest compliment! He's said what he likes about me is I'm young but with all the allure of experience!!'

'My dear how clever of Richard,' Mrs Weatherby drily rejoined.

'No not all that,' Miss Jennings appealed to the wine waiter who was filling her glass to the brim once more only she didn't lift it to stop him. Mr Pomfret slightly raised his eyebrows, then Jane and he descended back into their own conversation to the exclusion of all else.

'But I think it's one of the nicest things have ever been said to me,' she purred at Mr Abbot. 'I feel just like one of your cats when you've given her cream.'

'True right enough,' he stoutly averred.

'It had the ring of truth,' Miss Jennings said. 'Everything you say has, I think that's my real reason why I like you so. You're such a wonderfully honest person Richard.'

'Can't understand people saying what they don't mean. Doesn't make sense.'

'And honest about yourself,' she continued 'which is the rarest thing in the world, pure gold.'

It was almost as if, in time, the party had leaped forward between those mirrors so much had been recorded only to be lost, so much champagne had been consumed while, as day passes over a pond, no trace was left in any of their minds, or hardly none, just the vague memory of friendly weather, a fading riot of June stayed perhaps in their throats as the waiters withdrew though three or four remained to serve coffee brandy and port.

This was the moment chosen by Philip Weatherby to make his empty tumbler ring to a stroke of the knife, to rise with one hand of Mary's in his own while she stayed seated, to look so white as he examined the guests from the advantage he had taken, that of surprise and the five foot ten of height.

'Oh the dear boy,' his mother said to John Pomfret. 'He's going to propose my health, or so I do believe the saint.'

'I – ah – er' her son began while Miss Pomfret squeezed Philip's fingers.

'But who put it in his sweet head?' Mrs Weatherby asked entranced. 'Darling was this your idea?' she demanded and had no answer.

'I – well you see – that is . . .' Mr Weatherby began again while all the older people looked up at him with smiling faces, with that kind of withdrawn encouragement we use by which to judge how much better we could do this sort of thing ourselves, and Jane beamed as if in a seventh heaven. 'Ladies and gentlemen,' he tried once more, 'we are here tonight to celebrate my twenty firster.' He now started to speak very fast. 'My mother which is kind of her gave this party,' he went on, 'and I'm sure we've all very much enjoyed things, the festive occasion and so on, but Mary and I thought now or never which is why we want to announce that we're engaged.'

He sat down. A hum of fascinated comment was directed like bees to honey in his direction. Mary hardly glanced at her father but darted quick looks about the room while Jane turned to John Pomfret, one hand pressed on the soft mound above her heart and hissed,

'Is this your doing? Did you know of it?'

'Good God good for them. First I've heard,' he said.

'Oh my dear,' she cried. 'I feel faint!'

Not that Mr Pomfret appeared to pay heed. A pale smile was stuck across his face while he looked about as though to receive tribute. But the attention of almost everyone in that room was still fixed on the awkward happy couple, and Elaine Winder smacked their backs and generally behaved as if she were in at a kill.

'Oh my dear,' Mrs Weatherby groaned rising majestically from her place.

This movement repeated a thousand thousand times on every side brought each one of those present to his or her feet, except at Philip's table where they sat on transfixed in their moment and Miss Winder's exuberance. Mr Pomfret stood up also. As Jane began to make her way towards Mary he followed and the guests started clapping.

A naturally graceful woman Mrs Weatherby was superb while she crossed the room afloat between one tall mirror and the other, a look of infinite humility on her proud features. The occasion's shock and excitement had raised her complexion to an even brighter glow, a magnificent effulgence of what all felt she must feel at this promise of grandsons and, at that, from the daughter of what most of them knew to be an old flame with whom she had continued the best of old friends.

Tears stood in many eyes. Some men even cheered discreetly.

And when Jane came to their table she folded Mary Pomfret into so wonderful an embrace while the child half rose from her chair to greet it that not only was the girl's hair not touched or disarranged in this envelopment, but as Mrs Weatherby took the young lady to her heart it must have seemed to most the finest thing they had ever seen, the epitome of how such moments should be, perfection in other words, the acme of manners, and memorable as being the flower, the blossoming of grace and their generation's ultimate instinct of how one should ideally behave.

Mr Pomfret pumped Philip's hand.

Jane was whispering to Mary, 'Oh aren't you clever not to have said a word, you clever darling.'

One or two of the male guests called for a speech.

Mrs Weatherby disengaged herself with infinite gentleness, held her future daughter-in-law at arm's length as a judge holds a prize lily at the show, then turned to Philip. She leant forward offering a cheek. When he pecked this once, she did not push it smartly back at him. She held firm while John kissed his daughter on the chin. Next she linked arms with both the intended while Mr Pomfret hung at the edge. A fresh storm of clapping greeted this group and now most of the men called for a speech.

Mrs Weatherby nodded like royalty right and left. She wore what might have been called a brave little smile.

But once the appeals for her to say a few words with many a 'yes do darling' from the ladies, the moment this clamour grew too insistent Jane whispered to Philip and, with an arm still under Mary's she walked through the uproar back to her table. Philip and John followed, each with a chair. It was noticeable how frightened the girl looked, as was perhaps only natural.

Liz kissed the four of them in turn, the applause rose to a crescendo, and the family group, if Miss Jennings could be said to be of the family, sat down. Once they were all seated it was seen that Richard Abbot had effaced himself, had joined Elaine Winder and her young man at their table where, however, he was now without a chair. This a wine waiter fetched him.

John was first to speak.

'Champagne,' he cried to another servant. 'We must all have a toast.'

'My dear the bill!' Jane said in a low voice.

'Oh will you ever forgive us?' his daughter tremulously asked.

'This is on me,' Mr Pomfret explained. 'Bring the champagne glasses back,' he ordered. 'Order another dozen bottles. We shall have to toast 'em,' he shouted to the room. Cries of 'Good old John' greeted his yell. One of the male guests, rather drunk, seemed about to become dazed.

'Oh my God where's Richard?' Mrs Weatherby demanded in the same low tones.

'He's sat himself down at our table Mamma.'

'I still feel quite faint, John.'

'You'll be right as a trivet Jane when you've some more wine,' Mr Pomfret reassured. 'You'll see if you aren't.'

'But oh my dear aren't toasts unlucky?'

'Well my boy your mother's a bit bowled over. Ah here we are, and fill them up. All round the room, mind! Now haven't you been a minx keeping this to yourself,' he said to his daughter.

'Oh I did worry,' she cried to Jane. 'But you see it was Philip's twenty firster and people marry younger these days you know, if you see what I mean?'

Mr Pomfret rose to his feet.

'I'm going to ask you all to rise, be upstanding, and to – ah – lift your glasses and drink to – ah – the happy couple.'

Which, when done, set the party off again. And such a number of people came up to their table to offer congratulations, to twit Jane with not having dropped the least hint, to kiss Mary and to slap John on the back, that it was not for some time later they were able to have private conversation.

When they did find themselves alone once more at this table, John Pomfret incoherently took control,

'Well what's it to be?' he cried to the four of them 'a white wedding Mary my love with the old organ and a choir of course?'

'We hadn't got that far yet Daddy.'

'But when, how soon? Now you know the party we were to have, you remember I told you Jane, we'll make that into an engagement one, cocktails or something with the few intimate friends to stay over to dinner?'

'How wonderful for you both,' Liz cried. 'What a bewitching minute this is!'

Jane smiled a trifle sadly, gazed at each in turn. 'Isn't it?' she agreed with Miss Jennings. 'So much in the one wonderful evening. Oh dear very soon I really quite simply believe I shall have to go home to my bed.'

'Jane you'll do nothing of the kind,' John Pomfret insisted. 'Besides we none of us work tomorrow, we can lie in all day if we wish. It is a terrific occasion! I've been wondering the whole of my life what this moment would be like.'

'Dear boy,' Mrs Weatherby said to Philip but in tragic tones as she laid a white hand on his arm, 'if you only knew how your poor mother had dreamed and prayed, yes prayed!'

'But where are you proposing to set up house?' John demanded.

'We haven't actually discussed that have we Philip?' The young man did not answer, moistened his lips with a tongue.

'When I went to see Arthur Morris he told me once he was out of the clinic the doctors had advised him to get away in the country. So his flat at least will be on the market,' Miss Jennings suggested.

'Good Lord Liz poor old Arthur has three whole rooms. They'd never be able to afford it.'

'The sweet things mustn't start life in too big a little way,' Mrs Weatherby approved. She gave her son's arm a squeeze. The young couple frowned what could have been a warning at one another.

'Bless me I don't know when anything ever before in all my time has given me such a crazy lift,' the father exclaimed. 'Who's to be best man Philip?'

'I couldn't say I'm sure.'

'And the bridesmaids Mary?' John Pomfret insisted. 'We'll have to be very careful there you know. Of course Liz here must be chief one. You'll do that won't you Liz?'

'Oh John dear you are sweet but you should be serious once in a while,' Mrs Weatherby interrupted dolefully and fast. 'He simply doesn't understand about these things,' she explained to Miss Jennings then seemed to catch herself up. 'Oh goodness listen to me,' she laughed 'the interfering mother-in-law just like you hear about all the time! No John the darlings will have to settle that for themselves.'

'I'm too old,' Miss Jennings wailed. 'Besides poor Liz's been bridesmaid so often. And I always seem to bring such rotten bad luck. They invariably divorce after I've been in the aisle.'

'But now we are on the subject,' Jane announced 'Philip I'm certain your father would've liked you to hold the wedding under our rose window, darling, if he were alive. I know we have practically no connection with the village now but in a way it's still our very own precious church. I shall be buried outside under the yew by his side, I've put that in my little will.' She brushed at her eyes with a handkerchief.

'Now Jane,' Mr Pomfret expostulated, 'this is no time to speak of mourning, top hats and side bands. What next good God? But where are you choosing for the honeymoon?'

'We hadn't quite got round to that yet either,' Mary answered.

'Well you haven't thought of much then have you?' he said.

'Really John,' Liz exclaimed. 'When you're in love you can't make plans about one's plans.' She drank another full glass down.

'I don't know when else you plot things out,' he replied in obvious delight.

'John,' Mrs Weatherby cried. 'You're a changed creature! I hardly think that's quite nice do you darling?' and she turned to Liz.

'He's so thrilled,' Miss Jennings explained.

'No but to talk of children, nurseries and so on at such a moment, – why my dear you'll be positively indecent in a second!'

Philip Weatherby stifled a yawn.

'Who said a word about nasty sprawling brawling brats Jane?' John Pomfret demanded.

'You did my dear,' she said in a dry voice. 'Not more than a minute ago. Didn't he darling?' she asked of Liz.

'It's all sho wonderful I don't know whether I'm on my head or my toesh,' this lady explained.

'All right then we'll hold a ball, a dance.'

'John there's so much to discuss,' Jane said.

'I realize you'll say I'm crazy me dear,' Mr Pomfret said to his daughter 'but ever since you were grown up I've wondered what it would be like talking over marriage settlements with a middle-aged stranger and as I've often told you there's so little in the old kitty that I thought I'd have to take your future father-in-law out and make him drunk. And now good Lord it's going to be Jane that I've known all me life. I can't get over it.'

'John do behave yourself,' Mrs Weatherby sadly smiled.

'Well we shall be bound to have a chat one of these days won't we Jane?' he demanded.

'I expect you'll know where to find me,' she replied and Miss Jennings winced, only she did so very slowly.

'But we shan't want any money,' Miss Pomfret claimed with a weak show of determination.

'Nonsense monkey everybody does,' her father said.

'Then hadn't you better discuss it with me?' Mr Weatherby asked.

'Philip darling do think before you speak like that,' Jane cried.

'Well but you're a woman after all Mamma.'

'And I should hope so too indeed. No but your Daddy and I will have to have a little talk shan't we you angelic creature,' his mother proposed to Mary with some firmness.

'Of course Mrs Weatherby. I'm sure Philip never meant . . .'

'Now who are you "Mrs Weatherbying" dear. And you're never to call me "mother" because I would simply rather die that's all' she laughed. 'You do agree with me don't you Liz? John you'd never like Philip to call you Father?'

Mr Weatherby began to show signs of distress. Before he could open his mouth Jane went on rather fast and anxiously.

'No it's all Christian names these days isn't that so, and very sensibly too in my opinion. Anything to do away with the gulf between generations. Oh whenever will these sweet tiresome guests of mine drag themselves off to bed at last. John it's been such a day and a half and I'm so tired!'

'Bed? You think of bed on a night like this?'

'I truly am so tired John dear!!'

'Well I feel I could go on somewhere. What d'you say Liz?'

'Can Philip and I drop you back?'

'I can't very well go before the people I've invited can I?' Mrs Weatherby answered Mary in a sharp tone of voice. 'Oh do you think I could send for the bill?'

'Really Jane,' Mr Pomfret protested. 'You'd never hear the last if you did.'

She looked round the noisy party, the people who went from table to table with laughing flushed faces.

'They wouldn't notice you'd hardly think?' she hazarded.

'Shall I get hold of Richard?' Miss Jennings volunteered.

'Perhaps he could go tactfully round Liz to drop a word here and there but not so much that anyone would actually realize.'

'No no both of you,' John said. 'Jane can't break up her own party.'

'I don't know,' Mr Weatherby suggested, 'but Mary and I don't feel quite as if we wanted to go home yet. And if we went on somewhere it might start the others off.'

'Of course you darlings want to be alone. Oh don't I remember! And who wouldn't't!! But Richard has most cruelly deserted me all evening.'

'I shouldn't wonder he just found he couldn't intrude,' John explained.

'Then you maintain I should have gone to that beastly bitch's daughter's table,' Liz almost shouted. She seemed to have difficulty focusing her eyes.

'My dear Liz,' he replied with gentleness, 'I regard you almost as one of the family.'

'Thanks,' she said and appeared to subside. 'OK' she said.

'A woman needs another by her at a time like this,' Mrs Weatherby murmured.

'Well parents,' Philip began. 'What say if we simply pushed off?'

'Certainly not,' Jane sharply reproved him. 'Not now you're the guests of the evening. And before this surprise started it was your twenty firster after all. Please remember, if only to please me please remember that!'

'Why of course,' Mary Pomfret agreed and seemed most nervous. 'We wouldn't dream of the slightest thing . . .'

'Hm . . . m,' Mrs Weatherby replied. 'That's settled then.'

'You know Mary,' her father pronounced 'this is a great moment in a woman's life. You must be extra nice with Jane, it has quite bowled her over.'

'But I am Daddy.'

'Of course you are you angel,' the older woman agreed. 'Now John don't butt in between, we shall manage our own affairs perfectly shan't we dear? Still I can't tell why all these people shouldn't go. I really feel I almost hardly know them now. I'm so tired don't you understand John? No of course you two must stay at least for the present, dreadfully dull as it must be for you both. I've such a tearing headache. God what a day!'

'Anything I can do Mamma?'

'Just don't let poor darling Penelope the little saint into this secret, promise me will you? I know her better than anyone in the whole wide world but even I couldn't tell what the results might be now, I wouldn't dare.'

'I say, she could be one of our bridesmaids,' Philip said.

'I should hope so indeed,' his mother took him up. 'If not then I can't possibly imagine who else. And when we've just got her over the man in chains down at Brighton! Oh my dear if you didn't ask the child why she'd simply rather die.'

'Well it's not exactly secret now is it Mamma?'

'But we must break it gently don't you understand,' his mother answered. 'We've had this wedding trouble before with the sainted little sweet. Oh I blame myself but really John wasn't it wicked of you and now only four months later we're to go through this all over again! And when I told her the facts of life a year back, she was just five and a half then, will you believe me but she's forgotten every word, she must have done from what the little angel's said lately. Oh isn't parenthood confusing! I always tell these girls when they get engaged they simply can't guess what they're in for.' At which she gaily laughed 'Now there I go again,' she went on, beaming at Mary 'I do declare I'd quite forgotten for the second! What will you think of me? Oh Philip your stupid Mamma!'

'When they began giving sex instruction at Council schools,' Philip told them, 'there was a woman wrote to say the lesson had taken ninety minutes each week off her daughter's mathematics and surely maths must be more important.'

'My dear boy,' Mrs Weatherby approved, 'that was almost witty.'

'Good for you Philip!' Mr Pomfret said. 'Well then mum's the word where Pen's concerned eh?'

'Yes, you must all and every one of you promise faithfully,' Jane agreed. 'In fact the less spoken about this secret engagement the better, so it doesn't get to her sacred little ears poor soul.'

Later on, when John Pomfret's excitement drove him to circulate among the other tables with Liz and Mary in tow, Richard Abbot came back to his rightful place at Jane's left hand.

'Where have you been?' the lady cried 'and what d'you mean by it just when I wanted you!'

'Family matter I thought. Felt an outsider!'

'Well Liz didn't did she? She stayed. Oh Richard you do let me down at times of crisis.'

'Now my dear this's been a great day for all. Only natural to be overwrought a bit.'

'Oh I am,' she wailed, her large eyes even more enormous. 'Don't you think Richard you could persuade them to go so I can get home to bed?'

'My dear Jane, can't do that! Let me fetch you a black coffee.'

'In a moment. No, sit here,' and she patted the chair next her. 'Oh Richard I'm worried about little Penelope. You remember how she was after she imagined she'd married John? Well what will it be like when she realizes her brother has got engaged to what she must truly believe to be her own stepdaughter, have you thought of that?'

'She'll have forgotten everything about it.'

'But how can she I ask you? Richard do concentrate, this is important to me. Her little sanity's at stake.'

'She'll have forgotten about that tomfoolery with John I meant.'

'If you say so, then you pit yourself against the psychoanalyst. I asked Maud Winder's advice who'd such a lot of trouble with her girl at one time and I went to the best. He told me it might have bruised Pen's soul, he couldn't be sure he said until he had seen the child but I wouldn't allow that, don't you think I was right, I mean one never knows where these clever famous men will end does one, playing politics with my own precious darling's very being, Richard?'

'Don't hold with 'em myself.'

'Yet I'm not trying to say the chief responsibility doesn't rest with me, it must of course, it always will, oh my dear the load devilish Providence has put on my poor bended back! No I have to guard her against her sweet self. And when she hears and starts one of her things the desperate brave little martyr, I shan't be able to turn everything off as I did to finish the escapist at Brighton by giving the child a bag she liked to hang from the elbow she would insist on holding. Still if I have to I shall think of a ruse, it's what I'm here for after all. But the strain Richard!'

'Shouldn't wonder if Philip's a bit worked up too eh?'

'Oh the boy's all right. Not normal of course but in absolutely no need of help I can tell you.'

'Don't know Jane. Big moment in a young fellow's life, must be.'

'How can you judge? You yourself have simply never even risked it.'

'Not from want of trying.'

'My dear how utterly sweet you can be!' she said. 'In spite of this deplorable habit of yours of not being there when you're wanted. But don't you see Richard you're older, tougher. Oh dear have I been horrible, torturing you all this time?'

'If I were you I'd decide Penelope was all right for the moment and concentrate a bit on Philip.'

'How can I make up my mind against my better judgement?'

'Then there's Mary to consider,' he reminded Mrs Weatherby. 'Tricky few days this in a girl's life, always will be. She'll need making a fuss over.'

'Does one never have a rest?'

'You ought to have a man about to take some of the load off your shoulders.'

'To put a greater weight on, you mean! Oh I didn't intend to be beastly, you must believe. But I'm at my wit's end Richard.'

Later still Philip and Mary made good their escape, got away to a nightclub.

'Well,' he said 'I told you! It went quite all right.'

'Oh Philip darling,' she cried above but somehow under the music so that she sounded hoarse, 'they'll never let us marry, I know they won't, isn't it awful!'

'But see here,' he objected 'everything worked like a dream. I swear this was the only way to deal with my mother. I learned by watching Pen as a matter of fact. When she wants whatever it may be she just takes it; as soon as she feels ill she doesn't just say she feels something coming on, she is ill and Mamma loves the whole business.'

'We should've got married first. There's what we ought to have told them, not that we were only engaged.'

'I know but it's so rude to the relations when people elope.'

'Yes you're right,' she gulped.

'And then eloping's out of date, it went out with horses.'

'Oh dear now they're all eaten poor things.'

'Too many people on this island keep carnivorous pets Mary,' he replied. 'The waste is fearful.'

'But what happens next Philip?'

'With our parents? Well you know how it is. They'll argue, there'll be no end to the amount they're sure to squawk which they'll love. And Mamma will weep once or twice and your father will act pretty idiotically for quite a time.'

'Don't say anything against Daddy darling, please.'

'OK then lay off Mamma.'

'What d'you mean, I haven't said a word about her!'

'It was just I thought you seemed a bit unenthusiastic when you made out she'd try and stop us.'

'I said "they". I didn't say anything against her.'

'Well who is "they" in that case?'

'All of them.'

'But look here it passed off awfully well didn't it? I mean they seemed overjoyed to me. As a matter of fact I thought my speech went rather grandly didn't you?'

'Oh you were wonderful darling,' she warmly assured him. 'Heavens though I do feel I'd been put through a mangle.'

'Poor sweet,' he said and squeezed the hot hand he was holding. 'Shall we dance?'

They danced. Eyes closed, cheek to cheek, better than ever before. When they had had enough for a time they came back to their table.

'That's the way to do the rumba,' she told him. 'See that man on the left, how he makes the girl go round while he stays in the centre.'

'Should I do that with you?'

'Of course darling.'

'I doubt if I ever shall be able.'

'Then take lessons silly.'

'I say,' he said 'you do feel better now, you must?'

'I think so, yes.'

'Can't find out yes or no.'

'But no one can. First something inside says everything is fine,' she wailed, 'and the next moment it tells you that something which overshadows everything else is very bad just like an avalanche!'

'I'm so sorry,' he said. 'I truly am.'

They danced again and again until, as the long night went on they had got into a state of unthinking happiness perhaps.

A week later Mrs Weatherby asked John Pomfret to dinner.

'And how is dear Liz?' she enquired as she brought the man a glass of sherry.

'Quite well I trust.'

'Aren't you seeing so much of her now then John?'

'But of course,' he said. 'The fact is this news about our respective children has rather thrown me out of my normal gait.'

'So it's become a question of striding between you and Liz,' Mrs Weatherby commented. Her look on him over the decanter was one of sweet compassion. 'Oh my dear,' she continued 'you must be careful. Don't let it end as our love did in great country walks.'

'Really Jane when do I ever get away?' he cried. 'All my work in town here, and now this engagement! Philip and Mary are going to keep us pretty well occupied you know. Lot to arrange and so on.'

'I'm sure,' she agreed. 'Just sit back and relax.'

'And how is little Penelope?' he enquired.

She made a beautiful flowing gesture of resignation. 'Oh my dear,' she said. 'Sometimes I bless Providence I have a man like you can share my problems.'

'Isn't Richard much use then?'

'I don't know what I should do without him but he has that failing John of the absolutely true, true to one I mean, of being almost completely unimaginative poor dear.'

Mr Pomfret laughed. 'I see,' he said. 'Sometimes I have just wondered what you found in Richard.'

'Loyalty,' she breathed and smoothed her skirts.

'Which you never came across in me?'

'Don't let's rake up the past darling. What's over's over.'

'Enough's enough you mean?'

She let out a gentle peal of laughter, leaning back on the sofa.

'Oh John aren't you horrid!' she cried.

'Good sherry you have here,' he said.

'I'm so glad you say that. Ned makes me go to his man and I wouldn't know.'

'While Maud Winder sends you to her psychologist about Penelope?'

'No but John who told? Oh don't people talk!'

'You yourself did.'

'I'd quite forgot. No one must know darling, it would be unfair on my sad long suffering angel. Who'd want to marry a girl later who'd been analysed?'

'Would it make any difference?'

'Who can tell my dear? It might quite disgust Pen with all that side of life. So you won't breathe a word John will you? Besides I never did let him set his terrible hypnotizing eyes on her, no I guard my poppet too well for that. The thing is, she's heard!'

'Heard what?'

'Why that they're secretly engaged.'

'There's not so much secret now surely after the public announcement? It must be all over London.'

'But we've put no announcement in the Press yet John?'

'That's just one of the matters I wanted to have a word about.'

'Yes there's so much to discuss,' she sighed.

'Then you don't think Penelope ought to be a bridesmaid? Over-excite her or something?'

'My dear one she'd simply die as things are if Mary didn't ask her.

It was Isabella. Penelope absolutely jabbers in Italian now, so wonderful, while I can still hardly put two words together. And you see I don't understand what they say all the time. I spent hours with the dictionary to warn the woman not to breathe a word.' Mrs Weatherby merrily laughed. 'I must have looked a sight poring over it and in the end perhaps I said the opposite, as one does, even gave her orders to tell Penelope at once. Oh John what it is not to understand a syllable of one's only servant's beastly tongue! But the child knows, she babbles of the wedding all day and I'm afraid for her.'

'You know Jane,' Mr Pomfret interrupted 'I think I'm going to grow very fond of Philip.'

'I should hope so too. He's such a splendid bull of a boy.'

'I seem to have got really far with him the last few days.'

'What d'you talk to him about? My brother-in-law?'

Mr Pomfret appeared to ignore the dryness of her tone. He was peering at the sherry in his glass.

'We shall make friends. I always wanted a son,' he said.

'I'd so like to give Mary just a touch of advice about her clothes,' Jane suggested in a small voice.

'Then we seem ideally suited as in-laws,' Mr Pomfret laughed. 'Though you must not mind if the girl has thoughts of her own; she can be very pigheaded about dresses I believe.'

'Why how d'you mean John?'

'Liz took her round the various establishments some time back and didn't get her own way much so I understand.'

'But isn't that natural? You can hardly say darling Liz has any taste at all.'

'I never notice what a woman wears. Liz always looks very nice and neatly turned out to me.'

Mrs Weatherby smiled.

'Neat is not quite the word!'

'Well for the matter of that I'd like five minutes with Philip about the cut of his jib.'

'He goes to the best tailors.'

'It's his hats dear Jane.'

'He's never bareheaded is he? I should hate him to be.'

'So wide brimmed.'

'Now John you're not to put the poor boy into one of those bowler things or I'll never speak to you again.'

'Do you notice what men are wearing?'

'Of course.'

'Then did I get the suit I have on now from off the hook or was it made for me?'

'You ask me that when you wouldn't know if I was in one of my beloved mother's Ascot dresses this minute!'

'What tailor does Philip patronize?'

'His awful uncle's.'

'Well of course I haven't the advantage of knowing your brother-in-law well enough to have been acquainted with his cutter.'

'It's Highcliffe I believe, in that little passage off the Arcade.'

'Never heard of the man.' There was a pause. Then Mr Pomfret went on 'What made Philip choose Ned Weatherby's man?'

'Family reasons. Philip feels all men who are closely related should go to the same place for everything.'

'That's what must lead one to think he's in livery then.'

'But John the boy never wears striped waistcoats.'

'We shall have to change all of it Jane. Who'd d'you say your wine merchant was?'

'Ned's.'

'Curious. Remind me to ask you the address some time. So has Philip gone traditional with the trades-people? Can't say I remember anything of the sort in my family.'

'Then you've forgotten your Aunt Eloise.'

'What about her?'

'Wasn't it she who insisted on everyone getting everything on the route served by such and such a bus?'

'Extraordinary memory you have Jane. Whenever did I tell you that?'

'On one of those despairingly long walks you took me, dear.'

They both laughed. There was a short pause.

'Well I think all this business is rather marvellous,' he began again. 'It's given me a new lease of life Jane. Takes me back to the days we were walking out! I'm sure I couldn't think of anyone more perfect for Mary than your Philip.'

'What a sweet sentimental person you can be,' she replied. 'I believe most men are.'

'No seriously,' he said 'it's all I could've wished.'

'I never imagined, who would, I mean think of you and me sitting here like this after all that's happened, and in a discussion how we're to become related by the back door so to speak!'

'Not at all,' he objected. 'The main entrance.'

'D'you really think so? Don't you find your children, your own girl so remote?'

'Why should I Jane?'

'But Mary's a girl!'

'And what difference does sex bring to the relationship?'

'You see I'm forever making allowances for Philip because he's a man,' she explained. 'And the more so by reason of my not having a husband any longer of course. It's the same with you John. If you were married now you'd be so greatly critical, no not that, shall I say choosy about Mary.'

'Would I?'

'Well I mean about her clothes and everything.'

'Why?'

'Because you'd get some advice I suppose. I'm sure I don't know. What d'you expect me to say?'

'I couldn't tell you Jane,' he said smiling, and seemed very comfortable in the chair with his sherry.

'I hope Isabella's not to be late again like she was last time, or is each time if I'm not to tell a lie,' Mrs Weatherby said. 'Supposing I shouted to her in the kitchen?'

'I'm quite all right. Never been more comfortable in my life.'

'Well you did arrive a weeny bit early didn't you? The thing is, as I've already explained, ever since she told darling Pen all about the secret engagement I've been terrified to say much to Isabella in case unbeknownst I'm telling the woman the opposite. Never mind, I expect we can wait a bit. Then are you quite easy in your heart of hearts about Mary and Philip?'

'My dear,' he said 'I can't remember when I've been more pleased.'

'It just crossed my mind, only a moment ago to tell the truth, John I have almost wondered and you are the one person in the world to whom I'd bring myself to mention this, but don't you feel they both might be rather young?'

'Young? My dear girl what age were you when you married?'

'Eighteen months younger than your lovely Mary I know, oh I know!' she cried. 'Still wouldn't you agree we were different then?'

'Different? In what way?' An edge had come on to his voice.

'It's so difficult to look back to those golden wonderful days,' she

moaned, 'to feel back to how we felt then! I don't know but I sometimes think I was simply insane marrying when I did so I missed all
my fun.'

'Nonsense my dear,' Mr Pomfret said firmly. 'You never lived
until you met me and that was years later.'

'Oh why didn't I wait?' she murmured gently with a brilliant flattering smile full on him. 'That was when I made the greatest mistake.
And how about you? What d'you think?'

'Me? Oh I've been an absolute fool all me life.'

'There's not many would say that about you John. But, if we were
complete idiots is there any reason why we should let the children
fall into the selfsame trap?'

'Yes Jane and who's to stop 'em?'

'Ah,' she said 'ah! Yet these runaway affairs?' she hazarded.

'That's what I like about our two. They haven't eloped.'

'Not yet, sweet Providence forbid!'

'My dear,' he remonstrated. 'I say nothing against Mary when I
tell you she is far too level headed. And Philip would be frightened
of what his uncle's tradesmen might find to say.'

She narrowed her great eyes.

'John,' she warned him 'that's not funny!'

'Have I said something?' he exclaimed with what seemed to be
genuine innocence. 'Look here I do apologize. Now that the children
have got engaged I suppose I'm wallowing in intimacy, there you are,
thinking out aloud no end of illconsidered things. There's been so
little time to adjust oneself has there?'

'No no,' she agreed 'I was only absurd for a minute and ridiculously touchy. Forgive me dear John! Oh yes it has all been hasty
quick hasn't it?'

'Then you really think they're too young though you admit there's
very little we can do and that we married younger?'

'But John we had money. It didn't have to be love in a cottage for
us.'

'Quite out of date nowadays,' he laughed. 'Most expensive things
in the world, cottages! It's the old garret for the nonce all right.'

'And can you see Philip in one?'

'No Jane to tell the honest truth I can't, yet that's Mary's affair I
suppose? And then I imagine you and I'll be able to help a little.'

Mrs Weatherby covered her face with her fat white fingers in rings.

'Oh there you go,' she moaned 'and I've been dreading it all evening! I shall have to see Mr Thicknesse which I do terribly tremble at always!! I'm such an absolute fool over money matters John!'

'Thicknesse the family Oliver Twist?'

'Yes the lawyer. You remember him,' she said, still from behind her hands but in a stronger tone.

'Never had dealings with the man myself.'

'But you did. When we were wickedly threatened with cross divorces.' Her voice dropped to a whisper. 'Don't tell me you've forgotten even that?'

'Oh old Thicknesse,' he cried cheerfully. 'Yes I've got him now right enough. Lord I'm sorry for anyone who has to call on that fellow! And you say he's still alive when a fine chap thirty years younger like poor old Arthur Morris lies dying in bed?'

'No don't,' she wailed. 'No one, simply no one is to mention Arthur again in my presence! I told Penelope. I forbad her.'

'Yes I expect you'll have to call on Master Thicknesse. Unless you'd rather I went?'

'Oh well wouldn't that look rather queer?' she cried, lowered the hands from her face and looked at Mr Pomfret with a tiny smile at the corners of those magnificent eyes. 'Besides I'm afraid it may turn out to be quite like those Egyptian tombs they're always finding and are so proud of, quite empty, robbed.'

'You mean the sly old devil's got away with some?'

'Mr Thicknesse?' she gasped and actually glanced over a shoulder. 'Hush my dear, do think what you're saying!'

John roared with laughter, put his drink down, even leaned right back to let himself go. She caught the infection, or seemed to, and soon in her turn was dabbing at her eyes.

'Darling,' he brought out at last, a few tears about his cheekbones 'you're wonderful! I don't know what I'd do without you!'

Mrs Weatherby stopped laughing at once.

'You've managed without someone an unconscionably long time John.'

'Dear where do you get these long words suddenly?'

'My old governess,' she replied in a tart voice. 'What were we talking about?'

'Lord knows,' he said. 'That's the effect you have on me. I forget time and place.'

'Then I don't,' she gaily laughed. 'And I think I know what it may be. Isabella must have misunderstood again and is waiting for us in the dining-room. Let's go along, shall we, if only to try, anyway?'

John Pomfret invited Mr Abbot to have a bite to eat with him at the Club.

'I asked you to drop over because I'm worried in my mind to do with this business about my Mary,' he told Richard.

'Young love not running smooth eh?'

'I shouldn't say that for the simple reason I've no means of finding out. They look happy enough bless 'em but they don't let on much. Tell you the truth I wanted to enlist your help with Jane.'

'You've known her longest, John.'

'I'd like to put the whole thing before you. Basically I think a man's no right to stand between his child and her happiness.' He laughed. 'Lord that sounds a pompous pronouncement but you follow what I mean? And it's damned hard to get down to arrangements with someone like Jane you've known all your life.'

'Expect it may be,' Mr Abbot agreed.

'Good, I thought you'd catch on. The fact is I've been uncommonly careful not to rush Jane in any shape or form and then this week the summons I'd been awaiting came and she asked me round to dinner. Well we did have a bit of a chat while that Italian woman of hers kept us hanging on for the meal but I can't say we got anywhere. After we'd sat down to eat and later back in her room again it was hardly mentioned; to tell the truth we got laughing over old days and there you are.'

'Wonderful food Jane gives one. Can't imagine how she does it these days.'

Mr Pomfret turned on Richard Abbot a long considering look.

'Food's not been too bad in the Club lately,' he said at last. 'Richard are you with me about all this?'

'Completely ignorant of the whole issue,' Mr Abbot answered.

'Well I can't promise there is an issue,' John pointed out. 'Only perhaps that Jane doesn't seem wildly keen on the engagement. It's not so much what she puts into words as everything she doesn't mention and for somebody who's never been exactly silent all her life that may or may not be significant. How do you weigh things up?'

'She might be a trifle upset about Penelope?'

'I know but don't you think Pen's often a blind, Richard? Doesn't Jane use the child as a shield?'

'She has no need that I can see.'

'Of course not,' Mr Pomfret concurred. 'Never met anyone better able to look after herself than Jane.'

'Wonderful manager. Marvellous party she gave!'

'Superb! A trifle unfortunate though the way the children brought their marriage in.'

'As a matter of fact I a bit felt that,' Mr Abbot agreed. 'When all's said and done it was Jane's show. Speaking as Philip did he stole the thunder considerably or so I fancied.'

'Wasn't it his twenty firster?'

'May have been,' Richard Abbot admitted. 'But a mother has the right to celebrate having raised her own son to man's estate surely?'

'Admitted,' John allowed him. 'All the same we celebrated by ourselves didn't we when you and I ceased to be minors?'

'No doubt Philip did so.'

'I fancy they're a bit short, wouldn't run to two entertainments. Who could these days?'

'Don't know at all. None of my business John.'

There was another pause while Mr Pomfret studied Richard Abbot.

'D'you like Mary?' he asked at last. 'Forget I'm her father. Well of course you can't. But tell me what I ought to do. They seem very much in love. I don't say I've been particularly keen on Philip in the past but Mary's chosen and that's enough for me. Besides, now I've seen a bit more of him as one does on these occasions I find there's a lot in the boy. I'm not saying a word against Jane mind but he's missed having a man about the house. Have you run across him in one of his hats?'

'Bloody terrible. Don't speak of 'em.'

'Aren't they?' Mr Pomfret agreed in a relieved sort of voice. 'Later on I may be able to manage something about it. But are you on my side about those two or aren't you?'

'Not for me to take sides. You know Jane better than me John. Comparative newcomer is all I am.'

'You'll excuse my saying this but you aren't. Why I hardly ever see old Jane now, and then only at the cost of a row each time with Liz. No, all I want is the children's happiness and how to get it, that's what I'm after.'

'Won't they marry in spite of anything either of you may say?' Mr Abbot asked.

'Of course Richard. Simply I'd like to avoid the sort of un-pleasantness which could follow, shortage of cash, no help from Jane because she's been rushed or feels hurt, the hundred and one things to dog them once they're back from the honeymoon.'

'Don't ask me how Jane's fixed for money.'

'Which is not the point with great respect old man. There's every kind of support Jane can bring if she wishes. But look here if she didn't agree,' Mr Pomfret pointed out 'matters might go sour, all sorts of awful things, trouble and so on. Oh we shall be out of it right enough, you and I. I'm thinking of Mary.'

'Grandchildren do the trick d'you consider?'

'Well naturally. Still supposing there aren't any at first. And how can anyone carry it off in a single room, if they have to live in the beginning with practically no more than a single room, and on what they earn?'

'As I know Jane she'd never resist a baby,' Mr Abbot said.

'But good God Richard have they to breed like rabbits to get recognition?'

'They've always got you haven't they?'

'What's the use? I've no money left! Who has?'

'Well thank God I'm not in your shoes.'

'It's not as bad as that is it Richard? D'you mean you think Jane actually opposes the idea?'

'Me? How should I know? She doesn't discuss anything with me, good God no. Damned if I can say what I'd advise.'

'You don't sound very cheerful old man I must say.'

'It's like this John,' Mr Abbot explained 'and by the way I wouldn't care for anyone to know what I'm going to tell you now. The fact is Jane and I may see a bit of one another from time to time but she doesn't confide in me, never has. Damned self-reliant woman in my opinion Jane and always was.'

'I don't know I ever found her any different,' Mr Pomfret agreed. 'So you can't say what she's driving at?'

Richard Abbot considered his host in a long expressionless stare.

'D'you suppose Jane knows herself?' he asked in the end. 'Probably got a violent sensationalism over this marriage business. Except she'll hide it under sweetness and light if you follow me. Then when she's ready,' and Mr Abbot jerked his hands up from his knees 'out it will all come. Just like that.'

'Oh my God you appal me,' John Pomfret cried with signs of agitation.

'Could go either way with her, for or against,' said Richard in what seemed to be great satisfaction. Upon which Mr Pomfret took his guest to the bar, they fell in with friends and dined in a party. No more was said of the engagement that night.

Mr Weatherby and Miss Pomfret were in the saloon bar of the public house they used in Knightsbridge. Their becoming engaged to be married had not made the smallest difference in either's manner or appearance. As usual they sat over two light ales and, when they talked, spoke for a time almost in asides to one another.

'You know my blue hat darling?' she asked.

'Which one?' he vaguely said.

Mary gave a short technical description.

'Well I might,' he admitted but did not seem as if he could.

'Your mother doesn't like it.'

'I don't know that I care for many of hers.'

'D'you think I dress horribly badly darling?'

'Why Mary you must be sure I don't.'

'Because you see I'm wearing everything I've got for you now darling or almost, and I'd like to get some idea of what you feel suits me if we are to buy all these clothes.'

'What clothes?'

'Frocks. Dresses. Trousseau. Getting married you know.'

'Sorry darling. I've never done this sort of thing before. I wasn't thinking.'

'Nor me! The trouble is Philip these older women have and do, they've got us at a disadvantage.'

'Your father doesn't like my headgear either.'

'Daddy? He's never said a word.'

'He has to me.'

'How did he object?'

'Artistic was the word he used.'

'Oh dear I'm really sorry darling because I always think Daddy's the best dressed man I meet, of his own generation of course.'

'Well I rather fancy the way Mamma gets herself up sometimes.'

Miss Pomfret laughed.

'I'll tell you what,' she said. 'This conversation's becoming almost barbed isn't it?'

He gave a wry smile. 'Might be,' he agreed.

She took his hand under the table, stroked the ring finger with her thumb. A silence drew across them.

She watched a couple up at the bar with a miniature poodle on a stool in between. Its politeness and general agitation appeared half human. But when a man came in with a vast brindled bull terrier on a lead as thick as an ox's tail the smaller dog turned her back to the drinks, ignored her owners at once, and gazed at the killer with thrilled lack-lustre eyes. For his part the bull terrier lay down as soon as the man on the other end of his lead let him, and, with an air of acute embarrassment gazed hard at the poodle, then away again, then, as though he could not help it, back once more. He started to whine. Miss Pomfret smiled. The other occupants began paying attention to these interested animals.

'Rather sweet isn't he?' she said.

'Who? Your father?'

'Oh no, Daddy always is. The bull terrier I mean.'

'So long as he doesn't take it into his head to murder that other wretched brute in front of our very eyes.'

'But he won't Philip. She's a lady.'

'I've known it happen.'

'The man who's with him's got him safe.'

'They'll do something crazy to let them meet before the evening's out. We'll see blood spilt yet,' he opined.

'Philip darling do you like dogs?' she enquired.

'I do and I don't,' he said.

'Because I was thinking when we were married I'd rather love to have one for my own.'

'Might be a bit awkward if we both went out every day to work.'

'Oh I expect the landlady would look after things.'

'I wonder,' he said.

She dropped his hand.

'You're in rather a filthy mood this evening,' she remarked.

He drew himself up to finish his glass of beer.

'I'm sorry Mary,' he said and appeared to be so. 'I say I saw Uncle Ned at tea today.'

'What, did he come round?'

'To Mamma's? Good Lord no. I went to him.'

'Was he pleased about us?'

'D'you know I didn't dare tell.'

'Not dare tell him!' she echoed. 'That's not very nice to me, now then!'

'Oh it wasn't that. It simply seems he detests Mamma and won't have her mentioned in his presence hardly. Seemed very surprised when I sent up my name. Even told me he'd been in two minds whether to say he was at home. Me, his own nephew!'

She laughed. 'But perhaps he was busy darling.'

'No Mary it's no laughing matter. And when I can't remember ever having met the man. You'd think he'd have some family sense! And then when he started on Mamma like that!'

'Oh I am so sorry Philip. What on earth did he say?'

'Nothing much actually. I came away with the idea he really must be rather mad. In fact of course I had to stand up for her and so on. But that it should happen at a time like this, with marriage on our hands! After all a wedding is a family affair isn't it?'

'Of course darling,' she agreed with every appearance of concern, took his hand back in her own under the table and began to squeeze it hard. 'Oh dear you mustn't get upset.'

'It all came as a bit of a shock,' he said in a calm voice.

'But Philip you'd seen him before?'

'Never that I remember.'

'And there was Daddy telling me you went to your Uncle Ned's tailor.'

'Well I do.'

'Then you must have met Uncle first for him to recommend you.'

'Mamma gave me the name. My father went there too.'

'Oh of course darling. How silly of me!'

'What on earth was your parent doing to talk about my tailor?'

'Oh nothing really.'

'Doesn't he like the suits I wear either?' the young man asked.

'You mustn't bother about Daddy darling. He's tremendously of his own generation can't you see? I expect in their day it was only possible for them to get their clothes from the one man.'

'But my father went to Highcliffe too.'

'Of course he did. I'll tell you what,' she announced. 'The next time I think of it I'll ask Daddy what he really meant.'

'And you might get him to give you the address of his tailor.'

'Oh Philip darling shall I really?'

'I've been rather disappointed in Uncle Ned,' the young man said. 'I don't see why I should favour his tradespeople any longer.'

A day or two later, in what for once was brilliant sunshine, Mary Pomfret and Philip Weatherby were sitting on a Sunday afternoon in Hyde Park.

'D'you mind what part of London we live in?' she asked.

'Wherever you like,' he said.

She frowned. 'That's not quite what I meant,' she pointed out. 'If you had your dearest wish just which district would you prefer?'

'I don't mind,' he replied.

'Because darling I think we ought to start looking about you know?'

'I leave it to you,' he said, his eyes out over the Serpentine as a dog swam to a thrown branch in the foreground. 'I shan't interfere. A home's a woman's business.'

'But Philip before I begin to search I shall have to know what we can afford.'

'I'll hand over my salary every week less ten cigarettes a day. I've decided to give up beer. If we like to go to the pub you can take me on the housekeeping money.'

'Oh darling aren't you making it all sound rather grim?'

'I think marriage is. We'll have a lot of responsibilities.'

'Philip don't you want to marry me?'

At that he turned and took her hand. He did not say anything but there must have been something in his eyes or expression for she sighed as though satisfied.

'Oh darling,' she said. 'You had me quite worried for a moment.'

They sat on in silence for a while. He gazed at his feet. She searched every cranny of his face with her eyes.

'Because I don't think we need be right down to the bone,' she began again. 'I mean Daddy's said he'd be able to help a bit.'

'D'you believe one ought to accept anything from one's parents Mary?'

'They haven't much I know, that is compared with what they were once accustomed to,' she said. 'And yet what they've been allowed to keep is family cash isn't it? Savings handed down from father to son?'

As she put this forward she allowed a small smile to play almost imperceptibly about the corners of her mouth.

'That's a sound point certainly,' he replied. Then he stopped. He did open his lips once more after a minute but relapsed into silence instead. She waited. At last he went on,

'As a matter of fact Mamma has been to see the dread Mr Thicknesse.' He laughed. 'You don't know who he is now, do you?'

'Of course,' she gaily answered. 'Your family lawyer.'

'How did you find out?' he demanded and looked sternly at her again. Meeting his eyes she stuck her chin up in rather an attractive manner.

'Daddy told me!'

'You discuss quite a lot with your Father don't you?'

'If you talked over things more with me I mightn't have to.'

There was a silence.

'Oh Philip don't be so absurd. You're forever speaking about the family though I notice you don't ever seem to mention we might have children of our own, and now you object to my going into things with my Father. I think you're beastly.'

'I'm sorry,' he said 'darling truly I am,' and took her hand once more. 'The fact is I get worried. You were dead right just now when you pointed out people of our parents' age had the experience over us. You see I'm not sure it's right to accept money from them.'

'But your father may have left you some Philip.'

'Oh if he had they'd tell me. They could hardly not could they?'

'Still why don't you go and see Mr Thicknesse?'

'Me?' he echoed. 'But Mamma's been.'

'I see,' she said in an unseeing voice.

'It won't be a great deal cheaper for her with me gone,' he went on. 'There's Penelope to consider. I mean I don't see how we can afford Arthur Morris' flat do you? Three whole rooms!'

'We might have to if we had children.'

'Oh I don't suppose it will ever fall vacant,' he answered. When she did not say anything he continued,

'As to the little Weatherbys they'll have to wait till they arrive.'

She gasped and then she laughed.

'Little Weatherbys,' she cried. 'How extraordinary! All this time I've been thinking of them as little Pomfrets. Darling Philip I am absurd. I never even imagined I'd have to change my name!'

'Well that's the idea isn't it?' he said.

'Then if I must I'd like to sooner rather than later darling.'

'Whenever you say,' he said.
She frowned and bit her lip.

A few days afterwards Mrs Weatherby had John Pomfret to dinner alone for the second time since their respective children had become engaged.

The meal was announced almost before his sherry was poured and now he found himself seated by candlelight in front of some fried veal and unable as yet to start discussing arrangements.

'Me dear,' he broke in as soon as he decently could 'I'm very flattered. Here I am enjoying the most delicious dinner. But we have a lot to go over. Time is never short I know. All the same I should be glad to get down to things.'

'Darling John you were always so tempestuous.'

'Thank you Jane. I don't know that I usually let the grass grow under my feet. But this has to do with Mary's happiness.'

'Well then I went to see Mr Thicknesse like I promised.'

'And what did the old fool say?'

'Oh my dear,' Mrs Weatherby began as though a roll of drums had preluded a performance which was late only owing to the negligence of the conductor out of sight in the prompter's box 'it was terrible, I never thought I should survive. You know he always seemed to take such a curious view in the old days about our case John. I'm sure if they had ever come to court I'd've had more real true sympathy from the judge, although we were paying Mr Thicknesse weren't we?'

'Damned expensive he was into the bargain.'

'Well I went,' she repeated. 'When I got back I had to take one of my little tablets and lie down. It's really too bad Philip is so young and can't help out with these business things. As for you John dear Mr Thicknesse's manner to me was so strange once you might almost have knocked him down if you'd been there. Oh how does one change one's lawyer?'

'Simply by leaving him.'

'Leave Mr Thicknesse, I'd never dare! After all I've been through with him! But do you know I can't understand a word he says.'

'Hasn't he a clerk then?'

'Oh yes. A young one. He's sweet. He'd do anything for me. When I've something very urgent and I get on the telephone they put me through sometimes to Mr Eustace. Isn't it a queer name? I suppose that's only when the old devil of a man is engaged. Really isn't one's life too awful, to be at the mercy of men like Mr Thicknesse!'

'Don't beat about the bush Jane.'

'It's simply I can't be hurried. John do be sensible dear. I won't be rushed, just won't.'

She left her veal, went over to the sideboard and fetched a china dish of chocolates across to Mr Pomfret.

'Beautiful bit of meat you have here,' he said.

'It's always such a pleasure to entertain you John,' she replied. 'No but I mean what can all the hurry be?' she went on. 'Only three weeks ago when they so startled us all and now their whole lives in front of them!'

'You do feel they're too young?'

'I may have done at first but it was you, surely, confounded us both with my own marriage as though you were prosecuting me darling. We went to Folkestone for the first night of the honeymoon.' She sighed. 'My beloved mother sent her maid until we crossed to France next morning and the woman got so excited when she unpacked for me I couldn't get rid of her, so awkward. No I don't say they're over young now though Philip of course has a lot still to learn, not too young exactly, but where's the violent haste in all this John dear?'

'Oh none. But before there may be there's so much to discuss.'

'You don't mean . . .?'

'Of course not Jane. Only engagements often end in a race. Nerves turn ragged.'

'All right but don't you get cross!'

'Jane darling I'm not. Of course we must take our time.'

'That's much better,' she said, giving him her great smile. 'Because I think Mary's the sweetest child in the whole world. So lucky for dear Philip. But we must be practical. After all we are their parents. Oh who would've ever imagined darling us sitting opposite each other like we are solemnly eating our dinners with the children's marriage to decide!'

'It's a sobering thought certainly.'

'Aren't you pleased then?' she asked.

'It makes me feel so old,' he replied in a bantering tone of voice but with evident caution. 'Something like this can happen before one is ready for it.'

'Then you do think they're rather babies?'

'No no,' he said quickly. 'What I meant was I'm the one who's too young. And I know you are.'

She laughed. 'One can forever be certain you'll make delicious fun out of serious moments and I love you for it darling. Though I don't say I did always.'

'We never made a joke of our affairs in the old days. It might've been better if we had.'

'How d'you mean?' she demanded sharply.

'Well we were very very serious weren't we?'

'I should hope so too,' she said.

'It was most painful at the time though.'

'Oh I thought I would die,' she sighed.

'And did we get anywhere by waiting Jane?'

'No don't,' she moaned. 'We must simply never go over all that again.'

'It's a thought what I've just said just the same.'

'Oh dear I sometimes feel men must be wildly insensitive. If I knew enough of the language I'd ask Isabella if it's like this in Italy.'

'You wouldn't want a fat man about the house always singing opera.'

'I might be able to put up with it.'

'Now Jane you know how quick-tempered you can be, particularly when you've those headaches of yours and won't stand any noise.'

'I'm not like that now,' she answered. 'But we mustn't talk over ourselves and the old days tragically sweet as they were. We're here to be practical and I think we have been John.'

'Well well,' he said with an edge of sarcasm on his voice.

'My dear what's the matter with you now?' she asked at once. 'I thought I was being exactly as you wished.'

He laughed. 'You're too many for me Jane,' he admitted.

'And just don't you forget it,' she replied, once more beaming upon him.

Upon which she changed the conversation and in spite of one or two halfhearted efforts on his part he was unable to discuss the children further that evening.

A week later Philip Weatherby sought his mother out in the living room of their flat. He blurted,

'Mamma I don't think I want to be married after all.'

'What's that?'

'I don't think I want to be married Mamma.'

'But how about Mary, Philip?'

'I don't know.'

'You mean you haven't told her?'

'Not yet.'

'Oh my dearest!' his mother cried. 'And what are we to say to John?' Nevertheless there was something in her voice which could not be discouragement and when he replied it was in stronger if still bewildered tones.

'I thought you might have him round Mamma.'

'Me?' she asked. 'Tell him instead of you Philip?'

'Well of course it's for me to see Mary.'

'But dear boy are you sure about all this?'

'I don't know.'

'You don't know!' she echoed. 'Oh my God where have things come to?'

'Mamma why is it Uncle Ned won't have anything to do with us?'

'Ned? You poor child he's simply an idiot and always was. How does he enter into this?'

'Not really.'

'Oh my dearie,' she announced, albeit almost gay 'I feel quite faint. Tell me though! Why must you turn round like you are doing?'

'I'm an awful nuisance I suppose?'

'Nuisance?' she exclaimed. 'I hope I shall be the last to say that ever, your very own mother! No it's the shock.'

'Somehow I didn't imagine you'd be altogether surprised.'

'What was I to think?' she demanded. 'Getting to your feet as you did in the middle of my party to my friends. I backed you up you must admit and I should hope so too, who would if I couldn't!'

'Oh you've been wonderful' he said with conviction. 'You always are.'

'I love you when you're like you're being,' she said with fervour.

'Well, there's no closer family relationship after all.'

'Yes but when you get to my age, have my experiences, though heaven forbid you should, my dear you'll realize I really do believe, that you only truly meet people even your nearest and dearest once or twice in a long long while and this is one of those minutes. I just never could feel you were suited to Mary.'

'I don't think myself I'm right for her.'

'Philip there's not a soul else is there? It can't be Bethesda?'

'Don't be so absurd Mamma.'

'Forgive that,' she said 'I must be wandering. Oh I know Mary's a sweet child. But no one will stop me saying marriages between the children of old friends are so often a quite disastrous muddle.'

'I hadn't worried about that side of it,' he protested.

'Very likely not,' she agreed. 'All the same I did.'

'In what way?'

'In no way at all Philip,' his mother told him sharply. 'Call it knowledge of the wicked world, call everything what you will, instinct might be the best name, but something whispered to me this would be wrong.'

'You really have all along?'

'Oh I never interfere,' she cried. 'You can't say I've once come between you and something you've really wished. My dearest hope darling is to see you happy. Of course Mary's young. She'll soon get over things when the disappointment's gone. But what will John say?'

'Does this make it awkward for you?'

'I wouldn't say so quite,' she replied. 'I've known him now a great number of years. Still everything has to be done in a civilized way, I hope you realize Philip. Have you spoken to anyone yet?'

'Not a soul.'

'That's so much gained then' she said. She paused, got a mirror out of her handbag and began to remake her face. Those great eyes were limpid with what seemed to be innocence.

'I mustn't be rushed,' she announced at last.

'I know Mamma. I only came for advice.'

'A little late for that?' she said tartly. 'Now are you certain sure you've made up your own mind?'

'Well I'm not.'

'Philip how can you say so when the girl's very sweet I know but a simpleton without a penny and not even really pretty.'

Mr Weatherby became very dignified.

'Say what you like,' he protested in sulky tones 'I shall respect her all my life whatever happens.'

'Which means that for two twos you'd wed her now?'

'I didn't say did I?'

'All right my dear,' she said. 'But you seem very touchy about this. She's a nice girl I agree yet I also know she's not nearly good enough for you. What are we to do about it, that is the question?'

'To be or not to be Mamma.'

'Philip don't dramatise yourself for heaven's sake. This is no time for Richard II. You just can't go into marriage in such a frame of mind. Let me simply think!'

'What did you feel when you were getting married?'

'Is none of your damned business! Now leave me be, please my dear. I've got to use what wits I have left.'

There was a silence while she covered her eyes with fat ringed fingers and he watched like a small boy.

'I shall have to ask John here to a meal,' she decided at last.

'I don't somehow feel I could face him Mamma.'

'Alone with me,' she explained still from behind her hands. 'Oh dear,' she moaned 'it's horribly like.'

'What is?' he asked.

'Something years ago,' she answered.

At this moment the door opened without a sound and her daughter crept through, a forefinger to the lips, obviously in the middle of a game.

'Hi-ya Pen' Mr Weatherby gravely said.

Mrs Weatherby screamed. Her hands went to her ears. 'You sweet darling,' she cried 'what time is it? You mustn't come down now! So important. Philip and I are talking.'

The child considered them out of her enormous eyes. Then she as softly withdrew still signalling silence.

'Mummy'll come up and read to you when you're in bed,' the mother called after her. 'God forgive me,' she said in a lower voice 'the little saint coming down like that has driven every idea right out of my poor mind.'

'But Mamma you can't truthfully blame Mary for having no money of her own. Who is there has these days?'

'What's that got to do with it?' she asked from the midst of an obvious abstraction.

'Just a moment ago you said against Mary she didn't have a penny to her name.'

'Philip,' she cried 'don't clutter me up with detail. Besides I always imagined you must keep some rags and tatters of family feeling left, of keeping up the name. No you'll please let me think.'

He bit his nails.

'John has his awkward moments you know,' Jane murmured at last.

'Always seemed fairly straightforward when I've seen the man,' her son wearily protested.

'Which is all you know about people Philip. Oh dear for the matter of that what do we all of us know about anyone?'

'Well Mamma you're able to read me like the palm of your own hand.'

'I'm not sure I can now Philip.'

There was another pause.

'Then do you truly think I should go to a fortune teller?' his mother asked.

'If you feel it might help,' the son replied.

'They sometimes give such bad advice and it's cruel hard to go against what they've said,' she muttered. She removed the hand she held to her forehead, shading her eyes. He anxiously examined her face. But it could not be said there was any change in the expression. Sweetness and light still reigned supreme with perhaps a trace of mischief at the corners of a generous mouth.

'You'll have to tell Mary first,' Mrs Weatherby announced. 'Then and only then can I ask John to dinner. But what if he won't come?'

'Oh I know I shall have to see him Mamma!'

'You're to do nothing of the kind dearest until I've got my little oar in. I'll manage John I should hope after all these years, or I very much hope so. No I shall have to be ill. Not that I won't be really ill by that time, sick to death in my poor mind.'

'I'm dreadfully sorry.'

'Nonsense,' she cried gaily. 'Come over to me,' she ordered. When he sheepishly rose she kissed him on his forehead then made him sit by her side. 'What am I here for after all? Oh dear but isn't it going to be rather exciting and dreadful!'

Then she must have had a return to an earlier fear.

'My poor boy you're sure you haven't interfered with the girl in any way?' she asked with averted head, laying a hand on his arm.

'Interfered? What d'you mean? She was the keenest on the whole idea as a matter of fact.'

'Knowing you oh so well as I do I'm almost certain you've misunderstood me Philip. No I meant you haven't made love to her in that way have you?'

'Me? God no. It wouldn't have been right.'

'I thought so,' and she sighed. She turned her eyes back on him with a sorrowing look. 'Yes,' she said 'you make some of it ever so much easier. I wonder if any of this would have happened if I'd married again and there'd been a man about the house.'

'What difference could he have made? It's my life surely?'

'For you to live if you want to live,' she answered.

'Of course I wish to. I'm not ill am I?'

'Now dearest you're not to turn sour and desperate just because you've got yourself into rather a silly little mess and have to come to me to get you out of things. How would everything have looked if we'd had it announced in the Press, tell me that?'

'Oh don't!'

'Quite Philip dear and I think you've been very wise, almost clever when all's said and done. But you've not breathed a word even to Liz are you sure?'

'Me? Why should I?'

'Or Maud Winder's girl? What's her name?'

'Certainly not.'

'That's something certainly then!'

'You know I always tell you first Mamma.'

'Bless you and so you should.'

'But how does Miss Jennings come into this?'

'Dearest you'd never understand,' she said. 'Not in your present mood.'

'Oh if you want to make mysteries,' he objected.

'Now Philip I simply won't have it,' she protested in a bright voice. 'You get yourself into a desperate tangle without a single word to me, you come out with things in public as though you were the only one concerned and at last you come to your mother and who wouldn't, oh I don't blame you there, to extricate yourself from whatever it may be; then you ask what's what, who's who and details of everything passing through my poor head, — have some consideration dearest for the poor person you're speaking to,' she said happily 'or I'm very much afraid you won't be able to do much with your life.'

'Sorry,' he muttered.

'After all I shan't be here forever,' she added with a quick shadow of distaste passing across her lovely features.

'Don't,' he groaned.

She patted the arm she had been holding.

'You mustn't take all this too seriously Philip,' she comforted. 'Not since you've promised me no actual harm's been done.'

'But I've been so worried over little Pen,' he wailed.

'God bless the little soul,' Mrs Weatherby replied. 'What about her, the saint?'

'When she was dead keen on being bridesmaid!'

'Bridesmaid? Who to?'

'Why Mary and me of course. You know how Penelope was!'

'Now really Philip,' his mother protested and showed the first true signs of impatience she had displayed, 'if I can't manage my own daughter who can, what use am I? We'll soon snap her out of that,' she said stoutly. 'You'll see if we don't.'

The next Sunday John Pomfret and Miss Jennings were seated at their usual table. There was as yet no sign of Jane Weatherby or Mr Abbot. Thick fog curtained from without the windows that looked over the Park.

'But my dear,' Liz was saying 'what d'you propose?'

'In which way?' he asked.

'I mean how are you going to live?'

'Just the same as ever I imagine. We're all slaves to this endless work work work nowadays aren't we?'

'Then who will look after you?'

'Oh I expect I shall get by Liz. After all at my age it's the children's happiness is the thing.'

'What nonsense you do talk John! It's even disgraceful from a man who's in the prime of life, and the more so when as I believe you realize yourself there's not a word of truth in all this you're saying.'

He laughed. 'Well,' he reasoned 'the children have to marry some time haven't they, sooner rather than never – I mean later,' he corrected himself and gave Miss Jennings a short cool stare which she returned. 'And when they do or while they're doing it we have to take a back seat with the best grace in the world.'

'I don't think Jane is, John.'

'Now you know how fond old Jane still keeps of the limelight.'

'That's hardly what I meant dear. No she's telling almost everyone she'll stop this marriage by any means fair or foul.'

He laughed louder. 'Now darling whoever even suggested that?'

'It's all over London John.'

'Be damned for a yarn,' he said and a certain grimness underscored his voice. 'I've seen this happen before. When the tongues start clacking then's the time for all good men and true to look to their powder and see it's dry.'

'And make sure it isn't blank shooting or whatever that's called,' Miss Jennings sweetly said.

He frowned. 'Which sounds ominous. Did Jane speak to you Liz?'

'Oh no I'd be the last person, surely you realize dear! But she did get hold of that beastly Maud Winder which is why I was so careful just now to say Jane was telling almost everyone.'

'But the whole thing is totally absurd Liz darling. I only had dinner with Jane last Tuesday and we discussed arrangements for literally hours on end.'

'Did you go into detail?'

'Well no not exactly.'

'Then there you are you see!'

'But you can't rush these matters Liz. There's every sort and kind of point to settle. And after all the children have really got to think their own problems out for themselves. Our or rather my function is to assist where I can, God help me.'

'What did Jane actually say John?'

'Oh I don't know. She may be a bit confused of course, which is only natural but I know my Jane, she's fundamentally sound. Nothing wrong with her here,' he said tapping the waistcoat pocket over his heart.

Miss Jennings made a noise between a groan and a snort. He did not seem to listen.

'I'd never mention it darling,' he went on 'but as I expect you've already heard, Jane and I had quite an affair once years ago and I think I know her as well as any man ever does know a woman.'

'Which is why I asked what you meant to do with yourself.'

'How d'you mean Liz?'

'Well I've realized all along you wouldn't put up with Jane's plotting so I was sure the marriage would go through you see.'

'Thanks,' he said in a dry tone of voice.

'And now I want to know how you propose to manage?'

'Thanks again,' he repeated.

'No John don't be beastly,' she protested. 'Surely I've the right, or haven't I? Who is going to look after you?'

'When all's said and done Mary never did the cooking Liz.'

'Oh I realize if anything happens to one of your poor faithful women like happiness or marriage or both, if that should conceivably be possible, then you can go and eat in your club where you'll get better food than ever we can provide you with, but who's to send your suits to the cleaners?'

'They have a weekly service.'

She laughed. 'No John you're not to be loutish,' she cried. 'You know exactly what I'm driving at.'

'Who's to put my slippers in front of the fire you mean?'

'Well yes if you like.'

'My dear no one's ever done that for me in my life and it's too late now.'

'Which just shows you simply won't have comfort even at the smallest price,' she said. 'You are all the same. You'd rather be miserable alone in a hovel of a room than put up with having a woman about to make it home.'

'How little you know,' he replied and gave what was obviously a mock sigh.

'But you'll find yourself terribly lonely, you know you will.'

'Be nothing new in that,' he said with a sort of bravado.

'You'd rather stay by your own on a desert island than give in to Jane wouldn't you? Now tell me.'

'I suppose they must have been held up in the fog,' he replied looking for Richard Abbot and Mrs Weatherby.

'Heaven pity me,' she sighed. 'Oh but you can be maddening sometimes!'

He leant forward, put a hand over hers.

'I'm so sorry darling, you see it's not my life, I haven't the right but Jane and I went slap through things when I last saw her and of course she's simply delighted with Mary. Strictly between you and me she's been worried about Philip and as a matter of fact I didn't much care for the boy myself at one period if you remember. Marriage'll be just the thing for him.'

There was something in his speech which did not carry conviction, nevertheless Miss Jennings said 'Go on, do. This is a distinct improvement.'

He laughed. 'Don't all you women get excited over weddings!'

'Well of course. What else d'you expect? Now go on.'

'There's not a syllable more to tell just this minute. The second I have anything like a date or the name of the church, even where they propose to live I'll pass it on at once. But you know how jealous Jane can be, how particularly cagey where her own or her children's affairs are concerned. Why some days I myself hardly dare ask how little Penelope happens to feel. No, the less said at the moment the better.'

'Then what about Maud Winder?'

'Oh this will cook her goose with Jane right enough. You just wait till she hears.'

'But you promise if things won't run smoothly you shan't let Jane ride rough-shod over all your plans.'

'My darling Liz I've known her for literally ages. I might even understand Jane better than you.'

'Don't keep on John throwing that beastly old affair of yours with the woman plumb in my face. I really rather wish you wouldn't!'

'OK I won't.'

'Because heaven knows I'm no prude but there are parts of that story which aren't even, darling, for my tender ears.'

He laughed. 'I'm so sorry,' he said.

'Well you'd better be,' she answered and looked as though she sulked. There was a pause while he drummed on the table with his fingers.

'And have you got a list out, of the presents sweet Mary will want?' she asked.

'Not yet as a matter of fact.'

'Blankets bathtowels and so forth? It makes such a difference because otherwise in spite of two wars she may get nothing but glass.'

'I'll remember,' he promised.

A few days later Mrs Weatherby had John Pomfret to dinner alone for the third time after Philip had announced the engagement.

'Well Jane,' he asked 'have they said anything to you? Because I'm still without news at all.'

'My poor heart goes out to them,' she murmured.

'They seem to be taking their time certainly. But as you said the other day perhaps that's no bad thing in itself.'

'It's not the two of them I worry over my dear so much as yourself.' Her manner was unusually restrained, serious even.

He laughed uneasily. 'How's this?' he cried.

'What on earth's to become of you when your girl goes?'

'But Jane Mary's not my cook.'

'No John you're not to make a joke about it,' she said although there was little mirthful in his attitude. 'You owe your own self the sacred duty of seeing to yourself,' she argued with a sweet sincerity. 'I know children must marry some day bless them, but we do have the right to ask what is to become of our own lives.'

'Yet not the right to ask that question of them Jane.'

'My dear you are so much cleverer that you must bear with me. I never suggested anything of the kind I'm sure, now did I? I simply want to be told what you propose to do with yourself, that's all.'

'Carry on as usual I suppose.'

'Changing maids every eight weeks John?'

'Oh don't!' he cried. 'No I had the idea I might drift along to the Club perhaps for a bit.'

'And what sort of life is that for a man?' she demanded. 'Besides you know you can't afford standing drinks to all and sundry every hour of the day and night.'

'They have their licensing laws too you know.'

'Stuff and nonsense! Don't tell me those men pay the smallest attention to stupid little regulations. No it would be so bad for you John.'

'Then how d'you propose I should live?'

'I've simply no idea darling which is why I'm so terribly worried.'

'Well I'm most flattered. Everyone seems to want to be told how I can manage. I just hadn't considered it, that's all.'

'And you'll have had offers of help no doubt?'

'My dear if ever you hear of a responsible woman, what we used to call a cook general in the old days, who'll have nothing whatever to do in the daytime on vast wages, then you'll be my saviour.'

'That wasn't what I meant in the least.'

'But Jane I can't run to the expense of a married couple.'

'And have the husband drinking your gin and rowing with his wife all day, I should think not indeed!'

'What did you have in mind then?'

'Marriage John.'

'There can't be a double ceremony, they're so vulgar. Besides who'd have me?'

'Are you going to marry your Liz my dear?'

'Now Jane what is all this?'

'You should grant me certain privileges my loved one,' she said

115

staring at him until he looked away. 'The years as they roll on give me a sort of wretched right,' she announced. 'And I'll not sit idly by and see you make yourself miserable just because Mary says she must leave home.'

'There's no question, none at all!'

'But yes! Oh my dear you're going to be so lonely!'

'About Liz I mean.'

'Are you sure?'

'No Jane how can you say am I sure? I still know what goes on around me I should hope.'

'Does one ever?'

'I swear to you not a word's been said.'

'Now John that makes not a scrap of difference, does it?'

'Yet to get married you have to say so don't you?'

'It's the final thing you say, yes.'

'You will go on talking in riddles Jane.'

'My dear I give you simple plain common or garden sense. You are like all men, lawyers every single one. You think there's no contract until you've said yes or had your answer but the chances are you've unofficially sworn yourself away for ever all unbeknownst quite months before. Which makes it so wicked when men try and back out.'

'Now Jane to what is this referring?'

'Nothing my dear, at all.'

'You were.'

'On my honour. The past's past. The little I'm saying is she has her heart set on you.'

'Well I suppose I might do worse at that.'

'There you go, utterly sweet, completely deceitful!'

He laughed. 'But you just put the idea right into my mind,' he objected.

'I did nothing of the sort. And John don't bridle in that delighted way when I suggest someone might like to be married to you. I can't bear false modesty, which can be one of your little faults my dear. There are literally thousands of unattached women sitting by their telephones this very minute waiting waiting for the call that never comes.'

'I wish I met 'em.'

'Don't be so tiresome please,' she said. 'Who d'you think you are anyway?'

'Well who then?'

'A most attractive man whose family life may just about to be broken up from all accounts.'

'You flatter me.'

'No John you simply shall not take this stupid silly line. To all sorts and kinds of horrors waiting in their lairs you're a whole line of goods freshly come into the swim.'

'Oh now you must grant me some powers of choice.'

'But that's exactly it, I don't. How can I? You're only making fun while they're in wait there with the dread wretched lives they lead – no to give the present government its due they always did though it's not for me to praise politicians God help us, – those frightful endless days and nights have taught them so they're on watch for the slightest sign of backsliding.'

'Now Jane you really can't make poor Liz out into a harpy or a pike!'

'Can't I!'

'You may not like her, she might not be the sort of person for you but at least she's not that kind.'

'Well my dear,' she agreed 'you know how I always do go rather far. Mr Thicknesse has often told me. "Dear lady" he's said and isn't it fantastic there are still people to call one that, "your tongue will one day cost a deal of money". It never has yet you know but then perhaps one's friends are more loyal than sometimes we suppose. You see I expect they must be. Because when I say what I do about Liz I don't really mean anything, only that she's such a horrid beast who simply oughtn't to be alive.'

'No Jane there are occasions you can go too far!'

There was a pause which she filled by getting him more sherry.

'I'm sorry John but I mean every word for the best.'

'Doesn't one always? Is that a valid excuse?'

'She doesn't.'

'Then what exactly do you hold against the poor woman?'

'She's not poor, she's even very attractive in her own way, though of course she must have been to have the success she had. Oh what it takes to keep on learning one isn't the only pebble on the beach!'

'You don't suppose Dick Abbot is enamoured?' he asked with a degree of sarcasm in his voice.

'Richard?' she cried. For a moment she returned to her usually gay manner. 'That sweet man! Never in the whole wide world!! How could he be?'

'Then Jane you just can't really accept any soul who sees Liz?'

'What d'you mean? That I care who she sees?'

'No quite,' he agreed in a small voice.

'All I said was,' she went on 'and presuming oh yes I am on old friendship was that she couldn't, mustn't be the one for you, – I think I mean mustn't, really John darling!'

'And why? How mustn't?'

'But the woman drinks.'

'Now Jane that's most unfair. You know she never has.'

'I'm very sorry to say I know nothing of the kind.'

'Good God then where and when?'

'My dear John! In the bedroom I expect.'

'How can you speak of her bedroom?'

'Why should I know? I don't get in it.'

'No Jane this is honestly almost unpleasant. We might, we may from time to time have had something for each other, Liz and I, but really I don't feel you have the right . . .'

'Don't I darling?'

'In what way then?'

'If I see you take a wrong turn, after all these years can't I say what I feel?'

'But we're here tonight to talk about the children.'

'And isn't that just what we are discussing John?'

'No we never seem to get away from my own marriage which I give you my word is the first I've heard and which seems to be Liz all the time.'

'Do you maintain she doesn't drink then John?'

'Well she certainly wasn't bottled at Eddie's as Maud Winder said she might be.'

'How can you tell?'

'But I was there Jane.'

'I'm going to say something darling may make you rather cross. It's simply that when you're out with her you sometimes are inclined to take a drop too much yourself.'

'Oh now Jane this is preposterous! I wasn't that way at Eddie's.'

'How can you possibly judge my dear? Oh I'm not trying to make out you are a soak like poor William Smith, so much so that his wife had to leave him, you remember sad Myra – what's happened to her

– couldn't face pouring the whisky down his throat when he lost his arms? I'm not pretending anything. I only maintain which I shall until the day I die that when you're out with the woman, and it's not necessarily anything noticeable, you aren't sometimes a very good judge perhaps of how much someone else has taken.'

He swallowed air three or four times.

'I still don't see how all this has to do with Philip and Mary,' he objected.

'I do,' she said.

'Well how then?' he almost shouted.

'Now you're simply not to bully me in my own house,' she announced in a small voice. 'I have such a headache into the bargain.'

'I'm sorry Jane,' he said, quieter.

There was a pause. After which she said in low tones,

'I had no call to tell you what I did either.'

'Oh I know you meant it for the best,' he smiled.

'I not only meant it, it was best,' she rejoined.

'Very well,' he agreed. 'But you might admit you could be wrong about Liz.'

'Of course I may. Yet I'm not.'

He swallowed air again. 'All right darling,' he admitted.

'That's better,' she said.

'Still I don't get drunk Jane.'

'No there I admit I went too far dear John. I got upset!'

'Dear me!' he smiled. 'What we all go through when the children want to settle their lives for themselves.'

'What we go through to avoid what we might have to go through,' she took him up at once.

'Yes very well Jane,' he agreed.

'Oh my headache is so bad,' she said visibly wilting.

'You ought to lie down.'

At this moment Isabella flung the door open to announce something in a flood of words, presumably that dinner was served. Mrs Weatherby thanked her.

'It's hammering round my head,' she wailed.

'Why don't you go along then Jane?'

'D'you know I simply feel I must. But whatever will you think of me?'

'I'll bring you yours in on a tray.'

'You'll do nothing of the kind,' she objected. 'What would Isabella simply think? No when I get one of my sick headaches I just can't eat anything. I must shut my poor aching eyes in the dark. But what will you do John dear? Oh how rude I am!'

'I can get a bite at the Club.'

'Certainly not. No you'll dine here I insist. Not that it'll be worth having. Oh dear!'

'I'm so sorry Jane and I hope you'll be better tomorrow. Sure there isn't anything I've foolishly said?'

'How could there be? No you'll simply have to forgive.'

While he kissed her cheek as she prepared to leave he ventured once more,

'And you've heard nothing fresh from the children?'

'Not a word,' she replied, then disappeared tragically smiling.

Soon after this, with the day's work done, Mary Pomfret came to her father when he was alone over an evening paper.

'Daddy is there any news?' she asked.

'Of the wedding stakes?' he cried. 'But I have none.'

'Because oh dear it's not going well I think Daddy!'

'Engagements never do my dear.'

'You are such a comfort,' she said. 'And it's so complicated. Still I suppose everything always is.'

'I nearly went mad when I became engaged to your mother.'

'Did you? Oh Daddy what I want to know is the line Mrs Weatherby's taking?'

'Funny you should ask. I took old Dick Abbot out and put him that very question. I should think he sees more of Jane than anyone these days. He rather seemed to be of the opinion she hadn't quite made her mind up yet. Now you know I consider I can read Jane as well as the next man and I'd say myself she was enthusiastic, hand on my heart I would.'

'Then you haven't heard this extraordinary story that Philip and I are really half brother and sister?'

'What?' he yelled and nearly shot out of his chair, crushing the newspaper in the process.

'Here let me do that,' his daughter said and picked those sheets up to pat them flat again. She kept her eyes from off his face.

'If you would only tell me who'd said it then I'd have the law on 'em,' he panted.

'My future mother in law,' she murmured.

'Jane did! You can't be serious Mary!'

'Daddy, do say it isn't true!'

'True! You must be insane. Good God! Good God!!'

'Well is it?'

'No of course not.'

'How can you be sure Daddy?'

'Because I am.'

'I'm terribly sorry but you see this means rather a lot to me.'

He controlled himself. 'Of course, must do monkey,' he said.

'And you couldn't possibly be?' she insisted.

'Oh well you know how things are,' he lamely explained. 'Jane and I certainly saw quite a bit of each other about that time, the time he was born I mean. But the thing's utterly preposterous.'

'Because if it was true I don't think I could ever speak to you again.'

'I do realize that Mary. Look you've got to listen to me. I know you'll think I have a special reason for telling you this but you must believe your father!'

At this point she handed the newspaper back neatly folded.

'Oh thanks,' he said. It seemed as if his train of thought had been broken for when he went on he said,

'Jane surely never told you?'

'No she didn't. I went down to ask her at Brighton as a matter of fact and when I got there I simply found I hadn't the gumption.'

'I'm not surprised Mary.' He tried a laugh. She actually giggled a moment but still kept her eyes from his. 'I must say!' he added and laughed louder. She did not respond however and he returned to his serious manner.

'Who's been hinting?' he demanded.

'Well as a matter of fact Philip mentioned something.'

'Philip,' he echoed in noticeably brighter tones. 'How can he know at his age?'

'No Daddy you're not to laugh! You remember what I told you, I'd never speak to you again.'

'I'm not laughing,' he defended himself. 'But you'll agree my dear it isn't a very pleasant thing to be confronted on without a word of warning.'

'And not nice for me either under the circumstances?'

'Frightful,' he agreed. 'My God I've never heard anything like it. But where did your Philip get this extraordinary notion?'

'From his mother I fancy.'

'So that's how it originated! She didn't tell you then?'

'Oh no I've just said haven't I? I went down to see her in the hotel and then couldn't screw up my miserable courage.'

'You're not to blame monkey good Lord! I should say not! But d'you mean to tell me Jane actually put it in so many words?'

'I'm not sure.'

'Then darling you must make doubly certain.'

'Why should I when you told me not a moment ago it could be.'

'Could be what?'

'True Daddy.'

'But my love I never said a word of the kind!'

'You did.'

'How did I?'

'Just now when you admitted you'd seen a lot of her about that time.'

'But the idea's perfectly ridiculous,' he replied in blustering accents. 'Why doesn't he come and ask me himself? I'd soon tell him.'

'For the same reason I expect I couldn't bring myself with his mother. But oh Daddy do say all this isn't true.'

'I've already told you. It's utterly ridiculous! I've never in my whole life heard such awful nonsense!'

'Then why did you say what you did?'

'Earlier on? For the simple reason this was the first time such an insane idea had ever been put to me. I was flabbergasted, absolutely stunned! And I'm so accustomed to the worst that for a second I even considered whether it mightn't be a fact. But I tell you what. You know about that time things were pretty strained between the four of us, I mean he wasn't even born then and his father began throwing writs about and cross-petitions, – we won't go into all the business now, what's over's over, enough's enough, – but if there could be a word of truth in this tale don't you agree Weatherby would have used your story? And he didn't! If you don't believe me go and ask Mr Thicknesse.'

'Oh Daddy so you really don't think there's anything?'

'Of course not my dear. Lord but you had me thoroughly rattled for a minute.'

'I'm such a nuisance,' she wailed, gazing straight at him, her eyes full of tears.

'You aren't,' he said. 'Besides why don't you ask the others?'

'I have.'

He looked at her very hard.

'And what did they say?'

'I went to Arthur Morris and Philip did too, separately of course. He told us both the same or so Philip swears.'

'There you are then! With the poor fellow dying he'd surely never dare tell a lie.'

'But Daddy how simply dreadful! He isn't is he?'

'So Liz says.'

'He simply can't. He's so sweet!'

'That's the way things are my dear I'm afraid. Well we've all got to come to it. When he didn't turn up at Jane's party I thought he must be pretty bad. What's the ring you're wearing?'

'It's mine. I mean the engagement ring.'

'Oh I say,' he cried 'and you never told. Here let's have a good look.'

They bent their heads together over her left hand.

'Well well,' he said. 'This is quite pretty isn't it? How much did he pay?'

'That's my secret Daddy. We talked everything over of course. We decided we'd be insane to spend a lot of cash on what is out of date tripe. I never meant it to be more than just something to go on that especial finger.'

'One bit of jewellery I always did swear could be worth a bust was the engagement ring.'

'Oh I know you don't like it or him,' she wailed, sharply withdrawing her hand.

'Now my dear,' he interrupted 'we can't have this! You're overwrought. Good God you've your own lives to lead haven't you? I think the good ring very suitable, so there.'

'Do you,' she murmured seeming mollified. 'And you won't so much as breathe to Mrs Weatherby about the other business?'

'See here what sort and kind of a parent d'you take me for? Why naturally not,' he replied.

Knowing his daughter was to be out of London the next forty-eight hours on some trip in connection with her Government job Mr Pomfret at once got on the telephone to Jane and asked the lady round the next day to what he called a scratch meal at his flat.

After giving her a drink he led the way into the next room where a spectacular supper was laid out and which began with caviar. Once she had exclaimed at this and he had been able to sketch in the devious methods he employed to lay hands on such a delicacy, he so to speak cut right down into the heart of things by saying,

'Well I've seen the ring.'

'Oh my dear,' she replied 'so have I!'

He considered Mrs Weatherby very carefully at this response but she was eating her sturgeon's eggs with a charming concentration that was also the height of graceful greed, her shining mouth and brilliant teeth snapping just precisely enough to show enthusiasm without haste, the great eyes reverently lowered on her plate.

'Did you help Philip choose?'

'Me? Dear no,' she answered, carefully selecting a piece of toast. 'I know better than to interfere ever,' she said. 'But you make me feel such a perfect fool John,' she continued. 'There was I the other evening wanting so much to be told how you would manage when you had to live alone and now you put me to absolute shame with a lovely choice meal like this.'

'Oh we don't do it every day,' he laughed then turned serious once more. 'And do you like the ring Jane?'

'No' she said 'who could? I was so vexed.'

'I would only say it to you my dear,' Mr Pomfret announced 'but the boy must have gone to ——'s' and he gave the name of a shop which extensively advertised cheap engagement hoops.

She raised her eyes to his from the caviar with reluctance and a charming smile.

'One has to be so careful never to butt in,' she explained 'or rather, and am I being wicked, never to seem that one is arranging their little affairs for them. I tried to make him give dear Mary a solitaire darling Mother left me in her will and that somehow I've not had the heart to sell.' She now looked down at her plate again and went on unhurriedly eating caviar. Then she squeezed some more lemon with an entrancing grimace of alarm, presumably lest a drop lodge in the corner of an eye. 'How delicious and good this is,' she sighed.

'And Philip wouldn't have it?' he asked.

'Philip simply wouldn't,' she confirmed.

There was a pause.

'Then I had so hoped,' she calmly went on at last 'for you know what he is about family feelings, – well I don't say this ring of Mother's was enormously valuable or of course it would have gone long before now, one can't go round London barefoot after all, – but in a way the thing's an heirloom and he'd only have had to get it lined because of course Mother had such small bones.'

'You don't think Mary's fingers are like bananas?'

'John!' she screamed, eyeing him in alarm. 'I don't find that funny do you?'

'Well all right then,' he said. 'But what are we to do about this ring he's given her?'

'Doesn't she like it?'

'You know how you felt just now yourself Jane.'

'Oh yes but we mustn't make everything more difficult for them dear. You realize it's not going to be easy for those two sweet loves our being such old friends you and I. But has Mary actually put it into words about the thing?'

'No. How could she?'

'She's wonderful! So d'you think we would be absolutely wise to interfere?'

'Yet you can't let her walk round with that on her left hand Jane.'

Mrs Weatherby faced him squarely at this.

'Wait a moment John please,' she said in a level voice. 'Exactly what have you on your mind?'

'Awkward,' he grumbled. 'Damned awkward! It's simply as an old friend I feel that it may reflect on you and yours,' he said.

She pushed away from in front of her the plate which by now was dry as if a cat had licked it.

'But my dear,' she cried 'on me? After all I've done? When he wouldn't have darling Mother's which I'm almost sure Mary has never even seen. You mean poor Philip's one's too cheap?'

'I do.'

'I don't call fifteen guineas cheap.'

'Not for what he got.'

'Oh my dear I can't think when I've been so upset in my life,' she gasped but not altogether convincingly.

He laid a hand over hers which she did not withdraw.

'To do a thing like that might come back on us both,' he said.

'You mean our friends . . .?'

'Yes.'

'What does Liz say?' she asked.

'I don't know for the very simple reason that I haven't enquired,' he answered. 'And I shan't.'

'So you're just guessing, is that it John?'

'I've lived enough in our lot not to have to ask.'

He proceeded to serve Mrs Weatherby with lobster mayonnaise.

'Well if it all doesn't come back on my poor shoulders ...' she murmured. 'When I've done nothing but my best.'

'All the same Jane we must find something.'

'But oh they're so independent,' she wailed.

'Can't he give her another?'

'What with?'

'How d'you mean Jane, what with? You could sell the solitaire couldn't you and let him have the proceeds?'

'And he does go on so, that they must live on what they earn.'

'Well my dear,' he said 'we haven't been into that together yet have we? The last time you'd just come from seeing Thicknesse and didn't feel like it if you remember.'

'No more I do now John.'

'All right. I don't wish to press you. But we shall have to take some step about this engagement ring or we might be a laughing stock.'

'John,' she announced after a pause 'sometimes I feel rather inclined to say "damn the children, they're more trouble than they're worth".'

'Well I don't know about that Jane.'

'Don't you? But why can't they do things the way we did?'

'Money I suppose. Besides I wouldn't care for 'em to get into the mess we got into.'

'Now darling you're not to speak so of what is still absolutely sacred to me. How delicious this lobster is! Where did you go to find it?'

He told her.

She ate with evident appreciation.

'You don't care for Philip's hats either I hear?' she said sweetly.

'No more I do,' Mr Pomfret replied.

'On the whole wouldn't you say John it's rather best for them to make their own mistakes?'

'It all depends.'

'In what way dear?'

He turned very white.

'I don't want us to look ridiculous Jane!'

She raised her eyebrows and stared coolly at him.

'I'm not sure what you mean?' she said.

In a trembling voice, with an obvious and complete loss of temper he cried all at once,

'By trying to stop this marriage by saying as I'm told you are that Philip is my son.'

She put knife and fork carefully down on the plate, turned her face half away from him, closed her eyes and waited in silence. Within twenty seconds two great tears had slipped from beneath black lashes and were on their way over her full cheeks, shortly followed by others. But she made no sound.

He blew his nose loudly, his colour began to come back. He watched. Soon his breathing became normal again.

'I'm sorry,' he muttered at last.

'Excuse me,' she said getting up from the table and hastened out of the room. He waited. He hung his head to listen, perhaps for the front door. When the bathroom lock clicked he appeared to relax.

Eventually she returned like a ship in full sail. He stood as she came in the door. She stopped close enough to hit him.

'How dare you!' she hissed.

'Oh my dear I do apologize,' he said and wrung his hands. 'Last thing in the world I wished to blurt out.'

'How dare you John!'

'Look here sit down once more Jane. That silly remark slipped from me I swear it!'

'I oughtn't to stay here another minute,' she announced and sat in her place. He seated himself. He mopped at his face with a handkerchief. She watched her plate of lobster mayonnaise. 'This is Liz's doing,' she added.

'No Jane don't,' he implored.

'Well that was her wasn't it?'

'Yes I suppose so.'

She took up knife and fork again, began to push the food around the plate.

'I say it for your own good John,' she said. 'You should have nothing more to do with that young woman before she ruins you!'

'Now Jane,' he cried raising a glass to his lips with trembling hands.

'Because when you allow the squalid girls you choose for your wicked selfish pleasures to interfere between my son and your girl then you aren't fit.'

'And Richard Abbot?' he muttered.

'Is one of nature's gentlemen,' she royally replied. 'Now not another word of this or I leave at once never to step over your doorstep again.'

After which the conversation limped for some time then she laughed and in another thirty minutes he tried a laugh and in the end as old friends they parted early without another mention of the children.

A week later Miss Jennings did something she had never done before, she asked Richard Abbot round for a drink.

'Have you heard about poor darling John?' she said and giggled. 'His doctor's told him he's got a touch of this awful diabetes.'

'Good Lord, sorry to learn that.'

She giggled again.

'No one knows. Of course he told me. I'm so very worried for him. Isn't it merciful they discovered about insulin in time?'

'No danger in diabetes nowadays,' Mr Abbot agreed. 'Rotten thing to catch though.'

'How ought he to look after himself Richard?'

'Just take it easy and they can give themselves the injections.'

'Themselves? Injections! Oh no surely a woman must do for them. I mean you can't jab a needle into your own arm surely?'

'Or a leg. That's what they say Liz.'

'Of course there's Mary,' Miss Jennings continued. 'She could be the one until she actually marries Philip. But once those two get away on their own how will John manage Richard?'

'They can do it for themselves,' he repeated.

'Does Jane know?'

'The way to give hypodermics? Couldn't say I'm sure.'

'No no I naturally didn't mean was Jane a nurse. Has she heard d'you think?'

'Couldn't be certain. Not mentioned a word to me.'

'Because I'll tell you what. John's having diabetes like this alters everything. There is bound to be a change in Jane's whole attitude to the children's marriage.'

'Can't follow you at all.'

'Oh but of course you do. Don't play the innocent Richard. She's been simply fixed on stopping it by every means. But now he'll need looking after, she won't leave Mary home to do the nursing.'

'And d'you imagine John will have no say in that?' Mr Abbot enquired. 'He's got you hasn't he? You'll have to take lessons Liz.'

'He's got me all right' she said. 'Yes. But have I got him, there's the question' and she laughed outright then at once grew serious once again.

'Then will he have terrible pricks all over his poor arms and legs?' she cried.

He gently laughed.

'Oh come Liz,' he argued. 'That's only a detail.'

'A detail? Will there be something else as well?'

'No but what's the matter with a few dots on his skin?'

'I thought you meant he might have to have some other ghastly treatment Richard. I was so nervous for a minute. I believe you're teasing me you horrid man.'

'You're all right Liz.'

'I wish I was. Has Jane really said nothing to you about the marriage?'

'Not to me.'

'Because she'll force it on now, you mark my words.'

'Whatever she does is perfect by me Liz.'

'Has there ever been anyone as loyal as you dear Richard! You are so good.'

'Mind if I say something?'

'Of course not. How could I?'

'Might be you make too much of things.'

'Oh come now Richard you aren't going to say "mountains out of molehills", not as late in the day as this surely?'

'I could.'

'But don't you see what's going on under your very own nose?' she goodhumouredly demanded.

'Cheer up,' he said. 'It needn't happen.'

'And shan't if I have anything to do with things. I used to love old John. I can't bear to stand by and see him ruined.'

Mr Abbot's eyes widened. He watched the woman with plain amazement and some cunning.

'Don't look at me as though you'd seen a ghost,' Miss Jennings softly said. 'I've been around all this time even if you have only just noticed.'

'Sorry,' he said at once. 'But you're a surprising person Liz.'

'Of course I am,' she replied.

'You were keen enough on the children's marriage once,' he pointed out.

'Well naturally,' she answered.

'And now you want a girl of nineteen to stay at home single so as to give her father injections?'

'But John dines with Jane every other night already!'

'You and I couldn't stop them even if we wanted to.'

'Perhaps not Richard,' she admitted. 'Still we might try and keep it at that and then they could conceivably quarrel over the arrangements even yet, who knows? Because I won't have those two children made into pawns, their whole lives I mean, their own futures, just for Jane to play sicknurse to poor John.'

'I thought you were the one who was so keen on Philip marrying Mary.'

'I was,' she wailed.

'Well then why change when the wind seems to blow the other way? We aren't weathercocks after all.'

'I am where John's concerned.'

'But you just said Liz . . .'

'I know,' she interrupted 'but I simply can't bear the thought of that woman sticking needles in his arm.'

'Liz!' he warned.

'Oh what must you think of me?' she cried. 'Yet I just can't help myself and you know she'd give him blood-poisoning.'

'If he won't learn to manage by himself why shouldn't you be the one for the chap?'

'Would you like that best Richard?'

He paused and looked about.

'Me?' he asked at last.

'Yes you.'

'How do I come in?'

'Oh well if you won't talk' she replied with a small voice. 'Of course I've no right to go on like this. Yes well there you are.'

'Hope I didn't seem rude at all,' he said at once. 'Excuse me will you? Fact is I've got a feeling no one has any right to interfere with the lives of others.'

'But don't they interfere all the time in yours.'

'Shouldn't be surprised.'

'Well then!'

'There's no "well then" about this' he protested sharply. 'Can't be too grateful to old Jane,' he muttered 'and I like those two kids.'

'Richard you are sweet and wonderful,' she said with apparent sincerity shortly after which, and time was getting on, he went off alone to dine at the Club.

Upon which Mrs Weatherby again asked John Pomfret to dinner.

'Oh my dear I'm so worried about little Penelope once more,' she began as soon as he came in.

'Why how's that?' he asked.

'It's all to do with this horrid new thing you've got,' Jane explained. 'The poor sweet will insist on sticking pins into herself now.'

He laughed rather bitterly.

'Oh dear,' he said.

'I know it's dreadful of me,' she admitted. 'There you are chock full of diabetes so to speak yet I can't but worry my heart out over the little saint. What d'you suppose will stop her?'

'How d'you mean?'

'Well she can't just go on pretending to inject herself all of every day can she? It's even so dangerous. She might get blood-poisoning. And oh my dear in what way will you manage yourself? Have you thought of that? Because after a little while there won't be any free space left?'

He laughed once more.

'There is the diet treatment,' he suggested.

'Then do tell Pen so with your own lips,' she pleaded.

'But Jane you wouldn't want the child to starve herself?'

Mrs Weatherby chuckled.

'Good Lord what a perfect fool I am not to have thought of that,' she admitted. 'If you hadn't said we might've had her really on our hands! Now darling how about you? Are you all right?'

'Well yes I imagine so,' he conceded. 'Of course it's a bore but one has to be thankful it's not worse I suppose.'

'You're perfectly wonderful the way you take everything John,' Mrs Weatherby insisted.

'But who told Penelope about me?' he asked.

'I did,' the mother wailed. 'You know how truly fond of you she is, why, she dotes on you John, and I wanted to make Pen a little bit sad – you see at that instant minute she was creating such a dreadful noise and racket, so I told her your news the little pet, and my dear it came off all too well, she's been quiet as a mouse jabbing great pins in her leg ever since.'

Mrs Weatherby gaily laughed and so did John Pomfret. Then she went on quite serious again,

'And if Pen let go, should one of those pins get inside her, it might even travel right to her little heart, darling isn't that too awful just for words?'

Jane turned her eyes, which immediate fright made still more enormous, full on him.

'Don't you worry,' he said smiling.

'Yet darling mother had one in her all her life. It entered through the seat.'

'She sat on a pin?' he interrupted, broadly smiling now.

'Yes she was one of the first to be X-rayed,' Mrs Weatherby continued, 'it travelled all over, just think, and then when she died she had pernicious anaemia after all, poor wonderful darling that she was.'

'I expect Pen will be all right,' he comforted.

'She'll have to be,' Mrs Weatherby replied with great conviction. 'John tell me about yourself. How serious is it really?'

'Well I have to take things easy for a bit you know. I can't throw up the office worse luck but I'll have to be careful in the evening.'

'It's extraordinary my dear your saying what you have just done about the office,' Mrs Weatherby exclaimed. 'I was only thinking the other day over your sweet Mary and how bad all this working life is for these girls.'

'Why Jane what on earth do you mean?'

'Oh nothing, certainly nothing which concerns the ghastly talk we had last time about their plans or rather the endless lack of plans they seem to have. But John don't you think she should get right away before she settles down?'

He turned rather white.

'Rid ourselves of her for a bit?' he enquired.

'Now don't turn so damned suspicious,' she said equably. 'I wouldn't be in the least surprised if my little plot didn't bring precious Philip up to the boil though poor darling I don't really know how much else he can do when he's already proposed and given her a ring.' At this Mr Pomfret seemed on the point of speech but Jane waved him down. 'No,' she gaily cried 'I won't allow you, just let it pass, I was only joking. But you know what things are for a girl. And whatever we may do to help them, in the end there probably won't be much money. No I think she ought to have a change first.'

'She's only just out of the nursery Jane where she's rested all her short life so far.'

'Then they often start a baby so much too soon,' Mrs Weatherby went on imperturbably, 'terribly exhausting after all the excitement of the wedding. No John no you really don't understand about girls, how should you? And after that it's just one long grind darling until they're too old to enjoy a thing. I think you should send her to Italy for at least two months.'

'But the money,' he cried.

'Sell a pair of cufflinks,' she sweetly suggested. 'As a matter of fact I had a letter from Myra Smith only yesterday. She's been in Florence all this time, fancy that! She wants to hear of an English girl to stay with her and as a return she asks to be taken in herself over here, she wants to see London again she says.'

'But good God I couldn't put Myra up at my place. It wouldn't look decent!'

'With Mary not there, married to Philip you mean? Oh well I'd negotiate my fences as they came if I were you John. Still, if it amounted to all that I could take the woman in here.'

'I can't quite seem to see . . .' Mr Pomfret began when Jane interrupted him.

'I know you can't,' she said 'but you must remember you've been so fortunate all your life and now you have a touch of illness I simply shall not allow it to warp your judgement. Or Arthur Morris now? He has no use for his flat while he's at the clinic. He could lend it to Myra.'

'My dear Jane we've to get Mary out in Italy for two months first surely. In any case I'm sorry to say there's bad news about poor old Arthur. He's not so well at all they tell me.'

'No no John,' she cried 'I simply don't want to hear!'

'Yes,' Mr Pomfret went on 'it seems they've told him he'll have to have his leg off now above the knee.'

She covered her ears with two fat white hands.

'Too too disagreeable,' she moaned. 'And now that all one's friends have reached middle age is there to be nothing but illness from now on, first Arthur then my dear you? Oh tell me are you really all right?'

He laughed. 'There's nothing the matter with me compared with poor old Arthur,' he assured Mrs Weatherby.

'That's all right then,' she replied lowering her hands. 'Let me get you another drink.' When she had brought this and placed it on the table by his chair she leant down and put her cheek against his own. Not for many years had she done the same. He closed his eyes. Her skin was the texture of a large soft flower in sun, dry but with the pores open, brilliant, unaccountable and proud.

'You swear you're all right?' she murmured.

'Oh yes.'

'Because you of all men just must be,' she said, gently withdrawing. For the rest of the time she did not mention Liz or the children and was particularly attentive.

A few evenings later Mr Pomfret said to his girl Mary,

'Monkey I've been thinking things over and I should like you to go to Italy for a bit.'

'Italy Daddy? Whatever for?'

'Oh nothing in particular. I thought it might be a good idea that's all.'

'But why?'

'Wouldn't you care to travel then?'

'Daddy, did Mrs Weatherby also think of this?'

'Good Lord no Mary. Whoever put it in your head?'

'I just wondered that's all,' she explained rather grimly.

'Myra Smith would have you at her place in Florence,' Mr Pomfret went on 'and you could do the picture galleries and things.'

'Be serious Daddy. However could I get leave from my job?'

'I've thought of that too,' her father replied. 'Why don't you simply throw it up? You slave frightfully hard all day at menial tasks; there's no future there Mary as you yourself said the other day.'

'Give up my work!' she gasped.

'But they pay you so badly. When you're married you may have to find something that brings in more.'

'I'm glad someone has mentioned the marriage at last,' she said. 'Just recently there's been almost what I'd call a plot of silence about it.'

'I was only talking to Jane on the subject the other night dearie.'

'When she suggested I should go?'

'Now monkey I've already told you. It was my plan and she thoroughly agreed as a matter of fact. Indeed it was herself said there could be no manner of fun in getting married these days, I mean things aren't easy still, girls have an awful grind to put a home together. Take a few weeks off before you settle down.'

'But could you afford it?'

'Oh we'll find ways and means I suppose.'

'Wouldn't it be better though to save for the honeymoon if you're so keen for me to go to Florence?'

This silenced him a moment.

'No,' he replied eventually. 'Venice for newly marrieds, Florence for girls before they become engaged. Next time you go round to see Philip just ask their Isabella!'

'I'm not sure I want to go Daddy.'

'Oh go on and have some fun.'

'I don't wish for fun, or rather that kind of gay time. I'm not sure it would be enjoyable.'

'But you haven't ever been abroad dear, you've not seen anything in your life. As things are you may never have the chance again.'

'What made you get this idea Daddy?'

'Nothing. I just had it,' he said in rather a surly voice.

'You didn't speak to Philip about Italy?'

'I promise not.'

'Because he mightn't like my throwing up the job. He's funny that way you know.'

'But if he heard you were to go to a better paid one?'

'My dear you don't understand at all. He's very serious-minded Daddy. He thinks we ought all to be in Government jobs.'

'What's so odd about that? Practically everyone is.'

'Well I'm not going to try and explain Philip to you! Who is this Mrs Smith anyway? Would she like me?'

'Oh we all knew her at one time. Can't say I saw much of Myra ever. She was more a friend of Jane's to tell the truth.'

'There Mrs Weatherby comes into it again,' his daughter murmured.

Mr Pomfret seemed to ignore the comment.

'Rather a sad story,' he mused aloud. 'Drove poor William hopelessly to drink then left him when the poor fellow was done for. She's quite different now of course from all I hear, settled down quite remarkably from many accounts. You ought to ask old Arthur Morris. He keeps in touch I believe.'

'But has she a flat or what?'

'My, aren't you being practical all of a sudden love! I suppose it's this wedding business.'

'Now you of all people are not to laugh at me! I'm sure someone in this family must be sensible and it won't ever be you darling as you'll admit.'

'All right poppet,' he laughed. 'So anyway you don't say no to your Italian trip.'

'I haven't said yes have I?'

'I don't want you hanging about while there's still so much to be decided Mary,' he declared and was serious. 'Everything's going to come out the way you want, you'll see my dear but it might be best if you kept out of the picture a few weeks.'

'Oh Daddy you do think so?'

'I do.'

'I see. Well I'll try and get after Arthur Morris. When all's said and done I can't make up my mind without I know something about this Mrs Smith can I?'

At which Miss Pomfret retired to bed.

Four days later Miss Jennings was giving Mr Abbot dinner at her flat.

'Yes there she went poor child,' Liz wailed 'right through the teeming rain to ask him and when she got to the clinic she walked straight into that lift large enough to take a hearse. Dear Mary rose all the way to his floor and you know the long passages they have there, well she wandered down and knocked on Arthur's door just as she had done so often.'

'Were you with her?' Richard Abbot interrupted.

'No Mary told me. Who else has she got these days the darling? And when the child knocked a nurse happened to come from a next room and cried out "oh but you can't go in now". Anyway Mary was shown to one of those alcoves off the corridor with three armchairs and the occasional table. There she sat thinking Arthur was to be washed or something when at last the sister came. It makes one's heart sink Richard to picture it, the poor love thrown over by her own father, oh she has told me all, waiting to ask so much she shouldn't know of the one person who could give it as she thought, poor Arthur, then the nursing sister saying she was afraid Mary could go in no more!! When the child wanted to be told why, it all came out of course, he'd just died Richard, not an hour ago, wasn't it frightful!'

'Yes I heard at the Club. I'm very sorry,' Mr Abbot said. 'What was the cause?'

'Well the extraordinary part is they didn't have the address of a single one of his relatives, they wanted Mary at the clinic to give them names but he was absolutely alone Richard, if you'd been at the grave this afternoon with me you'd have seen there wasn't a soul except old friends, isn't that perfectly awful? Of course Jane cried enough for his mother and sister combined if they'd been spared, – oh I know what you're about to say,' and she solemnly raised a trembling hand to restrain him 'I expect she may have been quite genuine, minded Arthur being dead I mean, but naturally John had to make all the arrangements just as though he was the next of kin.'

There was a pause while Liz got out a handkerchief which she pushed with a forefinger at the corner of her eye.

'So what did Arthur die of?' Mr Abbot enquired in a neutral voice.

'The clot. Flew straight to his heart,' she replied tragically. 'Oh Richard it makes one wonder who will be next?'

'These things happen,' the man answered. 'But what did Mary wish to know?'

'Well I suppose you'll think this is none of my business,' she said. 'At the same time, fond as I am of John and Jane, I'm not so blind Richard I can't see all that goes on right in front of my own nose. I don't care what you say my dear but Jane's sending the child away to Italy and making her throw up the job for it, must be clearing the decks for action like they do in the Navy.'

'How can Jane send Mary?'

'But Richard by working on John. I never even see him now. The moment those two children tried to get engaged Jane has had the man living in her pocket.'

'I know what you mean,' Mr Abbot admitted at last, though he seemed to speak with reluctance. 'No more than natural all the same.'

Mr Abbot appeared ill at ease.

'Natural?' she cried. 'Yes I suppose so in a farm yard sort of fashion.'

'Then you think it's all come to life once again between them.'

'If I said "over my dead body" then I might be six foot underground this minute,' she replied and they both laughed.

'Sounds bad,' he muttered.

'Well every word's true isn't it Richard?'

'Shouldn't be surprised,' he answered with a return to his usual manner. 'As that film star said when he landed this side of the Atlantic and the reporters asked about the lady in his life, "I'm just a thanks a million man". Damn good you know.'

'But are you all right Richard?'

'All right?'

'Yes, in your own health and strength? Here's John with diabetes and Arthur Morris gone. Who's next?'

He laughed. 'Me? I'm fit as a fiddle,' he protested.

She laughed. 'Now don't you just be too sure,' she warned. 'Though one of the things I so like about you Richard is you keep your figure beautifully, still look really athletic I mean.'

'Pure luck,' he replied. 'Some are born that way. Well then about Mary? What did she want of Arthur?'

'They're sending the child off to this sort of Mrs Smith in Florence. I never knew the woman so Mary couldn't ask me though she has since. All I could tell the child was, Myra used to be a great friend of the whole bunch while I was still doing French grammar in my rompers. So you see Richard, Mary the poor angel doesn't know what's up. Frightfully wicked they are.'

'Expect everything's for the best. After all Liz whoever can tell what may come?'

'Oh I agree more than you'll ever realize. Yet how wrong to play with one's own children's feelings!'

'They don't. They're thinking about themselves and I don't altogether blame 'em.'

'I realize everyone does,' she admitted. 'I quite see even with a baby in arms a great deal of oneself comes into it. But they really ought not to work on Philip. They'll ruin his life, what there is left.'

'D'you reckon John realizes what he's up to?'

'Not consciously of course, yet he can't be so reckless he mayn't take advice. Oh Richard he's gone back so the last few months! Was it his diabetes d'you suppose?'

'Diabetes?'

'Weakened him my dear. I can't abide men who turn wet. He's come to be like a sponge, going round to her place every other day, sometimes twice in the twenty-four hours as he does.'

'Nothing we can do.'

'There is then!'

'How's that Liz?'

'Just you wait and see Richard.' She laughed light-heartedly.

'Well you've been wrong once and you can be again,' he said.

'When?' she demanded.

'Not so long ago you told me since John had diabetes Jane would hurry the marriage along between Mary and Philip for reasons of her own.'

'I also said she'd been against it Richard.'

'All right,' he agreed. 'On the other hand you tell me now Jane is packing Mary off to her father's old battlefields so that she can marry John.'

'Because I've begun to see Jane must have it both ways. She'll prevent the wedding so that when poor sweet Mary travels home it'll be too late and the child'll have to look for a room on her own or in a wretched hostel.'

'Come Liz you could put the girl up at a pinch what?'

'I might have my own plans Richard.'

'General post eh?'

'I don't know what you mean,' she said in a stern voice.

'I say,' he exclaimed. 'Dreadfully sorry and all. It was nothing.'

'That's better,' she agreed, smiled sweetly at the man.

Now that the meal was done Miss Jennings got up from table to switch on lights and draw curtains to hide heavy rain pouring down outside. He rose to help. As she straightened the heavy folds he came behind, turned her with a hand on her shoulder and kissed the woman hard on the lips.

'Here,' she cried drawing back. 'What's this?'

'Oh nothing Liz.'

'I like that after all we've discussed.' She gaily laughed. 'Anyone would think you'd taken our little gossip seriously.'

'Must have been this excellent meal you've just given us,' he grumbled in a goodhumoured voice.

'That's better,' she approved, patted his cheek and led the way next door to the sitting-room.

At the weekend John Pomfret asked Mrs Weatherby round for drinks at his place. When he had settled her in, she immediately began.

'My dear isn't it absurd and wrong the way those two flaunt themselves nowadays all over London?'

'Now Jane their engagement hasn't been announced yet, at least in the papers, and for all we know it may never happen but there can be no earthly reason why they shouldn't have a little time together to make up their minds, all the more so since I believe Mary is really off to Florence at last.'

'You are sweet,' Mrs Weatherby pronounced with marked indulgence. 'I was speaking of Richard and Liz of course.'

'Don't be absurd Jane!'

'D'you actually pretend you hadn't heard my dear?' she cried. 'Why I thought everybody knew!'

'Knew what?'

'Just that they've started the most tremendously squalid affair. In one way I'm so glad for Richard, even if I do pity the dear idiot.'

'Nonsense,' he said. 'I don't believe a word. And why are you glad?'

'You ask simply anyone,' she replied. 'But as to Richard in some respects he's even dearer to me than myself. I'd give almost anything to see the sweet man happy.'

'Then is Liz the only future for his happiness?'

'John dear you are so acute. D'you know I'm really rather afraid she is.'

'I thought his allegiance was elsewhere,' Mr Pomfret suggested and gazed hard at Mrs Weatherby.

'Oh no,' she admitted with a cheerful look. 'All that became over and done with ages back. Isn't it dreadful?' she giggled.

'Could you be having a game with me Jane?'

She grew serious at once.

'Me?' she asked. 'I wish I were.' She watched him. 'Why,' she said after a pause 'd'you mind so dreadfully?'

'I?' he demanded and seemed to bluster. 'Been expecting it for weeks.'

'Well then,' she sighed.

'But why can't people come and tell one themselves when they've had enough?' he asked. 'Not that you yourself did so with me more years ago than either of us probably cares to remember.'

'Now John don't be disagreeable. Besides I was such a giddy young fool in those days.'

'A very beautiful creature whatever you may have been,' he gallantly said.

'Oh darling,' she wailed 'just don't remind me of how I look now!'

'You haven't altered at all,' he protested. 'Why do you speak as though you could ever be a woman my age.'

'Because I see you such a lot perhaps,' she said.

'Good God if what you say is true well I don't feel as if I shall be able to speak to Liz again. And with due respect to you I can't seem able to think of her with Dick Abbot. Why I should have thought he'd have one of his choking fits.'

'Don't be silly John,' Mrs Weatherby cried in a delighted voice. 'Besides for all we know he may have had several over her already, poor sweet.'

Mr Pomfret laughed with some reluctance.

'Really Jane,' he protested 'what you could ever have seen in that pompous ass I shall never comprehend.'

'Speak for yourself darling,' she said. 'And when I take you in hand, if I find time, you're going to lead a far more regular life let me tell you. Which reminds me. How are you in yourself?'

'Oh I still go for these tests and they give me the injections and I have to wear a little tag round my neck like during the war.'

'Is there much in the injection part?'

'Nothing at all. Falling off a log!'

'John you're being so sensible and I do value you so very much. And have you any more news of the children?'

'Not so far as I can tell. I never seem to come across Mary for a chat these days.'

'Ever since you put to her your idea she should go to Myra in Florence?'

'My idea Jane? I thought that was your suggestion.'

'I still think it such a wise notion of yours John to give the dear girl time to look about. But isn't Mary a little bit rash to throw up her job?'

'Well once they are to marry and will insist they must live on what they earn she might in time have to find a better paid one if Philip can't bring in more.'

'Ah we shall have to wait and see,' Mrs Weatherby replied. 'You are so practical! Still you do think she is going?'

'As far as I know.'

'Doesn't she discuss it with you then John? How very wicked and ungrateful of Mary!'

'Oh she hasn't much reason to be grateful has she? No she's talked everything over with Liz.'

'Don't be absurd my dear, why that girl has to thank you for all she's got. And I'm really very surprised she should go to dear Liz. What Liz might dig up to say could hardly be disinterested, would it?'

'Well Mary went round to Arthur as you know Jane.'

'To Arthur Morris? But . . .' and Mrs Weatherby gaped at him.

'Hadn't you heard? It was she found him dead.'

The tears after a moment streamed down Jane's face. She might have been able to cry at will or it could be that she dreadfully minded.

'No John no . . .' she spluttered, struggling with a handkerchief. 'It's been such a shock . . . you mustn't . . . poor Arthur . . . oh isn't everything cruel!'

She covered her face and broke into sobs.

'Now darling now,' he said coming across to sit on the arm of her chair. He put an arm round Mrs Weatherby, took firm hold on a soft shoulder. 'You mustn't let it get you down,' he said. 'Poor old fellow he didn't suffer, remember that. There dear . . .'

He sat in silence while her upset subsided. After a few minutes she excused herself and went along to the bathroom. He lit a cigarette. He waited. When she returned her fresh face wore a peculiarly vulnerable look.

'Do please excuse me darling,' she announced, entering as once before like a ship in full sail. 'It was because you see he was alone when it happened!' She swallowed prodigiously. 'But I can never in all my life mention this again! You do understand?'

'Of course.'

She settled back in her chair.

'Philip said anything of late?' Mr Pomfret enquired.

'No. What about?'

'This engagement of theirs.'

'No' she repeated. She paused. 'John my dear,' she began 'sometimes I rather wonder if we don't discuss the children much too often. After all they have their own lives to lead and that at least we can't do for them! So I've simply given up asking. Do you mind?'

'Whatever you say Jane,' he agreed and they settled down to a long nostalgic conversation about old times, excluding any mention of Arthur Morris.

When the day's work was over Philip Weatherby called on Miss Jennings. She answered the door and said,

'Philip! Really you should not drop in on people like this in London!'

'I'm so sorry why not?'

'Because they might be occupied that's why. Never mind, come along.'

'Then you are free?'

'I always am to you,' she replied, waving him into the flat.

'I wanted to ask what you thought about all this?' he asked, turning round in the door of the living-room.

'All what?' she asked from the passage.

'Why Mary and me you know,' he answered, and made himself comfortable in the best armchair.

'How d'you mean exactly?' she wanted to be told as she fetched the half finished bottle of sherry.

'Well Liz,' he said with assurance, 'I look on you as almost one of the family.'

'Yes,' she replied 'I'm nearer your age than your mother ever will be.'

'I don't know,' he said. 'All I wished to ask was, are you on my side or not?'

'Well thanks very much,' she retorted drily. 'Now would you like a glass of sherry?'

'I wouldn't mind.'

'You'll find one day,' she put forward 'it's odd how like their fathers some sons are.'

'But you'd never met Daddy.'

'No perhaps I hadn't.'

'Then d'you mean ...?'

'Now Philip are you going to have a glass of this or no? I'm not here to argue will you understand.'

'So sorry,' he agreed at once. 'I mean I'm in rather a hole with my

143

own personal affairs and as you're a distinct friend of the family's I wanted to get your point.'

'In what way?' she asked pouring the wine neatly out.

'About Mary and me,' he said.

'Why of course I wish you the very best of everything,' she replied.

'Well thanks,' he murmured and seemed doubtful. 'But does my mother do you think?'

'Jane? She dotes on you Philip. What makes you ask?'

'And Mary's father? I believe you see quite a bit of him. How does he look on us both?'

'Dear John? Now you mustn't assume every sort of silly thing Philip. You don't imagine he discusses the two of you with me do you? Oh he may have done simply ages back but he's stopped. He's not that sort of man that's all.'

'I wish I could see my way through,' Mr Weatherby complained almost fretfully.

'How d'you mean?'

'No one tells me anything,' he said.

'What d'you want them to do Philip quite?'

'Explain to me the way they feel,' he elaborated. 'When I went to Uncle Ned he wouldn't say a word.'

'But what d'you expect them to feel?'

'After all,' the young man said 'when you go and get engaged you don't just look for silence. It makes one wonder. Does Mary's father approve or doesn't he?'

'Has it ever occurred to you Philip that more than half the time John may just be wondering about himself?'

'Well naturally. But he can spare half a thought to his own daughter can't he?'

'In what way?'

'How do you mean? It's her marriage isn't it?'

'He might be thinking of his own affairs mightn't he?'

'Mr Pomfret? At his age? Why he's a million.'

'Good heavens,' she said 'how old d'you imagine I am?'

'Then you don't mean . . .?'

'I certainly don't,' she replied with finality. 'All I say is everyone has a right to their own lives haven't they?'

'In what way?' he enquired.

'You're one of these talkers Philip,' she announced. 'You don't go out and do things.'

'I may not but I work surely?'

'Well there's more to life than working for the Government.'

'I don't see what you're getting at' he objected. 'How you spend your day is a part of your life, you can't get away from it.'

'But Philip one's evenings are a means to get right apart from what you and I have to do for a living in the daytime.'

'D'you know,' he said 'I can't see why.'

'Then oughtn't you to go into politics Philip?'

'I might at that.'

'Oh no my dear,' she protested 'you're hopeless.'

'I've got no chance?' he cried.

'I didn't say so at all. What you and Mary decide is none of my concern. You've simply got to take the plunge, there you are, and hope for the best.'

'Without Mamma's consent?'

'Why yes Philip if needs be. Doesn't Mary see this my way?'

'I'm not sure. I haven't much experience of women. That's the reason I came round if you want to know.'

'You're not asking me to give that to you?' she asked and he blushed. 'I'm sorry Philip,' she went on. 'Forget it. But the truth is I fancy there's going to be another wedding in your family soon if I'm not very much mistaken.'

'You and Mr Pomfret d'you mean?'

'Since when were you two related? At any rate you haven't married Mary yet have you?'

'I see you're against Mary and me as well,' he said.

'I'm not,' she protested. 'But you've no right to link my name with John's. What on earth d'you know about it? Of course I'm not going to marry him ever, not that he's asked me. Grow up, be your age for mercy's sake. All I was trying to say is he'll wed your mamma or bust.'

'My mother! He can't! She's too old!!'

'No older than he is.'

'You can't be serious.'

'I am Philip. Never more so.'

'Will they want a double wedding then?'

'With Mary and you? Listen Philip if you take my advice you'll rush that nice girl off to the Registry Office always supposing she'll still have you, and get the fell deed done without a word more said to a soul.'

'But that wouldn't be straight,' he objected and after a good deal more of this sort of argument during which however Liz became somewhat nicer to him, Philip Weatherby took himself away no nearer a decision, or so it seemed.

In a few days time Mrs Weatherby again had John Pomfret to dinner following which, after a gay discussion of generalities all through the meal, she led the man into the next room to settle him over a whisky and soda, and immediately began,

'Oh my dear isn't it too frightful about one's money.'

'I know,' he moaned.

'John even little Penelope's overdrawn now!'

He roared with laughter while she smiled.

'No Jane you can't mean that? Not at her age!'

'But yes,' the mother insisted. 'Only a trifle of course, the tiny sum a great aunt left the little brigand for her beautiful great eyes. Yet she had a letter from the bank manager Tuesday. I read it out to Pen and we both simply shrieked, she has such a sense of humour already. Still it is dreadful isn't it?'

Mrs Weatherby did not seem greatly disturbed.

'Well Jane,' Mr Pomfret beamed 'she's started young there's no getting away from that.'

'I wish everything didn't go on so,' she continued. 'Oh John I went to see the awful Mr Thicknesse again who makes me quake in my shoes whenever I meet him like one of those huge things at the Zoo.'

'Yes I suppose we must have a talk about the children some time,' Mr Pomfret said without obvious enthusiasm.

'No no, damn the children if you'll please excuse the expression. Just for tonight let's be ourselves. I mean we still have our own lives to lead haven't we? No but what is one to do with these Banks?'

'Exactly what I ask myself three or four times a week.'

'I never learned to cook, isn't it terrible, and if I started now I'd be so extravagant you see. Honestly I believe I save by having darling Isabella. With the price things are, you can't play about with what little food you do get can you?'

'I'll fry an egg with anyone but not much else,' he said.

'And then there's Pen. Even if darling Mother never saw I had cooking lessons she did at least leave me an inkling of essentials from her beloved sweet example, so I do realize it's no earthly use to experiment over a growing child's food. Once I started that I wouldn't be playing the game with my little poppet would I?'

'Oh quite,' he agreed, relaxed and smiling.

'So what is one to do?' she demanded. 'Just go on in the old way until there's nothing left?'

'I decide and decide to make a great change in my life but I always seem to put it off,' he said.

'Don't I know darling!' she cried. 'Oh I don't say that to blame, I spoke of myself. But those children we've agreed not to mention John, have changed my ideas. I believe my dear I'm almost beginning to have a plan!'

'Never start a hat shop,' he advised. 'They invariably fail.'

'You are truly sweet,' she commented with a small frown which he did not appear to notice. 'You see it wasn't that at all, something quite different. The simplest little plot imaginable. Only this. Two people live cheaper than one! They always have and will.'

'You're not to take in a lodger Jane,' he said sharply.

'But mine is a very especial sort of one,' she murmured. 'He's you!!'

Mr Pomfret sat bolt upright. There was a pause.

'Look here you know,' he protested at last 'you've got to consider how people'll talk.'

'I can't think of the sort of person you imagine I'm like now,' she said. 'We'd have to be married of course.'

There was another longish pause while they watched each other. At last a half smile came over his face.

'And Penelope?' he asked.

'Why she dotes on you John,' Mrs Weatherby cried.

'You know what you've told me ever since that unfortunate affair when I married her in front of the fire here?'

'Don't be absurd darling. This is real. Besides it's me who's marrying you, remember. The sweet saint would never even dare to deny her own mother anything.'

'But didn't she get very worked up over Mary and Philip?'

'This is precisely what will put all that right out of her sainted little mind don't you see? Oh John do agree you believe me!' Mrs Weatherby cried.

'Of course if you say so Jane, about Pen. Yet you did once just hint how jealous she was.'

'Then she'll simply have to get over it,' the mother replied with evident disappointment in her lovely voice. 'In any case I'd, oh, pondered sending her away to boarding school. She's young but I've begun to think it's time.'

He came over, sat by her side on the sofa, and took her hand.

'You're wonderful my dear,' he said softly.

'Oh John how disagreeable,' she murmured. 'So you don't feel you can? Is that it?'

'I hadn't said so. Then do you wish a double wedding?'

'Certainly not. Never!'

He kissed her hand.

'And Mr Thicknesse?' he enquired.

'Oh John you're laughing at me!'

'I'm not,' he said and squeezed her hand hard. 'I've been over this so often in my mind! But couldn't it be rather late in the day?'

She tried to draw away but he held her fast.

'So you think I'm too old now?' she protested in a low voice.

'That's the last thing Jane. If you only knew how often I'd dreamed of this.'

'Oh you have!'

'Yes again and again.'

'When?' she demanded with more confidence it seemed.

'Here there and everywhere,' he replied.

'Only that?' she reproached him.

He gently kissed a round cheek.

'And Dick?' he whispered.

She jerked away.

'Really,' she said 'it's too much. You are almost becoming like my Philip.'

'I'm sorry Jane.'

'But there's nothing, there never has been anything between me and poor dear Richard.'

'Yes darling,' he agreed.

'So what?' she demanded.

He kissed her on the mouth. She kissed him back almost absentmindedly.

'Will you?' she asked.

'Yes darling,' he replied.

'You mean to say you've actually asked me to marry you after all these years?' she crowed, taking his face between her hands and beginning to kiss his eyes.

'I have,' he answered half smothered, and plainly delighted.

'But this is wonderful!' she cried.

After an interval during which they kissed, held one another at arm's length, looked fondly on each other and kissed again Mr Pomfret exclaimed,

'I can't hardly believe everything.'

'Nonsense, don't say that John. Think how much more it means to me.'

'You? Anyone would be proud to marry you!'

'Ah how little you know my dear. But there is one matter,' she warned, drawing a little away for the last time. 'We aren't to have the old days over again if you please. You'll have to give up Liz.'

'I never knew her then,' he protested.

'I know that already,' she said. 'I mean now.'

'Well of course,' he promised. 'We hardly ever saw one another anyway except at Sunday lunch and that was only because I was sure to see you there.'

'It was!' she cried. 'No how truly sweet! Not that I believe you!'

He laughed. 'We're going on like an old married couple already,' he propounded.

'Who is?' she demanded. 'Speak for yourself my sweet old darling. Oh you'll have to look out now!'

'Oh Lord Jane have I said the wrong thing?'

'I should say so,' she answered and then she giggled. 'But there I expect you'll learn in time. Not that you'll get any other alternative will you, except to be taught by me I mean?'

'I suppose not. Back to school is it?'

'Oh yes yes,' she murmured beginning to kiss him again.

He spent the night with her, whispering part of the time because of Philip Weatherby, but they had no more serious conversation.

The next Sunday John Pomfret took Mrs Weatherby to lunch at the hotel and was shown to the table he had been given so often when entertaining Liz. As he sat down he looked round and saw Dick Abbot playing host to Miss Jennings, again at the very spot where Jane had so often been a guest of the man's.

'See who's here,' Mr Pomfret invited Mrs Weatherby.

'Oh, don't I know it,' she sighed and kept her eyes lowered. 'I spotted that couple John as soon as we came in and was so afraid you'd go over with that heavenly good-heartedness of yours.'

However he waved in their direction upon which Jane had to turn round, put on a look of great surprise and blow two kisses. Richard and Miss Jennings replied with rather awkward smiles.

'Can't cut 'em anyway,' Mr Pomfret muttered.

'There,' Mrs Weatherby laughed 'we've almost got through that and dear me I was so dreading it!'

'Don't smile Jane for heaven's sake,' he implored 'or they'll imagine we're laughing at them.'

'I could cock a snook at her, the horrid creature,' she replied 'only I'd never do anything to upset sweet Pascal.'

'Oh well if they set up house together, that rather lets you and me out surely.'

'Speak for yourself,' she said grinning at him. 'I haven't a bad conscience.'

'Which means you don't have one at all,' he laughed.

'I expect yours may be just as clever,' she answered.

In the meantime Liz was protesting vigorously to her companion.

'But it disgusts one Richard that's all. To flaunt themselves like this! I asked you particularly to bring me today just in case they might be here. Looking down their noses at each other, simpering like mad.'

'Careful now,' he said.

'I don't know we've anything to be careful about. Not us!'

'Don't want them to crow.'

'Oh they'll do that in any case Richard.'

'Then we'd better quickly crow over them.'

'So what am I to do?' she smiled. 'Stick my poor tongue out at John?'

'When did you get your letter?'

'Three days ago.'

'Got mine twenty-four hours before yours at that rate Liz.'

'Which only goes to prove he's under her thumb completely. Can't you just hear Jane nagging at him to find out if he'd written yet?'

'Military discipline eh? Oh well I don't suppose a bit of that again'll hurt him.'

'A taste of the old Scrubs more likely,' she replied with a pure and apparently genuine Cockney intonation. He glanced curiously at her.

She beamed on Mr Abbot.

'My darling,' she said. 'I almost rather feel I may have had the most miraculous escape.'

'How's that?'

'But haven't you often noticed the way some people seem doomed to bring terrible great trials on themselves? Dear old John, I can admit now, is just one of those.'

'You're arguing against yourself Liz.'

'How dear?'

'You meant Jane would be his trouble didn't you?'

'Well who else? Saving your presence of course.'

'And was he also doomed when he kept company with you?'

She laughed.

'How about yourself then, now darling?' she demanded.

'Prefer to choose my own disaster,' he replied.

'And have you?'

'Looks very much like,' he agreed. She laughed delightedly.

'Oh I'm truly beginning to feel as if I'd escaped,' she cried.

'Careful Liz, they'll think we're despising 'em.'

'Well aren't we?'

'I'm not.'

'Oh cheer up Richard. They can't eat us.'

'No but we should keep things in decent order,' he explained.

'Whatever you say my dear,' she agreed. 'Mayn't I even smile?'

'You've got a lovely smile Liz.'

'Good heavens a compliment at long last and from you Richard! Now I don't wish to pry but how exactly did Jane write, when you know, what we've just been talking about?'

'Four days ago you mean?'

'When else?'

'Why d'you want to be told Liz?'

'Because of course I'd like to find out if she dictated John's letter.'

'Couldn't say,' he objected.

'To compare yours with the one John wrote me,' she explained.

'Compare notes,' he said with no apparent enthusiasm. 'I'm not sure Liz. I mean we were both given our marching orders in those letters weren't we. If we put our heads together it might be like a dog going back to his own sick almost.'

'Don't be disgusting! I'd like to be sure, that's all.'

'But of what?'

'Why Richard I explained. To make certain Jane told him every word to say.'

'Oh I don't know Liz,' he temporized.

'I don't know about you I agree,' she rallied him. 'Of course long before I'd received this ridiculous screed from John I'd told the man till I was blue in the face that it could be no go between us where I was concerned and what he wrote really only took notice that at last he'd had to admit I was right.'

'Never was good enough for Jane,' Mr Abbot admitted with a show of reluctance.

'My dear Richard sometimes you actually fish for compliments.'

'I'm not, on my honour.'

'Oh yes you are and on this occasion you'll be unlucky. All I'll say is, you may never recover from the shock of Jane Weatherby throwing you over and your life may be finished.'

He laughed. 'Oh well,' he said.

'That's better,' she laughed. 'So now what?'

'They don't look too cheerful at that do they?' he observed, watching the other couple.

'Oh they won't find it all a bed of roses,' she assured Mr Abbot. Upon which she saw Pascal hurry towards John Pomfret's table.

'Watch this,' Liz begged Dick Abbot.

'Don't stare too hard,' Abbot implored.

'Ah Madame and Mr Pomfret,' Pascal cried in his voice which did not travel beyond the table he addressed. 'So great my pleasure to me Madame. It is so long since Madame and Monsieur lunch together here on this day like this.'

'Pascal!' Mrs Weatherby cried in turn and her tones carried so that one or two looked up from their meals near by. She reached a jewelled right hand across to where he stood bent forward and he took it. Her great eyes seemed to melt. 'Why are all the happiest hours of my life bound up with you here Pascal?' she almost purred.

He bowed. 'You are too kind,' he said. 'And is everything as you wish Mrs Weatherby?'

'More than you'll ever know,' she answered.

'Then can one hope?' the man began and paused to let go of her hand with a pleasing appearance of regret. 'My English is still not so good . . .' he went on. 'Can we look forward to many of these luncheons with you and Mr Pomfret Madame?'

'I think so, yes Pascal,' Jane beamed upon him.

'Because you understand it makes like old days to see Monsieur here again with Madame.' At which he bowed once more and withdrew dexterously backwards with his startling gaze fixed on the lady as though he might never see another promise of heaven.

'Oh John I do feel very happy,' Mrs Weatherby exclaimed in a low voice. John Pomfret could see tears in her eyes. 'Oh darling isn't it nice that everyone cares about us?'

He smiled with evident affection. 'Pascal knows,' he announced.

'Of course he does!'

'But how Jane, so soon?'

'From my face naturally you great stupid,' she laughed and got the mirror out of her bag to study her great eyes. Under the table he pressed Mrs Weatherby's ankles between his own. 'Don't you think I look different? My dear my skin is a new woman's.'

'Nonsense,' he said lovingly 'it always was.'

'Oh I do sometimes thank God you're blind and I pray you'll keep so.'

'My eyes are all right Jane.'

'They're beautiful ones,' she assured him 'and beautifuller still while they don't know what they miss by staring at me with your particularly sweet expression.'

'Why?' he asked with a smile and began to look about him. 'Am I missing a lovely girl?'

She laughed and then she sighed. 'There you go again, hopeless!' she said with great indulgence. 'But I do love you so,' she added 'although you can tease me so dreadfully!'

A few days later Philip Weatherby came back to the flat after work to find his mother alone over a finished cup of tea.

'I say Mamma,' he began 'what's this about Mary throwing up her job?'

'I wouldn't know dear. She never talks much to me.'

'I thought Mr Pomfret might've mentioned, perhaps?'

'Philip,' his mother said equably 'when will you realize that John and I could have other topics besides Mary and yourself.'

'Sorry,' he put in at once. 'I just had a thought.'

'Would you mind if she did?' Mrs Weatherby enquired in a lazy way.

'Be quite surprised that's all.'

'Why?'

'I don't know really except our work does seriously mean something to us. Not like Mr Pomfret with his absolutely endless complaints every time you meet him.'

'Perhaps he's been at this task longer dear,' the mother said. 'Anyway I do wish you wouldn't stay quite so critical of my friends as you've seemed to lately. What's come over you?'

'Am I being tiresome? I apologize. It's just that I don't appear to know what's going on around any more much. Nobody tells me a word nowadays.'

'I do.'

As he leant against the fireplace he smiled down on her in what might have been a superior manner.

'Oh you're different,' he assured Mrs Weatherby.

'But what makes you wonder about Mary throwing the job up when only a few weeks ago you stood there and told me you didn't care to marry the poor girl?'

'Did I go so far? I'd forgotten. I don't think I'd quite say it now Mamma.'

'Well Philip for all your generation being so serious while we're just flighty in your eyes, you certainly seem to have more difficulty in making up your minds than we do.'

'Oh come,' he replied. 'Are you fair? Couldn't it be at my age that one has more opportunities, and anyway we don't have responsibility yet.'

'Yes,' she sighed 'I expect you're right. I didn't mean to be nasty Philip. Yet things do still happen to my generation you understand.'

'They certainly would to you if you let them?'

'What are you insinuating now Philip?'

'Just that you look more like a sister than my mother. I bet you could marry again whenever you wanted.'

'You're very sweet,' she approved. 'As a matter of fact, and I spoke of this before, I've a good memory and I remember it very well, I actually am about to marry again, so there you are.'

She turned a radiant and delightfully embarrassed blushing smile on her son who said, 'And I haven't forgotten the mess I fell into when I asked you who. I suppose I mustn't try to find out now?'

'To tell the utter truth Philip,' she admitted 'I was not quite straight with you then, just for the once. Darling you must please be glad but it's my angel John Pomfret.'

'Well I say! Oh splendid! When's the ceremony to be?' he burst out, then a sort of cloud seemed to cross his face and his voice dropped. 'But now look here Mamma will there be a double wedding? Would Mary like that?'

'She can have whatever she says,' Mrs Weatherby said, steadfast.

'And Uncle Ned? Is he pleased?'

Jane moved smartly on the sofa to get a cigarette.

'I don't know and I couldn't care less Philip. Oh my dear boy do rid yourself, oh do, of this family complex!'

'I'm really sorry. I'll try and remember,' he promised.

'All the more so when there are mercifully so few of them left,' Mrs Weatherby added.

'That might be one of the principal reasons you see,' her son pointed out. 'But never mind. I say though this is marvellous! Have you broken it to Pen yet?'

'Oh my dear promise me you won't so much as breathe a single word. D'you think I ought to get hold of some doctor to tell her, not Dr Bogle of course? And Philip we ought even to speak of this now in whispers.' She suited the action to the word. 'Isabella listens at keyholes I'm almost certain, then tells Pen in an Italian only those two can understand; but isn't she simply miraculously clever, darling Penelope!'

He laughed. 'I promise,' he said.

'Don't you think it the most dreadful thing you've ever heard and in one's own house, each word noted down but what can one do, she's such a marvellous cook dear and my little growing love does benefit so from that?'

'You know Mamma Isabella's English is far too bad.'

'Don't you be sure while Pen's teaching the woman our sacred language all the time. Oh but we shall never get at the whole truth. I often think we're not here below to find that out ever, till I believe the truth's even stopped having any importance for me in the least. Which is not to say I go about all day telling lies myself, you're my witness! No I meant generally. But Philip darling do promise you are pleased over John?'

'Of course I am. And have you told Mary?'

'My dear that must be for her Father! And don't you dare breathe a word to the sweet creature till he's spoken.'

'Oh quite,' Philip promised. 'I'll be most discreet.'

'You swear!'

'Well naturally Mamma, anything connected with you!'

'You're sure? You're quite certain? Because I'd simply die! If she heard before the proper time I mean!'

'Whatever you say darling,' he reassured her and smiled so it seemed with all his heart upon his mother. After which they discussed Bethesda Nathan and soon went off to bed.

That same evening Mr Pomfret had tea with his daughter in their flat.

'I don't know what you'll think of me darling,' he began 'but the fact is I really might marry once more this time.'

'I know Daddy,' she smiled. 'You've said before.'

'But not who,' he insisted.

'I've learned never to ask again,' she replied. 'Can I now though?'

'Well I suppose you'll make out I'm a fool at my age Mary, it's Jane.'

'Now how wonderful!' she cried with every appearance of genuine enthusiasm. 'Oh I'm so glad for you!' She kissed him.

'You truly are?'

'Of course I am Daddy. And when's it to be?'

'Tell you the truth,' he said, still with some embarrassment 'we haven't quite got down to dates yet. Are you absolutely sure you're pleased?'

'But of course,' she assured him and seemed altogether wholehearted. Then she started frowning. 'D'you promise you haven't tried to get me out of the way for the wedding?'

'My dear child what on earth do you mean?'

'The Italian business,' she said.

'I don't follow, monkey.'

'Why you remember you were so keen I should throw up my job and go out to Italy?'

'Oh that! I swear to you I hadn't even considered it.'

'You hadn't!'

'Well this thing about my marriage wasn't on the cards then.'

'But you do want me at the ceremony Daddy?'

'Naturally! What sort of a father d'you imagine I am? Couldn't you fly back?'

'That's all right then. All the same why did you wish me away?' she asked.

'It's simply . . .' he began when she interrupted.

'Oh all right,' she cried smiling once more. 'Whatever will you think? Here's you getting married and I have to talk about myself!'

'Then you don't find the idea disloyal?'

'Daddy!' she brought out with a dazzling grin. 'That's something must be entirely between you and your conscience.'

'So you do,' he reluctantly put forward.

'I said nothing of the sort,' she protested.

'You see it's never easy to explain . . .' he tried once more.

'I didn't suppose it was,' she agreed. 'Lord there was me a few weeks back trying to tell about Philip and now the roles are properly reversed,' she cried. 'You're the one stuttering and stammering now,' she said.

'I've meant to ask about Philip, Mary . . .'

'No,' she cut in on him 'this is not the moment. Let's talk about you darling.'

'You are sweet,' he said. 'How can I oblige? What d'you wish to know?'

'Well all of it of course! And right from the beginning.'

'Oh that's rather a long story,' he objected.

'Whatever you say,' she agreed. 'So we'll keep everything for another time, very well.' Then her face clouded over. 'And where d'you both propose to live?' she demanded.

'I'm not sure my love. We hadn't really considered that yet. Wherever will be cheapest of course,' he added with the whine of a guilty conscience in his voice. 'In fact,' he went on 'Jane has been making pretty much of a point how things come cheaper for two people than they do for one.'

'Oh I'd have to find somewhere else naturally,' she admitted with what seemed to be amused if guarded acquiescence.

'Why good Lord monkey you surely wouldn't think we'd turn you out! Besides there's your own future to consider. No the little I meant was it's less expensive for the three in one flat than to live split up in two of them.'

'And there's Philip, and Penelope.'

'Well yes so there is! Bless me we may have to take a larger place that's all. And while we're about it we might move to a less disgusting neighbourhood than what Jane and I both live in now. I must speak to Jane. Because the way this particular quarter has gone down lately is too frightful.'

'I shouldn't bank on Philip and me setting up shop so very soon Daddy.'

'Why what are you trying to tell now dear?'

'Very little. Anyway don't let's talk about me just this minute. Today belongs to you. It was only for when you make your plans, that's why I said what I did. Anyway I'll have to get a room of my own. But still, enough of that darling.'

'However you wish Mary.'

'Well doesn't everything seem very strange to you?' she demanded. 'Your going to be married I mean?'

'Oh my love I'm so worried about dear Penelope!' he brought out at once.

'Yes Daddy?'

'She needs a man in the house.'

'Have a heart! She's not seven yet.'

'I've such a responsibility towards Jane regarding the poor child,' Mr Pomfret insisted. 'There's no getting away from it, cardinal errors have been made with that little thing. She's just a mass of nerves. I owe this to Jane to get her right.'

His daughter laughed, not unkindly. 'Pen will be a match for every one of you I'm afraid.'

'No monkey I'm serious,' Mr Pomfret declared. 'Marriage has certain responsibilities as you'll find in due course when your time comes. I've taken on quite a lot where Penelope's concerned.'

'Oh I'd be inclined to agree with you there Daddy.'

He laughed a bit shamefacedly in return for the broad smile she gave him.

'Am I being ridiculous again?' he asked.

'Perhaps you are just a little,' she replied. 'Well now I ought to go out and meet Philip. Goodbye for now darling,' she said and kissed him hard. 'I wish you every single thing you deserve and you're wonderful,' she ended.

'You'll have me crying like Pen in two twos,' he laughed.

Mary joined Mr Weatherby in the bar of the public house they always used in Knightsbridge.

'Sorry I'm late,' she excused herself. 'My father was making his announcement.'

'So he's told you,' the young man said and pushed one of two glasses of light ale towards her. 'Seems rather extraordinary that they could marry!'

'Well why shouldn't they?'

'After knowing each other all those years!' he objected. 'When we're engaged?'

'I'd not be too certain if I were you,' she said looking away from him.

'Why how do you mean?' he demanded.

'Just what I say Philip.'

'No one tells one anything,' he complained. 'Are you trying to make out we're not to be married any more?'

'You know Daddy wants me to go to Italy?'

'How does that really alter our plans?' he asked.

'I simply can't apply for leave from the Department for any length of time,' she answered as she twiddled her glass of beer round and round on the table and watched it closely. 'It's rather sweet in one regard if you wish to know,' she added. 'He'd prefer me away to let him get adjusted, I'm sure that's why.'

'Mary I don't follow you at all.'

'Well put yourself in their position, or in my father's if you like! He's embarrassed of course he must be, marrying an old flame at his age. He doesn't care to have a grown daughter around while he adjusts himself to your mother, and marriage is tremendously a matter of adjustment you must admit Philip.'

'I never said it wasn't did I?'

'Quite. I'm glad you agree. Which will make everything so much easier. For you know we've got to have a bit of a talk you and I one of these days.'

'What about for heaven's sake?'

'Everything Philip.'

'Oh dear,' he cried, but with a smile 'this does sound ominous of you!'

'I don't know,' she answered. 'All I am almost sure of is you won't mind.'

'You're giving me marching orders?' he enquired as he watched the toe of his shoe.

'I might be, yes,' she replied.

'You mean to say you aren't absolutely certain?' he asked with a sort of detachment. She turned to face Mr Weatherby.

'Philip you mustn't laugh!' she warned.

'I'm not,' he assured her with a straight face.

'For a minute I thought you were,' she admitted and from the tone of her voice she could have been near to tears. 'I'm not sure you mayn't even have worked for this,' she added.

'In what way?' he demanded.

'Oh why are you so difficult to know Philip?' she asked transferring her attention back to the glass she held and did not drink from. 'I think that's the whole trouble. I can't make you out a bit.'

'Don't get worked up Mary.'

'But part of all I'm trying to tell you is, I'll have to leave the Department; I've just explained I can't ask for extended leave. If they gave it me they'd be bound to take as much off my holiday periods and so in the end I'd never get away again for ages which would be impossible even you will agree Philip.'

'Really your Father is the most selfish man,' he burst out and raised his voice in indignation. 'Entirely because he's bent on marrying my mother all of a sudden, a thing he's not thought of for years, he insists that you throw up a job which is a whole part of your life . . .'

Miss Pomfret interrupted and had to shake his elbow to do so.

'Quiet Philip you'll have everyone listening in a moment. And anyway less of all this about Daddy please!'

'I can't help but . . .'

'No Philip I mean what I say. I never bring up anything against your mother so why should you start about my parent?'

'I wasn't blaming him so much as I was the way he treated you.'

'Where's the difference?' she asked.

'Very well then you win,' he replied in a calmer voice. 'So you're to chuck the whole career up in order to give your father time to get to know Mamma when they've lived in each other's pockets ever since we were born!'

'Go on I'm listening Philip,' she commented acidly.

'But dear my only thought is of you!' he protested with what seemed to be some unease.

'Why?' she demanded.

'How why?' he enquired.

'Did you think of me suddenly then?'

'Well Mary isn't that natural?'

'Except this. When you could have done something for me, for us both if you like, you'd insist time and again, Philip, you mustn't upset your family! It's they who've come first always, isn't that so?'

160

'I don't know what you're referring to,' he said.

'You made one great mistake Philip,' she explained in hushed tones. 'I told you once but you wouldn't listen. And that was we should have married, then told them all at your mother's beastly party, and only then.'

'Now who's being offensive about parents?'

'Oh Philip I only said about the party, I didn't breathe a word against your mother though probably I might have if I tried. No, and now it may be too late!'

'What may be?'

'Our engagement Philip!'

'You don't mean to say you agreed to go through the ceremony with me just to stop our parents' marriage!'

'Don't be disgusting! Of course not.'

'See here Mary,' he said with what might have been firmness 'there's no good in your getting cross. The fact is you're not a bit clear at the moment and I can't make sense out of all you say.'

'I meant things might be too late now for us to marry Philip.'

'No, look, of course it's for you to decide, but don't rush this! You're all on edge which is only natural. Go to Italy by all means, give yourself a chance to think everything over. But I'm bound to tell you throwing up your job on a whim as you are must affect me. I mean to say, what serious man wouldn't consider, well you know - Honestly that does seem childish!'

'There you are!'

'Where am I?' he demanded.

'But you don't think of me in the least, ever,' she angrily protested. 'If I talk of giving up my job you merely make threats about the effect it will have on you! Not that I care my dear in the least, so there!'

'I was trying to suggest what was best.'

'So you believe my interests lie in marrying you Philip?'

'Not at all,' he answered warmly. 'I've nowt to offer. I've never been able to believe you ever would. From your point of view it must be madness.'

'Well well!' she said and smiled on him. 'Oh I know you'll think me awful but I must have more time. Still I wish you could have been decided like this all through. Oh Philip I have been miserable, truly I have! At moments.'

'I don't suppose anything's been very gay for anyone except our sainted parents,' he replied.

'There you go again!' she wearily complained.

'Sorry. Forget it. Now how shall we leave all this? I know you will be annoyed but one thing I do bless my lucky star for, that we didn't put our engagement in the papers. No,' and he raised a warning hand at the expression on her face 'don't say it! If marriage is a long grind, as they make out, of give and take then my feelings for my family are just one of those bad patches you'll have to get used to. And I warn you there's no one will ever get me out of them. Anyway go to Italy dear and see how you feel when you do come back.'

'Oh no Philip,' she burst out, turning scarlet, 'you're not to be so bloody to me!! Here take your beastly ring, I'm off!'

She almost ran out. He went rather white and cautiously looked round the saloon bar, presumably to see if anyone had noticed. No one appeared to be watching however. After which he finished both light ales and then left with much composure.

'Well she's given him back the ring Richard,' Miss Jennings announced as she opened the door to Mr Abbot.

'Good God, can't have been worth much then!'

'No, no Mary has to Philip, not Jane to John.'

'I thought all was settled between those two,' he said carefully as he folded his overcoat on a chair. 'The children that is at least,' he added.

'Why my dear you haven't heard anything about John have you?'

'No Liz but after what's happened to the couple of us nothing in human nature can ever surprise me again.'

'You are sweet. I like you so much better when you begin to be cross with Jane and John. And once upon a time I really thought you never would be!'

He coughed and rubbed his hands together before her fire.

'Rotten summer we've had,' he said.

'Yes Mary's given him back the ring,' Miss Jennings insisted.

'And has Jane had hers yet?' he wanted to be told.

'I don't know. Oh d'you think so? I would really terribly like to see it. Because if he can't do better for Jane than Philip was able to manage for John's daughter the fur will simply fly my dear, you'll see.'

'Would she go as far as to chuck the thing back in his face?' Mr Abbot enquired smiling.

'Jane? Why you don't want that surely Richard? Not now any more you can't?'

'Not sure my old wishes will have a great deal to do with anything you know, not where they're concerned anyway.'

'Why did you ask in that case?'

'Curiosity never killed a cat in spite of all they say Liz.'

'But if you're so curious, then you do still care what happens to Jane! Oh Richard you can give yourself away at times so terribly!'

'Well don't you mind about John?'

'I just won't let myself.'

'Nonsense my dear of course you'd like to know if he'd made up his mind not to marry Jane.'

'I could still do with a small little satisfaction of my own if that's what you mean,' she answered. 'But I won't allow myself to care about how the man behaves afterwards.'

'Not much between us then probably,' he admitted.

'Now what are you getting at?' she demanded, smiling with obvious pathos.

'We're in the same boat right enough it seems.'

'Then don't you start to rock the thing by yearning after Jane!'

'Oh Liz as I told you once before I'm "just a thanks a million" old soldier now.'

'Well I say it's John should be thankful all his life to me and so should Jane be for you.'

'Why?' he asked. 'What've we done towards 'em in the long run?'

'But my dear,' she cried 'I'm ever so clear about it all!' Her voice was genuinely light and gay. 'It was we who rendered everything possible for those two, which made me so restless and cross at one time. They'd simply got into the habit of getting old, Jane even gloried in letting herself go, now don't protest, and when she saw I was beginning to make something of John she grew so jealous she just couldn't stand anything.'

'Where do I come into it then?'

'Why by being the sweetest man in the whole wide world and so enormously modest you can't even lift a thumb! Don't tell me she'd have been able to carry on once again with John if you'd as much as raised your little finger!'

'Did you let John off without a fight Liz?'

'Oh I'm different,' she admitted in honeyed accents. 'There's a fate on me Richard darling! Whenever I get involved with a man he always goes back to some first love old enough to be my mother.'

'Never heard such poppycock in all my life,' he gallantly protested.

'Ah but you don't know, you can't.'

'A lovely creature like you,' he insisted.

'Then why aren't I married now?'

'Often wondered and then by Jove one day I saw the whole thing in a flash! Fact is Liz you're so damned honest and that's a wonderful quality, rarest thing on earth nowadays! You just frighten 'em off when they can't measure themselves up.'

'Richard is this a compliment?'

'Certainly is!'

'If you go on like it you'll make me cry,' she beamed upon him. 'Because you're the kindest sweetest man I think I've ever met. Oh you'll make a woman so happy one of these days!'

'D'you believe that?' he demanded almost fiercely.

'As much as anything I've ever uttered in my whole life!'

'Because when Jane won't have me I doubt anyone else will now,' he muttered.

'Don't be so absurd! I tell you any woman would be proud and honoured Richard! And what d'you dare to mean by "now"?'

'I'm no' getting any younger Liz.'

'I can't make you out at all,' she protested. 'D'you feel old?'

'Can't say I do,' he replied.

'Well where's the trouble then Richard? As I've told you before but you simply won't listen!'

'I don't remember exactly Liz?'

'Why so far as I'm concerned I prefer older people, older than myself I mean. And you once said such a sweet thing to me when you were on the subject.'

'I did? You do?'

'There you go again,' she said cheerfully. 'Oh I might have known this! Then was it just one of those things you throw off at a party?'

'Dreadfully sorry . . .' he began but she interrupted.

'You should be more careful what you say to women,' she complained with a laugh. 'You're almost impossible Richard. And I did set such store! You told me at the engagement party what you liked where I was concerned was my special blend of still being young and yet that I'd all the allure of experience.'

'Good God I've always felt it Liz.'

'Then why couldn't you recollect?'

'I did,' he insisted. 'I do.'

'After all that's happened how can I believe you now?' she asked, her back to the fire.

'Never could manage to be much use at explaining,' he said, moved over, put his arms about her waist and gave her a hug and a long kiss. She drew back but not away from his arms.

'Oh no you don't!' she laughed upon which he embraced her again.

'Look here . . .' she said seriously when next he allowed her to come up for air but at once his mouth came back on hers. After a moment she went noticeably limp and then, while he still pressed his lips on her tongue she raised her arms and tightened these around his neck.

'Oh Dick!' she said at last. 'Oh Dick!!'

Upon which for no discoverable reason he began to choke. He soon had to let go of her and if at first she seemed to smile good naturedly, then as his face grew more purple and at last black, as his staring eyes appeared to fight an enemy within so frightful was the look of preoccupation on them, so in no time at all she was thumping his back, breaking off to fetch a glass of water, letting off small 'oh's' of alarm until, when his red eyes were almost out of their sockets he began to be able to draw breath once more and what was plainly a glow of ease started to pale him, to suffuse his patient, gentle orbs. Upon which, before this expression had time to grow positively hang dog, she got him in the bedroom on the bed. As he lay watching her and she unbuttoned his collar he found his voice again.

'Dreadfully sorry but quite all right now,' he gasped.

'What was it then?' she cried.

'Always have often swallowed the wrong way all my life.'

'I was so frightened. Oh Dick!' she said laying her soft cheek along his face.

He stayed the night and next morning she seemed entirely jubilant.

A week or so later Mrs Weatherby entertained John Pomfret once more at her flat. It was dusk and as they were seated next each other on the sofa, his arm around her shoulders while she held his free hand moist in both of hers; as the fire glowed a powerful rose and it rained outside so that drops on the dark panes, which were a deep blue of ink, by reflection left small snails' tracks across and down the glass in rose, for Mrs Weatherby had not drawn the curtains; as he could outline her heavy head laid next his only in a soft blur with darker hair over her great eye above the gentle fire-wavering profile of her nose, and, because he was nearest to this living pile of coals in the grate, he could see into this eye, into the two transparencies which veiled it, down to that last surface which at three separate points glowed with the fire's same rose; as he sat at her lazy side it must have seemed to him he was looking right into Jane, relaxed inert and warm, a being open to himself the fire and the comfort of indoors but with three great furnaces quiescent in her lovely head just showing through eyeholes to warn a man, if warning were needed, that she could be very much awake, did entirely love him with molten metal within her bones within the cool back of her skull which under its living weight of hair was deeply, deeply known by his fingers.

'Oh dear,' she murmured for the third time 'darling d'you think we should close the shutters?'

He did not answer but tightened hold, to keep her. At that she leant a little more against his shoulder.

They had been talking by fits and starts, not so much in reply one to the other as to make peaceful barely related statements which had advanced very little what they presumably meant by everything they said because they now seemed in all things to agree, in comfort in quiet and rest.

'So you don't feel dearest you should be married in church?' she sighed as though to sum up a long discussion.

'Registry office, or might look ridiculous! At our age,' he almost whispered to an ear he could not see.

'However you say,' she agreed. There was another pause. 'I'll think about it,' she added.

'What was that darling?'

'The Registry office' she explained.

'I know. Go on,' he mumbled, yawning.

'I said I'd think it over, aren't you sweet,' she sighed again and silence fell once more. After a long pause she murmured,

'D'you realize I can hardly believe Mary's given him back the ring, dearest?'

'Which ring?'

'Why the engagement! You're not to fall asleep on me yet,' she commanded in her softest voice.

'Yes she did,' he murmured 'or so she said.' He yawned again.

'But Philip's never mentioned a syllable John.'

'Can't hardly think Mary'd actually go as far as pawn the object,' he muttered.

'Oh darling the poor child could not get much for what it was, would she,' and indolently saying this Mrs Weatherby chuckled. 'Oh no she simply's not made that way, Mary'd never do such a thing. Now she's gone to dear Myra in Florence, Philip's taken Bethesda out twice, yes twice, two whole times did you know?'

'Never heard of her. Who's she?'

'So unsuitable dearest, a girl at his work.'

'Well Jane,' he said with a sort of low-pitched assurance, then yawned a fifth time, 'our children will just have to work their own lives out, we can't do everything for them.'

She gave no answer. They relapsed into easy silence. After quite an interval he began again,

'But Jane my dear as I've explained before this very evening, I'm worried about your Penelope. I feel I've a real responsibility towards you there darling.'

He spoke so softly she could not have heard for she asked,

'A real what my heart?'

'Responsibility, love. Always told you a man about the house is what the child needs. Now just when she's going to have a stepfather you speak of sending her off to ah . . .' and he yawned yet once more 'to one of those sleeping places, how d'you call 'em . . .' and he came to an end.

'Boarding schools,' she gently prompted.

'Yes . . . thick ankles . . . hockey, Jane.'

'Oh no the poor angel, then I'd never allow it,' the mother protested comfortably but with a trifle more animation.

'There you are . . .' he mumbled. 'Always knew you couldn't send her away . . . when things came to the point.'

'Oh no,' she quietly said 'I'd stop her playing those games at school then.'

'Expect you know best,' he commented, yawning a last time.

There was a longer pause while his eyelids drooped.

'And how's your wicked diabetes my own darling?' she whispered.

'All right,' he barely answered.

'And is there anything at all you want my own?'

'Nothing . . . nothing,' he replied in so low a voice she could barely have heard and then seemed to fall deep asleep at last.

Doting

'Pretty squalid play all round, I thought!'

His son only grunted back at him, face vacant, mouth half open, in London, in 1949.

Smiling with grace the mother, the spouse, leant across to the fourth of their after-the-theatre party, who was a girl older than this boy, aged almost seventeen, by perhaps two years.

'But could you conceive of the wife?' Mrs Middleton cried.

The girl, the Annabel Paynton, smiled.

'Oh wasn't she!' this child agreed who, as a favoured daughter of a now disliked old friend, was invariably asked to make even numbers at what had come to be the immemorial evening out, on the boy's first night of his holidays.

So they were three in full evening dress apart from Peter's tailored pin stripe suit in which, several weeks later, he was to carry a white goose under one arm, its dead beak almost trailing the platform, to catch the last train back to yet another term.

'Pretty fair rot to my ideas,' Arthur Middleton insisted, 'rot' being a word he did not use except in his son's holidays. But he had no answer save a long roll of drums, because, at this moment, lights throughout the restaurant were dimmed.

'Not quite ideal for eating,' Diana Middleton complained.

'Here, I am truly sorry,' the husband apologized, then switched their lamp on to cast violet from the shade upon their table, at which the girl's sweet features turned to no less than wild mystery in the sort of dark he'd made. Perhaps she was aware of this, for she laughed full at Peter until, at last, the boy squirmed.

'And have you been here ever before?' she demanded.

'What, at his age!' Mrs Middleton cried.

'Well in that case he's managed it at last,' the husband commented as he watched Miss Paynton's face, her eyes. Then, to yet another roll of drums, violet limes were switched on the small stage, a man hurrahed, and Annabel bellied the corsage of her low dress the better to see between elegant shod toes, the party being seated to supper up on a balcony at this night club and hard against wrought iron railings – she did this the better to watch what now emerged, an almost entirely naked woman who walked on to scant applause, and who carried with some awkwardness, within two arms thin like snakes, a simple wicker, purple, washing basket.

'Well but just look at that,' the father said and turned his gaze back to Miss Paynton, while the son opened his mouth as if he could eat what he now saw.

'Now, who's being stuffy dear, please?' Diana asked.

Peter shushed both as, following the drums, a dirge of indigo music rose then sank, or rose, to a single flute with repeated, but ever changing, runs or trills.

'Would you call her pretty, Peter?' the mother asked in a bright voice.

'Fairly awful,' he replied. At which Mrs Middleton smiled her fondest.

'All right by me,' his father said to Annabel to be snubbed by yet another 'sh'sh' from Peter.

For the lady had begun to dance.

All she wore was a blue sequin on the point of each breast and a few more to cover her sex. As she swayed those hips, sequins caught the light to strike off in a blaze of royal blue while the skin stayed moonlit and the palms of her two hands, daubed probably with a darker pigment, made a deeper shadow above raised arms, of a red so harsh it was almost black in that space through which she waved her opened fingers in figure of eights before the cut jet of two staring eyes.

Mr Middleton did not seem able to leave Miss Paynton be.

'How old would you say she was?' he demanded of the girl in what sounded a salacious whisper. 'Every bit of sixteen?'

'Heavens no! Twenty-three at least,' the young lady answered, in a matter of fact voice, as she continued to watch.

'Come now,' he said, louder, and appeared confident. 'Any girl with a figure like that could only be a child!'

'Yes, I suppose,' Miss Paynton seemed to agree, yet obviously doubted, and flicked him a look.

'Sh . . . Arthur,' his wife implored.

'Sorry of course,' he answered in a kind of stage whisper upon which, to another, shorter, roll of drums, the spectacle changed, those lights turned to a pink which flushed Annabel's forehead to rose while the woman below stood still, and seemed to swell as saxophones took over to welcome heads of what, it soon became plain, were mechanically operated snakes thrust forth on springs from the now apricot coloured washing basket, and which did not sway their blunt heads, but kept quite quiet to a sudden return of flutes.

'Perpetrated a bit of a bloomer, surely, when they turned their lights full on as she staggered in with the old property basket?' Mr Middleton suggested.

He had no answer. Now, to a crescendo, in which the whole band joined, the woman began to waggle with extreme violence and the limes went red till she seemed almost about to melt in flames beneath.

'Oh God when are we to get something to drink?' Peter protested and turned his face away, frowning.

'I know old chap,' Mr Middleton agreed.

'A pint of shandy!' the son wailed.

'And here's poor Annabel been without a drop the whole evening,' Diana reminded everyone.

'All in this place's own good time,' her husband explained, leaning forward as if he had only now begun to appreciate the good flesh, slopping to music, close below.

'But really, Arthur,' his wife grumbled.

'It's all a part of life,' he said, without looking back. 'They're Sicilians, each one,' he said, eyes fixed. 'There not a waiter here will stir before this is over. To them it's a kind of bonus.'

'Could I have a cigarette then, d'you think?' the son demanded, almost as a right it seemed, and Diana at once began to rummage in her bag.

'Steady on,' his father moaned, but no one paid the least attention.

And Annabel, who had been lending a sort of tolerant amusement to the dance, turned to the boy and said,

'Then you do already, is that it?'

Peter did not trouble to reply.

His father started to watch Annabel again.

'Strange how much nearer in age you two are, both of you, than to Diana or me,' he said, looking for a moment, as if in self pity, at his wife who chose to ignore this; thence back once more on Annabel, the Paynton, who was growing yet but was full grown already, lush.

Mrs Middleton having tossed her son a cigarette, passed him her lighter.

'Why not smoke occasionally?' Peter asked the girl. 'What's wrong?'

'Plenty of time yet, thanks.'

'If you go on saying that, you never will.'

His father interrupted. 'Yes, my dear, have you ever considered,' he said to his wife, 'only two years between him and any girl who's "out"?'

'Of course,' she replied with a fond smile at Peter. Upon which the act beneath they'd ceased to watch, came to a close in thin applause.

'And then can't you even drink?' Peter asked the girl.

'But I don't want.'

'I remember when you used.'

'You'd better not,' she said, and smiled.

'Now we must and shall get down to serious business,' Mr Middleton exclaimed, it can only have been to draw attention to himself again. Rising forty-five, on the way to stoutness, he added, 'I starve for food after a theatre.'

His wife put on a loving, superior smile. 'If you were just not so greedy you wouldn't gain all this weight,' she said, 'all the time.'

In reply he winked at Annabel, an act which Peter did not miss.

'I needn't bother, not at my age,' he boasted.

'You don't!' the girl exclaimed. 'You can say that and mean it?'

'Now Annabel!' he cried, delightedly laughing. 'You shan't make out I ought to bant. My life's half over!'

'Well, I do eat anything and it won't upset my stomach,' she boasted.

'Mine's like an ostrich, too,' he claimed.

'Poor dear, it's his liver,' Mrs Middleton told them.

'Thanks darling,' her husband said.

'The doctor keeps on repeating he must slim down for his own sake,' Mrs Middleton insisted, with a worried frown.

'Now really, my dear, we needn't go over all my ailments, not so much in public.'

'You know what Dr Adams said, Arthur!'

'Well, where is our waiter? Anyway, these young people don't have to consider the size of their meals.'

'I could eat a whole steak,' Peter announced. 'Was that real food they had at the play, d'you suppose?'

'The whisky's forever cold tea,' his father told him over a shoulder as he pushed the bell again.

'No honestly, Arthur,' Mrs Middleton appealed. 'Not whisky, remember! Dr Adams specially warned us.'

'Now dear, couldn't you be making me a trifle ridiculous before the children?'

'We aren't children,' his son objected, in a bored voice.

There was another roll of drums.

'Why, we're going to have something else,' Miss Paynton exclaimed, leaning forward again. Once more the elder Middleton looked down her dress, but, this time, his son caught him at it. And Annabel herself glanced sideways up, to pin the older man down. Upon which the father looked guiltily away, lights were dimmed, so he chanced a quick return to the girl's eyes and, in this half dark, it seemed she steadily regarded him.

'Hard to see down there from here,' he remarked to Diana, his wife.

'Is that so?' Annabel sweetly enquired. 'Then why don't you lean under the rail like I'm doing?'

Mr Middleton must have blushed, for, in the half light, his face seemed to go black, just as a juggler walked on the small stage.

The man started with three billiard balls. He flung one up and caught it. He flung it up again then sent a second ball to chase the first. In no time he had three, fountaining from out his hands. And he did not stop at that. He introduced, he insinuated one at a time, one more after another, and threw the exact inches higher each time to give six, seven balls room until, to no applause, he had a dozen chasing themselves up then down into his two lazy-seeming hands, each ball so precisely placed that it could be thought to follow grooves in violet air.

'Well surely our Sicilians will find nothing to admire in this,' Mr Middleton said, and pushed the bell once more.

A waiter, with little English, came at once and when Diana could not read the bill of fare in this dark, her husband had to raise his lighter like a torch, which caused a commotion because the lady was afeared for her great eyelashes. Chattering away, having fun with the Sicilian who, on being asked how their lobster would be cooked, said 'in rice very nice, in the shell very well' they altogether ignored, as they decided against this lobster, miracles of skill spun out a few feet beneath – no less than the balancing of a billiard ivory ball on the juggler's chin, then a pint beer mug on top of that ball at the exact angle needed to cheat gravity, and at last the second ivory sphere which this man placed from a stick, or cue, to top all on the mug's handle – the ball supporting a pint pot, then the pint pot a second ball until, unnoticed by our party, the man removed his chin and these separate objects fell, balls of ivory each to a hand, and the jug to a toe of his patent leather shoe where he let it hang and shine to a faint look of surprise, the artist.

But in spite of all this and another roll of drums Miss Paynton insisted on asking Peter,

'D'you know Terence Shone at your place?'

'Who?' he said. 'No one of that name!'

'He is there,' Annabel assured the boy.

'Well yes, there is a Shone,' Peter admitted. 'But he's Captain of Games.'

'The very one!'

'Not our Prefect,' the boy muttered. 'Why, how on earth?'

'Oh he's always asking me down.'

'What's he like then, Ann?'

'All right.'

When the girl said this Mrs Middleton allowed her eyes to come, as though casually, to rest on Annabel's guileless features, where they stayed, with her own great eyelashes batting every now and then like slow, purple butterflies.

'Oh Terry's all of a piece, I suppose,' Miss Paynton continued. 'Gives me tea in that sort of a club they have.'

'The Prefects' Lodgings!!' he cried out. 'So what's it like there?'

'So so,' she assured him.

'I've never seen you about,' he objected.

'Well then, you can't have looked while I've been having tea, that must be it,' she replied, and sent a short, sweet smile towards his mother.

'You could introduce them,' Mrs Middleton suggested.

'Oh really Mother, would you please mind not being so insane!'

'I know Peter, I know,' she apologized. 'Arthur, were you as difficult at his age?'

'What's that?' he asked. 'Just for the minute I happened to be thinking of all the papers I'd brought back in my case from the office.'

'Poor darling,' his wife cooed, in a genuinely soothing voice, while Miss Paynton was continuing to Peter,

'Terry's really rather sweet on the whole. He writes.'

The boy gave a scared, hoarse laugh.

'Old Shone?' he cried. 'Why, he's only the best half back we've had in fifteen years.'

'But he does write poems all the same. Though I feel Terry rather lately's taken a wrong turning.'

'Are you feeling all right?' the younger Middleton protested. 'Here, have a glass of water, won't you? I mean, you must be having me on a bit. Because, since you say you do go down, and I've never even seen you, in the street that is, what sort of a meal do they stand people at their Lodgings?'

'Oh, fried eggs and all the rest.'

'That's where the food goes, then!' the boy said, and looked moodily away.

'Well I call it very decent of you not to say straight out that I'm telling lies. For I do know him, you know, and visit.' She wore a mysterious smile.

'You were a Prefect when you were at St Olaf's, surely Arthur?' Mrs Middleton interrupted.

'Of course,' the man replied, and his son squirmed.

'Then did you have girls down from London in your day?' she enquired.

'Who else?' the father answered, at his most casual.

'Bet you couldn't have,' was all Peter said to this.

'Don't contradict so, darling,' Mrs Middleton protested. 'Who ever heard of anyone being a Prefect at seventeen! It's absurd! And Arthur,' she went on, 'poor love,' she comforted. 'Are you beginning to remember all that work? Can't you let it ride, just for this one evening?'

'My dear,' he replied, 'I really do think we ought to eat now, if we're to get home in anything like reasonable hours.'

'But we've ordered, Arthur! You know what these places are, my darling!'

'Why do you think I couldn't be friends with Terence Shone?' the girl pressed the young man again.

177

'No reason at all,' he said in sulky tones.

'Because I am, you understand,' she insisted.

'Well don't let him know you meet me, then! That's all I ask.'

'We might possibly have other things to discuss,' she assured Peter. 'No, you needn't get worried,' she added with a smile. 'Honest, I shan't tell.'

'I'm not the worrying sort,' he said.

Then the parents' wine was served, Peter drank his shandy in one long soundless gasp and another was ordered, a dance band below struck up, soup was brought, and they began to seem as if they were enjoying themselves a little more.

'Oh it's so lovely to have you back,' Diana exclaimed to her son. 'Isn't it, Arthur?'

'This soup's marvellous all right,' Peter announced. 'Wonderful to be here,' he agreed.

'Thanks to the soup!' his father laughed.

Peter laughed back. 'If Ann will come down, so we starve . . .'

'But Peter!' Mrs Middleton cried out.

'I'd say they have to be bribed with all our food, the Prefects, or they'd never get anyone to take their job on.'

'Oh, if you imagine I just go down to gorge,' Miss Paynton laughed, dropped her spoon on the plate, and shoved the dish away.

'Then they must get all they do, just to spoil,' Peter said, greedily eating.

'In an agony of despair about their figures?' Mr Middleton suggested.

'Haven't I already told you we needn't worry?' the girl reminded him. He laughed. 'Oh everyone eats too much,' he insisted.

'But you can't at Peter's age. No boy can,' Diana announced gaily.

'Oh Mother, now!'

'And so who's the greedy one?' Miss Paynton asked, delighted.

'Once my soup's gone, I'll be happy to take on yours,' the boy proposed to Annabel, and winked.

'Go ahead. You're welcome,' she replied.

'Oh Peter, no, you can't,' his mother claimed in haste.

'But, my dear, why not?' Mr Middleton asked.

'In front of all these other people, darling?'

'Yet there's hardly anyone here,' the husband pointed out, with truth.

'Go on, you disgusting hog,' Annabel encouraged the boy with a fond smile. 'And when you've your mouth full I'll make you laugh so you'll do the nose trick!'

'No, but honestly,' Peter complained with what seemed great good humour, and leant across to take her soup plate.

'Because I've just had a bad go of trench mouth,' she shyly added.

'That's done it,' the boy said, then pushed her portion finally away.

'Oh you poor dear, you haven't,' Mrs Middleton cried.

'And where did you learn about trench mouth?' the father demanded of the girl.

'From a cracked cup in her office canteen,' his wife protested.

'All in all, that was probably a close shave,' said Peter.

'But you don't really believe I've got it, really?' the girl wailed in mock despair.

'I'd heard those Prefects have been raising hell about their crockery lately.'

'Now, see here Peter, I'll let you look into my mouth, if you wish. Why, only the other day, when I went to see him, my dentist said I had the most perfect gums.'

'All right, let's have a peek, then,' Mr Middleton demanded.

'Now Arthur, I've never heard such nonsense. No Annabel . . .!'

But, in spite of Mrs Middleton's appeal, the girl, with a 'here you are' leant over to the husband and opened wide the pearly gates. Her wet teeth were long and sharp, of an almost transparent whiteness. The tongue was pointed also and lay curled to a red tip against her lower jaw, to which the gums were a sterile pink. Way back behind, cavernous, in a deeper red, her uvula seemed to shrink from him. But it was the dampness, the cleanliness, the fresh-as-wet-paint must have made the man shut his lips tight, as, in his turn, he leant over hers and it was then, or so he, even, told his wife after, that he got, direct from her throat, a great whiff of flowers.

He drew back. He sighed. He shrugged his shoulders.

'Expect you'd pass in a crowd,' he said at last.

'Here Peter,' Annabel went on, and bent her head his side so the boy could see inside.

'God, thanks no,' he exclaimed, then held his nose.

Annabel let out a peal of laughter. 'You're the absolute limit,' she complained.

'Really, my dears, you shouldn't,' Mr Middleton said to all.

'I'm sorry but I properly asked for that, didn't I?' Miss Paynton exclaimed. 'Look,' she interrupted herself, 'there's Campbell Anthony come in.'

'And who may he be?' Mr Middleton enquired.

'Only the best poet we happen to have.'

'My dear Annabel, how thrilling! Where?' Mrs Middleton demanded.

The girl pointed out a most carefully dressed and neat young man who had just settled down below with another of his own age.

'Peter, let's dance,' Miss Paynton quickly suggested.

'Not on your life,' the boy said. 'Besides my steak is due now, any minute.'

'You're just a greedy brute,' the girl laughed.

'He's no soul beyond his food, you'll find,' Mr Middleton agreed. 'But I'll try if you like, Annabel,' he added.

'Why of course,' she replied, after just a glance at the wife, and then they were gone.

Peter leant over the better to see them come out beneath, on the floor.

Diana laughed. 'She only wants to show herself off a little before her poet,' she translated.

At which moment their steaks arrived. 'I don't think we need tell them to keep these hot,' she said. 'Let's eat ours and leave theirs get cold.'

'Why not?' the boy echoed, already digging a fork in his. Then, for a while, they discussed what he should do in the holidays.

Arthur Middleton was dancing well, but not too close to Miss Paynton, over an almost empty floor.

'Nice of you to come out with us again,' he said. 'No great prize in all of this for you, I'm afraid.'

'I wouldn't know what you mean,' she replied. 'Tell me, don't you think he looks quite terribly tired tonight?'

Mr Middleton saw she watched the poet.

'He could be not entirely fit,' he agreed.

'Oh it's not that,' she said. 'Or, not always. Campbell will work so hard.'

Arthur glanced down once more at the girl in his arms to catch her in a small nod of recognition sideways at the young man and also noticed that this Mr Anthony, who was busy talking, had missed it.

'How long hours does he labour then?'

'You see it's every day at the Ministry of Propaganda,' she explained. 'And now he's all taken up with this thing he's got on dance music so he has to go out to listen almost every evening – oh things are so exhausting and expensive for Campbell!'

'The writer's day is never done, you mean?'

'Why, quite,' she replied.

They danced in silence through another few moments. Then Mr Middleton saw the poet at last wave negligently in their direction. Upon which, with a happy smile, Annabel Paynton moved closer within her partner's arms.

'Now, how awful of me,' she exclaimed 'I've just remembered! Peter says you simply slave at your business.'

'Peter says?' he demanded, with some astonishment.

'Oh you've someone really special there, all right,' she went on, enthusiastically bright. 'He's going to be terrific.'

'Well, thanks,' Arthur Middleton said drily.

'So here I go again,' she lamented. 'I suppose nothing can be a greater bore than having virtual strangers talk to one about one's own children.'

'I wouldn't have thought we were quite that, Ann.'

'No more did I, but you seemed ... Oh I don't know, I expect I misunderstood. But I imagine people must be talking to you about Peter all the time.'

'Not always,' Mr Middleton smiled.

'Then tell me,' she demanded. 'D'you, yourself, get these awful depressions, too, from one day to the other?'

'Peter's never given me a moment's anxiety,' he replied stoutly.

'No, no,' she said 'I thought you wanted to get off the topic of your son. I meant in yourself. Do you still have them?'

'Of course.'

'But why? What's the purpose in one's always being depressed?'

'I should say it may have a lot to do with sex,' he replied, with a nervous laugh.

She looked down her nose. 'Would you?' she asked. 'I wouldn't know, especially about sex, of course. No, Campbell worries so terribly over his health.'

'You don't though, Ann. You look blooming.'

'Yet I'm always in the dumps and there's nothing wrong with me, is there?'

'Not that I can see.'

'And you say you do, as well? What is it, then?'

'The times, perhaps.'

'But at the time everything has always seemed awful. You've only to read those bits in the newspapers quoting what they said a hundred years back. Their one idea is, the end of the world's in sight, even then!'

'What does Peter think about this?'

'But I mean he's much too young isn't he? Being a boy he's got at least another full two years to go yet, surely?'

'Oh, I was only curious to learn, if I could, whether he had these depressions too,' Mr Middleton explained.

'Is that how things are by the time you have grown children?' she enquired. 'That you're always more taken up with them than with other people?'

'No,' he told her. 'It's embarrassment, pure and simple, inclines one to lead any conversation back on them, away from oneself.'

'Why away from you?'

'As they grow older they make you feel so aged.'

'Oh I'm sure!' she obviously mocked. 'But listen. Isn't this quite your favourite tune?'

'Well yes, rather,' he admitted.

'I only wish everyone danced as well as you . . .' she said.

Up on the balcony Peter turned to his mother.

'Would you say she was having me on, when she made out she came down to St Olaf's to see Shone?'

'But why should she, darling?'

'That's exactly it. Annabel can't want to see him. He's not her brother.'

'Oh well, you know Peter . . .'

'And she doesn't, in the least, care what position he holds in the School, you must admit.'

'Perhaps she finds the boy attractive, dear.'

Peter burst into happy laughter. 'Oh now, that's absurd,' he crowed. 'Sorry and all that, but she couldn't. Why, she might even get him sacked!'

'It's no use going on at me!' his mother said equably. 'Perhaps your Terence Shone is rich, has money.'

'Oh d'you think?'

'A girl's got to look after herself, you know.'

'I'll bet!' he laughed. 'Poor old Annabel! And to think she has to! Have you any idea when all this started?'

'Not the least. But I expect it could be very recent or, darling, you would be bound to have heard!'

'Yes I would,' he solemnly agreed. 'Marvellous steak,' he added. At that moment the music stopped and the band filed out.

'Are they going to have meat, too?' he asked.

Arthur Middleton and Annabel came back gaily calling out for their own steaks, all laughter, and it was plain they were delighted. At which Peter asked the girl,

'Is Campbell the Campbell Anthony that used to be at St Olaf's?'

'Yes, the identical one!'

'Oh he's hopeless, then! He left at the end of my second term. Everyone breathed a huge sigh of relief.'

'So what?' Miss Paynton demanded.

'Nothing,' the boy replied.

'Steak's cold,' Mr Middleton grumbled.

'Darling, Peter was so hungry,' his wife explained.

An hour or two later Mrs Middleton, who had lit the coal fire in her grate because it was chilly, waited in her double bed, waited for Arthur with the lights off. At last she heard him coming, undress in the bathroom and then, almost before she knew it she lay so comfortable and warm, he was climbing cautiously in between the sheets.

'Finished darling?' she murmured when he had settled.

'All finished,' he answered.

There was a pause.

'Asleep?' she asked in a low voice, without turning over towards him.

'Not yet,' he said.

'So wonderful,' she immediately went on, 'really wonderful to have Peter back! I'm afraid of burglars, alone in the house by daytime.'

'Stupid,' he said and sighed with sleep.

'I know, darling,' she insisted. 'But I can't help myself. You don't mind?'

'Course not,' he muttered, then yawned.

'Such numbers of them,' she continued in a reflective sort of murmur. 'Running through the house all day whenever it creaks. You mustn't think I'm stupid to be nervous.'

'Go to sleep,' he whispered.

'I will, oh I will,' she replied. 'But I do love going out with you and Peter so!'

'Me too,' he said.

'Love it when he's back and dear Annabel,' she continued.

'Sweet,' he murmured.

'Poor darling, are you very tired?' she asked. On which he turned over on his back, watched firelight whispering on the ceiling while she rolled herself to his side and put a lazy arm warm across his throat.

'I'm so happy, dearest,' she said.

'And so you ought,' he answered.

'Just think of being her age again with this Terence Shone!'

'Questioned me if she should go on seeing him,' he told her.

'Why didn't Ann ask me?' Diana wondered.

'Don't call her that. Annabel's the name.'

'What Peter uses is good enough,' the mother whispered.

'She doesn't like it.'

'Who cares, darling?'

'Oh yes,' he replied, mumbling agreement. 'Who cares?'

'But I adore her,' she went on. 'The girl's fun, they laugh together,' Mr Middleton went 'mm . . . mm.'

'So good for Peter. And she's got no airs.'

'Not a great deal to her,' the man groaned.

Diana stirred. 'I don't know how you can lie there and say that,' she sleepily complained. 'Why Annabel's sweet.'

'I'll say,' he agreed.

'Then are you a little bit enamoured of her darling?' In reply he laid a heavy fist across her legs.

'Stupid,' he mumbled.

'Oh but I'm keeping you from your precious sleep,' she exclaimed, her breath now a balm upon his neck. 'Still it does amuse me terribly to see them together since she's almost grown up and he's such a tremendous schoolboy yet. You know there's lots of girls wouldn't at all be nice to him once they were "out", in spite of having seen such a lot of each other when she was in the schoolroom.'

'I'll bet,' he mumbled.

'It is so,' she insisted. 'And frightfully good for Peter! Why I bless her. Believe me,' she ended.

'Lucky young chap,' he agreed, and yawned again.

'So well grown,' his wife added.

'Wonderful,' he mumbled.

'Oh I know you! I saw someone watching her!' she said. 'And I do mean just a word of serious blame here, dear. It would be tiresome if Peter took it in his head to notice.'

'Who're you referrin' to?'

'No one but you, Arthur darling. My wicked old darling. You won't too much, will you?'

'Dunno what you mean.'

'You must go to sleep now, you're tired. Yes, you must. Go to sleep. Oh you'll never know how much I love you.'

He snored.

'There, sleep darling,' she murmured, she yawned.

A few days later Arthur Middleton, who had begun not to take a midday meal because he was getting fat, went to a News Film at one p.m. and ran slap into Annabel when he came out an hour later.

'I was just thinking of you,' she greeted him.

'You were!'

'And how hard you worked!' she laughed.

'I skip lunch most days,' he explained. 'So once a week I go off in desperation to one of these places.'

'Oh but oughtn't you to eat occasionally?' she cried. 'You must be worn out by the time you get home.'

'Well it seems to suit me. As someone once said – when you get to my age you can't digest any more, you simply ferment your food.'

She laughed again. 'Oh, don't you of all people start off by being disgusting!! And besides you aren't old! Whoever said so?'

'Diana for one.'

'I'll bet she never can have.'

'Look,' he said. 'We mustn't stand here like this all day, and hold up the foot traffic. Where are you bound for?'

'Well mine, thank goodness's as strong as an ostrich,' she replied. 'What's more I, for one, have to have food.'

'Alone?'

'I am so it happens, yes, as a matter of fact.'

'Then let me provide.'

'Oh all right,' she accepted without enthusiasm. 'Yes, thanks.'

He took Miss Paynton to the nearest expensive restaurant.

'You don't strictly need to spend all this amount of money,' she exclaimed with more animation, brightening. 'Really and truly,' she added.

'Not every day I take you out.'

'Yes, it's the first time alone,' she agreed. 'Oh don't allow them to put us anywhere but in the window! I might miss someone I know pass.'

'I haven't any pull in this place,' he warned her, but despite this modesty the headwaiter knew him by name, took a 'Reserved' card away, and sat them down where she could overlook the pavement.

'After anyone in particular?' he enquired.

'Who?' she vaguely asked, as though she had not heard.

'That you're looking for?'

'Why of course not,' she grumbled. 'Oh, but you are nice and kind to bring me here!'

'Because I've an idea that a certain Mr Shone doesn't live in London.'

'You don't say! Oh now promise, you must, you can't think it awful of me to go down to see Terry,' she pleaded, making her eyes very large at Arthur.

'My dear, it's not for me to stick my ugly nose into your affairs.'

'Because I do get so terribly depressed sometimes,' she explained.

'You are now?' he demanded in rather a gallant manner.

'But coming out as you did, you simply saved my life,' she cried. 'It was the luckiest thing! Just when I was so low I could hardly see out of my own eyes.'

'Everyone gets fed up now and again, Annabel.'

'What reason could you possibly have?' she protested. 'You're married after all!'

'Yes.'

'Well then!'

'Oh none, I suppose,' he said, with some vagueness.

'Or do you think I shouldn't have expressed that last bit,' Miss Paynton seemed to apologize. 'I can't explain, only something made me bring to mind my grandfather, just now. He used to go out hunting twice a week, Mondays and Fridays, and travel back to the office Monday nights. And towards the end of his life he simply made a duty out of following hounds! Now that's absurd, isn't it? I mean what can it all have been but one more of his hobbies?'

'I don't hunt myself,' Mr Middleton gently complained.

'Of course not,' she agreed. 'But just going to a cinema suddenly depressed you, you know it did!'

He smiled on the girl.

'You can't make out I look on that as a duty when I never do so more than an hour each week, at most.'

'Don't assume everything so,' she protested. 'Or am I being an added curse on you? But dear Campbell say we wear ourselves out trying to fill in odd moments.'

'How should I get through my lunch hour, then?' he asked. 'Just continue to sit behind the old desk with clenched fists?'

'Well I don't see how you can pass the time if you can't eat and only go to the News Film once a week.'

'Actually I walk round looking after all the pretty girls.'

'Oh you don't!'

'Why not?'

'But it's . . . it's . . . it's wrong!! Mind, I'm not saying people never do, nice people I mean as well, only you've no earthly need, have you, you can't have like this, as you are, if you understand . . .'

'There's nothing wrong in that, Annabel,' Mr Middleton complained.

'So you consider I'm just being childish!' she cried out, with a sweet expression of despair. 'How then shall I ever explain? No, it's simply that you've no right to feel depressed, the happiest married couple in London and a lovely son, whilst look at me, I've absolutely nothing, hopelessly in love with someone years younger than I am who's still at that beastly St Olaf's, me who'll probably never get married, ever!'

'You've still got everything in front of you.'

'What good's that?' she cried. 'It might turn out to be cancer.'

'Oh come,' he said. 'Anyway I could have cancer in store for me, too.'

'But you've had your whole life,' she muttered.

'Oh well,' he said dryly. 'Now let me try and get a waiter to carry on with our meal.'

'You're bored,' she accused him, with a pout.

It took some time to attract the man's attention. Miss Paynton meanwhile looked around the restaurant but did not seem able to hit on anyone she knew. During which, when Arthur Middleton casually began his story, she did not at first appear to listen.

'My office never opens Saturdays,' he said. 'When I rise up out of bed I go to buy the weekly Reviews, get some cigarettes for myself, change a library book and so on. Now you're familiar, of course, with the Arcade, aren't you? Three weeks ago I was just passing through when I saw a girl in a red coat coming, her eyes so hard on me they made me raise mine to hers. She really was rather pretty. Dark. Well I looked away, you know how things are – I thought she imagined she must have met me somewhere which I was fairly sure she hadn't, though I couldn't be quite certain – but when I took a second glance, by which time she was much closer, I saw she was still gazing full at me with a wonderful shy expression on her, but no smile if you follow what I mean. And then, when we came level, and I took a third look, she turned her face right away so I could see only the line of the jaw.'

'And what was that like?' Miss Paynton demanded.

'Really rather terrific,' he replied.

'Well, there you are then.'

'If your suggestion is, she just wanted me to see the angle of her chin, then I can't agree. No I think she must have been watching in the reflection of a shop window.'

Annabel laughed. 'And did you speak to her?' she asked.

'That comes later,' he explained. 'So we passed each other like I told you,' he went on, 'and I got the various bits and pieces I'd gone out to get. But when I was going back to my house I passed by the Arcade once more, purely in case, And d'you know, there she still was, or anyway it was her again!'

'Well naturally.'

'Why, you don't hang around like that yourself, Annabel?'

'I might.'

'Is that the case? Anyway I wasn't so sure by this time I'd never seen the woman previously. I should have explained she had her back to me on this second trip but I recognized her, or thought I could, by the colour of the coat she had on and by a sort of droop to the shoulders I spotted when I'd seen the girl from in front; I can't explain, I don't know, it was submissive and patient, rather wonderful on the whole, attractive – and as I was walking the faster, in the end I went by. I didn't like to turn my head but when I got to the street and had to go left I just looked round and there she was, standing at the greengrocer's, staring at me out of her huge eyes with all her heart!'

'And was she, all the time, this woman you'd already seen?'

'No, she can't have been, because I didn't spot her again till the Monday when I was waiting for my bus at the bottom of the Arcade. She came through and went across the road into the photographer's opposite – you know the Polyphoto people.'

'But what is it makes you think she can't have been the other woman?'

'Oh, if it had been Mary she'd never have gone into a Polyphoto. Besides this girl was in the selfsame coat.'

'But I believe you said you didn't know at all well this Mary you took her for.'

'No more I do.'

'Then how can you be so sure it wasn't the person it might have been?'

'I can't say. But I am,' he replied.

At this point their next course was brought them in a procession. They stayed silent until the waiters had departed.

'I hardly thought you were that kind,' Miss Paynton said at last in a wondering voice.

'But I never spoke to her once,' he objected.

'Somehow, though of course I don't know you at all well, I wouldn't have expected it,' she murmured and did not look him in the eye. 'Who could ever imagine you might turn out to be the sort to go chasing.'

'Now Annabel,' he protested 'I wasn't.' He seemed amused. 'She was the one who did all,' he defended himself.

'But it takes at least two to make a hunt, when everything's said and done, doesn't it?' she said. 'The hounds and the foxes.'

'In that case no man should ever go out of doors, even,' Mr Middleton supposed.

'Well yes, perhaps so,' she admitted. 'Yet I do still think you were most to blame.'

'For just looking at a strange woman, you mean?'

'When she was obviously trying to pick you up. Wasn't she?'

'I don't see it yet, Annabel. She may have spotted something about me which reminded her of someone, or even that she liked!'

'Of course it was the way I met Terry,' Miss Paynton admitted in a dreamy voice.

'How? You just smiled in the street?'

'Yes. I'd gone down with some other people to see someone quite else.'

'Well, where did I go wrong then?'

'Oh but you're married!'

'Just you wait until you are,' he protested. 'Can you see yourself out for a morning's shopping with your eyes on the flagstones like a young nun? I ask you!'

'Oh I know,' she seemed to agree. 'But I'd never, never tell a soul when I did the other.'

'You still hold it's disloyal to one's wife or husband as the case may be?'

'Not exactly.'

Mr Middleton studied the young woman, expressionless.

'What then?' he insisted.

'Well perhaps it makes one liable to be unlucky?' she suggested.

'In which way?' he asked, as if to drag this from her.

'The next thing could be your wife would, or my husband when I'm married.'

'But it's life, dear,' he said, with some impatience. 'Nothing will ever stop people meeting each other's eyes.'

'Oh don't I know that!' she muttered. 'Sometimes I could just strangle Terry; and at other boys, too, as he does. But, Campbell says, only to mention things makes them grow bigger.'

'They grow far more from being kept secret, surely?'

'Oh I don't think that, I'm sure, at all.'

'Then why say what you do about your Shone?'

'Because I love him,' she replied at once, and immediately added, 'but I know I shouldn't speak it out loud.'

'I can't see why you mightn't love him, Annabel. We're all human, after all.'

'No, I mean about his catching other boy's eyes,' she said. 'I simply ought not to mention that again. I must remember!'

'But it can't matter if you do with someone my age, Annabel.'

'I expect not. Oh I don't know. Come on,' she said with a challenge. 'Let's talk of doting. Tell me how you first met Diana.'

'At a Hunt Ball,' he told her, plainly reluctant.

'Well?' she insisted.

'That's so long ago now.'

'So do go on,' she urged. 'It's become important for me to learn all about first meetings.'

'My parents had a party,' he said. 'They were alive then. We all went and I danced with Diana, of course, and the three other girls who were staying. I don't remember anything especial except, later on, I did notice the four of them had rather got together at a round table in the supper room and it seemed to strike me a bit that they weren't with any of our party any more, my two brothers I mean or the one other man we'd had down to stay, who was a Rowing Blue called Humphrey Byass. I saw the girls were pretty animated, not talking to the partners they were with at the time. But I don't think I thought much about it till next day, when the story broke.'

'What'd happened?' Miss Paynton demanded.

'Well, I warned you, all this was quite a while back,' Arthur Middleton explained. 'It seems when Byass chose to dance earlier with one of our party, though not with Diana as it happened, he said the hair of her head had the most wonderful natural perfume.'

At this point Mr Middleton paused as if at some enormity, and gave a bitter, embarrassed bark of a laugh.

'All right then, why not?' Annabel wanted to be told.

'You well may ask,' he replied. 'Anyway once we got back to the house about four in the morning and the girls went up to bed – they didn't; that is to say, while we were having a night-cap down below, they hid themselves in Humphrey Byass' room, made an apple pie bed, filled his wash basin with water and balanced it on the open door, and so on.'

'Was he cut about when it all fell down on him eventually?'

'Not in the way I expect you mean, yet he was a shy man and came to be considerably hurt. Left next morning, a day too soon.'

'But I mean, how sad and odd!' Miss Paynton exclaimed. 'What could be wrong with the poor boy's saying that?'

'Just the way Diana and I argued. We rather got together over the whole thing the following afternoon as a matter of fact, out shooting.'

'Are you sure he didn't actually say a good deal more?'

'Not according to Diana. Of course she'd taken no part in the horseplay. Oh, how my wretched brothers were delighted! And the other girls would hardly speak to Diana after! Well, that was the start of Peter.'

'All I can say is, I think your generation's extraordinary,' Miss Paynton murmured. 'Or was,' she added.

'Of course we didn't have the boy till we'd been married a year, but it does seem strange what comes of things when one looks back,' he said.

'No really!' Annabel protested. 'Peter's sweet. And it's so un-dignified for him to have the whole of his having been born into this world, wished on to some old quarrel at a houseparty.'

'You asked for it when you wanted to know how Diana and I first came to look at one another, after all!'

'So matter of fact,' Miss Paynton grumbled.

'Well, did your parents ever tell you about themselves?'

'Now don't be horrible! Did yours?'

'Come to think of it, never,' he admitted.

'All right then. So treat Peter like a human and not just an accident which came of someone else's apple pie bed.'

'Here!' he demanded, the edge of anger on his voice. 'I don't need instructions over my own boy. After all Diana and I were absolutely in the right.'

'Now I'm being a real curse on you once more, aren't I?' she sweetly rejoined. 'I'm so sorry! I got excited. Let's talk about other things, shall we?'

He was silent.

'I apologize. Was rude,' she added in a low voice.

'I didn't want to start this, you know, Annabel.'

'Of course you never did. It was all me. Let's get back to Mr Byass, Arthur. I mean, he simply must have said something else.'

'Diana and I have often gone over it,' Mr Middleton replied. 'I don't now believe he can have done, even if you do think the others were very strange. Maybe he put his nose down into her hair for a moment while they danced. People weren't demonstrative in those days.'

'I don't consider your generation is now.'

'That's a matter of opinion,' he commented dryly. 'But there's no question the other girls did take grave offence. And to take up your last remark I've often felt the incident stopped me afterwards paying those great luscious compliments to women which seem to be all the rage nowadays.' He laughed selfconsciously.

There was a pause which she broke by saying, in the most natural manner,

'If I wished I could be married. Now! Any time I like!'

'Good,' he replied.

'Yes, and to either of two people.'

'Well, that's splendid Annabel.'

'Oh, but not yet. All the same they both would propose any evening

I let them.' She was still speaking in a dreamy, reflective tone of voice.

'You don't wish them to yet, then?'

'I can't tell,' she answered. 'Perhaps I'm just waiting for something.'

'What?'

'A sign like you two had over Mr Byass.'

'But Annabel, Diana and I agreed about the others' behaviour.'

'I bet your wife knew she was going to marry you.'

He cleared his throat. 'No Annabel . . .' he began in a warning voice.

'I hate false modesty,' she interrupted. 'Any woman would be proud.'

'It didn't come about the way you think in the least,' he protested.

'Don't try to stop me blurting what I feel.'

'Well thanks,' he said bitterly.

'Or have I said something awful, yet once more?' she cried in what appeared to be scorn. 'I just prefer men older. Can I help that? There, now you know my secret.'

'Annabel, then you'll have to find a widower.'

She gazed at Mr Middleton, large eyed. 'Oh never. They're too cunning, must be,' she protested. 'But that's what's the fault with Campbell and Terry, so unformed!'

'You're going to have a job on your hands then.'

She laughed at his last remark. 'Isn't everything too tragic,' she giggled. 'Aren't I all kinds of a fool! But there it is, and nothing will ever change.'

Soon after this he paid the bill and they left without arranging to meet again.

Some days later Annabel rang Peter Middleton and asked him out to lunch. They went to a cheap Indian curry place near where she worked.

'Did your father happen to mention he'd taken me out the other afternoon?' she enquired.

'No,' the boy said in an uninterested voice. 'Should he?'

'We ran across one another in the street. I'm afraid I can't afford anything like the gorgeous meal he provided.'

'But curry's my favourite,' Peter claimed. 'I wish I had it every day. Decent of you to ask me.'

'No, because I do truly enjoy seeing you. It takes me out of myself. And you've little idea how few there are I could say that of. Though, d'you know, it could be true about your Father. He's so terribly handsome, Peter.'

The boy broke into mocking laughter, with his mouth full.

'Look out for the curry,' she warned. 'You'll blow it all over me and the table.'

When he had composed himself he said,

'Well I once ate a green fig looked precisely like Dad's face.'

She giggled. 'Oh dear I suppose you could on the whole say that of him, some days,' she admitted.

The younger Mr Middleton at this point changed the subject.

'I say,' he said 'you don't actually know Terence Shone do you?'

'You're talking now just like the boy out of a school story book,' she objected. He grinned. 'Of course I do. And he's not, anyway, so exciting a person as perhaps you might think. Come to that, he's dull as ditch water sometimes. I'm a bit off Terence. But I didn't ask you out to lunch to discuss private affairs. Let's go on more about your Father. Look, I'll tell you about mine if you wish.'

The boy seemed to pay not the slightest attention.

'Are your parents still in love?' she asked.

'My mother and father? God, I suppose so. Are yours?'

'Not a bit. No.'

Peter went on eating.

'They don't even share a room,' she added.

'D'you mind?' he asked at last.

'Well it makes things rather wearisome at times,' she said. 'They have endless rows, going into the same old grouches over and over again. What's so extraordinary is, they never seem to say anything different. Are yours like that?'

'Well I expect they are Ann, yes. Of course I'm not home much, only in the holidays. They're pretty average I should say.'

'How long have they been married?'

'Lord, don't ask me. I wouldn't know.'

'All in all I'd imagine they were still very much in love,' she suggested.

'I expect so,' he said.

'You won't tell them I mentioned this, will you?'

'What d'you take me for?' he protested. 'I don't discuss anything with my parents.'

'And can't you, then, ever talk over your own father?' she demanded suddenly with some petulance.

'On occasions,' he replied with calm. 'At St Olaf's.'

'Why there?'

'Didn't you go to school?'

'No,' she said. 'I had governesses.'

'Wouldn't you discuss your parents with them?'

'Heavens,' she cried with a shrill laugh. 'You've never seen mine or you couldn't say that.'

'No,' he agreed. 'I'd be too young.'

'I don't think you are, Peter. It wasn't such ages ago. I say, in your own mind, would you consider your mother beautiful?'

'Yes,' he said, rather gruff, 'as a matter of fact.'

'Me too,' she echoed, but in a sad little voice. 'She has everything, Hair, teeth, skin, those wide apart eyes. By any standard your father's a very lucky man.'

'Why?'

'To have such a wife of course. Would you say she liked me, Peter?'

'Fairly, yes. No reason not to, is there?'

'Oh none,' she agreed, casually.

'She was jolly pleased with you as a matter of fact for coming along again the other night, to the play and afterwards.'

'But I loved to, Peter.'

'Shouldn't have thought it could have been much fun for you.'

'I adore them both, you see.'

'Well look out then, Ann! If you go on being so intense about it, you'll get nerves or something.'

At which they began to giggle at themselves, then over the Indian waiter who was a melancholy looking man, at the hot curry and saffron coloured rice, and then over the sweet which looked like little dog's turds, under the pink paper carnations in a dry, dusty vase.

The same evening Arthur Middleton worked as usual on the papers he'd brought home from the office. When he did come at last he found the fire lit, lights extinguished and Diana in bed, humped beneath the clothes, motionless, hardly breathing.

He undressed quietly, as usual, and climbed with stiff knees between the sheets. Mrs Middleton again had her broad back towards him, the dark hill of her thigh was across his sight.

'Finished darling,' she murmured, when he had settled down.

'All done,' he mumbled.

There was a long pause.

'Gone off yet?' she asked in a low voice.

'No, my dear,' he replied.

'Wasn't it sweet of darling Annabel,' she said.

'What's the girl done now?'

'Taken Peter out to lunch.'

'Did she,' he murmured in an uninterested voice.

'So good for him at his age,' Diana added.

Mr Middleton gave a grunt.

'I daren't think what they can have found to talk about, though,' Mrs Middleton wondered. 'Of course I chatter away to him and he's so jolly with me always – that's only natural, but wasn't it generous of anyone in her generation to take the trouble?'

'Yes indeed,' he faintly assented.

They were lying back to back. Diana turned over, settled the sheets about his chin. He brought a hand up and put these back the way they were.

'Sleepy?' she murmured.

'A bit,' he admitted.

'Well you can talk just a few minutes more,' she said, in almost a brisk voice. 'What d'you think they find to say to one another?'

'Discuss us?' he suggested.

'Oh we'd have no earthly interest for them, Arthur. Besides darling Peter would be too loyal.'

'Children do compare notes, you know.'

'Dig out things in common between me and Paula Paynton. Oh, no dear!'

He mumbled unintelligibly.

'What Arthur?'

'Only saying I've not much in common with Prior Paynton either.'

'Oh, that fool of a man,' she said. 'There could be no earthly resemblance at all, darling.'

With a slow heave Arthur Middleton levered himself over on his back. Diana rearranged the sheets under her chin. Firelight whispered on the ceiling.

'Well I can't say what the children discuss,' he admitted in quite a strong voice. 'Anyway, it won't be wine women and song, not at his age.'

'But d'you think she could be a little old for him, Arthur?'

'You just said . . .'

'Now I'm asking you, dear,' she interrupted.

'What exactly is it you mean, Di?'

'Of course it's good for Peter to see life, but I was wondering if I liked his going out, quite so soon, with older girls.'

'Jealous of Annabel, darling?' Mr Middleton enquired with a smile.

'Well yes, I suppose I am, perhaps, a bit.'

'But Di, this has got to come sooner or later with the boy.'

'I'm not sure, you see, if this is not too soon. I don't mind your asking her out to lunch, of course, as you did when you ran into the child, but don't you understand, she couldn't have you back, she had to invite Peter instead. And those beastly, cheap curry places are dangerous with the food they serve. Besides he might get hashish there, or hemp, or whatever it is these Indians take.'

'Oh my love,' he said 'no! I promise they're most respectable.'

'All of them?'

'Certainly.'

'Every single one?'

'Well of course, Di, I couldn't say.'

'There you are then . . .'

'So I mustn't ask out anyone we've entertained here, to come to lunch, if I stumble into them on the street, for fear they may invite Peter to a meal in return? Is that it?'

She chuckled.

'Yes,' she said.

He laughed.

'I see,' he said.

'Do you, Arthur?'

'Well yes. In a way,' he answered.

'Which means you aren't going to pay the slightest attention?' She laughed with great good humour. 'Is that what you mean, my wicked old darling?'

His reply was to turn over and give her a light kiss on the nose.

'Well, you may be right, though I'm sure not,' she said. 'I expect you think I'm just being silly!'

'I love you,' he murmured, shutting his eyes.

She put a lazy arm warm across his throat. He laid a heavy fist over her legs.

'There, sleep my darling,' she mumbled.

And in a moment or two he snored.

Some days later Mr Middleton rang Annabel first thing, soon as he got to the office.

'Oh it's you,' she answered in a neutral voice when he reached her.

'Look,' he continued. 'I don't know how you expect a man to pass his lunch hour, but I was wondering if you wouldn't do me a favour and come out, for once, today?'

'To lunch?' she asked in an expiring voice. 'Well, I might.'

'Same time and place?' he enquired in what seemed elaborately casual tones.

'Oh yes, very well. Yes, thanks a lot,' she said.

Yet, when they met in the restaurant, she was all smiles.

'This is sweet,' she said in her clear piping voice, and seemed to draw Arthur forward while shaking his hand. 'And in this glamorous, expensive room again. You are kind!'

'Nice of you to turn up,' he answered.

'Why, I'm not late, am I?' she asked. 'Oh, if you only knew,' she added without waiting for the reply, preceding him to the bar.

'What?'

'Simply no one invites me anywhere, any more,' she complained.

'Rot.'

'No longer now, it isn't, alas,' Annabel insisted, then had three cocktails, one after the other.

So it was with sparkling eyes that she reached their corner table, in the end. This time they didn't overlook the street.

'I've been through such dire trouble with Mummy,' Miss Paynton began, as soon as they had ordered.

'Not the first or the last time I presume,' he smiled.

'No,' she said 'but this is serious. Of course I'm really much closer to Mummy than I am to Dads but I can't remember her ever being so cross with me, ever before.'

'What about?'

'You see I went down to visit someone in the country.'

'Shone?' he asked.

'Well yes,' she said. 'For the first and only time, as a matter of fact. And Terry's parents turned out to be really quite odious people. So rude, when I did go as a guest, after all!'

Miss Paynton made her eyes very large and round at Arthur.

'Oh quite,' he said with an encouraging smile.

She began to giggle.

'Terry didn't altogether invite me,' she went on. 'But when he phoned and wanted to know what I was doing with myself these days, I said, "why on earth don't you just come up to London for an evening?" and he said he simply hadn't the money. Oh Arthur,' she cried, using his Christian name for the second time, 'how squalid it can be to fall in love with a schoolboy! So then I had to journey to him! I made Bill Allen take me in his car.'

'Who's he?'

'Nobody. He has a big car. I bet Mrs Shone was surprised to see me in anything so terrific.'

'How old is this Allen?'

'About twenty-four. What's that got to do with it?'

'Nothing,' Arthur said. 'But you've this to consider; if you were both young then Mrs Shone could have been seized with jealousy, Ann.'

'Well of course. She can't expect to be any other way from now on, can she?'

'Unless she does you down, in the end.'

'Oh how beastly even to dare suggest such a thing,' Miss Paynton exclaimed while she smiled fondly on Arthur. 'What'll you bet?'

'No thanks,' he smiled back. 'You can't be serious, though, when you say you expected a warm welcome from this woman.'

'Did I say that?' she objected. 'Because it turned out, in the end, Terry had been too frightened to tell his mother we were coming. So Bill and I couldn't have done worse when we roared up the drive in good time for lunch. It's a Dagonda. In addition to which, Sunday comes as a very quiet day for them down there. But you must agree, all in all, it was perfectly disgraceful on poor Terry's part.'

'Well, I can't entirely see that.'

'If you'd only heard him on the phone! He sounded so low, poor dear.'

'Which is the only one reason you felt you had to go?'

'Why else?' she asked.

'And the father then? What sort of a man is Mr Shone? Didn't he like you?'

'Oh, he's much older than you.'

'I thought you once said you preferred older men!'

'Terry's father would be too sweet if he wasn't so dim with his wife,' Miss Paynton answered with a bright smile. 'But although there wasn't enough for his lunch because of Bill and me, I could tell he was quite thrilled. The worst of all this was, Sunday is a considerable day for them into the bargain, as I said before. They go to church and that.'

'Yes,' Arthur agreed. 'Granted.'

'But I'm a bit off Terry at the moment,' she went on. 'I was, already, if you remember, a week or two back, only for a different reason. Then when Bill had to lug me down halfway to the sea, all that distance and he can't afford it any more than Terry can, coming up to London, well, I mean, I don't see how I could be expected to stretch my loyalties between two boys as if I was a bit of wonderful elastic, do you?'

'I'm sure you gave joy to Shone, anyway.'

'That might be,' she agreed. 'But if only he wasn't so meek,' she answered. 'He was struck dumb at not having told his mother about lunch. That's what must have brought all the stuffiness out in her. Oh,' she said, and her eyes filled with bold tears, 'isn't everything really too terrible, sometimes? One goes down to the rescue of a fellow human being of whom one's frightfully fond at the moment, he sends out an SOS for help, and they treat you like a thief, a baby snatcher.'

'The best way,' Arthur said 'is to give advice only over the telephone and then never find out if the advice has been taken. Above all, don't follow up in person.'

'In that case how's a girl ever to get married?'

'In what way, d'you mean?' he asked.

'I hope I never fall so low as to receive my proposals, if I should get any, on long distance, with women in every exchange between where he is and London comparing notes on how he pops the question.'

'Yes, I see,' Arthur admitted. 'I suppose you must face the men concerned.'

'In the end I imagine the one thing will be to fall in love just with those one can meet naturally, without all this perfectly ruthless parent trouble.'

'Your men would need to be much older, then.'

'Yes, they would,' she agreed with a smile. 'Arthur, you're sweet. In fact I don't know how I'd manage without you, and Diana, and dear Peter. But what made it worse was, when I told Mummy of the disastrous trip down to see, she turned quite cross and said I oughtn't to have gone! Well I realize the way her mind works, how she looks at things through her generation's spectacles, but you do understand, don't you, I can't sit at home and simply wait, can I? Not as things are now.'

'Why not?' he argued. 'You've loads of time.'

'There never is,' she objected, and again her eyes filled with tears.

At this point the wine waiter came to take their order. Mr Middleton laid knife and fork down.

'Will you have anything, Ann?' he asked.

'Oh no thanks,' she answered with a sad smile. 'Just plain water, please.'

'D'you mind if I take a whisky and splash?'

'How could I when you're being so perfect.'

Arthur ordered the drink.

'You are inclined to flatter one a bit, you know,' he said when they were alone once more.

'Me?' she cried. 'All I can say is, I wish you were my parent!'

'What about your own father, then?'

'Dads?' she said. 'Oh he's sweet right enough. But Mummy and me don't see such a lot of him just now.'

'I know,' he gravely agreed. 'I'd heard something. Your parents are two of Diana's oldest friends.'

'Are now, or used to be?' she asked.

'Yes,' he admitted 'things can't have been easy for you since Prior and Paula began not to get on. Unhappy people are apt to be bores, Annabel.'

'That's exactly what so terrifies me about myself,' she exclaimed. 'I can't ever be sure, now, I'm not becoming one. Peter's lucky to have you, believe you me. Because, as you've just hinted things are truly a bit grim for us at home at the moment, so I have to watch myself the whole time to guard against the utter bore I may become.'

'What absolute rot,' he protested. 'Of course you aren't.'

'Oh, but yes!'

'Yet you've two young men up your sleeve, ready and glad to propose tomorrow.'

'I told you,' she said. 'They don't mean a thing.'

'But, Annabel, they must prove to you that you're liked.'

'I expect they only go to show I'm not entirely hideous,' she muttered.

'Don't sit there across from me and say your generation of males want to marry just because a girl's a good-looker, for I simply won't believe that,' he pronounced.

'Well, what d'you know about it?' she asked politely.

'In my time people didn't.'

'Of course you in particular never could,' she agreed at once. 'But if what you say is true, then how lucky you both are, don't you understand, I mean with the person you married.'

'No, honestly Annabel, if you're trying to make out men of your own age can't fall genuinely in love any longer, then I give up.'

'You see,' she replied 'you were all so much more high principled in your day. From your own lips I had that story about a Mr Humphrey ... Humphrey what's his name?'

'Byass. How does he come into this?'

'Yes Byass. Well those girls, as they were, just must have mobbed the man because they thought he wasn't genuine.'

'Good Lord no! I don't think that at all. They were only being objectionable and hearty. You can't make them out to be more than they were.'

'What have you ever known about women?' she demanded with some petulance.

'Enough never to discuss 'em,' he dryly replied.

'Yet you do all the time, probably.'

'Perhaps it's only when I'm with you,' he suggested, smiling.

'Now I'm boring you once more,' she exclaimed in obviously mock contrition. 'But I do apologize,' she said with a sort of humble rage. Then Miss Paynton added, self pityingly, 'What a way to entertain one's host over luncheon!'

'Nonsense,' he said, in what, it seemed plain, was some alarm. 'Exciting for a man my age to be out with anyone as pretty as you.'

She left her eyes on his face and looked sad.

'Care was taken in those days,' she said. 'Girls were looked after, you yourself protect them still. I don't mean only you, but your whole generation.'

'Perhaps it is girls won't take the trouble, now,' he suggested.

'Don't take trouble?' she echoed with indignation.

'Oh you mustn't think I can't realize how good you are to come out and bother with me,' he put in quickly 'but I . . .'

'Please stop now, at once, being so modest,' she interrupted. 'I'm sure you can't mean that. I like to be invited by you. I dote on when you ask me. Now then!'

'All right, thanks. I'm sorry,' he said. 'But you'll ruin your whole life, believe me, if you insist that everything was better in the days you're too young to remember. People don't change much and if one wanted to find them distasteful then, it used to come quite easy.'

'How can I wish to dislike anyone?' she pouted.

'Well, if I may say so, you're going the right way about it now.'

'Why? I'm kind to everybody.'

'Kindness doesn't count, Ann.'

'Sometimes I think I'm too nice,' she went on as though she had not heard. 'I know Mummy thinks so. She says I shouldn't try to comfort people when they get miserable.'

'I suppose it's a question of degree,' he said.

'Well they will ring up, and will be desperate, and then I manage to go round, or motor down if I possibly can. Could any fellow human do less, Arthur?'

'Isn't Shone a bit young to be getting so desperate?'

'Oh I wasn't thinking of Terry just for the moment. No, sometimes, when Campbell's distracted, he telephones, when he's stuck in his work, and so on.'

'What's he at now?' Mr Middleton asked.

'An anthology of love poetry he's to call "Doting". Don't you agree it's a marvellous title?'

'Well, you know doting, to me, is not loving.'

'I don't follow,' she said with a small frown.

'To my mind love must include adoration of course, but if you just dote on a girl you don't necessarily go so far as to love her. Loving goes deeper.'

'Well,' she suggested 'perhaps the same words could mean different things to men and women.'

'Possibly,' he said. 'Perhaps not.'

'So anyway, quite often, Mummy and I are sitting alone after dinner, and you can be sure her poor heart is full of where Dads is, and then the phone rings so that we race each other. I always win. After which, as likely as not, it only turns out to be Campbell who's got stuck in his work, and wants my company.'

'Yes,' Mr Middleton admitted. 'I sympathize with you. Things can't be easy back home at present.'

'You are sweet, you really are. Am I being an awful bore?'

'Of course not. But tell me, how can this Campbell get stuck over an anthology?'

'Well, it wouldn't be cut and dried to choose among so many poems after all.'

'So he reads them out to you for your opinion?'

'Oh no, we play records, as a rule, to take his mind off. He has this thing, too, about jazz, you see.'

'So I understood,' Mr Middleton said, in a wondering voice.

'But he can't listen alone.'

'Why not?'

'Campbell says jazz is written for crowds and so mustn't be heard if you're one in a room.'

'I see. Then has he asked you yet to share his loneliness for good?'

She frowned. 'I don't think that's very nice at all,' she said. 'It might be almost nasty,' she added in a sad voice 'or else you're not so understanding as you seem. But of course Campbell would love to live in sin with me and I might adore it too, yet I'm not going to. Although, as I said, he could really be rather wonderful.'

'I'm sorry,' Arthur apologized. 'I was confused.'

'What about?'

'Everything Ann.'

'Who's to blame you,' she suddenly laughed. 'Look at me! I get so tangled up over my own feelings I often don't know where I am myself.'

'Wouldn't it help to talk this over with your mother, then?'

'I couldn't bother Mummy now, just when she's so worried.'

'And yet that might take Paula out of herself, a bit,' he suggested.

'In which case you don't know my mother,' she said. 'Anything about me could only be yet another great worry for her.'

'Yes I see. All right. But to go back to what you were saying, Annabel. Aren't you taking things too seriously? Because you needn't think your emotional life will ever not be in a tangle, dear.'

'You say I'm so crazy I shan't once be able to snap out of it?' she demanded with what appeared to be humble indignation.

'Of course not,' he pleaded with her. 'Take my own case, now, for example. Half the time I don't know where I am, in my emotional life I mean, whether I'm coming or going.'

'If you ask me seriously to believe that,' she objected 'then all I can say is your memory must be short, or else you intend to forget. I don't know the sort of life you used to lead but, just for a minute, look back to what it must have been before you married and had Peter.'

'I often do.'

'You do!' she cried. 'And you say you're worse off at the moment? Well, of course, I'm sorry,' she corrected herself 'that's not your argument, but you maintain, because this is what you're saying, isn't it, that you have a worse time now than me who's simply got no one, or anything!! Or have I gone too far again?' she asked in a contrite voice. 'Still, I don't feel you can remember properly. Because I won't agree. So long as I live I won't!'

'The fact is,' he explained with calm 'the minute one begins a discussion of mutual troubles or miseries, it invariably becomes a kind of fierce competition as to who, in effect, is the worse off.'

'Well, why not?'

'But Ann, I was trying to help.'

'I'm sure you were. Only how?'

'What I was after was an attempt to show that you were not alone in your old boat.'

'Even if I wasn't, in which way would that alter things?' she demanded.

'Then you won't have any comfort?'

'What do you mean?' she muttered with a lost look. 'Here you are, married with a lovely son, what can the matter be?'

'How about your own parents, then? There's plenty wrong with them.'

'But you're happily married!'

'Are you trying to make out you know, better than I do, what's the matter with me?'

'Well, all right, then,' Miss Paynton crossly announced. 'And to think that you even own your own house,' she added. 'But, because you at least see I do realize what my trouble is, just admit, then, I've simply no one, and nothing.'

'I remember a working man once said to my face "what have you to worry about, you're rich" ' Mr Middleton told the girl.

'Oh, how could I mean money?' she protested.

'I don't either,' he assured her.

'But you must understand,' she protested. 'Compared with my case you're well off beyond the dreams of avarice.' Then she laughed. 'Or perhaps not beyond my dreams,' she added, suddenly gay. 'Because, of course, I do want such a vast great deal.'

She leant across and squeezed his hand on the table cloth. Then changed the subject. She began to take infinite pains, and soon had him smiling at a long story about one of her girlfriends.

When it was time for her to go back to work she said 'Do please ask me again. You've done such a lot of good. Promise!'

'I will, if I may,' he replied as he raised his hat.

That same evening Mr Middleton worked as usual, after dinner, in the study, while his wife sat with Peter in the living room of their flat. The boy was seated opposite Diana on a sofa with the whole day's newspaper piled around him, the sheets separately strewn about to left and right halfway up to his shoulders. Two table-lamps were lit, one for Mrs Middleton to read by in her armchair and the other, so placed as to command the empty chair sacred to his father between this sofa and the fire, gave the boy but little light, although he had tilted the shade so that the bulb shone into his mother's eyes. And, as he was done with the day's news, he now breathed heavily over a catalogue of gramophone records.

'Why don't you change to where Arthur always sits, darling?' Mrs Middleton suggested. 'Then you'd be able to see better.'

'But he'll come back any time,' the young man replied.

'I don't think so, not yet,' she said. 'He does work so hard, he has such a lot to do. Because you'll ruin your eyes like this.'

'No I won't.'

'What's the matter with you tonight?'

'Nothing. Why?'

'Oh Peter, are you getting bored with London again?'

'Not more than usual.'

'Where would you like to be, then? In the country?'

'Well it might make a change.'

'We go through this every holiday,' she lamented. 'But there's no one to visit! And hotels are so expensive! Look, if you're desperate why won't you take someone out? I'm not sure you're old enough yet but I've my number two account for your expenses, and I'd provide the wherewithal.'

'There's no one to go with.'

'How about Annabel?'

'Oh, not her!'

'Then why don't you ring up one of your school friends? What are they there for? Some of them must live in London.'

'God no.'

'Which doesn't exactly make anything easier, does it?' Mrs Middleton commented ruefully. 'Peter, don't say you have something against Annabel now?'

'When did I ever even like her, Mother?'

'But she's been such a companion for you all these long years!'

'Well there are chaps at St Olaf's say they don't particularly care even for their sisters.'

Diana laughed. 'Yes,' she agreed 'I can remember my brothers were the same. Still Annabel does adore you darling. Why, she took you out only last week!'

'That was no more than to pay Father back for all he had spent.'

'And I don't think so,' Mrs Middleton protested, in an unconfident way. 'In any case Arthur asked her out to lunch this afternoon. You wouldn't wish to rely on her inviting you again, surely?'

'He did? He does see quite a bit of her now!'

'Why shouldn't your Father stand lunch to whosoever he likes?' Diana enquired patiently. 'I'm glad he can relax at times, with all that work of his.'

'But, I mean, Ann's young enough to be my sister.'

'That's no reason for him not to invite the child, is it?'

The boy gave a disdainful hoot, at which Mrs Middleton laughed a bit, with a show of confidence. 'I know your Father,' she said. 'You must at least allow me that. Nonsense!'

'Well I think it's silly at his age.'

'Now Peter, I'm not going to have you get tiresome over the holidays. Oh I realize it can't be easy here in London but we've nowhere else to go that we can afford, have we, and in any case this is not the right time of the year for shooting.'

'No, I know.'

'You've got to learn to take your pleasures where you find yourself,' she went on equably. 'You can't suppose I like to sit here alone, while you're away, night after night, with Arthur at work downstairs.'

'Well, why does he?'

'Someone's got to earn the money to keep you at school and pay for all this, Peter.'

'But doesn't he invite you out to lunch sometimes?'

'Of course. Yet, if he wants to ask Ann, one's only too pleased that he should be getting his mind off a bit. Now why don't you take your gun to the shooting school and put in some practice?'

After which they cheerfully discussed this and other methods for him to get through the holidays, till it was time for bed.

The next Monday Arthur Middleton was sitting opposite Miss Paynton at the same corner table of that restaurant they used every week for lunch.

'Now we've established a habit by coming here, what shall we talk about?' he gaily enquired.

'Tell me of when we first met,' she said.

'You were six.'

'Go on. Then how was I dressed?'

'With a pink bow in your hair.'

'Oh I expect. But which time of day was it?'

'Lunch.'

'Well, don't stop. What frock did I wear?'

'I'm sorry but all this was a long time now. Twelve whole years, you know.'

'I can remember all my dresses,' she replied. 'Then how did we talk?'

'Di was busy with Prior and Paula, whilst I sat next you,' he began. 'We discussed cleaning our teeth and got on, when no one was looking, to making terrible faces at each other.'

She sniffed. 'That doesn't sound terribly exciting,' she announced.

'Can't you really remember, Ann?'

'But there's nothing to remind me, surely?'

'No, I meant before lunch that day. The rabbit hutch.'

'All this is news to me,' she assured him. 'And you mustn't expect a girl to bring to mind everything. That was so long ago.'

'Well, thank God,' he said, in what seemed a strained voice. 'I know I shan't ever forget and I've been afraid all these years you might have taken a turn!!'

'What is all this?'

'You see, you brought me out alone with you before lunch, to inspect your rabbit.'

'Nip? Or Tig? No, this must have been earlier. Why you can't mean Doughnut?'

'How should I remember at this distance?'

'Well, continue Arthur. Tell!'

'It was a big rabbit and a large hutch,' he began with obvious reluctance. 'About three feet off the ground. You'd fixed a sloping plank so that when you turned your Doughnut out he wouldn't have to jump down. D'you recall where the hutch was, because that's everything. In the ruined chapel, on a lawn which used to be the floor, the greenest grass. I suppose you could get used to most of it but the walls, the extraordinary brick and blue ivy and stillness, absolutely not a sound, because I remember the sun was very strong that morning – well, I imagine, I shan't ever forget your rabbit twitching its nose at you while you got down on hands and knees to show me how it had to climb to get back. I thought the ladder would break under your weight, it was only elm. Then you clambered on top of the hutch, to simply become your rabbit. You crouched on the roof to show me how Doughnut, or however it was called, crouched, and the damn animal was beneath you all the time so I thought the whole thing must collapse under your weight and kill the wretched thing. All of which made me say for you to come down, but you paid no attention, and, in the end, I caught hold of your ankle to pull you off but, Ann, you screamed! Can't you remember?'

'How stupid,' she commented. 'Why on earth should I do that?'

'It was most significant,' he gravely said.

'So what?' Miss Paynton asked.

'You yelled like a stuck pig. I thought your parents would be on me in a flash.'

'Why Arthur?'

'Well I did have your ankle in my fist. You wore blue cotton socks.'

'I'll bet I didn't. Not blue at any age.'

'Yes, it is so. I shan't ever forget.'

'And so, then?' she demanded. 'After all, what makes this very serious?'

'Embarrassment, Ann,' he replied.

'Good God,' she said. 'Then you are really a mass of nerves inside?'

'I'm allergic to children if you want to know.'

'You mustn't even pretend you are about your Peter.'

'I am with little girls,' he said, in a satisfied voice.

'Up to what age?' Miss Paynton asked.

'Now don't you poke fun at me,' he said, and changed the subject.

That same week, on a summer evening, Mr Middleton walked a friend home from his club.

'No, but what do you really think about them?' he was persisting.

'Not much,' Mr Addinsell replied.

'All right,' Arthur Middleton admitted. 'But one thing you must agree, that they simply wave it about in front of one.'

'Females always have and will,' his companion said.

'You know what happened to me? Took my wife out with this girl and she leans on a balcony on purpose so I can look right down the front of her dress.'

'What might her name be?' Mr Addinsell demanded.

'Is none of your damned business,' Arthur Middleton laughed. 'But things are very different now, aren't they, to when we first went out in London.'

'I don't know, I wouldn't be too sure,' his companion demurred.

'Meaning I could be at the dangerous age, Charles? Oh well, all the same, really young girls never have behaved like that in the whole history of the world.'

'What do you care, after all?'

'Because she's simply destroying me, the little tart,' Mr Middleton sang out in indignation. 'I can't sleep at night any more when I think of her,' he said. 'In a week or two I'll even be obsessed.'

'Oh get it over with, Arthur, and go to bed with the child.'

'I could, of course, with a bit of luck, only I'm so upset it might make me worse. But Charles, your own boy's only eight, isn't he?'

'Rising nine, Joe. What difference is there in that?'

'You see this little bit is the one we almost always bring along, each time we take Peter out and about London. She's nineteen, or a trifle over.'

'Well then, she's two years ahead of him, isn't she?'

'About that. But look here, I wouldn't! You must see that. I couldn't! Not with the girl we trot out for Peter.'

'You'd get between the sheets in five years' time with your boy's own wife, if I know you, old man,' Mr Addinsell guffawed. 'Yet why d'you suppose Diana asks this nameless young lady along? Tell me.'

'I've told you already. To bring the lad company.'

'Not on your life Arthur. The purpose is to keep you gay.'

Mr Middleton gave a snort. 'But not for me to be gay in bed with, you can count on that.'

'Perhaps you may be right there,' Charles Addinsell admitted. 'Still, I've never known such a trifle hold a good man down before, not yet at all events.'

'The girl never would.'

'How can you tell, Arthur, if you haven't tried? There's all sorts of things come into bed, where they're concerned, at their age. Curiosity for one. Impatience. Anything. And then, they imagine men as old as we are won't be a bother afterwards.'

'I suppose I do seem like a grandparent in her eyes.'

'So what? When you were nineteen didn't you consider your aunts' lady friends?'

'No, honest to God, I don't think I did.'

'Then you were the only one, is all I can say.'

'Now Charles, what would you do if you were in my shoes?'

'Run like a hare.'

'There you go again,' Mr Middleton laughed. 'Can't you ever be serious?'

'I'd have to meet the sweet little thing first, Arthur.'

'God forbid, where you're concerned, old man. And yet, in the end, you'd simply make yourself scarce if you were me, is that it?'

'You alarm me Arthur, that's all. You're losing sleep over this, you say?'

'I am a bit.'

'And you, so serious as you've always been about your damned work. No, you just listen. Run like a hare.'

'I might, at that,' Mr Middleton said. 'But, somehow, I don't think I can.'

Her day's work done, Annabel Paynton had a drink in the pub outside the office with her confidante, Miss Claire Belaine.

'Oh Claire,' she said. 'Can you imagine, but it's happened again!'

'Another?'

'Yes. Don't laugh. He's married and middle-aged.'

'Well, that does make for a bit of variety!'

'There! You are laughing. I knew you might,' Miss Paynton rather breathlessly exclaimed although her companion, who was short and fat and ever wore an expression of comfortable wisdom, did not even smile. 'All right, then, just wait till this happens to you, Claire. Everyone has their turn.'

'I will. What's his name?'

'I don't think it would be fair to tell.'

'Have I met him?' Miss Belaine demanded.

'Shouldn't think so,' Miss Paynton said, after which there was a pause.

'So you say he's married?'

'Of course.'

'So are you in love with the man?'

'But Claire how can one tell, and when I've not described a thing about him yet?'

'I'm sorry. Go on, darling.'

'It's simply I'm very much afraid the whole old rigmarole is about to start all over, once more.'

'Like Terence, or like Campbell you mean?'

'No. This one's so much older, you see.'

'Well, in that case, avoid getting tangled with the wife then, Ann.'

'But sometimes I'm terribly sorry for him, darling.'

'Why? Does he complain?'

'Never! Arthur's not that sort at all.'

'Arthur?'

'There I go! My dear darling, you're to forget I ever once let the name slip. In any case you can't know, can you? I mean there are so many middle-aged Arthurs. But should one stop oneself being sorry for people? I don't see how one could, do you? Seriously, are we to go round, for ever, just being careful against our truly better feelings, or judgements?'

'Well then, exactly what d'you expect to get out of this?' Miss Belaine asked judicially.

'How should I know? Ought we to reckon on a profit?'

'You might lose.'

'But, Claire, I don't think so; only why not, if it comes to that? Because these endless Campbells and Terences just don't exist yet, they haven't even any feelings still, they're damp. All they do is to use you with their parents. One's an excuse to borrow the car.'

'Won't this Arthur make use of you, whoever he is?'

'I expect he will,' Miss Paynton laughed. 'But Claire, look, at our age we must be fairly expendable.'

'Why?'

'Simply because we have our own lives to make and you just can't prepare for that dressed in white muslin, a dummy in the shop window, the wonder bride-to-be.'

'How serious are you, Ann? You wouldn't invite me to meet him?'

'The only thing is, we can't see each other except where he has to pay.'

'Hotels?'

'Restaurants,' Miss Paynton replied with a kind of satisfied calm. 'And that's one thing in his favour. One does get the most delicious food. Not like sitting over a tired sandwich with poor Campbell, to listen to a cheap band, thanks very much.'

'Well, everyone to her own taste, Ann.'

'Then you do think it dreadful in me?'

'All I say again is, what about his wife?'

'Oh I know, I know,' Miss Paynton cried. 'Yet why in the world should a thing go as far as that?'

'Yes, but won't it?'

'I can't help the gentleman falling in love with me, can I?'

'You needn't see him.'

'Even when he doesn't know he is in love with me? Oh, I don't suppose he is. But Claire, he's all right. Takes me out of myself. I've told the poor man all about Terence, even a good deal about Campbell, and he's so truly sweet and understanding. I've actually been sleeping well, once again.'

'There's worse things than lying awake.'

'Oh Claire, darling,' Miss Paynton called out in a bright delighted voice. 'I knew you'd disapprove. You're out to make my poor flesh creep is that it?'

'Well of course, Ann.'

'I suppose we must be the only two close friends in the whole world could sit here, utterly different from one another, and still not agree, yet remain the closest of close to each other.'

'But, my dear, I don't admit we are so very dissimilar,' Miss Belaine objected.

'Why, how d'you mean?'

'Of course you're a hundred times prettier than me, naturally, yet I'd say quite likely we wanted the same things in the end, Ann.'

'Without knowing what those were? Except the obvious ones, I mean?'

'Well, darling, now you are talking in riddles.'

'In what way? I'm being flippant, is that it?'

'Not yet.'

'I'm sorry Claire. You'll have to forgive. The truth is, all this I've been telling you will probably come to nothing, of course, And will end in tears probably, anyway. That's not the point. Oh dear, will you please look at the time. I must fly.'

On which they kissed and left.

Arthur Middleton was giving Miss Paynton dinner in his flat. They were alone except for the cook who served them, and who was to go home as soon as she had washed up.

'Why didn't you say, when you asked me, that Diana and Peter weren't to be here?' Annabel demanded, a trace perhaps of severity in her tone.

'Didn't I?' Mr Middleton queried. 'Possibly I forgot.'

'I wouldn't think one could forget a little thing like that!'

'Really?' he enquired. 'As a matter of fact, Peter gets most awfully hipped in London. After all there's not much for a boy here, is there? So Diana's taking him up for a spot of salmon fishing with her brother in Scotland.'

'Oh dear,' the girl said. 'I could do with a bit of that myself.'

'Yes, he is lucky, isn't he! But I didn't know that you cared about fishing, Ann?'

'I might if I ever had some,' Miss Paynton answered. 'Anything to get away from London, anyway.'

'Why, aren't you happy here?'

'Who is?'

'What's the matter then?' he asked. 'Your young men giving you trouble?'

'Oh I don't allow them to bother me,' Miss Paynton replied with spirit. 'No it's simply that you've been everywhere and I've never got even as far as Scotland, all my young life.'

'Well in that case Ann, you must come up with us some time.'

'Fat chance there is, I'd say.'

'Why on earth not?'

'Peter's a bit young for me, you know,' the girl propounded and gave Middleton a sad-seeming, long, low look.

'All right if you won't come with Peter you shall with us. One day,' he added, virtuously.

'Oh I don't think so, no,' she said and laughed.

'I thought you said you wanted to see Scotland.'

'I did and I still do,' the girl assured him.

'So we'd bore you?' he asked, with obvious petulance.

'Who's fishing for compliments now?' she demanded.

'What on earth do you mean by that, Ann?'

'You know perfectly well,' she said. 'There's no one in the whole wide world I'd rather go with than you,' she averred, 'and darling Diana,' she added, with a limpid look.

'Well then?'

'But you can't just cart me around as an extra daughter, can you?' Miss Paynton objected.

'It wouldn't be that sort of thing at all,' he said.

'What else could it be then, Arthur?'

'What could it be?' he echoed. 'D'you know what you're saying? As a matter of fact ... Oh Lord ... No, you're out to make difficulties, aren't you? If we wanted to take you along, we would because, because we wished.'

'So I expect! But Arthur, how might it look?'

'Well there, I'm afraid, I can't follow,' he said, with a hard note in his voice.

'Oh won't you understand there's nothing I'd like better, nothing,' the girl insisted in a sort of wail. Upon which the cook came in with two grilled cutlets.

'No you simply shouldn't!' Miss Payton protested. 'Not your whole meat ration. Really it's too sweet!'

'Well they don't bother with regulations, up where Diana and Peter are going, so I thought we might just as well eat theirs this evening. Isn't that so, Mrs Everett?'

'Got to take what you can get these days,' the cook replied and left.

'You are luxurious,' the young lady said softly, to the closed door. 'Mummy has to cook for all of us now their wages have gone up so terribly. It's awful not having even one servant sleeping on the premises. Mummy lives in terror of burglars when the house is left empty.'

'We're in the same boat,' Mr Middleton explained with what seemed to be elaborate unconcern. 'When Mrs Everett packs up and goes home each evening, we're completely on our own. We've only dailies, too.'

'But why didn't you say when you asked me?'

'Tell you what Ann?'

'That this was going to be like a Victorian melodrama. Me, all alone, with you, here!'

'Don't be so absurd, darling,' he protested in a hard sort of voice. 'You can't suppose, if you started screaming now, that someone like Mrs Everett would rush in to help.'

'What?' Miss Paynton wailed.

'Nonsense, Ann. Of course she would. And I told Diana I'd asked you. In fact Diana ordered the meal herself.'

'Oh I was just only thinking of Mummy,' the girl said in a petulant, dissatisfied tone of voice.

'Then if Paula's got any complaints she can take them to Mrs Middleton,' the man said dryly.

'Now you are really going all Victorian,' Miss Paynton cried, and laughed in almost a wanton fashion.

'How so?' he demanded.

'Why, when you talk of darling Diana with that absurdly formal voice.'

'I like to show respect where respect is due,' the husband objected.

'I know,' Miss Paynton said, with a sad smile.

'What do you know?'

'If I told, Arthur, you'd only say I was trying flattery.'

'I can't find out, my dear, until you consent to put whatever it is, into words.' In his turn he smiled gloomily at the girl.

'It's so difficult to express,' she at once informed the man. 'Something people my age simply don't seem to have for one another. Respect' she ended.

'The only way to gain that, is to live with another person long enough.'

'What an extraordinary idea, darling,' and she gave a disagreeable sort of laugh.

'Why?' he demanded.

'D'you honestly mean you would have to live with me for years before you could ever bring yourself to respect me.'

'Oh I wasn't being personal, Ann.'

'I might have known you wouldn't be, where I was concerned,' she said in a most petulant voice.

'Here,' he protested. 'Steady on! How could I have given you that idea?'

'I know what you meant,' she insisted.

'If I've been very tiresome, well then I apologize,' Mr Middleton announced with a small smile.

'Oh you haven't! It's all in me . . . in me,' she wailed at once.

'I always seem to produce this effect,' he went on, still smiling as if to apologize.

'Oh, do you?' she asked. 'That makes everything much better.' She smiled mischievously at him now. 'Then it isn't just only me! Tell about the others you have here,' she continued. 'How do they put up with it?'

'Don't be absurd, Ann,' he protested. 'How often, after all, does Diana go away?'

'How should I know?' she countered. 'But do you have to get a girl alone then, do you, to have that effect on her?'

'It wouldn't be very amusing for Diana if I entertained girls here with her.'

'So you don't have "girls" as you call them to dinner every night,' she said, it seemed almost in triumph.

'Of course not, Ann.'

'Then what did you mean when you said you always had that certain effect on the poor dears?'

'I suppose it was just a figure of speech,' he said.

'I bet,' she crowed. Her face was now alight with what was obviously amusement. 'Because it's only right that I should be very interested in marriage,' she went on. 'Tell me, what does happen?'

'In marriage? Pretty well everything you can imagine.'

'No, now don't be disgusting,' she demanded with a straight face. 'I'm not like you, I really intend all I say. What I want to know is, can you take out the people you want, separately I mean.'

'Diana and I never felt we should sit down and mope when chance left either of us on our own.'

'So you're just not sitting down and moping now?'

'Exactly.'

She laughed a gay laugh, and looked at him.

'And you?' he smiled back.

'Oh me?' She replied, instantly serious. 'Why, you're simply saving my life!'

'Now Annabel!' he protested. 'What is this?'

'But it's true,' she insisted. 'You can't imagine what things can be like when one goes out with Campbell!'

'Who can't?' Mr Middleton demanded. 'I can.'

'So you're just going to be nasty,' she pouted. 'No, he talks of himself, nearly all the time. And he's so depressed, poor sweet! It's not that I don't love him, I do, I dote on him, but he's a rainmaker, stay with Campbell a couple of hours and heavy clouds at once begin to gather.'

'That doesn't sound very gay.'

'My dear, it isn't,' she said, rather glum.

'Well, shall we have our ice now?' he asked, and rang. 'I'm afraid there's nothing more. Hasn't been much for you, has there, worse luck.'

'Oh Mrs Everett,' Miss Paynton cried, as this lady immediately came in 'I've had such a delicious dinner. And now an ice! No, it's too much!'

'Not enough to keep my old parrot pecking,' the cook dryly replied, without a glance, and left again.

Arthur Middleton went to the door.

'Mrs Everett,' he called 'we'll have our coffee in the sitting room.' Then he shut the door and sat down.

'I can't imagine why Diana ordered ices,' he complained. 'She knows very well my teeth are too shaky to eat them.'

'You ought to go to a dentist then.'

'That's just it, Annabel. You were asking a moment ago about marriage. Well, it consists in one's having teeth too uncertain for certain foods and no attention paid at all, none in the least! In fact one seems to get those dishes all the more often.'

'Poor you.'

'I say, Ann, that's a very attractive dress you've got on this evening!'

'D'you really think so?'

'I do.'

'You don't think it's too low?' she asked in a matter of fact voice.

'Why not at all,' he protested. 'Besides, it lets one see your shoulders.'

'All the same I daren't hardly laugh in it,' she said and giggled.

'Go on, try,' he encouraged, with a sort of fixed grin.

'Now that's not nice,' she reproved Mr Middleton.

'You have the most lovely shoulders, Ann.'

'I do! You promise?'

'Yes.'

'Oh how nice! And what very good ices your Mrs Everett makes.'

'They come from round the corner.'

'They can't!'

'You can buy eatable ices anywhere over the way, but one doesn't come across someone like you in a month of Sundays.'

'I don't think that's very flattering,' she objected in a bored voice.

'Well then, now you've finished, shall we go and have coffee Ann?'

'Yes, let's,' she said, rising to lead a way into the next room.

Here they found a deep sofa drawn up to face the fire.

'Arthur,' she almost accused him 'you've been pulling the furniture about. I don't remember this, here, before.'

'I felt it was rather cold tonight. So I moved everything out from that bookcase because I thought we'd be more cosy.'

'I see,' she said and sat down on it.

'What d'you have, white or black?'

'Oh black please. Don't you remember?'

The tray with their coffee things stood on rather a high trolley. When he had served Miss Paynton and sat down at her side, the pot stood almost at the level of his eyes.

'I've never been out to dinner alone with you before,' he excused himself. 'I know you take white at lunch, of course.' He gulped his down at one go.

The young lady sipped hers. 'You give one such a lot to drink,' she announced.

'Nonsense' he said and then they both fell silent.

But when she had drained her cup, she reached up to put this away on the trolley and as she leant back once more it was to find that he had put an arm along the back of the sofa and that she was, so to speak, sitting against it. His hand closed on the bare shoulder. Without looking at him she reached her far hand over and put it over his. Then, when she felt him pulling at her she said 'Arthur,' expressionlessly, and half turned her head away.

He was seated beside the girl but rather too far off. Also this trolley, between the two of them and that fire, was hard by his knees. It seemed he could not move over easily. So he went on pulling, and, as she tilted towards him, he put his far hand round her chin to turn this in his direction. She quietly rubbed this chin against his palm. Then she gently subsided on the man's shoulder.

They kissed.

'Darling,' he murmured. 'So beautiful. Delicious.'

'Oh Arthur,' she said in just that expiring sigh she used to bring telephone conversations to an end.

They kissed again.

Then, probably because he was uncomfortable, for by the looks of it he had too far to reach to get at her, he dropped the far hand under her legs to lift these over his knees. He drew them unresisting to him, but must have forgotten the trolley. For the slow sweep he was imposing on her legs engaged her feet with that trolley and the coffee pot came over on to both.

'My dress!' she exclaimed in a loud, despairing voice.

'Damn,' he said.

The girl at once jumped to her feet. The trolley almost went into the fire and that coffee pot rolled off their laps on to the floor.

'Hot boiling water,' she cried out.

'Oh God, and to think Mrs Everett's gone home,' he yelled.

They started together, fast, for the passage. Once outside, he shouted 'in here' throwing open his and Diana's bedroom. There was a bathroom opened out of this, but, because the space was small, a basin with hot and cold water had been fitted by Diana's bed. It was to this that Miss Paynton ran. Turning the hot tap on, she zipped off her skirt, and stood with her fat legs starting out of lace knickers.

'Here, let me,' he said, and knelt at her side.

She picked the handkerchief out of his breast pocket, drenched it in that basin, and then, putting her hand inside the skirt she had discarded, she began to rub at the stain.

And it was at this moment Diana entered.

220

She stood at the door with a completely expressionless face.

'Arthur,' she said 'when you've done, could you come outside a minute.'

After one scared glance, Annabel went on rubbing.

Mr Middleton left the bedroom immediately, closing the door behind him.

'What on earth do you think you are doing?' she demanded of her husband in a low voice, then went on. 'It's about Peter,' and she seemed to choke. 'A taxi smash. He's in hospital, Arthur! On the way to that beastly train!'

'Hospital? Taxi smash? Why didn't you tell me?'

'We never caught it, you see. Oh, he's all right. But, poor sweet, he was unconscious. I thought why bother you when the doctors said he was in no danger – before the X-ray. Though if I'd known how you were behaving – I must say!' All this Diana said in a level, hurried voice. Then she slowed down. 'Now they've seen the prints, nothing's cracked and he's conscious again. Oh my dear!'

'Peter?' he stammered. 'On the way to the station? But why didn't you tell me?'

'Would it have made any difference?' she replied. 'Though he has an awful head, now,' she added with a smile. 'The poor darling!'

'Well what are we waiting for?' he demanded. 'Let's get to him!'

'And how about that little bitch in there?' Mrs Middleton asked, in the same level tones.

'She's just getting a coffee stain from off her dress,' her husband told her.

'Quite so, Arthur, but I saw your hand.'

'Damn my hand. Now about Peter . . .'

'I saw your hand,' she repeated in an awful voice.

'What about my hand, don't be so childish . . .?'

'We won't discuss this any more, if you please,' she calmly interrupted him.

'I wasn't doing nothing,' he protested.

'Never mind about that now.' His wife raised her voice. 'Are you going to stand here all night with your son in hospital?' Then she added, most severely 'I saw you.'

'Oh God!' he cried.

He opened that bedroom door a crack so he could not see the girl inside, and announced 'Oh Annabel, Peter's been in an accident but he's quite all right, and we're off to the hospital.' To this he got no reply. He shut the door. 'Come on!' his wife insisted with great impatience, and they hastened off together.

Mr Middleton, next morning, did no business at all before he had persuaded his friend Addinsell to throw over a previous engagement to lunch.

'I'm in trouble, Charles,' he said.

'How's that?'

'Well Diana was taking Peter in a taxi to catch the train for Scotland when they had a smash and Peter was knocked out. The boy's all right now, though, no bones broken, or even a fractured skull, as we feared at first.'

'I say, I am sorry. What a rotten thing to happen!'

'Yes, and that's not the whole of it, as a matter of fact. To tell the honest truth, I'm in a spot of bother with Diana, Charles.'

'How so?'

'Well, of course, all my silly fault,' Mr Middleton explained. 'I'd asked this Paynton girl alone to dinner.' At this point Mr Addinsell laughed. 'Don't do that,' Arthur Middleton exclaimed. 'I told Diana; in fact she ordered the meal. But what happened was a stupid accident.' Here he paused.

'Your wife came back to find you tucked up in bed together,' the other man suggested.

'For God's sake don't be so foul,' Mr Middleton appealed. 'There was nothing of that sort. No, we had a slight accident. Ann spilled some coffee over her dress. God, I don't like to think of it, even now!'

Again he paused.

'And so what?' Addinsell demanded.

'And so Charles, Diana came in while Ann was dealing with this stain I told you about.'

'Well come on, Arthur.'

'As a matter of fact, Ann had whipped her skirt off,' Arthur Middleton explained in a peculiarly shamefaced way.

'You old devil!' his companion commented.

'Oh there was nothing of that sort,' the husband protested. 'Well, to be truthful, I won't pretend there mightn't have been, but only, so to say, thirty minutes later. If you know what I mean. No, all this was

222

as innocent as the day, at the time I'm talking of. Then here's Diana all at once in the room when she should by rights have been steaming past Rugby at sixty miles an hour and so upset about Peter, as was only natural . . .'

'Did she herself get hurt, at all?'

'In the smash? No, thank heavens. But she decidedly cut up rough over Ann's skirt being off.'

'Not to be wondered at, Arthur, really.'

'No, I know, and in her own bedroom, too. Yet Charles, I've never been a jealous husband. Even my worst enemy would grant me that.'

'So if you came back unexpectedly,' Mr Addinsell opposed 'you'd ignore her dinner guest who'd happened to find himself without his trousers.'

'Well I don't know about overlooking it, but surely to goodness I wouldn't make the scene Diana made!'

'You forget she was naturally upset about Peter.'

'That's what I told her this morning, Charles, when we went into the whole thing again.'

'And what did she say?'

'She wouldn't bite.'

'Great mistake to hold inquests, Arthur. Greatest mistake there is, in life.'

'You wait until you're married again! You'll find you have no choice.'

'All right, all right.' Mr Addinsell admitted. 'Well, what do you want me to do?'

'You see, I've a dinner to the general managers Tuesday,' Mr Middleton said, almost in the voice of conspirator. 'And I was wondering if, for old sake's sake, for my sake, you'd ask Diana out to dinner that evening. With any luck she won't discuss it. But if she does, just remind her, will you, old man, there's never been anyone else in my whole life, really! You know that! You know me almost as well as I do . . .'

'OK' Mr Addinsell said, 'I'll try. Though it's a bit of a tall order!'

Later that same afternoon, when he got back to the office, he was just in time to take a call from Miss Paynton.

'Oh Arthur,' she sighed, in her signing-off voice.

'Peter's absolutely all right,' he said quickly. 'Of course he's got a stupendous headache, but there's nothing broken, and they're even getting him up tomorrow.'

'Splendid,' she said with a doleful tone.

'Yes, isn't it,' he hesitantly agreed.

'And darling Diana?' she breathed.

'There's been a spot of bother, there,' he admitted. 'In fact I'm in bad odour for the moment. But it was mainly the shock. She was in the taxi too, you know. She escaped by bracing herself back on the seat.'

'It's too awful,' Miss Paynton exclaimed, with a firmer voice. 'One never knows where one's safe these days.'

'Yes,' he admitted.

'And is she still very cross with you?' she enquired.

'Yes,' he said. 'And with you a bit, too, as a matter of fact.'

'Me?' she fluted. 'But why ever over me?'

'Well, of course, she'd just been in rather a nasty smash,' Arthur Middleton explained. 'Poor darling. And she was worried stiff about Peter.'

He paused.

'Arthur!' Miss Paynton said. 'D'you think I could see you for say five minutes, after work. I'm fussed.'

He did not answer at once. 'Well' he at last replied. 'I'm not sure that would be an altogether good notion, Ann. Just at the moment,' he added.

'I see,' she said.

A click then told him she had rung off.

Mrs Middleton was having her third conversation with her husband on the subject of Annabel Paynton. The attitude she adopted appeared to be one of pained surprise, of grieving bewilderment.

'No, Arthur, I shall never understand,' she said. 'Just when Peter was lain like dead in the ambulance and there was I imagining him gone.'

'You're not to give this another thought,' he murmured in a reassuring voice.

'But I can't help myself, Arthur!'

'Now, my dear, you'll make yourself ill if you go on visualizing Peter unconscious.'

'I'm not,' she objected, as if to a child. 'Arthur, I saw your hand!'

'My darling, we've been into this so often,' he implored. 'To my last breath I'll always maintain I'd done nothing with my hand.'

'I saw.'

'Then, come on now, which hand was it?'

'What difference does that make?'

'Tell me, Diana,' he begged. 'The left or the right?'

'Oh no,' she broke out 'this is too brutal. Why must you torture me so?'

'I didn't bring the subject up, darling.'

'But you see,' she said, her eyes very wide 'I smelled you, Arthur!'

'You smelt me? This is something new! And what d'you mean by that?'

'Why the powder she had on, or the scent she used, Arthur!'

'Now my dear, which? You know you've always prided yourself on your sense of smell. If this is right, what you're saying, you ought to be able to tell one from the other.'

'Don't try and dodge,' she informed him in the same sad voice. 'I did, I tell you.'

'I can't make this out at all. What am I supposed to have done now?'

'You'd put your hand on her leg, Arthur, and I can't, I shan't, ever, get over it.'

'Look darling,' he said, most reasonably. 'Will you believe me when I say I have absolutely no recollection of anything of the kind.'

'Are you trying to tell me, then, that you didn't?'

'Well, really, I'd say I might remember a little thing like that!'

'But Arthur, I smelled you!'

'Oh damn this famous sense of smell of yours,' he exclaimed with warmth.

'I can't help it, can I,' she suggested, in a voice of resignation. 'I was born that way.'

'Look darling,' he said and seemed to whip himself almost into a sense of eagerness 'be reasonable about this, don't let's get carried away. You can't call to mind which hand of mine it was, and you don't know what I'm supposed to have smelt of.'

'Why, of that horrible little Annabel, of course, Arthur!'

'Now darling,' he said again 'let's just face things. Coffee does get spilt you know.'

'Yes, but how? You've never even once told me.'

'Oh, in the way coffee always does get spilt.'

'There must have been something happened to make it, Arthur.'

'Well, you see, darling, I'd drawn the sofa out across the fire . . .'

'Yes, and what for, thank you?'

'I simply thought we'd be more cosy; then . . .'

'You're never to turn the furniture round again,' she raised her voice at last. 'It's my house—'

'I live here too,' he broke in.

'I'm in all the time,' she expostulated.

'So I only wish you could have been present, Di, and seen with your own eyes how truly innocent the whole thing was.'

'D'you suppose I wanted to be at that awful hospital?' she demanded in a calmer voice.

'Good heavens no, darling! No, in getting my coffee I stupidly, clumsy fool that I am, just jogged her elbow.'

'Well then?'

'Well then, I don't suppose she has much of a dress allowance, if there is still such a thing these days, and she called out, "hot boiling water" was the phrase she used, and of course I lost my head and rushed her into our bedroom, meaning to get her in the bath.'

Mrs Middleton at this moment let out a laugh in which there was very little fun.

'Well, as a matter of fact, she may have been first, before me,' Mr Middleton corrected himself. 'Because once Ann had seen the basin she wouldn't go any further, she peeled off her skirt at once.'

'But, Arthur, what could have made you kneel?'

'My dear, can't you see? I was in an agony of embarrassment.'

'Not at her fat legs, I don't suppose?'

'Now look here, my dear, there's no need to be insulting, is there? How d'you suppose it would look, to Paula, if at my age I bought her girl a new dress.'

'There are such things as cleaners and I've got no clothes,' his wife told him in an expressionless voice.

'Then I give up,' he said wearily. 'All I did was for the best, darling. I seem to have made a complete ass of myself and there it is.'

'She did of you, you mean,' Mrs Middleton corrected him. 'Well darling,' she added with a tired smile 'don't bother your old head too much. You see, I love you. There . . .'

He came over. They kissed as though they had been parted a long time.

226

'I do love you,' she repeated. 'And I've been upset. But don't let me ever catch you, even once, again . . .'

'Now darling!' he protested.

'All right, we won't talk of it just now,' she ended. She then told him Addinsell had asked her out to dinner. When he expressed a sort of resigned pleasure, they animatedly discussed Peter's splendid progress out of his concussion.

'What's the matter with Arthur these days?' Mr Addinsell asked Diana as he drove her away for the dinner they were to have together. 'Lately he's seemed a different fellow.'

Mrs Middleton laughed selfconsciously. 'I'm afraid I may have been a bit difficult the last few days.'

'In what way, may one ask?'

'Well, there was that terrible accident Peter and I were involved in. You see, Peter has been kept in hospital with a bit of concussion, but we are getting him back tomorrow, so things are looking up again.'

'Yes, I was sorry to hear. Is Peter going to be all right?'

'Oh absolutely! The doctors are delighted. But of course, as you can imagine, Charles, I didn't know, not at first. In fact, I nearly worried myself out of my poor mind.'

Mr Addinsell had to draw up rather suddenly at some traffic lights. She put her hands against the dashboard.

'Oh, do be careful,' she cried, then seemed to recover herself. 'I'm terribly sorry. But I've been nervous ever since we were in that awful smash.'

'Only natural!' he said.

'Yes I'm afraid I've made myself such a bore to Arthur the last day or two,' she went on in a nervous voice. 'Of course he can be maddening sometimes, who isn't, ever, in married life? And I only say this to you because you are Arthur's oldest friend.'

'Go on,' he said when she paused.

'Well, maddening is not quite the word I should have used, perhaps. But, Charles, although it's natural, after so many years of being married, it is sad, isn't it, when the man begins to look elsewhere?'

'Old Arthur? My dear, I can assure you . . .'

'No Charles,' she said 'I've had proof. And I never intended to say a word of all this. So dull for you!'

'Why!' he exclaimed, and drove with great caution. 'You two are my greatest friends. Nothing dull where you're both concerned.'

'You are sweet, Charles. Still, this is not a topic to go out to dinner on, is it? Let's talk about you, for a change. Why did you never marry again?'

Mr Addinsell accelerated past a taxi.

'I honestly don't know,' he replied. 'Never found anyone who would have me, I suppose.'

'Now that's just not true. It can't be! But there are times I lie awake, Charles, and wonder, and think how terribly wise you've been.'

'Me?' he asked, with what seemed to be genuine amazement. 'My dear I seem to have done nothing but lose money all my life.'

'No, don't joke about this,' she reproved him. 'Just think of it all. There are the children. Sometimes I thank Providence we've only one. They get ill, they nearly die and you're almost out of your mind, Peter has this terrible affair, and, the whole while, your husband is getting tired of you.'

'Now Diana . . .'

'I know,' she interrupted 'but that's only natural, isn't it? This is the way things are, Charles!'

'I'm sure Arthur—'

'And we can't change them,' she insisted. 'There are moments I feel it would be almost presumptuous to try. One has to learn one can't go against the laws of nature, and that can be a very painful experience, as I've just discovered, to my cost.'

'My dear,' he asked 'what is this?'

'He's found another girl,' she told him in a very small voice.

'But that's preposterous,' Mr Addinsell began, when she cut in with,

'Oh damn, I think I'm going to cry.'

Upon which he drew in to the side of the road, put his arm round her shoulder. While she turned her face away, he demanded,

'Now Diana what is all this?'

She held her breath while two tears came down each side of her nose. She did not answer.

'There are days I wonder,' he said in low tones 'if we aren't, every one of us, at our lowest, this time of the year.' He looked to his front, the windscreen wiper clicked and hissed to and fro. 'Wet streets, rainclouds down to the tops of the houses, this awful damp, and if you get a cold you can't seem to throw it off – there's nothing worse than our English winter,' he concluded.

She blew her nose, seemed to get herself under control. Then he put his far hand over, under her chin, turned this towards him and gently kissed her wet mouth. She as quietly responded.

'I'm sorry I'm such a fool,' she said.

'You weren't,' he replied. 'Now we'd better get under way, again, before a policeman catches up.'

'Drive slowly, won't you,' she begged. 'While I repair the damage.' She got out her bag.

'Of course, and don't talk of what's bothering you, unless you want.'

She spoke in a smothered sort of voice from under her powder puff.

'I swore I wouldn't, but now I can't seem to help myself,' she said.

'Then come out with it,' he encouraged.

'Only that I came home and found him in bed with that horrible little Annabel Paynton,' she lied.

'It's not possible, my dear!' Mr Addinsell protested, in a shocked voice.

'Oh yes, and stark naked, of course. Oh whatever am I to say to Paula, if she should get to learn?'

'I can't believe it,' Arthur's best friend said. 'The silly juggins!'

'And I, who'd come back to tell him his own son was unconscious in hospital!'

'Didn't they say anything?'

'What was there to tell me?'

'No, quite. But he made out to me she'd spilt some coffee on her dress.'

'So he's spoken to you?' she said, still working on her face. 'Oh I expect they began like that, but it's how this thing ended,' she lied and did not look at Addinsell. 'You won't mention this to a soul, of course?'

'Me?' he asked. 'Rather cut my tongue off first!'

'So now I've told you,' she exclaimed. She put away her bag again. 'You're a great comfort, Charles,' she said and put her hand rather heavily on his arm. The car swerved. 'Oh,' she cried. 'Oh Charles, I'm sorry,' she added 'all my own hysterical, silly fault!'

'That's all right,' he reassured her. 'No harm done at all.'

'Ah, but there might have been,' she responded. 'That's the way tragedies happen.'

'So how did all this end between you and Arthur?'

'Does anything ever end?' she objected. 'I called him out, of course. I had to tell him about Peter. Then I went back to the hospital and didn't show a thing to the boy, I can at least say that for myself.'

'Good for you Diana!'

'Now we must be somewhere near the restaurant you are taking me to and I absolutely refuse to talk about myself any more, or to allow you to.'

And she kept him to this. Once or twice in the evening she made him swear again he would not tell a soul, but, beyond that, she would not let him refer to what she said she had seen.

When he drove her back home she permitted him to stop the car a little distance from her door and kiss her quite hard. She cried a bit again, then, but said no more before she left him.

The next day, when Peter was discharged from hospital, his parents received the young man almost as though he were back from the dead.

'Well, my dear boy,' the father cried aloud 'this really is something!' and shook him by the hand.

'But how are you, darling?' Diana insisted.

'Bloody awful,' the boy said.

'Sit down at once. Now tell me, quite calmly, are you still in pain?'

'God yes,' the young man answered. 'And the nights are agony.'

'Really Arthur!' the wife, his mother, broke out in ringing tones 'have they any right to let patients out in his condition?'

'I suppose they need the beds,' Mr Middleton remarked in what was, probably, too casual a tone.

'Then they are murderers,' she said with firmness. 'Arthur, should he go to a nursing home, d'you think?'

'Now, hang on a minute,' the boy protested. 'It's death in those places, they nearly kill you. You can't want to send me in again?'

'But you don't seem well at all, to me, darling.'

'Oh I suppose I've what they call recovered,' her son admitted with obvious reluctance. 'But, d'you know, three people died in my ward, while I was there?'

'Don't, darling,' said his mother.

'I really think you might have put me in a private room.'

'Where was the money to come from?' his father asked.

'There you go again, Arthur,' Mrs Middleton complained. 'When Peter's all we have!' Then, in a sinister voice, she added 'Now!'

'Thirty guineas a week?' the husband queried.

'Three days,' she answered. 'And how much in that time do you spend on gin?'

'Oh come, Diana darling, you like your glass as well.'

'I need it,' she replied, emphatically.

'Yes, at least three people died,' Peter interjected.

'No, don't,' was Mrs Middleton's earnest plea.

'What time of the day or night?' his father wanted to be told.

'Usually it seemed about four or five in the morning.'

'But weren't you asleep then?'

'God, you don't sleep in those places.'

'Curious,' Mr Middleton remarked 'it always seems that resistance is lowest at that hour of the night.'

'And this time of year,' his wife murmured.

'You wouldn't joke about it if you'd just seen three people die before your very eyes!'

'I wasn't joking, Peter,' Mr Middleton explained.

'What I can't make out,' the boy went on 'is why, at my age, you send me to a place like that.'

'Because I thought you'd been killed,' his mother told him in a great voice. 'I had to get you somewhere at once,' she added.

'Well, it was absolute hell,' the boy said.

'But are you all right now?' Mr Middleton demanded.

'Yes, fairly.'

'Does it hurt you still?'

'Of course.'

'Then are you enough all right to go up with your mother to Uncle Dick's?'

'Oh I'd still like to get in some fishing.'

'It's so dull for him in the holidays, this time of the year, Arthur.'

'Don't I know,' the man exclaimed, almost with vexation. 'But it would be unfair on your brother to send the boy up to him if he was going to be ill, even if you were there to nurse him.'

'But, darling Peter, you'd get along all right without me?'

'Aren't you going now, then?' her husband demanded.

'Well naturally I'll travel if Peter needs me,' the mother promised. 'Surely, darling, you'll get along all right, alone with Uncle Dick?'

'Why, don't you want to come up with me?'

'You see, my dear, I've had really rather a shock!'

'You were hurt in the smash?' her son asked her, with what seemed to be distaste.

'Well, perhaps,' she said, looking hard at the husband.

'And are you all right now?' the boy enquired.

'Yes and no,' she answered.

After which it was agreed they should get their doctor's opinion on Peter's travelling. When this turned out to be favourable he journeyed up alone next day.

On the Monday Mr Middleton rang Ann Paynton. She blandly agreed to meet him that morning, at the usual time and place, for lunch.

She was first, and, when she shook him by the hand, 'I thought I was never going to see you again,' she said.

'Oh now, hardly as bad as that,' he answered.

She laughed. 'I don't know, Arthur. At the time I thought things were pretty fierce.'

He simpered. 'Nice of you to make a joke, Ann.'

'Though it wasn't very funny, then, after all,' she countered, in what appeared to be disgust.

'Perfectly appalling for both of us,' he agreed.

'Oh, Arthur, I do so want to apologize,' she nervously said. 'I can't think what came over me to take off my skirt, except of course, panic.'

'And if I hadn't been such a damn fool to spill coffee all over you, as though I, at my age, didn't know how to kiss a girl, then none of this would have happened!'

'Don't let's talk of that,' she implored, examining her shoes. 'But I have so few clothes. My one idea was to get the stain out. Honest!'

'Yes Ann, I know,' Mr Middleton earnestly agreed.

'So there was trouble?'

'Yes.'

'Bad trouble, Arthur?'

'Pretty bad.'

'Oh dear. I think perhaps you'd better give me a drink.'

They went to the bar. After a moment or two she giggled.

'What's that for?' he asked.

'Your face,' she replied.

'What's wrong with it?' He twisted until he could see himself in a mirror.

'Not now,' she giggled. 'Then.'

Mr Middleton looked ruefully at himself. 'When I was down on my knees?' he queried, watching his own reflection.

'Oh yes,' she said, in plain delight.

He turned back to the girl.

'Diana's been giving me some of that,' he told her.

'Oh you poor dear,' Miss Paynton cried and patted his knee as he sat beside her, up at the bar. 'What do I want to bring that up for, just when you have at last asked me out again? So Peter's all right?'

'Yes, thank God.'

'And they're both off to Scotland?'

'No. Diana wouldn't go.'

'Is it serious then, Arthur? About Diana I mean?'

'I don't know,' he said. 'I can't make out.'

'Why, whatever's happened?'

'Well, we've been married eighteen years, Ann, and I've never known anything like this, ever.'

'Like what?'

'It's hard to describe. You see, I love my wife,' he announced in a low voice, with unction. 'We've always trusted one another. Now, all on one side, that seems to have evaporated, and in a night!'

The young lady said nothing. She watched him.

'I don't know whether it wouldn't be a good idea if you went to her and explained, Ann.' He did not look at Miss Paynton as he suggested this.

'I'd not be too keen,' she replied, still closely watching the man.

'D'you think?' he murmured.

'Mightn't work out at all,' she said.

'Oh well, if you feel that way, Ann.'

'D'you mind?'

'No, it was just a thought. But I don't fancy the idea of Diana going to Paula.'

'To Mummy?' the girl cried. 'Oh things are really serious, then!'

she wailed. 'Why she couldn't! That would be really the end!'

'I mean if you could somehow apologize?'

'But what for?' Miss Paynton demanded with spirit. 'For being kissed by a person who then went and upset all the coffee over my dress? Oh Lord, now I shall really have to tell Mummy.'

'Now for heaven's sake, Ann, don't you go to Paula with this!'

She bit her pretty lip.

'I must get in first,' she explained.

'But listen, you can . . .'

'Has Diana actually said she was going?' the daughter interrupted. 'Not yet.'

'Oh, it's a disaster,' Miss Paynton exclaimed, with extreme symptoms of disquiet, although she kept her voice down, and only an acute observer of this scene could have noticed the untoward. 'Then my whole reputation's at stake?'

'But this was all an accident, Ann.'

'Fat lot of difference that will make when Mummy hears,' the girl said, with what might be described as indignation.

'But has she actually said she was to go to Mummy?'

'No.'

'At the same time you think she will?'

'Not really.'

'Now look, Arthur. This could be vital to me. Is she, or isn't she? If you've been married for eighteen years you ought to know! Will she go or not?'

'Probably not.'

'That's no great comfort,' the young lady objected.

'I'm sorry I started this,' Mr Middleton proclaimed. 'Diana never said she had that in mind, even. I expect I have too vivid an imagination. I just wondered if it mightn't be a good idea if you dropped in to see Di.'

'Has the same sort of happening happened before?'

'Ann, what is this?'

'Has she been to anyone else's mother?'

'No, of course not.'

'Then I'll tell you what. I won't go to Mummy if you swear, swear mind, you'll let me know in good time beforehand if she actually threatens to.'

'But of course, Ann. What d'you take me for?'

'I'm sorry. I got upset.'

'It's I who ought to apologize,' he said with an air of considerable relief. 'When all's said and done, I started this.'

'Then what made you imagine Diana was going to?'

'She's been in such a curious way lately,' he replied.

'How?'

'Well, by not travelling with Peter to Scotland, for one.'

'I expect she may wish to keep an eye on you, Arthur, just over the next week or two.'

'I'm not sure of that,' he said. 'And there's this whole business of Charles Addinsell.'

'I don't know about him, do I?'

'Old friend of ours, Ann. But, dammit, she's been out with Charles three times in five whole days.'

'You mean he's a flame?'

'Of course not, Ann. Don't be ridiculous, if you'll excuse the expression. As a matter of fact he's a very old friend of mine and I asked him myself, when this happened, to take her out.'

'Well then! Everything's perfect, isn't it?'

'That's exactly what I don't know.'

'Arthur!' she demanded. 'Are you, yourself, jealous now?'

'I don't know,' he dully repeated.

'You are!' she insisted.

'And if I am, why shouldn't I be?' he asked, with some signs of irritation.

'Yet she hasn't been caught with her skirt off too, has she?'

'Really, Ann,' he protested. 'You go too far!'

'I'm sorry, truly I am,' she replied with a show of great conviction. 'But what makes you think, then, the way you do?'

'Well, you know, three times in five days! When they'd hardly before been out together more than once a week! What d'you suppose they're saying all those hours?'

'I've simply no idea,' she answered, with a straight face.

Then their barman asked if they had any further orders and they realized that lunch must be almost over. Hurrying into the restaurant, they ate in haste and did not again refer to Mrs Middleton. In fact they cheered up, teased each other, and became quite gay on lager beer.

The next evening Mr Addinsell was driving Diana Middleton home after he had given her dinner.

'Come up to my rooms and have one for the road,' he suggested in a casual sort of voice. 'Before I drop you back.'

'Oh I've had so much to drink already, Charles,' she said and giggled.

'Nonsense, Di. Do you good. Only just round this corner here.'

'Well then, if it's only the one,' she agreed. She yawned. 'You're such a help to me,' she added.

'Got to get out of oneself, every once and again,' he said. 'And you know, you're a very, very attractive woman.'

'Now Charles,' she reproved with a kind of lazy indulgence. 'If we have any more of that, I'll take a taxi off the nearest rank. Besides, you don't begin to mean it.'

'Have things your own way. Here we are,' he announced, drawing up.

Upstairs, as he poured gin into her glass, she called out, 'Stop! That's quite enough. D'you want to make me drunk?'

They sat side by side on a sofa. He took her hand. After squeezing his once, she removed hers.

'Let's be serious a moment,' she suggested. 'I've been awfully good this whole evening, haven't I? Never even mentioned Arthur and my wretched affairs a single time. But just tell me this one thing. D'you think I should tell Paula?'

'Paula Paynton? What for?'

'Well, to warn her!'

'Would that help?'

'But Charles, in fairness to herself she ought to know her daughter's going to bed with men old enough to be the little creature's father.'

'If you do that,' he objected 'you'll have Prior Paynton round to horsewhip Arthur.'

She gave a delighted laugh.

'Oh I don't think so, Charles! Prior's not that sort of man at all.'

He took a gulp at his gin.

'Can't be too careful. Could make quite a lot of talk,' he said.

'Yes, I expect there might be a bit of a sensation. I see what you mean,' she conceded.

'I'm thinking of you,' he told Diana Middleton, and put his nearest arm around her shoulders. She laid the glass down.

'Oh Charles!' she said, in a grateful voice.

They kissed for quite a time. Then she drew away, and he allowed this.

'I simply must come up for air,' she announced. 'Oh Lord, how can I look?'

'Lovely as always,' he answered, drawing her into another kiss.

This time she withdrew after only a moment.

'You do more than something to me, Charles,' she said, in what seemed to be wonder.

He put his mouth close to her ear.

'Let's go upstairs,' he suggested, in a flat voice.

'But, my dear,' she objected 'you're all on the one floor in this place!'

'Next door,' he levelly corrected.

She pecked a kiss at him.

'No, Charles. Two wrongs don't make a right, do they?'

Mr Addinsell relaxed his hold.

'Bother Arthur!' he complained.

'Oh don't I know, darling! Oh Charles, you are sweet, but can't you see it wouldn't be right?'

'This is just the two of us,' he argued.

She briefly kissed the man once more.

'I'll say so,' she conceded. 'And then, no, Charles! You are one of the few people in the world I'd do it with, and yet I can't! You see that, don't you?'

'Suppose I must.'

'And you won't be terribly cross?'

'Whatever you say, Di.'

'Not exasperated, or anything?'

'No.'

'Then, Charles, kiss me once again, because I have to go.'

They kissed.

'I'll run you back,' he announced as, without lingering, he rose from the sofa.

'Even after I've behaved like this? Now you are truly being noble,' she said, on which they left.

Nothing else of consequence passed that night between them.

The next afternoon Miss Paynton met her confidante in the pub, after work. They drank light ale.

'The plot thickens,' Annabel announced.

'I thought it might.'

'I was caught by his wife with my skirt off whilst he knelt at my feet.' This account was met in silence. Miss Paynton then let out a sort of scared giggle.

'Well, go on, Ann. There must be more.'

'Oh he ran! She'd come back unexpectedly to fetch him. When she burst in on us she called him out and they both went off without another word to me.'

'And have you seen the chap since?'

'Of course.'

'Ann, you are a perfect idiot! What were the repercussions?'

'Fairly severe, I fancy,' Miss Paynton replied in a satisfied kind of voice.

'Look out that nothing boomerangs back on your head, then.'

'But how d'you mean? I couldn't help his spilling coffee over my dress, could I?'

'Well, anyone could dodge being caught.'

'What can you mean, Claire?'

'Why actually take the skirt off, Ann, in where you were?'

'Because it was fairly on the way to being ruined. His maid was gone. We were alone. There wasn't even a kettle on. What else could I do?'

'Not be found there with him,' Miss Belaine proposed.

'If you think I went to his flat for a purpose, then you're very much mistaken, Claire.'

'Well, for the matter of that, why did you go?'

'You say I oughn't so much as go out to lunch in public with Arthur? Because one thing leads to another? Is that it?'

'You're being promiscuous, Ann.'

'I'm not!' Miss Paynton protested in ringing, confident tones. 'I only know Campbell and a schoolboy, and how am I to meet any-one if I don't show myself.'

'Yet just because you do go out to restaurants with Mr Middleton for lunch, here you are having to come back to his flat alone after dinner.'

'I'd only been the once.'

'Yet you'll find yourself there again, if he asks you?'

'I don't think he will, not now,' Miss Paynton said. She giggled.

'And what does go on when you're with him?'

'We talk,' the girl said, it seemed with satisfaction. 'Mostly about his boy, Peter. You see I'm so much nearer to Peter in age than his father is. And he simply dotes on him. Of course he kisses me every now and again.'

'Does he?'

'All right, when you go out, doesn't your Percival kiss you?'

'I suppose so. Then he isn't married!'

'But this is just like a Victorian melodrama, once more.' Miss Paynton exclaimed. 'What's a kiss between friends, good heavens?'

'And supposing his wife tells your mother?'

'She couldn't!'

'She might.'

'Why? What for?'

' "Hell hath no fury like a woman scorned",' Miss Belaine quoted.

'But she hasn't even been scorned, Claire.'

'Why not?'

'He dotes on her! I must have told you. He honestly does.'

'Well, he may. But being the person he obviously is, Ann, don't you think she may end up scorned?'

'Of course, it depends on what you mean by that extraordinary word. Still, I'm almost sure not.'

'If he asked you, would you marry him?'

'He's married, isn't he?'

'Suppose he said he'd get a divorce?'

'Oh, now then,' Miss Paynton protested quite quietly 'there's been nothing like that, you know!'

'I see,' her companion said, following which they talked clothes, then went their separate ways, seemingly well satisfied with one another.

After Mr Middleton had come home, the day's work done, his wife waited till he'd had his tea and read the papers, she delayed until he'd taken his bath, and even so she did not speak before their dinner was over. Just as he was about to make himself scarce in the study with what he had brought back in his briefcase, however, Diana stopped her husband.

'Darling,' she said 'I know the other night I almost promised I would never mention this whole business again, but something else has happened now.'

'Yes?' he answered in a resigned tone of voice, sitting down once more.

'Paula Paynton's been to me, exactly as I told you she probably might.'

'If I remember, Diana, it was you proposed to call on Annabel's mother.'

'I may have said so, dear. But if I did, the other was what I really expected.'

'And I suppose she didn't just drop in to discuss this awful weather we've been having.'

'She may have mentioned the rain, now I come to think, Arthur.'

'Then out with it, Di. I've more than enough work to get through this evening. And don't torture me,' he pleaded. 'You know I'm on tenterhooks over the whole of the wretched misunderstanding.'

'Oh you needn't be alarmed,' she told her husband. 'You can be sure I saw Paula off, quite politely too, of course.'

'Then what in the name of God, Di . . .?'

'Now, now,' she interrupted. 'All in my own good time.'

'I won't listen to any more of this nonsense,' Mr Middleton announced, almost with passion. 'Nor have I the leisure, even if you think you have.'

'Very well,' Diana told him, giving nothing away in the tone of voice she used, 'Paula only came to ask weren't you seeing rather much of her precious little girl.'

'But just because there has been a stupid accident, am I then to see no more of the child?'

'Oh you told me you've been having her out to lunch, darling. I admit that.'

'Really, I must say very heavy weather is being made over some spilt coffee.' Mr Middleton appeared to sulk. His wife closed her eyes and sighed.

'There was no mention of the skirt,' she said at last.

'Who's been talking?' Arthur began again.

'You don't suppose I was so foolish as to ask Paula' Mrs Middleton replied. 'No, naturally enough, when one goes out, one's seen.'

'Doing what, good heavens?'

'Oh, Arthur, don't tell me there's been something else?'

He put his face in his hands.

'I shall go out of my mind,' he said in a frantic voice. Mrs Middleton watched her husband with a quiet, appraising look.

'Don't worry,' she told him. 'I know my Paula. I've dealt with her, at least for the time being.'

'So what's the position now?' Arthur demanded, rather more calmly.

'I suppose it all depends, quite a lot, on how much you intend to go on seeing the girl,' his wife replied.

'Now look here, Di,' he said. 'You know how hard I work. I don't visit the club at night. I don't fish, I don't shoot. My one relaxation is to take a friend to lunch. And I always secretly wanted a daughter. Oh I'm not blaming you! Everyone realizes what you went through having Peter. But what's wrong with my taking Ann out to a public place occasionally? It's all above board, surely? There's nothing clandestine about that, is there?'

'Well, I imagine Paula might prefer you to be more secret, anyway she said so.'

'No, Di, this is a wild paradox you're putting forward.'

'Well think, dear, and now go back to your briefcase. Try and see if you can do with perhaps a little bit less of Ann.' She got up. She kissed him on the forehead. 'There,' she said. 'But you do understand I had to warn, don't you?'

Mr Middleton asked the Paynton girl out to lunch at the usual time and place. He waited until they were seated at their table before he started.

'Your mother's been to see Di,' he said.

'Oh?'

'About my taking you out to lunch like this.'

'But how terribly disloyal of Mummy,' Annabel wailed. 'All I can say is, I hope you never treat Peter like that.'

'In what way?'

'Because she's never said a word to me on the subject.'

'Could it have made any difference if she had, Ann?'

'Of course not. But she would only have been polite if she did, don't you see?'

'A bit,' he seemed to admit, with a measure of diffidence. 'And do you think her going to Di has altered the situation?'

'What situation?' the young lady enquired, open-eyed. 'There isn't one, is there?'

'I mean about your coming out to lunch occasionally,' Mr Middleton explained.

'What does your wife say?'

'That we ought to be more secret.'

'Here's a fine thing,' Miss Paynton protested. 'I shan't come at all if you even start to talk like this.'

'Honestly, she did.'

'Then I don't want to hear. I shall have to forget all of it, and I'm afraid I shan't find that easy.'

'I'm very sorry, Ann.'

'So you should be, for sure.'

'What else can I do but apologize?'

'Just never mention it again.'

'All right. But Ann, who's been talking, then?'

'How could I know?'

'D'you tell your mother when you come out with me?'

'I do not,' she said. 'Certain things have to be observed in family life,' she announced, as though lecturing. 'And if a girl's to say to her parents where she is every moment of the day, then there's absolutely no end to things.'

'How did your mother find out then?'

'Perhaps Diana told her.'

'No,' Mr Middleton objected, in steadfast tones. 'Di and I don't fib to one another.'

'Well, I haven't said a word to a soul, no one,' the girl maintained. 'I can't understand it.'

'And Arthur, have you spoken about us?'

'I have, yes, once,' he admitted, obviously reluctant. 'To a man.'

'Who?'

'Oh, a very old friend,' he said, airily. 'Charles Addinsell . . .'

'The one who's taking Diana out five times in eight days?'

'Yes,' he admitted, in a low voice.

'But how could you?'

'It was before he'd asked Diana out so often, you see.'

'And what about my reputation?' she demanded.

'Now Annabel,' he said. 'We haven't done a thing, have we?'

'I'd like to get hold of that Mr Addinsell and tear his odious, prying eyes out, that's all.'

'Because there's no harm in us, is there?' he went on.

'I'd thank you to know what you mean, Arthur.'

'Well Charles talks, then Diana says this and that to me, she goes on about your reputation just as you do – good heavens, to listen to 'em, we might spend all of every weekend in bed together.'

'I must confess I don't think Diana's one to speak,' the girl commented, thin lipped.

'How's that?'

'When she obviously does, with this Mr Addinsell.'

'Now look here, Ann, you go too far!'

'All right, but have you asked her?'

'Of course not!'

'Don't you discuss things with your wife?'

'Not those,' he answered, beginning to seem shame-faced.

'I don't know about marriage,' she protested. 'Not yet! Still I can't think what could be better to talk about?'

'You will,' he replied, almost with a smile, and appeared to regain his composure.

'But it's so important, Arthur.'

'What is?'

'Sex. D'you honestly mean to tell me you don't know who your wife goes to bed with?'

'Listen, Ann,' the man said in a tired voice. 'You've got the whole of this wrong. All I maintain is, that one must be wicked to become jealous. D'you agree?'

'No.'

'Very well, but I say it is so. We're all entitled to our opinions. And if, as I say, I'm wrong to be jealous, then I'd better not know whether I've grounds for jealousy. Do you see my position now?'

'I just can't understand why a man, like you describe you are, ever marries.'

'But, Ann, the ideas one marries with, soon merge into the ideas one remains married on.'

'I wouldn't know,' she said.

'Perhaps not, but possibly you can imagine that.'

'Well, I'm not sure, Arthur. And still, if a day or two ago you'd told me this Mr Addinsell would have been the one to tell darling Diana, and we can't know how much he's simply invented yet, then, with all your experience, I'd've said you were crazy.'

'So would I,' he admitted.

'Then it must be frightful to be married!'

'At times, possibly. Although things can be almost as bad when you're single, you must admit.'

'So what ought one to do, Arthur?'

'Go on seeing each other.'

'No, about marriage I mean, stupid!'

'Nothing, darling. Drift.'

They both laughed. She told some funny stories about Campbell, after which both went back to work.

That night Mr Middleton failed to go off to his own room after dinner, as he usually did, but stayed by his wife, fidgeting with a newspaper on her sofa.

'What's this?' she asked. 'Darling, have you stopped being married to your briefcase?'

'I can't make you out at all these days, my dear,' the man complained.

'How's that?' she peaceably enquired.

'Di, I want us to have a little talk,' he said.

'Well, all right.'

'You're sure you won't mind, darling?'

'Why should I?' she asked. 'I never interfere with your work, you know, and, if you wish to discuss anything, then here I am, as always.'

'Yes,' the husband assured her, in almost a reverential tone of voice. 'But sometimes I wonder if it mustn't be most infernally dull for you.'

'Oh well, what's best for Peter's sake suits me,' she said. 'I mean, your working so hard is to educate the boy, then give him a start in life. I keep the house going, there's a home for him when he's back in the holidays. That's all!' There was something defensive in her tone.

'But the way I'm wondering tonight is, do you have enough in your life, Di? What I've on my mind – well look, we're not getting any younger, are we? I've such an awful lot to plough through every evening, that's my job, yet how about you? Can't be very gay for you, when I am at last back from the office?'

'Oh well, my dear, I suppose by now I've got used to it.'

There was a pause. And then, quite suddenly, he spoke in what seemed to be acute annoyance.

'Yes, certainly,' he said. 'And all the same there's no call, is there, to go out five times with Charles Addinsell in eight days?'

'But, Arthur, I haven't,' she protested with spirit.

He ticked the occasions off on his fingers, aloud.

'I'm rather sorry I told you, now, about when I did meet him,' she answered. 'Yet that's what we arranged, that we should tell each other, and we've kept it up for eighteen whole years,' she said. 'Still I don't agree going out to tea can be meeting someone, not in the sense we've continually used.'

'Now, Di, you're deliberately trying to aggravate me.'

'I'm not, darling. You know what we've always agreed. That we should each of us go whenever the other was invited.'

'But I haven't been asked out! Not once, when you were with Charles.'

'Please not to trip me up when I express myself,' she said in a calm, collected voice. 'Of course I meant, we ages ago settled that if one was asked without the other, then whoever was invited, accepted and went.'

'But five times in eight days?' He sounded almost tearful.

'I haven't Arthur,' she reasoned. 'We never did count teas.'

'What have I done?' he demanded.

'Only you know, my dear,' she said.

'And what may that mean?'

'Just all it says,' she answered.

'But darling, this is wrong, somehow. You're different suddenly. It's fantastic! What have you got against me all of a sudden?'

'Well, my dear,' she explained, as though to a child 'I didn't particularly want to say this, or perhaps not so soon, but Peter's growing up now, and we don't wish him to come back home to find what I did the other night, do we?'

'Diana, leaving everything else out for the moment, Peter's away at school when he is there, isn't he?'

'He won't always be,' she replied. 'When he's finished with his studies he'll live with us in the flat, until he finds a nice girl, settles down, and marries.'

'Still, in fairness to me, whatever I may be supposed to have done, this is the holidays, now. He's away in Scotland or isn't he?'

'I know very well Peter's up fishing, Arthur. My very loneliness tells me that. All I'm trying is to keep a home together, for him to come back to.'

'Well you won't do that if you're never in, yourself.'

'Giving you your little opportunities, you mean?' she asked.

'Diana, you'll have me lose my temper in a minute.'

'I'm sorry, darling, truly I am! But I didn't start this, did I?'

'Oh, everything is always my fault?'

'Now why do you say that?' she indignantly demanded. 'So what have I done?'

'Only practically left home,' he replied.

'I like that!' she complained. 'Aren't I sitting in front of the fire here, now then?'

'You know how I mean.'

'But I don't!' she protested. 'You say I'm different, yet it's you who always are. And I can't imagine what I've done to deserve it!' There was a trace of tears in her tone.

'Oh forget everything,' he said in a careless sort of voice. 'I suppose I'm just upset.'

'Now look, Arthur,' she suggested. 'If you feel like you say you do why not have a word with Charles?'

'To tell the man he's seeing too much of my wife?'

'And what's wrong with that?' she demanded. 'You're the husband, aren't you?'

'But he'd laugh me out of the club!'

'I don't understand, dear. Not one little bit! You say you're upset over my going to see Charles occasionally, and yet you don't care to discuss it with him?'

'I've already told you, Diana, haven't I? What more should I try and do?'

'But there's our old arrangement,' she most reasonably argued. 'We've always said, in fact you've just admitted, that whichever of us was asked could go without the other. So he invites me, and I accept!'

'Meaning you won't refuse unless I stop taking Ann out to an occasional lunch?'

'Well, what's wrong with that, Arthur?'

'It's inconceivable, that's all! Just goes to show the whole old mutual trust and confidence in our marriage has gone, the very thing I always thought and said was rather fine in us!'

'I'm not so sure about trust and confidence,' she objected. 'You don't seem at ease about what you appear to think Charles and I are doing.'

'Well, now then, how are you behaving?'

'I don't know what you're attempting to impute, Arthur, but I don't like any of this, I may tell you!'

'Any more than you cared for what you dreamed up about Ann and me?'

'Which is entirely different,' she quickly put in, with warmth. 'You forget, my dear. I saw you! And with my own eyes.'

'I don't know how else you could have seen?'

'Now, Arthur, enough, you're beginning to upset me! Oh why do you have to be so? Just when Peter had the ghastly accident and I come back and find you like I did!'

'Then you do admit all you're doing with Charles is so much retaliation?'

'I admit nothing of the kind,' she replied with spirit. 'He happens to be a very old, dear friend.'

'And yet I introduced you originally?'

'Oh Arthur, you can be so aggravating. What difference does that make?'

'I should have thought a lot.'

'Then go round and see him.'

'We've been into that already,' he wearily protested. 'I can't. You'd have me a laughing stock!'

'I don't suppose any more than you've already made yourself with this Ann Paynton.'

'What d'you maintain we ought to do, then? Separate?'

'Arthur!!' she screamed. 'Arthur! You're never to say that again, d'you hear, even as a silly joke!'

'Very well,' he said in a level voice. 'I apologize.'

'Oh damn,' she remarked. 'I think I'm going to cry.' Which she proceeded to do.

'Now darling,' he said in the same voice. He came over. He began to rub a hand up and down her spine.

Through her tears she spluttered, 'Why are you so horrid to me?'

'I'm sorry. There,' he said, still rubbing.

She began to recover. 'Forgive me. I never meant to' she announced and blew her nose.

He kissed the nape of her neck, tenderly.

She fumbled in the bag she had on her knee for a lipstick and came on Peter's latest letter.

'Oh I never showed you this, did I?' she asked in a voice already almost unmarked by tears. 'It came by the second post. He's caught a fish.'

'Not a salmon?' her husband fiercely demanded.

'Why, I'm not sure, what else? I mean that's what Dick has up there, isn't it?'

'A fifteen pounder' Mr Middleton quoted. 'Why it's terrific! And only seventeen! This is wonderful news.'

'Darling Peter,' the mother said. 'I always knew he would make a fisherman.'

'His first salmon!' the father echoed.

'Darling,' she next said to her husband. 'You don't have to work tonight, do you? Let's go up now.'

'Go up?' Mr Middleton laughed. 'We're all on one floor here, you know.'

She turned. She kissed him on the lips and took her time.

'Silly,' she said, smiling. 'Well, all right then! Next door.'

After two nights and a day, Arthur Middleton got his friend Addinsell on the telephone and persuaded him to lunch at their club.

'I'm in trouble, Charles,' he began, over a martini.

'Again?' Addinsell seemed rather guarded in his manner.

'Nothing's ever the same,' his host groaned.

'Then have you been to bed with that girl, whatever her name is?'

'God, no. Who d'you take me for?'

'Why don't you? And get it over?'

'But I don't suppose she would, Charles. Look, old man, all this is beginning to get so serious it even affects my work.'

'Things are bad, then! Always said you worked too hard, Arthur.'

'What would you suggest? The bills have to be paid, don't they?'

'Relax.'

'And how can I? See here, your wife died early, very tragic thing and all that – oh I know it was hell for you at the time – but, my God, after eighteen years of married life, you don't know how they can become!'

'I might be able to guess.'

'Yes, Charles, but you can't tell until you're actually married to them for long,' Mr Middleton said in a dry voice.

'Very possibly,' the man agreed. 'And so what's biting you at the moment?'

'Has Diana said anything?'

'Not a word.'

'Well I asked you to take her out . . .'

'Which I have done,' Mr Addinsell interrupted.

'Oh, I know, and thanks very much. But she hasn't said a word?'

'She wouldn't, Diana couldn't,' his guest lied in a flat voice. 'Her loyalty's like an oyster, and you'd cut yourself if you tried to open it with an opener.'

'Yet there are men who deal with dozens a minute out of a barrel.'

'Oh,' Mr Addinsell objected 'then, I imagine, they've all got their cards, are members of the Union. Any pearls they may find have to go to the credit of the Benefit Fund.'

Arthur Middleton laughed, almost harshly. 'Then Di's said nothing about Ann?'

'Never once referred to the girl.'

'She has to me, Charles!'

'Only to be expected, after all.'

'Yes, I suppose so,' the husband admitted. 'Yet, when you come to consider, just a coffee stain!'

'Difficult to see into a woman's mind, Arthur.'

'It isn't for me, not where Ann is concerned with Di. Di tells me.'

'Only natural after all.'

'You think so? Even when there's nothing to it?'

'Isn't there?'

'Well, not so far. I mean, there's been nothing yet.'

'Couldn't there be?'

'Not on her side. Honestly, Charles, you're becoming too much of an old cynic. The child's sweet!'

'Careful how you go, Arthur.'

'What's your point now?'

'The sweeter they seem, the harder we fall.'

'Well yes,' Mr Middleton admitted, weakly.

'Now look around this room,' Charles Addinsell appealed. The tall windows, leaning against rain, seemed to filter light back to dark bookcases from floor to ceiling to make a number of men, older than themselves, seated in deep, black armchairs with two waiters in attendance, appear as wraiths, thin before illness, and bloodless as cardboard. 'Look at them. D'you suppose there isn't one not ready to think, or talk, of sex.'

'By God, you alarm me!' Mr Middleton said lightly. 'Well, all right,' he went on 'I admit I dream of going to bed with her all the time, morning, noon and night. So what?'

'Go on and do it. Get her off the system.'

'But this might not be right for the child?'

'Let the girl decide that.'

'And have Prior round one morning with his horsewhip?'

Mr Addinsell laughed. 'She won't tell,' he reassured. 'They never do, they're always too ashamed.'

'But I don't want her ashamed, Charles. That's just it, you see.'

'You may not, but whether you like or not, one day she will be. And surely it's better for her that that shouldn't happen in wedlock?'

'Wedlock? Where did you get the frightful phrase?'

'In marriage then, which I always thought you took seriously.'

'My God, I do,' Mr Middleton admitted. 'So much so, I've begun to think I ought to see less of Ann.'

'How much d'you meet now?'

'Less, probably, than you imagine,' the husband said with a dry voice.

'Which means?'

'Oh, about once a week.'

'Only that!' Mr Addinsell cried, with the first sign he had shown of animation.

'Yes, I'd imagine it could sound seldom to you,' Mr Middleton said, with some unction.

'Well, you can't see the girl much less, then.'

'I'm beginning to feel I should cut down.'

'But there's competition, must be.'

'Don't!' Mr Middleton implored. He seemed genuinely upset. 'I can't bear to think, please! I thought perhaps I might begin to forget her slowly, damn the child.'

'I'm afraid you've got it rather badly.'

'That's what my wife seems to suggest, as a matter of fact,' Arthur admitted.

'And how d'you propose to go about this?'

'Precisely why I asked you out, Charles. You could do a damn good job of work for me here.'

'Look, Arthur, you know from experience you can always count on me,' the man said, without a smile.

'I thought I could ask her to a restaurant for a drink, and plead a very important lunch appointment. Then I'd look round and I'd see you having your drink near by. I would introduce you. And you could take her in for a meal. As a very old friend of Diana's you might tell her Di's been blowing off. Of course I would arrange with the headwaiter to settle it, if you signed the bill.'

'Now Arthur. None of that! Although I can't ever forget what you did for me over that business with Penelope.'

'No, I insist, Charles.'

'We'll see,' his guest said. 'But Di's told me nothing, as I informed you.'

'She has to me.'

'And what am I to say to this Paynton girl?'

'You see, Charles, I can't speak to her, because nothing's happened yet! It would be presumption on my part. We just talk about the wind and the weather, now. I can't go to her and say my wife objects. She'd think I was insane.'

'And I expect she'll slap my face!'

'She won't. But don't make her cry! Promise.'

'Still don't know what I'm to say to her, old man.'

'Tell Ann I have to meet her less, until this blows over. Make out you're an old friend of Di's, in whom she's confided. Why, old boy, to someone like you, it will be simple as falling off a log. It's just I can't discuss things with Ann because nothing's happened. After all, remember what you had me say to Penelope!'

Mr Addinsell left it that he could, and again, that he might not.

On their usual day, and the accustomed time and place, Arthur Middleton and Miss Paynton forgathered at the bar. It was cold and wet outside, but he seemed hot, almost bothered.

'I say, Ann,' he said. 'A frightful thing has cropped up. There's been a call from the Ministry and I've got to go today to lunch with the Permanent Secretary.'

'Then where am I supposed to eat?' she cried.

'You know how things are,' he apologized. He looked sharply

round the room, could see no sign of Charles Addinsell. 'Who can tell, we may run into someone,' he added.

'Palm me off?' she wailed.

'Now you must forgive this. Of course I mean nothing of the kind, Ann. It's simply that I can't ignore this summons I've had, although I'm aware beforehand it will be a complete waste of time. Look, I could see the headwaiter and have him send your bill along.'

'Oh Arthur,' the girl broke out 'I feel so awful, I really do! I can't imagine why I started to grumble. Somehow I felt as if I would never see you anymore!'

'Now, Ann, what is this? Aren't you well?'

'I'm quite all right, thank you,' she said, rather severely. 'Then when d'you have to go? At once?'

'How is the time?' he asked, glaring at the electric clock. After which he searched through that bar once more, from his stool. 'Good Lord,' he announced, so it seemed in great surprise 'see who's here, old Charles! D'you know Charles Addinsell?' he asked the girl.

'The same one?'

'Yes.'

'Of course I don't. Except what you've told me, Arthur.'

'Then let's give him a drink.'

After cordial introduction, plus some fervent small talk, Mr Middleton excused himself, without further explanation, and made off.

'Have another?' Charles Addinsell suggested.

'Oh, but I ought to go.'

'Well then, one for the road.'

'You are so kind. Might I really?'

'Good. Waiter, two more medium sherries. Waiter! Waiter!! Good God, am I to have to shout? That's better. Yes, two medium sherries.' He turned back to the girl. 'Terrible job to get attention these days.'

'Are you telling me,' she agreed.

'Though, looking at you, I can see you don't suffer,' he said.

'Oh, can't I!' she bridled, seemingly delighted. 'Yet suppose I went up with you to a glove counter staffed by the usual girls, I'd let you do the asking.'

He laughed. 'You might be right at that,' he said.

She frowned, stayed silent.

'Often come here?' he tried again.

'I always lunch out,' she said, very grandly.

'Well, good luck,' he proposed, raising the full glass.

'Thank you,' she answered over hers.

'Known old Arthur long?'

'Ages!' she said. 'I was practically brought up with the son Peter, who's much younger than me, of course.'

'At St Olaf's, isn't it, where I was with Arthur?'

'Then you have known him a long time!'

'Doesn't seem like that.'

'Really?' she asked in a cool, grand tone.

'So you've known Diana, too, for quite a bit?'

'Darling Di,' Miss Paynton assented.

'Wonderful woman,' Charles mused aloud, in a reflective sort of voice.

'Then you've been friends with her for a whole long while, as well?'

'The usual thing,' the man told Ann. 'Arthur was just about my best friend, and I was in love with Di before he married her.'

'But how extraordinary!' Miss Paynton exclaimed, in a warmer manner than she had yet assumed.

'So so,' Addinsell grunted.

She smiled with obvious malice at his eyes.

'You still don't sound very pleased!'

He studied the girl coldly.

'I suppose that's a thing could happen to any one of us' he replied.

'I'm sorry,' she said, almost humane. 'I didn't mean to seem as if . . .'

'Don't worry,' he interrupted, giving Ann his first smile. This always seemed to make an impression of extraordinary charm and frankness, because it broke up his somewhat severe, handsome middle-aged features.

'One never sees anyone one knows, any more, in these places,' he tried once again.

'Well, to be absolutely truthful,' she admitted in a gayer voice 'I've not met many. I simply haven't had time yet.'

'Yes, pretty few dances these days.'

'It's quite a problem for a girl, oh yes.'

'Yet I suppose Prior and Paula still have young people in?'

'Of course you know Mummy and Dads! But who can afford much of that nowadays?'

'Your parents can't be as expensive as you make out, surely?'

She gaily giggled.

'You are awful!' Miss Paynton protested. 'Don't dare to pretend my remark meant anything of the sort!'

He smiled. 'Sorry, and all,' he said.

'And so you should be,' she commented, indulgently forgiving.

'Have one more?'

'What about you?' she temporized.

'I'm going to.'

'Well perhaps. Then I'll simply have to fly.'

They were silent while he ordered, and obtained, the drinks.

'But you can't tell me that a man like you, with all your friends, ever has a casual, empty moment?' she proposed, in what appeared to be genuine friendliness.

'Oh, don't I,' he objected. 'What with the last show and all, many of 'em are dead by now.'

'Yes, with two wars and everything in between, your generation's had quite a pasting.'

'Not quite so old as that, just yet,' he told her, with a smile. 'Arthur and I were still at school in the first do.'

'Oh, what can you think?' she cried. 'How ridiculous!' She blushed.

'Not at all. Most natural; forget it. Look, what about a spot of lunch. Do one very well at this place.'

'Oh, I often come here,' she boasted. 'But after what I said? I mean I don't deserve . . .' she went on in a more natural way than previously. 'And I did ought to be getting along. As a matter of fact we've rather a marvellous arrangement at our office about the lunch hour.' Talking hard now, she proceeded to tell Addinsell a good deal on the subject of her work. In the end they walked through to the restaurant without another mention of their lunch.

'What would you like to have?' he enquired.

'Oh no, I couldn't.'

'Not even lion's drink?'

'No, no, I'd be drunk!'

'It's water.'

'Oh you are silly,' she giggled. 'I never heard that one before. Yes, I think I'd better.'

'All right far as I'm concerned.'

'No, water really, please!'

'Suit yourself,' he agreed, then proceeded to order an expensive meal.

'Saw old Diana the other day,' he began once more, but this time without looking at the girl.

'You did?'

'Yes,' he agreed, eyes averted.

'Well what's strange about that?' she demanded, in rather a nervous voice.

'Seemed a bit upset,' Mr Addinsell pronounced, gravely regarding the young lady for once.

'But how extraordinary,' Miss Paynton exclaimed. 'She's never said anything to me.'

'Hasn't she?'

'What d'you mean?' Ann almost quavered, then seemed to recover. 'Oh well she wouldn't, you understand. Not a woman who is, after all, of another generation. Look,' she broke out. 'Over there. No, there! Isn't that the film star, Jack Cole?'

'I wouldn't know. Don't go to 'em.'

'Oh Mr Addinsell, what you miss,' she almost cooed, and yet seemed alerted, defensive.

'Now, why don't you just call me Charles?'

'May I?'

'And can I reciprocate with Ann?'

'Of course.' She spoke with complete unconcern. 'Everyone uses Christian names nowadays, at least in my generation. It just doesn't mean a thing,' she threw in. 'D'you know, I think he is Jack Cole!'

'Who's he appeared with?'

'Oh Jack Cole's simply too terrific for words. He's slaying!'

'How d'you find Arthur's been these last few days, Ann?'

'Why just splendid, Mr Addinsell.'

'Charles.'

'Charles!'

'Thought he could have been a bit upset, I think myself.'

'Oh, poor Arthur! And, now, is that Cicely Amor, can it be, he's talking to?'

'The blonde?' Charles demanded, with animation. He looked round at once. He saw this actor, whom he knew by sight, was talking to the cigarette girl, a negress.

Miss Paynton began to giggle, eyes brimming.

'By Jove,' he said, and laughed.

The young lady giggled still more.

'Aren't I a silly juggins?' he exclaimed, apparently delighted. 'Well, we won't talk about them any more, shall we?'

'What d'you mean?' she asked, serious again at once.

'That, dammit, that this fish is really rather good, though as host I say as shouldn't.'

After which they got along very well, talking on indifferent subjects.

When she thanked him and was about to leave, Mr Addinsell said, 'Meet again?'

'We'll see,' she replied smiling.

'Ring you up?'

'How will you know my number?'

'I could ask Arthur.'

'No. don't do that,' and she then and there gave it to him. 'Now I must fly. So thanks so much! Goodbye,' she told him in expiring tones, and made off fast.

Her day's work done, Annabel Paynton had a drink in the pub outside the office with her closest confidante, Miss Claire Belaine.

'Well darling!' she said. 'Only imagine, but I rather fancy it's happened all over again!'

'My dear, you're impossible,' the girl replied, with calm.

'Aren't I? But you don't really think I am, do you?'

'Well, first tell me more.'

'As a matter of fact, he's a friend of the other.'

'Of the middle-aged one?'

'That's right.'

'Then are you being handed on, Ann?'

'Nothing like it!' Miss Paynton laughed, with confidence. 'No, Arthur – there I go once more – was called away to a sudden conference at the Ministry, you know how terribly high up he is, and this friend happened to look in at the bar of our restaurant and I was introduced, to this second one I mean, the one I'm telling you about.'

'Married?'

'I've made a few enquiries. No, as a matter of plain fact he's a widower with a child, a boy of eight.'

'And dark and handsome?'

'Oh Claire,' Ann breathed 'you've no conception!'

'Have I met him?'

'I'm almost certain you never have, but of course I can't give you his name, not just yet!'

'If he's unmarried there's no harm, surely?'

'Why, I suppose so. Claire, I hadn't thought! How odd,' she mused aloud. 'But I keep this passion for secrecy. Mummy, I expect.' Then she whispered the name.

'I've never even heard of him,' Claire announced.

'Is there any reason why you should, darling?'

'I don't know, Ann. I didn't mean to sound important. Then how d'you feel about this Arthur, now?'

'I can't be sure,' Miss Paynton replied with caution. 'You see he hardly ever seems to talk about himself, which rather makes me weary, if you know what I mean.' She laughed selfconsciously.

'Oh I like someone who can manage to listen.'

'And so do I, of course. But he doesn't so to speak tell one.'

'Unlike Campbell?'

'Most,' Ann laughed.

'Perhaps it's his age?'

'But he isn't really old, Claire.'

'Possibly not. Still he may find that holds him in.'

Miss Paynton glanced in a wary way at her companion.

'No, as he's talking, he compares everything with about twenty years ago,' she said, rather fast.

'Well, it may be he gave up being alive that long ago.'

'When he married? Shall I find it in all my middle-aged men? How grim!'

'I think they batten on one.'

'Why, you dark horse, how d'you know?'

'Don't your parents batten on you?'

'I seem to see what you mean, Claire dear. Oh, it's not much of a prospect, then, or is it?'

'Which has been my point all along!'

'But one's got to do something,' Miss Paynton protested and laughed. And they went on to discuss underclothes, with spirit.

That night, after Mr Middleton, having dined, had retired to his own room with the briefcase, Diana several times approached the telephone without, however, actually taking the receiver off its cradle.

She also moved around her room, picked up illustrated papers only to put them down again, opened two novels but to throw these away, and at last did something she seldom used to do, bearded her husband in his den before she went to bed.

'I'm so bored, darling,' she said, entering without apology. 'So flat, down!'

'Hullo,' he greeted Diana quite warmly. 'Now what does this mean? Servant troubles getting less?'

'Don't be absurd, my dear,' she answered. 'Why does a wife, who copes, have to listen to such silliness? No, I've nothing to do. I'm bored stiff.'

'Haven't you a book?'

'Arthur, I'm quite constipated with all the novels I read.'

'Then why don't you go out?'

'Who with?'

'Charles Addinsell not rung up of late?' he asked, keeping voice and face straight.

'Don't be ridiculous, darling,' she said, and sat down rather heavily opposite.

'I see,' he answered, with a small show of irritation.

'Well, if you do, I don't,' she objected, in a flat tone. 'Arthur, listen to me! Can we go on like this?'

'Why, what is it now?' he cried irritably. 'What on earth d'you mean?'

'Oh I know I'm being vile,' Diana wailed. 'But can all your terrific work be worth the candle?'

'You don't suppose I like slavery for its own sake, surely to goodness!'

'Sometimes I simply wonder, Arthur.'

'Is that all the thanks one gets?'

'We've our own lives to live after all, still, haven't we?'

'And what about Peter? He has to be paid for, and educated; you know it as well as I do!'

'Occasionally I ask myself if the darling wouldn't be better off in a council school.'

'Diana! Stop! He'd never in after life forgive us if I didn't give him the start I got from my father.'

'And where did that land you?'

'No really, Diana,' her husband protested, but with some signs, at last, of unease 'what are you trying to insinuate? That we've been failures?'

'Not at all,' she protested. 'Just, we might have gone somewhere further, that's all!'

'Where then?'

'Don't ask me. It's for the man to choose his own job.'

'And how much choice is there, nowadays?'

'I couldn't say, of course, Arthur,' she admitted with a certain show of reason. 'Yet, d'you really think we are making the best of our lives?'

'Darling,' he said 'I'm doing all I can!'

'I know,' she agreed. 'But couldn't you do something else?'

'Such as?' he demanded, in a weak voice.

'How can I tell?' she protested once more.

He came over to sit on the arm of her chair.

'Darling, what is this?' he asked gently.

'Oh just nothing. I'm so bored,' she repeated, almost in a whisper.

'Di, you don't really mean all you've just said?'

'Yes, darling, I do, but it doesn't matter, you're to pay no attention.'

'On the contrary,' he protested 'if that is so, then everything matters very much. What concerns me is your happiness, your welfare, my dear.'

'Does it?'

'How d'you feel in yourself?' he elaborated. 'Every day!' he added.

Picking up his hand from off her shoulder, she kissed the wrist.

'Darling darling,' she said.

'Of course that's so,' he consented. 'Have I ever given you cause to fear, or even doubt? You mustn't be down like this. Why not go out? You know I'm stuck here.'

'Who with?'

'Well, after all, as I said before, there's old Charles.'

'He hasn't rung up in a week, Arthur!'

'Then just you ring him!'

'Oh but Arthur, that's to make oneself cheap!'

'You cheap? My dear, you couldn't, not with that man,' he protested.

'Now you shan't grow nasty once more about dear Charles,' she sadly told her husband. 'No' she added 'I must not get on to him. I still have my pride.'

'Then what do you propose, dear?'

'Arthur, couldn't we have an early night tonight? Won't you come along to bed, now? I get so hipped lying there, waiting for you!' She smiled up into his eyes. 'Come on, then,' she said, and squeezed his hand.

He kissed her with what seemed to be restraint.

'Very well, for this once,' he agreed, upon which they went off arm in arm, immediately.

Some five days later the two girls met, by appointment, in their usual pub.

'Then how are you going along, Ann?' Miss Belaine enquired.

'How is who getting on?' she countered.

'I'm sorry,' the confidante apologized. 'What I meant was, have you heard any more of Arthur?'

'He's not quite the point he was, is he, darling?' Miss Paynton replied. 'I believe I told you he has a friend who's newly appeared on the scene.'

'Well anyway, what's your news?'

Ann giggled. 'I've been dropped,' she said. 'Like a hot brick.'

'By both of them?'

'Oh, the other had me to tea at a hotel since I saw you last, and he, at least, does show signs of being able to talk about himself, but of Arthur, not a word!'

'He may have the wind up.'

'Of his wife?'

'No, about himself.'

'I only wish he could,' Annabel Paynton tiredly complained. 'He's nothing but a bore the way he is now, or was, because, of course I haven't seen him.'

'So he's out, where you're concerned?'

'Out? I never said that! All I say is, we should have as many people round us as we can, to pretend to choose from. You always maintain one must keep oneself to oneself and I expect you skip a lot of pain and worry that way. My theory is, I'm expendable, up to a certain point, of course.'

'So you've said before, Ann. But I argue that if you pursue this, you'll make the men you go out with expendable, too.'

'The moment they invite me, they let themselves in for that, don't they?'

'And what do they expect in return?' Miss Belaine enquired, with a small frown.

'Why bed, of course.'

'Do they get it?'

Miss Paynton giggled. 'Strictly confidentially, no,' she said. 'At least, not yet, with me. You know that.'

'Which is where we disagree,' Claire announced, but in rather a doubtful voice. 'With precautions, of course, I don't see what difference it can make.'

'And you who always swore you never did!'

'I don't, Ann.'

'So where are you, if you go out with a married man?'

'I haven't.'

'Then d'you think one ought to pay them for the dinner by going to bed with them, supposing you accepted?'

'Not necessarily, Ann. You're too literal. It might only make them miserable.'

'Well, darling, I don't believe things quite work out like you've just described.'

'I dare say not,' Miss Belaine assented. 'Yet, whichever way one goes about things, one makes the creatures expendable.'

'Which I say we are, too. In any case, they ask for what they get by inviting us out, as I've just told you.'

'For bed?'

'Oh, I expect. No, what I meant is, they make themselves expendable the minute they ask one out.'

'And supposing one falls in love with them?'

'But, Claire, we mustn't run away from life, not at our age! If we've got to fall in love, we just do.'

'D'you think this Arthur's in love with you?'

'Doesn't look like it, does he, and frankly, at the moment, I couldn't care less.'

'Oh well, let me know what happens in three weeks' time, Ann.'

'Three days, you mean! You don't propose to suddenly stop listening, do you?'

They laughed, finished their drinks, and went separate ways.

＊

Miss Paynton had agreed to meet Charles Addinsell for lunch and somehow they, almost at once, got into a discussion. He'd been speaking against wives.

'The whole thing's no good,' he wound up, after being very vague.

'But, Charles, I can't follow at all,' she protested. 'This might become very important for me, some time. Why not?'

'You wait.'

'What on earth for, Charles?'

'Almost impossible to describe.'

'Excuse me if this is personal,' she put forward 'but did your wife leave you, or something?'

'No.'

'Then how?'

'She died.'

'Oh, good heavens, I do apologize. What was her name?'

'Penelope.'

'Now that's an absolutely heavenly name! So well?'

'She just died, Ann.'

'Surely to goodness you can't have it against her, Charles?'

'You've never been left with a child on your hands, have you?'

'Well, no, I suppose not.'

'So there you are.'

'But you mustn't hold it against your wonderful Penelope.'

'Don't know what you mean. No one's fault when they die in bed, is it? Can't see how that could be?'

'Then why not marry a second time?' Ann asked in a bewildered voice. 'Another mother for your child?'

'Might die again,' the man replied, with obvious distaste.

'Oh, no!' she cried.

'Not much use for poor little Joe if she did, after all?'

'I suppose not, Charles. Yet there's no reason she should, is there?'

'Oh none,' he appeared to agree. 'Still, that's all a part of what life has in store for one.'

'Now Charles!' she protested.

'You're young still,' he said, in a menacing sort of fashion.

'But it's so hideous!'

'Yes,' he assented.

'About your wife, I mean. How did she die, if I may ask?'

'In childbirth.'

'Yet that's the finest sort of death for a woman, surely, or so they used to say, didn't they?'

'Don't know.'

'And you just blame her for it? Oh, Charles! Really, then, we can't ever seem to do right in life, can we?'

'Of course I never have blamed,' he said, with obvious petulance. 'Poor darling, she couldn't help going like that,' he explained. 'Not her fault, good God! If anything, might have been mine, or equally the fault of each of us, in actual practice. No, what I have against living, is the dirty tricks fate has in store. No good blinking facts. Do better to realize, they probably will be coming to you. I couldn't stand a second kick in the pants of the kind.'

'But if you've already had one really terrible misfortune, aren't the chances against another, Charles?'

'Same as with roulette,' he answered. 'When you're at the tables, identical numbers will keep cropping up!'

'Oh, surely that's most terribly gloomy.'

'Depends on how you play,' Mr Addinsell replied. 'If you're on a number and there's a run on zero, where are you then?'

'I've never even seen the game.'

'Well you can back any number up to thirty seven, and in combinations, but if the ball falls into a slot on the wheel which is marked nought, everyone loses who hasn't betted on zero.'

'I still can't seem to see why a person should want to put their money on nothing.'

'Because it's precisely what they may get, Ann.'

'Oh, I didn't mean at your silly gambling game. In life, I was talking about.'

'I'm no Omar Khayyam,' Mr Addinsell gravely told this girl. 'But the spin of the wheel is all any one of us can expect.'

'So you say that I, for instance, oughtn't to marry on account of what so tragically happened to you and yours?'

'Of course not!' he protested with warmth. 'Never in the world! Was speaking selfishly.'

'Terribly sad for you, then,' she murmured, eyes downcast.

'One gets used to it,' he said. 'To anything.' Then he added with a sly smile 'Can even have compensations, sometimes.'

'That you do realize, once and for all, things for you can't ever become worse?' she asked, looking at him again.

'It could be better than that,' he dryly answered.

'How then, Charles?'

'Persistent, aren't you!'

'I'm sorry! I realize I become an awful bore, soon as ever I grow interested. I didn't intend to be a nuisance!'

'Hey, what are you saying?' Charles demanded. 'Come off it! If I spoke out of turn, let me apologize.'

'You didn't.'

'Pretty sure I did. Look, I take it all back! I've a mistaken sense of humour.'

'Then you're just laughing at me?'

'Don't follow what you mean, Ann.'

'I can't see your jokes, that's all,' she announced, in a most dignified way.

'My dear, I do apologize, I do really,' he said, in the nearest approach to the abject he could probably manage.

'For what?' she enquired, and seemed mollified.

'For anything and everything,' he handsomely replied. There was a pause.

'So you don't feel you can be happy ever again, is that it?' she asked.

'Hardly.'

'But it's outrageous!' she protested. 'Look at you! With so many years to see forward to, to live a full life in!'

'Maybe you misunderstood,' he said, in a flat voice. 'I told you before there could be consolations, Ann.'

'D'you mean to sit and tell me to my face you're referring to just squalid affairs?' she cried with a great show of indignation. 'You, a man with a boy of eight!'

'Not guilty,' he replied, and seemed quietly amused. 'All I tried to say was, one could still have friends.'

'Oh friends!' she broke out. 'I have tons of those, and yet what earthly use are they to me?'

'The salt of life,' he suggested with a sly smile.

'Are you honestly trying, after all your experiences, to propose that I've nothing more than friendships in the years I still have to live?'

'My point was and is, stay chary of your commitments, Ann.'

'Well, of course. Who isn't?'

'And don't believe it's to be a bed of roses.'

'How could I? What sort of a person d'you suppose I am? Charles, I'm surely still all right in my head!'

'You're always getting away beyond me,' he mildly complained. 'All I meant was, I suppose, just don't expect too much.'

'And mustn't I even hope for the best?' she wailed.

'Can't stop people hoping,' he agreed. 'Don't advise you to, all the same.'

'You are wonderfully cheering, aren't you, Charles?'

'Only speak to the truth as I know it,' he answered with a sort of dignity.

There was another pause.

'I'm sure I don't know where I'm going to be, now, with my life,' Miss Paynton at last complained, in a child's voice.

'Never let anything get you down,' the man advised.

'In which case, you can't remember much of what you felt at my age.'

'Not sure I do, at that.'

'Weren't you ever miserable then, Charles?'

'I expect so. Tolerably.'

'And so what has anyone to live for?'

'Blessed if I know.'

'But supposing you were a girl?' Miss Paynton demanded, with insistence.

'I'm not.'

'Well, I imagine I realized that,' she countered. 'Yet, if you were, would you really warn a woman against looking forward to her own children?'

'They can always die, too.'

'In a bomb explosion, you mean?'

'Not necessarily,' he said.

'Oh but fifty years ago they died like flies, quite naturally!' Ann exploded. 'Doctors have changed all that! I don't suppose any number of bombs nowadays could kill the millions of people that used to go just from disease.'

'People still die, all the same,' Mr Addinsell objected.

'Then am I not to love anyone because, like all of us, they've got to die some time?'

'Don't know.'

'But, please, you do truly love your Joe, don't you?'

'Certainly.'

'And he's still alive and kicking, isn't he?'

'Well, yes.'

'Then are you going to love him less for that?'

'I am. You see, Ann, on account of if he died.'

'But, Charles, are you saying I oughtn't to have children because they might die?'

'My point is, love no one too much, in case they do.'

'No, no,' she protested. 'I'd be bound to love my own children.'

'Anyway,' he said, with a sort of finality 'there's very little anyone can do about things.'

His face, which she was watching, took on a look of great sadness. She then changed the conversation adroitly and they talked of musical comedy until the time came for her to go back, late, to work.

Diana Middleton persuaded her husband to take her out to dinner, a thing he was usually unwilling to do.

'I'm sorry to be disagreeable again, darling,' she said, as soon as they'd had a few drinks at the restaurant to which he'd taken Ann 'but I've gone to see Paula myself, this time.'

'You have?'

'Yes, darling.'

'Well, what on earth for?'

'It's simply this,' she told Arthur. 'I felt I had to warn Paula that Charles was seeing too much of her Ann.'

'And you got me out to tell that?' he asked, in level tones.

'I did, darling.'

'Well, what did you say to the woman?'

'But I've just explained!'

'I mean, how did you put it?' Mr Middleton demanded, as if wearily, of his wife.

'I thought you might be rather angry with me,' she admitted.

'What have I said now?' he enquired.

'You're being a bit difficult, you know, darling,' Diana announced.

The husband rubbed the palm of his hand all over his face, starting with the forehead.

'In what way?' he asked.

'Oh, am I being very tiresome?' she wanted to be told. 'No, but I feel I do have a certain responsibility to the child.'

'Why?' he asked.

'Well, Paula's my oldest friend, although we aren't quite that, perhaps any more, now, and you did, forgive me, seduce Ann, after all!' Diana sounded rather breathless.

'You mean you've quarrelled with Paula?'

'So you don't deny it?'

'With my last dying word!' Mr Middleton informed his wife, in a voice which could have been called expiring.

'I'm sorry, my dear,' his spouse brought out, with what, she obviously thought, was sweet reasonableness. 'But I had to, didn't I? One has certain duties, after all.'

'I can't make a word of this out, Diana.'

'But you must understand how I did. I don't want you upset, all the same.'

'It would be so much easier if you consented not to talk in riddles, dear.'

'Oh,' Mrs Middleton commented in a gay, bright voice 'I don't wish, or choose, to go into the whole old business anew. Above all, I wouldn't want you provoked, darling. Yet you should admit it was the only thing I could do.'

'What, I'm getting almost hoarse with asking?'

'Why, tell her, of course.'

'In which way?'

'How can that matter?' Mrs Middleton demanded innocently of her husband. 'I'm trying my best to keep calm, dearest. Oh, was it so very awful in me to drag you out like this?'

'After nineteen years of married life,' he commented 'I've learnt to let you take your time.'

'Eighteen years,' she corrected him.

'Yes, dear,' he replied with patience, and what seemed to be humility.

'Well of course all I said was, it had come to my knowledge that Ann was going out so much with Charles, and that much as I dote on the man, I could only think the whole thing quite unsuitable, and although I'd resented her coming to me earlier about her girl and you, which I know to be true but how was I to admit that to Paula, what wife would – where am I? – oh well, all I said, was, and you must admit I couldn't not, was simply that Ann would set all the old tongues wagging.'

'And has she?'

'Not perhaps yet. But she will.'

'And how often does she really go out with Charles?' Mr Middleton enquired, in obvious disquiet.

'The whole time.'

'Then she's a little bitch,' the husband pronounced. 'That's all I can say, a little bitch,' he repeated, firmly.

'Oh, I'm sorry about all of this,' the wife wailed.

'Why?'

'Well, of course, I wasn't exactly heartbroken to be able to go to Paula after she'd been to me originally in that peculiarly reprehensible way, but how else can one prevent things turning out in quite such a revolting fashion?'

'And I who imagined Charles Addinsell my dearest friend!' Mr Middleton remarked in a grieving voice, it seemed almost at random.

'D'you blame him, then?' his wife asked.

'Who'd have ever believed it?'

'So, Arthur, you openly confess you're jealous, is that it?'

'Hey, what's this?' he demanded as though he'd had a rude awakening.

'I don't know yet,' she announced, with menace in her voice.

'All I mean is,' her husband patiently explained 'it must be an entirely different matter, my taking the girl out and a man like Charles to do so. I'm married, for one thing. Everyone knows I'm safe as houses. Whereas Charles, well, he's just a voluptuary.'

'What's that, darling?'

'Oh well, let it pass. I'm sorry I ever introduced them, now.'

'You did! But how tiresomely stupid of you, Arthur. You should have known you'd lose her by so doing!'

'You can't lose what you haven't got,' the husband objected.

'We won't go into that again. Not in this crowded place! Yet why are you still sorry?'

'I am for little Ann, because Charles is the man he's turned out to be.'

'I see, Arthur. So you don't meet Ann, now?'

'No. And do you ever see Charles?'

'No more, no more!' his wife wailed comically. At which they both laughed in a rather shamefaced way at each other.

'In spite of all your tricks I love you, darling,' Mr Middleton told his wife.

'You're a wicked old romantic,' she said, beaming back at him.

'Enough of a one to put a spoke in your works every now and again.'

'Oh don't worry,' she announced. 'I haven't done with Charles yet, not by a long chalk!'

'Steady on! You're playing with fire there.'

'I wouldn't mind if it was hell's own flames, dearest. It seems someone thinks they're making a donkey out of me.'

'But you can't imagine I introduced an innocent little thing like Ann to Charles just so you should see less of him?'

'Innocent? Ann! No, it's she is at the back of all this.'

'How, darling?'

'How would you feel, if you were a woman, about the girl who was trying to take away your husband and your friend, all in the one go?'

'Much as I do feel about Charles,' he answered reasonably. 'With you,' he added, to make doubly clear, perhaps.

'And Ann?' she demanded.

'I was referring to Charles,' her husband countered.

'But, my dear, we always had our great arrangement,' Diana said. 'The one could go out when the other wasn't asked.'

'So what, my dear?'

'Why, simply that you never kept to it, and I did, which is all!'

'Now, my love,' he protested, with heat 'you know this simply isn't true! When did I ever take Ann out to lunch any time you and I were both invited?'

'Have you once rung me up, before, to see if anyone had phoned?'

'But I used to ring Ann first thing, soon as ever I got to the office after seeing you over breakfast.'

'Oh Arthur, first thing! What can your telephone girl have thought? Just warm from our bed!'

'She wasn't.'

'No please, don't try to laugh this off, I'm serious! Didn't you even open your letters first?'

'When all's said and done, it was only once a week. And I always used to read them while I was talking with Ann.'

'You can't have had such a lot to say to each other then?' Mrs Middleton asked, in a doubtful voice.

'Only to invite her out to lunch, Diana.'

'And once, which is the only time I know about, to dinner, exactly when I was supposed to be on the train to Scotland with your own son.'

'So you maintain you've never been to dinner with Charles?'

'That's an entirely different kettle of fish.'

'I'll say it is,' the husband protested, almost with violence.

'Now, darling,' she begged him. 'Don't let's go into all this yet again. You're entirely in the wrong, and it can be so painful.'

'Oh very well, dear,' he said, as if in resignation.

'Then what d'you propose to do about things?' she demanded.

'After all that's occurred I must say I obviously can't take Ann out, even once more. If anyone can be said to have learnt a hard lesson, then it's me,' the man said.

'How, darling?'

'But my dear,' he protested 'your suspicions even over the ordinary accident Ann and I had, have simply made me ill!'

'And so they ought! Yet you don't intend to sit idly by under this, do you, Arthur?'

'Then what do you propose?'

'I don't know,' she said.

'Isn't there something I could do, darling?' he pleaded.

'I must think,' she answered, then immediately went on. 'You should ask Ann out again,' Mrs Middleton propounded. 'Not at night, of course. Never that! You must promise me faithfully, Arthur, you'll never again invite her on an evening?'

'Certainly,' he said.

'You promise?'

'I swear.'

'Very well then, you will have to give Ann lunch. And don't enjoy it, mind! Because I shall simply have to go up to Dick's for a few days to be with Peter, too unfair to leave the boy alone any longer. So let me tell you, dear. If, when I come back, I find any funny business, I shall just be distraught, darling, and you know from experience what that can mean! I might even try reprisals.'

'Yes, dear.'

'Then just remember! Yes, I feel you should take her out to lunch, once more. We owe as much, at least, to Paula.'

'Yes, darling. And what do I say?' the husband asked.

'Not too much,' Mrs Middleton replied. 'Of course, for a start, you should warn Ann against Charles.'

'And then?'

'Isn't that simply enough, Arthur? What else could you wish?'

'It wasn't me,' he explained. 'It happened to be you, I thought, wanted that I should do more.'

'Do more? Please be careful what you're saying!'

'I simply imagined you had a plan, I'd an idea you knew what else you wished me to put over.'

'Well of course I do,' Mrs Middleton admitted. 'Only I find it so difficult to say in words.'

'Should I suggest I'd not be able to face old Prior, if he came after me with a horsewhip, for introducing his daughter to a man like Charles?'

'My dear,' she protested 'please don't be so ridiculous! How can you imagine she'd care two hoots even if poor Prior tarred and feathered you!'

'I see, darling,' he humbly admitted.

'At one time I thought you could say Charles was ill, had TB, or something. And then I saw, at once, that that would be no good, the desperate little thing would go like mad for a sick man, she'd think her chances even better. No, tell her Charles is only interested in women very much older than himself, that he had this passion when he was a boy, as so many of them do, and, of course, in those days, his women weren't so very old yet. Then, Arthur, you must explain how he has never been able to grow out of this peculiar habit, that he's been to all sorts and kinds of psycho-analysts, and the only advice they've any of them been able to give the poor man, was that he should, so to speak, try himself out, every now and again, on a girl who is very considerably, even absurdly, younger than he is, now.'

'Will Ann believe me?'

'Why not, if she has before, dear? In any case, who's she got to check up with? She can't go to Paula, at this late date.'

'I suppose not.'

'Besides, Arthur, think how ridiculous she would look going to any older woman to ask a question of that kind. It would give her whole squalid little game away.'

'She told me she only liked older men.'

'Oh she did, did she?' Mrs Middleton snorted. 'Then, if she's said anything else of that sort, I'll thank you kindly not to tell your own wife, which I still am! One has to keep certain standards in married life, after all.'

'Very well, darling.'

'You will, then?' she asked.

'I shall,' Mr Middleton replied, without any show of enthusiasm. After which his wife changed the subject. She spoke at length, and with fervour, of Peter, and, afterwards, of their friends, in both of which topics Arthur Middleton joined wholeheartedly.

When they came home, it was plain the two of them had had, on the whole, a very pleasant evening.

The next day, therefore, Mr Middleton directed the telephone girl, as soon as he was in his office, to ring Ann Paynton and ask if the young lady would speak with him.

When the instrument tinkled at his right hand, he raised its receiver rather slowly. He listened into a silence.

'Ann, this is me,' he said at last, in an almost panic-stricken way.

'Oh hullo!' her voice came loud and unattached, then broke into a carefree, boisterous little laugh.

'You're different,' he announced.

'Am I?' she replied.

'Sound cheerful enough!'

'Good,' she said.

'What have you been doing with yourself, dear Ann?'

'Oh well, I've been up and about.'

'Had yourself a nice time?'

'As a matter of fact, quite, thanks.'

'Splendid,' the man said, soberly. 'Seen anyone I know?'

'You're a stranger these days,' Miss Paynton countered at once.

'You don't mind my ringing up like this?' he then asked.

'Why no, how should I?'

'Perhaps I just thought you didn't sound too pleased.'

'I'm always glad to hear from you, Arthur,' she said quietly.

'D'you think we could possibly take lunch together again?'

'I might.'

'You don't, quite, seem what is called impatient, Ann.'

'It isn't that at all,' she explained, with her far away voice. 'I happen to be rather full, you see.'

'Could you manage Tuesday?'

'This week, or next?'

'Tomorrow.'

'Just let me look at my book. Yes, as a matter of fact, I find I can.'

'Fine. And same time and place?'

'That will be heaven,' she said, in a disinterested way. Then with a suggestion of laughter, she asked 'Are you sure it will be all right?'

'Yes,' Mr Middleton said.

When he put back the receiver he was frowning.

By the time they were seated at their usual table in the restaurant, Arthur Middleton was palpably nervous, while Ann behaved with what was, for her, an unusual calm.

'I never apologized for leaving like I did, the last time,' he began.

'No, you haven't rung up, have you?' Miss Paynton replied.

'I've been rather rushed lately, Ann.'

'I envy the way you can telephone in your office, merely by telling the girl to get any person you want. Where I am, one has to go through a perfect rigmarole, over private calls.'

While she told him this, she was examining the other guests with a very languid eye.

'D'you do it much, then?' he enquired.

'Arthur,' she asked, and still did not seem to bother to look at the man, 'would you advise me to move, change over into something better?'

'Hard to say. Most people get fed up with their jobs every so often. Haven't you been out much lately?'

She gave him what appeared to be a reproachful glance.

'Well, I must say,' she said 'you don't seem very interested in my problems.'

'Why, I'd just asked, Ann, if you'd led a gay life of late!'

'Which might be a peculiar way of putting things, or isn't it? Oh, if you mean have I been out,' she explained, back again now at her scrutiny of the people in this great room 'if that's what you're trying to say, well yes, I have. No, as for a gay life I was referring to my career.'

'But for someone as beautiful as you, that must mean marriage.'

Miss Paynton turned her eyes on him, began to show a trifle more animation.

'Which I always think is a bit patronizing to say to a girl,' she complained, with a long-suffering air. 'Don't men get wed? Isn't that just as important for them, too?'

'I'll say it is! Ann, you misunderstood me.'

'How did I?'

There was a pause in which he gazed at the girl with obvious anxiety, and she looked down at her plate.

'Oh you do look so wonderful, I'd forgotten!' he said at last.

'Had you?'

'No, no, not that,' he corrected. 'I don't think it's ever been out of my mind, not since the rabbit hutch. Ah, Ann, you're ravishing, this afternoon!'

'Am I?'

She gave him a long look of some sweetness, and he seemed stricken.

'Am I always?' she went on.

'Yes,' he said.

'But I was only a child, then, the time you were speaking of.'

'Yes!'

'And you found me so, even at that age?'

'You were to me, Ann.'

'Then swear!'

He gave a heavy sigh. 'Oh yes!' he affirmed.

'I'm beginning to like this better now,' she announced, and gave the man almost a warm smile.

'Oh Ann, I've been so distressed about it all!' he at once pleaded.

'About what, dear heaven?'

'Leaving you, like I did, with Charles Addinsell, of course.'

'Well I must say I do think you might have rung up, after, to find how I was!'

'But, good gracious, nothing happened, surely?'

'I don't know what you mean,' and she began staring round the restaurant once more. 'Still, you would have been polite if you had.'

'I most humbly apologize, Ann.'

At which she gave Mr Middleton a true, warm smile.

'Then you're forgiven. There!' she said. 'Arthur, tell me more about him.'

'Charles?'

'Of course.'

'Well, darling, it's hard to know where to start.'

'Have you known him long?' she prompted.

'For years and years. Charles is a strange fellow.' Again Mr Middleton fell silent.

'He said you'd been at school together?'

'Yes indeed. He was an odd sort of chap, even then.'

'In what way, Arthur?' Miss Paynton appeared quite intrigued.

'Well I don't want to sound arch, and it's really very difficult to explain . . .' he began once more, at which she let out a screech of amused interruption.

'You're too shy to admit that when he was at school Charles used to look at other boys, like Terry does? Is that so?'

'Good God, no!' Mr Middleton protested. 'No, as a matter of fact, he always did on older women, very much older.'

'But that's only natural, surely? Couldn't you, then?'

'Now why should you think I'm that type?'

'I imagined all little boys were seduced by their aunties' old girl friends.'

'Really Ann!' Arthur Middleton sounded quite shocked.

'Then how did it happen to you? Arthur; don't be so puritanical, now please!'

'Well, I'll save that up for another place, and a different time of day, if you like.'

She gave him a look and let out rather a deep laugh.

'All right! So go on, do, about Charles,' she commanded.

'You may be right when you say all boys start with an older woman,' he began once more. 'I wouldn't know and I can't admit I myself did, but we aren't talking about me now, we're discussing Charles. And, in his case, it was that.' Mr Middleton came to a full stop again.

'Oh, who was it, then? You must tell the name, Arthur.'

'I don't know.'

'Are you just being horridly discreet?'

'Honest, I'm not.'

'Then how can you be sure about him?'

'I wouldn't be certain if she'd told me herself, whoever she may have been.' He sighed. 'People lie like troopers over these things,' he added. 'Amazing to think she's probably a grandmother, if she's still alive today. Well, Ann, you can just take it from me, in his case, he always did prefer very much older women.'

'You're talking about the first time he fell in love? All right, then. Perhaps.'

'I don't know so much about the love part,' Arthur said, with a smile.

'Don't laugh!' she commanded, sharply. 'This is serious.'

'I'm sorry, Ann. But the odd thing is, it has always been older women with old Charles, ever since.'

Miss Paynton snorted, in evident amusement.

'Like me, then!' she announced.

'How on earth?' he demanded.

'I've always doted on older men.'

'Oh doting isn't loving, at all, Ann!'

'I couldn't say, of course,' the girl rejoined. 'But this quite gives me a fellow feeling with Charles if all you tell is true. Yet, you know, I'm afraid, you're wrong.'

'How am I?' he asked.

'I just do know, that's all,' she announced in a dreamy sort of voice.

'You do, eh?' he demanded, accusingly.

'I can't simply guess what you mean, Arthur!'

'Well, you see, I've been friends with the man all these years, and you haven't, darling.'

'Ah, but how well have you watched him?'

'Did he ever tell you of Penelope, Ann?'

'Penelope, his wife?'

'Then he hasn't.'

'What about her?' the young lady pleaded.

'I'll leave Charles to speak for himself,' Mr Middleton said with firmness. 'No, it was just that I was able to help the chap a bit over Penelope. When he comes clean to you with the whole story, as he must in time, he always does, you'll agree it bears out what I say.'

'Which doesn't sound very nice, Arthur.'

'Oh that tale's all old history, now.'

'I'm beginning to wonder how much you two are fast friends,' the young lady suggested, with a hint of laughter in her tone.

'You ask him. Very grateful to me, Charles is.'

'Of course, you did introduce us. He's got that to thank you for, Arthur dear.'

'He certainly has,' the man agreed, seemingly without much conviction.

'Oh, Charles may have been like that, once,' she went on in a cheerful voice. 'But he's not any more, believe you me.'

'I've known him a long time, remember.'

'We won't argue,' Miss Paynton commented. 'Now tell me your news. How's Diana?'

'Well, she hasn't been too well the past two weeks.'

'I'm sorry.'

'Yes. But there's been a distinct improvement. To tell you the truth, she's going up to Scotland tonight to be with Peter a few days. He's caught three fish.'

'Good for him! Big ones?'

'The biggest was a fifteen pounder. But, I say, Ann, I'm going to be very lonely the next day or so!'

'I expect so.'

'I was wondering whether you'd consider dining with me to-morrow?'

'Not if it's going to be like the last time!'

'Well within the next eighteen hours Diana really will be at her brother's.'

'If you are going to be horrid like it, I certainly won't come,' the girl told him, and made her eyes large with what looked to be re-proof.

'I say, I am sorry, Ann! I meant nothing.'

'Perhaps you didn't, at that. All right.'

'You will, then?'

'Let me look in my book first, please.' She did this. 'Oh, I'm sorry, I can't.'

'And not the night after, either?' Mr Middleton pleaded, with a very hurt expression.

'Yes, I could then,' she said, quite gay. And more seriously 'But, I'm sorry, we'll have to go out somewhere. I shan't dine in your flat.'

'Very well,' he agreed. A few minutes later they parted. As he walked away he seemed, from his expression, to be quite pleased with himself.

That same evening, as soon as Mr Middleton got back from work, his wife arose from her packing to ask:

'And so have you seen her?'

'Yes.'

'You are good, darling! I was afraid I was laying too much on to you. What did she say?'

'Not much.'

'Then how could you have put it?'

'Well, I told the girl I had known Charles a long time, ever since school days, in fact. That he was a peculiar fellow, always had been.'

'And what did Ann say?' his wife enquired when Arthur came to a full stop.

'She laughed.'

'She would,' Mrs Middleton commented. 'But it's one of the last jokes that little thing will get out of this whole affair, I can promise her that,' she said.

'How shall I give you the picture?' her husband complained. 'It seemed to me her laugh came from sheer disbelief even, darling. That generation simply prides itself on knowing better than ours, don't they? Look at Peter.'

'We mustn't mention him in the same breath,' the mother objected. 'There are certain standards, after all!'

'Oh, quite. Yes, Ann laughed out loud. So I can't quite tell how far this all sank in.'

'It will in time, no fear,' his wife announced, and went back to her packing. Mr Middleton sat down on a hard chair.

'And did you make an appointment to meet Ann, once more?' the wife enquired, without looking at her husband.

'Of course not.'

'Are you sure, Arthur?'

'Darling, what is this? Are you in one of your moods when you're about to claim second sight again?'

'I might be. Yes.'

'Well, Diana, you're wrong, that's all.'

'Am I? Because I might only be going to the nearest hotel, you know, instead of Scotland.'

'Now really! What are you saying, dear?'

'And don't you forget it!'

'Yes, darling.'

'That's better,' she said in an approving tone. She dropped a nightgown into her valise, straightened up, came over, and gave him a deep kiss right into his mouth, where he sat on the hard chair.

'Yum–yum' he remarked, as soon as he could.

'I do rather love you,' she announced, lowering her bulk on to his knees. 'Fancy remembering, and keeping up that word all the way from when we were engaged.'

'How could I forget?' he demanded, as she kissed his eyes.

'Now, you're not to laugh at me! Particularly not just when I'm being so heavenly with you.'

'I'm not,' Mr Middleton protested, in a most virtuous voice.

'Oh heavens, how I love you, God help me,' the wife said. While she kissed his mouth with repeated little kisses, she undid a button on his shirt and slid a hand on to his naked chest.

He moaned.

'And you promise?' she murmured, then kissed him again. 'No, don't do that!' She kissed him. 'You do promise?' And she went on kissing him. 'No, Arthur, I told you, no.' She kissed him still. 'Oh Arthur!' she whispered, in tones of love.

'Let's go to bed,' he said.

'But there's no time, oh darling!'

'Two hours.'

'I do love you so,' she told him, and let her lovely body be undressed.

The next night Arthur Middleton took Miss Paynton to a restaurant they had never yet visited, where they ate, they danced, they drank, they danced and drank again until he told the girl he was not like her, no longer her age, that he must go home. He asked Ann back for another drink. She neither accepted nor refused the invitation, even when he'd given their driver his address. And, in the taxi, she let him kiss her with abandon.

Once they were in his flat, he asked 'What will you have? A gin and lime?'

'Just the one,' she replied. And when he'd mixed this, she said 'You know, Arthur, you dance divinely, you really do! And I'm sorry to say you've my lipstick round your mouth. You must hurry and wash it off while I repair my damage.'

'I will,' he answered. 'Do you want to go anywhere, Ann?'

'No thanks,' she said. As he hurried out, she began to put her face to rights in the mirror above Diana's fireplace.

When the man came back Miss Paynton asked,

'Why d'you not wish for me to step out with Charles, Arthur?' As she said this, she settled back into cushions with a sort of easy confidence.

He hesitated in front of her.

'Now, Ann, I never said that, surely?'

'But you meant it.'

'Did I?'

'You know you did. No, sit away over there, Arthur, I want to talk.'

'Why?' he asked.

'Because this is important,' Miss Paynton went on. 'It's my life, after all. I must meet people, you do grant me that?'

'Of course, Ann.'

'And if I am to meet them, I can't pick and choose, can I? I mean it's impossible for me to ask gentlemen out, I haven't the money, for one thing. So I go where I'm invited.'

'But that doesn't prevent someone, surely, putting in a word of warning?' he objected.

'Yet why? I can't see the good. I don't imagine you think I'm blind to how people are?'

'I never thought so for a moment,' Mr Middleton protested in what seemed to be some confusion. 'Only that with much more experience ...'

'And I'm earning mine!' she took him up. 'Then you do admit, Arthur, you tried to turn me against Charles?'

'Well yes, I suppose.'

'But why? Please never think I mind, I don't. I value your interest in me, Arthur, truly I do! Just tell me. What are your intentions?'

'Pure,' Mr Middleton answered, with evident amusement.

'That's not very flattering, is it?' the girl laughed. 'No, stay where you are now, be a dear! You tell me this elaborate story against a man you introduce one to, and who has since become a special friend, and you won't explain?'

'Jealousy, Ann,' the man replied, with a show of modest candour.

She laughed, almost nervously.

'Very soon I shan't believe you, any of the time,' she said.

Now he did come over to sit at her side. He took her nearest hand, which she left in his.

'I adore you,' he assured the young lady, in a bright voice. 'I love you.'

'You're sweet,' she replied at once, without the note of conviction. 'But Arthur, you should realize my main concern must be with marriage?'

'Of course.'

'You see, I've been wondering if I'd marry Charles. In case he asked me.'

'Yes, Ann.'

'Don't pretend to be so glum, then!'

'I'm not!' he groaned.

'Oh dear, I am sorry, have I said the wrong thing again?' she wailed. 'But I love your interest, truly I do! Yet won't you understand how difficult it is to be a girl?'

'Yes,' he gently said.

'Oh I think I could dote on you if I once allowed myself,' she cried out with plain enthusiasm. 'You are so sweet to me, you truly are! What would you advise? If he did propose, I mean.'

'Turn the man down, Ann.'

'But what on earth for?'

'He's got a child already.'

'Why shouldn't he, poor sweet?'

'Well, it must be a complication, after all,' Mr Middleton suggested.

'No, I fancy there's something much more wrong with him than this little Joe that I've never yet seen,' the girl confessed.

Arthur kissed her hand, which she then hauled away.

'No, listen!' she implored. 'If only for a short time longer. This is important.'

'I am,' Mr Middleton protested.

'Then why is it, Arthur, you don't even wish me to stay happy, enjoy myself?' she asked.

'Surely those two things are quite distinct and separate?'

'How could they be? If anyone is happy she enjoys herself, no one can get away from that!'

'Yet if you are enjoying yourself, you needn't necessarily be happy,' he objected.

'Well, I think you're just splitting hairs.'

'I'm not, Ann,' he assured the girl.

'Then I imagine that must be the difference in our ages.'

'What?' he cried out. 'D'you honestly mean to sit and tell one there's a difference between happiness at forty and at nineteen.'

'From all Charles and you have told, I'm beginning to think so, Arthur.'

'And what has he said?'

'Well, you see, poor Charles's had a very unlucky, unfortunate life, with a lot of sickness which turned wrong.'

'But you're bracketing me with him, Ann, and I haven't!'

'I don't know, and this is not personal, mind, but I find your generation so sad; no, not sad, that's not the right word. What I mean is, you seem melancholy, all of you.'

'Can't say I've ever noticed it in old Charles! I'd have thought he was a bit of a gay dog, myself.'

'When he can't bear to marry again because his new wife may die like his first one did!'

'My dear!' Mr Middleton protested.

'And he won't really let himself love his little Joe in case the boy goes the way the mother went!'

'No, Ann!' he protested once more.

'You see, Arthur, I'm beginning to think I've come upon a very different side of Charles.'

'Is it his true one?'

'Well, his wife did die in childbirth, didn't she?'

'Yes, poor Penelope.'

'And you say he oughtn't to mind still?'

'I've said nothing of the kind, Ann.'

'Yet, weren't you trying to tell me it was stupid, if you'd already lost one wife, to fear losing another?'

'It's unnatural, that's all.'

'You mean it's natural for women to die that way, even now? You're saying they're expendable as regards babies?'

'How d'you intend "expendable"?' Mr Middleton demanded, with obvious bewilderment.

'I don't know,' the young lady wailed. 'It's a phrase I use, about myself, with my great friend, Claire, and I'm never sure, quite, just what it means.'

He drew away from her.

'Because I could not consider things natural for a moment if anything happened to you while you were having a baby,' he said.

'I should hope not, Arthur!'

'Exactly.'

'You're just like everyone else,' she said, with some apparent bitterness. 'You want the best of both worlds. A succession of poor, beautiful women who bear you babies and die of them. Which is intolerably selfish!'

'What makes you think I do?' he appealed.

'Because Charles is afraid for his life to marry a second time, and you aren't,' she told Mr Middleton.

'Oh, come here,' the husband demanded, putting his nearest arm around her shoulders, and the far one about her lap.

'Arthur!' she said, in the expiring voice she used to close telephone conversations.

He started to kiss the girl all over her face.

'Arthur!' she exclaimed in the same tone. She put her left hand into his right, on her lap, and laced the fingers into his. Apart from that, she let him kiss her, freely.

He got quite out of breath in the end.

'Oh, let's go next door!' the man murmured, at last.

'No, Arthur,' she said, in a different voice.

'D'you mean that?'

'I'm afraid so,' Miss Paynton answered, and slewed her mouth away from his.

'How can one tell when girls mean no?' he whispered, kissing the lobe of an ear.

'By believing them, dearest,' she told the man. He seemed to credit this, for, after a moment, he drew away and began to fiddle with his tie.

Not so long after, he dropped the young lady home, with a polite ill-humour which she did nothing to dispel.

The same evening Mrs Middleton rang Charles Addinsell on long distance from Scotland.

'Oh Charles,' she cried, once he had answered 'he's already got four fish!'

'Splendid!' the man replied.

'Charles darling, I must see you,' she demanded.

'Where?'

'Oh not up here, of course. I'm coming South.'

'So soon?'

'You see, Peter's in the seventh heaven with all his success. I can quite well leave him. And I don't trust Arthur out of my sight another moment. Besides, I want to see you, darling.'

'Yes.'

'I must say you don't sound so very delighted,' she wheedled.

'Haven't been able to sleep at nights for thinking of you,' was Mr Addinsell's response, in a voice which carried conviction.

'Oh you shouldn't do that, darling!'

'Can't help myself, Diana,' he said.

'Then could the evening after tomorrow suit, for drinks before dinner?'

'Of course!'

'You are kind! I've been thinking of you such a great deal, Charles!'

'Damn this telephone. Wish you were here,' he said.

Following which, they spoke of the weather for a few sentences, and she rang off.

When the day came Mrs Middleton went round to Charles' flat at half past six. She kissed him on the cheek but moved her mouth away as he tried to put his lips to hers.

While he was mixing a drink, she asked 'Did you really miss me, like you said on the phone?'

'Too true I did.'

'I missed you, as well.'

'Why, Diana?'

'Well, for one thing, you are the one person in the whole wide world I can confide in about Arthur.'

'That's a reason. Why else?'

'Which is my secret,' she responded briskly. She accepted the drink he brought over and sat down on the sofa at his side. He at once put an arm around her shoulders.

'No, Charles,' she murmured, pushing it off with her free hand.

'Whatever you say,' the man agreed.

'Now, Charles, I want to ask you over Arthur,' she began. 'Has he been out with Ann, d'you think?'

'Don't imagine so.'

'Have you?'

'I believe I did run into the girl for a moment.'

'So you asked her if she had, Charles?'

'No.'

'And when it meant so much to me!'

'She'd never have told me true,' Mr Addinsell protested.

'But you could have told from her face, darling!'

'Doubt it.'

'Now don't be false-modest, Charles. With all your experience!'

'Well, if she had said something, and I thought her lying, and reported to you she'd done the opposite of what she told me, where would I have been with old Arthur?'

'Then you're his friend, not mine!' she mourned, in a low voice.

'You know that isn't so, Di.'

'It looks very much like it. Oh anyway, I told him he could take her out the just once more, to get rid of the girl!'

'As a matter of fact I believe I remember someone did seem to say he'd seen them out together.'

'Morning or evening?' she asked, in level tones.

'Wouldn't know, I'm afraid.'

'Charles, you're lying to me . . .'

'Now I . . .'

'No, don't interrupt, I can see it in your dear face,' she cried. 'Oh how you could! And for him! It was at night, wasn't it?'

'Well . . .'

'Oh the brute,' she whispered and began to cry softly, not even bothering with a handkerchief. 'And at a time I promised reprisals if he did,' she added, almost under her breath. 'Oh damn, Charles, I'm going to cry,' although a tear was already on her chin. 'I feel simply awful! Oh dear, sometimes I almost hate Arthur.'

'Whatever you do, don't tell the old chap I told you!'

'Oh no, I won't, I promise. Oh damn. Look, Charles, I'm afraid I shall have to go to the bathroom. There's nothing else . . .'

'Well of course. Sorry about all this.' He opened the door. 'You know the way?' She did not answer. She was sobbing over her glass as she went.

Mrs Middleton did not come back for ten minutes. In that time the man put down two stiff whiskies.

When she opened the door to rejoin him she thrust her finished drink forward. 'Get me another, darling, I need it, and please forgive that little exhibition.'

'You look more lovely than ever,' he said, to which she replied, but gently 'Don't be so absurd, dear Charles!'

He rattled the cocktail shaker.

'Forgive me,' she repeated.

'For what?' Mr Addinsell asked.

'Because, you see, I simply must know. Has he gone to bed with Ann again?'

'Even if she'd told me she had, Di, I wouldn't believe a word she said.'

'So then she has!'

'How can I tell?' he implored.

'How he could! After eighteen years' married life!!'

'Don't let yourself get upset,' Charles pleaded, bringing her drink over. 'People do, you know.'

'Does that make it any better?' Mrs Middleton demanded, not looking at him.

'Nothing ever gets better,' he replied. 'Not at our age,' and he put a hand round her waist, at which she moved just out of reach.

'It'll have to, that's all,' she announced, with a sort of resigned conviction in her voice. 'I can't go on with my life like this.'

'Relax,' he told the woman, as he came after her.

'No, really Charles, we mayn't dodge one another round the chairs and tables. Now, just you sit down, over there, and think about me for a while.'

'I am,' he replied, obeying her.

'Then what ought I to do to him?'

'Take things easy, Diana.'

'How can I?'

'Have your own fun, for a change. Be yourself!'

'But myself is just what I am being, at this moment.'

'And teach old Arthur a lesson.'

'Oh, I think mothers, of grown up boys, who go to bed are pretty squalid, don't you?'

'People do.'

'Which is no reason why I should,' she calmly objected. 'Besides, it's so long now, I really believe I wouldn't know how.'

'Then you should let someone remind you.'

'You, perhaps?' she asked, with a half smile across the six feet of space which separated them.

He gave a gay laugh.

'I'd like nothing better,' he asserted. 'What man wouldn't. But I know enough to realize I'm out.'

'Why, Charles?'

He got up, as if to come across to her.

'No, go on sitting there, Don't spoil everything just when you're about to fascinate me.'

'Only wish I could, Di.'

'Tell me, then.'

'We've known each other too long.'

'Why?'

'Well, I mean,' he said, in what appeared to be a perplexed voice. 'You're the wife of my oldest friend.'

'But you're telling me that ought to make no difference!'

'Only it does, sometimes,' he explained. 'No, all I said was, you should teach old Arthur a lesson.'

'Very well, perhaps I ought. But who with?'

'Don't you know anyone?'

'Not in that sort of way, Charles.'

'Then how about me, in the end?'

'Yet you've just said we've been friends too long.'

'I might be mistaken.'

'I don't think one ever is, not on instinct.'

'So you won't.'

'No Charles.'

'Can't say I blame you.'

'You're rather sweet,' she murmured, only she now wore a distant expression. 'Oh, my God, will you just please look at the time. I'll be late for his dinner.'

'And this is the man you were going to discipline?' he asked nodding in the direction of the flat she shared with Arthur.

'Oh well,' she laughed, came up and kissed him on the mouth. 'One's still to keep up appearances, after all! Hasn't one?' She laid her cheek against his.

'So it's goodnight?' he softly enquired.

'I'm afraid so, my darling,' she said, and left.

That same evening, once their cook had left them alone with the food, Mrs Middleton, white faced and in a voice that trembled, said to her husband,

'So you took her out at night, after all?'

'Ann? I don't know how you found out, but I did. Yes.'

'Why?'

'Because when I thought it over, my dear, I came to the conclusion your suspicions were rather absurd, if you'll excuse the expression.'

'Then nothing's sacred to you, now. Is that it?'

'Oh, Di!'

'You promised so faithfully, you know you did!'

'But a promise dragged out of one when you're in a state . . .'

'Is not binding? Oh, Arthur, you've grown double faced!'

'How?' the man asked.

'You say so when I haven't arrived back in London more than half an hour before I hear you've been around with her on an evening out?'

'Who told you?'

'Your own best friend.'

'And who would that be?'

'Only Charles Addinsell.'

'Oh, don't please believe a word he says.'

'Then you deny it?'

'No.'

'Well, in that case, where are we?'

'Where we've always been.'

'Don't be so sure, Arthur. You might try me too far.'

'And how about our old arrangement?' he asked, with an obvious show of indignation. 'When one of us gets invited he or she always has gone, irrespective of what the other may be doing.'

'Oh darling, you promised, you know you did!'

'Under duress.'

'Under how much?'

'That promise was forced out of me, Diana, when you were so upset.'

'But it's only once one is truly miserable that one makes people make promises.'

'Oh, my dear, you aren't!'

'What?'

'Miserable.'

'Could you be insane, all of a sudden? Of course I am!'

'And why?'

'For the simple reason you take out that little creature, Ann, the instant my back is turned, when you swore on your sacred oath you wouldn't, ever again!'

'It seems to me Charles Addinsell is playing a very curious part in all this.'

'Now Arthur, I'll not have you draw red herrings across your tracks.'

'The first person you see when you come back to London must be Charles? Before you've even said how d'you do to your husband!'

'Of course!'

'I can't spot any "of course" in this, Diana.'

'Really? But I had to find out what you'd been up to, you'll at least grant me that?'

'To do which you were obliged to go to my best friend?'

'Naturally.'

'Then how did you get it out of him? By sitting on his knee, I suppose.'

Mrs Middleton laughed. 'Almost,' she said.

'But that's simply disgusting,' the man protested angrily. 'And what's more I don't recognize my Diana in any of this!'

'Can't you?' she asked, with great calm. 'Oh, perhaps it wasn't so bad as all that, though it wouldn't do you any harm to get your imagination going some time. No, I did worm the story out of him, which is the important thing.'

'So you admit, Di, that what he told you was just a story?'

'He said the truth, my dear,' Mrs Middleton announced with solemnity. 'I could read it on his poor face.'

'I'm glad it's poor.'

'Charles is to this day a very handsome man, Arthur.'

'Unlike me, I imagine.'

'He still takes trouble,' she told her husband, in a dreamy voice.

'What rot this is!' the man protested uneasily.

'How rot, when you've already confessed?'

'When on earth am I supposed to have done that?'

'Oh not often, I'll agree, Arthur! No, you did just now, when you admitted you'd taken Ann Paynton out.'

'But, my dear, it was yourself asked me to.'

'Now don't play the innocent, and when I'm so tired with the horrible journey. The sky is my witness you swore you would never invite her out at night, again.'

'Oh Lord, what have I done now?' he moaned.

'And, in addition,' she went on 'I may be forced to do what I warned you I might have to. Reprisals!'

'Now, look here, Di . . .' he pleaded.

'Something with, say, Charles which I could afterwards regret.'

'With my best friend?' he burst out. 'Why, you'd make me a laughing stock!'

'Oh, I expect you'd quite soon get over that.'

'How could I, Di? What d'you want? To torture me, or something?'

She smiled pleasantly. 'How I wish I just could,' she said.

'Well then, everything's hopeless then, isn't it?' he muttered.

'It might not be, Arthur!'

'How's that?'

'I don't want to make you swear, or promise now, any more, but if you just come over here this minute and say faithfully you won't ever again . . .'

He went to her at once. 'Oh darling!' he said, it seemed almost in tears as he kissed her. She kissed the man back briefly. 'There, that's enough,' she murmured, pushing him off. 'Now let me tell you about his last fish. It took all of three quarters of an hour to land . . .'

Mr Middleton did not do any work that night. They went to bed soon after.

Miss Paynton had one of her sessions with Claire Belaine.

'Well, how's everything going, Ann?'

'If you ask me I don't think I'm getting anywhere, my dear. I haven't seen Campbell in weeks.'

'Oh him!' Miss Belaine commented, with plain disgust.

'I won't give anyone up, Claire, which has become a principle of mine.'

'In case they grow what you call expendable?'

'I forget what I meant by that silly phrase. I was miserable then, when I made it up, but now I'm just plain desperate.'

'Why? What's happened?'

'Nothing. Simply nothing! Which is the whole point.'

'How much did you expect?'

'Why, to fall in love of course,' Miss Paynton protested. 'Don't you?'

'But there's lots of time still, surely?'

'Is there, Claire? Can you be honest and say that?'

'You aren't twenty yet.'

'I think there must be something the matter with me, you see.'

'Why on earth?'

'Because I can't love anyone, and I don't remember a soul I have. Not even once!'

'Everything comes with time.'

'No, look. There's even the one who fell in love with me, or so he says, and I believe him, when I was eight and kneeling on a rabbit hutch at home.'

'Would he be this Arthur?'

'Yes.'

'And you don't love him?'

'No, I simply can't,' Miss Paynton muttered.

'Then how about Charles?'

'Oh, my dear, a hopeless neurotic.'

'But I've heard of people who go mad for love of those.'

'There you are, you see, Claire!'

'Well, I only wish I had the chance!'

'Why, d'you want to be introduced to him?'

'Me? Good heavens, no,' Miss Belaine protested, in a virtuous sounding voice.

'He's quite nice looking, you know.'

'Maybe, Ann. But I don't.'

'Have it your own way, darling. Then you do think I'm choosy not to fall in love with the first man I see, even if he's old enough to be my father?'

'Well, I've always been in love, Ann.'

'I know! You've told me.'

'And I haven't even had to speak to them, thank goodness.'

'Oh, you are lucky!' Miss Paynton sighed.

'You see, I never meet anyone,' the other girl complained.

'Yet you do all day, in the office.'

'I know,' Claire wailed. 'There must be something wrong with the both of us then, in that case. Only, of course, we're at opposite poles.'

'And just what d'you mean, dear?'

'That they ask you out and you can't fall in love with them, while they won't invite me, and I do!'

At which the two girls fell into a fit of giggling. When they'd got over it, they talked of other things, then left.

'People can be so extraordinary,' Miss Paynton was saying as she sat to dinner with Charles Addinsell in his flat the same night. 'There's a girl I know, rather a friend of mine, who simply falls in love with everyone she sees.'

'Better bring her up here some time, then.'

'Why, would you like to meet Claire?'

'I was only joking. Shouldn't know what to do with the girl.'

Ann laughed. 'I'll bet,' she commented. 'There's just one major snag. She can't talk to the person she falls for.'

'I might prefer that.'

'Are you serious?'

'No.'

They both laughed.

'Isn't it peculiar,' Miss Paynton began again. 'But they say some odd things about you into the bargain.'

'Such as?'

'You won't be cross, or offended?'

'Not me.'

'Well, they pretend you only like persons much older than you are.'

'Men or women, or both, Ann?' he asked, smiling.

'Well, ladies.'

This time Mr Addinsell roared with laughter.

'What absolute bilge and bunkum,' he said at last, when he could.

'I don't know so much, Charles.'

'You mean to say you believed that?'

'What do we ever really learn about other people?' she reasoned. 'Not to trust the way they look, and that's about all.' She paused.

'No, go on,' he said.

'But don't you see, even if you made the most violent love to me the next moment, which you won't,' she went on, although he had not risen from his seat 'which you won't because I shan't let you, I'd never know?'

'Couldn't you feel?' he asked.

'Do you trust your feelings then, Charles?'

'Of course.'

'And ought I to?'

'Yes.'

'Well, if I did, I'd have to admit there's something horribly peculiar about me.' She paused.

'Which is?'

She gave a giggle that sounded embarrassed.

'It's only I can't fall in love at all, and never have yet.'

'Much better not,' he said, in a sombre voice.

'Oh, you can be so discouraging at times,' she cried. 'Now Charles, just try not to head me away from the experiences my life must have in store. I've got to go on living. Don't even attempt to put me off with all the fearful things that could happen.'

'All right. But why do you think it is so necessary to fall in love?'

'Well, mayn't that be so?'

'No. If you wanted to marry, you could, and have a baby daughter, then get to love him much later.'

'Marry without love,' she said, in a shocked voice.

'My wife, who I adored, couldn't make up her mind to marry me, poor dear, so I took her along to see my old grandmother, who was alive then, and she told Penelope it didn't matter who you married in this life, you came to love them in the end.'

'Oh, but then she must have been one of those fearful Edwardian parents who never had children except by some other man than their husbands.'

'No, she was born in eighteen fifty.'

'Honest?'

'It's true.'

'Well then, Charles, I think that's the most extraordinary thing I've ever heard.'

'What's odd about it?'

'Everything.'

'Why? Human nature's much the same from one person to another. So long as you don't expect to be happy, you can get to love anyone. Ours is still a very small proportion of the world that chooses their own wives.'

'What a man's point of view!'

'You've got to take life as you find it, Ann.'

'Well, I don't find that, anyway.'

'How d'you know you won't, in time?'

'I'll take the risk, thank you.'

As the meal was over now, he suggested they should have their coffee in the living room. When she had settled in an armchair and he was sitting six feet away, he asked,

'See much of Arthur these days?'

'He's a friend of yours, isn't he?'

'My oldest.'

'Then perhaps you'll explain him. I think he's really rather strange.'

'In which way?'

'Well, he seems so frightened of and yet so fond, about dear Diana, all at the same time.'

'Old Arthur's not the divorcing sort.'

'I should hope not,' the girl said with some animation. 'We weren't discussing anything of the kind, not as far as I'm aware. No, I can't see how love and terror can run together.'

'Fear of losing what he has, I suppose.'

'I'd only say this to you, Charles, but he doesn't seem to have much, would you think?'

'Well, a home, a wife and child. After all . . .'

'Oh I realize that could be everything,' she rather quickly agreed. 'Almost all one should ask of life. But would you say he was still in love with darling Diana?'

'Does he have to be?'

'Then, if he isn't, why does he go on living with her?'

'I suppose he's afraid of something worse,' Mr Addinsell suggested.

She laughed.

'I expect I'll understand some time,' she said.

'Well I hope you don't learn the hard way, as I had to.'

'Now Charles, you're not to go gloomy on me again,' the young lady rallied him. 'In any case I'm rather cross with Mr Middleton, let me tell you.'

'Oh?'

'Yes. I never seem to even see him any more.'

'Why's that?'

'Which is what I was hoping you'd be able to explain.'

'Perhaps he's had the red light.'

'Of course not. Be serious. I don't think people ought to drop you suddenly after taking one up, do you?'

'Diana may have read him the riot act.'

'Over me?' Miss Paynton giggled. 'Oh I don't think so. As a matter of fact she's been round to Mummy and said it was you was seeing too much of me.'

The man seemed astounded.

'I? Diana?' he asked, in what could have been an offended voice. 'Who told you?'

'Mummy.'

'When was this?'

'A fortnight ago.'

'But, Good Lord, I'd hardly known you then!'

'Arthur first introduced us, Charles, three weeks and two days back.'

'Diana? I can't believe it!'

'Yes, she did. But you don't appear to be very interested in what Mummy thinks.'

'What does she think?'

'She didn't believe, either, after I'd talked to her for quite a bit. But in the course of our conversation she said a curious thing. Oh, heavens, there I go again! I'd sworn to myself I'd never mention this.'

'Go on, I'm like the grave, I don't talk.'

'Oh no, I couldn't. Why you'd never speak to me for ages.'

'Come on, Ann. You can't avoid telling me, now.'

'Well then, if you swear you won't be cross, and since you're practically forcing me on, you see, she said you'd actually been having an affair for months and years with Diana.'

'Damn the woman!' he exclaimed, with obvious irritation.

She gathered up her bag, made as if to rise. 'If you're speaking of Mummy . . .' she began.

'No, it's Di I meant,' he assured the girl. 'Who else?'

Miss Paynton settled down again.

'Yes, I thought it was pretty good cheek,' she said.

'More than that! She's been outright nasty. And I'd never have expected it of her.'

'Wouldn't you, Charles?'

'No. Imagine knowing a woman all these years and then to come on a piece of nastiness like that!'

Miss Paynton kept very quiet.

'Oh, I suppose Diana was just jealous,' she said, in a satisfied sort of voice.

'Jealous, what of?' Mr Addinsell demanded. 'When nothing's happened to make her jealous?'

'How would she know? Perhaps she just imagined.'

'I'm always imagining,' he objected violently. 'We all are. But that doesn't make me into a snake in the grass!'

'No, of course,' Miss Paynton sweetly agreed.

'I'm glad you see it,' he said, in a pompous voice.

'All the same I wasn't exactly delighted to have all that told me, Charles.'

'I'll bet you weren't. Perfectly rotten for you, I agree.'

'Oh, I got over it.'

'Jolly decent of you,' he responded with sincerity. 'What hell everything is!'

'Don't take things too seriously, dear Charles. I'm pretty sure no great harm has been done.'

'Oh, I'm all right. It was you I was thinking of.'

'You are sweet!'

'And so are you, good heavens! I wish to God, now, we had done something to give them a bit to gossip over.'

'Charles,' she exclaimed, in an unsurprised voice.

He got up. He came across. He sat on the arm of her chair. He put a hand into her far armpit.

She shrugged. 'It tickles,' she complained.

He dropped a leg over the side of the chair, began sliding down towards and underneath her.

Miss Paynton let out a small cry. 'You're squeezing me up,' she said.

'Come, sit on my knee a minute,' he demanded, in a small, authoritative voice.

As she settled on his lap, she asked 'But aren't I an awful weight?'

'I want to kiss you,' he answered, which he did.

'Oh Charles,' she said in the expiring breath she used to sign off telephone conversations.

He slid a hand down along her leg, where the skirt ended. She put her free hand to meet it, and laced the fingers into his. Her arm was rigid.

She snapped a kiss at his mouth. 'Oh Charles,' she repeated once more, into his silence.

'Might as well be hung for a sheep as a lamb,' he whispered to the girl.

'No, Charles.' She moved away.

'What's the matter with me, then?'

'Why you're perfect, you're sweet,' she announced, rather loud, and fetched the mirror out of her bag.

'Oh God,' she said, once she had had a look. 'No, Charles,' when he tried to kiss her again. And within twenty minutes, she'd got out of that flat, and left him behind, as though she'd done Mr Addinsell the greatest imaginable favour. Indeed, from the expression on his face, while he handed her into the taxi for which he'd phoned, it seemed he was fully conscious of his merit. He looked old and sad.

The same night Mrs Middleton was saying to her husband,

'Arthur, I thought I'd ask Ann to tea.'

'Who?'

'Ann Paynton.'

'What for?'

'And her friend Claire what's-her-name.'

Mr Middleton went back to his papers, even hid his face inside the dispatch case.

'Belaine,' he faintly said.

'It would be so much easier if you asked them, darling,' Diana propounded.

'Oh?' he echoed, in a muffled voice.

'Yes, and then didn't turn up, so I could have both alone for a change.'

'But I've never even met Claire.'

'That need make no difference. Just get your secretary to ring Ann up as you do first thing in the office every morning and ask her to bring the friend along.'

'I know, and what for?' he demanded, showing his face once more, which had a look of panic.

'I just want to be friendly,' his wife replied.

'And you don't wish me to be present?'

Diana smiled at him without replying.

'But mightn't that seem rather rude?' he enquired.

'You could be detained at the office, like you so often are.'

'What for?'

'Oh, I'm sure you can think something up.'

'No, darling,' the husband wailed, and wore a frown between his eyes 'I meant, why d'you want to see them?'

'Only I never see Ann except when Peter's up in London. And I thought of asking her friend because Ann might feel rather strange alone with me.'

'How could she?'

'I think she may.'

'What are you trying to start now?'

'Nothing, darling,' Mrs Middleton assured the man, with a bright smile. 'Now hurry up with all that stupid work,' she said, and gathered her knitting together. 'Then come to bed.'

'Yes.'

'So you will?'

'I shan't be long.'

'No, invite them to tea here, and not turn up, I mean.'

'All right.'

'There's a wonderful darling,' Mrs Middleton said, and kissed him on what looked to be a puzzled forehead, as she left.

'This is Claire, Mrs Middleton,' Miss Paynton announced, it seemed rather carelessly. 'She just saves my life at least once each day at the Ministry.'

'I've heard so much about you,' Diana told Miss Belaine as they shook hands. 'Ann's been so angelic with Peter always, when he's back in London, that I simply felt we had to meet.'

'He's been catching salmon, I hear,' the girl said, with a shy smile.

'Yes, up at my brother's in Scotland. Such a relief! I can't tell you how difficult it is for children to get even one, the gillie explained to me. And he's had five already.'

'Good for Peter,' Ann Paynton commented with an obvious lack of conviction while she accepted a cup on its saucer.

'Will you hold yourself ready for his last night, Ann?'

'Of course. As always.'

'And how about you, my dear?' the mother asked Miss Belaine.

'I think I'd love to!'

'Wait a moment and let me explain. Every holidays on his last night we take the boy out, and try to show him a bit of life. You're sure you wouldn't be bored?'

'I'd like to see a bit of life myself,' the girl assured her.

'Oh dear, but you must always be going out?'

'I don't.'

'Of course in my day there were all those dances.'

'You should never believe the half of what Claire says,' Miss Paynton interrupted, in a negligent voice. 'She sallies off with some young man almost every night.'

'Darling, I don't.'

'I'm not so sure.'

'Well if you will consent to come,' Mrs Middleton put in 'we must think of a boy for you.'

'No no! Please, you shouldn't bother.'

'But of course! Oh dear I don't know any. Haven't you someone you'd like to bring along?'

'I could think, of course,' Miss Belaine announced with what seemed to be studied modesty. 'As a matter of fact,' she went on 'I hardly know anyone. I don't know the reason, but I do of course, know why, I mean. The thing is I hardly go out at all, I never seem to meet a soul.'

'Then that must be set right at once,' Mrs Middleton pronounced with firmness. 'A lovely creature like you. Oh dear, but of course, for the evening we're supposing, Peter gets so shy with grown up lads just out of school, so many boys his age are like that, and if we brought one along, well I'm afraid Peter would just dry up, and not say a word. So, for this particular evening, my dear, would you say no to an older man, one of my contemporaries, in fact?'

'Why you are sweet and kind. Of course not!'

'Who were you thinking of?' Miss Paynton enquired, as she raised a piece of cake to her mouth.

'Charles Addinsell,' Mrs Middleton told the girl, with great calm. 'A very dear friend of Arthur's and mine from the old days,' she explained to Claire Belaine.

Miss Paynton laid the slice of cake back on her plate, untouched.

'Oh you are kind!' the other young lady exclaimed. 'Why should you go to all this trouble over me?'

'I want to do something for darling Ann here; pay her back for all these evenings she's come out with us and Peter.'

Miss Paynton's jaw had slightly dropped.

'Oh my dear,' Mrs Middleton exclaimed to the girl, with a sweet, blank expression. 'I'd quite forgot you knew Charles already. Won't it be very dull for you if we invite him?'

'Not really,' Ann almost gasped. 'I mean it would be quite all right. That's to say I don't mind who you ask. I so love coming always, you see.'

'So sweet,' Mrs Middleton commented, in fervent tones. At this point her husband burst into the room with his briefcase.

'Hullo, hullo, hullo,' he cried, shaking Miss Payton's hand with both of his.

'Darling you said you'd be late,' his wife reproved him.

'Couldn't resist seeing Ann again,' he said.

'You don't know Claire, do you?' the young lady asked. He greeted this girl.

'Did the meeting get through quicker than you expected, then?' Mrs Middleton insisted.

'Yes,' her husband answered. 'And what have you wonderful creatures been up to?'

'Why, we were talking of Peter,' Diana told him.

'He hasn't caught still another fish, has he?'

'Not yet. Now here's your tea.'

'Ta. Ann, you look lovely.'

'Thank you very much,' she replied, in a small voice.

'I'd just asked Claire, here, to come out with us on Peter's last night, Arthur.'

'Splendid,' the man said, heartily.

'Oh darling,' Miss Paynton interrupted, in the direction of her friend 'don't you think we should be on our way, now?'

Miss Belaine seemed rather disconcerted.

'So early!' Arthur cried, with obvious disappointment.

'Yes, must you go?' his wife murmured, but it was hard to tell if she meant it from the tone of voice she used.

Nevertheless Ann had her own way quite soon, and took the other girl with her when she left.

'Well, the two of them didn't stay long, did they?' Mr Middleton remarked as he came back from showing the young ladies out.

'Your fault for returning so soon,' his wife responded, and seemed dissatisfied.

'My dear, I'm sorry,' he said. 'We got through quicker than I'd expected.'

'Sure you didn't just long to see Ann once more?'

'Don't be so absurd, Di please!'

'Well you won't have much time in the end to wait. Peter'll be going back to school, quite soon now.'

'I say, since you've invited this Miss Belaine, my dear, we'll have to find a man for her?'

'I've settled all that, Arthur. I told them both I'm getting Charles.'

'Addinsell? Oh dear, darling, what is this?'

'Nothing.'

'But it must be, Di.'

'Very well, then. I only thought for a moment that if you couldn't have Ann, it was only fair Charles shouldn't. Miss Belaine, unless I'm very much mistaken, will create almost a diversion where he's concerned.'

'Now look!' Mr Middleton vigorously protested. 'You've become almost insane when that man is mentioned.'

'And I have certain obligations to Paula, even if you don't think so!' his wife added, in a virtuous voice.

'No, why should you do this to me?'

'What am I doing, then?'

'Oh, I know,' he agreed. 'But won't it be very awkward?' However, after a certain amount of humming and ha-ing on his part, she cut him short to run his bath, and soon afterwards led him to it.

As the two girls walked away, Miss Paynton explained herself.

'Sorry to drag you off, darling, but all that was too sinister for words.'

'Why, in what way d'you mean?'

'Then you didn't spot how Diana announced she was determined to ask Charles?'

'No.'

'But it was the reason she invited us to tea. She's off her head in love over Charles.'

'Oh, come now!'

'She is! And if she can't get him to take her out any more alone, she plans to use you and me as stalking horses.'

'Well, why should we mind, Ann?'

'Yet I do, darling. Oh, I could sue that woman for libel if I cared. The things she's been to say about me to my own mother!'

'You never said.'

'Didn't I? I expect that must have been because it all became too petty and trivial for words. Just an older woman's jealousy.'

'I see. But I should've thought that might be quite formidable.'

'My dear Claire, it's like water off a duck's back where I'm concerned! Luckily Mummy has a sense of humour, otherwise I assure you I'd have been away to the lawyers at once. When women get to the age Di is, they're desperate.'

'What's so odd in asking me to meet Mr Addinsell?'

'Or d'you think,' Miss Paynton mused 'she could be having us along to divert suspicion from herself? Poor, downtrodden old Arthur could have put a word in, at last, and forbidden her to see any more of Charles, except in public.'

'I never realized things were as tense as this, Ann.'

'But my dear, it's quite fantastic what goes on!'

'You mean they actually go to bed together all the time?'

'At least I know they try to. You wait until the first moment you're alone with either Charles or Arthur.'

'Heavens,' Miss Belaine exclaimed, in a calm voice.

'Look, Claire darling, I've an idea. Diana must not get away with this. Suppose you pretend to make a pass at Charles?'

'If I did, I couldn't very well in front of her!'

'To please me,' Miss Paynton begged. 'Look, I could ask him round for a drink before this party for Peter.'

'In front of you, then?'

'Oh, I could go out of the room, for a moment. Yes, that might be much better, to get you to meet Charles first, I mean. I don't trust that woman any more than I can see the nose in front of my own face without my mirror, and she may have something up her sleeve when she asks us both to meet the man. No, Claire, look, it's a most wonderful idea to get him to us, before. Think of her face when she learns you've already met.'

'But what exactly am I supposed to do?'

'Darling, if you so much as let Charles lay a finger on you I'll claw the heart right out of your pretty chest. Remember you are my special friend, and that he's mine, until I decide what I want with him.'

'Of course.'

'I warn you he's terribly attractive.'

'Well don't make me nervous, Ann. I expect I'll get by.'

'And you promise?'

'Oh yes.'

'Because I'll think something up. Diana's just a viper, and she simply must not be allowed to get away with this.'

Upon which they kissed and parted. And, as Miss Paynton hurried off, Claire Belaine watched her go, with a frown.

After some discussion the two girls had decided to ask Mr Addinsell to a drink in Claire's room.

'Well, well,' he said as Annabel introduced him to his hostess.

'It's so nice of you to come, dear Charles,' Miss Paynton murmured.

'Decent of you to take pity on me like this,' the man gallantly replied, and seemed to pay great attention to Miss Belaine's roundnesses.

'Claire saves my life every day in the office,' Ann explained.

'Is that so?'

'Oh I don't. But you see, they're a queer crowd, and Ann and I rather hang together.'

'I thought you should meet Claire,' Miss Paynton then explained. 'Because, I understand we're all going to be asked on a party and I decided we might have a get together first.'

'When's this? No one's said anything to me.'

'Haven't they, Charles? How remiss of Arthur.'

'Is the date fixed, Ann? Might be going somewhere else.'

'It's one of those special do's they lay on for Peter the night before he goes back to school. Oh Charles, you shan't cry off! I've had to carry the torch alone for ages.'

'Could be my Joe's last evening.'

'Then why don't you bring him along, as well?' Claire asked.

'Too young.'

'Oh damn, you're not to drop out of this now?' Miss Paynton protested. 'Just when, for a certain reason, it's become quite important.'

'Heavens, we haven't even given you a drink yet,' Claire cried and left the room.

'Don't you think she's sweet?' the other girl whispered.

'I certainly do, Ann.'

'Then be very nice to her. She's had a bad time.'

Mr Addinsell was just saying he was sorry to hear that when Claire returned with a tray of every imaginable savoury, on toast.

'What's so sad?' she asked, brightly.

'Oh a little thing to do with old Prior,' Mr Addinsell said, at once.

'Your father?' the girl enquired of Ann. 'And you never told!'

'Oh something's always the matter now with Dads. No darling, it's nothing.'

'I'll get the drinks,' Claire announced, and left the room again.

'Please leave Dads out, Charles,' Ann demanded with spirit, in a low voice.

'Sorry,' the man muttered. 'Couldn't think of anything else on the spur of the moment.'

'He shames us so!' she almost wept.

'Now Ann!'

Upon which Miss Belaine came in once more with a second tray, a bottle of gin, glasses, lime juice, water and ginger ale.

'Sit down, why don't you,' the young woman cried. 'I must say, Ann, you're not looking very festive! What are you groaning about now?'

'Not over this spread!' Mr Addinsell exclaimed.

'Go on, then. Mix your own drink, why won't you?'

Upon which the man poured himself out a very stiff gin. Into it he put a little water.

Both girls cried out, wouldn't he like something else, orange or coca cola?

'No thanks,' he replied. 'As it is, now, anyone who didn't know would think I was on the waggon. So Arthur's to ask us all out together, then?'

'He told me he was.'

'What did Di say, Ann?'

'Oh she just stood there when he said, Charles. In fact I fancy it may have been her suggestion.'

'Then we shall get asked all right,' the man announced.

'I fancy we will. Whether we like, or not.'

'Don't you want to go, then?' he enquired.

'I love being taken out, I live for it,' Miss Paynton explained. 'Only I don't know, but I somehow feel Diana is up to something.'

'She almost always is,' Mr Addinsell agreed.

'Oh, d'you realize, I'm so glad you've admitted that, Charles. There are times she genuinely frightens one.'

'Don't get me wrong,' he warned. 'I suppose she might be my oldest friend.'

'Well, what's wrong with that, after all, Charles?'

'Nothing.'

'No, with what I just said?'

'I was only being loyal, I suppose. Diana's all right. Known her years.'

'She may be for you, but if you happen to be a girl . . .'

'Very well then, how's she behaved now?' Mr Addinsell wanted to be told.

'Look. She had Claire and me to tea. She'd never even set eyes on Claire before. And she goes out of her way to invite her out, on this end of the holidays party, when Claire has never been asked previously.'

'I don't see, quite, why Mrs Middleton shouldn't,' the girl objected.

'Di may have wanted to make the numbers even, you for Peter, with me for Claire.' He smiled at the young lady.

'Why not?' Miss Belaine assented.

'Because, my darling, I still don't know if I should bring you in on this extraordinary imbroglio,' Ann answered promptly. 'After all, I still have some responsibility towards yourself, you must admit.'

'I might be able to look after myself, Ann.'

'Yes, don't make old Arthur and his wife into ogres,' Mr Addinsell agreed.

'I still can't see why she's inviting us all,' the young lady insisted.

Charles coughed. 'Aren't you making rather a mountain out of a molehill?' he asked.

'I suppose I might be,' Miss Paynton agreed. 'Oh dear, I must leave you two for a minute. Where is it, Claire, on your landing?'

'Yes, darling, and remember not to try and lock the door. It inclines to get stuck, and you'll never get out again.'

Once Ann was gone, Mr Addinsell turned to Claire.

'Doing anything tonight?'

'No, I don't think so.'

'Then how about a spot of dinner with me?'

'But what of Ann?'

'I rather wanted to have a word with you about her, as a matter of fact. She's an old friend of mine, Ann is, and to tell you the truth I'm a bit worried.'

'Oh, I wouldn't know anything on that!'

'I wanted to ask your advice,' the man explained. 'You'd arranged to go out this evening?'

'Not exactly.'

'In that case, come along, why don't you?'

'But how?'

'Look, I'll leave, and after a decent interval, I'll ring up and say where you're to come.'

'Will it be all right?' Miss Belaine wondered aloud.

'Well, why on earth not?'

'I might,' she conceded with a show of reluctance, and then Miss Paynton came into the room.

'Well, my dears,' she cried. 'Why so glum? What have you two been up to?'

'Talking about you,' he said.

'Oh no, but how sweet!' Ann cried. 'You shouldn't.'

Then, for a time, they went on with indifferent subjects until, despite their joint protests, he made his way off.

'That's that,' Miss Paynton said to Claire, when they heard the front door shut. 'Mummy's out, so I said I'd find myself a meal somewhere. How about you?'

'Darling I'd love it, but I can't. They've changed the date of my club, and tonight's the night, this week.'

'Oh well.' Miss Paynton yawned. 'So what did you think of him, darling?'

'Definitely attractive.'

'So do I. Now I shall have to get going.'

They kissed, and Ann left.

That same evening, Addinsell greeted Miss Belaine at the bar of the very restaurant in which Middleton used to give Miss Paynton lunch.

'Well, well,' he said. 'Nice of you.'

'It's sweeter of you to ask me,' she replied.

'This is the place old Arthur brings Ann.'

'Does he?'

'Didn't you know?'

The girl laughed. 'Perhaps,' she said. 'Is that why you think it suitable for me?'

'Not in the least. I come here because I consider the cooking's best.'

'Goody!' Miss Belaine exclaimed. 'Although I must watch my figure.'

'What on earth for?'

'Fat.'

'Good Lord, you aren't.'

'Thanks,' she said. 'But you see, if I didn't pay attention I might be, even more so.'

'Never in the wide world!'

'D'you bring Ann here?'

'Now why should you ask?' he demanded.

'I suppose I'm curious.'

'May have done.'

'Oh, you are discreet!' she remarked, as she sipped her drink.

'Like the grave, Claire.'

'Heavens, you do sound sinister!'

'It's not that,' he protested. 'But it's no great shakes, for you, to be seen here with me.'

'Why d'you say this?'

'Call me Charles, do,' he said. 'Well, you can't much enjoy yourself with a man old enough to be your father. You surely feel you must be polite to him all the time, like you're being now.'

'Am I? Then how ought I to behave?'

'Laugh a bit.'

'I have. After which you suddenly went serious on me.'

'Here, I'm sorry, I do apologize. I didn't mean anything, you know.'

'No more did I. There.'

'You ever met Diana Middleton?'

'Only the once.'

'What did you think?'

'Me? Why, I thought she was sweet.'

'I suppose I've known that woman all my life; since I was grown up, of course,' the man said.

'Lucky for you!'

'You think so. I don't know. Anyway it's very decent on your part to consent to come out with me.'

'Why on earth?'

'Well, isn't it?'

'When I have to go without if I want to buy anything for myself!'

'How d'you mean?' the man demanded.

'Consider for a moment,' Claire begged him. 'I have the room to pay for. I only earn a few measly pounds a week. It's simply heaven to be asked out to a real, genuine meal.'

'Is it?'

'Well, wouldn't it be?'

'I suppose. Yet, believe me, I'm still very grateful.'

'Then we both are, one to the other. Which is a reasonable basis to be on.'

'Yet you say you actually don't get enough to eat?' Mr Addinsell declaimed.

'Up to a point,' she admitted.

'Better order yourself a pretty decent dinner tonight, in that case,' he said.

She laughed. 'I will!'

'But can't you go round to your parents when you're short of a square meal?'

'They're dead.'

'I say, I am sorry! What time did that happen?'

'When I was twelve.'

'It's a terrible object lesson, having a father and mother.'

'I've never thought so,' the girl complained.

'When they die.'

'I hadn't seen it like that before.'

'Simply rotten on my little boy when his mother left him!'

'You mean she went so far as to run away?'

'No. She died. As yours did.'

'Oh I do apologize. Truly!'

'Quite all right,' he conceded. 'Then who brought you up?'

'My aunt.'

'And you don't care for her?'

'If I were you I'd marry again to save your son going through what I did if something should happen to you.'

'I'd never seen things in that light!' the father exclaimed. 'You mean it might be selfish not to?'

'Yes. Judging by my experience.'

'Good Lord. You don't know how interesting all this is to me.'

'Of course I may have been just plumb unlucky,' the girl explained. 'I was a most tiresome, boring child, I shouldn't wonder.'

'I'll bet you weren't!'

'But yes, Charles dear.'

'You mean you can't go back to your aunt at any price, even for a square meal?'

'Of course I can!'

'Sorry, have I said the wrong thing again?'

'No, no,' she cried. 'It was me. I suppose there was something in the way you put it!'

'I'm a clumsy old fool.'

'You aren't old or clumsy. I don't like it when you put on these airs, dear Charles! But what d'you suppose I left my aunt for, as soon as I felt I was old enough to get a job, with only a pound or two a week to my name, which Mummy left me.'

'Are you saying this relation of yours was actually cruel to you?'

'No, only that I got in her way.'

'A child! In your teens. Orphaned! How could you?'

'You see she couldn't have friends to the house.'

'My dear Claire, and why on earth not?'

'Men friends, Charles. I was always in the light.'

'Oh!!' he said, in a loud voice.

There was a pause.

'I didn't mean to shock you,' the girl began again, in an apologetic voice. 'But that's how things turned out.'

'What a rotten time you must have had,' he said, in muted tones. 'No, of course, you didn't shock, I've seen a bit of the world. Tell you the truth, the more I do witness things, the less I like 'em, but then I'm a bit of a cynic, I imagine.'

'Does that go for the people you meet, Charles?'

'You mean, what I said about not liking persons? No, not for all of them, no.'

'Which is something, then,' she said, in a satisfied voice.

'And how d'you find most of those you run up against, Claire?'

'But I've already told you, I meet absolutely no one, ever,' she wailed.

'I see. And Ann?'

'Oh, she's just a girl friend.'

'I understand, Claire. Yes, quite.'

'You can't imagine how it can be for me at my age in a big town like this.'

'Then you must do me the great pleasure of coming out again some time.'

'Oh now,' Miss Belaine objected. 'I haven't been saying all I have, so as to get you to invite me.'

'It would be a privilege,' the older man insisted.

Upon which they argued a bit, and eventually she agreed to sally forth with him once more, on Wednesday, the evening after next. After that, when the meal was over, he took her to a club to dance. They had a merry time.

He dropped her back in his car. Claire was quite passionate when she let him kiss her. But she did not ask him up, not on this occasion.

The next day Mrs Middleton rang Charles Addinsell early in the morning.

'You doing much tomorrow night, Charles?'

'What's tomorrow? Wednesday? No, I don't think so. Let me look at my book.'

'You see, Arthur's just told me he has to go to some agent's dinner. So inconsiderate to leave it so late, but there! You know what I have to put up with.'

'Lord, I'd forgotten, but I'm afraid I can't this time, Di. Here it is, written down,' he lied. 'I swore I'd take old Edward Dallas to the club.'

'What's "this time" meant to mean?' she demanded disagreeably.

'Why, Wednesday, Diana, that's all.'

'I see. Then why don't you put him off?'

'Couldn't do it. The man only comes up to Town once in a blue moon.'

'I think I'll ring Barwood and check with Edward myself about this little trip of his.'

Mr Addinsell laughed, in a tone of great good humour.

'You may,' he replied 'but you know how terrified old Ed still is of girls. You won't get the truth out of him.'

Diana giggled. 'Is he still? After all these years?'

'Most certainly so!'

'And you swear you're not taking out that little creature Annabel?'

'Ann Paynton? Never in the world!'

'Her real name is Annabel, as you'll find if you try long enough. Very well, I suppose I'll have to let you go, this time. Goodbye for now, dear.' And Mrs Middleton rang off.

Wednesday night Charles took Claire out. After eating they visited another place to dance, where they drank, they danced, they laughed; and laughed, and danced and drank again until at last she said she must go. He squeezed her wrist. 'Wait for me, please,' she begged as she disappeared into the cloakroom, and when, afterwards, they stood at the top of the stairs until they got a taxi, each soberly leant his or her weight against the other.

'I love you,' Mr Addinsell murmured.

'You don't,' she protested, in as low a voice.

'Oh but I do,' he said, and she sighed.

As soon as the doorman had a taxi, Charles gave his own address, in an undertone, while she climbed in. He tipped more than he need.

Once they were on their way, he put an arm round her waist and kissed the girl, at length, on the mouth. She was passive. And the moment he withdrew, he said,

'To go back to what you told me about going to bed . . .'

She responded with a 'Sssh—' and set her lips on his, so that he might not talk.

As soon as he could, he went on,

'But you know you said Ann did?'

'I'll bet she does with you,' the young lady answered.

Charles did not paw Miss Belaine. He kept an arm loose around her waist and occasionally kissed the soft, moist corner of her mouth.

'Never in the world,' he protested.

'Aren't you discreet!' She seemed to mock.

'Just truthful, Claire.'

The girl laughed. She kissed him. 'You're all right,' she said.

'How much all right?'

'Just a teeny bit.'

He laughed. They had been laughing a lot. 'That's something, then,' he said, and gave her a long kiss.

Eventually she broke away.

'See here,' she exclaimed with calm. 'This isn't anywhere near my direction. Where on earth are we going?'

'I owe you an apology, I said the address of my flat,' Mr Addinsell told her in a soothing voice. 'Fact is, I just couldn't see the last of you, all of a sudden.' He kissed her. 'You're so extremely sweet.' She kissed him back.

'We'll have to see about this,' she dreamily announced.

At which moment they drew up outside where he lived. He kissed the girl at great length. The taxi driver looked to his front.

'Come up just for a minute,' Mr Addinsell said at last.

'No, Charles darling.'

'Not even for a second?'

'I can't, you see.'

'Why ever not? When I promise I'll behave.'

She gently laughed.

'You know I can't,' she said.

'I just don't, Claire.'

She laughed and pecked a kiss at the man. 'Oh, very well,' Miss Belaine agreed. 'But only on the condition you won't be cross if it is only an instant.'

He kissed her. 'I solemnly promise,' he affirmed.

Upstairs there was a sofa drawn up before the fire. He mixed the girl a drink, out of which she took one sip.

'Oh no, Charles, mine is too strong!'

'Give it to me,' he demanded, and watered the thing down.

Then he came to sit beside her, setting his own glass, the contents untasted, on a stool to the right.

'I must kiss you once more,' he said.

'Charles,' she gently replied, and held her mouth tilted.

Shortly afterwards, when she was half naked, with her eyes closed, Mr Addinsell carried her to bed in the next room.

Two hours later, he ran the girl back in his car to her digs. She still seemed just as wordlessly contented.

The next morning, when she had telephoned her place of work to say she would not be in, Miss Belaine accepted the flowers which he had sent and which arrived about eleven, but, as soon as Mr Addinsell rang her towards a quarter to twelve, she pretended to be someone else on the line, and, when the man had rung off, she phoned Ann at her office.

'Tell them anything,' she told her friend 'say I'm ill, I leave it to you, but I must see you. Could we meet later in the pub?'

'You seem a bit wrought up, darling. Nothing dreadful, I hope?'

'No, rather the reverse. Only you may be cross with me, Ann!'

'I shall be? Oh, I don't think so.'

'I'm not sure I'll be able to tell you, even,' and, as she said this, Miss Belaine weakly giggled.

'Can't you now, over the phone? All of a sudden it seems so long to wait, darling.'

'No, I couldn't, not possibly!'

'All right then. At half past five, Claire.'

Upon which they rang off.

As they settled down to their drinks in the saloon bar that same evening, Claire began,

'Well I've news about Charles.'

'I might have known,' Miss Paynton said.

'What can you know, Ann?'

'I guessed.'

'Is it obvious as that, then?'

'I'm not aware of what passed, of course! But everything was fated from the first, I'm sure.'

'D'you think?'

'Oh Claire it's my fault for ever introducing you two. Yet I don't know. D'you sometimes believe that nothing in the whole wide world matters?'

'Oh Ann, but surely simply everything has supreme importance, if it happens.'

'I've a feeling that everything is relative.'

'Between people?' Miss Belaine exclaimed. 'Well of course!'

'No, as to what occurs between people,' Miss Paynton said in a doleful voice.

'But how can you evaluate what's happened, Ann, when I haven't even told you?'

'Thanks very much, I don't think I want to know.'

'Then you seem very sure it must be on the dingy side, Ann.'

'Isn't everything always?'

'Have we nothing to look forward to, at our age, in that case?'

'Just treachery, I suppose.'

'But, darling, what makes you talk like this?'

Miss Paynton laughed in a nervous way. 'Oh, put it down to the weather,' she said.

'That's not good enough, Ann.'

'Very well, then what d'you want?'

'Me?' Miss Belaine expostulated. 'But I'm asking nothing.'

'So aren't you, darling?'

'My dear Ann, what is all this?'

'Oh Claire I was such a fool to act like I did.'

A look of great patience came over Miss Belaine's fat features.

'I blame myself entirely. I should never have done it,' the Paynton girl went on.

'But do what, dear?'

'For the most despicable of reasons, too! You see I was so dead jealous of Diana.'

'Yes?'

Miss Paynton beat a knee with her hand.

'When that horrible Diana asked you for Peter the other evening, I thought . . . I thought she was up to something – and when is it by the way, in three days' time? I knew you wouldn't mind, so I . . . Anyway, you both went out; oh you had my blessing, up to a point, of course, because it came to me Diana has some plan which I can't possibly know, and it was only fair that you should get to meet him first in case he tried anything. And now you look radiant and I feel miserable.'

'I still can't understand what this is, Ann, but I'm sorry, I truly am.'

'Oh well, as I was saying, nothing really matters.'

'But my dear, why not?'

'Or I suppose it doesn't. I don't say I put much money on Charles, but I did hope he'd turn out a friend.'

'He is, Ann.'

'I must go. We'll see. Goodbye.'

She left without a smile, and had not even finished her drink. Miss Belaine sat on with a small, guilty and contented grin across her face.

That night the telephone rang in Arthur Middleton's flat about nine o'clock, just when he had started work on the contents of the briefcase. His wife answered, as a matter of course.

'It's for you, Arthur, and I'm sorry to say it sounds like that little Ann Paynton, though of course she won't give her name.'

Mr Middleton groaned.

'Hullo there,' he said into the phone. 'No. Yes.' Then after a pause 'What? When, last night? I can't believe you.' After which he had another bout of listening. 'And to think I used to call that man my friend,' he said at last. 'Yes, thanks, this is very bad,' he ended, and rang off.

'To think of it,' he said to his wife, in a rather excited voice, as he came back from the instrument. 'I'm afraid you're not going to like this. There's more about Charles now.'

'I dote on him, and nothing you can say will alter that fact,' the woman promised.

'Wait till you hear,' he told her, almost with satisfaction.

'And why should I believe?' Mrs Middleton demanded. 'Because it was Ann, I recognized her hypocrite's voice, didn't I?'

'Ann rang up then, yes.'

'The nerve! So what did she pretend, dear?'

'Only, Diana, that Charles has been out with her best friend, Claire Belaine.'

'Which must be just an idle, lying tale,' his wife announced most indignantly. 'Why, he doesn't even know the little thing.'

'Ann says she introduced them.'

Mrs Middleton gave a stricken cry.

'Oh but,' she announced 'then this may indeed be serious.'

'Darling,' her husband reasoned, 'I sensed it could provoke you, but hardly . . .'

'There's no loyalty left in the wide world!' she yelled.

He came over. 'Now darling, what's upset things?'

Diana put the pink knitting down and closed her eyes.

'So you get Ann back and everything's perfect, then, isn't it?' she said.

He laid a hand on her shoulder. 'I don't even begin to understand,' he told his wife in a patient tone of voice.

'I did what I had to with the best of all possible intentions,' Mrs Middleton began again, shut-eyed still. 'It was all for Peter.'

'But how, my love?'

'To keep a home together for the darling boy!'

'Now, Di, just you leave Peter right out of this nonsense?'

'I couldn't be expected to go on seeing you make such an utter ass of yourself over Ann, surely?'

'So you brought Miss Belaine in?'

'Because of Charles! Aren't I to have my friends too? Oh darling, I'm so truly miserable.'

He slid down the arm of her chair until, with a practised movement, she wriggled on to his knee.

'Still, if you are happy, that is all I care,' she murmured.

He kissed her closed eyes.

'You of all people have no cause to worry,' he said, with great conviction.

'Yes, Arthur, but I must lead my own life after all.'

'I always did think Charles a cad,' he muttered.

'More than you could be, my dear?'

'Now, Di, what is all this?'

'When I loved you so!'

'And don't you still?'

'Of course.'

'So why does what Charles has so wickedly done, affect you in this way, my dear?' Mr Middleton asked.

'Are you then to have everything?' she demanded, and opened her eyes at last, in an accusing stare. 'Ann Paynton, as well as Claire Belaine, if needs be, the whole time?'

'But I don't even know the other girl!'

'My dear Arthur, your intentions were very evident when you met her over tea in this very room.'

'And what did I do or say to make you think so?'

'It was the way you looked, Arthur.'

'What nonsense, Di,' he protested vigorously. 'You're mad!'

'I'm saner than you know,' she said, and shut her eyes once more.

'Now have you been all right in yourself, lately?'

'Thank you, Arthur, I'm fairly well, I suppose.'

'I mean you aren't in the middle of your change of life without knowing, are you?'

She opened her eyes very wide, looked away from him, and drew herself apart.

'Arthur,' she said, in a low voice 'are you insane?'

'I only wondered, my dear.'

'Why do you do this to me?' she whispered.

'My dear darling, what am I doing?'

'You know I'm not!'

'Well, you've got to face things, Di. It will happen some day and I thought this may have started, that's all.'

'But why, Arthur, is all I ask?'

'Because you're so peculiar about this whole business.'

'How peculiar, when I'm naturally upset for you if your young mistress who has been trying to ensnare the one friend I still have, starts him off with another girl? What would you feel if you were me?'

'I admit none of this, but for purposes of argument I see your point,' the husband confessed.

'Oh fiddlesticks, Arthur! And I could think of a stronger word.'

'I see, dear,' this man said, in his driest voice.

'And you're going to blame me for it?' Diana cried, seeming on the verge of tears.

'How could I, my darling?'

'You simply don't know about yourself, any more,' she told him.

'Very well, then,' he said. 'Let's call this whole party off.'

'But with Peter down from Scotland tomorrow night!' Mrs Middleton protested.

'Why not when you seem so frantic with each one of our guests?'

'Well, my dear, wouldn't you be?'

'Quite possibly, Di,' he replied 'if I was in your position.'

'Which is?' the wife indignantly demanded.

'Now darling,' he said, with a show of caution. 'I just said what I did because you seemed fed up with the people you'd invited, perhaps with reason.'

'But how could I, when I've written to darling Peter who we're to have!'

'There was no way I could have guessed that, is there?'

'You might.'

'How, then?'

'If you truly loved the boy!'

'Now, Diana, I promise you I simply won't have this! We are not to enter into a competition as to who dotes on him most!'

'Oh, doting!' the mother cried, in tones of disgust.

'Whatever you care to call it, I don't mind,' Mr Middleton exclaimed. 'Can't I love my own son, even?'

'And do you?'

'Now, Di, I'm not excusing a single word of this! Kindly pull yourself together!'

'To call off the party we've told him about, and on his very last night! Oh, Arthur!!'

'I said not a word of the sort, I'm certain.'

'Oh Arthur!'

'Did I? Well, all right then, I take it back, that's all. And you can't stop me!'

'When have I ever said I could?' Mrs Middleton murmured.

'You're hounding me, trying to drive me off the face of the earth!' he cried.

'I don't know what you're speaking of,' his wife answered.

'But when all's said and done, how will it be when I go out with you, and those two girls, and with Charles?'

'That must come down to a matter between you and your own low conscience,' Mrs Middleton told the man. Shortly after which they went to bed, where they made love apologetically.

Next morning, Arthur Middleton arranged to meet Addinsell at lunch.

'So you went out with this friend of Ann's?' he began as soon as they were settled.

'Yes,' Charles replied.

'At night?'

'Yes.'

'And you went to bed with her, after?'

'As a matter of fact, I did.'

'You didn't!' Mr Middleton accused, in obvious agitation. 'You can't have!'

'But of course I got her into there. It was what she was asking for, surely?'

'And yet, Charles, she's only eighteen?'

'Well, they've got this coming to them, sooner rather than later, haven't they?'

'Why her, after all?' Mr Middleton demanded, as though he was a loss.

'You'd prefer I'd pick on Ann, and not on Claire?'

'Oh I suppose Ann's old history by now to you, Charles!'

'No, and not by want of trying, let me tell you, either.'

'So how about Di?' the husband hazarded.

'Now look here, Arthur, you must take a hold on yourself,' Mr Addinsell firmly told him. 'Try not to go on like this. I'm saying, you'll get ill! There's not a thing to any of it. My own tragedy is, I wish there could be something. And you sit here, and make mountains out of soft molehills!'

'A little girl like Claire!' Mr Middleton groaned.

'She's not little, she's a great big creature,' Charles objected. 'Come off it now, Arthur!'

'I wish I could.'

'Then you blame me, old man?'

'I? Not the least bit in the world,' Middleton said, with evident sincerity. 'No, if you want me to put my finger on the spot, I'd say it was taxation.'

'By making everything more expensive?'

'Precisely, Charles. They don't get asked out any more.'

'Except for the old, old reason?'

Mr Middleton laughed. 'How then are they to meet anyone nowadays?' he demanded.

'Arthur, my dear, I dine out on that, and I can't afford to, either. One should be able to put the little things down to expenses.'

'Well, Charles, all I can say is, you're hopeless!' Mr Middleton announced in a most genial voice.

'My dear boy, it's me who thinks you are!'

'But look here, I'm still married.'

Charles Addinsell winced. 'Don't rub in about Penelope,' he asked.

'I apologize for that,' the husband said, with sincerity, and there was a pause.

'Then you want to call the whole evening party for Peter, off, is that it?'

'No, I don't, at all.'

'Come clean, Arthur. You know that's the sole reason you've asked me for lunch.'

'I'll admit the idea had crossed my mind. But Di won't hear of it.'

'Yes?' Mr Addinsell asked guardedly.

'On account of Peter,' Middleton explained. 'The boy's liable to dry up if we put him with people his own age.'

Charles roared with laughter. 'So that's why you're still asking me?'

'Yes,' Arthur Middleton admitted, and laughed, in his turn, with a shamefaced air.

'Well then, I'm very glad,' Mr Addinsell said, with evident sincerity. 'Because, for the life of me, I can't see why this sort of absurd misunderstanding should be allowed to come between two people like us who've, in the past, been through so much together.'

'All right Charles, and I'm not trying to rake up old sores, but it's plain you forget what it's like to be married.'

'Maybe so,' Addinsell said, with an air of distaste.

'You don't hold it against me that I said that?'

'No . . .'

'Or when I told you I'd thought to put you off for Thursday?'

'So Thursday's the evening? Let me look at my book, Arthur.'

'No, see here old man, you shan't cry off now, how can you? What would my wife say? She'd think I was at the back of it!'

'All is well, Arthur, I'm free.'

'You mean Di hasn't asked you properly, yet? Oh, how careless of her! Honest, I don't know what she does with her time, all day!'

'That's all right. I was invited. Only Diana didn't seem so very sure it was coming off, this party of yours, Arthur.'

'Not going to happen!' Mr Middleton cried. 'Why Peter would never speak to either of us again! Well no, as a matter of fact, to be entirely truthful, I don't suppose he lays such great store. In a manner of speaking you could say it was mine, and my wife's, show to show him off.'

'I only wish I could do the same, but Joe's too young yet,' Mr Addinsell said with great sincerity. Shortly afterwards they left, went their separate ways, without anything else of significance having passed.

That same evening Peter arrived home off the train from Scotland. While his mother laughed wildly as she kissed him and Arthur called 'well, there you are' the boy, in a shy voice, said,

'Oh hullo.'

'And have you got another fish, darling?'

'Well, yes. As a matter of fact I did.'

'Wonderful!' his father cried. 'Any size?'

'Ten pounds two ounces.'

'That makes eleven you caught, then?'

'Don't be so silly, Arthur! If he's had one more, that makes twelve in all. I must write to Dick. He's been too kind! And did you remember to tip the gillie?'

'Angus? Of course. Actually, because I'd brought in really rather a lot I thought I ought to give him a bit more.'

'And how much was that?'

'Stop it, Arthur! D'you suppose Dick won't ask the boy again if he doesn't tip properly.'

'Yes, my dear, I do.'

'In any case, when you talked over the original amount with me, I thought that was much too small.'

'Oh, let it pass!' Mr Middleton begged of his wife.

'Who's coming to the party?' the son demanded.

'Well, darling, we've got Ann, of course. I wrote you.'

'Oh yes,' he said, as if bored.

'And this time,' the mother went on 'we've asked a friend of hers, Claire Belaine.'

'Who's she?'

Mrs Middleton laughed. 'You well may ask!' she agreed. 'Then I've invited Charles Addinsell, for myself.'

'Oh God,' the boy commented.

'But didn't you get my letter?'

'Which one?'

'Telling you who we were to have?'

'No.'

'Wasn't that the one I told you to post, Arthur?'

'How should I know, my dear?'

'I truly believe it's becoming impossible to call on you for anything, these days!'

'I'm sure I put every single one you told me into the box, Diana.'

'You can't have done, dear, if Peter never got it.'

'Did you see anyone besides Dick when you were up there?' the father asked his son, perhaps to change the subject.

'Yes, there was a chap from school.'

'Oh, what a bore for you!' Mr Middleton sympathized.

'As a matter of fact I rather liked it.'

The parents exchanged a glance.

'Who is he? Shall we invite him to stay the next holidays?' his mother demanded.

'Oh God, no! Not that.'

'I see, darling.'

'What's Ann up to these days?' the boy asked.

'Much the same as usual,' Arthur answered.

'Not engaged to be married yet?'

'So far as we know, darling,' Diana said, in a most peculiar voice.

'Are you off her too, then?'

'No. Why?'

'You sounded as though you might be.'

'Why should I?'

'I never liked the woman,' he told his mother.

'Oh but Peter, you know you've always doted on Ann! For Heaven knows how long you've simply insisted she should come out on our last evening of the holidays.'

'Not me.'

'I sometimes say we go through this rigmarole of the first and last nights for our own and not Peter's benefit,' Mr Middleton diffidently suggested.

'Who to?' his wife at once asked.

'Oh, I think Charles.'

'Have you been seeing him again, Arthur? What for, this time?'

'Well, he's a friend of both of us, isn't he?'

'You never told me!'

'Is there any reason why I should?'

'No, about your taking him out, I mean,' she said.

'Who is, after all, this Belaine woman?' Peter wanted to be told.

Both parents began to speak at one and the same time, then each broke into gay laughter.

'She's just a hussy,' his mother told the boy at last.

'What's that?'

'Something almost unmentionable, my darling.'

'Then why do you choose her as suitable to meet me?' Peter laughingly asked.

'Look, Diana, can't we call the whole thing off?' Arthur Middleton demanded.

'And how would we look if we did, at this late date?'

'Not go out at all! On my last night? That would be pretty grim.'

'No, of course we're going, darling. Pay no attention to your father. Now tell me more about your fishing. Did you get your last salmon in the Uil pool?'

After Peter had gone to bed, Mr Middleton returned to the charge.

'No, but seriously Di, why should we have this evening which no one is going to enjoy.'

'When it's tomorrow night?'

'What's that got to do with things?'

'I certainly hope you're not going to be disagreeable even over this!' his wife told him. 'Just kindly indicate to me how we're supposed to put them all off now?'

'We could say he had 'flu.'

'Well, Arthur, I for one am not going to lend the boy's name to a low lie.'

'There's that, of course,' her husband seemed to agree.

'And I should hope so too, Arthur!'

'Yet if Peter doesn't seem to be looking forward to it, as he so obviously isn't?'

'You heard him, only half an hour ago, my dear, say with his own lips it would be pretty grim if we didn't.'

'I know but it's borne in upon me we may have asked the wrong people.'

'Oh, darling, can one ever do right with children?' Diana declaimed, in a sad voice.

'I agree, Di. This is all a question of numbers, surely?'

'And what d'you mean by that?'

'Simply a matter of how many people come that Peter doesn't want ever to meet.'

'Are you sure all this isn't a fear, on your part, of being in the same room as me with certain members of our party, Arthur?'

'You mean I'm capable of anything?'

'Yes.'

He laughed, with good humour.

'You may be right at that,' he said.

'Darling,' she announced 'whatever they may say against you, you're in a way a reasonable sort of husband.'

'Who does?'

'Oh, not many people!'

'You're telling me you've been at your old game of discussing me again?'

'I can't always talk about the weather.'

'Then I think it's disgusting, that's all,' he burst out. 'There must be a sort of standard of loyalty in married life, when all's said and done.'

'Yet you take Charles out, unbeknownst to me?'

'Why shouldn't I?'

'And you discuss with Charles who should and couldn't be asked on a party for your son's last night, without even a word to me before!'

'It just happened that way,' Mr Middleton admitted, wanly.

'How could it have?'

'What can you mean by that, Di?'

'Show me how it's possible to go over such a subject, with Charles, without meaning to!'

'Now, look here . . .'

'No,' she interrupted in a violent voice. 'You did that on purpose, Arthur! After all, Charles is my friend!'

'Of course,' he agreed, in evident distress. 'But, before you came along I'd, in actual practice, known Charles a fair while.'

'He's loyal to me,' she cried out, on the verge of tears it seemed. 'He'd never have allowed you, if you hadn't forced the discussion on him!'

'Oh, do let's call it all off!' her husband begged.

'What, in heaven's name?'

'This party, the people we know like Charles, Miss Belaine if you like, the whole bag of tricks.'

'And Ann?'

'I must be left with some of my friends,' Mr Middleton objected. 'We haven't been married nineteen years just to look across a table at each other each night, you and I.'

'Eighteen,' his wife corrected him.

'Eighteen or nineteen, how does that make a difference?'

'Then you are truly tired of me?' she wailed.

'I do so wish you'd not speak such nonsense,' he said, in a flat voice.

'And I could, where I'm concerned, put up with a bit more consideration from you in the expressions you use!'

'But what is it, after all, that you need from me, Di? When all's said and done, I work all day at the office, I come back tired out at night.'

'When you aren't taking your girls to luncheon.'

'You know we have our arrangement.'

'Damn our arrangement!'

'Very well,' he said, in his weariest voice. 'All this is simply wearing me out! I wouldn't be surprised if I wasn't ill. What say if we just didn't see any of these people any more, even Ann?'

'But that would mean utter defeat, dear.'

'Now what's this, Di?'

'All I'm trying to say is,' the wife appeared to explain 'if we turned our backs on these people, never saw them more, then we'd have failed in our married life. Paula would be able to say she was right.'

'What has she said?'

'Nothing to the point, yet, when has she ever?' Mrs Middleton enquired. 'But if we did that, she will. I know about these things, and you don't,' she insisted. 'I know, Arthur!'

'Very well,' the husband said, as though exhausted. 'So what's the next step?'

'You'll see, my dear old darling,' the woman told him, kissing his mouth. 'Now come to bed, do, you look so tired,' and they went.

The whole party, on the night, settled down to their table in an establishment which had just recently been opened in the West End of London and where, whilst having dinner, you could watch all-in wrestlers, dancing or a floor show, at one and the same time. This was made possible by the fact that supper tables had been placed on a balcony the walls of which were of plate glass. The corridor for service was on the wrestling side of their table but left a good view of that ring in which two men were to pretend to pull each other apart to the sound of a good dance band, for the diners were drenched, through open windows on the other side, with a great rhythm from two bands that played alternately, while the yells, the groans-to-be opposite would be totally unheard through plate glass which did not have one opening. This place was called 'Rome'.

'Oh heavens,' Mrs Middleton announced, as she took her seat 'but what if I feel giddy?'

'I'm so sorry, my dear, yet I did think we might try something new, just once,' her husband answered.

'Over there's where they'll gouge one another's eyes out in precisely twenty minutes,' Mr Addinsell informed Peter, nodding at the empty ring.

Meanwhile both Ann and Claire were leaning out of an open window on the dancing side.

'No Charles, or I shall feel quite sick,' Diana implored the man, plainly nervous at the sight.

'Now girls,' the husband called to those two young women. 'Come back to your responsibilities.' Grave-faced, Claire and Ann then sat down to table.

'Poor Campbell is here,' the first one said.

'I wish I could do all my work in these places,' Arthur laughed.

'My dear, if you did, with your health, you'd be dead in three weeks,' his wife told him.

'Now look, Di,' Mr Addinsell protested. 'What's this? I thought we were all out to have a jolly evening.'

'You don't know about Arthur, Charles darling!' was her reply.

'Well I must say, there's no call to bring my health into question right now, surely?' the husband countered.

'Campbell has been very ill, too,' Miss Paynton told them, in a doleful voice.

'Would you wonder at it, in this atmosphere!' Mr Middleton demanded.

'The doctors were very worried over him,' Miss Belaine volunteered.

'Who was, and why?' Ann sarcastically asked.

'You told me yourself,' her one time friend answered.

'Now illness of whatever kind's a serious thing,' Charles Addinsell pronounced. 'My experience is, don't ever laugh about it. Can always end in the tragic.'

When Claire giggled, Miss Paynton followed suit.

Upon which, Peter intervened. 'I say,' he said 'd'you think I could have a shandy?'

'But of course, darling,' his mother told him. 'Arthur, when will you just begin to look after your guests?'

'You know what the help is like, in these places, my dear,' this man replied, and began to click with his fingers.

'Oh God,' the son commented.

'What's wrong now?' his father asked.

'Nothing.'

'How have you been?' Miss Belaine enquired of Charles.

'Are you all right?' the mother wished her son to tell her.

'We shall never get a waiter!' Arthur wailed.

'Steady the Buffs,' Mr Addinsell said. 'Di, you'll feel a new woman once you've had a drink.'

'Who'll dance?' Miss Paynton demanded.

'When does the wrestling start?' Peter wanted to be told.

'This is a divine tune,' Miss Belaine assured Addinsell at the same time.

And Mrs Middleton put her own view forward.

'Why shouldn't we just leave?' she asked.

'Go? But nothing's even begun yet!' her son protested.

'It is his evening, after all,' the father said.

'I'd love to dance,' Charles told his girl. 'Only, let me stoke up with a drink first.'

'I'm doing all I can!' Arthur Middleton complained, and waved violently.

'I know you are, old man. Forget it.'

Upon which the near miracle occurred, an attendant came to take their order. Better still, he brought the drinks almost at once. Their host thereupon ordered another round, then champagne for all.

As he raised the martini to his lips, Mr Addinsell gave Claire Belaine a long slow wink, to which she replied by wrinkling her fat nose. Mrs Middleton must have become aware of this, for she reached over and drove a thumbnail hard into her husband's wrist.

Possibly he took it as a love token, because he murmured back to his wife two little words,

'My darling!!'

'Better now?' Charles Addinsell asked his girl.

'Of course,' she said.

'When you get down to a drink you seem to want to withdraw your funny nose right out of the glass,' he went on.

'Now, Charles, don't start being a bore,' Claire answered.

'I'm still not sure I feel all right up here, Arthur,' Mrs Middleton complained. 'It must be what it's like to be parachuted.'

'Drink your cocktail up,' the husband urged her.

The next lot of cocktails came, with shandy for Peter, and buckets of champagne.

'Better now, I am,' Mr Addinsell announced.

'Oh Charles, you are being rude,' his girl informed him.

'Arthur, I feel at last as if I were coming back to earth,' Mrs Middleton told the husband, already at her second cocktail.

'Splendid, my dear,' Arthur said in an enthusiastic voice. 'Now, who's going to dance?'

Peter asked 'When do the wrestlers start?'

'Shall we?' Addinsell demanded of Claire Belaine, as he drained his second martini down.

'Yes,' she answered, getting up.

They went, and the waiter uncorked their bottles in the buckets.

'Just a minute and I expect they'll be coming,' Mr Middleton answered his son. 'Darling, will you join me on the floor?'

Diana gave him a sweet, loving smile. 'Well, I might,' she said, and got up.

Thus were Ann and Peter left alone.

'I rather hate this place, don't you?' she asked the boy.

'I don't know yet.'

'I suppose it's useless to invite you to dance, Peter?'

'Good Lord, you surely don't mean that, do you?'

'All right,' she responded. 'It's your evening. Forget what I said.'

'Isn't it bad enough to see my parents making a sight of themselves in front of everybody?'

'But Peter, they aren't! They dance too sweetly.'

Mr Middleton junior laughed.

'You'll have to one day, you know,' Miss Paynton told him.

'I'll wait until I marry, then.'

'What for?'

'Well, my father did.'

'I thought you were like me,' the girl complained. 'Still everything my parents aren't.'

'You know I'd only make you look a fool, Ann. I've never even had lessons.'

'I might just want to see Campbell for a minute. Please Peter!'

'You'll get plenty of chances later on,' this boy told the girl, and finished his second shandy.

'Then how about some champagne?' Miss Paynton suggested, looking at her empty glass.

'You can't want to, before it's cold!'

'Now look, Peter. It's me who's going to drink the stuff, isn't it?'

'Oh all right! If you will wish to be different, I'll get a waiter,' and the boy turned to look behind him.

'No, you pour.'

Which he proceeded to do. Because he had not dried the bottle with a napkin, iced water began to drip on his thighs. She saw this.

'You'll get all wet!' she objected.

He laughed and said 'But I quite like that.'

'Yes, stuffy in here,' she agreed. Then she giggled. 'Such a fisherman, you can't do without cold water on your legs?' she asked, in a teasing voice.

'Damn sight better on a river than at one of these places,' she was answered.

At that, the tune having ended, the rest of their party returned.

'Champagne, gracious heaven! Arthur, you are doing us proud!' Charles said.

'All in darling Peter's honour,' Diana told him with a meaning look.

'And is he not going to be allowed any?' the man went on.

'Now Charles, behave yourself,' Mrs Middleton protested looking angrily at Claire.

'Can't stand the stuff, thank you,' Peter said.

At this there was one of those short pauses, into which Claire's voice soared.

'Just one of those girls who make her young men take her to the same restaurant each night only to show the waiters how many men she has,' she was saying to Charles.

'Oh, how people can change!' Ann moaned to Mr Middleton.

'Who? Me?' he demanded.

'Yes, I expect,' she answered. 'But I didn't exactly mean you this time.' Then Miss Paynton whispered to the man. 'No, it's Claire. Why, she's become absolutely revolting!'

'When, in the end, are they going to start?' Peter asked his mother.

'Who, darling?'

'Why, the wrestlers of course.'

'In their own good time, I suppose. Like everyone else.'

'And what is that supposed to mean?' her son almost disapprovingly rejoined.

'Oh, my dear!' Mrs Middleton answered. 'As you go on in life, I fear you'll find people come more and more only to consult their own convenience.'

'But if they're paid to appear?' Peter wanted to be reassured.

'Aren't we all, in one way or another, darling, being paid, the whole of the time? Take tonight. Don't we all have an obligation to your father because he is taking us out in this expensive place?'

'I haven't.'

'And nor you should,' his mother laughed. 'But these girls! D'you think they feel it?' Mrs Middleton said this into a clamour of conversation, so that she would probably not be overheard. 'D'you suppose anything means anything to them?'

'I don't know what you're talking about,' her son told her in a bored voice. 'Why don't you ask Father?'

'I will, at that. Darling!' she called across the table to her husband.

'My dear,' he almost shouted back. 'Ann here's just been telling me the most extraordinary piece of gossip.'

'I'm sure,' his wife dryly said. 'Come on then, let's have it.'

'You remember Charlie So and So,' the man went on delightedly. 'Who got rid of Dorothy in order to marry one of Ann's contemporaries? Well, now he's reduced to this . . .' and Mr Middleton retailed aloud some really quite scabrous details of the jealous life this couple led.

Diana beamed with obvious pleasure.

'Aren't some people utter idiots,' she cried.

'Charlie'd better look out for his health, then,' Mr Addinsell commented.

'Oh Arthur, you are a bore! After all, I told you not to say,' Ann grumbled.

'Darling, this is very nice champagne,' the wife told her husband.

'But I don't see this story of yours,' Claire expostulated to Miss Paynton 'I mean, does it get anywhere?'

'Only as far as one wants to, I suppose.'

Arthur Middleton laughed exaggeratedly.

'Good for you, Ann,' he crowed.

'Now, dear, there's quite enough of that,' his wife checked him.

'Can't one ever tell anything private any more?' Miss Paynton demanded, smiling.

'Oh I'm beginning to enjoy this!' Diana said, with an enchanted expression. She raised her glass again.

'Wonderful champagne,' Mr Addinsell announced, as he followed suit.

'No, just watch yourself, then! You know how terribly acid it can be for you,' Mrs Middleton warned.

'Oh surely,' the man complained. 'Just once in every so often?'

'I'm threatening you for your own good.'

'But, Di, no one can say I drink!'

'Who has?' she replied, taking another gulp.

At which all the lights were lowered, their table was lit by one small yellow cone aimed at them through a hole in the ceiling and below, on one side, the dance hall was turned, by more switches, to a deep, glowing violet. The wrestling arena was dead empty, darkened.

Charles Addinsell asked Diana 'Will you waltz?' She rose and the extremely soft expression on her face was lost as, in sailing to her feet, she escaped the faint light which was directed on their table.

'Ann?' Mr Middleton appealed.

So, in no time, Claire and Peter were left alone, which was the moment the waiters chose to serve melon all round.

'You never dance?' Miss Belaine enquired of the boy.

'No, I don't,' he rather nervously answered.

'Well, why should you, if you don't want.'

'That's exactly what I say.'

'Because if I keep to that, not being critical, if you understand me, it means I can do what I wish when I want, and no one can say a word of blame.'

'It kills me to dance,' Peter said in an indistinct voice.

'Why not,' Miss Belaine murmured, as she watched the dancers.

The cornices, the window embrasures had been decorated with what seemed to be rope fixed to the wall. This feature had, of course, disappeared in this new darkness. But then, just as Peter was starting on his melon, someone, obviously very late, turned another switch and all this, which had looked like rope, broke into colour from within, a pale rose, which framed everything.

'Oh God,' young Mr Middleton exclaimed.

'Would you like some of my champagne?'

He nodded, and drained her glass.

'Let me pour you some more,' he suggested.

'All right,' Miss Belaine agreed. 'There's a clean one on the next-door table and no one will notice your dirty glass in this light, even if somebody comes.'

This Peter did, and came back to what was now his goblet several times, when unobserved, later in the evening. This time he managed not to wet himself with iced water.

'Thanks a lot,' the girl said. They both watched the dancers circling below. No more was uttered for a time. Then hardly turning her head, she added,

'You might do one thing for me, though, Peter. I fancy I'm in Ann's bad books. If you see her beginning to start in on me try and head her off, will you? You know her so well.'

'All right, but why?'

Miss Belaine, however, did not explain, and, soon after this, the music stopped. Diana came back to the table with Charles much noisier than she had been when she was her husband's partner. And Ann was exuberant on Arthur's arm.

'Oh, poor Campbell,' she laughed.

'Why, my dear, doesn't he seem to be enjoying himself?' Mrs Middleton indulgently enquired.

The young lady smiled, then sighed.

'It wouldn't be fair to tell,' she said, straight at Arthur.

'I enjoyed that dance,' Charles Addinsell informed the mother.

'I truly love dancing with you, my dear,' she exclaimed, and then to all 'Oh, darlings isn't this becoming gay,' she cried out, in an exultant voice.

'Certainly is, Di. Haven't had an evening like it, not for ages,' Charles responded.

'We'll never have any wrestling,' Peter said, in despondent tones.

'My dear boy, of course there will be,' his father told him.

'But it's all dark!'

'What then? Don't you know all wrestling audiences stay in the bar till the last minute?'

'Do they?'

'Don't be tiresome, just when we're beginning really to enjoy ourselves.'

'Look Peter,' Miss Paynton suggested. 'You're way ahead of the others with your meal. Why don't you and I go down and see what the form is? I'm not hungry.'

'Not to dance.'

'I didn't even mean that. Let's find this bar?'

'You're not to have a drink there, mind,' his mother said.

'Come on, Peter,' Ann encouraged him, and they went.

'Like a nursemaid when the kid's crying and takes the sweet little creature behind a tree to wee-wee.'

Mrs Middleton laughed. 'Now Arthur, don't run the boy down. It's natural he should be disappointed.'

'Good champagne, this,' Charles announced.

'Good heavens, your glass is empty. Here, fill up. Well, you know, Di, I'm wondering if there is to be any tonight, when all's said and done.'

'Oh no, Arthur! After you promised those wrestlers to Peter?'

'But, if they are to show up, they're being a bit slow about it, surely?'

'In any case, he can't have everything. Now should he, Charles?' the mother said, using a suddenly bored voice.

'Got to learn to go without,' Mr Addinsell agreed.

'Charles, I believe you're only a great humbug,' Claire Belaine announced.

'How's that?'

'Well, I mean, you don't yourself lack for much, do you?'

Mr and Mrs Middleton exchanged a long look.

'Quite right, my dear,' Arthur guffawed. 'Go for the old hypocrite, why don't you?'

'I say, what's this?' Addinsell cried, in what was possibly mock dismay.

'Now, I can't have my dearest old Charles teased,' Diana said with a smile towards her husband. 'I just won't stand for it.'

'I wish I had the friends you seem to have,' Miss Belaine told the man.

'Here's how,' Middleton said, raising his glass to the girl.

They each of them drained theirs, which were at once filled again. And then, for no apparent reason, they all burst out laughing.

Giggling now, Mrs Middleton announced,

'And, oh my dears, I'd meant to say something to that young woman tonight!'

'Who, Ann?' her husband protested. 'Dearest, be careful. You'll get yourself into dire trouble.'

'Yes, I had. But knowing myself as I do, I don't suppose I will.'

'Did you?' Miss Belaine asked, with what was plainly intense interest. 'Oh good! What was it going to be?'

Mr Addinsell emptied his glass and then, unbidden, refilled it from the nearest bottle.

'I have my little plans at times,' Diana told the girl. 'And then I so seldom carry them out, which I'm inclined to regret, always!'

Addinsell hiccupped, almost pompously. 'Very wise,' he said.

'Charles!' Mrs Middleton gaily protested.

'Oh come on, now do!' Claire Belaine encouraged her.

'No, Di. Enough,' her husband said. 'Why, look who's back so soon,' he went on, of Ann and Peter, as they came up to the table.

'There isn't going to be any!' the boy accused them all.

'Any what?' his father demanded.

'Wrestling, of course.'

'But it's advertised, Peter.'

'I know! What can you do!'

'Oh well,' Charles Addinsell commented, and hiccupped once more. 'Bad luck, is all I say, bad luck!'

'Now Di, what could I?' her husband asked, in a high voice. 'With this in all the papers. And on the bills outside. Wasn't it, Ann?'

'I don't know. Oh, all right!' the girl agreed.

'Now you're not to be tiresome,' his mother told the young man.

'If there isn't to be any, there just won't be even one wrestler, that's all! When you've been having such a divine time in Scotland after salmon, I do think it's rather hard you should try and spoil our heavenly night out by wishing anyone, even anything, could be at all different.'

'I wasn't,' the son protested. 'Only you said . . .'

'Now Peter!' Mr Middleton warned. 'Don't try and put the blame on your mother when it's my fault.'

'In what way yours, darling?' his wife wanted to be told.

'There is a bar downstairs, but hardly a soul inside except for one or two old soaks,' Miss Paynton interrupted.

'Sounds interesting,' Charles announced. 'Come and dance, then you show me this place of yours.'

The young lady made no move.

'Why not take Claire, dear?' Mrs Middleton put forward with obvious malice. 'She's been sitting out up here for ages.'

'Come on then, somebody, for heaven's sake,' Mr Addinsell demanded, swaying on his feet.

'Oh very well,' Claire said. They left.

'He's dead drunk,' the boy pronounced.

'Now Peter,' Mr Middleton objected. 'Watch yourself before you cast adzpersions 'pon my guests!'

'Yes certainly, darling,' the wife backed up her husband. 'Since you've been out with that gillie you've simply become a bore, that's all!'

'I'm sorry. D'you think I could have some more shandy?'

'Another one?' his father cried. 'Won't that be your fourth?'

'No, I've only had two. And I took too much salt with this steak.'

'Oh, go on, Arthur,' his wife commanded. 'Why be so mean, on his last night?'

'I'm not, darling! But we don't want him drunk, do we?'

'Poor Peter,' Ann said. 'Not much fun for you, at this rate.'

'Now, please keep out of this!' Mr Middleton commanded Miss Paynton. 'Or rather, come and dance?'

'What!' his wife declaimed. 'And leave me here all by myself? My dear,' she went on to the girl 'I was just going to say something to your little friend she wouldn't forget in a hurry.'

'Oh good! What?'

'But Diana . . .' her husband warned.

'Yet, knowing myself as I do, I don't suppose I ever shall,' Mrs

334

Middleton continued. Then she paused to drink deeply from her glass. And all, except Peter, did likewise. The mother actually gasped.

'There's been the most extraordinary change in Claire, lately,' Miss Paynton told them, in confidential tones. 'I don't know if I can describe it, but she's become so ordinary, that's the only word.'

'You're telling me!' Mrs Middleton took the girl up, warmly. 'Yet, don't you think she always was a little bit, even?'

'It's my fault!' the young lady wailed. 'Always has been. One gets so taken in!'

'D'you think Charles is?' Mr Middleton wanted to be told.

'Would you say poor Charles could now be in a condition to tell his head from his toes?' Diana demanded.

At this all, except Peter, drained their glasses. Mr Middleton filled them up again.

'Let live, and let live,' he pronounced.

'Charles gets so tired,' the wife added.

'But he doesn't work, does he?' the girl asked.

'It's the boy of his,' Mr Middleton explained. 'Oh sorry, Peter. Of course he's years younger than you! Nine, I believe, in fact.'

'Oh God!' his son told him.

Ann Paynton, unseen, reached across and took his hand. But Peter shook her off.

'And Terence Shone?' he asked the girl.

'No don't mention him!' the young lady cried. 'He's out! I'll never once again speak to that baby-in-arms, ever! No offence to you, Peter, of course.'

'Yes, quite,' Middleton junior answered.

'Oh really, Peter!' his mother objected. 'When there isn't anyone at this table wouldn't give their eyes to be your age again.'

'I couldn't,' Miss Paynton told them.

'Oh well, my dear, you're different,' Mrs Middleton admitted, in a grudging voice. 'And long may you so be,' she added.

Meantime, on the floor below, Claire managed to dance with Charles Addinsell by holding him safe in her arms.

'Comin' back to my place afterwards?' he thickly enquired.

'You're dead tight,' she answered.

'Not so much so I can't see that friend of Ann's, the wet poet.'

Miss Belaine laughed. 'Good for you,' she said.

'No, but sheriously, Claire,' the man went on. 'There's something in this whole evening, you know. Domesticity, what?'

'How on earth d'you mean?'

'Only I might've been wrong when I said I'll never marry again, that'sh all.'

The girl giggled. 'And what's brought you to this?' she asked.

'Just being with old Arthur, and Di, out on this night out with their Peter. And you,' he added.

'Why is it special?'

'Don't sh'you shee it the way I do?' the man demanded. 'When I go out with my son we have to trail round the Zoo.'

'Yes, but one day he'll be older, Charles.'

'I dunno but sometimes you dishappoint me,' Mr Addinsell said. 'Impersheptive!'

'Now you are being rude, Charles darling,' the young lady answered in a glad tone of voice, which seemed to show she did not mind.

'Oh, I feel miserable suddenly,' Miss Paynton told Peter upstairs, and his father overheard.

'Why's that, because you mustn't be,' the man said.

'Well, Claire and everything.'

'You needn't go on apologizing for the girl. After all you never invited her tonight.'

'You mustn't, my dear, cry over spilt milk,' Mrs Middleton put in.

'Will you have some brandy, or something?' the husband asked.

'Oh, it's getting so late. I ought to be on my way home,' the girl answered.

'Now Arthur,' the wife and mother entreated. 'Not another word! I'm sure we've all had quite enough, and I don't want Charles to make any more of a fool of himself than he need.'

'How about you, Peter?'

'No thanks.'

At this moment the dance music stopped, and the players walked off, except for a drummer. A curtain went up and on to the stage came the identical conjuror Peter had watched on the first night of his holidays.

'Oh God!' he said.

Claire reappeared with Charles Addinsell, holding the man tight by the arm. He did not say a word. While Arthur paid the bill, the

336

girls thanked Mrs Middleton. Ann announced that she thought she wouldn't leave just yet, but sit below with Campbell for a bit. Then, while they awaited Claire and Diana outside the ladies' cloakroom, Charles did speak to Arthur, swaying a little,

'Will it be all right tomorrow, Arthur?'

'Of course,' the husband answered.

Soon after which, he left in a taxi with Miss Belaine, and the Middletons rode grumbling home.

The next day they all went on very much the same.

Blindness

Contents

to My Mother

Part one – Caterpillar

Laugh

Diary of John Haye, Secretary to the Noat Art Society, and in J.W.P.'s House at the Public School of Noat.

6 July (about)
It has only just struck me that a kind of informal diary would be rather fun. No driving as to putting down something every day, just a sort of pipe to draw off the swamp water. It has rained all the past week. We went to Henley yesterday and it was wretched: B. G. going off to Phyllis Court and leaving me with Jonson, an insufferable bore who means very well and consequently makes things much worse. Seymour went with Dore who was dressed in what would be bad form at Monte, and at Henley ¿¿. Had a row with Seymour, and refused to be seen with Dore.

Wonderful T. Carlyle's letters are, and his wife's too. One can always tell them at a glance. She is the best letter writer there has ever been, I am told by a modern authority. I should think T. C. runs this pretty fine, his explosive style going well into letters.

9 July
Two people in my absence just had a water fight in my room, which enraged me.

The usual question asked, 'Why not in anyone else's room?' and of course no answer: however, felt better after calling Brimston an animated cabbage. His retort was, 'Oh, cutting!' ¿¿.

Seymour, B. G. and I were seriously discussing the production of a revue here next term, as they do at the universities, but as Seymour said, the difficulties were insuperable, too many old men to surmount.

19 July
Walk with Seymour today, who was very charming. Fell in love with a transparent tortoiseshell cigarette case for three guineas, very

cheap I thought. He keeps his band of satellites in very good order. When he told them to leave the School Shop they did. They positively worship him. He is an extraordinary creature, I don't believe he could get on without them: keeping them as some people keep a dog, to let off steam at. A rift between Harington Brown and Seymour, very amusing to watch: H. B. much the same as Seymour but lacks his charm. Seymour furious because H. B. has brought out a bad magazine called the Shop Window. Seymour thinks it is a challenge to his precious Noat Lights. If it is one it is a failure.

Dicky Maitland, who used to try and teach me science, has been writing to the Adjer to say that my Volunteer's uniform is always untidy; the Adjer says he has had several notes: did you ever hear such cheek? But then the poor man is a military maniac.

As a matter of fact I ought to look quite well tomorrow on the occasion of the Yearly Inspection, as my tunic is nothing but oil stains, and everything else is sketchy and insecure.

J. W. P. told me last night that I was a person who wanted to fail at Noat and who thought (and only he knew how mistakenly) that he was going to be a success in after-life. A typically House-masterish thing to say. But then he was in a bad temper.

Later – Have just announced that I go to the dentist tomorrow so shan't be able to play in the House match that afternoon: frenzy; 'I call that rather a shame,' etc. Isn't it funny what a good player one becomes on a sudden?

The dentist tomorrow will be the third time he has tried to kill a nerve, and it isn't nearly dead now, but still fairly active.

Tremendous excitement over Hutchinson's coming novel, everyone trying to get a first edition.

Thursday
Corps Inspection: all went well.

Afterward I went up to the dentist, and in the train met Mayo who is leaving early. Had a long talk mainly about Seymour and Co. As might be expected he did not like him, but what was more to the point, produced a most interesting reason and unanswerable to a person who holds views like his. Firstly, then, he has no use for a person who is no good at anything. He tolerates the clever scholar, he tolerates the half-wit athlete, but since he cannot see that any of us are remotely even one of these, he cannot bear us as a set.

What adds fuel to his fire is a person who glories in his eccentricity, which of course is true of all of us, in that we glory in ourselves. And of course the inevitable immorality touched on, which is always connected with eccentricities.

B. G. of course he merely regards as really and actively evil, and I don't blame him as he does not know B. G., whose appearance is well calculated to sow the seeds of doubt and dislike in any righteous person. Furthermore, he can't see what good any of us are going to do in after-life. He said that he was going into the army, he trumpeted that, and then because we were alone together he put me out of the argument by saying that I should be a future financier.

I could not answer him, there was nothing further to say, but in the course of the running fire that we kept up afterwards just to show that there was no ill-feeling, he actually said that Seymour went up in his estimation because he had won his House hundred yards. Extraordinary! Very interesting, and, of course, a view which is almost incredible to me, in fact a great eye-opener.

Had to return in a hurry from the dentist who has given up trying to kill the nerve in my tooth. He prophesied what he called a 'sting' in it tonight: he under-estimated it considerably. It is hurting damnably.

21 July
Am reading a very good book on the Second Empire with Napoleon the Third. It is in the Lytton Strachey style, which after Carlyle's is, I think, the most amusing.

The Volunteers' Camp and all its attendant horrors is getting quite close now: though I could get off whenever I wanted to with my hammer-toes, but I want to go just for once.

22 July
Bell's, across the way, have bought as many as seven hunting-horns. Each possessor blows it unceasingly, just when one wants to read. They don't do it all together, but take it in turns to keep up one forced note. Really, it might be Eton. They can only produce the one note during the whole day.

In addition to this trifling detail, it is 'the thing to do' now to throw stones at me as I sit at my window. However, I have just called E. N. a 'milch cow,' and shall on the first opportunity call D. J. B. a 'bovine goat', which generally relieves matters. These epithets have the real authentic Noat Art Society touch, haven't they?

24 July

No Art Society this evening. No one turned up except H. B. who was to have read a paper; he was rather hurt. However, I think it will be all right, he has about as much admiration for the satellites as I have.

Am too tired to do anything but write this. The House rather alarmed and faintly contemptuous to hear I keep this; they have given me up, I think and hope. Rather a funny thing happened while fielding this afternoon. I had thrown myself down to stop a ball and I saw waving specks in my eyes for two minutes afterwards. I suppose my blood pressure was disturbed.

'For those in danger on the sea' is at the moment being sung by Truin's at House prayers.

26 July

J. W. P. came in last night to say that I had bad reports, everyone saying that I took no trouble, which is not surprising on both sides of the question: says that next term I shall have to do all my work in his study with the half-wits, a song which I have heard before, I think, though it is so encouraging coming at the end of a term's boredom.

Camp at Tidworth will be delightful in this soaking weather.

27 July

Have bought the most gorgeous sun hat for a horse in straw for sixpence, and have painted it in concentric rings. Shall wear it at Camp, and have fixed it up so that it will bend when worn like a very old-fashioned bonnet. In the ear-holes I am going to put violently swearing colours, orange and magenta, in ribbon I got for nothing by being nice to a shop-woman at Bowlay's. Our little John is getting on, isn't he?

The hat is a masterpiece, and being so has, of course, started a violent controversy. Those who consider it merely bounderism, and those who think it amusing, talk very seriously together and stop when I approach, while the faithful come in occasionally to tell me what the others have said.

The most beautiful letter ever written is undoubtedly that of Charlotte Brontë's on her sister Emily's death.

28 July

No more work till the summer holidays. Have been relegated by the House selection committee to the dud tent at Camp, which amuses

346

me vastly. Apparently those who manage the affairs of the tent prefer Bulwer and Matson to myself; more amusing still. Shall I get elected into the Reading Room next term? Probably not. I think as a matter of fact they want a mobbing tent which they know I would not join in, anyhow I shall be much more comfortable as I am: at any rate that reads better, and sounds so for that matter.

Apparently I shall get attacked if I wear my straw hat, a fact I can hardly believe. I have had the most heated arguments as to why I should not wear fancy dress; the fact remains that people are more prim and hidebound there than here, except that, as far as I can see, all and sundry combine to be rude to other schools.

29 July
A sing-song in the Hall to-night, to which everyone but myself has gone: didn't go for two reasons; first, because the cinema part of it was certain to be lamentable; secondly, Fryer irks me when he sings songs, and the applause he gets, for no other reason than that he is everything at games, and so is profitable to applaud, maddens me.

What is bad is that this school tends to turn the really clever into people who pretend for all they are worth to be the mediocrities which are the personification of the splendid manhood phrase. And in the end these poor people succeed and lose all the brains they ever had, which is distressing, particularly for me who could do with a few more.

Sunday
Sing-song apparently a great success. There is an auction going on now, everything that has been handed down through the ages is being resold. I suppose some pictures have seen about forty auctions: the commonest are Thorburn's petrified partridges, or worse still, those most weird and antiquated pictures of horse-racing, the horse's neck being the length of its body.

Social ostracism which I am experiencing now for the first time for many terms is really incredibly funny. It begins with a studied vagueness when you address anyone, which means that he is frightened at being seen talking to you: it goes on, in direct ratio to the number of jaws they have about you, to a studied rudeness, and the lower and younger you are the more your room is mobbed. And then the whole thing blows over you on to some other unfortunate.

I suppose I have been rather tiresome lately, but all except T. D.

and possibly E. N. are so distressingly the athletic type, who sink their whole beings in the school and its affairs, and are blind and almost ignorant of any world outside their own.

31 July

The last flourish before Camp.

My room is a sight for the gods, piles and stacks of clothing to be packed, a bulging pot-bellied kit-bag filled with changes of clothing for the ten days' horror, everything upside down, and over all the frenzied maid as near suicide as she ever gets: her chief job is to look for lost garments, and as she regards me with the deepest suspicion over a pair of tennis shoes, I am not left long alone. The storm in the Chinese tea-service had died down, and once more I am anchored precariously outside the haven of the barely tolerated.

I hear that the only hotel where one can get a bath in Camp has been put out of bounds, which is delightful. How furious Mamma will be: apparently the reason is that people used to drink there.

In Camp: 2 August

Just a scrawl. It has been raining viciously as if with a purpose. At the moment I am lying on what is affectionately known as a 'palliarse'. Underneath is deal planking. Underneath that is a torrent as we are on a hill and the accumulated effects of two days' rain are flowing beneath. Above is a bell tent, long since condemned by the army authorities as unsound, so that the cloudburst which is pouring from Heaven penetrates freely. There is one spot under which lies Brown, the world's greatest grouser, and it is appropriately thread-bare. He was foolish enough to put soap on it; we had told him that if you soaped a bit of cloth it became waterproof, and now soapsuds drip down on to his face. We have also told him that his grousing is intolerable, and will be dealt with unless he suppresses it, so that he lies in a misery too deep for words, and is the only thing that keeps us happy.

There are, of course, rumours about our going home on account of the wet, but such a good thing could not possibly happen.

The food and the smell of grease in the eating tent are both very foul. The smell I was warned against by an old campaigner. Thank God my turn has not yet come for washing up, but I shall have to do it tomorrow. They are thinking themselves the most awful devils in the next tent with a bottle of port; perhaps if I had one I should feel one too.

Holidays: 11 August
The village fête here yesterday, and after a three forty-five awakening, reveille or whatever you like to call it, at Tidworth, I had to run about here when I arrived and be officious to all and sundry. An awful thing happened. It was towards the end when I was so tired I could hardly see. Mamma told me to go and find the young lady who ran the Clock Golf Competition and tell her to send in the names of the prize-winners. The young ladies who ran things were all surprisingly alike, disastrously so, and there were many of them. I went up to a girl I was sure had run the Clock Golf, and I asked her if she had done so. No answer. Again I asked, and again no answer. Somehow I felt only more sure from her silence that she had run it, so I asked her yet again, and more eagerly. There was no answer, but there came a blush like a banner which rallied all her friends to her, to protect her from the depredations of this young man. After that I hid myself in the house. I know what the neighbourhood will make of my reputation now. Mamma laughed; I have never heard her laugh so much before.

I have got the most vile and horrid 'bedabbly' cold – Carlyle again. Had one or two highbrow talks with Seymour in a small canteen with two cubic feet air-space for each savage human, which was rather wonderful.

29 August
I fished today and 'killed' two tiddlers, one was a minnow, and such a small one at that that I thought it too infinitesimal even for the stable cat. That was a record broken, if in the wrong direction.

Mamma tonight on religion. What effect it had, and how far it went, at Noat? They are effectively stifling mine.

During dinner I saw a man run across the bottom of the garden, so when it was over I took the dogs, and with an eye to theatrical effect I put the bulldog on a leash, and led him snorting, pulling, panting and roaring round the garden. He made just the noise, on a minor scale, that one is led to believe a dragon made. William waited with Father's revolver loaded with blank, awaiting a scream from me if I was attacked. He looked too ludicrous, with a paternal smile on his face.

2 September

To my mind there is nothing so thrilling as the rushing, hungry rise the chub have here; it makes me tingle even now to think of it, and the more spectators on the bank watching, after you have hooked your fish, the better.

At the present Mamma is in a great state over someone on the Town Council of Norbury. After swearing me to secrecy she told me all about it, and I have forgotten. But the main thing is that she has her suspicions only and no proof, but that, of course, only makes her more sure. But she had a splendid speech in the middle about dishonesty on town councils when she was at her best. But I wish she would not take these things so seriously. She expects me to too, and when I don't, she says, 'Ah! you are too young, John dear.'

9 September

Mamma not sleeping, so Ruffles, the chow, passed the night in my room, which he disliked intensely, so much so that when he did eventually doze off distrustfully, he had what is a rare thing with him, a nightmare of the most alarming and noisy order. I hope this Town Council business is not really keeping Mamma awake. Probably the wretched devil is quite innocent. It would be quite like Mamma to go up to him and accuse him of it. But then she couldn't.

Caught seven fish yesterday, which wasn't so bad. They were rising well.

Noat, Friday, 29 September

Back to the old place again, and very depressed in consequence: however, I am now a full-blown specialist in history, and am allowed to send small boys on errands as I am one of the illustrious first hundred in the school. But the football is going to be awful.

I came back on Wednesday. As usual, nothing is changed in the least: Bell's opposite have discarded their hunting-horns of accursed memory for an accordion and a banjo, just as painful.

What with the accordion and the cold and the noise and the discomfort and Cole, who I am up to in history, this has ceased to be a life and has become a mere existence. However, the outlook is always black at the beginning of the term.

Later – An excellent meeting of the Art Society: very amusing. There was a grand encounter between Seymour and Harington Brown and B. G.'s unrivalled powers of invective were used with great effect. His face, his voice, everything combines to make him a most formidable opponent in wordy warfare.

1 October
Since all my contemporaries spend all their time in the Senior Reading Room with a newly-acquired gramophone, I am left alone and undisturbed, which is very pleasant. Am feeling much more cheerful now, which I attribute to a cup of hot tea.

Am keeping up all the traditions by being the only person in the school with a greatcoat on. Why is it that when there is the hardest and most bitter frost no one wears a greatcoat here? I think it is so absurd, and get rewarded for my pains by catching reproving glances from the new boys, who, of course, are ultra careful, so much as to say, 'You are making an ass of yourself with that coat on.'

Seymour and B. G. are going to give the most immense and splendiferous leaving party, which is going to be wild fun.

3 October
This morning an outrage: I am eating my morning bun, given to me for that purpose by J. W. P., when my tooth meets a stone, and half of it is broken off clean. Result, an immense jagged cavity which I shall have filled, at J. W. P.'s expense, with platinum, and set with brilliants. I am furious.

Brown, a friend of mine, has hit Billing, who keeps the food shop where you get rat poison, in the stomach so that he crumpled up behind the counter: the best thing that has happened for years.

Billing had apparently hit Brown previously, and had sent him to the Headmaster for being rude, and he, instead of backing Billing up, had asked Brown why he had not hit him back: so when Billing hit Rockfeller today, Rockfeller being with Brown, Brown was rude to Billing, who attacked Brown, who laid Billing out. Meanwhile Brown has gone to his House master to ask that Billing's shop may be put out of bounds, and Billing presumably is going to the Headmaster. There will be a fine flare-up.

6 October
Rejoice, O land! My director on seeing my first essay, and a bad one at that, tells me I ought to do well with my writing. What fun it would be if I could write! I see myself as the English Anatole France, a vista of glory . . . superb!

I have fallen hopelessly in love with the ties in Bartlett's window. I shall have to buy them all, even though they are quite outrageous: the most cunning, subtle and violent checks imaginable.

Sunday, 8 October

This morning we had a howling dervish of a missioner who comes once a year. All his ghastly stories were there and his awful metaphors and his incredible requests. In this morning's sermon he asked us to give his mission a vision; last time it was that we should pray for it, and before that, that we should give up our holidays to work there. Today we were told that even cabbages had visions, and God knows what else. He was upset by our laughing at him and he broke down several times, Chris crowning himself with glory by going out in the middle of the man's discourse clasping a pink handkerchief to his nose which he said was bleeding. Really the pulpit is no place for self-revelation, but I am afraid the man has not learnt it yet.

9 October

Two youths have been insolent to me in the Music Schools. Am I considered the school idiot? If so I am not surprised; any way I was most polite to them – next time measures will be taken. The best way with these people is to ask them their names; it generally shuts them up. I believe my appearance is too weak; I shall have to grow mustachios. I am always the person the lost Asiatic asks his way from, and French come to me as fly to fly-paper, ditto the hysterical matron. Such is fame.

12 October

Guy Denver tells me the following: It is extremely cold, and he and Conway are walking together. Says Conway, 'God, I am cold!' Guy: 'Then why don't you wear an overcoat?' 'Oh! then I should be classed with the John Haye and Ben Gore lot.' That is what the fear of popular opinion drives the ordinary Public Schoolboy to; that sort of thing is constantly recurring like the plague.

15 October

This afternoon a delicious six-mile walk with B. G. The weather was perfect, a warm sun and everything misty, with 'the distances very distant', as Kipling puts it. Though we did not rock the world with our utterances, it was very enjoyable indeed.

20 October

Greene has ordered several chickens' heads, lights, etc., to be sent up to White, which we hope will be a nice surprise. It is rather a good idea.

Have been painting a portrait of Napoleon, cubist and about three foot square, with B. G., who has got it as a punishment from a new master. He will soon lose that most refreshing originality. Moreover he said that B. G. was not to do anything comic, which showed that he was already beginning to lose it. It just depends how much the others have instilled into him to see his manner of receiving our glaring monstrosity.

New phrase I have invented: 'To play Keating's to someone else's beetle.' Used with great success on Seymour who is enraged by it.

21 October

This morning, so I am told, Seymour and B. G. dragged a toy tin motor car along the pavement on the end of a string. How I wish I had been there: it is quite unprecedented, and seems to have outraged the dignity of the whole school, which is excellent.

Seymour created another sensation by quoting his own poetry for today's saying lesson, which caused much amusement. Everyone who matters athletically now thinks it is the thing to do to know Seymour, which is intensely funny, and into the bargain I feel I get a little reflected glory when I walk with him down the street. The Captain of the Rugger smiled at me the other day. I nearly spat in his face (but of course I really smiled my nicest).

Have written to several artists to ask them to talk to the Society. When we founded it we put in the rules that we must get men down to speak to it; it is the only way of keeping the thing alive. And I think if we can get someone down the Society will recover from its present rather dicky condition.

25 October

Have just had a letter from the biggest swell I wrote to, saying that he will come down to the Society on 14 November. It really is too splendid: he is the most flaming tip-top swell who has written thousands of books, as well as his drawings, which are very well known indeed. All these people are so nice and encouraging about the Society, which is splendid.

31 October

I am seventeen now – quite aged.

Last night was the gala invitation night of the Society, and was an immense success, where I had secretly feared failure.

All those invited came – all the boys, all the masters, and all today I have been hearing nothing but how pleased and interested they were. It was on Post-Impressionism, a subject which had the merit of being one which the Society knew more about than anyone else present. B. G. made the most gorgeous speech of pure invective which enthralled everyone. The Society is now positively booming, even T. R. C. having thawed into enthusiasm. I think it is a permanency now.

Fires on alternate nights now, which isn't so very, very bad, and the weather is slowly improving. Extraordinary how the weather affects my spirits. I had a telegram from Mamma who had remembered my birthday, which is splendid, for somehow I hate its being forgotten. She never remembers till Nan reminds her. But the football, it is enough to kill one.

Would you believe it – but J. W. P. gave me a long jaw on the 'hopelessness' of my having a bad circulation, because I habitually wore a sweater underneath my waistcoat: it's a filthy habit, I know, but he drives one on to it with his allowance of fires, and then he tries to blame one: it is an outrage.

1 November

It is freezing again, bad luck to it.

B. G. and I in the morning went up to Windsor and got some electioneering pamphlets from the Committee Rooms, and have posted them all over Noat, including the Volunteers' Notice Board and the School Office and the Library. Later I put them up all over the House notice boards, which scored a glorious rise out of 'those that matter'. These people are really too terribly stodgy; they have no sense of humour, though they did faintly appreciate the pamphlet on the maids' door which said that Socialism was bent on doing away with marriage.

This afternoon I had to read fifty pages of medieval history, which has left my brain reeling and helpless: it is too absurd making one learn all about these fool Goths and Vandals: they ceased to count in practical politics some time ago now, so why revive them?

11 November
Have just conceived the idea of having a gallery of all the people I loathe most at Noat to be pasted up on the door of my room, which has been denuded of the rules of the Art Society since I spent a frenzied afternoon changing the room slightly.

Smith, the master, crosses his cheques with a ruler. One comes across something amazing every day here.

This is the coldest day I have ever met at Noat, and a very thick fog thrown in, greatly conducive to misery, but strangely enough I am most cheerful, having written a tale called Sonny, which is by far the best I have done so far.

15 November
Quite the most wonderful day of my life. It was polling day, so after two o'clock (a saying lesson so we got out early), B. G., Seymour and I went to Strand caparisoned all over with Conservative blue and with enormous posters.

When we reached Strand, we found all the Socialist working-men-God-bless-them drawn up in rows on either side of the street, so we three went down the rows haranguing. We each got into the centre of groups, and expected to be killed at any moment, for there is something about me that makes that type see red. However, they contained themselves very nicely while we talked nonsense at them.

Then we went to the station and got a cab, and with B. G. on the box and Seymour and I behind we set off, B. G. with posters stuck through his umbrella, and dead white from excitement. We went by the by-ways shouting and screaming till we came to the top of the High Street. We then turned down this; by this time all of us were worked up and quite mad, and eventually came to the Cross again, where we passed the Socialists who were collected in a meeting. They cheered and hooted, and we went round the same way only shorter, and after going down the High Street, turned down towards Noat, where we soon picked up six or so Noatians. With them we returned, some running, with a rattle making a deafening din. We passed the Labour and Socialist meeting on the 'Out' road of the railway station, and went over the railway bridge, where we paid off the cab. We then returned in a body past the meeting, which broke up and followed across the crossroads, pelting us with rolled-up rags, etc. Then at the corner of the road to Noat we formed a meeting. I was terrified at moments, and wildly exhilarated the rest. The meeting lasted twenty minutes, questions being asked the whole time. B. G. did most of the speaking; Seymour and I did a little too. Woodville harangued the women; he was very good with them. They had their spokesman, an old labourer, very tub-thumpy, and the whole of this part of the entertainment is a blur. Looking round in the middle of it I saw that all the Conservative men and women were formed up behind us, which was touching. All this time messages were coming from the fellows on the outside that the people there were talking lovingly of murder (on us), and matters did look very nasty at one time, but it worked off. The police came at the end with an inspector and marched us off, I shaking every man's hand that I could see. So we returned shouting madly. It was too wonderful; never to be forgotten.

16 November

I now understand why men were brave in the war; it was because they were afraid of being cowards, that fear overcoming that of death. The crowd in Strand and having to go back into it again and have things thrown at one – it was terrifying at first for so great a coward as myself, but great fun when one got hotted up. The women were by far the worst. One old beldame screamed: 'You dirty tykes, you dirty tykes!' continuously.

Later – Another wonderful time. I went with Seymour up to the market-place of the town of Noat, outside the Town Rooms, and there we had another stormy meeting. I talked a very great deal this time; Bronsill and I went on the whole time to rather an excited crowd. Then he and I were dragged off and put on a balcony where the Press photographed us, and he addressed the crowd and I prompted him and hear-heared, etc. I would have spoken had there been time, but lunch arrived and we departed. It was too wonderful; it is tremendous fun being above a crowd, about 150 this time, and I wasn't a bit nervous. Nor was I terrified when the crowd became nasty again as on the previous day; it is the most exhilarating thing I know – far better than hunting. Meanwhile, a master saw me and J. W. P. knows. What will happen?

17 November

Nothing happened with J. W. P.; he didn't mind, and was vastly amused.

Have written another story all about blood; not impossibly bad but sadly mediocre. If only I could write! But I think I improve. Those terrible, involved sentences of mine are my undoing.

Fox was pleased at my admiring Carlyle.

18 November

Harington Brown asked me for an MS. for the magazine he is producing: gave him Sonny, but don't suppose it will be suitable, though I am sure it has some worth. The thing is only about 1400 words, and when he refuses it I am going to send it up to some London magazine which will take very short stories, and at present I don't know of one.

I rather hope that H. B. won't accept the thing. The ephemerals are always putrescent, and nobody with any sense reads them. There have been about three editions of it so far, one a term.

19 November, after lunch

Have been accepted by H. B., with mixed feelings on my part. However, his thing is a cut above the usual ephemeral and is quite sensible, but there is a sense of degradation attached to appearing in print. But I hope this means that I can write; it's not bad work as I'm only just seventeen. Perhaps it is too good, and I shan't do anything again.

Carlyle's flight to Varennes in his Revolution is almost too painful to read, so exciting is it to me. It is all untrue, of course, they did not go half as slow as he would make out, nevertheless it is superb.

Thank God there are only a few more weeks of this football.

Noat, 26 January

What a long interval, and what a very little has happened! The holidays were enlivened by two deaths in the village, which much excited Mamma, and one or two scandals in the neighbourhood, which she followed carefully without taking up sides.

The bulldog died, which was very sad; he was such a dear old thing. Mamma was very much upset about that too, in her funny way. She seems to spend more and more time in the village now, and to see less and less people. One comes back here looking forward to the fullness of the place.

We came back yesterday, and I feel absolutely lost without B. G. and Seymour, who have both left. They do make a gap, for we three understood each other, and we ladled out sympathy to each other when life became too black. And now I am alone, in a hornets' nest of rabid footballers.

At the moment I am reading Gogol's Dead Souls. His word-pictures are superb: better than Ruskin's or Carlyle's, and his style is so terse and clean-cut, at least it is in the translation, but it shines through that. I am an absolute slave. I shall keep this book for ever by me if I have enough cash to buy it with. He is wonderful.

He is at his best, I think, in description; I have met nothing like it. Almost he ousts Carlyle; not quite, though. He is a poet through and through.

29 January

But surely this is most beautiful:

The trills of a lark fall drop by drop down an unseen aéry ladder, and the calls of the cranes, floating by in a long string, like the ringing notes of silver bugles, resound in the void of melodiously vibrating ether.

He is a poet: and his book is in very truth a poem. It is Gogol.

30 January

Am reading Winston Churchill's biography of his father, which is very wonderful.

I hardly remember B. G. as having existed now. That doesn't mean to say that I don't answer his letters, but life goes on much the same.

Did I say that I had become the budding author at home? No, I think not. I have written in all three things, so that I am hailed as a Napoleon of literature. Such is fame. I only wish I deserved these eulogies, and must set seriously to work soon. Mrs Conder most of all seems impressed. Talks at tea of nothing but where she can take me to get 'copy' – which means Brighton, I suppose; not that horrid things don't happen there, though. But she is the limit. Since Conder died she has blossomed. At least, when he was alive, one could make allowances for her, because he was so foul, but now there is nothing to say. She is so gay, so devilish gay! But all this is very untrue, unkind and ungrateful. In all she has given me £5 in tips, and a cookery book for Boy Scouts.

17 February

In a moment of rash exuberance I bought a cigarette-holder about eight inches long. Have been smoking it all the afternoon. Caused quite a sensation in the middle-class atmosphere of the tea shop chez Beryl.

Am delivering an oration to the Arts Society on Japanese Art. I am going to speak it and not read it, which is bravery carried to foolhardiness. But it is good to get a little practice in speaking.

22 February

Just been to dinner with the Headmaster. I was put next him and occupied his ear for twenty minutes. In the course of that time I managed to ask for a theatre for the school to act in, and for a school restaurant where one could get a decent British steak with onions, and, if possible, with beer. I also advanced arguments in favour of this. The only thing we agreed on was the sinfulness of having a window open. He listened to it all, which was very good of him.

On Monday I got off my speech on Japanese Art all right, I think, save for the very beginning, which was shaky to a point of collapse. Tomorrow I go to tea with Harington Brown. Meanwhile at the tea Dore gave we arranged that the Art Society should give a marionette show. The authorities agreed the next day and gave us the Studio. Someone is busy writing the scenario, about lovers thwarted whose names end in io. Then we shall paint scenery. It will be such fun. Of course the figures will be stationary.

The only modern Germans who could paint are Lembach and Boechel.

24 February

Had tea with H. B. I have sent him a story for this term's Noat Days. It won't be accepted, I suppose. It is an experiment in short sentences. He read me the libretto of the marionettes as far as he had got, and it really was remarkably good. He is producing it in his ephemeral.

10 March

This morning occurred one of those incidents which render school life at moments unbearable to such as myself. I was raising a spoon-ful of the watered porridge that they see fit to choke us with, when someone jerked my arm – The puerility of it all, yet a wit which I, for my years, should enjoy according to nature. Of course there was a foul mess, as of one who had vomited, mostly over me. However, it only took an hour or so to regain my equanimity. Incidentally I had a little ink-throwing exhibition in the fool's room. I had always wanted to see the exact effect of throwing a paint brush at the wall to appreciate Ruskin's criticism. It was most interesting.

Later – What an odious superior fellow I am now! It is my mood tonight. Sometimes I think it is better to be just what one is, and not be everlastingly apologizing for oneself in so many words. To be rude when you want to be rude – and how very much nicer it would make you when you wanted to be nice. I am sure it is all a matter of relative thought. You think you are working hard by your standards, and to another man you don't seem to be working at all. Don't you work just as hard as the other really? Because, after all, it is only a mental question. I shall expound this to J. W. P. I have already done so to Gale with rather marked success. It is a very good principle at Noat.

11 March

I wish the world was not so ugly and unhappy. And there is so much cynicism. And why does Science label and ticket everything so that the world is like a shop, with their price on all the articles? There are still a few auction rooms where people bid for what they think most worth while, but they are getting fewer and fewer. And people love money so, and I shall too I expect when I have got out of what our elders tell me is youthful introspection. But why shouldn't one go through something which is so alive and beautiful as that? But they only say, smiling, 'Yes; I went through all that once; you will soon get over that.' I shall fight for money and ruin others. Down with Science. Romanticism, all spiritual greatness is going. Soon music will be composed by scientific formulae; painting has been in France, and look how photography has put art back. Oh, for a Carlyle now! Some prophet one could follow.

15 March

Spent a whole afternoon at work on the marionette stage. I carpentered while E. V. C. tinkered up the scenes he has painted. Between us we got through surprisingly little in a surprisingly long time.

My story in the new Noat Days will appear shortly. I read the proofs of the story at extreme speed and thought I had never read anything worse or feebler. The paltry humour sickened me, though the end did seem to have some kick in it.

19 March

The marionette show becomes more and more hectic. One hardly has time to breathe. There is a performance on Saturday: the day after the day after tomorrow. Nothing done, of course, and the Studio a scene of hysterical budding artists, mad enough in private life, but when under the influence of so strong and so public an emotion surpass themselves in do-nothing-with-the-most-possible-noise-and-trouble.

1 April

The marionette play continues to be an immense pleasure. We give a children's performance tomorrow at three. Answers from mothers pour in: I am afraid it may be too full. How well do little children see? They are so very low down when they sit. I think the life of a stage manager must be one of the most trying on this earth.

Good Friday

On a Pretty Woman, 'And that infantile fresh air of hers' (from Browning).

'If you take a photograph of a man digging, in my opinion he is sure to look as if he were not digging' (Van Gogh). Have been reading Van Gogh's letters. They are the hardest things I have ever taken on. He is so very much in earnest, and so very difficult to understand. I think I have got a good deal of what he means.

A wonderful postcard from B. G. in Venice:

We are here till Thursday, wondering who has won the Boat Race, the National, the Junior School Quarter-Mile and the Hammersmith Dancing Record.

Read a little Carlyle to a few of the House. What else could it be but incomprehensible to them? 'Mad,' they called it. Anything of genius is 'mad' in a Public School. And rightly so, I suppose.

4 April

One day more to the end of the term. How nice it will be to be back, to start life again for a day or two. The holidays are disgustingly short, though, only three weeks and a bit.

We have just given our third and last performance of the marionette play. It has been a wild success and should, if possible, be repeated. But the light in the summer would be too strong and everyone leaves at the end of next summer, so I don't suppose we shall have enough people to get one up next winter.

Oh, for tomorrow to go quickly!

Holidays: 10 April

Back again to peace, even if it is cotton wool and stagnation, but very pleasant all the same. Am reading George Moore's Ave with considerable relish and amusement. He is so very witty.

My reports have come in and are uninteresting: no one very enthusiastic, which is not to be wondered at.

20 April

'Polygamy is a matter of opinion, not of morality.' Montague Glass is undoubtedly the greatest comedian of letters. Potash and Perlmutter is superb.

At dinner tonight Mamma informed me in one of her rare pronouncements on myself, that I always kept people at arm's length. It sounds an awful thing to write, but I seldom meet anyone who interests me more than myself: my own fault, I suppose.

We have acquired a gramophone, and Strauss' 'Last Waltz' has bewitched me. It is such a lovely thing.

Noat, 4 May

Back to it again: good old Noat, bloody place! Have just seen a book entitled Up Against it in the Desert, which sufficiently describes my feelings at the moment.

It is so hot as to make writing impossible as my pen and style testify. I shall play no cricket this term, but will just read. I can get off the cricket on the score of health, which becomes increasingly bad. Last holidays we went from doctor to doctor. They look on one as an animal of a certain species, those people, than which nothing is more irritating.

5 May

The weather continues to be quite lovely. I pass the afternoon watching the cricket, with a book. It is the nicest thing to do I know. This evening I went on the river. What is it that is so attractive in the sound of disturbed water? The contrast of sound to appearance, perhaps. Water looks so like a varnished surface that to see it break up, move and sound in moving is infinitely pleasing. Also it is exhilarating to see an unfortunate upset.

I must work hard at writing. There are all sorts of writers I have never read; Poe, for instance, the master of the suggestive. I think my general reading is fairly good, but I have such an absurd memory.

2 June

Two portraits of me in the Noat Art Society Summer Exhibition. Not very good, but both striking.

29 September

Many things have come to pass since I last wrote in this. A distinguished literary gent has been kind enough to pay me a little praise for my efforts at literature. I am in the Senior too, now, and in the middle of writing a play that I cannot write. It is sticking lamentably. One last thing. They have given me a different room, and have put a new carpet into the new room for luck. And this smells rather like a tannery. Consequently I am being slowly poisoned. 'Ai vai!'

12 October

Really, Noat is amazing. Last night the President of the Essay Society, who is a master, wrote to ask me to join it. I refused; I am sick of Societies. This evening J. W. P. sends for me, and tells me he has heard about it and that I must join. Compulsion. Think of it — being made to join! Of course I can't go now. I shall join formally and never look at it. It is extraordinary.

Am reading Crime and Punishment by Dostoievsky. What a book! I do not understand it yet. It is so weird and so big that it appals me. What an amazing man he was, with his epileptic fits which were much the same as visions really.

20 October

About a week ago I finished Crime and Punishment. It is a terrible book, and has had a profound effect. Technically speaking, it is badly put together, but it cuts one open, tragedy after tragedy, like a chariot with knives on the wheels. The whole thing is so ghastly that one resents D. harrowing one so. And then it ends, in two pages. But what a finale! Sonia, too, what she suffered. And the scene when she read the Bible.

I have tried to read The Idiot, and have finished Fathers and Sons, by Turgeniev, but it was a dream only. It is a most dreadful, awful, supremely great book, this Crime and its Punishment. And the death scene, with her in the flaming scarlet hat, and the parasol that was not in the least necessary at that time of day. With the faces crowding through the door, and the laughter behind. What a scene! And the final episode, in Siberia, by the edge of the river that went to the sea where there was freedom, reconciliation, love.

What a force books are! This is like dynamite.

Extract from a letter written by B. G. to Seymour.

Sat., 7 April

'Dear Seymour,
'An awful thing has happened. John is blinded. Mrs Haye, his
stepmother, you know, wrote a letter from Barwood which reached
me this morning. The doctors say he hasn't a chance of seeing again.
She has asked me to write to all his school friends and to you. It is a
terrible story. Apparently he was going home after Noat had "gone
down," on Thursday, that is. The train was somewhere between
Stroud and Gloucester, and was just going to enter a cutting. A small
boy was sitting on the fence by the line and threw a big stone at the
train. John must have been looking through the window at the time,
for the broken glass caught him full, cut great furrows in his face,
and both his eyes are blind for good. Isn't it dreadful? Mrs Haye
says that he suffers terribly. It is a tragedy. Blindness, the most . . .'
etc.

Part two — Chrysalis

1 News

Outside it was raining, and through the leaded window panes a grey light came and was lost in the room. The afternoon was passing wearily, and the soft sound of the rain, never faster, never slower, tired. A big bed in one corner of the room, opposite a chest of drawers, and on it a few books and a pot of false flowers. In the grate a weary fire, hissing spitefully when a drop of rain found its way down the chimney. Below the bed a yellow wardrobe over which large grain marks circled aimlessly, on which there was a full-length glass. Beyond, the door, green, as were the thick embrasures of the two windows green, and the carpet, and the curtains.

The walls were a neutral yellow that said nothing, and on them were hung cheap Italian crayon drawings of precocious saints in infancy. The room was called the Saints' Room. Behind the glass of each were hundreds of dead flies, midges, for the room had a strange attraction for these things in summer, when the white ceiling would be black with them by sunset. With winter coming on they would creep away under the glass to pine on attendant angel lips. Perhaps the attraction was rather the hot-water cistern that was under the roof just above, and which gave a hint of passion to the virgin white-wash.

He lay in bed, imagining the room. To the left, on the dressing-table by the bed, would be the looking-glass that would never stay the right level. It would be propped up with a book, so that it gazed blandly up at the ceiling, mimicking the chalky white, and waiting for something else to mimic. On the chair between table and bed was sitting the young trained nurse, breathing stertorously over a book.

There came quick steps climbing stair carpet, two quick steps at the top on the linoleum, and the door opened. Emily Haye came in. She was red, red with forty years' reckless exposure to the sun. Where neck joined body, before the swift V turned the attention to the mud-coloured jumper knitted by herself, there glowed a patch of skin turned by the sun to a deeper red. She was wearing rough tweeds, and she was smelling of soap, because it was near tea-time.

He turns his head on the pillow, the nurse rises, and Mrs Haye walks firmly up the room.

'Well, how are you?'

'All right, thanks.'

'I'll sit by him for a bit, nurse, you go and get your tea. It's rainin' like anything outside. I went for a walk, got as far as Wyleman's barn, and there I turned and came back. Stepped in and saw Mrs Green's baby. It's her first, so she's making a fuss of it; beautiful baby, though. Have you been comfortable?'

'Yes, thanks.'

'Get any sleep?'

'No.'

'Is it hurting you much now?'

'Just about the same.'

'It's too wretched for you, this thing comin' right at the beginning of the holidays. I should be very angry, but you seem to be takin' it calmly; you are always like that, you know, John, always hiding things. I was talking with the specialist just as he was going – and he says that you probably will not be able to go back to Noat next term. So you will miss your last term, which is so important they tell me. It means so much to you in after-life, or something. I know Ralph always used to say that it had meant a great deal to him, the responsibility and all that. But I expect you're glad.'

'Of course. Father may have had some responsibility, but they would never have given any to me, however long I stayed there. I was too incompetent. Can you imagine me enforcing authority?'

'I think that you would be excellent in authority, I do really. But as Mabel Palmer was saying at tea the other day, you never seemed to have any of the ambition of ordinary boys – to be captain of football or cricket, and so on. I did so want to be a boy when I was a girl. I wanted to be good at cricket, and they never let us play in those days.'

'You would have made a fine cricketer, Mamma. But I don't think you would have thought much of school life, if you had gone there. You wouldn't have been as wretched as I was, but you would have seen through it, I think. You don't judge people now by their goodness at games, do you?'

'You know you weren't wretched, and – oh, well, we mustn't

argue. John, what's it like with that thing in front of your eyes so that you can't see anything? What's it feel like?'

'I don't know, everything's black, that's all.'

What was it in the air? Why were they talking in long sentences, importantly?

'I should go mad if I were like that, not to be able to see where one is going. John dear, you are very patient, I shouldn't be nearly as good as you.'

'I can quite imagine that. But it won't be for so very long?'

Why had he ended with a question?

'Well, we must be practical. And the specialist was telling me it would be quite a long time before – before you would be up and about again. But doctors always exaggerate, you know. And there's your poor face to get well besides.'

'But how long will it be before I shall be able to take this damned head-dress off in daylight? It was all very well when the old fool took it off in the darkened room so that I couldn't see anything, nor he either. His breath did smell nasty, too.'

'My dear boy, I never notice people's breath.'

' "May be the sign of a deep-rooted disorder." "Even your best friends won't tell you." "Halitosis is an insidious enemy," and so on. And an American firm has got the only thing on God's earth that will cure you. He ought to take it, really.'

'John, I do wish you would not swear like that. The servants would be very shocked if they knew, and it is such a bad example to the village boys.'

'But, heavens above, they don't hear me swear.'

'No, but they hear of it, don't you see.'

—Must talk. 'Rather an amusing thing has happened. You know Doris, the third housemaid. Well, she is little more than a child, and hasn't got her hair up. When she came, of course I insisted that she should put it up, which upset her terribly. Now, when she takes the afternoon off she puts it into a pigtail again. Silly little thing.'

'What's that in your voice? You aren't angry with her, are you? Because I think it's rather nice. I like pigtails, don't you? Do you know that bit of Browning, Porphyrias' Lover? But when shall I be able to see a pigtail again, that's the point?'

'What's that thing, John, a poem, or what?'

'He makes her lover strangle her with her own hair, done in a pigtail. I don't know what it means, no one knows, only I am quite sure I should like to do it. Think – the soft, silken rope, and the warm, white neck, and . . .'

'Now, don't be silly. I don't understand.'

'But when shall I be allowed to take this off? It will be fun seeing again. I suppose he gave some idea of a date?'

'Yes, but he was not very definite, in a way he was rather vague. You see, it is a long business. Eyes are delicate things.'

Dread.

'How long? – three months? I only thought it would be one, but it can't be helped.'

'Longer than that, I am afraid. Much longer, he said.'

'Six months?'

'Dear boy, we must be practical. It may take a – a very long time indeed.'

'In fact, I shall be blind for life. Why didn't you tell me at once? No, no, of course I understand.'

So he was blind.

She looks out of the window into the grey blur outside. Drops are having small races on the panes. The murmur fills the room with lazy sound. Now and then a drop falls from an eave to a sill, and sometimes a little cascade of drips patter down.

His heart is thumping, and there is a tightness in his throat, that's all. She had not actually said that he was blind. It wasn't he. All the same she hadn't actually said – but he was blind. Blind. Would it always be black? No, it couldn't. Poor Mamma, she must be upset about it all. What could be done? How dreadful if she started a scene while he was lying there in bed, helpless. But of course he wasn't blind. Besides, she hadn't actually said. What had she said? But then she hadn't actually said he wasn't. What was it? He felt hot in bed, lost. He put out a hand, met hers, and drew it away quickly. He must say something. What? (Blind? Yes, blind.) But . . .

'We must be practical, John darling, we must run this together.' – Darling? She never used that. What was she saying? '. . . bicycles for two, tandems they're called, aren't they? Work together, let me do half the work like on a tandem bicycle. Your father and I went on a trip on one for our honeymoon, years ago now, when bicycles were the latest thing. I wish he was here now, he was a wonderful man, and he would have helped, and – and he would have known what to do.'

'What was he like?' (So he was blind, how funny.)

'Dear boy, he was the finest man to hounds in three counties, and the most lovely shot. I remember him killing fifty birds in sixty cartridges with driven grouse at your grandfather's up in Scotland. A beautiful shot. He would have helped.'

'It's all right, I guessed it all along, you see. I knew it really when the man was looking at me in what he said was darkness. There was something in his manner. Christ! my eyes hurt, though.'

'Dear boy, don't swear like that. No, it can't be your eyes that hurt; if they did it would be a very good thing. It's your face that — that is cut up rather. Not that all hope is gone, of course, there is still a chance, there always is, the specialist said so. Miracles have happened before now. But I do hate your swearing like this.'

'I'm sorry.'

Why had she died, who could have helped him so much now? All these years he had thought so little about her, and now she was back, and she ought to be sitting by the bed, and she would be helping so much, and there would be nothing to hide, and it would be so much simpler if Mummy were here. Her hands would drive away the pain. It would be so different.

'But I will read to you, all your nice books. And then you will go on writing just the same; you could dictate to me. I shall always be there to help, we'll see it out together.'

Heaven forbid. She would never be able to read Dostoievsky, would never be able to understand. Besides, poor dear, it would bore her so except for the first few weeks when she would feel a martyr, and that was never a feeling to encourage. And how fine it would be to renounce her help in seeing it through, not as if it ever had an end, but how unselfish. Why was there no one else?

'Thank you, darling.'

What had he said? He ought never to have said that, it gave the whole show away. Why did one's voice go? But what was there to say? He was blind, finished, on the shelf, that was all. Still, he must carry her through. She must be dreadfully upset about it all. But what was there to say?

She was struggling.

'It's all right, it's not so bad as it looks, it's not as if we were very poor, it could — much worse, much worse.'

How wonderful he was, taking it like this, just like Ralph. She would like to say so many things, she longed to, but he did so hate demonstrativeness. She must try to say the right thing, she must not let it run away with her. And she must talk to keep his mind off.

'You are very brave, dear. I know it would have knocked me up completely, Ralph too. I don't know where you take everything from, I can't understand you half the time, you're not a bit like the family, though Mabel told me the other day that you are getting Ralph's profile as you grow older, but I can't see it. You know God gave you your sight and He has taken it away, but He has left us each other, you know, and . . .'

'Yes, yes.'

There, she had done it. But it was all true, it must be true. She must not make that mistake again.

It wasn't fair to say that as he was helpless. And what business was it of hers? – he wasn't hers. Why did these things happen? Why did she sit there? It was so hard. And the pain.

'Yes, Mummy, of course.'

Mummy, he hadn't used that for so long.

It would not happen again. Her feelings had betrayed her. The great thing was to keep his mind off. One must just go on talking, and it was so hard not to harp on it. A silence would be so terrible. There was always her between them. And it was not right, it was not as if the woman had ever done anything for him, except, of course, to bring him into the world. But it was she who had brought him up. He belonged to her.

'I am afraid I shall never be a good mother to you, John. I don't understand anything except out-of-door things, and babies. You were a lovely baby when you were small, and I could do everything for you then, and I loved it. But now you've outgrown me in a way and left me behind. As I was saying to Mabel the other day, I don't understand the young generation, you're too free about everything, though in many ways you yourself are an exception to that, with your secretiveness. I don't know how it is, but young people seem to care less about the country than they did. Now you, John, when you went – go for a walk, you mooch about, as old Pinch would say. And when you come back you don't eat a decent meal, but in that nice phrase, you are all mimmocky with your grub.'

She laughed tremulously, then hurried on. He smiled at the old friend, though his mouth seemed afraid.

'I believe it all comes from this cigarette smoking, that's what Ralph used to say, and I think it's true. Nasty as his pipe was, at least it was healthy. You are all either too difficult and unapproachable, or too talkative. That Bendon girl a few days ago at Mrs Pender's told me all her most private and intimate affairs for a whole hour after having met me for the first time. In the old days the girl would have been thought improper. She was the sort of girl your grandfather would have smiled at. He . . .'

'Mamma!' This was better.

'Eh?'

'Nothing.'

'He always smiled at something he could not understand, and what he could not understand he could not, and of course there was something wrong in it if he could not. In the old days . . .'

She was off again, and how the old days thrilled her generation, how blind they were not to see the glories of the present and future! Blind. Perhaps in years to come his memories would be only of the time when he had seen the colours and life through his own eyes. But he was becoming sentimental, and surely he had recovered from that phase of his Noat days. What is she saying? (Blind? Yes, blind.) What?

'. . . don't understand.' – The strain of talking to him of other things!

'But why try? Parents will never understand their children. Have you read Turgenev's Fathers and Sons? There's a wonderful picture there.'

He had not been listening. She had not been able to understand the bailiff's policy with the pigs. And here he was on to his books again, as if books mattered in life. But one must always show interest, so that he might feel he had someone who took a kindred interest. One had read all those Russian things in one's teens. One had loved them then, but one saw now what nonsense they had been.

'Yes, I read it years ago, when I married. I don't remember much, but I don't think it was a tremendously interesting book, do you, dear?'

There, they are always like that, 'Yes, I read it years ago.' Nothing lives for them but the new, they have forgotten everything else, life itself even! She has always read a book, any book you care to mention, and she has always forgotten all about it, save that she has read it. Irritation! She was dead, withered through not caring, and he was alive, how alive he was! Alive! Alive? And blind, a tomb of darkness, with all the carbuncles of life hidden away! Blind? Yes, blind for ever, always, always blind! No. What is she saying? Nothing, there is silence save for the silken rustling of the rain outside. She must be ill at ease.

'Yes,' he says, as one throws a lifebelt at someone drowning.

'Dear, I meant to help, and here I am, swearing away just the same. I'm not much of a mother to you, I'm afraid . . .' Was there no way to help him? When you tried to make him respond to affection he withdrew into himself at once. She would cry if she stayed here much longer. Why did these tragedies come like this? And they were like strangers.

'. . . don't, of course, not. Of course you help, because I can feel that there is someone there, someone standing by who can really help when I want it. That's what you are to me, a real friend.'

The weather had beaten all real sympathy out of her. She was so hard, so desperately rugged. There was a great deal to be said against going out in the rain. Hot-house flowers were better than hardy annuals, but then he would never understand the names of flowers now. Mrs Fane was the ideal, so tantalizing, so feminine. Mummy would have been like that. And now he would never see a painting, he would just become a vegetable like Mamma, a fine cabbage. And he would have had such a marvellous time with flowers, and with women, who were so close to flowers. But what was this? One must not slobber, sentimentality was intolerable. But how nice to slobber sometimes.

What's that she was saying, a story? Which one? As, yes, the new one, about the waste of pig-wash.

There's the rain outside, and the chuckling of the gutter pipes. It will be grey in the room now, or is it dark? Blind, so he didn't know. Light, no more light. And if he were to lift the bandages, surely there was only that between him and light, not a whole lifetime. There is a click.

'Is that the light on?'

'Yes, dear. Well, I must go to tea. Don't let it all worry you too much, dear.' She could not bear it any more.

And she was gone. What did she mean by her 'and don't let it all worry you too much'? Worry? Worry? He was blind. They did not seem to realize that he was blind, that he would never see again. Nothing but black. Why, it was absurd, stifling. He was blind and they did not mind that he was blind and would never see again. But it was silly to say that you would never see anything again, that was impossible. You could not see black for ever, you would have to see something, or you would go mad. Mad. So he was blind. He had always heard of blind people. But of course it meant absolutely nothing. It was silly.

There were slow steps up stair carpet, three wavering steps on the linoleum, and the door opened. Nanny comes in.

'Master John, I have brought you your tea.'

She puts something down that clinks.

'Thanks.'

'Did you have a nice sleep?'

'No.'

'Would you like a nice cup o' tea, Master John?'

Was everything nice and like her religion, comfortable?

'All right, Nan.'

He was being very good. Tea drinking was a vice in some walks of life, and in tea there was tannin, a harmful drug. But he was blind, he could not see. And the pain. So that he was like a blind worm in a fire, squirming, squirming to get out.

'Nice hot tea. You love your tea, don't you, Nan?'

'She likes her cup o' tea, your old Nan does, Master John. I always have been partial to a cup o' tea. All through the time when you was in the nursery it helped me along, for you was a bad boy then. An' before that, when you used to lie 'elpless in my arms with yer little red face. Lor', you would 'oller too if yer milk was so much as a minute late. I remember . . .'

She was remembering. Why were they all remembering? But perhaps it was an occasion to do so. They looked back into a past that lived only in their memories, they did not see the present, the birth of a new life, of a new art, and his life which had changed so suddenly. But he had lived his life, as Nan had lived hers, he must now look back. And it would be so comfortable being sentimental, and talking about memories. For to look back was the only thing left, to look forward was like thinking of nothing. Still, it could not all be over, there must be something in the future, something beyond these black walls! Romantic again. She too, '. . . with yer grasp in yer little hand . . .' she was maudlin. Magdalen, he was to have gone there. Oxford. No. Prehensile, that is all a baby is, and the nurse a ministrant at the knees of Moloch, the supreme sentimentalist. But her feelings were hurt so easily, and her tears were terrible. He must be good.

'. . . a lovely babby . . .'

'What is there for tea, Nan?'

'Well, I thought you might like buttered toast and bread and butter, you always was that fond of at nursery teas, and the Easter cake ...'

'I'll break the rules and have a bit of that first, Nan, please.'

She cuts a slice and begins to feed him bit by bit, at intervals putting the teacup into his hands. She loves doing it. For years she has watched him getting more and more independent, and now she is feeding him again. It is nice.

Her hand trembles, she has been garrulous and reminiscent, while she is usually sparing of unnecessary words. She has been told that he is blind, of course that's it. So that will mean more sympathy, if not expressed – which would be intolerable – at any rate only just underneath the surface. But how could you escape it? There were the people who had seen him grow up, and who inevitably had a possessive interest in him. They cared for him through no fault of his own, like dogs, and were sorry for the pain they felt in themselves at his blindness. They were busy dramatizing it all to him, while he wanted to be alone, alone to patch up his life. And now he was being theatrical!

'Would you like a sip of tea again, Master John?'

'Thanks, and some buttered toast.'

'I do so love feeding ye, Master John, like I used to with the bottle. I remember ...'

There would be red round her eyes, there would be a tell-tale weakness about her lips. He could see her looking at him with the smile he used to notice on parents' faces in Chapel at Noat, while they were saying to themselves, all through the service, that they had been through just what the boy was going through now, though what it was they didn't know. They were saying that they had read the book, years ago. And she was remembering him when he had hardly been alive, she was gloating, gloating that he was weak and helpless again. He would have to have her near him day after day, while she bombarded him with her sickening sentimentality. But what was he doing, eating like this, with this tragedy of darkness upon him? And the pain, the pain.

'No, no, take it away, I don't want any more, I couldn't.'

'Oh, Master John, don't take on so.'

And the poor old face is falling in, and he hears her beginning to sob. Then she is groping for the chair, to sit, bowed, in it. This was terrible, it bordered on a scene, and he was helpless. He shrank and shrank till he was shrivelled up. The whole creed was strength and not giving way. He gives her his hand, which she takes in her skinny, trembling ones, and tears fall on it, one by one, with little sploshes that he feels rather than hears. Poor Nanny.

But of course she must have been crying in the servants' hall before this, banking, minting on the fact that she had known him longer than anyone else there. The cook and Mamma's maid had been most attentive and sympathetic, the kitchen-maid had wept with her. Only the trained nurse did not listen, she would have sat apart reading, for she knew what youth was, the others had forgotten it. He could see the scene, with Nan babbling on through her tears. That fatuous line of Tennyson's, 'Like summer tempests came her tears.' But there was coming a serious Tennyson revival.

The trained nurse understood youth from the way her hand caressed his bandages, they had not trained it out of her yet, nor had life. But everyone else was like that, everyone except B. G. He wanted B. G., who would understand, who was the only person who would feel what he was feeling, and who would sympathize in the right way.

She struggled to her feet, letting go of his hand.

'You mustn't mind me, Master John, I'm only an old woman.'

And she went out slowly. So she had gone. But he was blind, everyone would be sorry for him, everyone would try to help him, and everyone would be at his beck and call; it was very nice, it was comfortable. And he would take full advantage, after all he deserved it in all conscience. He would enjoy life: why not? But he was blind. He would never be able to go out in the morning and recognize the sweep of lawn and garden again, and to wonder that all should be the same. He would never again be able to appreciate the miracle that anything could be so beautiful, never to see a bird again, or a cloud, or a tree, or a horse dragging a cart, or a baby blowing bubbles at his mother! Never to see a flower softly alive in a field, never to see colour again, never to watch colour and line together build up little exquisite temples to beauty. And the time when he had gone down on his knees before a daffodil with Herrick at the back of his mind, how he had grown drunk before it. And then the thought of how finely poetic he must be looking as he knelt before a daffodil in his best flannel trousers. What a cynic he was! That was another of his besetting sins. What a pity, also, to be self-conscious. The pain.

The misery of hating himself as much as he did. How unlucky he was to have been born like that, so infinitely superior to the common ruck. The herd did not feel all that he did, all his private tortures, and he was unfit to die like this, shut up in the traditional living tomb. A priest ought to have said offices over him as the glass entered his head and caused the white-hot pains there. And now the darkness pressed down on him, and he was not ready. He was not sufficient in himself. He did not know. He had been wandering off on expeditions in a mental morass before, and now all chance of retreat was cut off. He must live on himself, on his own reserves of mental fat, which would be increased a trifle perhaps when Mamma or Nan read to him, as steam rollers go over roads, levelling all sense, razing all imagery to the ground with their stupidity. And when he learned Braille it would be too slow. And it terrifies, the darkness, it chokes. Where is he? Where? What's that? Nothing. No, he is lost. Ah, the wall, and he is still in bed and has hurt his hand in the blow he gave it. The bell should be here to the left – yes, here it is, how smoothly everything goes if you keep your head. His hand tastes salt, he must have skinned it against the wall.

There are steps on stair carpet, four quick steps on the linoleum, and the nurse enters, prettily out of breath.

'Well, and how are we? Did you ring, Mr John? I am so sorry, I was having my tea.'

'Oh, nurse, I was frightened. Look, I have skinned my knuckles, haven't I?'

'Silly, whatever did you do that for? That was very naughty of you. Now I shall have to bind it up.'

She washes it . . . She has such a pretty voice that he would like to squeeze her hand as she is holding his. And he wanted sympathy. But it would be too terrifying, he had had enough awkward scenes today, he did not feel strong enough for another if she were to object. And a nice sight he must be with bandages all over him. Besides, being a professional, she would not be intrigued by bandages as others might. No, he could do nothing.

And she? Well, he wasn't a very interesting case, was he? It was not as if he had eyes left in their sockets, eyes that needed fighting to save. There was nothing interesting in his condition. How she loved difficult cases. She had only just graduated, so she hadn't had any. And he was quite healthy, he was really healing very quickly, and he hadn't a trace of shock. They had always told her in the profession that she would soon get out of it once she had had one, but her dream was a case of delirium tremens; to hear the patient describe the blue mist and the snakes, snakes crawling over everything. But she hadn't had one yet. They fought, there had to be two of you, it kept your hands full. She was sorry for the poor boy, but then he was not really suffering. Suffering made you a great well of pity, and that of course was love.

Her hand felt the bandages and then started work. The pain redoubles, torn face with white-hot bars of pain shooting across it. He was in agonies. He was like a bird in a white-hot cage, the pain pursuing him wherever he turned, and he began to squirm, physically now, in bed. Agony filled his head and his body and everything of him. She was changing the dressing, it would be over soon, and he must not moan, for that was not strong or beautiful. Aah. There, he had done it, and the pain died down again to the old glow. She had finished and he had moaned just a second before everything had been over. All for nothing, and it did not seem much now. She was despising him for moaning, he could sense it. And the athlete would have riddled his lips with his strong teeth before he uttered a sound, and then only to ask for a cigarette. Poor woman. And he was blind, was he?

So that he would grow on into a lonely old age. He would know his way round the house, and there would be his favourite walk in the garden. As all blind men he would do everything by touch, and he would have tremendous powers of hearing. He would play music divinely, on the gramophone. And the tears would course from behind his sightless eyeballs – but had he any? He had never thought of that. He felt with his hand, but the bandages were too tight. He remembered that men with amputated legs could still waggle the toes which by that time were in the dustbin. He squinted, and was sure that his eyes were there.

'Nurse, have I any eyes?'

'How do you mean? No, I am afraid they were both taken out, they had to be.'

It had been a dull operation, and they were now in spirits on the mantelpiece of her room at home in the hospital. When she got back she was going to put them just where she could see them first thing every morning, with the toes and the kidney. She had had an awful trouble to get the eyes.

Oh, so his eyes were gone. Now that was irritating, a personal loss. Dore had been furious because his appendix had been removed the term before last, he said it was a blemish on his personal beauty, but eyes were much more personal. Why hadn't they taken the eyes of one of the 'muddied oafs'? While he, he was blind. How had it happened? He had never asked; must have been some accident or something. He would ask.

'Nurse, how did it happen?'

'Do you think you can bear to talk about it?'

'Why not?'

'Well, a small boy threw a stone at the train, and it broke your window as you were looking out. It was very careless of him. But what I can't understand is your being unconscious immediately like that, and not remembering. But doctor said you could be told, and . . .'

A small boy. Damn him.

'And what happened to the small boy?'

'He was whipped by the police yesterday. Won't you try and get some sleep now?' and her hands smooth the pillow disinterestedly and tuck him up. Before, when he had remembered it, this had been deliciously thrilling. So a small boy in a fit of abstraction, or of boredom, had blinded him, a small boy who could not appreciate what he had done, at least only for so long as his bottom hurt him. Why, if he had the child, he would choke him. One's fingers would go in and in till they would be enveloped by pink, warm flesh. The little thing would struggle for a while, and then it would be over, you know, just a tiny momentary discomfort for an eternity of pleasure, for were not his god-parents shouldering his sins for him? It would be a kindness to the little chap, and one would feel so much better for it afterwards. He would be apprehended for murder, and he would love it. He would make the warder read the papers to him every morning, he would be sure to have headlines: BLIND MAN MURDERS CHILD – no, TORTURES CHILD TO DEATH; And underneath that, if he was lucky, WOMAN JUROR VOMITS, something really sensational. Mr Justice Punch, as in all trials of life and death, would be amazingly witty, and he would be too. He would make remarks that would earn him some famous title, such as THE AUDACIOUS SLAUGHTERER. All the children in England would wilt at his name. In the trial all his old brilliancy would be there. Talking. No more of those conversations that had been so tremendously important. No more snubs, no more bitternesses, for the rest of his life he would be surrounded by dear, good, dull people who would be kind and long-suffering and good, and who would not really be alive at all. How dull being good for ever, always being grateful and appreciative for fear of hurting their feelings. And never to see again, how important transparency was. His head was beginning to hurt again. Nothing but women all his life. Better to have died. Why didn't the pain go away?

What was the time?

2 Her, Him, Them

'Good morning, mum.'

'Grmn', J'net.'

And Janet, after putting the can of hot water in the basin behind the screen, went to the red curtains and pulled them back. The sunlight leapt, catching fire on her fuzzy hair, and the morning came freely in by the open windows. Mrs Haye, in the right half of the double-bed, had such a lost look in the eyes which were usually so imperious that Janet shook her head sadly.

She had had a bad night, the first since Portgammon over the fireplace there had fallen with her jumpin' timber and had broken his back. She would get up immediately, it was no use stickin' here in this ghastly bed. Pity she did not take her bath in the morning, a bath now would do her good, But there was more need for it in the evening.

'Janet, I will get up and dress now.'

'Now'm?'

'Yes, now.'

Later: 'Will you have the brown tweed or the green'm?'

'The heather mixture. Janet, these stockings each have a hole in the heel. I wish you would not put me out stockings that are unfit to wear.'

She was in one of her tempers today, and no wonder. But as cook had said at supper last night, 'No one to give notice till a year 'as passed by.'

She was washing behind the screen, splashing and blowing. Then her teeth were being attacked. Work and forget, work and forget, till some plan emerged. She would send for Mabel Palmer and they would talk it out.

She almost fell asleep while Janet was doing her hair.

Diving upwards through the heather-mixture skirt, she said, 'Tell William to ring up Mrs Palmer Norbury 27, you know, to ask her if she will come to tea today.'

'Yes'm.'

She struggled into the brown jumper and before the looking-glass put in the fox-head pin. There was old Pinch in the herbaceous border doing nothing already. She had never seen him about so early, it was really extraordinary. She looked a long time at Ralph in his photograph, but he was absolutely the same. His smile said nothing, gave her no advice, but only waited to be told what to do, just as he had been obeying the photographer then. He would have had more in common with the boy perhaps, would have been able to talk to him of pig-sticking out in India in the old 10th days. She could do nothing to distract him. But then he didn't hunt, he didn't shoot, he only fished and that sitting down, and he couldn't fish now. Perhaps it was just as well he had given up huntin', it would have been terrible had that been taken away from her suddenly.

How heavy her skirt felt, and she was stiff. She felt old today, really old: this terrible affair coming suddenly like this, just when the Nursing Association was beginning to go a little better, too. And she could do nothing for the poor boy, nothing. But something must be done, there must be some way out. Of course, he would never see again, it was terrible, she had seen that the first time the doctors saw her at the hospital, where that appalling woman was head nurse. She had not had a ward all through the war for nothing, she had seen at once. Some occupation must be found for him, it was the future one had to think about, and Mabel Palmer might know of something. Or his friends might – but then he hadn't any, or at any rate she had never seen them. There it was, first Ralph falling down dead of his heart on the stairs, and now fifteen years after the boy was blinded, worse than being dead. What could one say to him? What could one do?

She went downstairs. In the Oak Hall she found the dog, who rose slowly to greet her, looking awkwardly in her direction.

'You, Ruffles? Why have they let you out so early? Poor blind old thing. Oh, so old.'

She scratched his neck gently. Would it be better to have him destroyed? He was so old, he could hardly see any more, and it hurt him to bark. What enjoyment could he get out of life, lying there by the fire, asleep all day and hardly eating at all? Yet he had been such a good servant, for ten years he had barked faithfully at friends. And the only time he had not barked was when the burglars had come that once, when they had eaten the Christmas cake, and had left the silver. But it would be kinder to put him out of the way. One must be practical. But he was blind!

William came in by the dining-room door carrying one of the silver inkstands as if it had been a chalice. His episcopal face was set in the same grave lines, his black tail-coat clung reverently to a body as if wasted by fasting, his eyes, faithfully sad, had the same expression of respectful aloofness. William, at least, never changed. She remembered so well old Lady Randolph, who had known him fifty years ago when he was at Greenham, saying, 'I see no change in William.' But of course her eyesight had not been very grand, nevertheless William had shown distant pleasure when told. Still he was too aged, he could not do his share of the work, it must all fall on Robert; the boy was so lazy, though, that it would be good for him to do a little extra. But what could one do? He had served her for years, he had been a most conscientious servant, and it was only the night when the burglars did come that he had been asleep. However, they had only eaten the Christmas cake, they had left the silver.

'William, I should like breakfast as soon as possible.'

'Very well, madam.'

And he was gone. Yes, it was convenient to have him about. He was quiet, he never exceeded himself, and he understood.

Outside, on the little patch of lawn up to the drive, they were mowing already with the horse-mower. They had made a very early start. The same George, the same Henry leading the pony which had carried John across the open country behind the hounds before he had given up, and which was still the same. It was only John who had changed.

'George,' she cried, 'George.'

The pony halted by himself, the men listened.

'George, see that no stones get in the blades, it ruins them. Henry, you must pick them up and throw them back on to the drive.'

Both: 'Yas'm.'

And they went on mowing.

Of course they were going to keep her waiting for her breakfast now. But no, William came in and gravely announced it.

As she went in she looked gratefully at him, he was a symbol. He had come to them directly after the honeymoon, prematurely white and sad. Ralph used to say that he was a marvellous valet. Thirty years ago. Then they had gone to India with the 10th. Ten years after they had come back, and had found William again. It was extraordinary, that, and Ralph had said then that he tasted comfort for the first time in ten years. At the funeral William had sent his own wreath, on it written in his copy-book handwriting, 'To his master respectfully from his valet.' It had not been tactful, she had had to thank him. He had exceeded himself. His only lapse.

Nothing seemed worth while. Yesterday had tired her out utterly. First the doctors destroying her last bit of hope, and then her breaking it to him, which had been so terrible. She had gone up again after tea, and it had been frightful, his face underneath the bandages had been tortured, his mouth in a half-sneer. She had been frightened of him. And finally, as nicely as he could, he had asked her to leave him for the evening. The nurse had met her at the door and had whispered, 'He is in rather a state,' as if she had not known that. The woman was a fool.

This coffee was undrinkable. The cook had probably been gigglin' again with Herbert. That affair! You could not drink it, absolutely undrinkable. She would make a row. But was it worth while? She felt so tired today. But the house must go on just as usual, there must be no giving way. She rang the bell. They must find some occupation for the boy, he could not be left there rankling. Making fancy baskets, or pen-wipers, all those things blinded soldiers did, something to do. William coughed.

'William, this coffee is undrinkable. Will you tell the cook to find some occupation for ... to find some ... The roaster must be out of order. No, don't take my cup away. I will drink it for this once.'

Had he seen? At any rate he would not tell. She had not been able to give a simple order, it was terrible, without giving herself away. She must make inquiries about Braille books, and find someone to teach it to him. A knock.

'Come in.'

It was the nurse.

'Good morning, Mrs Haye. I came down because I wish you would come up to speak to John. He has refused to eat his breakfast, and there was a nice bit of bacon this morning. I am afraid he is taking it rather badly, he did not sleep much last night. But if you would come up and get him quieter.'

What right had she to call him John? She must be changed. Oh, the misery of it, and the tortures he must be going through. She could do nothing, if she spoke to him she would only say the wrong thing.

She rose from the table and looked at the coffee-pot.

'I can do nothing with him, nurse. I think it would be better to leave him to himself, he always prefers that. He will be quieter this evening.'

'Very good, Mrs Haye; I dressed his wounds this morning, they are getting on nicely.'

His wounds. The scars. And he would wear black spectacles. He had been so handsome. It would be better not to go up this morning, but let him quieten down.

She sat down and looked out of the windows in the bay. The big lawn was before her, they would begin to mow it soon. Dotted over it were blackbirds and thrushes looking for worms, and in the longer grass at the bottom she could see the cock pheasant being very cautious. They were pretty things to look at, but he and his two wives did eat the bulbs so. She would have to send for Brown to come down and kill them. And what good was it keeping up the shootin', now that all hope had gone of his ever holdin' a gun? But nothing must change. The lower border was really looking very fine, the daffodils were doing splendidly. It was just the same, the garden, and how well it looked now. He hadn't eaten his breakfast. No. Of course, once in a while a tree fell down and made a gap that would look awkward for a bit, but there were others growing and you became used to it. There went a pigeon, fine birds but a pest, they did more harm to the land than the rooks. She ought never to have made that birthday promise to John, that the garden should be a sanctuary for them; but going out to watch them had made him very happy in the old days, and now? What would he do now?

She got up heavily and left the dining-room. Going through the house she came to the sitting-room, which looked out on to the small rose garden surrounded by a high wall. It ought to look well this year, not that he would see it, though. She had a lot of things to do this morning, she would not let the thing come up and crush her. His was the sort of nature which needed to be left alone, so it was no use going up to see him. Plans must be made for when his new life would begin, and some idea might emerge out of her work. Being blind he could do work for the other blind, and so not feel solitary, but get the feeling of a regiment. Meanwhile there was the Nursing Association. She must write to his friends, too, they ought to know that he was blind. Would they really care? But of course anyone who knew John must care. Then their letters would come in return, shy and halting, with a whole flood of consolation from the neighbours, half of whom did not care in the least. She would have to answer them; but no, she couldn't. Then they would say that the blow had aged her, she had said that so often herself. Their letters would be full of their own little griefs, a child who had a cold, a husband worried by his Indian liver, one who had been cut publicly by Mrs So-and-So – but this wasn't fair. They would write rather of someone of theirs who had died recently or years and years ago, of the memory of their grief then, of what had helped them then, of prayer, of a wonderful sleeping draught. Not sleeping, that was what was so hard. And she would answer suitably, for of course by now one knew what to say, but it was hateful, people laying little private bits of themselves bare, and she being expected to do likewise. She could say everything to Mabel, but not to them. Still, it would be all over some day. Life would not be the same, it would go on differently, and yet really be just the same. But did that help? Could she say to the boy, 'You will get used to it in time'? It was ridiculous. Could she preach religion at him when she was not quite sure herself? Something must be done.

She took up the Nursing accounts. Five pounds in subscriptions, it was not bad. That Mrs Binder. She would have to write to her, it was ridiculous not to subscribe. She was the sort of woman to put spider webs on a cut. But they did not give their babies cider to drink any more as a substitute for mother's milk, she had stopped that. Yet perhaps Mrs Moon did, she would do anything, and her house was so filthy. The annual inspection had gone off so well, too, the Moon child had been the only one to have nits in her hair. What could one do? The house was filthy, the husband earned very low wages, you could not turn them out for being insanitary, they would have nowhere to go. And the house was losing value every day. John must learn to care about these things.

And her affairs were none too bright. It was as much as one could do to keep the house and the garden going, what with the income tax and the super-tax and everything. The car would have to go, and with it Evans. Harry could drive her about in the dog-cart, it would be like the old days again except when one of them passed her. It was terrible to see the country changing, the big houses being sold, everyone tightening the belt, with the frightful war to pay for. Now that he was blind there was no hope of his ever making any money. And the charities had not stopped. What would happen to John? Even if he hadn't gone blind it would have been difficult enough. There were more charities now, if anything; they came by every post. Her letters, she had forgotten. She rang the bell. That Mrs Walters had written for a subscription to a garden fête in aid of the local hospital. Of course she stole half the money you sent, but a little of it was fairly certain to be used by the hospital. The woman never kept accounts for those things, which was wicked. Then, again, Mrs Andrew and her Parish Nurse, the effrontery of it when she did not subscribe to the Barwood one. What a fight it was. Were there any blind boys in Norbury of his own age, nice boys whom he could make friends with? They could not afford to go to London where he might find some. They could, of course, if they sold Barwood. Sell Barwood! – No, and he would appreciate still having it when he grew older. To be blind in one of those poky little suburban villas, with a wireless set, and with aeroplanes going overhead, and motor bikes and gramophones. No.

William came in.

What had she rung for? Blank.

'It is all right, William, I have found it now.'

It was terrible, she could not even remember when she rang.

No, everything must go on just the same, the garden would be still the best in twelve miles, even if all the world went blind. They must find a companion for the boy, Mabel would be able to help there. Someone who would spend his time with him, her time, that would be better. It was so terrible, he would never marry now, she would have no grandchildren. The place would be sold, the name would die, there was no one. Ralph had been the last. 'Granny.' He would not meet any nice girls now, he could never marry. A girl would not want to marry a blind man. All her dreams were gone, of his marrying, of her going up to live in the Dower House – that was why the Evanses had it on a short lease. She would have made friends with his wife and would have shown her how to run everything. His wife would have made changes in the house, of course, and it would have been sad seeing the place different; but then the grandchildren, and he would have made such a good father. Why was it taken away quite suddenly like this? But then they might still find some girl who had had a story, or who was unhappy at home, who would be glad, who would not be quite – but who would do. He must marry. All the bachelors one had known had been so womanish, old grandfathers without children. John Goe. She could not fill his life, there would have to be a wife. Mabel might know of someone. Perhaps they would not be happy, but they would be married. And she ought to be happy here, it was a wonderful place, so beautiful with the garden and the house. It had been her real life, this place; before she had married she had not counted, something had just been training her for this. And she had improved it, with the rock garden and the flowers. Mary Haye had not known one flower from another. And she had got the village straight, there had been no illegitimate children for two years, and they were all married. It would be a blow going, a bit of her cut off, but the Dower House was only a mile off, and right in the middle of the village. And now perhaps she would be able to live here till she died if he did not marry. But he must, for his happiness, if there was to be someone to look after him when she died. And she would have grandchildren after all, it might turn out all right, one never knew in this world; there had been Berty Askew. If everything failed he could have a housekeeper. Yes, it was immoral, but he must have love, and someone to look after him. After Grandmamma died the Grandparent had had one at Tarnarvaran. Argyll and the heather ... Really, now that this trouble was upon her, Edward might write. But it was for him to act first.

She must order dinner. There was comfort in choosing his food, it was something to do for him. Going out she straightened a picture that was a little crooked. As she opened the door the sunlight invaded the passage beyond, and made a square of yellow on the parquet floor.

In front of the swing door into the kitchen she halted. Honestly, one did not like to enter the kitchen now for fear of findin' Mrs Lane gigglin' with Herbert. That affair. Well, if they brought things to a head and married, they would have to leave. She could not bear a married couple among the servants, they quarrelled so.

Inside it was very clean, the deal tables were like butter, the grey-tiled floor, worn in places, shone almost. Along one wall was hung a museum of cooking utensils, every size of saucepan known to science, and sinister shapes. Mrs Lane was waiting. Where was her smile? Oh, of course it was. How nice they all were. Mrs Lane began talking at once.

'I am sorry to say'm that Muriel has had some kittens in the night. We none of us suspected'm. In the potato box'm.'

What, again!

'Tell Harry to drown 'em immediately.'

One must be practical.

'If I could find a home for them'm?'

'Very well, Mrs Lane, only I cannot have them here. What with the stable cat and the laundry cat there are too many of 'em about. What is there this morning?'

'Very good'm. I've got a bit of cod for upstairs' – it was no use mentioning no name – 'an' would you like one of the rabbits Brown brought in yesterday, and the pigeon pie'm, with cherry tart for upstairs?'

'That will do nicely.'

'An' for dinner I . . .' etc.

As she was going out into the kitchen yard so as to gain the stables, Mrs Lane ran after her to stop her. She spoke low and fast.

'Madam, the nurse asked me this morning that she could 'ave 'er meals seprit. Didn't like to take them in the servants' 'all'm.'

'If she wants to eat alone, Mrs Lane, we had better humour her. Have them sent up to her room.'

'Very good'm.'

An' who was to take 'em up to 'er, stuck-up thing?

There, now there was going to be trouble about the nurse. Cook had been angry, although she had tried not to show it. Really they might leave her alone and not bother her with their little quarrels. Somebody would be giving notice in a week. Still, Mrs Lane would not go while Herbert was here.

'Harry, Harry!'

A sound of hissing came suddenly through an open window on the other side of the little yard. A head wobbled anxiously behind a steamy window further down. A hoof clanked.

There was the stable cat. 'Shoo!'

'Harry!'

'Yess'm.'

She inspected the horses and went out.

No, she would not go to the laundry this morning. The damp heat would be rather exhausting. Curry had been riding a nice bay last season which had looked up to her weight. She was getting rather tired of Jolly. She stopped, that had reminded her.

'Harry, you can take them both out to exercise tomorrow, I shall not go out, of course.'

'Very good'm.'

He would never ride now, all her hopes of getting him back to the love of it were broken, and he could not even go on a lead, for that was so dangerous. What would he do?

She went through the door in the wall into the kitchen garden. She called:

'Weston, Weston!'

There was Herbert pickin' lettuces just for the chance of going to Mrs Lane in the kitchen with them. He raised his bent body and touched his cap. She nodded.

Again she cried:

'Weston!'

A cry came from the other end, from the middle of the artichokes, the tops of which you could hardly see – it was a big kitchen garden. Weston appeared walking quickly. He took his cap off.

'How are the peaches getting on?'

Peaches were good for convalescents.

'Very nicely'm. Going to be a good crop, and the apples too. Was among the artichokes'm. Fine crop this year. Never seen 'em so high.'

'What beautiful cabbages, Weston.'

He would eat them, as he could not see flowers.

'Yes'm. Going to be a good crop.'

'Yes; well, good morning, Weston.'

'Good morning'm.'

Into the garden. Pinch was still at the same spot on the border as he had been when she had looked out of her bedroom window. He was too old, but he was a faithful servant.

Yes, his wife was going on as well as was to be hoped. Yes, it was bad weather for the farmers.

Pinch was the same, so why had he changed? What was the matter with Pinch's wife? Just age perhaps, any way they would be the next for the almshouses. When Mrs Biggs died they could go in, and that should not be long now. This would leave vacant their cottage on Ploughman's Lane, which that nice man from Huntly could have. How nice the trees were with their fresh green; whatever happened the seasons went round. If this warm weather went on he could get out to be on the lawn. but then you could never tell with the English spring. She would have to go in to write those letters, while it was so lovely out here. There was the moorhen starting her nest in the same place in the moat. Mrs Trench's baby would be due about now, her sixth, while that Jim Pender, earning excellent wages, only had his one girl, and she was five years old. It was ridiculous, she would have to speak to him about it, a great strong fellow like him with such a pretty wife. She must have some jelly and things sent up to Mrs Trench. He must take an interest in the village now that he had nothing to do. He could start a club for the men and teach them something, he would do it very well, talking about art or books, or one of those things he was so interested in. That would do something to occupy his time. There was a daffodil out already, it had planted itself there, it looked so pretty against the bole of the tree. How good a garden was for one! She felt quieter after the ghastly night she had had. The only way out of trouble like this was to work for others till you forgot, when a plan would emerge quite suddenly, that was what life taught one, and Mabel was the same.

Annie was weeding the gravel of the Yew Walk. In summer she weeded, in winter she swept leaves, and she picked up dead branches all the year round.

'Good morning, Annie.'

'Good morning'm.'

She was not quite all there, poor thing, but there was nothing to be done for her, she would always be like that.

The attendances at church were disgraceful again now, just as bad as when the Shame had had it. That had been the only time the village had been right and she wrong. No one had been able to persuade her till she had seen for herself. It was all part of this modern spirit, she had seen terrible dangers there for him, but now, poor boy, that he was blind she could at least keep him to herself away from those things that led nowhere. She ought to go back now to write those dreadful letters, but it was so lovely out here, with the sunlight. And it didn't look as if it would last, there were clouds about. She had been right to put on thick clothes. How pretty the little stone Cupid was, king of his little garden of wallflowers walled in by yews, it would be a blaze of colour. Now that the flagstones were down you could see what a difference it made.

She opened the door into Ralph's old study. It would be his now, as she had always meant it to be. It got all the sun in the morning, and there were no awkward corners. He would have a hard time at first in getting about, but she would lead him and teach him where the furniture was and all that, it was one of the things she could do for him.

In the Oak Hall there was a note for her. The parson's wife again. Oh, this time she wanted fifty cups and saucers for the Mothers' Union tea. Well, she could have them. What, again? No, no, not another. Yes, in the PS, 'I am going to have another darling baby.' That was too much. Would they never stop? And they could not afford it with the covey they had already. All it meant was that Mrs Crayshaw would not be able to do any visiting in the village for quite two months. Now there was another letter to write, of congratulation this time, and it was going to be hard to word. What did they call it, a quiver full? Tomorrow and there would be another letter from her, she would have heard about him by then, it would be full of earnest stuff. And she did not want sympathy, she wanted practical advice.

It was all so difficult. She had betrayed him this morning, she had not thought nearly enough about it all. She was beginning not to care already. This morning she had frittered away, excusing herself by saying that Mabel would think of something, while everyone knew that it was always she who talked while Mabel listened. Still, it was necessary to talk. But last night had been so dreadful, when she had lain in bed turning the thing over and over in her mind, and she had prayed too. She had thought of many ways to occupy his time, but they had all gone out of her head now. Those red curtains were getting faded, but Skeam's man had been insolent when last he came. That was what we were comin' to, a decorator's tout giving himself airs. Before all this she had meant to put John into a decorator's business, he was so artistic that he would have done wonders, perhaps even made a little money. But there, it was no use thinkin' of might-have-beens. He must marry, it was the only thing he could do. He must be a man, and not be left unfinished. They would have the marriage in the church, and a dinner for the tenants in the Great Hall. But he was so young. And she would spend the evenin' of her days in the Dower House.

She passed through the Great Hall. She buried her head violently into a pot of dead roses. In her room Ruffles was sleeping fitfully in his basket. She picked up a paper, glanced at the headlines, then put it aside. She sat in her armchair and looked vacantly at Greylock over the fireplace. Along the mantel-board were ranged a few cards to charities, to funerals, and to weddings. She picked up the paper again and looked through the Society column, and then the deaths and marriages, and then threw it on to the floor. She blew her nose and put the handkerchief away in the pocket of her skirt. She rubbed her face slowly in her hands, when she stopped it was redder still. Then she sat for some time looking at nothing at all, thinking of nothing at all. The specks kept on rising in the sunlight.

She got up. She rang the bell. She went to the writing-table and sat down. She opened the inkstand hoof, Choirboy's hoof, and she looked at her pens. She dipped one into the ink, and she drew a bit of paper towards her. Then she looked out of the window on to the rose garden for some time.

William came in.

'William, Mrs Crayshaw has written to say that she will want fifty cups and saucers . . . No, on second thoughts . . . It is all right, William, I will go and tell cook myself. And – oh, William, the letters, please.'

'Yes, madam.'

William held the door open for her. Mrs Lane might not like it from the butler. She would go up to see him after this. But you could not be too careful with servants nowadays, and . . .

How did one pass the time when one was blind? Six days had gone by since she had told him, days filled with the echo of people round occupying themselves on his account. Mamma had had three long conferences with Mrs Palmer, conferences which had reached him through vague references as to what he was going to do, with not a word as to what he was going to do now. Nan was struggling with an emotion already waning. Her long silences, in which she sent out waves of sentimentality, told that she was trying to freeze what was left into permanency. The nurse helped him grudgingly back to health, the new life was forming, and it was even more boring than the former. They read to him in turn for hours on end, Mamma talked of finding a professional reader. It was now so ordinary to be blind.

He was in the long chair, under the cedar on the lawn. He felt the sky low and his bandages tight. The air nosed furtively through the branches and made the leaves whisper while it tickled his face. Pigeons were cooing, catching each other up, repeating, answering, as if all the world depended on their little loves. It was the sound he liked best about the garden; he yawned and began to doze.

He was alone for the moment. Nan had left him to take a cup of tea. The nurse was taking the daily walk that was necessary to her trade union health, and Mrs Haye had gone up to the village to console Mrs Trench, whose week-old baby was dying. Herbert, leaning on the sill of the kitchen window, was making noises at Mrs Lane while she toyed with a chopper, just out of his reach. Weston was lost in wonder, love and praise before the artichokes, he had a camera in his pocket and had taken a record of their splendour. Twenty years on and he would be showing it to his grandchildren, to prove how things did grow in the old days. Twenty years ago Pinch had seen better. Harry was hissing over a sporting paper; Doris in an attic was letting down her hair, she was about to plait the two soft pigtails. Jenny, the laundry cat, was very near the sparrow now, by the bramble in the left-hand corner of the drying ground.

He roused himself – if he went to sleep it would only mean that he would lie awake all night. He fingered the letter that Nan had read to him from J. W. P., full of regret that he was not coming back next term, saying that he would get his leaving-book from the Headmaster for him. No more going back now, which was one good thing, and no more irritations with J. W. P. He had done a great deal of work, though, that last year; he had really worked quite hard at writing, and he would go on now, there was time when one was blind. J. W. P. had disapproved, of course, and had said that no one should write before he was twenty-one, but about that time he had come under the influence of the small master with spectacles, whose theory was that no boy should have any ideas before he had left school. Perhaps they were right, it was certainly easier to give oneself up to a physical existence. Healthy sanity. And here was weakness, in saying that they ever could be right. But he was in such an appalling desolation that anything might be right. Why had he taken that train?

He felt himself sinking into a pit of darkness. At the top of the pit were figures, like dolls and like his friends, striking attitudes at a sun they had made for themselves, till sinking he lost sight of them, to find himself in the presence of other dolls in the light of a sun that others had made for them. Then it did not work, and he was back in the darkness, on the lawn again. Nothing seemed real.

He said 'tree' out loud and it was a word. He saw branches with vague substance blocked round them, he saw lawn, all green, and he built up a picture of lawn and tree, but there were gaps, and his brain reeled from the effort of filling them.

He felt desperately at the deck-chair in which he was sitting. He felt the rough edges of the wood, which would be a buff colour, and he ran a splinter into his finger. He put his hand on the canvas, he knew that it was canvas, dirty white with two red stripes at each side. It felt rough and warm where his body had touched it. He felt for the red, it should have blared like a bugle. It did not; that would come later, perhaps.

He felt the grass, but it was not the same as the grass he had seen.

He lay back, his head hurting him. How much longer would he be here? The letter crinkled in his hands, reminding him of its presence. He ran his fingers over the pages, but he could feel no trace of ink. He came upon the embossed address. It might have been anything. A fly buzzed suddenly. Even a fly could see.

He was shut out, into himself, in the cold.

So much of life had been made up of seeing things. The country he had always looked to for something. He had seen so much in line, so much in colour, so much in everything he had seen. And he had noticed more than anyone else, of course he had.

But when he had seen, how much it had meant. Everything was abstract now, personality had gone. Flashes came back of things seen and remembered, but they were not clear-cut. Little bits in a wood, a pool in a hedge with red flowers everywhere, a red-coated man in the distance on a white horse galloping, the sea with violet patches over grey where the seaweed stained it, silver where the sun rays met it. A gull coming up from beneath a cliff. There was a certain comfort in remembering.

This would have been a good fishing day. There was no sun, yet enough heat to draw the chub up to the surface. The boat would glide silently on the stream, the withies would droop quietly to dabble in the water. Where the two met the chub lay, waiting for something to eat. And he would prepare his rod and he would throw the bright speckled fly to alight gently on the water, and to swim on the current past mysterious doors in the bathing green. The boat floated gently too, a bird sang and then was silent, and he would watch the jaunty fly, watch for the white, greedy mouth that would come up, for the swirl when he would flick lightly, and the fight, with another panting, gleaming fish to be mired in struggles on the muddy floor of the boat.

He would go down the river, catching fish. The day would draw away as if sucked down in the east, where a little rose made as if to play with pearl and grey and blue. There were chub he had missed, four or five he would have caught, and more further on. A kingfisher might shoot out to dart down the river, a guilty thing in colours.

More rarely a grey heron would raise himself painfully to flap awkwardly away. He would go on, casting his fly, placing it here or there, watching it always, and now and then, with little touches, steering it from floating leaves. And it would become more difficult to see, and the only sound would be the plops the fish made as they sent out rings in eating flies on the water. One last chub in the boat and he would turn to row back through the haze that was rising from the river. The water chattered at the prow, he would notice suddenly that the crows were no longer cawing in the trees on the hill, but had gone to sleep. He would yawn and begin to think of dinner. It was a long way back.

He would come to the ferry, where the boats were tied up, where they huddled darkly together. There would be the rattle of the chain, and the feeling that something else was finished. Voices would come from behind the lighted blinds of the inn; a dog would bark, a laugh perhaps, while the other bank was thick with shadows. He would carry the oars and rowlocks to put them as always in the shed, and he would climb the gate, the rod tiresome, the creel heavy. A quick walk home across the fields, for there was nothing to see in the dark. An owl perhaps and a bat or two.

Or again, the river in the heat of an afternoon, stalking from the bank the chub that lay by the withies, and being careful with his shadow. He would wade slowly through long grass with here and there a flower at random, or more often a bed of nettles. He would peer through the leaves that drooped in green plumes to where a chub cruised phantom-like in the cloudy onyx of the water. The sun made other smaller suns that would pierce his eyes and dazzling dance there. Bending low he would draw out as much line as he could. Stooping he would pitch his fly cunningly. The line might fall over the fin, and the fish would be gone.

The chub were hard to catch from the bank, and often it was so hot that the only thing to do was to lie in the shade. There was an alder tree under which lived a rat. He would watch for it sometimes: if one kept still it would come out to play, or to teach a baby what to eat, or to wash in the water. The cattle, bored, might bestir themselves to come and look at him, blowing curiously. The flies would always be tiresome. The water slipped by.

Why was it all over? But it wasn't, he would cultivate his sense of hearing, he would listen to the water, and feel the alder, and the wind, and the flowers. Besides, there had only been about ten fishing days every summer, what with the prevailing wind, which was against the current, raising waves, and the rain in the hills which made mud of the water. There would be no more railing against the bad weather now, which had been half the joy of fishing.

Sometimes, when he was rowing back in the dark after fishing over the sunset below, he had stopped by a withy that he could hardly see, to cast a white fly blindly into the pool of darkness beneath. He would strike by the ripple of light, he had caught two or three fish that way, and it was so mysterious in the twilight. Colours had been wonderful. But these were words only.

What sense of beauty had others? Mamma never said any more than that a thing was pretty or jolly, and yet she loved this garden. She spent hours in weeding and in cutting off the heads of dead roses, and there were long talks with Weston when long names would come out of their mouths – why had some flowers nothing but an ugly Latin name? But you could not say that she had no sense of beauty.

Harry looked upon the country from the hunting standpoint, whether there were many stiff fences and fox coverts. The Arts of Use. And there was Herbert, during the war, at Salonica. The only thing of interest he had remembered afterwards was that a certain flower, that they had here and that was incessantly nursed by Weston in the hot-house, grew wild and in profusion on the hills above the port. Egbert, the underkeeper, at Salonica also, had seen a colossal covey of partridges. That was all they remembered.

In the country one lost all sense of proportion. Mamma used to become hysterical over some ridiculously small matter. Last Christmas it had been ludicrous, she had been so angry, and it had led to one of her outbursts about his not caring for the life here, he, who was to carry on the house and the traditions, and so on. It had been about the Church Parochial Council. She had asked that at matins on Christmas Day there might be music. Crayshaw had answered that there would be music at Holy Communion which took place before, but that as no one ever came to matins on Christmas Day – (And whose fault was that, my dear?) – it was not worth while having music again. There had been a violent discussion, one would have given anything to be there, during which Mamma had said that if she was a child her Christmas would have been ruined with no music on Christmas Day. Crayshaw had replied that the children could come at six in the evening when everyone else came, and when there was music. Mamma had said that it was the morning that mattered. Crayshaw had parried by saying that the children could come to Holy Communion. Mamma had not liked that, 'it was bothering children's heads with mysticism'. Finally they had voted, and Mamma had been defeated because she had closed the public pathway at the bottom of the garden, a path which no one had used for nine years, and the gates were ugly and in the way. It had spoilt the drive, that wretched path. 'The first time, John, that the village has not followed my lead. It is so discouraging.' Oh, it had been tragic.

Behind the house a hen was taken with asthma over her newly-laid.

A bee droned by to the accompaniment of flies. He glided down the hill of consciousness to the bottom, where he was aware only of wings buzzing, and of the sun, that poured down a beam to warm him, and of a wind that curled round. Only one pigeon cooed now, and he was tireless, emptying his sentiment into a void of unresponding laziness. He was singing everyone to sleep. How dreadful if a cuckoo were to come. The sky would have cleared, it would be a white-blue. It was hot.

A woodpecker mocked.

He leant down and his fingers hurried over the grass, here and there, looking for the cigarette-box. He found and opened it, taking out a cigarette. Again they set out to find the matches, which they found. He felt for the end that lit, he struck and heard the burst of flame. Fingers of the left hand groped down the cigarette in his mouth to the end, and he brought the match there. He puffed, he might have puffed anything then. He felt with a forefinger to see whether it was alight and he burned the tip. The match blew out with a shudder, and he threw it away.

How intolerable not to be able to smoke, but people said that you came to appreciate it in time, and it was degrading to chew gum. Was it still alight? Again he burned his finger. He threw the cigarette away. Now it would be starting a fire; still he had thrown it out on to the lawn. What was that? A tiny sound, miles away, no one but a blind man could possibly have caught it. He sniffed, he could smell the fire, very small yet, but starting, just one flame, invisible in the sunlight, eating a pine-needle. What was to be done? To leave it was madness, but how to find it to put it out? Await developments, there was nothing probably. Stevenson's last match.

All the same the cigarette was not burning anything, it was an invention typical of the country. He was getting into the country state of mind already, with no sense of proportion, and always looking for trouble. And he would become more and more like that, when one was blind there was no escape. It was a wretched business. The life of the century was in the towns, he had meant to go there to write books, and now he was imprisoned in a rudimentary part of life. And the nurse was busy nursing him back to a state of health sufficient for him to be left to their all-enfolding embrace of fatuity. So that all he could do to keep his brain a little his own was to write short stories. Perhaps one on the nurse, with her love of white wards and of stiff flowers, they were sure to be stiff if she had any, and of a ghastly antiseptic sanity. With her love of pain and horrors, and of interesting cases, with her devastating knowledge of human anatomy. But that was rather cheap, for she wasn't like that. She was merely dull, with a desire for something concrete and defined to hold on to. But she was dull.

He would write a story, all about tulips. That time when Mamma had taken him one Easter holidays to Holland, when the tulips had been out all along the railway line. And the cows with blankets on in case it rained. But no, it would have to be in England, the tourist effect in stories was dreadful. It would be a Dutchman with a strange passion for tulips – that was rather beautiful, that idea. Yes, and he would have passed all his life in sending tulips over to England, till he had come to think that England must have been a carpet of them in spring – he would have to be uneducated and think that England was only a very tiny island. He would be just a little bit queer with lovely haunting ideas that drifted through his brain, and he would love his tulips! So that Holland in springtime would not have enough tulips for him, and he would sell the little he had so as to buy a passage, that he might feed his soul on his tulips in England. His place in the bulb farm would be to address the wrappers, and there would be an address in Cumberland that he was told to write to very often. Then there would be those hills to work into the story, and he would go on a bicycle, which he had bought with his last penny, and each hill would seem to hide his tulips, they might be there, just beyond, behind the next hill. Till he would fall down, dead, his heart broken! But perhaps that was a little flat. It must simmer over in his brain. He would be very queer, with little fragments of insanity here and there. It would work.

The laziness of this afternoon.

Mrs Haye crushed grass on the way to Mrs Trench. Herbert

stretched out a hand and made clucking noises, while Mrs Lane giggled. Weston shifted his feet slightly, and put his cap further back on his head, before the artichokes. Harry began hissing his way down another paragraph, and Doris was fondly tying a bow on the end of one pigtail. Jenny, the laundry cat, was two inches nearer the sparrow.

Nan put down her cup with a sigh and folded her hands on her lap, while her eyes fixed on the fly-paper over the table.

They were all standing round him on the lawn.

'Seven days old. I said what I could to Mrs Trench. A terrible affair. What can one do?'

'Poor little mite.'

'What was it, Mrs Haye?'

'Gastric pneumonia, I think, nurse. I am sure that Brodwell muddled the case.'

'To think of it!'

'Of course, Mrs Haye, gastric pneumonia with a seven days' child is very grave.'

'Was it a boy or a little girl'm?'

'A girl. How is he today, nurse?'

'Oh, I'm all right.'

'I think we are getting on very nicely, aren't we?'

'He has more colour to him today.'

'Oh, Master John, you do look a heap better.'

'Thanks, Nan, I'm sure I do.'

'Yes, Mrs Haye, he really has. In one or two days we shall be up and about again, shan't we?'

'I suppose so.'

'Of course you will, dear.'

'It did give me a fright.'

'Well, there's another fright over anyway, Nan.'

'Dr Mulligan is not coming again, is he, nurse?'

'Only tomorrow, Mrs Haye, for a final inspection. And I had perhaps be better getting ready to go back to town in a week or two, he is going on so quickly.'

—Thank God, the woman was talkin' about goin'.

—Time she went, too, airified body.

'Well, nurse, I think in about ten days' time it will be safe for me to take over the dressings, and then there would be nothing left for you to do except teaching him how to get about and so on, and we can do that, can't we, Jennings?'

'We can do that'm.'

Yes, they could do that. The nurse was intolerable, but at least she was alive, and now they were sending her away.

'Then, Mrs Haye, I can write up to town to tell them that I shall be free in, say, twelve days' time? That will make the 24th, won't it?'

'Yes, shall we say the 24th? Why, it's you, Ruffles. Oh, so old.'

'Poor dog.'

'How old is he, Mrs Haye?'

'Twelve years old. He ought to be destroyed. One must be practical.'

'That's right. Kill him.'

'But, my dear, it is cruel to let him live.'

'He is too old to be healthy, Mrs Haye. They are germ traps.'

Ruffles made confiding noises, wagging a patchy tail. An effluvia of decay arose.

'Perhaps it would be best.'

It was a pity to shoot him, after he had been so good. How sentimental dogs were. Nan would be having one of her waves of silent grief. Their breathing descended in a chorus to where he lay, hoarse, sibilant, and tired. Were they thinking of Ruffles? Did they all snore at night?

The evening was falling away and the breeze had dropped. A midge bit him on the ankle and a drop of sweat tickled him by the bandages. The pigeons were all cooing together, there seemed to be no question and answer, they were in such a hurry to say everything that there wasn't time. Birds twittered happily and senselessly all round. Through it and over it all there was the evening calm, the wet air heavy everywhere. The sky would be in great form, being crude and vulgar.

They were silent because it was the evening, though they could not keep it up for long.

'A pretty sunset.'

'It's that beautiful.'

'I do love a sunset, Mrs Haye, I think . . .'

'A sunset, John' – the woman was intolerable.

'Ah.'

'Is it not becoming a little fresh for him out here, Mrs Haye? We mustn't catch a chill.'

'Perhaps. Jennin's, could you just go and tell William and Robert to come here to help Master John back.'

'But I can walk by myself if one of you will give me their arm.'

'I don't think we are quite strong enough yet, Mrs Haye.'

She would write tomorrow to get her changed. It was too bad of them to send her this thing.

God blast the woman, why was he always treated as a baby? Oh, how they loved it, now that he was helpless.

'What time is it?'

'Eight o'clock, dear. Time for dinner. Ah, here are William and Robert.'

Ruffles licked his hand. My only friend. Oh, he was sick and tired of it all.

'Now, dear, put your arm round William's shoulder, and the other round Robert . . .'

'Would it not be better, Mrs Haye, if between them they carried the chair and him on it?'

'Stairs – narrow. Now lift him. That's right. You can get along like that with them on each side, can't you, John?'

The woman was insufferable.

'Yes, I'm all right. Goodnight, Ruffles.'

'I'll come up and see you after dinner, dear.'

William breathed discreetly but heavily, Robert full of energy. William's shoulders were thin.

'Mind, Master John, here's the step into the library.'

The nurse walked quickly behind. Mrs Haye was a fool, and with no medical training, even if she were an honourable. Of course it was bad for the patient to walk upstairs. If she had had her way, they would never have put him in a room two storeys up, even if he had been in it since childhood. These ex-VADs who gave themselves such airs.

Nan was drowned in a wave of silent grief.

To see him supported between Mr William and Robert with white bandages over his head and him so weak and feeble and who would never see again, and the nurse who was not fit to look after a sick boy she was that cantankerous.

She trailed away to a cup o' tea in the kitchen.

Mrs Haye went round to her sitting-room through the door in the wall of the rose garden. No solution yet, nothing found, nothing arranged. Only one or two letters of condolence left to answer. And the nurse was terrible. Terrible. The idea of carrying him up those narrow stairs. There might have been a nasty accident if the woman had had her way. And he was in such a difficult state of mind. You could not say a word to him without his taking it wrong. Really, the only thing to do was to watch him and await developments. And in two or three years' time they would marry him to some nice girl, they would look out for one. There was – well, perhaps.

She went upstairs to dress for dinner.

He sat on a chair while the nurse got the bed ready. His head hurt him, the stairs must have done that. Poor Ruffles, it was too bad that he was finished. His head was throbbing; how he hated pain, and in the head it was unbearable. And this atmosphere of women. There was no male friend who would come to stay, he had always been too unpleasant, or had always tried to be clever, or in the movement. And now there was no escape, none. A long way away there might be a country of rest, made of ice, green in the depths, an ice that was not cold, a country to rest in. He would lie in the grotto where it was cool and where his head would be clear and light, and where there was nothing in the future, and nothing in the past. He would lie on the grass that was soft, and that had no ants and no bugs, and there would be no flies in the air and no sun above his head, but only a grey clearness in the sky, that stretched to mountains blue against the distance, through the door of his ice-house. There would be pine trees in clumps or suddenly alone, and strange little mounds, one after the other, that grew and grew in height till they met the mountains that cut off the sky. A country of opera-bouffe. And little men in scarlet and orange would come to fight up and down the little hills, some carrying flags, others water pistols. There would be no wounded and no dead, but they would be very serious.

Why couldn't there be something really romantic and laughable in life? With sentimentality and tuppenny realism. Something to wake one out of an existence like this, where day would follow day with nothing to break the monotony, where meal followed meal and where people sat still between meals letting troubles fall into their lap. Nothing stirred.

'There, it is ready now. Take off your dressing-gown and lean on my shoulder. There we are. Would you prefer to have your dressings renewed now, or after dinner?'

'Oh, now, to get it over.'

He hated pain. He only half saw how pain fitted in with the scheme of things, and it made him afraid.

She was clinking bowls, and already the clean smell, far worse than any dung-heap, was all over the room.

Fingers began to unpin and to remove his bandages. It was hurting less today. No, it wasn't. Oh . . .

3 Picture postcardism

In the green lane between Barwood and Huntly there was a stile in the tall hedge. Behind were laurels, and brambles, and box trees, and yews, all growing wild. At the end of a mossy path from the stile lay the house, built in yellow brick with mauve patterns, across a lawn of rank grass. It had been raised in 1840 by a Welshman, the date was over the door. But this was hardly visible, it was early morning and a heavy white mist smudged the outline. Birds were beginning to chatter, dawn was not far. There were no curtains to the house, and no blinds but one, torn, hanging askew across a dark window swinging loosely open on the ground floor. A few panes of glass were broken, and brown paper was stuck over the holes. There was a porch at the near end with most of the tiles off; they had been used to patch the roof, which was a dark blue-grey. At the far end was what had once been a hot-house, its glass broken.

The garden was dishevelled, no attempt had been made to clean it for many years, and the only sign of labour was the cabbages that Father, in a burst of energy, had planted in a former flower-bed. There was one huge beech tree, most beautifully tidy, and the only respectable member of the garden. The others merely went round the edge, keeping the chaotic growth from the neat meadows. The whole garden gave the effect of being unhappy because it had too much freedom. It was sad. And the house was sadder still with its wistful mauve patterns, looking so deserted and forlorn although it was lived in. Nobody loved, and, though by nature so very feminine, it had to remain neuter and wretched. No one cared two farthings, and it felt that deeply. No one minded. The birds were chirruping heartlessly. From over the river the church struck a silver five.

At the back was a yard, in the middle a hen coop made out of an old army hut. A cock was crowing within, had been doing so for some time. There is a stable, with a rickety door off its lower hinge hanging ajar. A rat plays inside. There are holes in the red roof of the outhouse, gaping at the pink sky. Broken flagstones lie about, and weeds have grown through the cracks. The back door has lost its paint. The four windows stare vacantly with emptiness behind their leaded panes. The mist hangs sluggishly about, and the air is chill as the cock crows in his raucous tenor.

Then the sun lights up the top of the beech tree into golden fire, and there is a movement in the paleness. It begins to go, while the sky fades back into everyday life. The fire creeps down the beech till the tops of the overgrown laurels are alight, the mist has drawn off to the river just below there. Everything brightens and stretches out of sleep, the sky is blue almost. A butterfly aimlessly flutters over the cabbages, the flycatcher swoops down and she is swallowed; he was on guard already. A pigeon drives by, a bright streak of silver painted on him by the sun. The birds chirp in earnest as the sun climbs higher and begins to make shadows, while anywhere that a drop of dew catches the light he breaks into a gem. A gossamer web will dart suddenly across something, like a rainbow thread.

The chickens begin to make a great noise, scolding and crooning in their wooden prison, sounding very greedy. They want to be let out, for a late worm, who has come up to see the new day, may yet be left by the gobbling blackbirds and thrushes. The last mists are drawing out, a breeze is stirring, and the morning is crystal. The dew has made a spangled dress for everyone, and the weeds and straggling bushes are all under a canopy of brilliant drops of light.

A starling sits upon the chimney pot preening himself. A crow flies over the garden, glancing to right and left. The three yews are renewing their green in the sun, the laurels are shiny and clean. A rabbit hops out, looks round, and begins to nibble at the fresh grass, his last meal before he goes to bed.

The air is new.

All are one community, but it will not be for long. When the sun sucks up the dew and the moistness of the gossamer, everyone will be for himself again. Each bird will sing his own song, and not the song of the garden. 'Me, me, me,' he will say, 'I am the best.' And the nettles will whisper to each other, 'You or me, you or me,' laurels, yews, box trees and brambles too. Even the beech tree who has won to his great height and who has no rival in fifteen miles, he, too, will be straining, straining higher to the sun. It is all the sun, who has not climbed high enough yet.

The back door opened and she came out, pausing a moment before shutting the door behind her. She was tall and dressed in red slippers, a dirty blue serge skirt, and a thin, stale mauve bodice. She was so graceful! Her skin was unhealthy-looking, dark and puffed, her mouth small, the lips red. Her hair, black and in disorder, tangled down to her eyebrows. Across one cheek a red scar curved. Her eyes, a dark brown and very large, and a light that burned.

She felt alive, and she could see that the yard was dead – yes, she was like that this morning.

She stepped out into the yard, slammed the door behind her, and swept through the weeds that sprinkled her with dew. One big bramble twined so amorously round her skirt that her legs could not tear themselves free, and she had to bend to tear him off superbly. All over at the contact of her hands he trembled, and trembled there for some time. She went to the pump which stood near the outhouse, and the rat fled down his hole. She worked the pump handle till it chugged up water for her which she splashed over her face, wetting her dress as well. She went to the hen coop, opened the door, and stood waiting. The cock walked sedately out first and she hurried him up with her carpet slipper, laughing to see him flustered. Her voice was deep, and, of course, had a coarse note in it. And then she went back into the house, all wet, banging the back door behind her.

Snores, deep and thick, came down from an open window above into the yard.

The cock was angry and he watched his hens for a moment with a sense of humiliation, one claw stopped in mid-air. He did not know but he felt out of sorts. Not in actual ill-health but liverish. All the same, if there was anyone to look at him they would see a fine sheen to his feathers today. He cried out to attract attention, and Natacha, who was by his side, said duteously that his ruff was stupefying in its beauty, rivalling the sun with its brightness. After it was all over, leaving Natacha squawking, he fluttered up on to the top of the coop. He was feeling ambitious, in revolt, the world was all wrong somehow, too soft, not enough dust for a dust-bath. There was not even a dung-heap in this wretched yard. Everything was too soft – the sun, and the dew, and the gentle weeds. He wanted heat, heat. Between intervals of killing things on himself he stretched out his neck and told this to the world, and that he was king of this castle.

Joan upstairs is putting on her stockings. What a lot of holes there are in them, but no matter. Sunday today. How will Father take the church bells? Last Sunday he had not minded very much. It is going to be beautifully hot, and Father will hate that too, poor old thing. George hated the heat, only she loved it. The wonderful sun!

How red her hands are getting, and rough. That was the house-work, while nice, young, rich ladies kept theirs folded with gloves on, and they had coloured umbrellas to keep the sun off. To be fright-ened of the sun! Nice young ladies had never done a day's work in their lives. Why should she work and they be idle? Oh, if she were like one of them! She would have light blue undies. Wouldn't she look a dream in the glass! And stays? No, no stays. But perhaps, they must fortify you so.

But what was the good of dreaming? – dreaming never did anyone any good. There was George, he might be working in the meadow tomorrow, and then she would lean over the stile – climb over the stile? – and talk to him, and get a few shy answers back, perhaps. George was wonderful, George was so exciting. With his fair hair, with his honey-coloured eyes, with his brick-red face so passionate, with his strength, with his smell. The one that drove the milk fac-tory's lorry and that was always smoking a cigarette on his upper lip and that had that look in his eyes like a snake looking for his prey, she could not understand how she had seen anything in him. But George, with his honey-coloured ones, slow, but with it at the back of them, and with his shortness, and with his force, oh, it would, it must be something this time after such years of waiting. To find out all about it. 'Yes, George, go on, go on.'

What nice toes she had, except that the nails were rather dirty. But what was the good of keeping clean now? They weren't in the Vicar-age any more, and there was no one to tell her how dirty or how pretty they were, except Father when he was drunk, but that, of course, did not count. George would say all that. She would teach him, if he didn't know.

She moves to a looking-glass and wrestles with her hair. In the glass was the brown-papered wall behind, the paper hanging in strips, showing the yellow plaster beneath. Those holes in the roof. And there was the rash that broke out in the top right-hand corner of the glass where the paint had come off the back. She was so mis-erable. The only chair has no back, and the front leg is rickety, so that you have to lean over to the right when you sit down. The bare boards of the floor are not clean, the bedclothes are frowsy, the pillow greasy. Everything is going to go wrong today. It is close in here. She goes across the room and flings the window open.

By the window there was a small table, on it a looking-glass. She never used this one because you had to sit down to it, and that was tiresome. Draped round the oval frame and tied in wide, drooping bows to the two uprights was a broad white ribbon. Tied to the handles of the two drawers beneath were white bows also. On the low table were hair-brushes, a comb with three teeth out, a saucer full of pins and hair-pins and safety pins and a medicine bottle, empty, with a bow round the neck made out of what had been left of the white ribbon. Violets, in a little bunch, lay by the bottle, dead.

She goes through the door into the next room, which is his. He is lying noisily asleep, with the bedclothes half off his chest, and his red beard is spread greasily over the lead-white of his skin. One arm hangs down to the floor, the other, trying to follow it, is flung across his chest. His face has a nose, flat, hair red and skin blotchy. There is the usual homely smell of gin. The window was wide open to let out the snores.

And this was Father, Daddy, Daddums. Oh, he was pretty in bed. She couldn't remember him very well as he was at the Vicarage such ages ago, without his beard. It had been wonderful then: they had had a servant, which you could order about. And Mrs Haye, she used to terrify her, now she did not care two snaps of the finger although she had run away from her when she had seen her coming down the lane the other day; and Mrs Haye had called him Mr Entwhistle, the ordinary people, Passon, and Colonel Waterpower, whom they had met occasionally, had called him Padre. Silly all those people were with their silly ways, but they were so well dressed and the ladies too, those stuffs, so ... And it was his fault that they were like this. You could see what people thought by their faces as they passed, they always went a little quicker when they caught sight of you coming. And they might still have been in the Vicarage.

Poor Father, perhaps it was not all his fault. And after all she was the only person left now to look after him. And the life wasn't too bad, he left her alone except when he was drunk and wanted someone to talk to. And he told her the most wonderful things. He was really a wonderful man, a genius. All it was, was that he was misunderstood. He saw visions and things. And really, in the end, it was all Mother's fault for being such a fool, though of course Father had been fond of gin before that. Mother, when she lay dying, with Father and her at the bedside, instead of whispering something she ought to have, had cried out quite loud 'John' as if she was calling, right in front of the doctor and the village nurse and that. Then she was dead, and they were her last words. John was still the postman. She had been a fool, and Father had drunk much more gin ever afterwards. After Mother died Father had been unfrocked, that was soon after the beginning of the war, partly for the gin, and partly for the talk about Mother. Mr Davies died in time, and with most of the money that Uncle Jim had left them when he was killed they had bought this house here, only two miles away. It would have been nicer to go somewhere new, but as Father said, 'he was not going to run away from those that had hounded him from the parish'.

What was she doing standing still? She had to wake him and then get breakfast and then clear up. 'Here, wake up. Wake up.' and she picks up the clothes, flung anyhow on the floor, and smooths them, putting them at the foot of the bed. Roses on wallpaper, roses hung down in strips from the damp wall pointing. 'Get up, get up.' He was shamming, that he might give her more work to do. Yes, that was it. 'Do you hear? Get up.' She lifts his white shoulders and shakes him till the blue watery eyes open. She lets him flop back on to the pillow, the red finger-marks on his skin fading away again.

His eyes open painfully. He scratches, gazing vacantly at the ceiling.

'Another day?'

'Yes.'

'Oh.'

'I'll go and get you some water, if you'll get up.'

'Well, go and get it then.'

She goes to the pump, and he drags himself out of bed. He is short and thick-set, with bulging flesh. He has been sleeping in an old pair of flannel trousers. He sits on a box by the window. He looks out beyond the garden, over the meadow and the quiet river, to where the trees cover a hill on the other side. Their green dresses are blurred by the delicate blue mist that swims softly round them, the deep shade yawns the sleep away. In the meadows some cows lie in the open, it is not hot enough yet to drive them under the hedges. Below, a hen chuckles with satisfaction. How quiet it all was, nothing wrong in the best of all possible worlds. They thought that, all the rest of them, they did not care. And he was forgotten. Nature insulted him,

What right had the country to look like this, basking in the sunshine while he lived in the middle of it? He with his great thoughts, his great sufferings. Why didn't the State support him, instead of letting him live in squalor? He deserved as much of the money from the bloated capitalist as anyone else. It was their class that had brought him to this, they had never paid him enough, for one thing. It was their fault. Where was the water?

Today was going to go badly, it was going to be terribly hot. Sunday too, so that the church bells would ring and then he would remember Barwood church, the little altar, the roses – his roses – growing outside. He felt so ill today, not at all strong. He would weep when the bells rang, weep because so many things were over, the Colonel calling him Padre, the deference of the churchwarden. How great his tears would be. All that was so far and yet so close. Every day he thought it over. But there was no need to regret it, he was working out his salvation here, if he had stayed on in that Vicarage he would have been dead alive. He was so vital here, and then somehow the grasp of it would leave him.

He was ill today all the same, he felt it inside, something seriously the matter. Was it the cancer? There, turning over and over. Yes, there it was. Here no, there; no, no, there. Yes. Cancer, that he had been awaiting so long.

'Here's the water.'

He winced. The noise the girl made. Was he not ill?

'I am ill.'

'Again?'

'It's the cancer at last.'

There was a certain satisfaction now that it had come.

'Again. The doctor will cost you a bottle just for telling you it's imagination. I know them and you.'

'Go away, go away.'

She was essentially small in character, like that mistaken woman her mother. Oh, he couldn't any more. Cancer coming on top of it all. What a fine tragedy his was. And it would cut short his great work, before even it had been begun.

She opened the door downstairs and went into the kitchen. He was much the same today, a little stronger perhaps, but that would go till he stoked up in the evening. Poor, weak creature.

Through a small window in a small bay looking out on to the garden the sunlight comes in and washes the dirt off the worn, red tiles. There is a sour smell of old food, and underneath the two windows on the right lie some empty sardine tins which have missed the gaps in the glass when thrown away. She goes to the cupboard, which is on the left. On it is an almanack from the ironmonger in Norbury, ten years old, with a picture in the middle of a destroyer cutting rigid water shavings in the sea, with smoke hurrying frozenly out of its funnels, and with a torpedo caught into eternity while leaping playfully at its side, out of the water and into the air. She jerks the cupboard open. Inside are plates, knives and forks, cups, and a teapot, all in some way chipped or broken. There are tinned foods of every kind, most of all sardines, and three loaves. At the bottom are two pails and a mangy scrubbing-brush and some empty gin bottles. On the top shelf some unopened bottles and a few cakes of soap are jumbled up with vaguely folded sheets and towels. She takes out a sardine tin and a loaf of bread and pitches them with two knives on to the table in the middle of the room. A chunk of butter on half a plate she puts down, as well as two cups without handles, and the milk-holding teapot. He has an injured spout, poor thing.

She goes over to the bay window and flings it open. She rolls up the torn blind. Father liked going round at night occasionally, 'shutting up' as if he lived in a castle, but as he could never see straight enough by then to find the window latches it was not much good, but he always pulled down the blind. The range was disused and rusty, it had not been lighted since April. Before it was a tub of greasy water in which she did the washing up. The sun did not get far into the room. The paper here also was beginning to peel from the walls. An early bluebottle buzzed somewhere.

There was a movement in the sunlight, a scamper, and Minnie was arching his back against her leg, while his tail waved carefully at the end. Minnie, so fresh, so clean, the darling. Cat's eyes looked up at her, yellow and black. 'Minnie, have you killed anything?' In a rush he was out of the window – how like darling Minnie – his tail a pennant. Then he is back, the clever darling, and in his mouth a dead robin redbreast. How he understood. 'Oh, Minnie, the little sweet. Look at his crimson waistcoat and his crimson blood. Why, he is still warm. Shall we give him to Father for his breakfast? What a clever Minnie,' and Minnie purrs half attention. He paddles a paw in a speck of blood. She bends down, taking him in her arms. 'Oh, Minnie, what a clever Minnie.' But with a light jump he was out of her arms and was going to the window, and then was out of it. Joan follows, looks out, and Minnie is standing there, quite still, detached. Then he was off, slipping by everything, while the dew caught at his coat. How lovely cats were, she adored her Minnie.

A slow step came down the stairs, with a careful pause at the hole on the ninth step from the ground, and he comes in shakily. His face is baggy and fallen in, his black clothes have stains. He is wearing a dirty drainpipe collar, for it is the Sabbath, while round it a khaki shirt flaunts, without the black dicky. He stands in the doorway, his beard waggling.

'Sardines? Again? I tell you I can't eat them.'

'We ought to be glad to eat what is given to us.'

'Don't throw up quotations like that at me just to annoy me. Do you hear? Given, who said it was given? I paid for it, didn't I? You hate me, and everyone hates me.'

But that was as it should be, he ought to take a pride in the hatred of the world. It was ever so with the great. But sardines, he paid for them. There had been a time when he had thanked God for sardines, because he had always hated them so that he saw in them his cross. But what was the good? He paid for them, and ate them because it was better than eating dry bread. After all he had paid for them, and if he had not paid he would not have got them, so where did thanks come in? He ought only to thank that oil-well in Southern Texas where Hoyner the cinema-man came from. There had been a time when he had thanked God for oil-wells, wars and apples, while these were nothing but unfortunate mistakes, he having lost half his money in Mexican oil, and apples being bad for his digestion. Why did he keep that money in oil? – it would go like the other half had. But it was so awkward changing. It was all so difficult. But then if no one ate fish the industry would die and with it the fishermen. No, thank God, he could see nothing divine in anything now, whereas in the old days he had eaten even a sardine with considerable emotion. Yet how could one be sure? His reason, how it tortured him, how it pursued round and round, coldly, in his brain. He had a fine intellect, too. Edward had told him that thirty years ago at Oxford. And it had been growing, growing ever since in his hermit existence, even Joan could not deny it ... He was even more of a genius because he was recognized in his home, a very rare thing surely. And his reward would come, it must come. Yes, he would start work this very morning. But he felt so ill, weak.

'I feel so ill this morning, child. I have such a headache. And I am so weak' – physically only, of course; no, not mentally.

'Have a drop of gin in your milk. That will make it all right.'

'Yes, I think you are right' – but no more than one, really.

He was always like that before the morning one. Poor Father.

That is better, more comfortable. But still there may be something wrong with him. He swallows another gin-and-milk.

'It's the cancer, Joan, that's what I am so terrified about. I can feel it glowing hot. We can't afford an operation or morphia. I shall die.'

It would be nice to die; but no, it wouldn't be, and that was very unreasonable. But no, it wasn't, there was his book.

He was so clever that he had always been bottom at school – all great men had been bottom at school. Then he had lost his way in the world. No, that wasn't true, he had found it – this, this gin was his triumph. It was the only thing that did his health any good, and one had to be in good spirits if he was to think out the book, the great book that was to link everything into a circle and that would bring him recognition at last, perhaps even a letter from the Bishop. It would justify his taking something now and again as he did. But one doubted, there were days when one could not see it at all. How ill he felt. Some deep-seated disorder. How dreadful a disease, cancer. Why could not the doctors do something about it? Oh, for a pulpit to say it from.

Terrible, terrible.

'Father, where did you put the tin-opener for these sardines?'

'I don't know. My pain. Never had it.'

'But it must be somewhere. It isn't in the cupboard here.'

'Can't you open it with a fork? It's all laziness. Why bother me? Oh, here it is in my pocket. How funny.'

'You are drinking all the gin. No, look here, you mustn't have any more. There will be none for this evening at this rate.'

'But I'm not going to drink any more, I tell you. Leave me alone.'

'Oh, yes. Here, give me that bottle.'

'I shan't; I want it, I tell you. My health.'

'Give it me.'

You could be firm with him in the morning. She locks up the bottle in the cupboard, slips the key inside her dress, and begins to open the sardines. He is almost in tears, 'insulted, by a girl, my daughter. When it was for the good of my health, as I was ill.' But he wasn't such a fool, oh no. He had a dozen beneath the floor of the study. He had wanted to drink more lately, and the girl always regulated his bottle a day carefully.

'Damn, I've cut myself with the tin-opener.'

There is a gash in her thumb, and she bleeds into the oil which floats over the sardines. Serve her right, now she would get blood-poisoning, her hand would swell and go purple, and it would hurt. They would die in agony together. Think of the headlines in the evening papers, the world would hear of him at last: 'AMAZING DISCOVERY IN LONELY COTTAGE,' then lower down, 'UNFROCKED GENIUS AND HIS BEAUTIFUL DAUGHTER FOUND DEAD.' Beautiful. Was she? Yes, of course she was, as good as anyone's daughter anyway, except for the scar. The scar, it was like a bad dream, he had a hazy memory of her taunting him, of his throwing the bottle and missing, and of throwing one of the broken bits, and of catching her with it on the cheek. It was horrible. Still it was what a genius would have done. He was so weak this morning. What was he thinking about? Yes, suicide, and the headlines in the papers. But in any case it would be over in three days. What was the use of it all? And what was he eating, blood-stained sardine? He did feel sick. Cancer.

She had bound up her finger in a handkerchief, and was eating sardines on slabs of bread-and-butter, heads and tails, while he unconsciously cut these off. She eats with quick hunger, her chin is greasy with the oil coming from the corners of her mouth. She says thickly:

'I love sardines, and the oil is the best thing about them.'

No answer.

Poor Father, he was in for a bad day, for it was going to be very hot, and he must have had a bad night, he was a little worse than usual. And he did hate sardines so, but there was nothing else to eat, except the kipper in tomato sauce, and they were going to have a tin of that for lunch. Father was really not very well, perhaps this talk of cancer wasn't all nonsense. But it must only be the drink. He was such a nasty sight, with his finicky tastes and his jumpy ways. Think if George were there across the table, eating with a strong appetite, with his strong, dirty nails, the skin half grown over them, instead of Father's white ones, the last thing about himself that he spent any trouble over. They were one of his ways of passing the time, while she slaved. There would be something behind his honey-coloured eyes, a strong hard light, instead of blue wandering, weak ones. His face would be brick-red with the sun, his flesh inside the open shirt collar – there would be no starch about him – would be gold with a blue vein here and there; he would be so strong, it would be wonderful to be so frightened of him. Gold. While that weak creature over there, why even his beard was bedraggled and had lost its colour. Yet there were times when his body filled out and his voice grew, and when his beard flamed. Her fingers crept to the scar on her cheek, it had been wonderful that night. You felt a slave, a beaten slave.

But it was the scar that frightened George. His eyes would stray to the scar and look at it distrustfully; at first he had looked at her dress with horror, but she had not made that mistake again. Still he never spoke, which was so annoying but lately there had been more confidence and shrewdness in his eyes. But the others did use to say something, all except Jim, he had been worse than George. Of course, no one ever saw her with him, it would scare him if the village began to talk. But it was very exciting. It was incredible to think how the days had passed without him.

There were now two bluebottles busy round the head of a sardine about three days old. The head lay there, jagged at the neck where Father had pulled off the body, a dull glaze over the silver scales, the eyes were metallic. There was blue on the two bluebottles who never seemed content, they buzzed up and down again so. Minnie had come in by the little bay window, and the bluebottles seethed with anger at being disturbed by someone besides themselves.

She rises sideways without stirring her chair, whispering hoarsely:

'Minnie, Minnie, come here.'

But he slips by her hands. The key slipped down her leg to tinkle on the floor.

'That cat. Ah you, go away, go away,' and he gets up, his chair screeching along the red tiles. He throws his knife feebly, it misses Minnie and makes a clatter. He is out of the window in a flash, and Father sits down again. She puts the key under the bread.

'I do hate cats, they frighten me so. There is something so dreadful about a cat, the way she seems to be looking at nothing. They don't see flesh and blood, they see an abstract of everything. It's horrible, horrible. Joan, you might keep her away from me, you know how I hate her. I can't bear any cat. And in my condition. I think you might, yes, I do think you might.'

'All right, but I don't see what you mean. Minnie is such a darling, I don't know why you hate her.'

'Of course you don't know cats as they really are. She is a devil, that cat.'

Poor Father.

Outside, on the right, a hen stalks reflectively, her head just over the weeds. Her eye is fixed, its stare is irritating, and the way she has of tilting her head to look for food is particularly precious. She goes forward slowly, often dipping out of sight to peck at something. All that can be seen of her is a dusty-brown colour, dull beside the fresh green round her, encouraged by the sun into a show of newness. He watches her one visible eye with irritation.

'A chicken, at six in the morning, and loose in the garden. That shouldn't be. A pen. I will build a pen for them some time. I will start today, but then there is no rabbit wire, and we can't afford wire.' Yet hens in one's garden. Degrading. Yet why not? They had to live, it was only fair to them that he should let them get food even if they were in his way, because they gave him food, and he did not deserve it. All the same, he did. And they were God's creatures, even if they did come out of an egg, and even more because they did so. But was that true? No. Yes. He couldn't see at all today. Scientists understood the egg, all except the life that entered it – and that was God; there, there you are. But an egg. He didn't know. There was something. He did not know. No, not in an egg.

He gets up and moves towards the door by the cupboard.

'You'll never build that pen, and you know it. Here, what are you going to the Gin Room for?'

'Don't use that tone to me. Can't your Father go where he likes? Can't he retire to his study for a little peace? You seem to have no – no feeling for your Father.'

And he was gone. That meant he had some gin in there, but you couldn't help it, there was nothing to be done, and he was better when he had drunk a little, he was more of a Man. And what was the use of worrying? and anyway it pulled him together. Blast this finger, why had she been such a fool as to jab it open? It hurt too, though not very much, still it would have been nice to have had someone to be sorry about it and to help her tie it up. If George had been here she would have been able to make such a lot of it. Those bluebottles, there were three of them round that sardine now, and three more over there, all in the sun. That was the one sensible thing about them; how she loved the sun. She put the key into the table drawer.

*

The clock in the village church across the fields struck twelve in a thin copper tenor that came flatly through the simmering heat. No bird sang, no breath of air stirred, nothing moved under the sun who was drawing the life out of everything except Joan. She got up slowly, damp with sweat, from the window-sill where she had been stewing in the white light. The wood of it was unbearably hot, and what few traces of paint that were left, blistered. She fanned herself with the old straw hat she had been wearing, and tried to make up her mind to go out and find the eggs for dinner. She loved the sun, he took hold of you and drew you out of yourself so that you couldn't think, you just gave yourself up. She loved being with him all round her till she couldn't bear it any more. You forgot everything except him, yet you could not look up at him, he was so bright. He was so strong that you had to guard your head lest he should get in there as well. He was cruel, like George. And he was stronger than George, but then George was a Man.

The air, heavy with the wet heat, hung lifeless save when her straw hat churned it lazily into dull movement. Three bluebottles, fanning themselves angrily with their wings at the windows, by their buzzing kept the room alive. She was lost in a sea of nothingness, and all the room too. From inside Father's room came low moans at intervals, the heat had invaded and had conquered Father. Oh, it is hot, she is pouring with sweat all over, and her hands feel big and clumsy and heavy with blood, there is nowhere to put them. How cool the iron range is, its fireplace gazing emptily up the chimney at the clean blue of the sky. Her hand on the oven door leaves a moist mark which vanishes slowly.

She must look for eggs, though how the poor hens can lay in this weather she didn't know. Think of having feathers, dusty feathers on you for clothes on a day like this. And laying eggs. Minnie would be hot too, in an impersonal sort of way. But the poor hens. Why they would die of it, poor darlings, and the old cock, the old Turk in his harem, what would happen to him, how would he keep his dignity? She would have to go and look, besides she was sticky all over, and it would be cooler moving about.

She leaves the kitchen and goes round to the back under the arch in the brick wall that went to the outhouse, and up which a tortured pear tree sprawled, dead, and so into the yard. The stench is violent, and with the sun beating down she drifts across to the pump, limp as if she has forgotten how alive she had thought she was. She works the

417

handle of the pump slowly till the water gushes reluctantly out. Then she splashes it over her face as it falls into the stone trough, and she plunges in her heavy hands – how nice water was, so cool, so slim, and she would like to be slim, like you saw in fashion plates in the papers, ladies intimately wrapped in long coats that clung to their slimness, they drank tea and she milk; Father said the water was unsafe, although it was so clear and pure and cool. It was hot.

The cock was lost in immobility in the shade of the stable, and she had forgotten about him.

She went round the side of the house, past the window of Father's room till at the corner she came to the conservatory, the winter garden, inside which the crazy hen sometimes laid. She was crazy because she would cry aloud for hours on end and Joan never knew why, though perhaps it was for a chick that a fox had carried off once. The broken glass about caught the sun and seemed to be alight, and inside it was a furnace. Standing quite still in a corner was the hen, but no egg. She was black, and quite, quite still.

In front the beech tree kept a cave of dark light, behind and on each side the tangled bushes did the same, each kept his own, and the giant uneven hedge. They were all trying to sleep through it. She ploughs through the grass and looks vaguely here and there, into the usual nests and the most likely places. Under an old laurel tree with leaves like oilcloth, into an arching tuft of grass. A bramble lies in wait, but she brushes him aside. Two or three flies come after her, busy doing nothing. She passes by clouds of dancing grey gnats in the shade.

Still no eggs.

Nothing of course under the yew, so old that he empoisoned and frightened young things. Drops of sweat fell down. Here was the box tree who kept such a deep shade. There were two eggs. She turns, and crossing a path of sunlight, enters the shade of the beech and sits down, her back against his trunk. If he were George.

She thinks of nothing.

Then she finds that the house is ugly, the yellow and mauve answer back so coldly to the sun. And it was so small and tumble-down. The life was so full, so bitter. If she could change it. There would be the long drive through the great big park with the high wall round it and the great big entrance gates, made of hundreds of crowns in polished copper. After that you would come suddenly through a wood of tall poplars upon a house that was the most beautiful in the world, made of a lot of grey stone. Standing on the steps to greet her as she steps out of her luxurious car would be the many footmen dressed in scarlet, and all young and good-looking. Inside would be the huge staircase, and the great big rooms furnished richly. On a sofa, smoking a cigar, would be the husband, so beautiful. He would have lovely red lips and great big black eyes. Like a sort of fairy story. It would be just like that.

But there was the other dream. A small house with a cross somewhere to show it was a vicarage, and a young clergyman, her husband, and lots and lots of children. She would be in the middle, so happy, her big dark eyes shining like stars, and they would be stretching out chubby fingers to her. But what was the good of dreaming? – dreaming never did anyone any good.

It was nicer to live as you were, and George might be somewhere near. There were the eggs to do.

She wriggles round and looks out, through the gap with the little gate, over the river sunk in her banks and invisible, to the trees on the hill that were soaked in blue, with sunshades of bright sun green on top. A pigeon moves, winking grey, through them; no sound breaks the quiet. It is a sleepy blue, and how the ground was bubbling, air bubbles rising that you could see. She would have to go and boil the eggs, and bubbles would come then. The oil lamp would make such a heavy smell. She liked them raw, but Father would have them boiled. It had to be done. Father was a great baby, and he had to be fed.

She gets up and moves slowly into the house without bothering to put on her straw hat again. From the cupboard underneath the stairs she takes out the lamp with a saucepan fixed above it and carries it into the kitchen. She fills the saucepan by dipping it into the washing-up water, and puts the two eggs in, then lights the lamp with a match from the box on the shelf over the range. Bubbles very soon appear mysteriously from nowhere in the water, and these grow more and more, till the eggs move uneasily at the number of them. Eggs, why do chickens come out of eggs? It was like a conjuring trick, darling little yellow woolly, fluffy things who were always hurrying into trouble! But she knew just how the hen felt with them, it would be wonderful. How long had they been in? Oh dear, the heat and the smell! Poor eggs, it was rather hard on them. This must be about right, and she turns the flame off. Now for the bread and the kippers in tomato sauce and plates and spoons and cups and – the milk, she had forgotten the milk. And she could not go to Mrs Donner's, it was too hot. Father would have to drink gin, he wouldn't mind, but she would, she hated it. She went to the door of his room and beat upon it with the palm of her hand, leaving damp marks wherever she touched it. 'Father, dinner is ready.' His voice answered, 'All right.' It was weary, but with a stronger note.

He shambles into the room dejectedly.

'Oh, it is hot, it is hot.'

'Yes. Father, here's an egg.'

'Thank you. Oh dear.'

They begin to eat, he carefully, and she roughly. He takes up his cup to drink.

'Milk.'

'There isn't any left.'

'No milk? Why is there no milk? We always drink milk at lunch, don't we? And Mrs Donner always has milk, doesn't she? Why is there no milk?'

'You know we can't afford it.'

'I don't suppose we can, but can't I have a little luxury occasionally, with my bad health?'

'I don't know.'

'You don't know, and what's more, you don't care, you don't mind that you make your poor old Father uncomfortable. Where would you have been without me? . . . Don't smile, shut that smile or I'll knock it inside out.' He is streaming with sweat, it falls in blobs on to the table. She just didn't care, didn't care. He'd make her care soon enough. But what was it all for?

'Any gin left for me?'

'Don't taunt me, don't taunt me, don't taunt me . . . don't . . .' and his voice rises, and his face crinkles into funny lines. She was taunting him, taunting him. Just when he felt so ill, too. He did feel ill. And these rows were so thin. Ill.

He gets up and goes to the door of his room, dragging his feet.

'Where are you going? More gin?'

'Yes, more gin. Why shouldn't I? Just one more.'

'But aren't you going to finish your egg? – and then there's the nice kipper and tomato sauce.'

'I tell you I can't eat, I'm ill,' and he pulls to the door of his room.

Silly old Father, he was ridiculous, and yet it must be horrid to be as unhappy as all that. Anyway, it would mean all the more for her. She finishes his egg and then opens and begins to eat the fish. She does not eat prettily. He is having no lunch. Is he really ill? No, it was the gin. Still, it was her job to look after him, if she didn't who would? And if he was ill and died she would feel just like the hen who trod to death a chick – yes, just like that. For he was hers, he was an awful child, and he had to be looked after, and he had to be petted when he cried. He had to be told how wonderful he was, and if you told him he was a genius he would at once cheer up and begin talking about birds and trees, and the sky and the stars. There was something queer about the stars, they were mysterious, like Minnie's eyes, only nice and small; and she liked nice small things, when she saw them. They were cool too. There were heaps of things she did like, but then she didn't have the time, she was so busy. What was a genius exactly? How hot it was, and she wanted a drink.

Everything was old and sleepy. The sun, who was getting very red, played at painting long shadows in the grass. The air was tired and dust had risen from nowhere to dry up the trees. Sometimes a gentle little breath of wind would come up moving everything softly, and a bird would sing to it perhaps. All was quiet. Gnats jigged. From over the river the clock struck a mellow golden eight. The sun began throwing splashes of gold on to the trees, even the house caught some and was proud to be under the same spell.

The air began to get rid of the heaviness, and so became fresher as the dew soaked the grass. A blackbird thought aloud of bed, and was followed by another and then another. The sun was flooding the sky in waves of colour while he grew redder and redder in the west, the trees were a red gold too where he caught them. The sky was enjoying herself after the boredom of being blue all day. She was putting on and rejecting yellow for gold, gold for red, then red for deeper reds, while the blue that lay overhead was green.

A cloud of starlings flew by to roost with a quick rush of wings, and sleepy rooks cawed. Far away a man whistled on his way home.

Joan came from the porch as the light failed and moved peacefully to the gate. She went through and crossed the meadow, the heavy grass dragging at her feet. Some cows ate busily near by and hardly bothered to look up. Then the river flowing mysteriously along with the sky mirrored in the varnished surface. Trailing willows made light smiles at the sides where the water was liquid ebony. An oily rise showed a fish having an evening meal. He was killing black flies. Joan sat on the bank.

Opposite, between sky and water, a fisherman is bent motionless over his float. He never moves except to jerk violently at times. Then, a short unseen struggle, a bending rod, and another fish to die. Joan thinks he must be a clever fisherman to catch so many fish, but it is silly to trouble about him while there is George to think of. Why, he has caught another, it is a big one too, it is taking quite a time to land. The reel screams suddenly like someone in pain, he must be a big fish. The little bent figure gets up and begins to dance excitedly about. A plunge with the landing-net, a tiny tenor laugh of pleasure, and then peace again as he leans over the net, doing things.

George, what if George were here now? He would say nothing but would merely sit, his great idle form. And then . . . yes.

The blackbirds had stopped. Blue shadows had given way to black. The little man was taking down his rod, and soon had gone off into the dusk on a bicycle, dying fish in his creel. There was the moon, reserved and pale but almost full. How funny to go up the sky, then down again. Aah. She was sleepy, yawning like that. And it was getting cold sitting out here. The river was ebony, and away in the west was a bar of dying purple across the sky. The trees had vast, unformed bulks. The moon shed a sickly light round her on a few clouds that had come up all at once. It was cold. She jumped up and began to walk back to the house. But she would not go to bed yet.

Yes, there was the light in his room, a candle flame, still. She closed the door carefully behind her and crept upstairs in the dark. The hole on the third step and the creaking board on the ninth, she passed both without making a noise. Then through his room into hers and she was safe. She jammed her door with the chest of drawers, a heavy thing which she moved easily, it had the four castors intact for some reason. Funny how some of the furniture kept up appearances. Old days almost. Below it was quiet. She sat on a box in the window, and the cool night air breathed gently in, softly, like a thief.

Barwood . . . no, why think of that place? Everything had been so cultured there and so nice, and now it had all been beaten out of her, so that it hurt to go back into it. If there hadn't been any milk left for lunch you had sent for it and it came, you didn't have to pay for it on the nail as you did now. And she had been so clean and pretty, it was filthy here, but that had gone, and there was only the memory of it to go back to. Not that they hadn't always let her run wild, though. But things had changed since then, Mother wouldn't know her again if she could see her now . . . Barwood Vicarage had been one of those houses that have white under the roof. An old wall went round. Little trees grew out of the wall, and their roots made cracks in it. One thick arm of ivy worked its way through just before the gate and made a bulge in the top. There was an old lawn and a gardener who looked much older, but then he can't have been. It was a deep green, and he mowed it lovingly twice a week with a scythe, he was so proud of his mowing, and it used to be such fun going up to him and saying how well he did it, to watch new wrinkles come out with his smile. His face always looked as if there could be no more wrinkles, and yet there were new ones. Swallows used to build under the roof and then used to show off, they flew so fast and so close. For hours she had watched them rush in a swoop to the door of the nest. They never missed.

The only party at Barwood, the huge lawn and the immense house, the footman in livery, the people, it was another world. There had been ladies on the lawn dressed in marvellous stuffs with brightly-coloured hats – like birds they were. They shook hands very nicely and kindly, then they rushed away to play before the men. Mother had sat talking to Mrs Haye, with her on the other side, and Mother had laid a restraining hand on her all the time as she half bent over Mrs Haye. The unhappiness of that afternoon. Who were these people who lived such beautifully easy lives, and what right had they to make you so uncomfortable? The men were such willing idols. A little boy, Hugh his name had been, had sat next her for a time, sent by his mother. He was at school then. He had asked her if she had been to the Pringles' dance and she had blushed – silly little fool – when she had said no. Then he had said something was 'awfully ripping,' how at ease he had seemed, and then his glancing blue eyes had fixed and he had gone off and soon was laughing happily with an orange hat. Yes, he had left her for that thing, but you couldn't blame him. How cool they all were, even when hot after tennis; Mother's hand had been hot, lying in the lap of her new muslin which Mother had made for her. It might have been yesterday. That hand had seemed to be between her and the rest. Tennis was a pretty game to watch, and the men had laughed so nicely at it, with their open collars. One had had a stud-mark on his skin where the stud had pressed. Then there had been cool drinks on a sideboard – everything was new. Sometimes one of the ladies would say something to her with a quarter of her attention, the rest of her watching the men, and she herself had been too shy to answer . . . She had had a little ear under a kiss-curl, that lady. Mother still talked to Mrs Haye. People would sometimes look at the three of them seated on the bench, and then they would look away again and laugh. Oh, she hated them, it was their sort that had brought them to this. Sitting on the bench there she had begun to long for the tiny lawn and the poor old broken dolly. A dream, those beautifully-dressed people who had been so cool, and whom mother had been so frightened at. Then they had gone, and she had had to say goodbye to Mrs Haye – 'What a fine upstandin' girl, Mrs Entwhistle' – and they had begun to walk the mile home. What a little fool she must have made of herself that afternoon. Mother had been so funny, she remembered her so well saying eagerly, 'Did you see the green dress that girl with the auburn hair was wearing? And the white one of the girl with the thick ankles?' That had been the first time they had talked dresses as if it was not Mother who bought hers without asking her opinion. That night she dreamed of a wonderful party with Hugh and his blue eyes and fat cheeks, when he had been terribly nice to her, and when they had had the sideboard to themselves. But behind it all lay the memory of the preparation, her hair being brushed endlessly, her longing to be off and her longing to stay behind, the interminable delays and the too short walk. 'Behave nicely, and for heaven's sake don't bite your nails.'

And the dolly. Thomas, the old gardener, used to say, 'Bean't she a beauty!' as he leant on his spade as Dolly was shown to him every day. He never said more than that, it was enough. Then there had been the time when she had dropped her, and one arm had come off, just as any grown-up's might. Fool, fool. She had cried for ages, and had given up all interest in her for a time because she had cried so much. But she went back to her, and Father glued on the arm so that it came off again; still they made it up and between them settled that she should have only one arm.

Then there had been Father's roses. They bordered the path from the drawing-room French window to the door in the wall. Just over it climbing roses scrambled up and hung down in clusters. And little rose trees stood out on each side of the path, and red and white roses peeped out from the green leaves that hid the thorns. Father was so proud of them, ever since she could remember he used to talk about them at tea. He planted more and more, till the vegetable garden was invaded and in the end was a jungle of roses. His duties had to wait while they were being sprayed, or pruned, or manured. Thomas, of course, was never allowed to touch, it was his grief, he longed to help look after them. She remembered him saying wistfully, 'Them be lovely roses, Miss Joan.' Roses, roses, all the way. Ro – o – ses.

There had been another side to the roses. She could remember the quarrels Mother used to have with him over them as if it was yesterday. The manure – best fish manure – cost money, and she would tell Father, in that funny high voice of hers that she used when she was angry, that one or the other would have to go, and then the rest was always whispered, sometimes less, sometimes more, but it must have been the gin or the roses. Father had not minded, nor had Mother after a time. John, the postman, must have begun about then. It was a pretty uniform. So it had gone on.

Mrs Haye complained that Father never visited until they were dead. Of course he had visited. And the Parochial Church Council had asked for more services, though, of course, no one ever came to church, only Mrs Haye, and she merely as an example to the village. The almshouse people came, but only because they were so nearly dead. The almshouses were built in dark blue brick, always in half-mourning, among the tombstones. Father had told her about these complaints over the rose trees. He had talked a great deal to her then. Poor Father. So he had planted roses to climb up the church, and they had given him a new interest there till Mrs Haye had made him pull them down. He had been running away.

There had been a queer light at the back of Mother's eyes about then – how she understood that light now! At the same time Mother had stopped taking any notice and would only smile tiredly at the things that had made her angry before. She took to painting her lips, and sometimes she would put one of the roses in her hair. Father never said anything about it to her, only, lying in bed with the owls hooting, she used to hear quarrels going on, quite often. Bed meant owls then, there were none here. He spent more and more time on the roses about the house. And in the summer he would dream himself away among them, sitting there by the hour while she played on the lawn, putting Dolly to bed in rose petals. Would it do if she painted her lips for George? No, it would frighten him. Tomorrow was Monday, he might be about. They had been all right, too, when they had blossomed, great bunches of them, red and white, all over the place. Just like those beautiful picture postcards Mrs Donner had in the window sometimes. They had been lovely, those days.

Joined on to the Vicarage behind there had been a small house with a farmyard and a few buildings. It was the lower farm of Mr Walker's. Henry had lived in the house, Henry who was her first love. They had kissed underneath the big thistle in the orchard hedge, only he had been rather dirty. She had seen him driving a cart two weeks ago, only he had looked the other way. Didn't like to own her now. Before he had always lifted his cap with a knowing smile. Or had he been sorry for her? How funny that first kiss was. She had only been fourteen. All wet. But he remembered. Mrs Baxter, his mother, with her nice face and her chickens. Mrs Baxter used to come in some-times to help Mother with the housework. She always used to say, 'God is good to us, Mr Entwhistle,' when Father was about. And Father used to look serious and say, 'Yes, Mrs Baxter. He is indeed.' He was, then. She used to call her 'Miss'.

Then the Wesleyan, 'the heretic', had started a rival Sunday school. He gave a treat once a year and Father never did, so all the children went to him and left Father. He had been angry: 'Bribery and corruption; I won't bribe the children to come to God.' Then they could not afford to give tea at the Mothers' Meetings, and Mother had lost her temper with Mrs Walker, who had insinuated that they were lazy. But the real reason why no one came any more must have been the gossip about Father which began about then. But they had become indifferent; they hadn't cared.

Mrs Haye had called and had stayed to tea. She, Joan, was allowed butter with her bread and jam. That was only on great occasions. After that the Mothers' Union started. Mrs Haye must have stamped on the gossip, for all the women began coming again, every month. Mrs Haye attended herself the first time. Mother put some cut flowers in a pot just by her. It was a special occasion, so Father's objection to cutting flowers was forgotten. 'Do you want the best rose tree to be the rubbish heap?' Later, there was a woman who tried to teach them how to make baskets, but she forgot how to make them herself in the middle, and nobody minded, they had gone on whispering just the same. They were great times, those.

A fat drop of rain plunked on to the window-sill. Rain. Then another, and another. The air became full of messages, a branch just underneath moved uneasily. There was a rumble miles away that trundled along the sky till it roared by overhead and burst in the distance. Thunder. Rain fell quicker. A broad flame of lightning – waiting, waiting for the crash. Ah. The storm was some way off. The rain walked up the scales of sound, swishing like a scythe swishes.

Quick light from another flash lit up the yard, and a bird was flying as if pursued, across the snouted pump. Darkness. The thunder. Nearer.

The air was cool, unloaded. Joan drew back from the window, for she was being splashed by the spray as the drops smashed. The rain fell faster, faster. A terrific sheet of light and all the sky seemed to be tumbling down, moving celestial furniture. Father's bass came up singing confidently, 'There is a green land far away.' Daylight, the sky fought. Darkness and rain. Sheet lightning never hurt anything, but how wonderful to be as afraid as this. Father was rising on the tide of knowledge, 'I know, I know,' he cried, and heaven saluted it with her trumpets. He sang a line of the 'Red Flag', but switched off. Swish, swish, said the rain, settling down to steadiness. Father was singing something and taking all the parts. The chickens in the hut made plaintive noises, the cock was being so tiresome. 'What a bore the old man is,' they were saying, 'but we are so frightened of him.' How wonderful, terror. Joan quaked on the box. Swish, said the rain.

Joan draws her blouse round her and hunches her shoulders. How much fresher it is now. The storm thunders away behind, it has passed over. Mumbles come from below. Laughter. All of her listens. His voice, 'Ring out, wild bells.' Always the church bells that he could not escape. Hunted by bells. Crash – the empty bottle. Then he is singing again. Mother had used to play. He is coming upstairs, toiling up, and Joan shivers. Into his room. Silence. Quietly he goes to bed and is asleep. The light in him had gone out. He had forgotten.

She feels cheated. He had been so mad underneath. Why hadn't he battered at the door? What a shame. All that trembling for nothing. He had forgotten her. She shuts the window and, lighting a candle, undresses and lets down her hair. She gets into bed. Sleep.

Eyes closed.

Sleep. Now she would go to sleep.

Turns over.

Sleep.

The lawn. The roses.

It can't have been sheet lightning because there was thunder. Then it had been dangerous.

A stands for ant. B stands for bee. C stands for cat. Sitting on Mother's knee tracing the tummy of a, her hand guiding. Later on Mother tried to teach her other things. It used to be a great game to get as many 'I don't know myself, dear's,' out of her as possible in the morning.

There was the Vicarage pew every Sunday, Mrs Haye to the left, crazy Kate just behind, then the churchwarden, sniffling, sniffling, and two or three almshouse people. Father always preached out of the green book on the second shelf in the old study, though sometimes he talked about politics. Mrs Haye would stir violently when she disagreed, which would make Father stutter and Mother angry. Sometimes, though not very often, her son John would come too, he who was blind now. She used to watch him all through the service when he was there. He was so aloof, and there was nothing, no one else to look at. Nothing happened, no one did anything except the organist when she forgot. The service would go slowly on. Weston, the head gardener at Barwood, the only person in the choir, would sing as if he did not care. Father's voice toiled through the service. Mrs Haye argued the responses. The organist was paid to come, Weston only came that Mrs Haye might see that he came. Outside, through the little plain glass window at the side of their pew, the top of an apple tree waved. In summer there were apples on it which she used to pick in her imagination, and any time a bird might fly across, free. The service would go on and finish quite suddenly with a hymn, and then the run home with the blue hills in the distance, with the glimpse, just before the second gate, of the tower of the Abbey church, the greeting of Mrs Green who was always at her door at the beginning of the last field – no, the last but one, there was the orchard; dinner. It had all gone. Why, since she loved it so? The summers were so wonderful, the winter nights so comfortable. Gone. Today had ended wrong and had started wrong. Forget in sleep.

The bed was too hot, the sheets clung, one leg was hot against the other. Her hair laid hot fingers about her face. She pulled aside the bedclothes and lay on top of them on her back, a white smudge in the dark. Outside tepid rain poured. This was cooler.

There was the clock that used to strike bedtime, half-past six. Had she heard the one stroke? Had she forgotten? But no.

'Bedtime, Joan.'

'No, I don't want to.'

'Now be a good girl.'

To gain time – 'Where's Daddy?'

'Now, Joan, you know your Daddy works all the evenings. Now go to bed, dearie. I'll come up and see you.'

Starting in on the gin more likely. Oh, everything was very proper then. Where had he put the empties, though? Of course he can't have been bad as far back as that, it was only much later. Just before the Mothers' Meeting she had found Mrs Baxter sniffing round Father's room. She herself had smelt the smell too. She had called Mother, who had not noticed anything, of course. After that Father had said that he would dust the room himself, as he could not have his papers being fidgeted with.

'Fidget, fidget, that's all a woman is when cleaning. Tidying up means hiding. There is an order in my disorder. Yesterday I spent half an hour looking for the church accounts which I found eventually, tidied away into the private correspondence. I can't bear it. You do understand, don't you, Mrs Baxter? Of course I am not blaming you in the least, but . . .'

'Very well, Mr Entwhistle. I understand, sir.' Sniff!

Something like that, but it was the sniff. It was the first sign of a mystery that had been so exciting till she had known.

His private correspondence. That can't have been anything. Only letters to Mrs Haye – oh, yes, and to the Bishop. He had scored off the Bishop one day. A great thing. Butter with her bread and jam that day.

But times had been hard. Really they were better off here. The food had dwindled, she had felt hungry a good deal.

'A wage less than a labourer.'

'Oh, yes.'

'What's that? Well, isn't it?'

'It wouldn't be.'

'Well then, approximately. And then there are your clothes to buy and the child's.'

'And your personal expenses. What you waste.'

'What? I suppose I can't spend a penny on myself?'

'Run along, Joan, and play.'

'Yes, Mummy.'

Then Uncle Jim, whose death they had waited for so long, died in France. Of fever or something. He had no child and had left all his money to 'the poor fellow he's a parson'. Lord, that joke. Father had seen it in the Evangelical Supplement and had used it for ever when he talked. However, things had become a bit easier then, and probably the spirit merchant had begun to give tick again.

Only one villager had been killed.

'And I said to them, I put it to them point-blank, "I won't sign the minutes when no member of the Parochial Council comes to church," I said.'

What was there to get for tomorrow? Milk, more sardines, and some more candles. Perhaps that book Mrs Donner had in her window for thruppence. She could put the thruppence down to the bread. The title was so thrilling, The Red Love of White Hope, Scioux, Matt.

She had not read many books in the old days. There was the Water Babies, and one or two others, but she had forgotten. And Robinson Crusoe. After that she hadn't read at all. She didn't really know what she had done. She had sat on the wall a good deal, asking why and how the world was here, and watching people go by. Silly to trouble about why the world was – it was, that was all. On Saturdays in summer dusty motor cars would clatter by on the way to the river-side pub. Birmingham people they were. There were other people sometimes. And four times a day the milk lorry came by with him driving it. Fascinating he was, he looked so wicked.

Was Scioux the name of a town, or did it mean that White Hope was a Red Indian? Mrs Donner might let her have a look inside. If it was only a town she would not buy it, but with a Red Indian it should be meaty. Then, again, she used to go up to watch the village blacksmith shoe the horses or repair a plough, and he would let her work the handle of the bellows and make the sparks spray out. The corners of his forge had been wonderful, all sorts of odds and ends of rusty iron, and always the chance, as he said, of finding something very valuable among them. Little innocent. But above all there was the blacksmith himself. He was very stupid but the strongest man that ever lived. It was wonderful, his strength. She had tried to lift the big hammer one day, and she had let it drop on her big toe, it was so heavy. Wouldn't be able to lift it now, even. He had had to carry her back to the Vicarage. Mother had been very angry. But then the days were gone when she kissed to make it well. Poor right big toe.

Occasionally they had gone into Norbury. There used to be the old horse bus along the main road to take you in, and then you were in the middle of the hum and bustle of it, hundreds of people hurrying along in town clothes. Norbury was wonderful with its three thousand inhabitants. And there was Green the draper's, Mother fingering the stuffs for her new dress – would it wash, would it wear? it did not look to her like very good quality. And the boot shop, Dapp's, with the smell of leather and hundreds and hundreds of shoes hung about, and the shop assistant's hair – like a cascade of glue, Father said once outside, but it wasn't, it smelt lovely – and his way of tying the shoe on, that little finger. Fool. He would be married now, and she, whoever she was, would have someone to wait for in the evenings, to kiss or to have rows with, and wear his ring. She would have his children, and they would watch them together. And the farmers, fat and thin, in their pony carts, getting down at the Naiad's Calf to have a drink. Father had hated the farmers; 'they are making a lot of money', was what he said. And as evening came on they went sometimes to tea at the Deanery, and she would doze by the fire, sitting very correctly in her chair, hearing the boom of the Dean's voice to Father, and Mother's shrill complaint to the Dean's wife, dozing after the huge tea that she had eaten when they weren't looking. They would have a fit if she went there now.

She hadn't been in Norbury for ages. There was Mrs Donner who sold everything. She was a one, that woman. Three and six for a bit of stuff which she wouldn't like to put on a horse's back to keep the cold off!

It had been hard work following Mother about. She had hurried so from shop to shop. She must have been hungry for town life again. Those that are town-bred hate the country. They used always to eat lunch in the Cathedral Tea Rooms. Mrs Oliver, big and fat, who looked after the customers, always came up and said, 'Ah, Mr Entwhistle, so you've come to see us townsfolk again, sir.' Mother would bring out the sandwiches. After they had eaten Mother and she would go off to the shops again, while Father went back to the Library. Mother used to call Mrs Oliver 'a designing woman' – sour grapes. And the chemist, mysterious behind his spectacles, in his shop made of shelves and bottles, and cunningly-piled cardboard boxes. The jolting ride home in the dark, with the walk at the end.

Then there was Nancy. All the last years at the Vicarage had been Nancy. What had become of her now? Married with children, most likely, but not to the baker's son she had been so gone on. Nancy, with her fairest hair and skinny legs, she was not nearly as good-looking as her. Her snub nose, and the small watery pink eyes.

They had met in a lane, had smiled, and had made friends. That is, they had never really made friends, she had been far too stupid. But Nancy used to giggle at her jokes, and she liked that. Dolly had been forgotten then.

They talked a great deal about men, with long silences, and Nancy's giggle and 'Oh you's'. They walked arm in arm, or more often with their arms round each other's waists, their heads bent, whispering. Lord, what fools they must have looked. Of course Mother was only too glad that she was out of the way, Father too.

They used to walk most in the lane, just outside the house here. She had been in love, oh, how passionate, with Jim who never spoke, and who worked for Mr Curry. He had been worse than George. But he used sometimes to come home by the lane in the evening, and they would pass him arm in arm. She would give him the sidelong look she had practised in the mirror, but he never did more than touch his cap. She had dropped her handkerchief once, as Nancy had told her they did in the world. They had talked and giggled for days before she had plucked up courage to do it. But of course he did nothing.

Nancy wore a ring round her neck on a bit of cotton. She said at first that Alfred had given it her, but that time under the honeysuckle when she had shown Nancy her birthmark on her leg, she had confessed that she had only got it out of a cracker at Christmas. Nancy used to think her awfully daring.

Then their walks when evening was coming on, when they wandered down the sunken lane. Thick sunlight and thicker shade, when they twined closer together, and walked slower, and were silent. There was the heavy smell of honeysuckle, sweet, which a little fresh air coming down between the banks would begin to blow away. The birds flew quietly from side to side, there were flowers whose names she did not know, and long tufts of grass full of dew. The flowers made dots of colour in the shade, the ground they walked on buried the sound of their feet ... Soon they would come to the gate, and they would sit clinging to each other and balancing, watching the horses scrunch up the grass and the cows lie chewing, idly content. The sky was always different, and the end of a hot day was sleepy. The flies buzzed round, the midges bit. On a piece of fresh manure there would be hundreds of brown flies, and a bee would hurry by. She used to watch the trees most often. There were so many of them, one behind the other, hiding, showing, huddled, alone. Far away a car would blow a horn, or a train would whistle, but it used to feel as if there was everything between them and it. Birds up in the sky that was paling would fly silently with a purpose. They were going to bed, and soon she would go back, have supper, and go to bed. Partridges talked to each other anxiously, as they gathered together, against the dangers of the night. The horses looked round calmly. A dog barked miles away.

Then, as it was getting dark, they would part to go home. Nancy up to the village, and she herself across the fields to the Vicarage. The cows would not rise, and the horses would give her barely a glance. Only a rabbit perhaps would sit up, drum the ground, and flee to his burrow. And he would not bother to go down it, for as soon as she had passed he would be back again nibbling. In spring there would be lambs, absurd and delicious on their long weak legs.

She would climb a warm gate and feel the wet of the dew soaking through her stockings. In front was the Vicarage, all the windows open, waiting, and her glass of milk and biscuits. She would climb the last gate and cross the dusty road, lift the latch of the door in the wall, and the roses, the white ones and the red ones, would greet her. Father might be sitting in the deck-chair on the lawn, smoking his pipe, the blue smoke going lazily up to the other blue of the sky. Mother might be sewing just inside the French window. The milk was cool.

And then she would go up the stairs into her room, the little white bed, the texts round the walls, the open window letting in the dim light and the roses. And she would go to sleep and – was she going to cry?

All gone, the lawn, the roses, the quiet, the protection, her little room, the glass of milk, Jack, the horses, the cows, the walks, for they were not the same, Nancy, those evenings. Fool. The peace, the untroubledness, the old wall, the . . . All . . .

She went to sleep.

'—College, Oxford

'My dear B. G.

'I saw you last night in the club, but you cut me dead. Come to lunch Friday to be forgiven. I wanted to talk about poor John. I am so sorry about it. Poor dear, amusing John. I must write to him, though what there is to say I don't know. Really, these letters of condolences are very difficult.

'But why did you cut me like that? I saw David Plimmer the other night and he spoke of you with enthusiasm. Don't forget about lunch Friday, if you cut that I shall know the worst.

'Yrs.—

'Seymour'

Part three — Butterfly

1 Waiting

He was in the summer-house. Light rain crackled as it fell on the wooden roof, and winds swept up, one after the other, to rustle the trees. A pigeon hurried rather through his phrase that was no longer now a call. Cries of rooks came down to him from where they would be floating, whirling in the air like dead leaves, over the lawn. The winds kept coming back, growing out of each other, and when a stronger one had gone by there would be left cool eddies slipping by his cheek, while a tree further on would thunder softly. Every wind was different, and as he listened to their coming and to their going, there was rhythm in their play. In the fields, beyond where the trees would be, a man cracked his whip, and a cow lowed. The long grass copied the trees with a tiny dry rustling.

But there was something new today; he had met her; he would meet her again, and the wind was lighter for it, the branches danced almost. He had been shy when they had met, and so had she, and he had laughed at himself for being shy, though that was all part of the game. For now at last he could play as the trees were doing now, advance, retreat, and it was a holiday, and she would be wild, so wild. Mamma was horrified at her life, she must have had a queer time, so that she would be interesting. And her voice had been afraid; she had been frightened at his lack of eyes. She would be fascinated later, as he lay by her side – oh, devilry – to listen to her hoarse voice, to weave question and answer.

There had been doubt in Mamma's voice when speaking about her, and it had only been through pity that she had brought her to the house. He was old enough to know now, she had said, that the girl lived a most extraordinary life with her drunken father, that she was not quite proper. As if he had not always known, as if he had not told at once from her voice. But she, Mamma, had met her in the lane, looking so ill, with her hand all swollen and the thumb tied up in a rag, a rag-an'-bone man's rag, and she, Mamma, had said to herself that after all the girl was a parishioner, and she had positively insisted on her coming back to the house at once, that the thumb might be properly done up. And at first the girl had been sulky and silent, and then the poor girl had become quite servile in her thanks. That dreadful man, her father.

So they had met. But Mamma's voice had been uneasy all through her account of it; she had been frightened. She had told him that artists married barmaids continually and were unhappy ever after. And he had said that unhappiness was necessary to artists, and she had called that stuff and nonsense. But they had met. For Mamma had feared before he had gone blind that he would marry beneath him – well, not quite that, but someone unsuitable; and just lately she had been talking a great deal about marriage, how he must marry, how he must make a home for himself here. Her voice had been full of plans.

Voices had become his great interest, voices that surrounded him, that came and went, that slipped from tone to tone, that hid to give away in hiding. There had been wonder in hers when he had groped into the room upon them both; she had said, 'Look.' But before she had opened her mouth he had known that there was someone new in the room.

Voices had been thickly round him for the past month, all kinds of them. Mamma extracted them from the neighbourhood, and all had sent out the first note of horror, and some had continued horrified and frightened, while others had grown sympathetic, and these were for the most part the fat voices of mothers, and some had been disgusted. She had been the first to be almost immediately at her ease, when she spoke it was with an eager note, and there were so few eager people.

Tomorrow June (her name was June) would come to have her poor hand attended to. She had cut it, and it was poisoned a little, poor little hand. 'Like white mice,' her fingers. They would not be white though, but hard and a little dirty with work. Tomorrow.

Today Mamma had gone into Norbury in one of her fits of righteous anger. On the road and in front of the town rubbish heap, just where you had the best view of the Abbey, the Town Council had allowed a local man to build a garage, in tin, painted red. Of course, she had said, there was jobbery in it, and there probably was. So she had gone to the Dean, and she would be talking to him now. The Dean would boom sympathy, and he would be tired, poor man, but he would write to the Town Council. They would do nothing. Poor Ruskin!

Still it was a pity, for the garage spoilt that view. But they had not tampered with the inside of the church. It was quiet in there as the country round, and all was simple, and the round pillars were so kind, and the echoes that blurred everything and so made the words more grand. The church music went round and round the walls, and then rolled along the ceiling till the shifting notes built walls about you till you were yourself very high up, so that you could see.

But Mamma always made one go to Barwood Church, where the service was out of tune and where there was not even simplicity, for Crayshaw lit candles and wore vestments. And outside always there were quiet fields and colour to show you how absurd it was to worship indoors. Crayshaw had just had another baby, a son, and he had so many. But Mamma said that they must go to Barwood Church that they might be an example to the village. So they went, and the few others they met there went to show that they went, and everyone realized that, and so on.

Last Sunday, the first time he had been after going blind, there had been voices singing in the county accent. Such nice, strong, genuine voices. But then Crayshaw had spoilt it all by preaching about blindness in the East, ophthalmia in the Bible, spittle and sight, with a final outburst against pagans. During the sermon he had fingered his prayer-book; it was longer and thinner than any of the rest. It had been presented for his first service in church. And he should have been sentimental over it; he should have thought how good he had been so long ago in the nursery, of how he had wanted to be a bishop, and of how Mabel Palmer had said how nice it would be for the neighbourhood to own a bishop.

Things were different now. The nursery was gone and the days at Noat, so full of people, were gone. There were other things instead. There was so much to find out, and, in a sense, so much to discover for others, for when one was blind one understood differently. A whole set of new values had arisen. And being blind did not hurt so long as one did not try to see in terms of sight what one touched or heard.

The wind was higher and the summer-house groaned now and then in it. The trees roared, when suddenly there would be lulls, strangely quiet, waiting for another wind to come up. Everything would be stopped short. The branches were still, and would be looking vacantly at each other, like children come to the end of a game. Then a wind comes up and covers the emptiness that had followed; a dead branch snapped and fell to the ground. It was getting colder; the sun had not been out all day, and one always knew when the sun was out. A blackbird warned as he fled down wind. The air round was stealthy.

It was all so full of little hints; the air carried up little noises and then hurried them away again. The silence had been so full. The rain had stopped falling now, and he was straining to catch the slightest secrets that were in the winds, and before he had never known that. In a way one gained by being blind, of course one did; besides he was happy today, for was not she coming tomorrow?

So that they would go for walks together, and he would get her to lead him to the top of Swan's Wood to look upon the view there and listen to her eager voice. What a pity never to see that view again – the river, the meadows, the town, the rubbish heap, the Abbey and the hills behind. And the one hill, a mound that came before the line of hills in the distance, and that had things dotted about on it, and through them a road, a quiet yellow line, which had clung to it and had shown off the hollows.

When they were there they would talk of everything and he would find out her life, why her hand was like that and why she trembled the air in a room. He would teach her the view, and she would be so bored with it as she would so want to go on talking about that. A wind would come down to wreathe rings about them – how lyrical! But June would be so charming; she must be, and she had such strong hands. Besides, her voice was lovely; there was something wild in it and something asleep there as well, as if she too had lived alone and had many things to tell. For she would be interesting at least; she must have suffered living in the cottage that was falling down now, and she would be able to tell of it, and she would have had some contact with horrible things so that she would not be vapid. So many of the young ladies he met were like Dresden china. And she would be ... well no; there was no word for it. But they would go on walking out together like any boy and his slut, and he would explore in her for the things that her voice told him were there, and that had never been let out. For no one saw her or would speak to her.

It was so necessary to talk; you had to and with someone who could understand or sympathize with your ideas. How they would talk, June and he, for she must and would understand how he needed someone young. When you were blind and beginning to make discoveries you had to tell them to somebody; besides, talking was the only thing you could do as well as anyone else. And surely she would not dance, for who was there to dance with her, unless there was another man? Perhaps there was, and then the whole dull round of country conversation would go round again, and when one had gone through it so often before. Let them talk about things, not people. And then, of course, they could talk about themselves.

Why had he never learnt to play the piano? It would be so nice to be able to sit down and make the lazy notes ripple though this echoing house, up the stairs and through doors and windows to be lost in the wetness of the garden. She had known how. She had played music wandering out to the gossamer, and so quiet; as raindrops gather on a twig and then slip off, so had her notes fallen in such a silver, liquid sound. But then the sun came out. It was changed now. The hut, the trees and each leaf suddenly had a spirit of their own. And the wind bore them down to you that they might whisper in your ear, and be companions as you sat in the dark. So that you were not really lonely; there were only the deaf who were really cut off. How dreadful to be deaf, not to hear this wind choosing out the leaves and carrying them down gently that they might rustle on the ground.

Would June be like this? So that she could sit still and listen. Surely she would not want to break out into a great screaming laugh to announce that someone had been hurt or something broken? She also might have dreams and be able to understand his, perhaps. And yet she would not be sickly, but rather like a sunflower, absorbing from the sun, and so proud, so still. Women were like flowers; it was silly, but they were. The sudden flutter of wings of a bird who was going elsewhere to drink more in and pour it out again to the sun brought the grass and trees together, and the earth that kept them both. Women understood like that. Their intuitions exalted them to the simple understanding of the trees, for trees were so simple; there was no remoteness in them as of mountains and their false sublimity. But he had not met any women who were women. Still, June felt like that, and her loneliness would have taught her silence, for she could not have met many people.

As long as she was not like Miss Blandair – but then how could she be? Miss Blandair, whom Mamma had had to stay, who played tennis so very well, who danced, and was so very suitable. She had been so bright as she cackled on, and Mamma had approved; her voice had been rotund with approval. She had made him very weary; hers was such wasted energy. What energy one had should be put away secretly for the thing in hand, not thrown to the wind in handfuls of confetti. For then one saw it in retrospect only, lying rather tarnished on the ground.

All June would be stored up.

But it was an anxious time for Mamma, waiting to see him settled. And it was the end, to settle down. He could not; one did not dare to. It was not fair to Mamma, but what could one do? She was not his mother; she had only made herself into one, though that was just the same. But he must go out with June; there was so much to talk about, so much sympathy to be sought after. For they were all so old, one could not talk to them; they did not understand, in spite of their always saying they did. Nurse had been young but too full of her trade.

And Nanny had not been so well lately. She had been more hesitating on the walks and her shoes had creaked more slowly. Mamma had said something about it, how Nanny must take care of herself, and she had given her some medicine. Nanny was talking more and more as time went on, that afternoon when he had been told she had talked far more than she would have done in the old days. She had a cough now that was becoming more and more frequent, a juicy cough, that seemed to tear her, and that was horrible to hear. Poor Nanny! For she was a link with so much that was gone; she had seen the house before he had come to it, or rather just after he had arrived. She had known those who lived in it, and she had known him so long that they were used to each other, so that they had a few worn jokes at which they laughed together, and that was all; there was really no conversation left, nor was it necessary. She had been so jealous of the nurse. The hours he had spent making it all right again!

She had known his mother, Mummy. She had a very few stories about her, such nice stories, and he would make her tell them again and again, when perhaps a new story would come out. Mummy must have been so charming, they had all loved her so.

She was like a dream, something so far away that came back sometimes. And now that he was blind he had come to treasure little personal things of her own, a prayer-book of hers, though that, of course, was mistaken; a pair of kid gloves, so soft to touch, and they had a faint suggestion of her about them, so faint, that gently surrounded them and made them still more soft. And she had died because of him.

There was so little that he knew about her, only what Nanny could tell. He never saw anyone who had known her, and Mamma was always trying, ever since she had told him by letter how he was not her son, to put herself in Mummy's place. How silly to go on calling her by that name; she had been dead nearly nineteen years now; it was so sentimental. But the word was fresh, it clung about the gloves. They had been cold so long, those gloves.

From what Nanny said she had been so happy in the house, going about lightly from place to place. One really did not know anything about her; Nanny had only seen her once and her stories were only what the other servants had told her. They would have been seated round in the kitchen waiting for the funeral, and they would have talked and talked, weeping in turns, and Nanny had learnt what she knew in that way. There were none of them left; he had never known them, for Mamma had sent them all away when she had married Father and gone to India. But apparently she had whistled most beautifully; Nanny's descriptions never went beyond 'beautiful', and he could hear her going about whistling gently till the house was full of shadows. She must have linked everything up with it. And then apparently she had played the piano quite beautifully.

Such ages ago he had been at Noat, only a few months, but still – the misery of those days, their dreariness, and with their strange exaltations now and then. So much depended on whether people were nice to you or not. And the Art Society with the marionette shows. There had been no one at J. W. P.'s to mind about such things. It was getting cold out here. Heat drew one out, one was with a companion. Just as their glow against each other would draw them out – June and he.

Mummy would have helped, then and now. She would have had such a gentle understanding, so that when he came back from Noat for the holidays they would have sat by the fire and talked it out. What evenings, and what quiet grey days with the colours in the fields washed into luminous clarity, and the calm in the trees. She would have understood all that with her tender whistling, and they would have walked, perhaps, silently happy together to the top of

Swan's Wood. Or down to the river with its surprises and the quietly-flowing water.

For she would have seen things by the light of intuitions, often wrong, but no less enchanting, and by discovering things in other people she would have shown herself. How silly people were to think a grey day sad; it was really so full of happiness, while the sun only made things reflect the sun, and so not be themselves. Dew came in the morning with the light sky above and sent pearl colours over the fields, and so made him think of her, who was so like that herself.

There were so many things to do, all the senses to develop, old acquaintances of childhood to make friends with again. To sit still and be stifled by the blackness was wrong; he had done that long enough. The temptation was so great, the darkness pressed so close, and what sounds one heard could only at first be converted into terms of sight and not sound. When a blackbird fled screaming he had only been able to see it as a smudge darting along, and he had tried in vain to visualize it exactly. Now he was beginning to see it as a signal to the other birds that something was not right; it was the feeling that one has in the dark when something moves, and when one jumps to turn on the light, and the light leaps out through the night. Why translate into terms of seeing, for perhaps he would never see again, even in his dreams? They might be of sounds or of touch now. The deaf might dream of a soundless world, and how cold that would be. There was the story of the deaf old man who had forgotten that the breaking waves of the sea on the beach made sound. He must not go deaf; one clung so to what senses were left. But sight was not really necessary; the values of everything changed, that was all. There was so much in the wind, in the feel of the air, in the sounds that Nature lent one for a little, only to take away again. Or was there nothing in all these? Why did everyone and everything have to live on illusion, that Mummy was really near, and as the meaning of everything? But one could not let that go.

June was an illusion – a lovely one. He had never felt anyone so alive. Coming into that room had been like a shower of sparks, or was it merely the mood he had been in? There were days when everything bristled with life, the mahogany table in the front hall almost purred when you stroked it, it was so warm and clinging. Great feline table. And the flowers poked their soft heads so confidingly into your palm, tickling. They must get another dog now that Ruffles was dead that he might have his hands licked. Stroking June, her skin would be so alive. There were days when everything was a toy, and when even the big flowers with heavy scents condescended, except the wooden lilies, and they stank of pollution. Violets were silly; they were not bold enough; they nestled simpering and were too frightened. But the others would play with you if you would only let them, gay exquisite things.

He would write about these things, for life was only beginning again, and there were many things to say. Besides, one couldn't for ever be sitting in a chair like this, and be for the rest of one's life someone to be sorry for. And perhaps the way he saw everything was the right way, though there could be no right way but one's own. Art was what created in the looker-on, and he would have to try and create in others. He would write slowly, slowly, and his story would drift as the country drifted, and it would be about trivial things. The man who chased tulips on a bicycle was silly as well as being an idiot, but the piano-tuner might make a story. He was of the type that had to feel over your face before he became confidential. Why hadn't he done that to Miss Blandair? Of all practices it was the most revolting, and far more for yourself. Faces were so deformed, your fingers strayed into hair suddenly, though shut eyelids were incredibly alive. Not that the piano-tuner ever became confidential. He was very unhappy and very secretive. He had been blinded in the war, and the injustice of it made his hands burn when he talked about it. He gave himself away so painfully when he played after the tuning was over. But he had a few interesting things to say, how you would find when you were blind a little longer that you could tell by a feeling in your face when a wall or a chair or even something so low as a footstool was coming. So that you could walk about alone and unaided as he did. It would be wonderful, this new sense, he looked forward to it so, and was often imagining objects in the way when there were none. It would give a new feeling of companionship with the world. The darkness would be more intimate.

But it would all be so different with her about. So that they would all go for walks together, all of them. There would be Mummy to take up to the top of Swan's Wood, and of course June to take there, too, and Nanny to go round the garden on his arm, and Mamma to accompany visiting in the village. What talks they would have, telling Mummy what June was like, Nanny how inferior June was, and Mamma how sorry he was for June, though she would see through that. So that this, perhaps, was a beginning with June and the birds and the trees. They were much nearer, and Mummy was, too. The days would have change in them now.

It was charming to think of Mummy being so close, but she wasn't. And June was so much more tangible. It was also charming to think of the trees as being in conspiracy with the birds to make life more endurable, but of course they weren't. One lived, that was all, and at times one lived more than at other times. But they were charming illusions, and they became real if you believed them. Oh! why did he think these things?

Those gloves and things of her, why did they have so much of her about them? And why did the trees and the birds conspire together so openly? And why when he was alone did some presence – some companion of days that were dead now, because he could not remember them – why did she come and walk with him and sit by his side and make him understand dimly through his blindness? Mamma would come upon them when they were alone together sometimes, and she would say that he must not become morbid. And she would talk and talk until the longing went away.

Was that what it was – a longing? Would he come upon it suddenly?

There was no pain in his memory of her; if there had been it would have driven her away. That was why it was so lucky he had never known her; another illusion would have gone. Why did he go on thinking these things? Then it was lucky perhaps that he could not see any more, that the little boy had taken his sight away. For she was nearer than she had ever been before, now that he was blind.

Evening was coming and with it the soft, harping rain, rustling, rustling. A bird was muttering liquidly, gently somewhere, and it was very like the night – kind, strange. And she was here with the feel of the air, and June was tomorrow, tangible as the sunlight. He shivered, and getting up he went into the house.

2 Walking out

'My name isn't June, it's Joan, and always was.'

'But do you mind my calling you June? I think June is such a lovely name, so much nicer than Joan. You are just like June, too.'

'Why should I be like June? You are silly. But I don't mind. You can have your own way if you like, though I don't know why you shouldn't like Joan, which is my name whether you like it or not.'

'That is the only reason why I like it.'

'You are clever.'

'But when June is your name I like it better than all other names, don't you?'

'No, I don't.'

'Oh, well, I will call you Joan, if June is not to your fancy.'

'No, have it your own way.'

'That is most awfully nice of you. I . . . No.'

It was not going too well. It was so hard to find anything to talk about, and she was not easy. There was a terribly strained feeling in the air, they were feeding on each other's shyness. But it would be better next time. The ice must break.

'Where are we now?'

'We're just coming to the stile into Mr Cume's orchard.'

'Then it was here that the bulldog attacked a cow. Most alarming it was. Flew at her nose.'

'No, he didn't, did he?'

'Yes, but I pulled him off. Do you like bulldogs?'

'I don't know, I haven't seen very many. I only saw yours once or twice, and then he rather frightened me.'

'He was so tame, really.'

There was a pause. They walked on.

'Do you like dogs?'

'I don't know. No.'

'You don't like dogs! Oh, June, I love them.'

'I like cats.'

'No, I don't like cats. They are so funny and mysterious, or is that just what you like about them?'

'Father doesn't like cats either.'

'Doesn't he?'

'No, he doesn't!'

'Have you got a cat?'

'Yes, he's called Minnie.'

'They are so nice to have about the house – pets, I mean.'

'Yes, aren't they?'

A pause. She was wonderful, so shy and retiring. What was there to say? He sought for words.

'Will you come for another walk with me one day?'

'Perhaps.'

'We could go to the top of Swan's Wood. It would be very nice of you. I am so alone.'

'Why do you want to go up to the top? What happens there?'

—What would? 'There is a view, that's all. A lovely view that I used to look at a great deal in the old days. And you can describe it to me when we get there.'

'All right. Though I don't know what you see in views.'

He was a queer person, but very exciting.

They walked. He guided his steps from the sound of hers. He felt awkward. Then he stumbled and almost fell, on purpose. She stopped and laid a hand on his arm.

'Take care. You mustn't fall down and hurt yourself.'

'There is no harm done. I say, June, would you mind dreadfully if I did put my hand on your arm? I should be able to get along easier then.'

'If you want to.'

They set out again. Was it imagination or did she press his arm under hers, close to her? Had she much on? His heart beat, one felt that one could never say anything again. Wasn't she wonderful!

'Do you like cows?'

'I don't know. Why?'

'They frighten me sometimes, although I live most of the time in the country. Don't they you?'

'No, I don't think so.'

'But they looked so fierce with their horns, and sometimes when they were frightened in Norbury market their eyes went purple and they slavered at the mouth.'

'They are very stupid, that's all.'

'I'm not sure. And bulls, of course, are really dangerous.'

'Bulls?' She laughed.

'I like calves, June.'

'Yes, calves are all right. They are so funny when they are young an' their legs go wobbly.'

He laughed. That was a little more human of her.

'But they are awfully dangerous when they are like that, for the mother is only too ready to attack you, isn't she?'

'Quite likely. Don't men fight bulls in Spain or some place like that?'

'Yes, they do. And in England they used to set bulldogs on to bulls, so it's in their blood. That was why ours went for Crayshaw's cow. But I should have thought that they ought to stage cat-and-dog fights.'

'Oh?'

Back to cats again. But his arm was in hers, and it was warm there.

'There's a gate coming.'

'The one into the road?'

'Yes, that's it. Mind, you mustn't hurt yourself.'

She guided him through, and his feet felt the stones.

'Well, this is where I leave you. I'll walk back by the road.'

'Will you be all right?'

'Yes. You will be coming tomorrow to have your hand looked to, won't you?'

'I expect so.'

'Poor hand, I am so sorry about it. Does it hurt very much?'

'It does rather.'

Here was someone to make a fuss over it, and it did hurt too.

'I'm so sorry.'

There was a pause. They faced each other in the middle of the road. His head was on one side and he didn't seem to know where she was quite. Poor blind young man, she was sorry for him. He must be looked after.

The awkwardness had fallen again between them. There was nothing to say. But she had agreed to come up to Swan's Wood, which was one good thing. She was very nice.

'Well, perhaps I had better be going back.'

'Yes, an' so had I.'

'Goodbye.'

'Goodbye.'

And he began to walk home. Their first meeting was over. It had been terrifying. But they had walked arm in arm anyway. The touch and the warmth were so much finer when one was blind. And one was more frightened; still, her voice had been kind. She would come again right enough. He touched his blue glasses, he must be a sight. His steps sounded hollowly on the road, and he thought of a dream when he had run and run and run. But there had been no birds then, they had all been hushed. For suddenly the sun came out, and, warmed by him, a bird began to sing in little cascades of friendliness. How good the world was. He wanted his lunch.

*

Nanny sat by the fire. Shadows ran up and down the walls of her room, and it was very quiet in there except for her breathing and the murmuring kettle. Kettles were so companionable. On the table by her side was a cup of tea which steamed up at the ceiling, broadly at first, and then the steam narrowed down till at last it was lost in a pin-prick. It could not get so high. On the table was a patchwork cover, the heirloom of her family. By the cup stood a tea-caddy and by that a spoon. The kettle spurted steam at the fender in sudden, angry bursts.

It was close in her room because she never opened the window. Her black dress rose stiffly up against the heat, and the whalebone in her collar kept the chin from drooping. Little flames would come up to lick the kettle, and then the shadows on the wall would jump out of the room. But she sat straight and quiet as the people in the photographs round. She was of their time. Only her breathing, tired and hoarse, helped the kettle to break the quiet of the watching photographs.

It wasn't right his going out with her like this. This would be the third time he had gone out with her, and it wasn't like Mrs Haye to allow it, it ought to be stopped. At that age they could so easily fall in love with each other. And what would happen then? Young people always went into those things blind, they didn't see what the conse-quences of their actions were. He ought to be more careful of whom he took up with. His daughter, indeed. What would everyone be saying? And that her boy should go out with that thing, him that she had brought up since he was a squalling babby, it was not right.

There had been the time when he had first been given to her – a wonderful baby strong as you could wish, full seven and a half pounds from the moment he was born, and since then she had fed him with her own hands just like as she was doing now, and getting up at nights constant when he was hollering for his pap. She had seen him grow up right from the beginning. And he had gone blind – it couldn't have been worse! – so that now he could never have a good time with the young ladies or nothing, poor Master Johnnie! But she would see him out of this thing that had come upon them, she had seen him out of many such – there had been the time when he had been taken with whooping cough a deal of trouble they had had with him, but they had pulled him through. Mrs Haye had been such a good mother to him better indeed than his real one Mrs Richard Haye would ever have been. There were stories the servants that were with her told but then, what was the good of believing stories but from what was said she was too free altogether. You can never trust men not even your husband's best friend but there it was!

And Master John had growed up and gone to college but that never had agreed with him, he was weakly ever since she could remember. It was what she said that had kept him from a preparatory school even if the doctor had said so too. Then they had had the governess who was not up to much with all her airs and graces. The way she used to carry on with that teacher in Norbury, undignifying. But he had been too weakly for college, he had never been happy there even if he had growed to the figure of a man he was. The other boys what were less well-behaved and brought up would have always been at him, she knew their ways. And there had come a time when he would hardly so much as throw a glance at her and say 'Hullo, Nanny,' and Mr William had said one day 'He is growing up,' and she had seen him going away from her when the only things she could do for him was to darn his socks and sew on buttons, but he was back to her now, she could help him again bring him up his food and take him out for walks. It wasn't right that hussy taking hold on him and everyone would be talking you see if they didn't.

Then the master had married again and a good thing too for the first one wasn't such as to waste breath over. Beautiful she had been, too beautiful they was a danger them lovely ones though what he could see in this hussy she didn't know but then he couldn't see, poor Master John that was what it was. There had been great goings on for the marriage, a servants' ball and the service in church had been lovely the bridesmaids being in pink and the clergyman having a lovely voice. She had been a good mistress to her Mrs Haye had been, only a hard word now and then from that day on. And she had made a good mother to Master John, always thinking of him and looking after him just as if he was her own boy. Then the master going to India with his regiment and leaving her with Master John to live with the grandparents, what was dead now some time, and where they didn't treat her proper they was half-starving the poor boy. They hadn't no illusions of his mother but it wasn't his fault poor little mite what she was. And then their coming back after she had wrote to tell them, though the regiment did come back too, and his falling downstairs dead as mutton his heart having gone sudden like. A lovely funeral it was and a fine corpse he made lying out on the bed. In the church it was the men of the estate that carried the coffin, and the church was draped in black, and there were officers from the regiment and wreaths that the officers had sent and some from the men. Everything had been done in style. And the mistress had been splendid. Quite soon after she had said to her 'Well Jennings it is up to us to bring him up' and she had said back 'We will'm'.

And then he had begun to crawl round the nursery, very fond of coal he had been, and always full of mischief. And they had all said then what a fine man he was going to grow up into, and so he is, but they none of them had the gift of sight so they couldn't have foretold this. When she had been told she was sitting in this chair as like as she might be now and she said 'Lord have mercy on us,' she remembered it as if it was yesterday, though it did seem an age away, and that only six months really. In the next room in the old day-nursery was all the toys he used to have and her first thought was that he would never be able to play with them again. You got a bit mixed up with time when you grew older. They were all in the cupboard there the tin soldiers scarlet and blue with some cannon and the spotted horse which he used to be that fond of and the marbles with colours inside that he always wanted to swallow, they was a peril them things, and the box of bricks as he grew older so that they said he was going to be an architeck, and what would he be now? He had loved his toys, she could remember his sitting on his heels and getting excited over the soldiers as if they was real and fighting a real battle. They were all there in the cupboard waiting. Nothing had been lost and now that her time was coming perhaps when she was gone they would throw them away or give them to some poor child instead of keeping them, maybe for his children if he had any. Waste that was.

Would he marry now? And would a young lady want to marry a blind young man? Ah, but if they knew her Master John of course they would. She ought to know him, she had known him longer than anyone now, and he was so good and kind-hearted even if he was a bit rough at times, but then all young people were like that. She would like to see his son but she might go off at any minute, the doctor said so, it was her heart, she wouldn't last on to see him. But it wasn't doing him no good to be following around of that girl with her father. That man, and him in the church too, it was a sacrilege that's what it was. And the shame on the village and on the house. They was the laughing-stock of the countryside. And him going and living quite near just to spite them, oh if the master was here, he would send him packing and that daughter of his parading of herself about. She would talk to Mrs Haye she ought to know what everyone was saying.

She had been sitting in this very chair when who should come in but Mr William and she could see something was up on account of his being out of breath and he had said 'The young master 'as been 'urt' he said, and she had been turned to stone so to speak, as it says in the Book, and he had gone on about the accident on the railway and how he would be blind for ever. And she had said 'Lord have mercy on us. Lord have mercy on us.'

To think that it should happen to him, him that was so good and kind. He had been good to her he knew what he had to thank her for. And he had been so brave through it all. Oh dear. Even when he was quite a mite he had been that kind-hearted. Mrs Richard Haye was like that they had said. In another way though it must have been. And she always going about whistling, never going to church, and so happy with all her men friends hanging around and the master too simple to notice or suspect. Folks as are that happy are dangerous. And her silly whistling so that you couldn't stir without hearing it, senseless it was. And everything in such a muddle so they said. She had only seen her once when they had taken her to be shown to the mistress as the new nurse. Too weak she had been to stir a finger but beautiful although so pale lying there on the bed propped up on cushions, the light shining on her face, blue eyes half-closed with long lashes and so thin with her last home-coming. She hadn't said a word just looked at her, they were beautiful eyes, too beautiful. But they was all liable to die like that all women. She had been near to marrying Joe Hawkins before she went out into service. She didn't regret it, she would do it again if she had the chance, though two Master Johnnies didn't come but once in a lifetime.

Getting up with difficulty she made herself some fresh tea, hanging up the kettle-holder on a brass-headed nail that goggled like a golden eye from the wall. The room was thick with warmth. A lifeless pennant of steam came from the spout of the teapot.

She lifted the cup to her lips with hands which trembled rather. She sipped. A cup o' tea did you a deal of good. Nothing like it so that the older you were the more you felt the need of it. And the cough was getting worse, it wouldn't go till it had killed her. But Mrs Haye would give her a fine funeral with a stone which would have an angel on it maybe. Beautiful she always thought they looked, them tombstones as had angels on 'em.

And when she was gone Master Johnnie would be still more alone and he was lonesome enough now. He hadn't a soul left as belonged to him except Mrs Haye and her. The master had been the only son of an only son so that if Master John did not marry the name would go. Mrs Haye had brothers and sisters, and many of them, but they wouldn't speak to her nor she to them. It had been a romance her marrying the master. Mr William had told her at one time and another what he had heard at table and it seemed as if her parents had not approved of her marrying the master, and he as fine a man as ever was. The marriage had been sudden enough certain. So that when she had married against their orders, as it might be, they wouldn't hear of her again. That was a shame. Scotland she came from and lived in a fortress, they was wild them parts. But there it was and he was alone poor Master John. It was funny how some families did seem to die out, and when you thought of her own sisters and brothers dead and gone now and their children. There was no sense or order in it.

There was Christmas coming and she would have to begin thinking of what he would like. Two presents each year he got, one from Mrs Haye and one from her and every year he gave her one. To think of his having no one else to give him one. And it was hard to think of something he would want and it took longer to make things up now as you were older. It had better be something warm, there was a hard winter coming, and she would make socks for Eliza's new baby her great-niece. He would want another muffler on cold days like this, and there would be more of them too, but then he would be wearing it with that hussy. What the world was coming to. To think of him walking out with her, that common thing.

And he had had a letter from that nurse only the other day, that was another one, stuck up she had been and not fit to look after anyone much less Master John. But he hadn't liked her, oh no she knew her Master Johnnie he didn't hold with her sort, and quite right too. The good Lord knew what she was. She hadn't liked to trust him a moment out of her sight when she was there. And she that would not take her meals in the hall and her no better than anyone. What did she think herself she would like to know. Oh it had been a mess-up everybody knocked off their feet, as it might be, by this happening. Mr William hadn't known which way to turn and it was the first time as she had seen him flustered. And she had not slept so much as a wink in three nights nor had cook with thinking of what he would want to eat what time he came back from hospital. Mr William had not known such a thing happen ever, and she was a knowledgeable man. And Mr Weston had worried himself about the fruit that he could 'ave peaches and grapes so that old Pinch could not remember anything like it ever, not that he was liable to, useless rude old man that he was. There had been the time when he had said to her quite sudden like 'I ain't a-goin' to die yet awhile so don't you worry,' which was all on account of her asking of him kindly as to 'is health, which no one could take offence at. But he was of the sort as drop down sudden. And there was Annie, poor body that was half-crazed, and for a week, when they had told her she said nothing but 'Deary me,' she felt it too poor soul, of course she did, as if they wasn't all fond of Master John. It was a mess-up.

But with Christmas coming on you really didn't know where you were, what with the happenings and everything, though it was all settling down now. But there was this girl he was walking out with which didn't bear thinking of. She would knit him a muffler that would keep him warm and there wasn't many as knitted as close and firm as she did if she didn't go quite so fast. And the socks for Eliza's new baby, Harriet they was going to call her and a good name it was, grandma had been a Harriet. Then there was Joe, who was to marry next month, he would want a wedding present, something useful as would be a standby. He was a good boy that and a good son to his mother, her twin, as was dead now. Twelve brothers and sisters, the good Lord had been favourable to her mother, and six of them dead and gone now and four nephews killed in the war one after the other. But there was eight left. Joe had been too young to go, but now he was marrying and was in a good position, and there would be children and she would knit them socks . . .

She sipped. The kettle threw out sprays of steam and bubbles bubbled angrily about the lid. Sometimes the lid would rise as if to let something out, and there would be a hissing in the fire and then it would fall back again. The room was full of movement with sudden still glowing colours here and there on the furniture where the fire caught it. A late fly dozed just within the half-circle of light thrown out by the fire on the ceiling and where the shadows crept up from the corners trying to choke the light. The room was so warm. And the figure in the chair sat straight and quiet with hands crossed on her lap, and the whalebone in her collar kept the chin from drooping.

*

'So we are going to Swan's Wood, are we?'

'Yes, do you mind?'

'No.'

He pressed closer.

'This silence with the sun and with the sharpness of the frost still on the ground and with you here . . .' he said, but she did not answer.

'The breadth and distance there is in the country today, June, don't you feel it?'

'I don't know.'

'The country is so full of the sun today, June, and I am away from them all, for you have rescued me from the house, so that I am with you. And we have hours of time, this will be the longest walk of all that we have had yet. It is such an adventure. Do you like walking with me, June?'

'Perhaps I do, perhaps I don't.'

'But you must, or else it will be so dull for you. And you are kind to take me out, for they are old in that house, so old. Poor Nan who is dying, and William the butler who is waiting for a pension, and old Pinch who is going to retire next week. Mamma is giving him a cottage rent free. He has worked in the garden for forty years.'

'Do they get pensions? How much?'

'Enough to live on, when they have deserved it. But listen to that cock, June, crowing so boastfully such miles away. And the car droning up Bodlington Hill on its way to Norbury, with the stream just near hurrying by over the stones. And the birds are singing to the fine day, there are so many of them. Do you know the names of birds?'

'No, an' I wish I did.'

'Nor do I, it does not really matter. But what luck that we should have the sun for our walk. We have had so much rain up to now.'

'An' I hate rain.'

'So do I! Listen to the starlings on that tree, screaming at us, perhaps. June, did you say the other day that you lived alone with your father?'

'Yes. Why not?'

'I did not mean that. It is a very excellent thing to do. But you must be very lonely sometimes.'

'Sometimes.'

'Then do you never see anyone? It must be so dull: I know how it is.'

'Oh yes, I see one or two.' She laughed.

'Who? But I never see anyone, except stewed people that Mamma serves up, when there is no way of keeping them out. And you are nicer than any of them.'

'You are a funny card.'

'Am I? Well, there are worse things to be. Isn't it funny, though, that we should never have met in all these years? I have never seen you, June, never seen how you are.'

'You have, only you don't remember. In church I used to watch you when we were both quite little, but you would hardly ever look at me, you were too grand. And afterwards.'

'But then I must have seen you. Why did you look at me?'

'There was nothing else to do.'

'No, I suppose not. Where did you sit?'

'To the left of your pew, just in front of the font. Don't you re-member?'

'And what was the church like? I never really noticed it. Oh, it hurts to try and remember. I can only see bits of it, the spaces are so hard to fill up.'

'Don't. I hate that church too, only through the window on the right you could see an apple tree.'

'Yes, I know. And there were birds.'

'And apples in the autumn. Do you remember?'

'Yes. Apples.' And he laughed.

'Why do you laugh?'

'I don't know. But I did hate being made to go to church – though of course your father used to preach really well.'

'Oh yes!'

'Mamma . . . He grew roses up the church, I think. I liked that very much. They were so pretty.'

'An' Mrs Haye made him take them down again.'

'Did she? I wonder why. Do you like roses?'

'Very much. There used to be so many of them in that garden at the old Vicarage. Father was always crazy on them, an' so was I.'

'The rose is lovely, June, don't you think? The poets sing so often of them. They call her the queen of flowers. "The damask colour of thy leaves." "Sweetness dwells in rosy bowers." "The blushing rose." '

'Oh yes. They were all over our garden.'

'Then you must have lived in a way dear to the lyrical poets of the seventeenth century. How charming!'

'I never read poetry. I haven't time.'

'Really? And the church must have been so pretty, buried in them. But then Mamma is very low church.'

'How do you mean?'

'Well, she does not like ornaments to a church. I think it is very silly of her, though Crayshaw goes too far with his lighted candles and so on.'

'But what does it matter?'

'It is popery, that is all. It is going to Rome.'

'What's that?'

'Oh well, why talk about it?'

'Father was so fond of his roses. Making him take them down like that was a shame.'

'Listen to those bells, June. The sound comes tumbling over the country from so far off. It would be Purley church, I suppose.'

'Father hates church bells. They hurt him.'

'Where are we now?'

'We are just coming to Mr Brownlee's farm.'

'I thought so. Brownlee's chickens are making such a noise.'

It was a shame the way they had treated Father.

'What a lovely material your dress is made of.'

'Do you like it?'

'So much. It is so soft, one's hand glides over it and then sinks down in the folds of it drowned in it, June. What colour are you wearing?'

'Blue.'

'Yes, it would be blue.'

'Poor boy, not being able to see.'

'Call me John, dear, "boy" is so young.'

'Poor John.'

'It has been awful without you.'

'Has it?'

'Everything is black. Before, even when one shut one's eyes the eyelids were red if one were outside, but light now has been cut off from within. Nothing but black. One gets desperate sometimes, you know. There are times when I would like to kill myself, really, I mean.'

'Poor John.'

'But your eyelids when you closed them would be such a delicious colour for the lovely eyes inside.'

'Would they? Oh, but then you have never seen my eyes.'

'Perhaps not, but I can feel them just the same.'

'Do you?'

'Yes, they are so calm, so quiet. Such a lovely blue.'

'But they are dark brown.'

'Oh. Then your dress does not match?'

'No, I suppose not.'

'But what does that matter? They are such lovely brown eyes. And sometimes they light up and burn, perhaps?'

'How do you mean?'

'Well . . . But have you ever been in love?'

'I don't know.'

'Maybe they are burning now?'

'N-no, I don't think so.'

'How sad. And mine, if they had not been removed, would have burned so ardently.'

'What's ardently?'

'You know, hotly, pas— No.' This was awkward. 'But I like your eyes, whether they are brown or blue.'

'You are really quite nice, John, an' I think I like you.'

'No more than that?'

'Perhaps.'

And his hands was in hers. Better to ignore it at first.

'Perhaps?'

'Well, I don't know.'

'You are strange, June, so distant, so cold. I don't believe you really like me at all, no, really not.'

'Mind, here's a gate. Be careful.'

'Where is the gate? You are cruel, you know. You don't care a bit. Oh, here it is; good.'

'Care about what?'

'What about? Why, me, I mean. But this will be where we have to cross the road. Then we go through the gate which should be to the right there. Shut this one; that is the home farm we are leaving.'

'Have you got a farm all of your own?'

'Yes, and why not?'

'You must be rich.'

'I am not so sure about that.'

'It must be wonderful to be rich.'

'It must be wonderful to be poor.'

'How do you mean? You've never been poor in all your life. So how can you tell?'

'But poor people are always much happier than rich people on the cinema. The cinema used to be the only way I had to see life.'

'But what do you think of scrubbing floors all day, and of cooking food, and of having to look after your father who is ill, and all that?'

'Is he ill, June?'

'Yes, at least he thinks he is.'

'I'm sorry. But you won't always be poor?'

'As far as I can see.'

'But one day a fairy prince may spirit you away to a place of luxury. Think of it.'

'Gracious, no! Why should he?'

'He would have every inducement. These things often happen, you know, here and there.'

'I don't think so.'

'But I do. One of these days ... we ... perhaps. Well; but I am so sorry he is ill.'

'Oh, I don't think he is as ill as all that. He is a poet an' imagines things.'

'A poet? Does he write poetry?'

'Yes. Leastways he doesn't write, but he talks beautiful. About stars and things. I can't understand him half the time, so I just say "Yes" or "No" to keep him company. He is a wonderful man.'

'And you must lead a most thrilling life all alone with a poet in that house. Mamma says that the garden was – is very beautiful.'

'Yes, it is full of trees and things.'

'So wild. Such a free life.'

'Free? Well, I don't know about that. But we have some chickens, only they have to be fed. And there's the cat. She killed a great big mouse the other day.'

'Did she!'

'Yes, an' there's the chicks that get lost in the grass, I love them, an' there's a starling that nests every year in the chimney, and my own mouse which plays about in my room at night, an' ...'

God, the boredom of this.

'... but sometimes I hate it all.'

'It must be horrid for you.'

'I've had no one else to tell it all to.'

'No, of course not. June, here we are in the wood. Do you feel the hollowness of it? For the trees crowd about us, and their branches roof us in slyly, with sly noises that one can just hear. And we seem to be in another world now, for the cart that is creaking along the road outside is so faint, floating through the twigs that urge the sound gently along as they are tickled by the wind. So that we might be on our way to some dark and dangerous spot. June, it is medieval.'

'What's that?'

'It means long ago. But we are happy together, aren't we? You know, you are the only person I would take with me to Swan's Wood.'

There was Mummy, but she did not count.

'Why?'

'Because I used to spend so much of my youth at the top there, thinking great thoughts.'

'But why only me?'

'Surely you know.'

'Perhaps I don't.'

'Oh yes, you do.'

'When I was little I used to tell everything to a friend I had then. We used to walk in the lane, down at Broadlands. One day she tripped up and cut her leg.'

'And I have never told anyone everything.'

'Tell me.'

'I will some day, it would take too long now. June, are we getting near the top now?'

And he would tell her, it would help, though she would not understand. But he would never tell her of his writing, that was too important.

'I see light behind the trees.'

'We are getting there. This must be near the top of the hill, and you are not a bit out of breath.'

'My! an' here we are. Is that your view? I don't see much in it, not that it isn't very pretty though.'

'Shall we sit down?'

'Yes.'

She lets go of his hand and they sit down.

'June, give me back your hand, it makes you so much more real.'

'There it is, silly.'

'And what do you see of my view?'

'There are fields an' trees an' the river an' behind that the hill with the waterworks' tower an' to the right there is the town with the Abbey, no more than that.'

'That is all gone for me, anyway. June, my hand is so comfortable in yours.'

'Is it?'

'Yes. Your hand is warm and so strong. But it is only just big enough to hold mine.'

'Shall we change round?'

'That is better. I have it captive now. It is like holding a bird.'

'Oh you!'

'Oh me?'

'You are a funny boy.'

'Do call me John.'

'Funny John.'

'How is your other hand, the one that was cut?'

'It is better now. But it did hurt.'

'Poor hand. I was so sorry.'

'Were you? That was nice. There was no one who cared.'

'Poor June. But didn't your Father mind?'

'No, he never would. He is always thinking of himself.'

'Well, he ought to have. It was . . .'

'No, no, he oughtn't, it wasn't his fault, he is a genius, you know. Great thoughts he has, not like you and me. Above it all.'

Not like you and me!

'But, poor hand. Give it me, June. Ah, now I have both your hands – so much and yet so little.'

'No, don't press it like that, you are hurting.'

'How much would you give me of yours?'

'Of mine? Why? Well, I haven't very much to give. But if you like I'll give you a brooch of my mother's which is broken so as I can't use it. You will remember me by that. But I expect you have a bad memory, John.'

'Only when I have nothing to remember.'

'What shall I give you, then?'

'What you like best.'

'And what will you give me?'

'A ring, and more, perhaps.'

'You are nice, John.'

'Aren't I?'

'Oh, well, I never. Don't you ever think of me? It's always you, you, you.'

'But, of course I think of you much more than you would believe possible. And you come to me in my dreams.'

'John!'

'Yes, dear. It's true, even if I haven't told you before.'

'How wonderful!'

'It is, and more than wonderful.'

He laughed, and there was a pause.

'No, it's not comfortable, your holding both my hands.'

'Here is one back, then.'

'John, the sun's come out and the Abbey has gone all gold.'

'And it has caught the trees as well, perhaps? When the sun came out for a moment it used to be a great thing for me, and I have sat here entranced, but when you think that all this doesn't bother itself about one at all, it is a trifle boring.'

'John, you are very like Father.'

'Am I? How?'

'I don't know. You talk the same.'

'Do I? Oh, well. But I used to dream here so. Have you never dreamed, June – about things, I mean?'

'Yes, perhaps.'

'And what do you do all day? There must be time to dream.'

'Oh, there's lots to do. But I do dream.'

'What about?'

'I don't know.'

'And this place would fit in with my mood. A view helps, do you find that?'

'Yes.'

'At last, something definite. You really think that?'

'I suppose I do, seeing as how I said it.'

'You are frightened of your feelings. But one soon grows out of that. I did a year ago.'

'An' then there is the river. I sit on the bank sometimes an' watch it going by.'

'I know. I love doing that. Do you fish?'

'No, I don't know how to.'

'I used to, but I can't now.'

'Poor John.'

'Poor me. But it will not be "poor me" if you are nice.'

'But aren't I being nice?'

'Fairly.'

'Well, I never! Only fairly? What more do you want?'

'Lots more.'

'You are a one. But it is nice up here.'

'With you. Say "with you".'

'Why should I? No, I won't.'

'Say "with you." '

'No – hi, stop! What are you doing? If you go on like that I shall go home.'

'But you didn't say "with you".'

'Why should I?'

'To please me.'

'I'm not sure I want to now.'

'Do.'

'I'm sure I don't see why I should. But as you seem to've set your heart on it, here it is – "with you," stupid.'

'It has no meaning now; how sad. You are very cruel, June. I used to think of cruel ladies and of kind ones when I was up here, but they were none of them like you.'

'Cruel ladies and kind ones? What do you mean?'

'Such as one used to see on the cinema. I used to grow so romantic over this view. I wanted to go into politics then. When you thought of all the people starving, there was nothing else to do. I became Prime Minister, of course, up here, and addressed huge meetings which thundered applause. Once, at one of those meetings, a lady became so affected by my words that she had a fit. She was carried out, and the commotion over it gave me time to drink a cup of water, which was most necessary. It was all very vivid up here. I was to lead a public life of the greatest possible brilliance. It is different now.'

'How wonderful that would be.'

'You know what I mean? One planned everything out on a broad scale, remembering little scraps of flattery that someone or other had been so good as to throw one and building on that. One was so hungry for flattery. The funny thing is that when one goes blind life goes on just the same, only half of it is lopped off.'

'Yes?'

'One would think that life would stop, wouldn't you? But it always goes on, goes on, and that is rather irritating.'

'My life's always the same.'

'Yes, I was on the crest of my audience and the woman threw her fit just as the climax was reached; but I repeat myself. I shan't feel that sort of thing any more now, there is so little to want.'

'Oh, John!'

'And it would have been so lonely without you.'

'Would it?'

'Say you like being up here with me.'

'All right, so long as it pleases you.'

'Pleases me? Only that?'

How slow, how slow this was.

'Oh, well. Nice boy.'

'Thanks. But now, do you know what I am going to do now? After all, one must have something to put against one's name. For I am going to write, yes, to write. Such books, June, such amazing tales, rich with intricate plot. Life will be clotted and I will dissect it, choosing little bits to analyse. I shall be a great writer. I am sure of it.'

'Yes.'

'But I will be. What else is there to live for? Writing means so much to me, and it is the only thing in which the blind are not hampered. There was Milton.'

'Ah yes, Milton.'

'I must justify myself somehow.'

'Funny John.'

'Yes, very comical. Blundering about in the dark yet knowing about everything really. I know I do. And I will tell the world.'

'Yes.'

'But do you understand?'

'Yes.'

'You see, June, no one cares enough, about the war and everything. No one really cared about my going blind.'

'Yes.'

'And I will write about these things – no one cares and I will be as uncaring as any. I will be a great writer one day, and people will be brought to see the famous blind man who lends people in his books the eyes that he lost, and . . .'

Poor John, he was properly off it now. She did not understand all this writing stuff; and how did one do it, it would be so difficult when one could not see the page?

'. . . but I am boring you.'

'No, you're not. Do go on.'

'It is getting cold out here.'

'Oh, don't let's go home just yet.'

'So you like being out here?'

'Yes.'

Why had he told her about his writing? Now everything was spoilt. And of course she did not understand. She was lamentably stupid. They had better go home.

'But you will catch a chill.'

'Why should I? We can make each other warm.'

And she pressed closer to him, and she laughed.

She would call that snuggling, he thought. There was a pause.

'John,' she said, pulling his arm, 'how silent you are.'

'I have just said so much.'

'How do you mean? Oh, John, will you write about me?'

'Perhaps.'

'Fancy me being in a book. Just think.'

'Would you like to be?'

'Of course I would. Father writes books too, only they never get written.'

'Does he put you in them?'

'Oh no, they are not that sort.'

'What sort are they?'

'I don't know. But he's always talking about his writing,' She paused. 'John, you'll make me the person your hero's in love with, won't you? and your hero'll be you, I suppose?'

'Perhaps.'

'You aren't very chirpy now, are you, John?'

'No, it is cold out here.'

'But don't I keep you warm?'

'It is my other side that is so cold.'

'Well, an' perhaps we'd better go home.'

'Yes, perhaps we had better go home.'

They get up. He staggers, then, arm in arm, they go down the hill through the wood.

'Mind, John, there's a fallen tree here.'

'Thanks. Where? Oh, here. June, how sad it is going home.'
'Yes, it is. But we'll go out again.'
'Of course.'

3 Finishing

'How minute we are.'

'Why?'

'Well, this does not seem to be a time of great feeling, perhaps we have had too many of them lately. And we are so small compared to the trees. Gods come and go, but trees remain. By "small" I don't mean "in height". They seem to me so lasting, so grave in their fat green cloaks, or in winter like naked lace.'

'There, an' I've forgotten to feed the chickens.'

'We are so petty, while time in the towns rolls by on well-oiled wheels with horrible efficiency. The machinery there goes on and on, and there are bits of it that are not right. The most horrible injustices.'

'There's no justice.'

'No, there is no justice.'

A long way beneath something in the town was dropped with a clang, while a tug coming up the river whistled to get through the lock, a long shriek which shivered through the trees. Birds circled in specks round the Abbey tower. There was no wind and on the hill smoke from a cottage fire drifted straight up towards the blue sky, for the sun was shining. Just in front, in the meadow by the edge of the wood, a rabbit was feeding quietly, trembling at being alive. And they sat together against a tree, he with his head on one side to catch what was going on, and she dozing, with the world drifting in and out of her mind.

'I hate this easy life with the millions toiling there.'

'I don't find it easy.'

'No, I suppose not. But I will do something, even if I am blind.'

She pulled a wisp of hair away from her face and rearranged the ragged scarf about her neck.

'I expect you will, John.'

'Do you think so?'

'Yes, I do.'

A confused shouting came from the lock, into which the barges were being packed. Several dogs were barking at each other while men ran about. The rabbit sat up and listened.

'John, there's a darling rabbit out there,' and the rabbit fled.

'Oh?'

'He's gone now.'

'Oh?'

And they were silent. From the other side of the wood a ploughman cried to his horses. Then from in front came a rattling of machinery and the lock gates creaked, painfully slow.

'Why are you so silent today, John?'

'I must go, I must go away.'

'What do you mean, away from here?'

'No, to the towns.'

'Yes, I know. You do want to get off sometimes. So do I. Minnie is getting very tiresome, he's been making messes all over the house, an' father does hate messes. I really don't know what to do.'

'What is Minnie?'

'Our cat.'

'Why do you give him a female name?'

'I don't know. Father always calls him she. Father hates cats.'

She had told him this before.

'An' Father's so nervy nowadays, you don't know what to do with him. It gets harder and harder to live there at all. Father spends so much money on – on small things we don't need. There often isn't enough to eat an' . . .'

He heard a train snort in the distance like a dragon, and the wood round reared itself in tall crowding shapes and dark images. A voice droned complaint and he saw a little figure at the foot of an image throwing words at the things which hemmed her in.

'. . . but he doesn't care, he never thinks of me, it's me who has always to be thinking of him, how to keep him alive, how to keep the home round his head, how to manage so's he won't starve. Always thinking of him, I am, and he with never a thought to me.'

'Poor June.'

'Yes, it is poor June. You don't know what it is with your easy life down there. There's times when you don't know if your own life's safe when the fit is on him, he's so dangerous.'

'June, he doesn't attack you?'

'Attack me? If you could see my – the bruises on my arm, you

466

simply wouldn't believe. And he was brought to it, brought to it.'

'I must go away.'

'It wasn't his fault.'

'We ought all to go away for a time. The country is poisoning us, June. Under all the smiles that one hears and the soft kindness that one sees at first, there is so much cruelty. We will go.'

'They brought him to it.'

'It's all so different in the towns, there is so much more going on.'

'But I don't want any more to go on. I've got enough as it is.'

'I'm so sorry.'

'Oh, it's all right. If it wasn't for Father's being as he is, it wouldn't be bad. He's worse than usual just now, and he won't have you do anything for him.'

'We shall never do any good in the country. What is the use of staying down here? I ought to go away.'

'But how can we?'

We? How awkward!

'I shall never do any writing down here. It's no good, one can't.'

'No, I don't suppose so.'

'Does nothing ever happen in the country?'

'Well, I don't know that you have much to complain of, poor darling.'

'What, you mean going blind like that? Yes, I had forgotten. Except for that, then, nothing has happened. Sometimes I see a pool shut in by trees with their branches reflected in the stagnant water. Nothing ever moves, the pool just lies there, day and night, and the trees look in. At long intervals there is a ripple; the pool lets it die. And then the trees look in the same as before.'

'Funny John.'

'I may be, but that is the country.'

'D'you know how I live in that house where there's everything to clean, and with not a soul to help me, mind you, with a man that throws anything away, anywhere, an' the chickens to feed and the meals to cook?'

'There would be food to prepare and boards to scrub in towns.'

'Oh, I know there would, but we could have a gay time there, what with dancing an' nice dresses an' everything.'

'Oh yes, we could have a gay time there.'

How different this was to the first time he had sat at the top with her a fortnight ago. Only two weeks and so many things had happened.

'You will take me, won't you, John darling?'

'Yes.'

Let in for it this time.

'But I can't leave Father.'

'But I thought you said you wanted to go.'

'I wanted to make sure of you. Besides, why can't I make believe?'

'Don't you want to go with me, then?'

'Yes. But I can't leave Father, he wouldn't be able to do anything without me. Poor Father, he's helpless, you know. He must have someone to look after him. And anyway you'ld have gone off.'

'June, why do you say that?'

'They always do. There was a story I read called The Love of White Hope. The young man in that left his girl whom he had promised to marry, and she committed suicide, which was stupid, and he was so sorry that he drank water for the rest of his life, or something, I forget, which was stupider still. Yes, that was it, he used to drink in his young days, and then after that he gave it up. He was lovely when he was young. You would never take me with you.'

'But I asked you to come.'

'Did you?'

'I said you could.'

'But you never meant me to.'

'Yes, I did.'

'I know you didn't.'

'Why don't you come, anyway? It will not be for long, probably.'

'Shall I?'

A cow bugled dejectedly. He thought that the neck would be stretched out with the mouth half open as though it were going to vomit. Idiotic cows.

'No, I can't leave Father.'

'Well, don't say now that I didn't ask you.'

'But you never meant me to go.'

Another cow answered from a long way off, and they exchanged dull grief across the hedges and the meadows. The hedges would be black at this time of the year, and the trees bare. The plough creaked leisurely, how slow everything was.

'I'm not blaming you. You're not the sort that are meant to stay.

Your sort can get rid of anything that displeases them, as Father says.'

'June, do come.'

'No.'

'Then I don't see what you have to complain of from me.'

'Poor John.'

'It's not as if you are going to have a baby or anything.'

'Don't.'

'Well, is it?'

'You don't understand.'

There was a long pause.

'Oh, to be in a town again, to hear a barrel-organ, for instance, across the street through gaps in the traffic! And all the rush there, and the thousands of people. I'd give anything to be there and just listen, so much would be going on, while here . . .'

'I couldn't leave Father, could I, now?'

'No, perhaps not. But I think it is really fine of you to stay with him, I really do.'

'Fine? I don't know about that.'

'Well, I mean, if he attacks you. And he has not done a great deal for you.'

'It isn't his fault – besides, I won't have you say things like that about him. Anyway I shouldn't have been here if it wasn't for him.'

'I am sorry. I did not mean that. Certainly I have much to be grateful to him for.'

'Why, how do you mean?'

'For your being here.'

'Nice John.'

Why had he made a compliment like that? And why had she swallowed it?

'What will you do, June?'

'I don't know.'

She never knew, perhaps that was the best. But he was beginning to.

'Well, remember, if ever you want to run away, come up to London and stay with us. We have not yet arranged to go to London; that is, I have not even broached the subject with Mamma, but I must go, and in the end she and I will go. So just you come when you want.'

'I will. An' may I bring Father too?'

'But – but yes, if you think he needs it.'

'I know you. An' what's wrong with Father? He's nothing to be ashamed of. You think I don't notice the way people pass us as if we weren't there when they meet us on the road? It's not his fault his being what he is. He was brought to it, and by your lot too.'

'June, what do you mean?'

'They were always criticizing him – d'you suppose I don't know how it was? – always carping away at him till his life wasn't his own and as if it didn't belong to him and no one else, and not to everyone as they thought, and finding fault with Mother for being in love with the postman, of course it was wrong, but why shouldn't she, and them saying that he didn't do his duty by the parish when he was worth the whole crew of them put together.'

'But, June . . .'

'Oh, I'm not blaming you, don't be frightened. But it was your lot that brought him to it, it . . .'

These scenes. And after all, flirting with the postman, it was unfortunate, and a squalid story. Now the man was so soaked in the whisky, or whatever it was he drank, that he was a topic of conversation. For that alone one ought to be grateful to him. But Mamma was right for once, it was disgraceful. But it was sad too.

'. . . poor, poor Father.'

'Yes, June, I am sorry.'

'You aren't really.'

There was a pause, and then he said:

'I think perhaps suffering is rather fine, don't you?'

Was it? He did not know. At any rate, it was a way out of blindness. She began again:

'But why wasn't I allowed to wear nice dresses and stay in the Vicarage and go to dances an' have some fun? Why have I got to scrub floors all day and cook meals and look after the house with never a word of thanks? It isn't fair.'

'But you and I are really rather lucky . . .'

'Lucky? You . . .'

His face, that awful face. He didn't know what scars he had, poor boy. You couldn't say anything to him, with his blindness an' all.

'. . . but not lucky, John.'

'I can't express myself. And I cannot understand how you endure your life if you don't see the fineness in its being as it is.'

'Endure it? Why, it just goes on. Oh, John, you will take me with you, won't you?'

'What is going to happen to Mr Entwhistle, then?'

'I can't leave Father.'

'Does he want to go to the towns?'

'No, he says that would be running away, I don't know what from, though.'

'You couldn't leave him, June.'

'No.'

'But you will one day.'

'How do you mean? When he dies? Oh no, he mustn't die.'

'I wish you saw that about suffering.'

What could one say to her? If one was in her position and did not make it into something, it was not worth its own unpleasantness, that must be so. So that if she was too small to understand, she had much better go on the streets and have a good time on and off, if she could get it no other way. She could not come to London with him, even if they went there, for she would only be unhappy. He could never introduce her to his friends, if he educated her she would only be genteel. Her value was her brutality, and she would lose that. Besides, there was the Shame, who was a fool from all accounts, almost an idiot. But you couldn't let her go back to him in this frame of mind, it was waste. And what would she do when the old man died? – not that he was old, either, but quite young. Probably marry a commercial traveller. He would talk to Mamma. Oh, he was tired, tired.

There was a roar in the distance.

'June, what was that?'

'It's a football match on the Town ground. Norbury are playing Daunton today, so Mrs Donner told me. She has a son that plays, wonderful they say he is.'

'That must have been a goal, then. Or a foul.'

'Oh, John, you mustn't go.'

'Where?'

'Why, to London, of course. What shall I do?'

A huge voice came as a whisper from across the river. ''ere!' it said, frenziedly, ''ere!' And another roar overwhelmed it, then a shrill whistle, and silence.

'It is no good, June, I must go. And June must go too, if there is anything in a name. Think of your August, and of how exciting that will be. It will come right one day.'

'Will it?'

'You see, you cannot leave your Father; what would he come to? It is your duty to stand by him. It is good for one, too.'

How unpleasant it was giving this sort of good advice. She ought to stay down here, from every point of view it was best that she should. And when the man died he would see what could be done. Yes, he really would.

'We will write to each other, June, and everything will seem better tomorrow.'

'It won't.'

'Yes, it will. Poor June. But think, we have had one good time anyway, you and I, haven't we? There is one good thing behind us anyway, isn't there?'

'Don't go, don't go-o.'

God, she was weeping. Well, that had finished it, he could not go. Poor June, and what a beast he was.

'All right, June, I won't go. It's all right, June, I'm not going. I'm not going, June, so it's all right.'

'I'm so mis-erable.'

'But I am not going.'

'It's' (sniff) 'not that.'

'Aren't you glad I am not going?'

'No. Yes.'

'Well, then?'

Why did one always talk baby-talk to someone who was crying?

'There, June, are you better now?'

'Yes.' Sniff. 'The chickens'll be starving.' Sniff. 'I'd better go home.'

'Oh, you must not go home yet. June, I love you so.'

'Do you?' Sniff.

'Yes, I ...'

'But, John, I think you'd better go to London, after all. It'll be better for you there. I was only crying because of everything. I'm better now ...'

What did she mean? What was in her mind? What was this, what was this?

'... fond of me, and I must help Father with his book, his wonderful book which will come out next year, we're hoping. An' you'll go to London and do whatever you're going to do there, I know you will. I expect you will be a great man one day. There's the chickens. I've got to feed them an' look for eggs, too, for supper. Shall I walk you back or can you get home alone now? For I've got to hurry.'

'No, I can get back alone all right by the roads. But, June, don't go like this. What does it mean, – I mean how do you . . .?'

'Oh, you go to London. Father an' I've got the book to write. He'll show you all what a mistake you made. So long, John.'

'Goodbye, Joan.'

Another roar came from the football crowd, an angry sound. A dog had been barking monotonously for ever so long.

'But, June,' he shouted, to the wood, 'June, what do you – June, I – June . . .'

But there was no answer, and he began feeling his way down the ride. How strange it all was, what could she mean? One's head felt in an absolute turmoil, one didn't know what to think.

He felt ill.

Heavy clouds lay above the house, mass upon mass. From the garden rose a black tangle of branches with showers of wandering twigs. And on these would hang necklaces of water-drops caught from the rain, shining with a dull light. Over the river in the dark pile of wood there showed frightened depths of blue, untrusting patches of it, lying here and there. The grass on the lawn was sodden, beaten to a lake of pulp. But over everything was a freshness of morning and of rain that had gone by, and there was a feeling that the trees and the house and the sky were washed, and that this day was yet another page, that there were more to be, so quiet it was.

She came down the stairs, pausing at the hole on the ninth step, and entered the kitchen, a song on her lips. The room was filled with a wet, grey light that made it kind, and she was happy, so that she thought of sweeping the floor. Father had been much better lately, those pains of his had gone, and perhaps he had been drinking less. How would he be today? It was not good for him, all the gin he drank, but he could not help it. How nice it was this morning. She was sleepy, so sleepy. A wonderful dream last night, about a young man who had made love to her, with blue eyes. Poor John. But it was dusty in here. She went to the cupboard under the stairs and took out the broom.

The broom swept a wrinkle of dust across the floor, with matches and crumpled paper and dried mud thrusting along together in it. She hummed contentedly and thought about her poor John. Her poor John who had no eyes. Blindness would be a terrible thing to come upon you, and he was so brave about it, always talking as if it were nothing. You couldn't help liking that in him. Oh, it was so wonderful this morning, and he was wonderful too. He was a gentleman, just as they themselves were for that matter, it was birth that counted, besides he hadn't treated her as anything else but the same as himself. But there was no going on with him. It wasn't as if times weren't difficult enough just with her own set of troubles, his into the bargain were too much. Though if she had gone with him it would have been a score over Mrs Donner. And what would have become of Father then? He had been so much better lately, quite different from what he had been before. Where was Minnie? And she hustled the dust through the door, driving it into the air in a fan-shaped cloud till it settled on the grass round the flakes of mud and the paper and matches which sat there taking a first look round.

Now there was no nonsense about George. How those cows did eat, all day long, and when they weren't eating they were chewing over again. And George had been quite nice lately. He had even said something, rather surly and rude, and she had been rude back. At any rate it was a beginning. Funny George, he was so powerful, his hands looked as if they could hurt you so, not like John with that awful face always screwed up with his scars; you were frightened of him in a horrid way. John was clever right enough, but there wasn't much to those clever ones. While George could do anything with those hands. The beech tree looked very big this morning, with the damp lying on his trunk in sticky patches. But the weather was clearing, and it felt so fresh this morning. There were the chickens to feed. Roses, roo-zez, all the way.

Getting some grain out of a cupboard in the kitchen, she went to the hut and let the chickens out. The cock was quiet and dignified this morning, rather sleepy. But as soon as he was in the yard he challenged the world and then scratched over a stone. The hens at once began to bustle about anxiously. When June scattered the grain they hurried to each fresh handful, while the cock asserted himself in the intervals of eating. She laughed at them as she always did, and cried 'Chuck, chuck,' and they clucked back with choking voices.

She sauntered away and stood looking at the trees over the river. There had been a new man on the milk lorry yesterday, which was exciting. He had such a nice smile, and all for her as she leant over the gate. He would be going by again about half-past two, she would be there. Perhaps he had come for good, and had taken the place of the one with the wicked face. He had had two lives, that one. But the new man was a dream, with fair, fair hair and his blue eyes that danced. It was nice to have somebody new. There was a lot new today.

Funny how sometimes you suddenly saw everything different. The chickens looked just like old women going round to tea-parties, and the cock like that old Colonel who used to call Father 'Padre'. They were well out of that. That was John's life, and – well, he was done with, anyway. Three weeks and not a word, but then that was like him. Probably there would be three letters one after the other in a week's time, he was all moods. Nice the way the wind blew the sleep from off you.

Father's voice from the window: 'Is breakfast ready?'

'In a minute.'

'Oh, it's all right. Don't hurry.'

'I won't.'

Oh, why was she so happy today? And he was too, you could tell by his voice, he never spoke like that unless things were going well. She hugged her arms. The way that hawk hovered. Where was Minnie?

She called: 'Minnie, Minnie.'

He would turn up in a minute or two. He was always coming from nowhere, so to speak. You looked down and there he was, rubbing his back against your leg, quite uncanny it was.

She turned and went back into the house. There was Father coming downstairs.

'Breakfast isn't ready yet. I've had no time.'

'That's all right. Let's go out.'

'It's fine,' he said, 'this morning, fine.'

They walked in silence along the path smothered in weeds. The dripping undergrowth was shining. A sparrow chirped. And there, suddenly, was Minnie.

'Oh Minnie.'

'So she has come out too. I don't hate her so much today. Puss puss.'

Darling Minnie, so sleek, and looking rather frightened of Father, the cold eyes watched him so closely. Webs of moisture clung to

Minnie's coat, making such a brave show, pearls on black velvet.

'Minnie.'

And he lifted a paw.

'Never mind, leave her alone. We've interfered with her hunting. Anyway she'll want to be killing. Come on.'

That was a good sign, Father not making a fuss when he saw him. His head was redder than usual, too.

'What about this Haye?'

'Oh, we parted.'

'Parted' had such a wonderful feel about it, and it had been so quiet. They had just said 'goodbye'.

'Good thing too.'

'He was quite nice.'

'I don't think much of that house.'

They walked on, round and round the old lawn. She had a fluttering inside.

'How did you know, Father?'

'Mrs Haye wrote.'

'Wrote? What to say?'

'That you were going out with him. What business was it of hers, what you were about?'

'She wrote to you?'

'Damn them all. But you would have done well to have married him. It meant money.'

'But I couldn't leave you.'

'Very good of you.'

She felt a kind of clearness, she saw her way. She was much, much happier than ever. She took his arm, but he seemed so uncomfortable that she let it go again.

'What'll you do, d'you think?'

'Stay here.'

'But you can't always do that, you know. You'd better go away.'

'Where to?'

'But you'll marry some day.'

'No, I'll stay with you.'

He pressed her arm. This time she did not try to press his, he was so shy.

'And there's your book to write.'

'Yes, my book.'

There was a pause, and then he went on:

'I tell you what, I'll fix up that hen-run today. But then there is no rabbit wire, and it is so expensive. Oh, well.'

'They're just as well as they are. Look, Minnie has just pounced.'

'I must go and have a drop of something.'

'Why not give it up for a bit?'

'Oh no, can't give it up, does one good, you know.'

'Then I'll get breakfast ready.'

He went through the kitchen and into his room while she began leisurely putting out the breakfast things. A sheet of chill winter sunlight lay on the floor, and some of it was spilled over the window frame as well. She dabbled her feet in it and it came up to her knees. In her hand was the teapot, and, in the other, half a loaf of bread. There came the sound of a cork being drawn in the next room, which sent a shiver pleasurably down her spine. It got rather dull here when he knocked off the drink. But still, it was bad for him. Turning, she put the things down on the table and then went over to the cupboard.

A cough came from the next room. Then the door opened and he came through, a faint flush over his face, and went out of doors. From outside he shouted through the window:

'It's great today.'

And there were patches of blue sky. Oh, it was going to clear up. Was there enough milk? Yes, just. Anyhow he wouldn't get angry, not yet awhile, at any rate. Marry? Who was there to marry? No one as far as she could see. They were all too difficult or too easy. George was only something to do, if she hadn't had someone to think of she would have gone mad. That new milk-lorry man was so nice-looking. But she ought to stand by Father, it was easier that way. Why marry, anyway? It would all turn out right in the end.

Mrs Donner said that the other night when the wind had risen so, a tree had blown down across the road and had prevented Mrs Haye getting to Barwood without wetting her feet, and that was a good thing. What did she mean by writing to Father? She would like to marry John now, just to spite her. She poured milk out of the can into the teapot, and then began to wash up the plates from overnight. Father did not like eating off dirty plates, and it wasn't really very nice either. She would have to change this water she washed everything in, it was so greasy that you couldn't do anything with it, and it smelt rather. They might as well have some of that tinned herring. They had eaten it once too often, but still it was good.

Father was better. He hadn't been like this in the morning for many a time. So pleasant to talk to, and he hadn't minded about breakfast. Yes, she would stay here and help him, he needed her, and look how much better he was already. And what would they do then? You didn't know. It was not as if he could have a living again. But he would find some job, sure to. She laid out the clean plates and put out the butter. Had a mouse or something been at it? They were devils, those vermin, they got into everything and ate all that they set eyes on. There was nothing to be done, you couldn't do away with them, there were too many. She put down the tin of herrings with the opener and looked contentedly at the table. She called:

'Father, breakfast is ready.'

He came in slowly and sat down.

'I'm so lazy.'

'So'm I,' said she.

Mrs Haye was sitting in an armchair in her sitting-room reading a volume of reminiscences that some hunting man had left behind him. Over the fireplace Greylock looked down upon her, while on the writing-table stood Choirboy's hoof, and there were sporting prints on the walls and an Alken in the corner. But all round were masses of flowers, the air was heavy with the scent of them, for her one extravagance was the hot-house, and Weston understood flowers. This book was interestin', she had never known that the Bolton had distemper in '08 and mange in '09, a most awkward time for them, and the bitch pack had been practically annihilated. Again, it appeared that in '13, Johnson, who used to hunt hounds so marvellously, had broken an arm, and on the very next day his first whip, the man that the Aston had now, had cracked his thigh. It was an unlucky pack. They had had foot-an'-mouth for two years now. Their own pack down here was gettin' impossible. Even the Friday country was infested with wire, which of course was young Beamish's fault; why they hadn't given the job to someone more experienced no one could tell, but then there was some money that went with it. And she would have to get rid of this groom of hers, Harry; he drank, there was no doubt about it, you had only to smell him. What could one do?

Mabel would be here soon, and then they could have a long talk about it all.

How dark it was getting. Putting aside the book she rang the bell.

Really it was becoming most tiresome, this affair between Herbert and Mrs Lane. All day long they were at it, she had seen them again yesterday, spooning in the back yard. And the cooking suffered in consequence, that beef had been positively raw three days ago, and there seemed to be nothing but vegetables to eat now, John had been complainin' about it. His appetite had returned, which was splendid. Where was William? She and Mabel could really have the business out, she knew she would approve. Ah, at last.

'William, bring the lamps, please.'

The old thing had aged lately. They were all gettin' older; and with Jennings dying like that, it was sad. Pinch retirin' too, the garden didn't look the same without him. But he was comfortable at home, and he had earned a rest.

There was somethin' the matter with Annie, perhaps she was getting really crazy, and they ought to send her to a home, but the other morning when she had said to her near the rubbish heap, with such a gleam in her eye, 'There will be new leaves soon,' it really was too extraordinary. And what did she mean, it wasn't even March yet? Why were there always idiots in a village? And there was nothing one could do for them, that was the annoyin' part about it.

Here were the lamps. Appalling it was, the way some people were installing electricity, oil was much more satisfactory. They had always had oil and always would. Electricity was so hard and bright that it was bad for your eyes.

'William, Mrs Palmer will be in for tea today.'

She was late, and that was wrong of Mabel, she knew how it irritated her to have to wait. She needn't have hurried so down from the village. That roof in Mrs Cross's cottage would have to be seen to, it was in a terrible state, she ought to have been told before. Would the next people take any trouble? But then that wasn't settled yet.

She was restless today, she hadn't been able to settle down to anything, this thing had been weighing on her mind so. And there were the household accounts to do, she was late with them, and they should be interesting this month. Mrs Lane would have been going through an orgy of waste, the affair with Herbert would be sure to make her careless. They would have to take sixpence off the income tax this time, things couldn't go on as they were, and the papers were full of it. Of course, giving this up would save money, but then there would be no flowers and no horses. So much of one would go with it. Mabel was late, late.

A motor. Ah, the Cadillac. Really, it was too bad of her, and it was not as if she ever had anything to do. Well, anyway, they could get down to business now.

The door opened.

'Mrs Palmer.'

'My dear Emily, I'm so sorry I'm late. You see, my dear, the Cadillac broke down on the way, so tiresome of it. How are you?'

'Very well, thank you, Mabel dear; and you?'

They lightly kissed.

'I caught a nasty chill at the Owens' dance, and I've only just thrown it off. My dear, such a bore! There are nothing but draughts in that house, you know how it is. I think they might let one have one window shut, don't you? Emily, it is nice to see you, I haven't come across you for a week.'

'To tell you the truth, Mabel, I haven't been about much this week. With the village and one thing and another I haven't had a moment. I wanted to have a talk . . .'

The door opened. John came in.

'Who is it?'

'Mabel, John.'

'How are you, John?'

'Oh, is it you? I'm all right, thanks. How are things with you?'

'Well, you know how it is, dear boy, one irritating thing after another. Only this afternoon on the way here the inside of the car went wrong, so tiresome. We waited for hours while Jenkins tried to find out what was the matter. And while we were there guess who should come by at the most appalling speed, my dear, so that it was not safe for anyone.' Pause. 'The young Vincent boy on his motor bike.'

'Was he going fast?'

'My dear boy, he shot by, I have never in all my life seen anything like it, you know.'

'John dear, would you mind leavin' Mabel and me for a short time? We want to have a talk.'

'Then I shall see you at tea, Mrs Palmer.' The door shut.

'What has happened, Emily, nothing serious, my dear?'

'Mabel, I wanted to talk over a very important matter with you. You see, it's about John.'

'What? He is not ill again or something?'

'Let us go straight to the point. Let me collect my thoughts. You see, Mabel, it's like this. But perhaps I had better begin at the beginning. You see, even before he went blind, I knew that he was not made for the country, you know how one can tell about one's boy. Well, anyway, from one thing or another I saw that he was not happy down here. You see, he has never liked huntin' or shootin' or any of those things, and now he can't fish. I don't know how it is, he is not in the least like Ralph or me. Where can he have got it from? And this writing that he is so keen about, of course I encourage it, my dear, it is so good for the boy to have a hobby, but no one has ever written on either side of the family. Ralph even found letter-writing almost impossible. So that it is so difficult to understand him, dear.'

'Yes, Emily, I have always felt that, you know.'

'And then one has had girls to the house so that he might see some nice young things, but he has never taken to any of them, Mabel. There was Jane Blandair, a charming girl, but he has told me, in confidence of course, that he definitely dislikes her. My dear, I asked him why, and he said that it was everything about her. What can one do? Jane would have made such a splendid wife and mother. And of the other girls who have been, there was not one of them I would not have liked for a daughter-in-law. And he is quite a catch, isn't he, clever and artistic, and he will have a little money. It was all very depressing, Mabel.'

'Yes, dear, I felt for you so.'

'Well, I was wretched about the whole business, and I slowly came to realize that he was not made for the country, like you or I. You see, he does not really care for the village, though he makes great efforts, poor boy. And then it is his future that matters. He gets terribly bored down here, he has no interests. He is always talking of the towns. He never actually says it, but I know he thinks we all get into grooves in the country, and so I suppose we do, I mean I personally am always fussin' about the village, but of course he is too young to realize that one gets into a groove wherever one is. But there is his writing. That is his only interest. He has been so very brave all through this business, and he is now writing as hard as ever he did; naturally I encourage it, I think everyone should have a hobby, and I am sure you agree with me in this Mabel. But he seems to think that one can't write books in the country. Though all the books that you and I used to read, Mabel, like Jane Austen, were written about the country. Still, he thinks that he can't, and I have always told him to try, but it must be so different when one is blind.

So what he wants is to go away, Mabel, that is what it all comes to. He had never said it, of course, but that is what he wants to do.'

'To go away, Emily? What for?'

'Well, he is young ...'

'Yes, but we all know the wretched life they live in town, you know how it is, dancing all night and only getting up for lunch, you know how it is. I never could stand it when I was a girl. My dear, I don't understand it.'

'I think I do. I'm his mother, you see. He needs a change.'

'Listen, Emily, why not take him to Eastbourne for a few weeks? Such air you get at Eastbourne.'

'It is not that, besides there are other things. No, he – we must go to London.'

'To London! For how long? But think of the noise. Do you mean for the winter and then come down here in the summer?'

'We could not afford it, Mabel. You see, so much of the money went in those shares which are worthless now. No, it would have to be for good.'

'My dear Emily, no, I cannot allow you to do this, you know. No. Think of the Town Council, and the Board of Guardians, what would they do without you? All it would mean is that the Walkers woman would take charge of the whole thing, Colonel Shoton is such a hopeless creature. And think of the village, Emily. Oh, you can't go. It is probably only a passing whim of the boy's, you know. Take him to Eastbourne to get over it, my dear. Don't do this thing recklessly. When you and I were young we had these moments ourselves when we wanted to get away. Why even now sometimes I say to myself that it is all too much and that I was happier at Allahabad, you know how it is, only a little restlessness, my dear.'

'It's more than that, Mabel. I've been so wretched about the whole thing.'

'Yes, my dear, I am so sorry for you, but don't let the fact of you being a little over-wrought influence you to ... Why, think of the village. You know better than I do that Mrs Crayshaw is so busy having babies that she has absolutely no time to attend to the affairs of the village. Why, it would all be indecent and disgraceful if you went so that there was no one left to look after it. You know how it is, illegitimate babies immediately, my dear. Oh no, Emily, you cannot go. Besides, what does the boy want to do in London?'

'Yes, but you see he is artistic.'

'But, Emily, painters always go to the country for inspiration. I have never heard of a painting of a town that was any good. And there is nothing to write about in a town. Don't let him ruin your life, Emily.'

'My duty is by him.'

'Yes, my dear, but does he know what he wants? He is only restless. And what would become of the committees and everything? And the Hospital Ball, Emily?'

'Yes.'

'And the Nursing Association, and the Women's Institute, just when it is beginning to go so nicely, you know. Without you it would collapse. You are absolutely indispensable to its welfare!'

'Am I?'

'Now don't be modest. Why, of course you are. Think of Mrs Walkers on the Board of Guardians. Emily, she isn't honest.'

'She is dangerous, that woman.'

'My dear, do you know what I heard the other day? That as a very natural result of the way she goes on and what with all the money she burns and the way she keeps that house open always, trying to get people to come to it, you know how it is, and of course no one will, she is in the hands of the moneylenders. Deeply involved.'

'Well, I don't know whether I should altogether believe that, but it is very interestin'.'

'Isn't it? All it means is that she will be misappropriating funds as soon as you are out of the way. And you know I've no head for figures.'

'Yes; well, I don't know.'

There was a long pause while outside the night drew in softly, peering through the windows at the fire and the pools of light kept by the lamps. Mabel Palmer was lying back in her chair worn out by what she had had to say, and Mrs Haye was looking vacantly at Greylock. Presently she roused herself.

'Shall we have tea now, Mabel?' And she got up and rang the bell.

'Is everything in?'

'All that I'm going to take, yes.'

'Well, I must go and see about the labels.' Mamma hurried out again.

John stood in the middle of the room, smoking a cigarette. So they were going. Lunch had been a hurried affair, he had hardly eaten he was so excited. He had a wonderful stirring in his belly, for they were going. A light feeling, a warning of change. They had packed all that was being taken. When they got there Uncle Edward had lent them his house till they should find one for themselves. Everything was packed and arranged. There was only the train now. It was nice of Uncle Edward. He sat down on his trunk.

Was there anything more dreadful than waiting to be off? When there was nothing left to do, and you were forced to sit about and wait? He did not dare to walk for the positions of everything had changed, chairs were upside-down in the middle of what had once been a path, there was a large packing-case with protruding nails in what had been the passage between the sofa and the fireplace in the Hall, and he had tripped over a carpet which was rolled up suddenly for half its length. Desolation brooded over each room, and there were clouds of dust driving along here and there on draughts. The flowers had been removed so that the house was cold and hollow. It was changed.

For of course they were moving. London was only six hours off now. Life would be quite different when they got there. Barwood would be wiped out, and he was going to begin again, on the right path this time. Think of all that one would write when one got to London, great things were going to happen there. He would hunt out B. G. and Seymour; they would introduce him to all the amusing people. How nice it was to be going.

He had thought that yesterday was never going to end. Sitting here all the afternoon and all the evening, with William moving about painfully, stacking what he was to take away in one corner, and what was to be left and sold in another. Mamma had shot in and then shot out again continually, and her voice had been breathless at the number of things left to do, with a high note of anxiety whistling through her sentences. Ever since that day three months ago when she had sent him away that Mabel might deliberate alone with her, the high note had pierced through her conversation. Mabel had come many times since then, almost every day, and lately her voice had grown hard towards him, as if she thought that he was ruining Mamma's life. But after all he had not made the suggestion first, it had been Mamma a month back who had said quite suddenly, 'We are going to London,' and he 'To London?' 'Will you like that, dear?' Everything inside him had been beating, beating. It was good of her. He had a sinking feeling now, the whole thing was almost too good to be true.

Spring was beginning here, and the hot rain that fell in short bursts made the room sticky. They said there was a haze of yellowy green over the black trees. He took off his tie and opened his collar.

Nothing had happened in those last three months, nothing had ever happened down here, or rather, nothing always happened. He had thought a good deal and little had come of it, only he had seen God as a great sea into which all goodness drained, and those who were good pumped the goodness out again and watered the desert to make the flowers grow. Trees drew it up. A pretty notion. And all the time expectancy had quivered in the air, making life unbearable, there had been so much going on behind the scenes. Poor William, he had been sad packing yesterday. He was not coming to London, he was too old, and he was retiring on a pension, like old Pinch. That was another thing, all the old people were being left behind to die, and Nan was dead. There would be a new start in London. Poor Nanny, but she was happy, nursing children who had died young. Would she remember him? On her character in heaven, 'Great experience of blind babies.' Oh, he was so happy today.

But Mamma would be happy in London, she would meet there all the people she had known in Scotland before she had married, and they both wanted to get away from Barwood. A town would be a great hive of houses where people were born and lived and died bitterly, there would be no dozing as in Norbury. They would be in the centre of things there, they would be on the spot, and the echoes of what was happening that one only heard faintly in these muffled fields would be clear up there, as a gong. Life was only nice in retrospect, and they could look back on the mists that coiled round Barwood and make them into an enchanting memory, with Joan rising through them, attracting a stray glance of the sun, and dispelling the mists a little.

The coal fire burned steadily with a brittle tinkling sound, as though flakes of glass were falling tiny distances. Far beneath something groaned at being moved.

The train, the first time since the affair. The same boy might sit and throw more stones, one of which might hit his window appropriately. Or there might be a collision, trains were unlucky for him. They would rush through the quiet fields while the telephone wires dipped beside them, over rivers where the fish lay under the bank, through villages where Barwood was repeated, through towns that were not big enough, till they crawled into the biggest town of all, dirtied by all the work that was going on there.

Far away a steamer whistled on the river, it was the first warning of change. He was so excited. The room was sticky with damp. The soft harping rain fell rustling, rustling, while from the eaves drops pattered down on to the window-sill.

Feet climbing stair carpet and Mamma came in.

'We're off in half an hour. Is everything ready?'

'Yes, I think so.'

She went down the stairs, more slowly this time, Half-way down she paused to look at her watch, then hurried on.

'William, they ought to be off now, if they are going to catch that train. Are all the labels on?'

'Yes, madam.'

One, two – five – seven, eight. Eight trunks. They were all there, piled on to two cars. Cars were so expensive to hire nowadays. Thirty shillings. Ruinous.

'Get in, Janet, get in. You have got the money I gave you? Don't forget to label them to Paddington. The stationmaster is expectin' you, and I will be there soon, so you'll be all right. Yes, drive away.'

Janet waved to William. He had aged, he looked so worn standin' by the door there. It was a terrible business gettin' people off.

'There they go, madam.'

'Yes.'

What did he mean? Of course they were going. What?

'They have not stopped, William?'

'No, madam.'

Janet was a capable young thing and she had travelled, so she would be able to manage. Besides, Smith had promised to look out for her.

'Are the labels on all the suitcases?'

'Yes, madam.'

'Well, we start in half an hour.'

Half an hour. Now what had she forgotten? Everything must be in. And anyway, Dewars would sent her the inventory, so that she could send for anythin' she did not want to sell. They could come by the furniture vans.

'William, if there is anything I find missin', you will send it up in the vans with the furniture.'

'Yes, madam.'

Well, that was that. She sank into a chair. A great sigh escaped from inside her. How terrible a house looked when you were gettin' out of it. And all the doors were always left open. She got up and shut them, then she came back to her chair. This rain was horrible, and there was no fire. Had she said a word to everyone? Of course she was not going away for good, but they were not to live down here any more, so that a word or two was expected of you. It was so difficult, too, to find anythin' to say. She had loved them all, and they loved her, but they did not understand her going away like this. They were always asking who was going to live here instead, and she did not know. It was a relief, though, now that they were really off, now that those endless discussions were over. Mabel was impossible sometimes, this business had estranged them almost. The clock had stopped. Really, William might have wound it up, even if they weren't going to be here this evenin'. She looked at her watch. Twenty-nine minutes.

It was nice of Edward to lend them his house with the caretaker and his wife. The two would quarrel, of course, that was the trouble about having married servants, but they would be comfortable there, and it would give one time to look round. 9 Hans Crescent. A German name, but, after all, the war had been over some time. Nine. But . . . And she had only counted eight, and she had let them go off. What was this?

'William, William!'

'Yes, madam.'

'Did you take Mr John's trunk?'

'Mr John? Mr John's box?'

'Oh, oh. I was afraid that would happen. I should have reminded you. Oh dear.'

'Will you take it with you, madam?'

'Yes, that would be best. Will you get it down now, and tell Mr John that we start in twenty minutes.'

How terrible all this was. There was William's voice calling for Robert. He was useless, that boy, quite useless. Why was he never there when he was wanted? He was a good riddance, worthless creature. And William was beginning to forget everything. What could one do?

They would have to take his box with them. And they would have to start earlier so as to have time to label it and everything. Really, John might have told them that he still had it in his room.

Ah, this sort of thing exhausted one. She was quite worn out. What with going through the village on a last round of visits and talking to everyone for the last time in one's official position, so to speak, one was worn out. Then she had given a farewell tea-party to the neighbours, a terrible affair. But they had said nice things on the Board of Guardians, and the Parish Council had presented her with an address, she would never forget that. Weston was going to Mrs Parks, only three miles away, which was a good thing, for the soil here suited him. Wait, there was Annie! She had not seen Annie. But what was the good, the poor thing was quite crazy? Crayshaw was going to take her on in his garden, so that she would be all right. It was good of him, he had the village at heart. She would send Annie ten shillings when she got to London. Mrs Lane, too, was only moving two miles away, which was because she wanted to be near Herbert, of course, as he was staying on here to keep the garden tidy, till someone came to buy it. The house was sure to be sold, it was so beautiful, and the garden was the best in twenty miles. With Weston, Mrs Parks would win all the prizes at the Norbury Flower Show. He was a good gardener, quite excellent with chrysanthemums.

It was stupid to forget that trunk. Why, he had been sitting on it when she went up. She looked at her watch, ten minutes more, they ought to be off. But no, not quite yet, perhaps.

It was nice of Edward, he must have understood how terrible leaving Barwood would be to her. Having a foothold up there made house-huntin' so much more comfortable. Goin' away was like leaving half one's life behind one, but then the boy would be so much happier. She would be able to look up Mrs Malinger, who used to live in Norbury years ago, she was such a nice woman.

Had she put in the medicine chest? There, she had forgotten. But perhaps it was in. She leapt up and hurried upstairs to her bedroom. Out of the window there was the view over the lawn. And there was the cock pheasant being cautious at the bottom there. He and his wives could eat all the bulbs now. That lawn, how beautiful it was. And in the wild garden at the side the daffodils were beginning to come out, such a mass of yellow. Well, they were going. What had she come here for, she had been round the garden yesterday? Yes, the medicine chest. She looked, and it was there still. She had forgotten. It must come up by the van. How stupid of her, for towns were so unhealthy and the boy might need a tonic. Oh dear, the garden. They ought to be off soon. She hurried downstairs again. There was William.

'The car is round, madam.'

'Very well.'

Wait a minute, just to show him she did not have train fever. But that was childish.

'John dear, get your coat on and come, or we shall have a rush at the station.'

His voice from above:

'Coming.'

'William, I entirely forgot about the medicine chest in my room. Will you send that on in the van?'

'Yes, madam.'

His voice, nearer:

'Coming.'

'Are the suitcases in?'

'Yes, madam.'

'Give me my coat, then.'

'And, William, come and see us in London some time. Your brother is there, isn't he?'

'I will, madam, thank you.'

Poor old thing, he was quite upset. It was rather terrible. Ah, here he was. How quickly he walked alone now.

'Be careful, dear.'

'I'm all right.'

'Well, let's get into the car. We have got plenty of time. Oh, William, the clock has stopped in the Hall there. I hope it isn't broken. You had better get Brown's man in to look to it.'

They were off now. What did the clock matter as they weren't coming back, but they sold better if they were going. John was waving. No, she couldn't look back.

'So we are going?'

'Of course, dear.'

He was so happy.

They were in the car on the way to the station, how extraordinary after so many weeks' work. Perhaps she had decided too quickly. Mabel, of course, had been right against it from the start. But the boy would only be happy in London, he wasn't made for the country, especially after he had gone blind like that. Only the other day and here they were. Oh, there was the Vicarage. How fast they were going.

'Hi! don't go so fast.'

'I love speed.'

'But it's so dangerous, dear.'

'Where are we now?'

'In the sunken bit. He has slowed down, that's better. Dear boy, are you nearly enough wrapped up?'

Farther away, farther away. Everything had been leading up to this. The road went by with a swish, the rain made the surface so wet.

'Are you sure you haven't forgotten anythin'? There may be still time to go back.'

'I don't think so.'

There was the dove-cote. They were leaving so much behind. How fast the man drove. What was the good? But it was tiresome forgettin' John's box like that. It would put the excess luggage out, they would have to make a new bill, and that would take time. It would be a rush. There was Mrs Trench. She hadn't seen them, they were travellin' so fast. She was about to have another baby. There must be something in the family, it was the only way to account for all the Trench babies dying as soon just as they were born. It brought the average of infant mortality in the village so high.

'Where are we now?'

'Why are you so jumpy, dear? We are just going under the leanin' oak.'

The leaning oak? There was a long way to go yet. The engine purred. London was the temple of machinery. It was hot in here.

'Shall we have a window down?'

'As you like. But it is rainin'.'

The air came rushing in, sown with raindrops that spattered coolly against his face. He drank the wind in gulps, half-choking at the volume of it cramming down his throat. This was good. And the horn on this car had such an imperious note, but after all, great hopes were driving with it. They must go faster, faster, but then Mamma did not like it. The station was so far away, they might not catch their train. The horn again. He would like to take it away and have it in London as a souvenir to blow when things were not going well.

'Oh, John, look. There are the village.'

'Which side?'

'There, to your left. Oh, you have missed them, they are behind now. How nice of them, how nice of them.'

'Yes, that was nice of them.'

'They were nearly all there. Oh dear.'

'We shall come down and see them again soon.'

'I saw Mrs Withers, and Mrs Hartley and old Mrs Eddy had come from the almshouses. I waved. They were waving. It would have been nice to stop, but we haven't the time.'

'No, that would only have made a rush at the station.'

Stopping like that would have been intolerable. Besides, it was better to break quickly with the old than to linger by it. The village would be all right. They must be on a hill now. How slow it was. They might miss that train. Then they could always take the next one. But it was this train that mattered, they must catch this train, he had thought so much of it, tearing across the country to the biggest town of all. Everything would give way to it, it was his train.

'We are just passing the last of your estate, dear'; for it was still his.

'Yes?'

Thank God for that. They were almost out of the circle now.

She did feel miserable, yes, it was being worse than she thought it would be. See how the corn was coming up, and the blossom just peeping through the trees. Two partridges, frightened by the car, shot away to curl over the hedge at the bottom of that field. Spring, and they were leaving. But then October was always the best month down here, they would come back for that, she had promised herself and Mabel. There was Norbury, quite close now, with some blue sky over it and a great rainbow, – over the station no doubt.

'Are you happy, John?'

'Yes, very.'

What a fool of a man that was who was driving the cart. Why couldn't he get out of the way? That kind of labourer went to sleep, so the horses did too, of course. What was that? No. Yes, it was the Vincent boy on his motor bicycle. Mabel had been right, it was mad the pace he drove. Look at him – no, he was gone.

'Here we are in Norbury.'

'Are we? Oh, well, it is not so very far now. Yes, I can smell it. Splendid. What's the time?'

'We have another ten minutes yet. Look, there's the Tea Rooms, and Smith the boot shop, and Green the draper's.'

The driver had turned out of the High Street. Only another minute. He could hardly sit still. That must be a coal dump they were passing. A train whistled. Joy. The car pulled up, he jumped out and then stood lost.

'Don't move a step without me, dear.'

'All right.'

'You might fall on to the rails or something. Where's Janet?'

That would indeed be an anti-climax.

'Here, John, come this way and sit on this seat.'

How quiet it was here. A cursed sparrow was cheeping foolishly so near. The station seemed asleep. But he was going away. Behind in the waiting-room a voice droned on, while another laughed at intervals. There was Mamma's voice coming. She had got hold of Smith, poor man. He was being allowed to speak, 'No trouble at all, Mrs Haye, at all. I will see to it immediately.' She stopped by him.

'They are making out the excess luggage, my dear. I think it is all going to be all right.'

'Good.'

This seat was hideously hard. That sparrow. Why was no one moving? A burst of laughter from the waiting-room, there were quite a number of people in it. They would be travelling by the same train.

'Janet.'

'Yes, Mr John.'

'How much longer, Janet?'

'Only five minutes now.'

Why did she speak as if he was a child? Here were steps coming towards him, boots clanking on the flags. The man had a smell of grease and leather about him.

'Porter?'

'Yessir.'

'Is it a through train to London?'

'Change at Bridcote, Swindon and Oxford.'

Why had Mamma not told him? So they were to travel provincially. Oh well. It was London, but it was not the express. They would crawl like a worm instead. Voices on all sides began to make themselves heard, growing louder and louder. Over them all was

Mamma suddenly thanking Smith. Then she came and sat down by him.

'I have done it all, I think.'

'Good.'

'It will be in soon now.'

'So we change three times.'

'Yes, dear, do you mind? Such a nuisance. But it was the only train in the afternoon, and I thought we had better have lunch at home, it is so much more comfortable, don't you think?'

'Yes.'

How funny that she had never consulted him. But she had always loved secrecy in her arrangements. A bell rang, steps began to make patterns of sound, and the voices rushed out of the waiting-room. They were off. A rumble which ran up to a roar and the train drew up. What a noise it was. But Mamma was dragging him along. A child's voice, plaintive, 'Mumma . . . blind, Mumma.' Yes, that was him.

'Here you are, dear, jump in. The corner seat. The carriage is reserved. I shall be back in a minute. Thank you, Smith. Now . . .'

So they were off. Goodbye. He had had so many. Where was Mamma? Oh, why didn't the train go?

4 Beginning again

London. He was sitting in the drawing-room of the house Uncle Edward had lent them. He was ill, ill. The sunlight streamed through the window by him, for it was spring, and ate stealthily into the plush which covered his armchair.

There was a sickly scent of flowers in the room. They had been sent up from Barwood and were fading, when once they had danced so wildly at the wind. The afternoon was heavy and the air thick with the sweetness of a dying lily just by him, a putrefaction drooping through the heat. The window was open and from beneath the noise of the street came in shafts, cutting through the steady sun. The ringing of bicycle bells shot up in necklaces of sound from the road, and jagged footsteps tore in upon his old life that was being left behind now with the song of that bird.

Oh, why had he gone blind? All these months now he had seen

nothing, and he had pretended to others and even to himself that in feeling things he was as well off as one who saw them, but it was not true. For in London so much went on that there was no time to separate or analyse your sensations, everything crowded in upon you and left you dazed. But in a sense life was beginning again, for they would be so happy up here. In time he would learn to understand the streets. Mamma had found a house which would do, and soon they would be moving in. That would make another rift, for he would lose Margaret, the wife of the caretaker here. She had kept him alive, she was so vivid, and then sometimes she would dream, falling into long silences when her hand lay as if asleep in his. Probably she was hideous, but then he could not see. She must hate him with his scars.

The glass had ploughed through his face, as his blindness cut into his brain now, and they had taken him to the hospital where even the nurses had been antiseptic. Everything had felt most wickedly clean with a mathematical cleanness. But this nurse had had wonderful hands that hovered and that touched so lightly and yet helped when it hurt. Her fingers had been so lithe. It was silly to talk of 'white mice' as he had with June, of how her fingers had scurried about in his; one needed strong unerring fingers. Margaret's were like that sometimes. But even the clean stench in that hospital had been better than this of the flowers, and anyway it had been quiet, not as here where these stabbing bursts of sound tortured you. But there was a whiff of tar in the air, and he liked tar.

Listen to that bird, singing as though there were nothing better to do in the world. Barwood was so far away now, yet, because he had seen there perhaps, he could not get away. The roar of the streets reminded one of the quiet which had been over it, where sounds came as if distilled by the great distances; and then Margaret was so different to June, June who had never known her place in the order of things – there was no place for her – and Margaret who knew her position exactly, and was so sure of herself. Why had that bird chosen this house on which to sing, little inconsequent notes being flung at the blue sky, crystal notes that shattered against the tawdriness of these dying flowers and of his own discontent? A car bore down and overwhelmed the song, but it emerged once more as the car sped away and made him ask if he had done right, to leave June like that, and to take Mamma away. For the garden at Barwood would be bursting into life just now, all the birds would be singing, and if Mamma were there she would be spying over the border and endlessly conferring with Weston. He would have been able to share in the spring as well, lying on the lawn in a chair he would have passed hours feeling the leaves come out and everything changing round him, while he was out of it in London, too lost, too tired to raise his head above the clatter of the streets, where everyone except himself had work to do. He must work.

He would write. At Noat he had thought about it, at Barwood he had talked about it, but he must work at it up here, there was nothing else to do, as he was left alone for hours, they were all so busy. In time he could get to understand the streets and so to write about them, for in time one would know more about them than people ever would who had sight. It was so easy to see and so hard to feel what was going on, but it was the feeling it that mattered. A bell rang downstairs. Someone was at the front door, coming to see him, perhaps; and then there was Mamma's voice with a shy laugh in it, saying:

'Why, it's Lorna! My dear, I recognized you at once. How nice of you! Just think, you after these years and years. I happened to be passing so I opened.'

And a strange voice was talking at the same time, then they both kissed – why need Mamma kiss so loudly in London? – and the strange voice rose over Mamma's and was saying:

'Emily – such ages and ages . . .'

But a motor bike passed and cut them off from him, he only heard the front door crash as they shut it. Someone to see Mamma, well, that would make her very happy. But he was forgotten up here, he was only allowed the echoes of all that was going on, and he saw himself waiting and listening here for the rest of his life. No one cared whether he was blind or not. But there were steps outside, it was Margaret, she minded, and he would fascinate her so that she minded all the more. There was a knock on the door, her knock, and she slipped in on a gust of cool air from the marble hall, and there was something cool about her as well, waves of gentleness breaking round him. Every time she came he was surprised at her quietness. She was so deft, but then she had been a lady's-maid. Her skirt touched his foot so lightly.

'I'm just going out, Mr Haye, and I thought I'd look in to see if I could find you anything.'

'Take me out.'

'Mrs Haye just said she would do that herself, she won't be long now.'

To be taken out! He was in everyone's way. And why shouldn't he go with Margaret? Now he would have to wait till that visitor had gone.

'Are you comfortable in that chair, Mr Haye?' and her hand arranged the handkerchief in his breast pocket. She was listless today, her thoughts were elsewhere. And she had scented herself, the first time she had ever done that since he had known her. It was very, very faint, but you could just tell it if you were near her. Perhaps it was meant for someone who would be nearer. He would be. He searched round his handkerchief for her hand.

'But your hand is burning. Well, I never,' and hers had escaped; 'I must be going.'

'Could you pull the blind down and shut the window, the noise is so frightful?'

The blind ran down and he thought of how to detain her. The window shut and the world became muffled.

'Oh, and this lily here, could you move it?'

She tugged, but the stand that held it was heavy, and her breathing grew deeper at the effort.

'Let me help. There is nothing in the way, is there?'

'I can do it, don't get up, Mr Haye.'

But he was on his feet and groping about when he met her hand again, calm and a trifle moist, which took his and guided it. His other hand meeting her shoulder slid down the dress (through which her arm glowed) till his finger caught on her elbow. How small it was, but it wriggled, and seized with a sudden despair he loosed it. Then, as he was groping forward again, the lily poked gently into his face, trying to tickle him, and shuddering, he pushed the thing away. He leant forward further to where he felt her presence and the stand. Her breath burned in his face for a moment and bathing in her nearness he leant further forward still, in the hopes of finding her, but she dropped his hand and it fell on the slick edges of the pot in which the lily grew. Despair was coming over him again, it was too awkward, this pursuit of her under a lily, when all at once her arm mysteriously came up over his mouth, glowing and cool at the same time, and the scent was immediately stronger, tangible almost, so that he wanted to bite it. But before he could do that her arm had glided away again and he gave it up, and was merely irritated when a stray bit of her hair tickled his right cheek, so different to the lily, as they were pushing the stand away. But when they had the thing moved and she was leading him back, he felt so glad at the touch of her presence that once again he could not bear the thought of her going.

'Don't leave me. Sit here for a little, I am so continually alone.'

'I must go, really, I shall be late already. My brother's come up for the day and I'm to meet him. Is there anything else you want?'

Her brother. It was no good, there was someone else, just as June would have someone else now. How could they like him with his scars? He raised a hand and slipped the fingers along them, smooth varnished things unlike the clinging life of his skin. The door shut, she was gone, and the coolness with her. He was alone. That child on the platform as they had been coming up here: 'Look, Mumma, ... blind, Mumma,' and the horror which had been in its little cursed treble because another little thing had thrown a stone at a passing train. Of course it had been his window the stone hit, of course. A motor horn kept on braying in the street outside. And now that the blind was down and that the window was shut he felt that he would suffocate, and that those flowers were watching him and mocking because they could do something that he could not.

He must go out, but he must wait first for Mamma as he could not find his way about. Their walks were terrifying very often, crossing a street Mamma would lose her head, pulling on his arm this way and that while death in a car rushed down on them and passed in a swirl, gathering the air after it, and all the time he was trying not to show how frightened he was. Then, when they were on the pavement at last, people had no mercy on you if it was crowded; you were always being jostled, and broken ends of conversation were jumbled up and thrown at you, and then presences would glide past leaving a snatch of warm scent behind them to tantalize. He was continually running into dogs, he trod on them, and they howled till their owners became angry and then apologized when they realized that you were not as others were. In the country you had been able to forget that you were blind.

Everything was pressing down on him today, crowding in on him, dragging him down. And now that the window was shut and the sun cut off by the blind he felt suffocated. A barrel-organ was thudding a tune through the window, beating at the threshold of his brain. He got up and groping towards the window opened it. As he did so there was a sudden lull in all the noise, he could only hear the clop-clop of a horse receding into the distance, and then mysteriously from below there floated up a chuckle; it was a woman and someone must have been making love to her, so low, so deep it was. He was on fire at once. Love in the street, he would write of it, love shouting over the traffic, unsettling the policemen, sweeping over the park, wave upon wave of it, inciting the baboons to mutiny in the Zoo, clearing the streets. What was the use of his going blind if he did not write? People must hear of what he felt, of how he knew things differently. The sun throbbed in his head. Yes, all that, he would write all that. He was on the crest of a petulant wave, surging along, when his wave broke on the sound of a motor horn. There were his scars, and the sun pricked at him through them. He drew back into the room, his face wet with the heat. Oh, he was tired.

As he searched for his chair a flower poked its head confidingly into his open hand, but he crushed it, for what had he to do with flowers now? Why did Mamma leave him alone, a prey to all his thoughts? They must go out, Mamma and he, but he felt so ill. And was she happy here, away from Barwood and all the worries that she had lived for? As for him, it was only that he was dazed by all these new sensations, he would rise above them soon, when he knew how to interpret them, and then he would have some peace.

A car was pulled up sharp, the brakes screamed and he writhed at it. He was imprisoned here, for somehow he could not learn to find his way about in this new house. Why didn't she come?

It was hot. It made him think of Barwood, where probably it would be raining, and of sitting in the summer-house while the cool rain spattered softly in washing away the scars, and where the wind brought things from afar to hang for a moment in his ears and then take away again. Years ago the trees there had been green for him, only months ago really, and here there was only dust and the dying flowers and tar. And he had fished where the sunset came to earth and bathed in the river. But there were voices coming up the stairs, Mamma's and a new voice. They must be glad to be together again, because the two streams of what they had to say to each other mingled as they both talked at the same time and purled so happily on. The door opened. He got up shyly.

'Who have you brought?'

'My dear, what do you think, it is Lorna Greene. Just think, we had not met since I married. Oh, Lorna, this is like old days.'

She was so excited and laughing, she must be happy. Then her voice dropped. 'Lorna, this is John.' All the life had gone out of her voice, but then why wonder at it, after all he was the problem and the millstone. Damn them! But he was saying:

'Oh, how do you do,' while a strange hand, languid but interested, took his for a moment and he felt many rings and much culture. He had never in his life held anything so cared for, she must bathe this hand in oil every night, it was so smooth, so impersonal. Then it coolly slipped away again, and she was saying something about his having known her son at Noat in an amused kind of drawl, her voice curling round her lips. It was almost as if she were laughing at him. She searched with her voice, it was sardonic, she would drive him mad. What was there funny about him, except that he was stuck here defenceless?

'Lorna, my dear, I can't hear myself speak. These appallin' motors and things don't give me a minute's peace. Why don't the police do somethin' about it? It is nice to have you here. I am shuttin' the window, John, do you mind?'

No, he didn't mind. Window shut, window open, you were boxed up just the same. They sat down, talking hard. Very long ago he remembered this woman at Noat, Greene's mother, she had been tall and he had thought her nondescript. And now there was so much in her voice and in her hand. In this way one gained by being blind. But she was talking and her voice was fascinating.

'Do you remember when I was staying with you that time, Emily, and the minister came to tea, the yearly tea your father gave him? And how we put mustard into all the cakes he was fondest of, and he noticed nothing and ate them all, then stayed talking longer than he had ever done before, all about how the family were like the cedar in front of the house?'

'And what Solomon's temple was made of . . .'

They were remembering, they all did.

'And oh, Lorna, do you remember . . .'

Mamma's voice was quite different, as if it had suddenly leapt into youth again, it was so happy and excited. So London was a success with her, she was really enjoying herself for the first time! There was only himself out of it, all the others were in the swim.

'And, Emily, when we fed the dog on chocolate and it was sick all over your father's room, how furious he was!'

Oh, naughty, naughty! This happiness of theirs was exasperating. How ludicrous to think that, but he could not help it. And then all the time this Greene woman was speaking she seemed to be gibing at him. They had no life, they lived only in what was passed, while June and he had carved great slices out of the future when they had been together. June, at any rate, had always been there ready to come when she was wanted, but Margaret's time was divided. Why couldn't Mamma and he go out for their walk, but then she was so happy talking. There was no air now that they had shut the window, they had muffled the room so that they might muffle him the better with this talk of theirs. On and on it went, dragging one back just when one was beginning to strike out into new ground. He must plunge into the tumult outside and find a place for himself. He got up.

'It is so hot in here, do you mind if I open the window?'

'Let me do it for you.'

'No, no, I can do it.'

Why couldn't they leave him alone? Of course he could do it, he was not wholly incapacitated. Where was the catch? He must look such a fool fumbling here.

Good heavens! the boy looked ghastly. Why hadn't she noticed before, it was Lorna's having come that had excited her so that she had not seen. And as she helped him raise the sash she looked anxiously into his face, she did not like it, he seemed from his expression to be seeing things which she could not. But then how could he? He was not going to be ill? She blamed herself, how selfish of her to be gossiping with Lorna when he was ill and needed her. All this noise must be bad for him with the window open, but then it was air he wanted, and it was rather sticky today. Lorna must go. But it was as if the dear thing had guessed, for she was saying that she must fly now and that she knew her way and that no one was to show her out. But you couldn't do that, Edward had left no servants, and as they went downstairs Lorna was told how the journey up a few weeks before had made the boy unaccountably seedy, how at first the noise seemed to worry him terribly, but that the new house would be quieter, and how worrying it all was. What could one do?

The soft sound of their murmuring at the bottom of the stairs and the roar of Oxford Street swept him away on a flood, but he was so tired that he seemed to sink in it to a place where the pitch was higher, the cars and everything more shrill as they darted along so far away, it seemed. The flowers were singing to themselves, or was it a bird? Birds lusting in trees which suddenly were round him, their notes screaming through the rich leaves. They were full of sap, hanging down thick hands to cover the nakedness of the branches on which birds sat mocking at him, for they could see and he could not. All Barwood was laughing at him because he had gone away, and by doing that had found out how helpless he was. He could not open the window, he could not go out.

Mamma was coming back, her footsteps rang heavily on the stairs, and as she came in and shut the door he roused himself, saying that he was only feverish and that it would pass with a night's rest. She came up to him and laid her hand on his shoulder.

'Are you all right, dear?'

'Yes, yes, quite all right.'

Why did they go on nagging him?

'Shall I shut the window? Don't you find this noise terrible?'

'No, please leave it open so that I can listen.' She sat down and took up some knitting. That doctor was a fool. What was the matter with the boy? She could only sit and watch, there was nothing to be done with him, he was in one of his moods. Their walk was out of the question now.

He passed a hand over his forehead, the skin was dry and burning, electric. Again he felt that he was being enveloped, this time by the close room and by the sun which throbbed outside. He was growing afraid at the way in which the walls pressed in and crowded the flowers together so that their scent rose up in a fog mixed with the turmoil outside and made to overwhelm him, when suddenly and for no reason, like a gust of wind through the room, purifying it, came the sound of bells from the church along the street, tearing through the room, bells catching each other up, tripping, tumbling and then starting off again in cascades. Theirs was such a wild joy and they trembled at it between the strokes so that they hummed, making a background for the peals. He loved bells and, inexpressibly happy, he was swept back to Barwood and June – 'Listen, June, how the sound of them comes over the country,' and her father being hunted by them through the mazes that gin had created in his brain, and their walks stretched in a gesture to the sky, they had been so unfortunate in their lives.

Then, for no reason, the bells began to stop one by one and the humming grew fainter, and he remembered an evening on the river when the sound of them had glided over the water, but a lorry mumbled along beneath, and one by one the bells stopped till even their humming had gone. Barwood was being sold, and after all, those walks of theirs had come to nothing.

He must ask B. G. and Seymour round to see him. But perhaps they would be bored and would laugh at his ideas after the time they had spent at Oxford. And he was not going to let them see him crushed under his blindness, they would despise him for it. He must first make out how he stood with life in general so that he could show them how much better off he was than they. He would start a crusade against people who had eyesight. It was the easiest thing in the world to see, and so very many were content with only the superficial appearance of things; it would teach them so much if they were to go blind, though blindness was a burden at first and he was heavy with memories.

Those bells, everything, brought them jostling back in one's mind. But there had been something different about the bells, they had left him trembling, and when he passed a hand over his chair he was surprised at how stolid and unaltered the plush remained, for he was certain that the wild peal of them had made a great difference, their vibration had loosened and freed everything, until even the noise of the streets became invigorating. He felt a stirring inside him; it was true, they had made a difference, he felt it, and in a minute something was going to happen. He waited, taut, in the chair.

Mrs Haye knitted. The bells carried one back to Barwood. He would have been better there, you could not breathe in London, and fresh air was good for one if one was feelin' seedy. But it was no use thinkin' about Barwood, one must be practical, and everything would change once they had a house of their own. This caretaker and his wife were impossible, it was so like Edward to have servants like that. You could not speak to the man he was so rude, and that woman was hardly any better, though she did seem to take some trouble with the boy. But there again you never quite knew, he might form one of his terrible attachments for her, and then there would be the old worry of the Entwhistle creature all over again. She ought to have stood up to him at the time and told him straight out that it was ridiculous and that she would not have it, it was wrong of her not to have done that, but then his blindness had come upon them so suddenly and it had been so soon after. You could not speak out to him when his life had been taken from him like that. Anyway, they had gone and it was done – so much of her was there, in the village and the Town Council and all those things, but of course one understood his wanting to get away from all the old places where he had seen, and he was so brave making a new life for himself like this. And she would make a home for him, they would start again up here, it was rather excitin' really, of course it was. She would get hold of Lorna and they would find some young things. He must marry. If he did, perhaps she could go back there?

Lorna had altered, she was so fashionable now, one felt shy meetin' her again. It had been good of her to come round, she was goin' to be a real help, for they must find something to distract the boy. She had bought that lily, one would have thought he'd like it, it had cost quite a sum being so early in the year, but he had pushed it away. Better not to mention that. These motor cars, it was a disgrace the noise they made. But he seemed to like it, for he was lookin' happy almost for the first time since he had been up here. He had said all the time that he was very happy, but she had felt that he had been worried really, and mainly as to whether she was happy in London, but of course she went where he went. It was difficult to understand his moods. Perhaps they could go for their walk now, and that she had only been imaginin' things when she thought he was ill.

Oh, these waves of sickness that came suddenly over him, stirring through his brain. And it was as if there were something straining behind his eyeballs to get out. He dropped his face into his hands, there was such a feeling of happiness surging through him.

Mamma's voice, a long way away it seemed, and anxious:

'What is it, dear?'

'I'm frightened.'

'Why? What is there to be frightened of? Why?'

But he was frightened at such joy. In a minute he felt it would burst out of him in a great wind and like a kite he would soar on it, and that the mist which lay between him and the world would be lifted by it also. Rising, rising up.

He was rising through the mist, blown on a gust of love, lifting up, straining at a white light that he would bathe in. He half rose.

'John!'

And when he bathed there he would know all, why he was blind, why life had been so to him. He was nearer. To rise on this love, how wonderful to rise on this love. He was near now.

'John!!'

A ladder, bring a ladder. In his ears his own voice cried loudly, and a deeper blindness closed in upon him.

As they carried him to his room, the bells suddenly broke out again from along the street. Probably they were practising for some great event. It was the first thing he heard as he came back to the world, and he smiled at them.

A letter

'*Dear B. G.*

'*They tell me I have had some sort of a fit, but it has passed now. Apparently my father was liable to them, so that anyway I have one behind me after this. But it is so divine to be in London again near to you, and with the sun shining down on me as I lie in bed as if it had never shone before, while underneath, in the street, the traffic glides past in busy vibrations, I am so happy to be in the centre of things again, and to be alive. How stimulating a town is – but perhaps you think me silly. You have led such a different life to mine, I hardly know what you think or feel. Come round and look me up again, you know how I love talking. I have had a wonderful experience. I am going to settle down to writing now, I have a lot to tell. Mamma read me your article in the 'New World' and it was wonderful – really, I mean, for that is not flattery. Why am I so happy today?*

'*Yrs.*
   '*John.*'

Henry Green
**Loving,
Living** and
Party Going £1.75

Three novels by the man hailed by W. H. Auden as 'the finest living
novelist'. Long neglected, the three novels published here deal with life in
an Irish country house during World War II – *Loving*; working-class factory
life – *Living*; and the comedy of manners of life in a London railway
station – *Party Going*.

'A spellbinder . . . a true artist' L. P. HARTLEY

'His novels are . . . unlike any others . . . assured in their perilous
luminous fullness' JOHN UPDIKE

edited by W. B. Yeats
Fairy and Folk Tales of Ireland £1.75

This volume, with a foreword by Kathleen Raine, contains the two books
of Irish folklore collected and edited by Yeats, published as *Fairy and Folk
Tales of the Irish Peasantry* in 1888, and *Irish Fairy Tales* in 1892. Yeats's
enthusiasm for the imaginary creatures of his own race produced an
extraordinary and exhaustive anthology: almost every aspect of Irish myth
and legend taken down by writers over two centuries finds its place in
the book.

'Yeats was scornful of the earlier folk-tale collectors, who saw little but
knockabout farce . . . These tales, by contrast, are full of strange events:
mortals cursed and killed by fairies, great fights between bulls and stallions,
funeral visitations by creatures of the sea' SUNDAY TELEGRAPH

John Cowper Powys

'The finest historical novelist in English literature'
G. WILSON KNIGHT

Owen Glendower £2.50

This extraordinary novel about the Welsh rising at the beginning of the
15th century brings to life the hero, Owen Glendower, and also tells the
engrossing story of the love affair between Rhisiart al Owen (the novel's
true hero) and the beautiful red-haired Tegolin.

'Beside *Owen Glendower*, with its Shakespearean largesse of recaptured life,
nearly all historical novels are charade' GEORGE STEINER

'A historical novel in the real sense . . . remarkable' ANGUS WILSON

The Brazen Head £1.50

This panoramic novel, set in 13th-century Wessex, displays Powys's genius
at its richest. The story of Friar Roger Bacon, of the love between Lil-
Umbra and Raymond de Laon, of the quest of the giant Beleg, for Ghosta,
the girl seen, loved and lost on the battlefield, is a shimmering tapestry of
history and magic. Dominating all is Friar Bacon's mysterious creation: the
bronze head which can utter oracles, the greatest of his world-changing
inventions.

'A book of wisdom and wonders' G. WILSON KNIGHT

'His pen is the wand of Merlin, his desk a Wessex cromlach, his light
the moon' SUNDAY TIMES

Gabriel García Márquez

'Latin America's most powerful writer' SUNDAY TIMES

No One Writes to the Colonel £1·25

'These tales of life in South America are the real thing: rich and full of incident and the dignity of men and women who have nothing else left' DAILY TELEGRAPH

'Masterly picture of despair and optimism . . . Márquez has insights and sympathies which he can project with the intensity of a reflecting mirror in a bright sun' NEW STATESMAN

Leaf Storm £1.25

'A second collection of stories . . . so brilliantly organized and well translated by Gregory Rabassa, that the eye is held to the very end . . . Márquez has enormous gifts of narrative, wit and irony' THE TIMES

'A celebration of the myth-making process . . . the prose of Márquez is plain, exact, subtle, springy and easily leaps into the comical and exuberant' V. S. PRITCHETT, NEW STATESMAN

'I take my hat off to him' P. J. KAVANAGH, GUARDIAN

Richard Brautigan
Dreaming of Babylon £1.50

When you're a deadbeat private eye with no car, no office, no bullets for your gun, no money and a mother you owe 800 bucks, dreaming of Babylon is maybe not the best way to earn a living. But C. Card, who hadn't kissed a girl since the day before Pearl Harbor, finished the 596 BC season with a 0.89 batting average, and had once had a fancy office just down from the Hanging Gardens...

'Established as one of the writers of our time'
NORMAN SHRAPNEL GUARDIAN

Thomas Pynchon
The Crying of Lot 49 £1.50

The death of her ex-lover sets Oedipa Maas on a trail of delirious weirdness through Dr Hilarius, Freudian shrink, Gengis Cohen, the eminent LA philatelist who likes his sex with the news on, not to mention Yoyodyne Inc, Randolph Driblette, and Mssrs Wistfull, Kubitschek and McMingus, Attorneys...

'The best American novel I have read since the war' FRANK KERMODE

'An exuberant, off-beat talent ... turbulent as storm-clouds' GUARDIAN

Italo Calvino
Invisible Cities £1.25

'This most beautiful of all his books throws up ideas, allusions, and breathtaking imaginative insights on almost every page. Each time he returns from his travels, Marco Polo is invited by Kublai Khan to describe the cities he has visited. The conqueror and explorer exchange visions: for Kublai Khan the world is constantly expanding; for Marco Polo, who has seen so much of it, it is an ever-diminishing place . . . Calvino is describing only one city in this book. Venice, that decaying heap of incomparable splendour, still stands as substantial evidence of man's ability to create something perfect out of chaos'
TIMES LITERARY SUPPLEMENT

'The cities correspond to psychological states and historical states, possibilities and transformations' LISTENER

Paul Monette
Nosferatu – the Vampyre 90p
based on the screenplay by Werner Herzog

Nosferatu . . . The Undead . . . Count Dracula . . . A lonely wraith-like figure, doomed to wander forever in the realm of twilight in search of an alluring and lovely woman, whose destiny is to defeat him only by submission . . . the giving of herself from dusk until dawn.

Nosferatu – the name under which the vampire legend first reached the screen – is now recreated by Werner Herzog as a sensual and haunting masterpiece of cinema. Eighty years after Bram Stoker's *Dracula*, Paul Monette's outstanding novel once more breathes life into the ultimate myth of evil.

Arthur Koestler
Janus: a Summing Up £2.25

'The human brain has developed a terrible psychological flaw, such that now it is working against the survival of the race. Something has *snapped* inside the brain. It is no longer necessarily a function which will lead to a better world, but something demonic, possessed' BOOKS AND BOOKMEN

'A summing up of a quarter of a century's study and speculations on the life sciences and their philosophical implications' GUARDIAN

'One of the major political *experiencers* and most widely informed spirits of the age turning to the crux of human survival on a ravaged planet' SUNDAY TIMES

J. E. A. Tyler
The New Tolkien Companion £2.95

The classic guide to Middle Earth, now revised to include *The Silmarillion*. An encyclopedia of every known fact, name, 'foreign' word, date and etymological allusion occurring in Professor Tolkien's completed saga.

A guide to the creation of Middle Earth and of the Ainur, the High History of the Elven Peoples (including an explanation of Elvish writing), the origins of Morgoth the Enemy, and the rise to power of his servant, Sauron, Lord of the Rings – the *Companion* details the long and heroic struggle of the Free Peoples against the Perils of the Ancient World.

'Rivals the work of the Dwarves in the *mithril*-mines of Moria' BERNARD LEVIN, OBSERVER